'Move over Dick Francis and John Francome – there's a new kid on the block, and it's a racing certainty she's heading for success . . . a compelling read . . . [it] will have you turning the pages quicker than a champion takes the jumps at Aintree'
Evening Telegraph

'A remarkably accomplished first novel from a woman who knows what she is writing about; the vicissitudes of being a woman in a man's world. It gives the reader a brilliant insight into what a trainer – especially a woman trainer – has to put up with'
Daily Express

'In terms of popularity Pitman's fiction is galloping hard in the hoofmarks of Dick Francis and John Francome but with rather less murder and mystery and rather more feminine subtlety . . . allows us genuine insight into the trials and delights of training horses'
The Times

'An assured, swift-moving piece in which the racing universe is sharply evoked . . . big, bold, page-turning'
Amazon

'The antics of this adrenaline-fired profession are utterly compelling. Pitman's expertise in the field not only illuminates the demands of juggling horses, jockeys and owners, but the netherworld of gambling and bribery that threaten this volatile sport'
Glasgow Herald

'Pitman writes from the heart, often giving the impression that she is imparting many of her own views and ideals as well as demonstrating a knack for engaging the reader . . . For racing fans, fiction fans, or both, the saga of Jan Hardy is sure to appeal'
Racing Pos

'Pitman has her hands firmly on the reins in this tale of love, determination and courage. It's a racing cert for anyone who loves horses and romance'
Lancashire Evening Post

Jenny Pitman is well known as the first woman of racing. She has achieved success in the world's toughest races and has landed two Grand Nationals. In 1984 she became the first woman to train a Cheltenham Gold Cup winner, which she repeated in 1991 with Garrison Savannah, who was ridden by her son, Mark. Jenny has also trained the winners of the Scottish, Irish and Welsh Grand Nationals. In 1998 she was awarded the OBE for her services to horseracing. She retired from training in 1999.

Jenny Pitman

On the Edge & The Vendetta

PAN BOOKS

On the Edge first published 2002 by Macmillan.
First published in paperback 2002 by Pan Books.
The Vendetta first published 2004 by Macmillan.
First published in paperback 2005 by Pan Books.

This omnibus first published 2007 by Pan Books
an imprint of Pan Macmillan Ltd
Pan Macmillan, 20 New Wharf Road, London N1 9RR
Basingstoke and Oxford
Associated companies throughout the world
www.panmacmillan.com

ISBN 978-0-330-45230-4

The Vendetta: The events and characters in this book are fictitious. Certain real locations and public figures are mentioned, but all other characters and events are totally imaginary.

1 3 5 7 9 8 6 4 2

A CIP catalogue record for this book is available from the British Library.

Typeset by SetSystems Ltd, Saffron Walden, Essex
Printed and bound in Great Britain by
Mackays of Chatham plc, Chatham, Kent

On the Edge

Acknowledgements

My husband David Stait,

Peter Burden,

Jonathan Lloyd at Curtis Brown Group Ltd,

David North, Maria Rejt and Peter Straus
at Pan Macmillan Ltd

and others for their support

1

The snow that had covered the Brecon Beacons for a week after Christmas was nearly all gone, leaving behind it no more than a faint tingle in the air.

Jan Hardy looked down on St Barnabas's church, where it lay in a fold of the bare hills surrounding it, circled by stout yews that gave added protection from the ravages of the Welsh weather. The squat building, with no spire or tower, had been constructed from stone and lime-washed more than seven hundred years before.

From the south, where the road snaked up from Painscastle over the brown bracken curves of the small mountains, the peaceful churchyard looked a suitable place for a man like John Hardy to be laid to rest.

'God knows, he needs a rest!' Jan murmured as she let the Land Rover coast down the hill towards the tiny hamlet where the church stood.

'Mumma?'

Jan wondered if the little girl in the child's seat behind her had recognized the bitter sorrow in her voice intuitively.

John's mother had told Jan not to bring the children to the funeral. They were too young to deal with it, she'd said. 'I'm not taking them for their sake,' Jan had replied. 'I'm taking them for mine. I need them beside me; I need to feel them there, to remind me that John's still alive in them.'

She tilted the driving mirror, caught a reflection of her own young, round face and glanced behind her, thrilled as ever at the big, beaming smile her daughter gave her. She smiled back as best she could. 'It's all right, Meg. There's nothing to worry about, I promise,' she said brightly, to back up the lie, while she wondered how much Megan would miss her father.

She looked at the old carrycot strapped into the passenger seat, where Matthew, just six months old, slept fitfully, as alert as his elder sister to the grief in their house, but unaware of its connection to the absence of the quiet, gruff-voiced person he sometimes used to see lying in bed. Jan couldn't tell yet how much he missed his father, or whether he missed him at all. For the last two months of his life, when he'd been at home, John had barely spoken – neither to the children, nor to Jan or his own mother.

Physically, he could have talked; he just didn't want to, as if he was ashamed of himself for letting them down – by promising to house them, feed them and keep them, then dying on them.

The hearse looked glossy and incongruous among the unruly gathering of farmers' vehicles, muddy Land Rovers and ancient saloons, all parked up the banks and in any slot off the narrow, sunken lane.

'They'll never all fit in that little church,' John's mother had said.

'It's too bad,' Jan had replied. 'There's nothing I can do about it; it's where John wanted to be buried.'

Olwen Hardy had crunched her old face into the frustrated expression she'd worn consistently since her only son had brought this independent-minded English girl back from the Three Counties Show at Malvern seven summers before.

It was hard to persuade sons to stay on the farms up here. They wanted so many things that farming would never buy them, especially not now, with twelve million ewes on the Welsh hills where once there had been four. It would take a full-scale disaster to restore the price of lambs, while the hill subsidies had quietly been whittled away.

Some farmers had tried to pretend it wasn't happening; they just put their hands over their ears when they found it cost more to produce a lamb for market than they'd get for it, especially with fuel prices soaring.

More and more of them were giving up. But John Hardy had always said he would stay. He loved the hills and the ewes. He understood the cattle, too, and had a real talent for growing corn in the few lower fields on the farm.

Even when he had faced a future that promised no more than permanent poverty, he'd shown no sign of wanting to give up. And by the time he'd reached thirty-five without marrying, Olwen had begun to hope that she would never lose him, that he'd be there to look after her, as he should, now her husband had passed on.

Jan thought about her mother-in-law's view of life as she reached the bottom of the valley and turned into the narrow cul-de-sac leading to the church. The only blessing she could see in the death of the man she loved was that she would no longer have to pretend that she liked his mother.

She found a space for the Land Rover just inside a farmyard beside the church. She stretched awkwardly over to the back seat and unstrapped Megan. She climbed down herself and went round to the passenger door to put Matthew on her shoulder while she waited for Megan to scramble out.

She was about to walk up to the church when another car pulled up and parked beneath a curtain of frosty lambs' tails on a hazel rooted in the stone wall. An old man and his wife, strangers to Jan, climbed out and looked at her with mournful sympathy. She wondered who they were. They would have needed only a tenuous connection with John Hardy to feel they had a right to attend his funeral. Jan had noticed since she'd arrived in the Welsh hills that funeral-going was a popular activity among the older people; there were so few other social activities to compete for their time, besides hunting in the winter, trotting races and village fêtes in the summer. She wondered if, like her mother-in-law, they would disapprove of her unfunereal outfit.

Jan had woken that morning and decided to wear her only good clothes – a well-cut green suit with a matching coat she'd found the year before at a shop in Hay. She had bought them with her own hard-earned cash from the hunters and point-to-pointers she kept in livery. She'd done it on the spur of the moment, which was totally out of character, because she'd had a dream that Rear Gunner, the best horse in her yard, had won the Foxhunters' at Cheltenham and she hadn't had anything to wear when she went up to receive her prize.

She remembered worrying how John would react, but he'd only admired her for her boldness and the way the suit flattered her rather less than willowy frame.

She didn't see why she should wear black to his funeral. It wouldn't mean that she missed him or respected his memory any more than she did already. Besides, he would have said it was a total waste of money to buy a new outfit just for a funeral.

The lane up to the church was lined with cars. The undertaker's men, in drab black suits, leaned against the crumbling wall of the churchyard and smoked surreptitiously, hiding their cigarettes in cupped hands.

Jan led Megan through the lychgate into the dark

circle of ancient yews. By the wall at the east end of the church, she saw a mound of earth that had been dug out to make room for her husband's coffin. Instinctively she clutched Matthew more tightly and walked a little faster to reach the church before Megan saw the hole and asked why it was there.

A dozen people were clustered outside the small porch and a few more were standing in the porch itself. They moved aside to let Jan pass. Some nodded and murmured words of condolence. One or two stretched out a hand to touch her arm or her back.

Inside, the tiny church was full and warm from a hundred well-wrapped bodies which had dispersed its normal, musty smell. The people outside were there because there was nowhere else for them to go. Jan thanked God – with whom she felt she was not on the best of terms at the moment – that, although there was a slight frost in the air, at least it wasn't raining for once.

There were two small windows in each side of the church, and a smaller one at the east end. These provided the only light apart from two naked bulbs dangling from the roof and the two candles which burned on the altar in the tiny, rounded apse. In front of the altar, John's coffin rested on two trestles. Ash with silver-plate handles, it had been paid for by some clause in an old, almost forgotten insurance policy John had kept up with the NFU. Two wreaths, *From your loving mother* and *With all our love for ever, Jan, Megan and Matthew*, rested on top of the box.

The front right-hand pew had been reserved for the family. John's mother was already there, in the seat beside the aisle. Jan thought Olwen should move along, to let her sit there, but knew she wouldn't and so carefully squeezed between Olwen's knees and the front of the pew.

It needed only one flash from the older woman's eyes to convey her views on Jan's green suit and Megan's floral, smocked dress. Jan settled Matthew more cosily against her shoulder and beckoned Megan to sit quietly on the pew beside her. But the little girl was craning her neck to look at the coffin.

Megan stretched up to put her mouth near her mother's ear. 'Dad's in there, isn't he?' she whispered.

Jan looked at her and nodded. 'Yes, he is.'

'Will he be all right?'

Jan took a deep breath and wished she knew the answer. 'I'm sure he will.'

Soon after Jan had sat down, the vicar emerged from the vestry at the back of the church. He walked slowly up the aisle to the altar, where he turned and stood, gazing around at the tightly packed congregation.

He was a tall man of sixty, lean as a vulture, with a haunted air, as if at some time in his life he'd been severely tested and found wanting. He looked at Jan with a thin smile of encouragement.

He's not a bad bloke, Jan thought. She had met him a few times before John had become ill, and then more often when he'd started to call regularly as John's illness progressed.

John had seemed pleased by these visits, although he had never actually said so. Jan thought he probably appreciated the vicar taking the trouble when he had such a large area to look after for the Church in Wales – eight churches, ten villages and a hundred farms.

After John had died, the vicar had come to see Jan. Without becoming all intense, he'd been kind and practical. 'Make sure you don't forget to look after yourself, now,' he'd said. 'To God you're just as important as the children, you know.'

As the vicar started intoning the funeral prayers, Jan looked at the coffin and imagined John lying inside it. But she saw him as he had been before the organophosphates in the sheep dip had, as she believed, introduced the cancer which had destroyed his inner organs.

She remembered him as she'd first seen him, showing a Welsh black cow and calf in the special section at the Three Counties Show. She didn't have a particular interest in cattle, but her eye had been caught by the small, pretty animals and then by the man leading them. John's good looks weren't obvious; they were somehow obscured by his own introverted nature. But there was an unmistakable strength and dependability about him. He looked as if he was always sure about what he was doing – in sharp contrast to her current boyfriend, who told everyone he knew everything, but was too lazy to do anything worthwhile.

The vicar was used to giving funeral addresses about people he'd never seen in any of his churches, but he had known John Hardy quite well, inasmuch as John allowed anyone to know him. Jan was pleased that the vicar talked about the special qualities in John which might not have been known to many of the congregation. She glanced at her mother-in-law, sitting rigidly a few feet to her left. The old woman was looking straight ahead, with her lower jaw firmly clamped to stop it quivering. Jan felt sorry for her despite the antagonism there had always been between them. Olwen had lost her husband, now her son, and she was probably well aware that her grandchildren might not grow up within easy reach.

Outside, in the crisp January morning, the crowd clustered around the grave. In the silence, two crows barked harshly from a tall ash outside the magic ring of yews, and a magpie cackled as it fled across the pasture beyond.

As the men from the undertaker's lowered the coffin on two broad straps, deep into the peaty earth, Jan gave in to tears. She clenched her eyes and clutched Megan's hand, while she squeezed Matthew to her chest. When she opened her eyes, she gazed through a hazy film at the vicar, who stood with his purple stole moving in the breeze, praying for the last time as the men in black suits solemnly withdrew their straps from the grave.

A small man in a long black coat held out a wooden box to Jan, with some earth to scatter on the coffin below. She didn't want to let go of Megan's hand. She shook her head and glanced down at the little girl, who stared curiously as a few other people dropped soil onto the box in which her father lay. Megan glanced up and gave her mother a little smile which seemed to say that she understood.

Jan walked out of a small stone building in the middle of Hay-on-Wye and closed the dark green door behind her. She shut her eyes, took a long, deep breath and exhaled with relief.

She glanced up and down the narrow, sloping street to see if anyone was looking at her, although she didn't really care. The solicitor she had seen was new to Humphries & Co; the partner John always dealt with had retired earlier that year. This young man knew nothing about the history of the Hardys; he had no idea of the implications of the will John had left. One of the older partners, he told Jan, had warned him not to ask Olwen in as well, but it all seemed straightforward enough to him.

The late John Hardy had left everything – Stonewall Farm, the house, the bungalow, the buildings, the stock, the tackle, and twenty thousand pounds, which were the proceeds of a life policy he had never been able to increase – to his wife, Janine Susan Hardy, with the proviso that his mother should occupy the bungalow, where she currently lived, free of rent until her death.

When he was alive, John had never told them what he planned to do and Jan hadn't dreamed of asking – not because she was frightened to, but because she knew he wouldn't have told her. She had always assumed, though, that he would leave his mother with a significant degree of control over Stonewall Farm and she was sure that Olwen herself had been certain of it.

Jan had not told Olwen where she was going that morning; the solicitor hadn't asked her to, and she'd needed somewhere to leave the children.

Now she wanted someone to talk to, someone to share her relief, who would understand that she was not celebrating her acquisition of the farm, but the freedom to do what she wanted, to take the children and bring them up where and how she chose.

But Jan had never had the chance to make friends, either in the narrow, introspective valley where they lived, or here in the town, where she and John came only once or twice a month. She could think of only one person who might be glad to see her. Harold Powell, she was sure, would welcome any excuse to talk about his horses.

She walked down the hill towards the big stone clock tower which stood in the centre of the town and stopped when she reached the door of a small office with a plain, gilt sign on the window – *Harris & Powell. Auctioneers, Valuers and Estate Agents*.

The woman behind the reception desk looked up.

She evidently recognized Jan. With a barely perceptible pursing of the lips, she stood up briskly. 'I'll tell Mr Powell you're here.'

Jan felt a sudden panic. Although she had trained point-to-pointers for Harold Powell for four years now, she had never been to his office. She shouldn't have come here. Not now, not just after John had died.

But Harold, forty-eight and six feet tall, came out of his office at the back, straightening a tie decorated with flying pheasants. 'Hello, Jan,' he said, an eyebrow raised in a faint question mark.

'Hello, Harold,' Jan said quickly, 'I was just passing, but I expect you're busy; I must get back home anyway. I've still got one of the horses to do.' She turned and started to open the door.

'Hang on, Jan,' Harold laughed. He'd had plenty of experience with coy women. 'I'm sure you've got time for a quick drink up at the Bull Ring.' He stepped quickly round the reception desk. 'You know – to cheer you up after everything?' His voice was deep, with a rattle of whisky in it. He was beside her now, smelling of tweed steeped in pipe smoke, and fresh shaving soap. His dark hair was thick and gleaming and he wasn't bad looking, even close to. His hand was on the small of her back. 'I never got the chance to talk to you at the funeral – there were that many people there.'

Harold spoke with a Herefordshire accent, unlike the people in her valley. He was the third son of a big farmer on the rich broad plain of the Wye valley east of Hay. She wanted to run back to her Land Rover, but that would have looked absurd and Harold confidently opened the door and ushered her back up the narrow street to a hotel on one side of a small square.

Half a dozen men, obviously with time on their hands, were already drinking in a gloomy bar. They nodded respectfully at Harold in his well-cut jacket and gleaming nut-brown shoes; they looked speculatively at Jan.

'Do you know Mrs Hardy?' Harold asked the oldest of them.

The man nodded. 'I was sorry to hear about your bereavement,' he said neutrally.

'Life must go on, eh, Jan? With all those horses to get ready for point-to-points. Jan's got four of mine,' he told the room in general. 'All good 'uns, too, aren't they, Jan?'

'They could win a few races,' Jan agreed.

Harold ordered drinks. 'Make that a large one,' he said to the woman behind the bar when Jan asked for a gin and tonic. He carried her glass and his tankard of beer to a table in the corner, between a lively log fire and the window. They could talk here without being too easily overheard.

'Thanks,' Jan said and took a sip, glad of the drink, if she was truthful, after the drama of the morning.

'What brings you into town, then?'

Jan thought he had probably guessed and that it would be easier to talk about it than to let him sit there speculating for as long as it took to finish her drink. 'I had to come and see the solicitor, to sort things out.'

'John had made a will, all right, had he?'

'Oh yes.'

'And everything's OK?' Harold prodded.

Jan looked back at him steadily, wondering why he should be particularly interested in her affairs, beyond professional curiosity, though that was more than enough of a reason round here. 'Yes. Fine, thanks.' She took a deeper breath. 'I'll be putting the farm on the market.'

He stared at her. 'What? Did he leave it all to you?'

Jan nodded. 'Yes, he did.'

'Didn't he make provision for his mother?' Harold sounded quite shocked.

'Yes, of course. She's to live in the bungalow, rent-free until she dies, but that's all right; it's well away from the farm.'

'Why do you want to sell up?'

Jan shrugged. 'What's the point of staying? I don't come from round here and they never let me forget it. And John had to work his guts out to barely make a living. I don't know how some of these people stick it.'

'But where will you go?'

'I'm not sure – nearer my mum and dad, maybe.'

'That's over Gloucestershire way, isn't it?'

Jan nodded. 'Dad's still got a bit of ground up on the hill.'

'What would you do there?'

'I'll get my own yard,' she said simply.

'You won't buy much of a place in Gloucestershire with what you get for Stonewall.'

'I don't need much of place – just stables and twenty or thirty acres would do me.'

Harold was looking at her with consternation. 'Look, Jan, you shouldn't do this without thinking about it a bit first, you know. You're probably just reacting to what's happened now, but I think you should stop around here. There's a lot of people who would be sorry to see you go.'

'Who?' Jan couldn't resist asking.

'Me, for one. You've done really well with those horses of mine.'

'I can still train them.'

'I don't want my horses in Gloucestershire. And as far as Stonewall's concerned, if you didn't want to farm it all yourself, I'm sure I'll find someone to rent the ground off you; that'd bring in a bit.'

'I just don't want to live in that valley any more; or that house.' She stopped for a moment and thought of all the lonely nights filled with bad dreams since her husband had died. 'It was all right when John was alive and well, but I can't live there on my own.'

Harold's face showed he was taking a calculated gamble. 'I doubt a woman like you'll be on your own for long.'

Jan stared back at him, deliberately looking more shocked than she felt. 'Harold, John's only been dead a fortnight! Have some respect.'

'I'm sorry, but I was only telling the truth. You're a young, healthy woman – ' he dropped his chin and looked up at her from below thick black brows ' – and very attractive.'

Looking at his big, shifty eyes, Jan wanted to laugh. Instead, she picked up her glass and tipped the rest of the drink down her throat. She stood up a little unsteadily. 'Thank you for the drink, Harold. I've really got to go now.'

Harold got up too. 'I'm sorry, Jan. I didn't mean to upset you.'

'You didn't.' She tried to smile. 'I've just got to go.'

She turned before he could try to talk her out of it, while the other men watched in silence as she walked out.

Jan felt as if she were floating over the brown hills as she drove back to Stonewall under a clear blue sky. It wasn't the grief still underlying every thought that made her feel detached, or even the gin: it was the prospect of freedom, triggered by her effectively public announcement that she would be selling the farm.

She wished now that she hadn't told anyone yet. Harold Powell's appalled reaction hadn't surprised her, but she knew it would be repeated across the local farming community, spiced with the view that they might have known someone like her from away would betray an old family by selling the farm.

I don't give a monkey's, she thought. They could

whinge and bicker as much as they liked; the sooner she was gone the better. She would offer to take Olwen with her and if her mother-in-law declined the offer – which Jan was sure she would – that was just too bloody bad!

She knew that she would have to tell Olwen right away. A rumour starting from the bar in the Bull Ring Hotel might easily take wings and reach her own valley before she did. And Olwen would have accumulated a strong advantage if she knew before Jan admitted it.

Jan went straight to the bungalow, where she had left Megan and Matthew.

Olwen opened the door to her dressed in a pinafore that looked as if it had been made from a pair of pre-war chintz curtains. With her snow-white, thick curly hair and steel-rimmed glasses, she looked deceptively like everyone's idea of a cartoon granny. She led Jan into a cramped and neatly cluttered sitting room. Matty was sound asleep in his carrycot. Megan leaped up from an ancient, dog-eared jigsaw on the parquet floor. The old woman eyed Jan suspiciously. 'Ain't you got more horses to do yet?'

'Yes,' Jan nodded. 'I'm sorry, I got caught up in town. It took longer than I thought.'

'What was you doing?' the old woman asked brazenly.

'Seeing Humphries's about John's will.'

Olwen stiffened visibly; she blinked rapidly a few times. 'Why . . . why did you go on your own?'

'Because they asked me to.'

'But I should have been with you . . . at the reading of my own son's will.'

'They said it would be better if I told you about it.' *The bloody cowards,* she thought to herself. She went on quickly. 'John wanted you to live here in this cottage for the rest of your life.'

The implication of what Jan was saying wasn't lost on Olwen. She looked behind her, groping for the high, moquette armchair she normally occupied, and lowered herself into it with quivering arms. She looked at the floor for a few moments while the idea sank in. When she looked up, Jan could see she was already defeated. 'He didn't leave me this bungalow, then?' Olwen said.

Jan couldn't bring herself to utter a straight 'No'.

'He said you've the right to live in it for the rest of your life.'

Olwen sighed with a noisy breath and looked down at her bony hands. She suddenly seemed a lot older than sixty-nine.

Jan went on, 'I'll be selling the rest of the farm – the house, the buildings and the land. But you'll still have your garden.'

There was a flicker of defiance in the silver blue eyes that glanced up. 'I'll be here a long time, I promise you that.'

'I hope so,' Jan said, though she knew she was fooling no one. 'Would you mind if I left the kids here until three? I've still got one of the horses to do.'

Olwen grunted. 'Yes, you carry on. What's a grandma for if she can't look after her son's children?'

Jan drove another four hundred yards up the track beside the bungalow until she reached the big stone courtyard of buildings that was Stonewall Farm. On one side of the yard was a run of five stables, with another five timber boxes backing onto it. Five heads were gazing at her by the time she had parked the Land Rover outside the front door and climbed out. Three dogs, a lurcher, a Border terrier and the farm sheepdog, emerged from the hay store and rushed over to greet their mistress.

For a few moments Jan stroked the old sheepdog and listened to a silence broken by a lone buzzard, keening as it circled high above to survey the land for unwary rabbits. Soon, she reflected, the air would be filled with the sound of lambs bleating and their mothers' answering grunts. And she realized she owed it to John to stay here at least until the lambing was done.

She glanced around. Philip and Annabel, who helped her in the yard, had both gone home, but Jan could see that they had done all that she had asked and left the yard as spotless as the old cobbles allowed – Annabel's doing, she guessed.

'Hello, boys,' she murmured to the horses as she walked over to the big grey head stretched over the first stable door. The horse gave a faint whinny and kicked the bottom of the door. 'Don't get so excited, Mister. I'm not going to feed you now, am I? You've got to do some work first. I'm sorry,' she added when the horse's head retreated, as if he'd understood and didn't like what he'd heard.

Jan took a head-collar off a hook beside the door and let herself in. The eight-year-old gelding had arrived from Ireland the previous spring, frightened and confused. He stood at nearly seventeen hands and Jan had to stretch her legs to the tips of her toes to fix his collar. She led him out and across the yard to the tack room, where she tied him with a piece of binder twine to an iron ring in the wall.

As always, she talked quietly to the horse all the time she was dealing with him. It was natural to her and she knew how much it reassured him. She fetched his bridle and an exercise saddle from the tack room and put them on. She left the girth loose, so he'd get used to having it there for a few minutes while she strode briskly up the steps and let herself into the house. Without a glance at the unwashed plates in the kitchen sink, she ran up to the bedroom and swapped her skirt and top for a pair of stretch jeans and a thick, scarlet fleece. On the way back down, she grabbed her well-worn chaps from a peg on the back of the kitchen door and walked out of the house still buckling them.

Within a few minutes, she had tightened the gelding's girth and scrambled onto his high back with the help of three well-worn stone steps. She headed up the bank behind the house, along a narrow cart track that led to the common grazing land on the top of the hill. Fred, her brindled lurcher, loped along beside her, weaving in and out of the scrubby thorns and gorse bushes like a snake.

With each long stride the horse took, the tensions of the day – the uncertainty, at first, of what the solicitor was saying, the obscure attentions of Harold Powell – released their grip on her shoulders. With her crop, she hooked open the gate at the top of the track, which let them out onto the open spaces where broad swathes of turf permanently cropped by a millennium of grazing sheep swept up between a thick growth of bilberry, bracken and heather.

She turned left and gee'd the big horse into a steady trot along a faintly rutted green track that followed the contour of the hill. The sun had appeared, gleaming through pink and silver streaks above the softly wrinkled face of the Black Mountains' grey-green bluff. She could feel the chilly wind rippling through the short blonde hair below her helmet, as if cleansing her of any wrong or selfish thoughts she might have had that day.

She would miss John, of course; she would miss him unbelievably. He had been completely dependable. Although, when fit, he'd been as strong as any man in the valley, he had been gentle and thoughtful and never pretended to know more than he did. John Hardy was as good a man as Jan had ever met and, while she might once have thought goodness in a man a guarantee of tedious wedlock, she'd never been bored by him. There had been nothing wrong in bed, either. All her memories of their love-making were happy – though there hadn't been much of that in the last few months.

But in his crass, man's way, Harold Powell hadn't got it so wrong. Life would go on for her. Although it seemed absurd at the moment, she didn't doubt that she would marry again and be able to live without being tormented every few minutes by a massive wrenching sensation in her chest.

Besides, John had left her two beautiful and infinitely precious children. From now on, their needs would come before any of her own. She owed that much, at least, to John's memory.

And that was why she was leaving Stonewall. Not simply because she felt alien and uncomfortable in the valley, but because, if she was going to see her children fed, clothed and nurtured in the way she wanted, she would have to make more than just a decent living. And she was never going to do that up here in the Brecon hills, where even the best farmers had drawn their belts in so tightly their stomachs were screaming.

But all Jan knew about was horses. They were all she had learned about as a child around her parents' small rented farm. She also knew that, while the

Cotswolds didn't offer the best soil in the land for growing corn, the cosy, picturesque hills could produce a healthy crop of rich, potential horse owners.

The Brecon men also liked their point-to-pointing, along with their flappers and trotters, but few of them had much money to spare on good thoroughbred stock or training fees.

Jan was sure that John would have approved of her decision to move. That was why he hadn't tied her to the farm by leaving it to his mother. He had never said a word against Olwen in Jan's hearing, but she had no doubt that he was well aware of the relentless barrage of verbal and mental abuse the old woman had dealt out to her over the past seven years.

Jan wheeled the big grey gelding to the right and turned him up a long, turf-clad slope. She sat forward out of the saddle and squeezed his sides with her calves. Within a few strides he was reaching out into a strong canter and Jan couldn't help smiling. Mister Mack was the sweetest-paced horse she'd ever ridden; when he'd arrived at her yard, no one, but no one, had been able to get on his back. It was bringing him round last summer, from rogue to gentleman, that had shown her that maybe she knew more than most about caring for animals who had been emotionally scarred at some point in their lives.

As the ground levelled at the top of the ridge and she asked him for more, the horse stretched his legs until she felt like a flyer in one of the gliders that often came soaring over the hills from Shropshire. As she reached the end of the ridge, before it dropped down on the dark, north side, she came up fast on a cluster of gorse bushes – serious obstacles, four feet high. She kept the horse straight at the first, shortened her rein and felt him find a stride. He stood way back and flew it with a foot to spare. Jan shrieked and whooped, intoxicated for a moment. It had been the first time the horse had really seen his own stride and it was by far the best jump he had ever made.

As she pulled him up to a trot, she steered him back the way they had come. She leaned forward to pat the horse vigorously on the side of his neck. 'Oh, well done, boy! If you keep jumping like that, you're really going to win a few races, aren't you.' Not for the first time, Jan wished she hadn't had to sell him to Harold Powell. Of the eight horses in her yard, this was the one she would have liked most to keep in her own name.

2

A week after John Hardy's funeral, Jan could still hardly sleep. The day after hearing his will, she tossed and turned and woke long before the first light glowed from the east, chilled by the perspiration on her pyjamas.

There was no shower in the old farmhouse and she had to wash herself in the one unheated bathroom. To keep warm, she towelled herself down vigorously and dressed as fast as she could.

In the dark corridor she listened, but heard no sounds from her children. Downstairs in the kitchen she put a kettle on the hob and pulled up a chair to sit as close as she could to the oil-fired Rayburn – the one improvement she had managed to make to the house and the only warm spot in it for six months of the year.

She'd lain awake half the night, thinking about what she had told Harold Powell, and in the morning she was sure she was right. Whatever the farm fetched, she had to sell; this house and its bleak, ungenerous land would have to go.

She must rear her children, made even more precious now by their father's death, and she didn't want to spend the rest of her life battling against wind, rain and thin soil before she could even think about making a profit. She had lived on a farm all her life and she was well aware that she had neither the knowledge nor the commitment to earn a good living from farming, wherever she was. As far as she could see, horses in Gloucestershire were the only option. It was a daunting prospect for a thirty-year-old, widowed mother of two, but she'd never been afraid of a challenge.

Her mother had begged her to be practical when Jan had first told her she was marrying a farmer from the Welsh hills. She understood, of course, when Jan insisted that, however tough it was going to be, she and John Hardy loved each other. They were both fit and resourceful and, one way or another, they'd make a living and raise children on his unproductive two hundred acres.

It had been tough all right, but for the first few years Jan had thrived, despite the lack of comfort or encouragement from John's mother, and had thrown herself into being a farmer's wife. When she had been there a year, though, and no child had yet appeared, she'd decided to make her own contribution by doing the one thing for which she knew she had some talent.

She told everyone she met that she was going to

make use of her experience by taking in hunter liveries and training racehorses to run in point-to-points. People had come to talk to her and look at the yard she had made from John's old stone barns and, eventually, some had sent her horses.

In her first year she'd had three wins from six horses and her name had echoed over the loudspeakers at the local courses. Over the next five years there had been steady success – eight or nine wins for each of the last couple of seasons. It didn't sound a lot compared to the big-time trainers under Jockey Club rules, but it was enough to make Jan the top point-to-point trainer in her area.

But, for all the work it took, and the difficulties of dealing with one, then two, tiny children, the stables had never brought in enough money to make up for the falling price of lambs and life in the hills had become seriously hard, until John had found himself working every hour of daylight and beyond to save the cost of an extra hand.

Maybe he'd been tired or careless with the dipping, but somehow, she believed, the regular contact with organo-phosphates had got to him and he hadn't quite reached his forty-second birthday when the cancer, undetected by their rural doctor, had finally claimed him. But, through it all, he had always praised Jan for her determination to add to their dwindling income. Now, though, she would have to more than double what she made from it – which gave her another good reason for moving on.

Revived by tea after her long night, Jan pulled herself together and went up to deal with her quietly burbling baby son.

Matthew was one of those children who had been granted the priceless gift of permanent cheerfulness. Jan didn't know how he'd done it. While he was still in her womb, until six or seven weeks before he saw the light of day, he'd regularly been galloped over the hill tops, leaping banks and gorse bushes on the way. But this seemed to have caused no pre-natal trauma and from the day he was born he had been an easy and contented baby. It was almost as if he had been determined to prove his grandmother wrong with his tireless good humour.

Jan picked him up and nuzzled him and his baby smells, kissing his chubby cheeks. The pleasure of being with him was like an elixir after her miserable night.

Megan seemed happier and bounced up and down on her bed to greet her mother. Downstairs, giving them breakfast in the now fuggy warmth of the kitchen with Terry Wogan on the radio, Jan felt much better. And at eight o'clock, as the first rays of a frosty sun beamed through the high kitchen window, Annabel came in.

Jan looked up at her and smiled. She couldn't help it. Annabel, with fine, pale chestnut hair that fell to her shoulders, was a willowy and quietly beautiful twenty-three-year-old, one of those serene people who never seemed upset or angered by anyone or anything.

She had turned up at Stonewall out of the blue at the start of the last season and asked if she could help Jan out.

She had worked without a single day off until the last race in June, when she'd left as abruptly as she had come. Jan guessed that was the last she would see of her, but at the end of August, when the horses started to return from their summer holidays, Annabel had turned up at the house and asked if she could come back. By that time John was so weak he could barely work, and Jan hadn't disguised her gratitude, for, though she had two other part-time lads, Annabel was in a class of her own.

Jan had been really glad to see Annabel anyway; she loved having her around the yard because she was always good company and in some ways, Jan realized, her calmness was a perfect foil to her own excitable vitality.

Their backgrounds, both rural, were otherwise very different.

According to Annabel, her father, Henry Halstead, an ex-cavalry officer, had come out of the army with nothing but his pension, only to find that he had inherited a three-thousand-acre estate from his aunt. Now he lived as far as he could in the way he imagined his grandfather might have done, just over the border in Herefordshire in a rambling, early Georgian mansion, which he never left unless he had to.

Annabel was his only daughter; she had one brother, Charles, who was five years older. She'd told

Jan that Charles didn't get on with his father and had gone to live in the States as soon as he'd left university. She had said no more about it, but Jan had the impression that there was an uneasy, love–hate relationship between Annabel and her father and it was mainly for her mother's sake that she was still living at home.

She had been sent away to boarding school until she was seventeen, then after a brief period at college in London she'd gone on to Bristol University, which she'd left during her first year.

Annabel had revealed this edited account of her life to Jan sparingly when she'd first come to work for her. She'd told her how she hated London and couldn't bear the hustling and the hordes of people who all seemed so superficial. Reading between the lines, Jan gathered that something had happened there which had left her with unhappy memories and that things had also gone wrong at university. But, despite Jan's inquisitiveness, Annabel wouldn't tell her any more.

'Do you want some breakfast?' Jan asked brightly as she always did, knowing what the answer would be.

'No thanks; just a little water and lemon.'

'For God's sake, girl!' Jan chided her, as she always did. 'There's no flesh on you. Do you want to fade away completely?'

'I ate before I left the house,' Annabel said.

Jan never knew if she was telling the truth when she said this, so shrugged. 'Help yourself,' she said.

Annabel took a lemon from the basket of fruit that Jan kept for her and cut a slice. She helped herself to a mug hanging from the large Welsh dresser, put the lemon in and poured boiling water over it. She sat down and smiled at Matthew, who was propped up in a wooden high chair being fed by Jan.

'Hello, Matty,' she cooed, and the boy gurgled back with a fat, dribbly bubble.

'Hello, Annabel,' Megan squeaked, anxious for her share of Annabel's attention.

Seeing the children with Annabel, Jan said, 'If we go from here, they'll miss you,' she said.

Annabel glanced at her, with a hint of worry in her soft grey eyes. 'Go? Why should you go?'

'You know I went to see the solicitor yesterday?'

Annabel nodded and, fearing the worst, her eyes clouded more.

Jan saw. 'No, it's not bad news. John left everything to me, except his mum's to live in the bungalow as long as she likes. So I'm going to sell this place.' She gave the house around her an unaffectionate nod.

'Where will you move to?'

'Back where I came from. I'm going to see if I can buy a small place in Gloucestershire – a yard and a bit of decent grazing.'

Annabel's face fell. 'Oh, Jan! I'll miss you – and these two.'

'Will you, really? Miss me with all my shouting and swearing and riding out every day, even when it's blizzarding?'

'Specially that,' Annabel nodded with a grin.

'Then you'd better come with us.'

Annabel gave her a look so enigmatic that Jan didn't have any idea what was going through her mind. 'I'll think about it,' she said.

Later Jan took Matthew and Megan to the bungalow for the morning, as she always did when there were horses to do. Her mother-in-law was as tight-lipped as always, but Jan refused to be cowed by her accusing eye.

'What are you going to do when you haven't got me to look after these children?' Olwen asked. 'You can't just leave them with anyone while you go gallivantin' around the races.'

'I've thought of that. I'll get my mum and dad in,' Jan retorted and immediately regretted the provocation. To be fair to Olwen, she thought, she'd looked after the kids a hell of a lot since they'd been born. But, then again, Jan knew she adored having them. 'No, I'm joking,' she said quickly. 'If I do move, I'll make sure I've got a good girl to come in every day.'

But as she drove back up the track to the farm, she found herself wondering if she really was right to be selling up so soon after she'd been widowed, and leaving her mother-in-law behind. However annoying and interfering Olwen Hardy was, she was always there to have the children, and in Jan's life just then, that was a vital support.

Annabel was already tacking up the first three horses to go out, and Philip, as lackadaisical as Annabel was reliable, had shot up the track behind Jan in the battered pick-up his father had given him for his eighteenth birthday.

Philip, stringy, shaggy-haired and already minus his right incisor, was the third son of a farmer from further up the valley. He had no intention of following his father into farming, even if the option had been there, but he liked his country sports too much to leave. While working for Jan didn't bring in a lot of money, it gave him the chance to kid himself and his friends that he was going to be a jockey. Jan knew he never would be, but she gave him the odd ride to satisfy his urges. Once, by default, in a members' race, he had won, and now thought of himself in the same league as the Herefordshire farmer's son who had just become the champion National Hunt jockey.

Out of respect for John's memory, Jan had cancelled her entries in the last three accessible point-to-point meetings. Harold Powell, the owner most affected, had said he quite understood, but now she intended to start again on the following Saturday; she was sure John would have approved.

Soon Jan, Annabel and Philip were up on the horses they were exercising first, two of whom were due to run in four days' time. Five minutes later they were jogging out onto the firmly matted turf of the hill behind the farm.

Jan watched Annabel on Mister Mack, and prayed that if she and the children moved Annabel would choose to come with them. She didn't underrate the value of a familiar trusted face in new surroundings. Besides, where else would she find someone with hands so gentle and yet so confident, for whom almost any horse would behave?

She sent Philip on ahead for a while and walked beside Annabel. 'Would you like to ride Mister Mack when he races?'

Annabel turned to her and a broad smile spread across her face. 'You know perfectly well I wouldn't.'

'Yes, I suppose I do, but I still wonder why not. You're easily good enough.'

'No I'm not. I've no killer instinct. Nothing would induce me to hit a horse with a stick; I'd feel guilty trying to make it give more than it chose. I hate telling anyone what to do.'

Jan chuckled. 'What are you going to do when you get a man, then? You can't just let them do whatever they want – they'll walk all over you.'

After a moment's silence, Annabel said, 'Not all of them, surely?' After another pause, she asked, 'Did you have a lot of boyfriends before you married John?'

'A few.' Jan laughed again and thought of the groping boys at Pony Club camps and the inept, hasty love-making of one of the lads in the Cotswold racing yard where she'd worked between leaving school and meeting John. 'I found most of them too childish; I think that's why I went for John. He was totally solid. Anyway, I was too keen on the horses to take much notice before that.'

'Don't you miss riding races yourself now?'

'A little. No – a lot. I can honestly say the biggest thrill of my life so far was winning my first point-to-point at the Heythrop when I was seventeen. But now sending out winners I've trained comes close. It's certainly more nerve-racking.'

'Which horse did you ride for your first win?'

Jan smiled at the memory. 'God, he was a lovely horse – at least I thought so at the time. I don't think he ever won another race after that though. He was called River Rocket – a big grey, a bit like Mister Mack.' She nodded at Annabel's mount. 'He belonged to my dad's landlord, Colonel Gilbert. His daughter was supposed to ride him, but she'd fallen off the week before and cracked her elbow or something. She was really pissed off when I won on him!' Jan laughed. 'Of course, she rode him after that, which is why he probably never won again.'

'Is that the Gilberts of Riscombe Manor?'

'You would know them,' Jan snorted. 'All part of the old boys' Mafia, I suppose.'

'I only knew their son, George. He used to be a friend of my brother, Charley.'

Jan sensed that Annabel knew George Gilbert quite well, and stopped herself from saying what an arrogant, spoiled little brat he'd been when she'd known him. 'Winning on Rocket was the best, but now I'm a mother riding myself wouldn't really be an option, would it? Anyway, I've got a feeling that training the winner of a good hunter chase on a real race course would give me just as much of a buzz, maybe more.'

'They still go well for you, though, don't they?'

'They seem to. That's why I ride 'em as much as I can.' She decided to confide in Annabel a piece of news she had been keeping to herself up until now. 'I'm thinking of entering Rear Gunner in a hunter chase at Ludlow at the beginning of March.'

Annabel turned to her with sparkling eyes. 'Are you? How brilliant – your first hunter chase! You must let me look after him there.'

'I'm glad you're so excited about it,' Jan said. 'Of course you can take him.'

'I'd love that.' Then Annabel's tone changed. 'I'm really sorry you're going to move, though. I can't tell you how much it's helped to keep me sane, coming over here every day.'

'I always thought working with me drove people insane,' Jan teased. 'And we won't be going just yet. I've decided not to be too hasty. We'll get near the end of this pointing season before I ask Harold to sell the place for me. It'll be a good four months before we finally move – plenty of time for you to think about coming with us!'

By the middle of February the point-to-point season was well under way and Jan was taking horses to at least one meeting every week. In order to qualify them to run, she'd hunted them all regularly with her local foxhounds, except Mister Mack who wasn't ready, and she was pleased to see how well they'd come through their winter training.

Annabel and Philip, despite his shortcomings, were good exercise riders, but Jan liked to do most of the fast work herself. She had no formal gallops on the farm, but was blessed with totally free access to the open hill tops, where the going on the sheep-grazed turf on its thin bed of peaty soil was nearly always good. It made her laugh to think how much it would have cost to make and keep a set of gallops like that down at one of the big racing centres. As it was, there were so many tracks over the hills they could vary the horses' work all the time, which stopped them from becoming bored.

She and her 'lads' took the horses out for regular road work, too, to keep their legs hard, and her little string was a familiar sight in the valley, when people passing would stop to ask which horse was which and how they were getting on, and, most importantly, when were they going to win.

At times like this Jan felt perhaps she was being unfair to the locals, until she reminded herself that the previous season, when things were beginning to go well, she'd had the chastening experience of hearing two people from her valley discussing her shortcomings as a trainer, when they didn't know she was on the other side of a display shelf in the supermarket in Kington.

As far as owners were concerned, point-to-pointing was only about sport, fun and honour. The prize money was negligible. As a result, the business was run on a shoestring, and relied heavily on the good will and enthusiasm of most of the people involved. Jan found it frustrating sometimes that she couldn't run her yard on a strictly business footing, and yet the need to keep everyone on her side had been a useful training in human management.

But one of the toughest aspects of trying to win point-to-points was finding the right jockey. Billy Hanks came from Riscombe, the village where Jan had lived until she was married. Six years younger than Jan, his elder sister had been her closest friend, and Billy had grown up in awe of the bouncy, green-eyed laughing blonde who could make any pony jump anything. Like the girls, he was horse mad and showed an exceptional natural talent from an early age. By the time he was eighteen he was one of the top dozen point-to-point riders in the Midlands. But he never forgot his earliest inspiration and now he would drive a hundred miles to ride for Jan if she asked him.

By the time March arrived, ushered into the Welsh hills with more than the usual amount of rain and bluster from the west, Jan had sent out nine runners, scored four wins, two seconds and a third, all ridden by Billy. *Horse & Hound* had already noted her success and a photograph of her had appeared in the *Brecon & Radnor Express*. But, as she'd told Annabel, running Rear Gunner in a hunter chase was going to be a completely new experience for her.

3

On the morning of 3 March, Jan woke at six-thirty. She'd only slept for an hour or two: the excitement of sending a horse to race on a real National Hunt track had kept her awake most of the night. But she sat up with the energizing tingle she always felt at the start of a race day.

She threw off the covers and swung her legs over the side of the bed. The air in her room was freezing and there was no sign of daylight through the curtains. She shivered, told herself to forget the discomfort and switched on her bedside light to dress.

Downstairs in the kitchen, she was making some toast and a mug of coffee to calm her nerves when Annabel arrived.

'Hi, Jan,' she said with her usual brightness. 'How are you feeling?'

'Bloody terrified, if you want to know the truth.' Jan wouldn't have admitted it to anyone else. 'Here, have some coffee.'

Annabel shook her head, and propped her slender

backside on the corner of the table. 'Did you sleep all right?' she asked.

Jan was trying to eat her toast and Marmite. 'I hardly slept a wink, and when I did, I kept dreaming that when I unloaded Gunner at the race course he was covered in mud and all the other trainers were laughing at me. Then, when he started to race, he was either falling over, or passing the post with no one else in sight – until I saw that was because he was so far behind the others.' She laughed. 'We've got to turn that horse out looking a million dollars. Everyone will be wanting to see what he looks like and what sort of condition he's in after all the point-to-points he's won. And they'll be looking at us – new kids on the block and all that.'

'I can't wait! What does Billy think?'

'He phoned last night to ask how the horse was,' Jan said. 'I told him he looks ready to win the National and he definitely wouldn't be wasting his time.'

'How does *he* feel about Gunner's chances?'

'He's been doing the job too long to say, but I should think he's pretty confident. He had that lovely win on him ten days ago at Garnons, when he beat two of today's field by six or seven lengths. Right,' she said, getting up to swill her crockery, 'we'd better get on with it.'

'Sure,' Annabel agreed. 'What are we doing first?'

'Barneby Boy wants some fast work. He'll be running next week. And I'd like to give Gunner a quick canter before he goes racing, as he can be a bit thick in his wind. We'll take out three more when Phil arrives, probably about half-eight, knowing him.'

'What time do you want to load Gunner?'

'His race is at two-forty so I want to get there by eleven-thirty to leave plenty of time to walk the course. It'll take us an hour to drive there, so we have to leave at ten to be on the safe side.'

Annabel nodded. 'We should be able to get everything done by then.'

'I've just got to go and get the kids dressed,' Jan said. 'Do you think you could take them down to Olwen's then? She's giving them breakfast and having them for the rest of the day.'

When Annabel got back from the bungalow, she and Jan walked down to the tack room and Jan pulled out her keys to undo the padlock which secured it. Even in a remote place like Stonewall, she thought horse tack was a popular target for opportunist thieves, despite John's old sheepdog, Fly, still standing guard, with Fred and Tigger the terriers, barking like mad every time anyone they didn't recognize walked into the yard.

They sorted out what they were going to need for exercise and what they would be taking to the race course. 'I want his bridle gleaming', Jan said, 'and his leather head-collar. I'll show you how to rub them down with glycerine when we get there, to make them really shine.' Jan knew that there would be people at Ludlow today who would notice her for the first time. She didn't intend this to be her last visit to a real race course with a hunter chaser and she was going to start as she meant to carry on.

She and Annabel took the exercise tack out into the yard. Barneby Boy was in the back row of stables and as Annabel disappeared round the end of the stone block Jan let herself into Rear Gunner's box and talked to him quietly for a few minutes to calm him.

Standing at 16.3 hands high, with a big handsome head and long ears, Rear Gunner had developed into a classic steeplechaser, bred by a local farmer using a popular stallion from over the border in Herefordshire. Harold Powell had bought the gelding from the farmer as an unbroken four-year-old and had sent him to Jan soon after she'd started up in business. She'd slowly brought the horse on through his sixth and seventh years without asking too much of him, watching him win his member's, maiden and intermediate races with ease, until he'd won his first open at the end of the last season. He'd won three more from four starts this season and was heading for a good placing in the regional championships.

Jan was very proud of what she'd done with him and though she didn't have the same affection for him as she had for Mister Mack, he was undoubtedly the most important horse in her yard. Having seen the overnight declarations, she didn't think he would win today. There were at least three better horses running, but there were quite a few worse ones, too, and if he showed some form it could be a boost to her new start in Gloucestershire.

After she had tacked him up and led him out of his box, she brought him over to her mounting block to help get her short legs over his high back. The tension of the day ahead had turned her knees to rubber, but she managed to heave herself up onto the saddle and walked him down the yard to join Annabel.

The horse Annabel was riding, Barneby Boy, was a half-brother to Rear Gunner, but a year younger and a slow developer. The same farmer had bred him, but he'd come to see Jan and told her he was sick of hearing how Harold Powell was boasting what a good deal he'd done with Rear Gunner and this time he'd decided to hang onto the horse, if she thought he was worth training. Barney, as they called him, didn't have the eye-catching good looks of his half-brother, but he had much the same temperament and a good turn of speed. He'd won a maiden race, which was for horses who had never won, and Jan had him entered in a restricted race the following week, with a pretty good chance, she thought.

But today she only had eyes and ears for Gunner.

She and Annabel walked their horses side by side up the green lane beside the farm and out onto the open hill. It hadn't rained since the previous evening, but the gusting westerly hit them hard from behind and got up the horses' tails.

'I don't want either of them to do much,' Jan

shouted over the wind. 'Just follow me up to the wide track along the ridge, then come alongside me and we'll give them a quick three furlongs to wake them up. Stay with me if you can.'

Annabel nodded, her eyes shining. Despite not wanting to ride in races, she loved giving the horses fast work. Jan guessed it was the high-speed jumping that daunted her, though she'd often seen her take schooling fences at full racing pace.

Jan trotted up the hill between the banks of gorse and last year's bracken, excited by Gunner's big bouncy stride. Once they had reached the beginning of a broad, gently climbing strip of fine turf, which the wind had already returned to its normal firm springiness, she turned round in her saddle to beckon Annabel up to her. When she could hear Barney's breathing she kicked her horse into a canter, until she reached the level ground at the top of the ridge and eased him into a steady gallop, all the time feeling for anything in his movement that might be cause for worry or optimism.

She was pleased with the way he was going and when she glanced back at the small thorn tree they used as a two-furlong marker, she wasn't surprised to find that Barney, though going strongly enough, was slowly losing ground to his half-brother. She knew she'd done enough and gently began to pull Rear Gunner up as Barney caught up, with Annabel grinning broadly.

'God, he went well!' she shouted, nodding her head at Rear Gunner. 'This chap couldn't get near him and I was flat to the boards.'

'I wasn't,' Jan laughed. 'I didn't want to knacker him. But he feels great.'

When they got back to the yard, Philip had arrived on time – a measure of his excitement at their first race under rules – and had done all the feeds. They took out the next three horses, and turned out the last three to get some air and exercise themselves in the paddock.

They mucked out, cleaned tack and cleared up the yard together, as they did every normal day. Jan wasn't going to make any concessions just because it was their first run on a regular race course. When everything had been done the way Jan liked it, Annabel spent the last half-hour before they left grooming Rear Gunner until he gleamed like the polished leather of his bridle, with a beautiful geometric pattern of diamonds on his quarters.

'They'll all rub off in the lorry under his rug,' Jan laughed when she saw them.

'So I'll do them again when we get there,' Annabel grinned back.

Jan tried not to let her arms shake as she crunched the engine of her old, grey lorry into first gear and turned down the farm drive. She felt an extraordinary mixture of elation and trepidation at what the day might hold. She thought it a good sign that the sun was beginning to show itself through small blue patches in the sky for the first time after several days of heavy rain.

'With this wind and a bit of sun, the going should be just about perfect for Gunner today. The course at Ludlow's on gravel, so it always drains well.'

'What does it ride like?' Philip asked, hunched on the seat of the cab between Annabel and the passenger window.

'Pretty good, I think; Billy says he likes it, anyway.'

'Has he won a hunter chase before?'

'Yes, three or four last season. He's a bloody good little pilot and we're lucky to have him.'

'What weight does he have to do today?' Annabel asked.

'Eleven ten.' Jan nodded at the paperwork in front of Annabel on the dashboard. 'You'll find all the conditions in there – the Shropshire Gold Cup.' Jan raised her eyebrows with a grin. 'Not quite the Cheltenham Gold Cup, but that's what it feels like to me.'

Annabel picked up the entry form. '"The Shropshire Gold Cup",' she read. '"Three thousand, five hundred pounds added to stakes; for horses aged six years old and upwards which before February 25th have been placed first, second, third or fourth in a steeplechase, or have won two open point-to-point steeplechases. Run over three miles, about seven furlongs." That's lucky,' she went on. 'I see he gets no additional penalties for point-to-points won since January the first last year. And he'd have got a five-pound allowance if he was a mare.'

'That's his bad luck,' Philip laughed.

Jan, Philip and Annabel continued to chat for the eighty minutes it took to wind their way along quiet country roads, through Knighton, until they emerged opposite Ludlow race course on the main road a few miles north of the medieval town.

Two hours before the first race was due to start traffic was already being sucked onto the course. Jan felt her bowels tighten as she turned into the lorry park and saw the gathering of large, expensive horse-boxes with some of the great names of National Hunt racing emblazoned across their sides. One of the big trainers from Lambourn had a runner in Rear Gunner's race. Jan had known she was up against this level of opposition, but suddenly it didn't seem very fair.

'Where's Billy?' Philip asked. 'He's usually waiting for us.'

'It's a bit different here from a point-to-point,' Jan said. 'He'll be in the jockey's changing room. I'll have to take his colours there.'

'What do we do first?' Philip asked.

'Find a place where I can park this and drop the ramp easily,' Jan muttered through gritted teeth, knowing that the tension was beginning to get to her.

'Don't worry,' Annabel said calmly. 'Look, there's plenty of space over there.'

Nobody spoke while Jan manoeuvred her unwieldy lorry into the place Annabel had pointed out.

'At least we got here,' Philip said when the engine was turned off.

'Is that supposed to make me feel better or something?' Jan tried to laugh.

'Do you know what we have to do now?' Annabel asked.

'First we've got to get this horse off and into the stables. Then, while you two are giving him a serious grooming and shining his tack with that bar of glycerine I gave you, I've got to go and declare. I think I have to sign the form up in the weighing room.'

'We'll get him off while you're doing that, Jan. I can ask where everything is.'

Jan thought Annabel with her willowy, innocent look might get more co-operation from the racing pros than she would. Besides, she had enough on her plate without having to worry about people looking down their noses at her for not knowing where to go.

'Thanks, Bel. I'll come and find you at the stables as soon as I'm done, then we can walk the course.'

As Jan went about the business of delivering Harold's newly made colours – scarlet with yellow chevrons, white sleeves and a black cap – and declaring her entry among all the bustle of a busy weighing room, she found it hard not to let her nervousness show. She couldn't help it – it was all much more brisk and businesslike than she was used to. At the point-to-points the officials in their temporary canvas billets were smiling, familiar faces with a healthy respect for her proven record of producing winners between the flags.

Here, she thought, she was right at the bottom of the pecking order and didn't they let her know it!

But she got through it all without making a fool of herself and was glad to be one stage nearer her debut under rules. She walked round to the race course stables, where the usual stringent security arrangements were in force, to find she wasn't allowed in because she couldn't find her security pass. She was very relieved when Annabel appeared at the stable-block gate and told her everything was fine.

'He's travelled really well,' she said. 'That little bit of work you gave him must have done the trick. And he looks brilliant now,' Annabel laughed. 'And I mean brilliant – really shiny. And the tack's gleaming.'

'Hmm,' Jan grunted, annoyed at not being able to get in to see her own horse without going through the rigmarole of getting a pass from the clerk of the course. 'I'll take your word for it for now. I'll have to get another pass after we've walked the course. Where's Phil?'

'Back at the lorry, I think, or in the lads' canteen. He bumped into a bunch of rather dodgy-looking friends.'

'Dodgy?' Jan asked sharply.

'I don't mean dodgy like that,' Annabel reassured

her quickly. 'Just all spotty with horrible spiky haircuts.'

'Let's hope so,' Jan said, still trying to sit on her anxiety. 'We'll have to walk the course without him, though, God knows, it might have taught him something if he really wanted to be a jockey.' Jan made a face. 'Which, let's face it, he's never going to be.'

'You can let him dream, though.'

'I do. I must be mad to encourage him, but I do.'

As Jan and Annabel walked towards the course, Jan pulled a race card from the pocket of her sheepskin coat. 'I'd better check where this bloody race starts from. I meant to look before we left, but I've been here enough times as a punter, so I should know, shouldn't I,' she chided herself.

'I don't suppose you thought you'd ever be sending a runner here yourself, not until last month when we realized how good Gunner was.'

Jan chuckled. 'Don't you believe it. I've been dreaming of sending out hunter chasers for years. You have no idea what a watershed in my life this is.'

'Yes, I have,' Annabel said quietly. 'And I really, really hope it goes well.'

They walked on in silence as Jan studied the map of the steeplechase course to identify the start of the race.

It took the two friends three-quarters of an hour to complete a circuit of the right-handed track, which the horses running in the hunter chase would do two and half times in under ten minutes. For the most part they walked in silence, while Jan studied the approach and the ground on either side of each fence. Between the fences she checked the firmness of the turf across the width of the track and made mental notes to pass on to Billy.

The strong wind of the early morning had dropped and there was a serenity about the round, wooded hills surrounding the course. Now only a mild breeze blew in from Wales and rippled the long grass between the fairways of the golf course in the middle.

As they walked the quarter-mile run in, they had a good look at the open ditch and then the water jump directly in front of the wrought-iron Victorian grandstand, which the horses would take in the earlier circuits.

'What do you think?' Annabel asked.

'He won't have any problems with these fences and the going will really suit him.' Jan shrugged. 'But who am I to make predictions?' Inside she was a lot more apprehensive than she was prepared to let on. She was beginning to realize that she'd had no idea how nervous she would be and she was beginning to feel queasy; she wondered how long she could hold it in. 'Right, let's get back and have a look at Gunner.'

Once she'd sorted out a stable pass, she went through the security gate with Annabel to find Philip hanging over the bottom door of Rear Gunner's temporary home. 'Everything all right, Phil?'

'Yeah, fine.' He swayed back from the door and Jan realized that he was already quite drunk.

'For God's sake, pull yourself together. I'm not having some drunken moron anywhere near my horses. Go back to the lorry and sober up.'

Philip looked shocked by her outburst. Jan was too, but she didn't feel like retracting anything as she watched him wander off towards the lorries.

In his stable Rear Gunner looked every bit as good as Annabel had said. 'Thanks, Bel, you've done a lovely job. You might even win twenty quid for the best turned out.' Out of habit, Jan felt the horse's four legs and his back, under his rug. He seemed pleased at the attention and aware that it was a big day for him. 'You show 'em today, Gunner,' she murmured into his big ears. 'You show all these big posh trainers what little hillbilly Jan Hardy can do.'

In the canteen Annabel ate nothing, as usual, and even Jan found it hard to swallow the thick ham sandwich she had bought herself. 'God, this running under rules malarkey is bad for my nervous system,' she murmured. 'It's much more regimented than I'm used to. Everything seems to be designed to make you feel inferior, when your only crime is never having done it before.'

'Stop getting a persecution complex,' Annabel said. 'I don't suppose anyone else has noticed that you're not sure of everything.'

'Don't you believe it. I bet this lot are past masters at reading body language.'

Jan didn't feel any better when, later, they tacked up their runner and Annabel led him to the parade ring twenty-five minutes before he was due to race. Jan had wanted the horse well loosened up and used to all the crowds and noise before he was asked to run. Once she was satisfied that he was settled, she started to look around for his owner.

Harold Powell had said he would get to the race course at least half an hour before the off and, sure enough, a few moments later Jan saw him, in a green tweed suit and a brown trilby, shepherding his reluctant wife through the crowd towards the nether regions of the race course buildings.

Jan knew that Sheila Powell had always been a little wary of her, and on the one occasion she'd talked to her since John had died, she'd made it clear that she didn't approve of her husband's preoccupation with keeping horses with a trainer who was a woman and now was alone. Jan guessed this, as much as anything, was the reason for Harold's objections to keeping horses in Gloucestershire when she moved.

As he leaned down to kiss her on the cheek, from the corner of her eye Jan saw Sheila purse her lips. She stepped back automatically. The last thing she wanted was to make owners' wives jealous, especially when there were absolutely no grounds for it as far as she was concerned.

Harold took it in his stride. 'How's my horse?' he

asked, a little louder than necessary, Jan guessed because he wanted anyone who could hear to know that he was an owner.

'He's looking fine,' she said, without too much emphasis. She'd learned early in her training career that it served no useful purpose to build an owner's hopes too high. 'I did a little work on him this morning and he's travelled well. Annabel's in the parade ring with him now to get him used to all the noise. Shall we go and have a look?'

'Let's get a drink first,' Harold said. 'I'll have a proper look at him when we go into the ring.'

Jan really didn't want one, but she realized that a lot of people thought it was one of a trainer's duties to drink with their owners.

The light, spacious bar, recently built to replace the old wooden clubhouse which had been burned down, was packed now with a jovial midweek gathering of sporting farmers and local businessmen. Jan sensed they were a friendlier crowd than she might have encountered at one of the great National Hunt courses and she relaxed enough to accept Harold's offer of a gin and tonic.

She felt quite green after the first sip, but she was damned if she was going to let Harold see what she was going through, so she told him what she thought of the course.

Harold nodded sagely and Jan suddenly realized

that he was also trying to hide his nervousness at his first experience as an owner under rules. He kept looking around the room, nodding every so often with a knowing smile at various acquaintances.

'What are you going to tell Billy?' he asked.

'I want him to keep his powder dry until the last six or seven furlongs. There are twelve runners declared and most of these amateur riders will go off like scalded cats – they usually want to impress their mums or their girlfriends by being in front for a bit. Billy's been at it long enough not to bother. So I'll tell him not to be in too much of a hurry and tuck in ten lengths or so off the pace, in eighth or ninth slot. Then he can move up the far side on the final circuit, and get himself in a handy position to track the leader over the last two before that long run in.' Jan paused. 'Then I'll tell him to kick on a bit.' She laughed.

Harold grinned back tensely. 'And do you think he'll do it?'

Jan finished her drink. 'I'll tell you later.'

'When?' Harold asked anxiously.

'When it's all over.' Jan grinned. 'Now it's time I went and checked your horse. Coming?'

Harold glanced at his wife. 'We'll see you in the parade ring.'

Jan watched proudly as Annabel led Gunner around the parade ring. He had been the first in and, seeing him, the public had begun to drift over to lean on the rails. He looked magnificent, gleaming with condition, and, as she'd promised, Annabel had redone the diamonds on his quarters, which seemed to accentuate their quality. As the other runners appeared, in varying standards of turnout, Jan thought her horse stood out, even beside the three runners from big yards who were more fancied.

Unknown at Ludlow, Jan was able to stop for a few moments outside the ring, as if she were another punter, and listen to the comments. It was very gratifying to hear a total stranger say, 'That Rear Gunner looks well, don't he? I'll have a few quid on him.'

When she saw Harold and his wife coming, she joined them and they walked in together. A few moments later the jockeys trooped in, a riot of colour among the browns and khakis of the owners and trainers.

Billy Hanks strolled up to them, unwilling to appear impressed by the prospect of riding in a hunter chase. He tipped his cap and gave Jan and her owners a broad grin, displaying the wide gap where his two incisors had once been, before he'd left them embedded in a timber fence three years before.

Jan had spoken to Billy briefly in the morning, on her way from the lorry to the weighing room, but once he was in the dressing room she'd seen him only for a few moments when he was being weighed out and she'd taken the saddle from him. Now she gave him the instructions she'd outlined to Harold, with the added information that the good ground on the back straight was on the outside. 'Remember, most of these other jockeys won't be able to hold their horses early on, but just let them go, OK?'

Billy nodded. He knew the form in hunter chases. 'How did the horse travel?'

'Fine. Doesn't he look good?'

Billy chuckled. 'If it was a beauty competition, he'd win hands down.'

'He should be fine and, for God's sake, if you're in contention at the last, give it plenty of welly and he'll go on.'

'He did last time,' Billy nodded.

The instruction for jockeys to mount echoed around the ring. Jan and Billy walked over to where Annabel was turning Rear Gunner in. Annabel held the horse steady while Jan checked the girth, pulled down the stirrup leathers and gave her jockey a leg-up. Billy dropped into the saddle with a grin and took the horse off to do a few more turns around the ring before they left for the race track. As she followed, Jan heard the course commentator announce that Rear Gunner's groom had won twenty pounds for the best-turned-out horse. She turned to Annabel. 'Well, at least we won't be going home completely empty-handed,' she grinned.

Jan didn't want to watch the race with anyone except Annabel, but she felt she had to be with the Powells for Gunner's first run under rules. However, she made sure that Annabel was with them as they crossed back over the course and climbed up into the stands to find a good viewing spot.

The course was laid out so that every fence was visible from where they were, and they all trained their binoculars on the start in the top left-hand corner of the track. The runners had already cantered the short distance from the parade ring and were gathering in front of the starter.

When she saw him raise his hand to the starting-gate handle, Jan took a deep breath; she wasn't conscious of taking another until the race was over.

As the runners set off on their trip over twenty-two fences in just under four miles, Jan didn't need any help from Harold's striking new colours to identify Gunner. She could tell him simply from the way he galloped.

The horse had taken a strong hold right away, but Billy wasn't panicking. Before they'd reached the first of the three plain fences on the back straight, he had Gunner under control and took it lying fifth, several lengths behind the leader, who looked as if he was running away with his jockey.

Rear Gunner's jumping was one of his strengths, and Billy knew exactly how to place him at a fence. Jan watched with satisfaction as they sailed over the next two comfortably and without any apparent strain. Before they started the long right-hand turn, the horse stood right off the open ditch and flew it, gaining a length and a half on the two inside him.

'Pull him back!' Jan muttered, concerned that her horse was seeing too much daylight already.

But Billy hadn't forgotten his instructions and allowed the two he had passed to cruise by him again. By the time they reached the water jump in front of the stand for the first time he was lying seventh in a closely bunched field. There were no fallers and the pack swung away towards the far side of the course.

When they reached the first fence for the second time, the early leaders were showing their tiredness. The third horse barely left the ground and didn't even get his front feet over the birch. In a terrifying cartwheel, he catapulted his jockey into the air and crashed to the ground in front of the favourite, who stumbled, depositing his own rider, and carried on without him.

Billy, on the outside, avoided the melee. He took the fence confidently and found himself lying fifth. Jan noted with satisfaction that her horse was going easily, on the bit but not fighting it, while his jockey sat motionless.

When they swung into the turn on the right-hand side of the course for the second time, they had already covered two miles. The two early leaders, never fancied, were weakening quickly and going backwards. By the time they reached the water again, one had pulled up and the field was much more strung out. Rear Gunner was now lying third of the nine still in the race.

Jan winced. There was a complete circuit left to

run. She was sure Gunner didn't perform his best when he was near the front. But other than taking a hefty pull, there was no way Billy could ease their position. Nevertheless, although he looked as if he could easily have passed the horse directly ahead, he managed to steady Gunner in third place all the way down the back straight for the final time. Then, swinging wide after the open ditch, he moved up to lie second, five lengths behind the horse from the big Lambourn yard, who was still going strongly.

Beside Jan, Harold was bellowing so loudly she thought Billy could probably hear him. 'Come on, Gunner boy! You can do it!'

As they turned into the straight with the last two fences ahead, the leader was beginning to tire. Suddenly, Jan found herself hot and sweating: reading his form in the morning, she'd thought that three miles seven furlongs might be beyond his distance.

Gunner, by contrast, was still going strong. He'd gained a length at the third last. But the Lambourn horse was fighting back. As he came up to the second last fence, the jockey pulled his stick through and delivered a full, forehand crack on his rump.

The horse read the signal wrongly.

He took off a stride too soon. His front feet got over, but his back end was never going to make it and he ended up straddling the fence with his rider hanging round his neck.

Jan thought she was going to explode. Rear Gunner came up calmly with plenty of room outside the flailing horse. He popped the fence five lengths clear of the next horse and galloped on strongly to the last. Jan closed her eyes as he came to jump it. Nothing but this fence could stop him winning now.

Harold was yelling himself hoarse; even Annabel was screaming. The whole crowd roared their approval. Jan opened her eyes to see her horse cantering the last four hundred yards to the winning post. For a moment, as he passed it, she thought she was going to faint, until self-preservation kicked in and kept her on her feet.

Harold was hugging her; even Sheila didn't seem to mind, and when he let her go Annabel's arms were around her.

'Jan, that was absolutely brilliant! You've done a fantastic job on him! You must be so proud. Can I go down and bring him in?'

Jan couldn't speak for a moment. She just nodded. She could hardly think. Only in her wildest dreams had she dared to imagine that Gunner might win. She would have been ecstatic if he'd been placed, or just completed the course. And even though there was a bitter-sweetness to the win because one favourite had dumped its rider and the other had fallen, hers had done neither and had run on strongly to the end of the testing race.

Annabel had already hurried away. Jan stood for a moment and watched her go out on the course with a lead rein to meet the victorious Gunner. All around her people on the stands realized her connection with the winner and, checking in their race cards to see who she was, offered their congratulations. As she and the Powells made their way down the stand to cross the course to the winners' enclosure, more people seemed to have learned who she was and called out to her.

'Gosh,' Jan thought, 'if it's this good winning the Shropshire Gold Cup, what must it be like to win the Cheltenham Foxhunters'?' And suddenly that looked an intoxicating prospect.

Annabel, conscious that all eyes were on the horse, beamed shyly as she led Rear Gunner into the winners' enclosure, where his owners would receive their prize. Billy's gappy grin seemed to cover his whole face as he rode to the winner's slot and jumped down. Jan hugged him and Harold, still almost puce with excitement, shook his hand vigorously.

Jan felt she was still in a dream as she helped Billy to unsaddle their horse, and watched him go off to be weighed in, praying that nothing could happen now to upset the result. She hugged Gunner's big head and fondled his ears as she started to rub his sweaty neck. 'You big, beautiful boy,' she murmured, and his top lip twitched in recognition.

The wife of one of the local Jockey Club stewards had been asked to present the battered old cup, which, after a century of handling, had lost most of its gilt.

Harold accepted it with unusual humility and Jan's hands were quivering as she took the small salver for the winning trainer.

Annabel had thrown a string rug over the horse and was wiping away the sweat on his neck. 'Shall I take him to the lorry or the stables?'

'Take him back to the stables first,' Jan said. 'Wash him down and I'll come and put his bandages on. It'll give him more of a chance to cool off before we load him.'

Annabel led Rear Gunner away from the enclosure and, now that the formalities were over, Harold was anxious to get to the bar and celebrate their win in the traditional manner. 'Come on, Jan. Champagne, and plenty of it – on me!'

Sheila Powell's eyebrow lifted, but tolerantly this time when she recalled that Harold would pick up a cheque for nearly four thousand pounds for his horse's win.

With some embarrassment, Jan felt a sudden surge of tears, but she had to hold them back. Before she could leave the enclosure a handful of racing journalists homed in on her with their notebooks at the ready and their pens poised. It hadn't even occurred to Jan that the press would want to speak to her, and suddenly all the tales she'd heard about misrepresentation and the tricks they played to get a story crowded into her head, and she found herself wanting to run.

'Well done, Jan,' said a man she'd never seen before

in her life. 'Did you think you had a chance when you were on your way here this morning?'

'Of course I did,' Jan managed to blurt out. 'I don't even take a horse to a point-to-point unless I think I've got a good chance.'

'But you were very lucky today, weren't you?'

Jan suddenly saw red. 'Lucky? What do you mean lucky? I trained that horse to go the distance; he did; the others didn't. And jumping's the name of the game.'

'The favourite was obstructed when he lost his rider, though.'

Jan wished she could be less angry with them, but why the hell were they trying to undermine her win – her first under National Hunt rules? 'That doesn't mean he'd have won. Our time was pretty good, too, if you'd bothered to check. I'm proud of Gunner. He's run a super race and you know it. If you don't believe me, come and see him next time he runs.'

Ashamed of herself for rising to the bait, Jan turned and strode out of the enclosure, trying not to look back, before she said any more.

In the members' bar the last thing Jan wanted to do at that moment was drink champagne; she thought it might make her sick, but she felt she should at least take a sip, for Harold's sake.

'I tell you one thing, Jan, now you've really shown

what you can do,' Harold took a sidelong glance at his wife, 'there's no way I'm going to take those horses away from you when you move.'

Sheila's lips tightened.

Jan wasn't going to be put off. 'That's great, Harold. I'm really going to need Gunner if I want to make any kind of impression and Lazy Dove's looking as if he might live up to his breeding before long.'

'You take them with you,' Harold said expansively, taking another massive swig of champagne. 'I wouldn't do better in any other yard in the country, not at this game.'

After a few more minutes of mutual congratulation, Jan had had enough. 'OK, Harold. I'm really pleased you're letting me take your horses with me, but don't forget I need to sell Stonewall for as much as you can get if I'm going to find anywhere half-decent to live.'

'I won't forget and we'll do our very best for you.'

'Thanks. Now I'll have to love you and leave you. I've got to bandage your horse's legs before I put him in the lorry.'

'Can't one of your staff do that? The lovely Annabel?'

'I'm sure they could, but I want to do it myself.'

By ten o'clock that night Jan had driven the lorry home, helped Annabel and the useless Philip to feed the horses, and picked up, fed and bathed her children. When she had put them to bed, she said goodbye to

Annabel and made herself a mug of cocoa. She carried it up to her room and lay on her bed, fully clothed.

She felt absolutely drained by the exertion and emotion of the day. She knew, of course, that she'd been helped by Billy and by Annabel, but in the end she was the captain of her own small ship and whether it sank or swam was her responsibility and no one else's. She had guessed it would be exciting to win a race on a real course against serious competition from big professional trainers, but she'd had no idea just how big a buzz it would give her. And although a couple of reporters might have tried to imply that her win was the result of luck, rather than skill, she knew differently and that she was right to be very happy indeed with the way her horse had performed. She couldn't have asked him for more, although, perhaps, he had even more to offer.

Most of all, she felt that she had proved to herself that she really did know what she was doing; that she wasn't mad to think she could go on and make a living by doing this job well enough to bring up the children John had left her.

And above all, she was certain that, if John had been there today, he would have been very, very proud of her.

4

Two weeks after Rear Gunner's glorious win, Jan sat with Harold Powell in the Bull Ring Hotel in Hay.

Harold was shaking his head sadly. 'To get a fair price for Stonewall you've got to be patient. It might take a year or two for the right buyer to come along. That's the way it is with these hill farms. There may be some family sitting at home right now, thinking it over, working out if they can make it pay and prepared to take their time.'

He sat opposite Jan at the table by the window which they'd occupied when they had last had a drink in the bar.

She leaned towards him across the table. 'But I could sell it quickly if I wanted?'

'Yes; we could auction it for you, but if there weren't at least two real bidders, you wouldn't get any kind of a price.'

'I could put a reserve on it.'

'If it didn't sell, you'd still have all the expenses of the sale.' Harold gazed at her like a benign uncle. 'I'd strongly advise you to stay put until a real buyer appears.'

Jan shook her head. 'It'd be too easy to sit around and do nothing about it, always waiting for the next better offer. If I'm going to do it, I've got to move straight away at the end of the season so I've got the whole summer to get ready for next year. I must make a living, Harold, and this is the only way I can do it.'

'I can't argue that you're not up to the job – not after what Gunner did at Ludlow. But I still don't see why you can't do it from where you are.'

'There just aren't enough owners here. I'll have a much better chance of finding them over there. That's the main reason for moving – that and being nearer Mum and Dad.'

'And further from your mother-in-law,' Harold murmured.

'Well, you know what she's like. Do you blame me?'

'No, I don't blame you. I just don't want to see you lose money by doing things in too much of a hurry.'

'How long would it take to get an auction sale organized then?'

'No less than five or six weeks, really, if we want to get it properly advertised.'

'That would take us to the end of April, just after Easter,' Jan mused. 'OK, I'm giving you my formal instruction to get on with it.'

'But, Jan, why the hurry for God's sake? You're doing all right where you are; nobody's forcing you to go.'

'That's why I'm forcing myself. I know what I'm

like; if I don't do it now I've made up my mind, I'll end up stuck in a rut and the whole idea will run out of steam; that's just the way I am. I've talked to a couple of agents in Tewkesbury; I've already had details of a place that might do very well. I reckon I could get it pretty cheap, which will help to get the new yard going a lot more easily. Now, what do you think I could expect for Stonewall?'

Harold was sitting gazing at her with dismay but, putting on his professional hat, he straightened his back and gave Jan a warning look.

'I don't think I'll jeopardize your chances of a good sale by discussing that with you here, but I will let you know in writing what our guide price would be.'

'And I'll want to hold a farm sale as soon as possible. There's the rest of the ewes, a load of tackle and feed and a whole lot of furniture I don't want to take with me.'

'That should realize quite a bit,' Harold sighed, making a note in the diary he'd pulled from his inner pocket. 'It's surprising what rubbish you can shift at a busy farm sale, and for the widow of a man like John Hardy I'd say it would be very well attended. Do you mind my asking – were there many debts to clear?'

'Only the bank, really,' Jan said with a quick grimace, 'but they know what the story is.'

'You know, I did read about a shepherd who worked for Lancashire County Council and sued them for damages for getting ill from organo-phosphate dips. He won eighty grand. There's a woman lawyer in this town who's been working on cases a long time; maybe you should look and see if there's anyone you can take to court over John's death.'

Jan leaned back in her chair and screwed up her face. 'No,' she said, shaking her head. 'I just don't want to go down that road.'

'But if you have some entitlement—'

'John wouldn't have wanted that. He hated causing anyone trouble.'

'But they caused him a bit of trouble – he *died* from it, for God's sake!'

'I'll think about it, Harold, I promise,' Jan sighed, although the idea of taking up arms legally over John's death appalled her.

By eleven forty-five on 21 April more than seventy people were gathered in the old assembly room on the first floor of the Bull Ring Hotel for the sale of Stonewall Farm, which was due to start at midday. Most were men for whom attending sales was an essential part of their lives, part of the mechanism by which judgements were made and decisions taken. They also liked to be present at critical moments in the macro-history of their land; changes of farm ownership in the area could have far-reaching effects.

The sale of stock and farm equipment on the ground two weeks before had gone well; a large, inquisitive crowd had come and everything had sold for reasonable prices. But the sale of the land was a different matter. It was still early in the year, too early to attract the leisure buyers who would sometimes turn up to pay a premium and create a stir. But generally it was a farm of only average potential, and as vulnerable at the moment as any other in the hills of mid-Wales.

Jan had set a reserve price on the sale of the whole which was twenty thousand pounds more than the minimum she thought she would need to spend on a Cotswold smallholding, to give her at least some buffer for the first few years in Gloucestershire.

Harold Powell, who was going to sell the property himself, looked well groomed and ill at ease.

'The trade's not good,' he had said to Jan when she arrived at his office earlier that morning. 'I just hope you haven't got yourself caught between the devil and the deep blue sea.'

'From what I can tell, at the reserve I've set, it should find a buyer all right,' she said. 'I'm not being greedy.'

'We'll do our very best for you, Jan, I can promise you that,' Harold said earnestly.

Jan recognized the words for the meaningless flannel they were. She didn't particularly mind; it was part of his job. She certainly wasn't under any illusion that she would be getting special treatment.

Jan had left Megan and Matthew with their grandmother. Olwen had made it clear that she didn't want to witness the disposal of the farm she had entered as a bride forty-five years before, when they still used a horse to plough the bottom fields, but Jan had refused to be moved by her sour tearfulness.

She was standing now in the sale room, behind and to the left of the rostrum from which Harold would run the auction. She felt detached, not at all nervous, as Harold stepped up onto his small dais and cleared his throat. The murmured conversation that earlier had filled the room subsided and a sea of faces turned towards him.

'Good morning, gentlemen . . . ladies,' he added, to a little laughter, as he acknowledged the handful of women scattered among the crowd. 'I'll not waste too much time with preamble; I don't doubt you've all already had a good look at the details of Stonewall and are aware that we are offering freehold vacant possession of the house, ground and buildings, all in one lot.'

There was a palpable tension in the air now, as there always was at the start of a sale. Jan thought that for a lot of people an auction held the same fascination as the spectacle of a group of men playing poker.

'So let's get the bidding under way,' Harold said in a businesslike manner. 'Who'll get me started at two hundred thousand . . .?'

There was a grunt from the back, which Jan didn't understand, but Harold pounced. 'Fifty thousand?' he said disparagingly. 'Oh well, I'll let you have your fun.' After that, with the help of a young man of twenty or so gazing around eagerly beside him, Harold started to spot bids from around the room and the bid price mounted in steps of five thousand pounds.

Jan had been to enough sales to know that these were mostly from men who wanted more than just the spectacle but enjoyed being part of the drama, at no real risk to themselves as long as the price was obviously way below value. She could imagine them standing around later in the pub at lunchtime, boasting. 'I put a bid in, nearly got it, too.'

But as the price crept up, closer and closer to Jan's reserve, the bids came more slowly. Harold Powell's gaze swept the room from side to side as he cajoled the remaining bidders. 'Come on, now. There's still two of you who want it, but only one of you's going to get it – whichever's got the nerve,' he teased until, at last, the bidding reached Jan's reserve. Now that Harold had definitely sold the property, Jan saw a slight relaxation of tension in his neck, but no amount of eloquence from him could raise the bidding by another increment. 'Is that it?' he finally asked a man invisible to Jan in the far corner of the room. He picked up his shiny, mahogany gavel from the shelf of the rostrum, raised it and knocked down Stonewall Farm at the reserve price.

'Davies!' he said, to identify the buyer.

Jan had no idea which Davies; there were twenty farming families called Davies in the vicinity. She found that she didn't care; she felt no emotion, no resentment that the farm to which her husband had dedicated his life had now moved irrevocably beyond her control. John was dead. It was John she had loved, John she missed, not the farm that had taken him from her.

Ten days after the sale, Jan left the children with Annabel and drove to Gloucestershire. Her first stop was at her parents' house on the edge of the honey-gold hamlet of Riscombe.

Reg Pritchard, in his seventy-fifth year, could not and never would abandon the habit of farming. Although his wife Mary pleaded with him regularly to give up before he did any serious damage to himself, he still insisted on shuffling forty ewes from field to field on his remaining thirty acres and into the tired old buildings to lamb each January. His state pension brought in more than his farming activities, but, for him, to stop farming would be to stop living.

Soon after Jan had married John and gone to live in Wales, Colonel Gilbert, her parents' landlord, had suggested that Reg might like to give up a hundred of the acres he farmed. Reg had seen the sense of it and Colonel Gilbert had said that he and Mary could stay in the house, with the thirty acres, for the rest of their days. From Reg's point of view, as the land was there, it would have been a crime not to farm it. The overproduction of lamb across the United Kingdom and the ecological arguments against farming the less fertile margins of the nation's land didn't affect his view one jot.

Jan always loved coming back to Riscombe, where she had been born and brought up. Although the farm had been bigger then, it had scarcely been more profitable, and little in the house had changed for as long as she could remember. The big beech tree which she and her younger brother, Ben, used to climb as children still stood, spreading its grey, green-clad limbs skyward, like a giant bodyguard beside the house.

She felt the usual aching sadness when she thought about Ben, seeing his sun-browned face, creased with laughter, beneath a stack of thick blond hair as he swung from the branches with strong, supple arms. She still couldn't begin to understand what had made him walk out of the house, the day after his twenty-first birthday three years before. He'd sent cards, three or four from different parts of the world since he'd gone, to tell their parents not to worry, but he had given no address and he had never phoned or come back to Riscombe. Once he had sent a postcard to Jan from Disneyland in Los Angeles. She'd gazed at his familiar writing with wonderment, scarcely able to imagine how her brother, who'd grown up with ponies, ferrets and fishing, could be happy anywhere as exotic as California.

At the same time, she'd always known that there was a side to his character that yearned, almost lusted after adventure; that his guitar and music had replaced catapults and rabbiting. The small sum of money left him by Mary's mother had been just enough to enable him to go. Jan only hoped that he wasn't aware of the deep, unremitting sadness it had caused their parents. Reg was so disappointed that his son had turned his back on farming, after more generations than anyone knew, that he hadn't mentioned Ben's name in Jan's hearing in the past twelve months.

Reg was waiting for her at the front door as she parked the Land Rover. Putting aside thoughts of Ben, Jan got down and gave her father a long hug, feeling that he had shrunk a little since the last time she'd seen him. She noticed with concern that he had missed a few swathes of bristle in his shave that morning, when once he had been so particular. His hair, though, was thick, white and wavy, and had been carefully combed, not, Jan suspected, without a little vanity.

'How are you, Dad?'

'Oh, pretty much the same. Can't do so much now.' He shook his head at the frustration of it. 'Them ram lambs are gettin' too strong for me.'

'If you can't physically manage it,' Jan said, 'you should give up the ewes.'

Reg was shuffling back into the house now. 'What would I do then?'

Jan sighed. It wasn't the first time they'd had this conversation. 'You're a stubborn old bugger,' she laughed.

Mary had been watching out for Jan's Land Rover from the kitchen window. She had already made a pot of tea and was cutting thick slices from a dark, gooey chocolate cake as they walked in. Although she was fifteen years younger than her husband, she shuffled across the kitchen on short, arthritic legs to hug her only daughter, before standing back to gaze at her proudly, as she always did. 'Dad says you're thinking of moving back over here!' she said with a breathlessness that was beginning to worry Jan.

'Yes, I hope so. If I can find something I can afford, where I can keep enough horses.'

'What's this place like you're going to look at with Dad?'

Jan took a sheaf of estate agents' brochures from the bag slung over her shoulder, and sat down with her parents at the old pine table she'd known all her life to look at the details of Edge Farm, Stanfield.

'There's not much to the place,' her father said, 'and all the ground's on a bank, if I remember right.'

'That'll help get the horses fit,' Jan justified.

'S'long as you never has to plough it. These buildings ain't much either and there's no house.'

Jan had already absorbed these obvious defects, but she knew from the research she'd done that this was about all she could expect for the money she'd got from the sale of Stonewall. 'Dad, I told you on the phone, the agents said I'll have no trouble getting planning permission for a house, then I can build it as I want when I've got the money. I won't mind living in a mobile home for a few years, so long as I know what I'll be getting at the end of it.'

'But will that be all right, with the kids?' Mary asked anxiously.

'They won't mind. Mobile homes are very civilized theses days.'

Mary pondered this for a moment, but didn't voice any more doubts.

'How many horses do you think you can keep there?'

'Up to twenty, I should think.'

'There's not the grazing for twenty.' Reg shook his head. 'Not on those banks. The pasture ain't much there.'

'Reggie,' Mary chided him. 'Stop trying to put her off. It'll be lovely to have her close, now I can't get out much.'

'It's OK, Mum. Dad's just thinking like a farmer and he's right to. But it's OK about the grazing – most people take their pointers home for the summer. They wouldn't want to pay me for grass keep anyway.'

'What'll you do for money in the summer months, then?'

Jan had already been asking herself that, but she didn't want to worry her father. She screwed up her small round face and shrugged. 'I'll be schooling and bringing on young ones; maybe trading a few.'

'With them two kids, you'll need something steady coming in. I can tell you, though me and your mum would have liked a few more of you, I did sometimes thank our lucky stars we only had the two extra mouths to feed.'

'I never thanked my lucky stars,' Mary protested.

'Well, Dad, I'll just have to do what I can do. I know I can train pointers. I've already won eleven this season, as well as Gunner's hunter chase – that's why Harold's letting me bring his horses with me. It shouldn't be too hard to find a few new owners for next season with that track record. I'm sure I'll get more wins from Gunner and Lenny's Lad next year, and Lazy Dove, so long as we can keep his mind on the job, and that should bring in more owners.'

'*If* they win.' Reg grunted. 'There's no certainty in your game and you know it. But if they do, you're right; there's plenty of money round here these days, though God knows where it all comes from or what'll happen when it stops.'

'It's all townies, Dad, you know that. All wanting to be the country squire. Anyway, are you going to come and look at this place with me or not?'

A big stone barn was perched on a ledge on the steep, western face of the Cotswolds that had given its name to Edge Farm at least two hundred years before. The farmhouse that had once stood beside it existed now only as a partially buried, two-dimensional floor plan of its former self. With the stone building stood a black iron Dutch barn and a cluster of Scots pines of about the same age, which increased the farm's air of bleakness, wind-whipped as it was just below the top of the ridge.

The land for sale stretched in a thin slice from the

bottom of the hill to the top, comprising six fields of permanent pasture, although the lowest and most level of them still showed the ridges and furrows of medieval cultivation. A rough track of limestone chips climbed two hundred yards from the lane up to the buildings. It was clear that the track often doubled as a stream in winter, to cope with the rain which fell when the clouds blown from the west were forced to rise after their passage across the broad Severn valley.

Jan parked the Land Rover in a yard that hadn't been swept for years. The big stone barn, picturesque from a distance, looked a serious liability close to, with a roof of rotting asbestos sheeting. The Dutch barn was fit for nothing but scrap. Jan turned to her father with a rueful face. 'I'm sorry, Dad. I shouldn't have dragged you out here.'

But she was surprised to see an eager light in her father's eye. 'We may as well look at the place now we're here,' he said and opened the passenger door to climb down.

Jan got out too and stood gazing at the dereliction all around them. 'I don't think I can handle this,' she said.

'Let's have a look at the ground,' Reg urged.

They spent half an hour walking the fields, assessing the grass, checking the fences and gates. Jan guessed the barn was two or three hundred years old as she stood in it and gazed glumly at the holes in the roof and the puddles on the floor.

'I tell you what,' Reg said out in the yard. 'This

place'll be cheap. No farmer would give much for it and it's too windy for any of them townies. It looks like it's been on the market for years. If they want to sell it, they'll take a lot less than they're asking.'

'But, Dad, look at the barn! I need somewhere to stable my horses right away.'

'They'll be out mostly, this time of year, but anyway you could tarpaulin the roof and there's room to knock up ten stables in there with three-quarter-inch ply. It wouldn't look pretty, but it'd do the job.'

'Dad, what are you talking about? This place is rubbish and you know it.'

Reg shook his head impatiently. 'Not with a few ideas. It's a lousy bit of ground, really, but I reckon it'd just about do the job you want. And I smell a hell of a bargain.'

'I just don't think I can handle it.' Jan shook her head.

'Yes, you can,' her father said with fierce conviction. 'If anybody can, you can.'

After lunch the next day Jan picked up the telephone from the time-blackened oak dresser that had stood against the back wall in the big, gloomy hall at Stonewall for the past two hundred years.

She dialled the estate agents in Evesham and offered half the asking price for Edge Farm, provided there was completion by the end of the month.

The man she was talking to smoothly declined her offer at once.

'Well, let me know how close they can get to that, if they want to get shot of the place in double-quick time.'

'I will, Mrs Hardy.'

Jan cleared the line and dialled her father.

'Hello, Dad. I just did what you said and offered half the asking price on the farm. I'd hardly taken a breath when he'd already turned it down.'

'They'll be back with a good price – just you wait. I've been asking around. That's the fifth agent the land's been with in the last three years and they wants to get shot of it.'

Jan was nothing like so confident as her father, but she was as aware as him that getting the place cheaply was the only option; that to buy it at anything above a bargain price would be no achievement at all. But she was determined that she wasn't going to let herself get wound up and irrational about Edge Farm. Yes, she wanted it – but only if it really was cheap and would allow her to start this new stage of her life with some kind of advantage. She knew that to do the deal she had to keep her cool. She was grateful for her father's support and guessed that Reg, who had never owned a freehold in his life, was determined to enjoy the buzz of the chase with her.

The next day was Saturday and Jan was going to the races, so she didn't have time to think about Edge Farm.

She woke at half-past five, just before her alarm clock started buzzing. The usual adrenalin rush she felt at the thought of running her horses was no less intense, despite her successes of the last few months.

She walked across a worn rug on the bedroom floor and opened the thick curtains covering the window. She was met with a glorious view to the south, lit by the silky glow of a gold and pink dawn. The larks were already trilling as they spiralled high over the heather on the hill behind the farm and Jan sighed at this strange, fickle country, so bleak all winter, but suddenly seductively beautiful when the weather allowed.

Dismissively, Jan turned her eyes away.

Too bad, she thought, no amount of summer beauty could make up for the misery of winter. Besides, she told herself, to run a profitable point-to-point yard she needed owners and even her dad had agreed there was a lot more potential in the Cotswolds than there ever would be here in mid-Wales.

She washed and dressed in stretch jeans, a T-shirt and a tan cord blouson she'd had since she'd started her first job. She tiptoed from her room and along the corridor to check on the children. They were both sound asleep and she went downstairs with a clear conscience. Her neighbours' fifteen-year-old daughter would be up soon to give them breakfast and take them down to their grandmother's.

As she opened the front door, she heard Annabel's Golf turn off the lane at the bottom of the drive. She smiled and wondered why Annabel, with all the things that should have tempted her away, was so committed to this little yard of hers and all the horses in it.

She walked down and stroked Mister Mack's big pink nose while she waited for the Golf to appear round the end of the buildings. When it did, Annabel parked neatly and swung her long legs out of the driver's door.

'Hi, Jan!' she called, not too loudly, knowing the children would still be asleep. 'What a heavenly day! Isn't it unbelievable here when it's like this? I had the most beautiful drive over the hills. It was worth getting up at six just for that.'

Jan grinned. 'I can see how lovely it is, but I'm still moving to Gloucestershire.'

'I know.' Annabel laughed. 'I was just trying to remind you of what you'd be missing, but I'm sure you're right really; this place must have pretty awful memories for you.'

They sorted the tack they needed and talked about their runners' chances at the Llandeilo Farmers' Hunt point-to-point. The races were being held on a broad meadow in the valley of the River Teifi, in a beautiful, distant corner of Carmarthenshire. It was a long way to go but, as Jan saw it, its very remoteness improved her chances of winning. And she'd been in racing long enough to know that most people judged a racing yard solely by its strike rate – the number of winners it produced in proportion to the number of horses it ran.

They were taking three horses that day – Barneby Boy, Lazy Dove and Gale Bird, which belonged to Jan and was the only mare in the yard. From their previous runs and the way they'd worked that week, all three had a chance. Lazy Dove was another of Harold Powell's horses. Jan had entered him in the men's Open, the principal race of the meeting. The small gelding came from a long line of winning mares who had blazoned their family name across National Hunt courses all over the country. Lazy had the same grit and stamina as his female forebears, but a quirk in his nature matched his name and had made him difficult to train and ride. Jan was only running him today because she had persuaded Billy Hanks to come all the way to west Wales to pilot him. She was flagrantly cashing in on their longstanding friendship and his gratitude for Gunner's win at Ludlow.

'It's a three-hour drive for him, mind,' Jan said to Annabel, making a guilty face, 'but he's got the ride on the other two; both of them could win and he says he's picked up another good one from a trainer in Pembrokeshire.'

'He won on Gale Bird in the North Cotswold, didn't he?' Annabel said, as they carried saddles and bridles across the yard to the horses they were going to exercise before they left.

'Yes, but he was lucky, remember? The leader

pecked after the last and went arse over head. Of course her five-pound mare's allowance will help.'

By seven o'clock they were on the top of the hill under a cloudless morning sky and the scene around them was breathtaking. The sun was already warm, but hadn't yet dispersed the pools of mist that lingered in the valleys below. There was scarcely any wind and the distant bleat of a late hill lamb drifted up the heather-clad ridge.

After the work, they stopped and dismounted to let the horses pick a little grass that the sheep had left. Annabel took off her helmet and shook out her long chestnut hair. She sucked in a deep breath of scented air and her eyes sparkled. She looked, Jan thought, as good as any girl in a glossy magazine.

'You really ought to go into fashion or films,' Jan said. 'You're wasted up here in the hills.'

Annabel turned to her. She seemed suddenly insecure and embarrassed. 'I thought you wanted me to come and help you set up the new place when you move.'

Jan laughed at her reaction. 'Of course I do, very much. But sometimes I just can't understand why you don't take advantage of what you've got.'

'You mean go to London and try to make money out of modelling or something? That's what my father's always saying. But I don't particularly need any more money. I've got all I want.'

'But what about boyfriends – men? You'd meet a lot more if you got into that world.'

'And the last kind of men I'm interested in.'

'What is it with you and men? You don't seem that keen.'

'It's not that I'm not interested, the trouble is all the men I meet only seem to want one thing and they just never stop banging on about it. I'm sure there's more to life and relationships than just that.'

Jan nodded. 'Even I came across that when I was your age, though I dare say I didn't have quite so many flinging themselves at me. And of course there's more to life, but you're right – it seems S-E-X is all everyone talks about these days.'

'That's why I love coming here, and talking about the horses and doing this.' Annabel waved a hand across the spectacular vista of hills stretching away to the distant shadow of Snowdonia in the north. 'Being in a place like this, at a time like this. This is what I call really special. And how many people are there up on these hill tops enjoying it? Maybe a dozen. It makes me feel really privileged.'

Jan nodded and gazed around her. 'Yes, I suppose you're right; in fact, you *are* right, but running my yard, even though it's so small, I always seem to have so much on my mind. Perhaps I just don't have time to appreciate it the way I should. Which reminds me,' she went on, changing her tone briskly, 'we'd better get back if we're going to get a couple more done before we load up. It'll take three hours to get there in the lorry and I've got to walk the course. They usually have this meeting a month earlier, but it was postponed because the course was waterlogged. I don't know what it'll be like at this time of year.'

No clouds blew in to change the outlook. Jan and her two 'lads' arrived at the small cluster of tents in good time to inspect the course, which lay in a pretty meadow among broad, parkland trees and set between steep wooded banks. It was obvious from the range of ages and types strolling in from the car park that the point-to-point was an important social event in this sparsely peopled corner of Wales. Jan couldn't help responding to the carnival atmosphere and she realized how much she enjoyed the meeting's informality and friendliness, compared to the serious, businesslike discipline of National Hunt racing. She was also quite relieved that Harold Powell had rung the evening before to say he couldn't come and see Lazy Dove run.

Gwillam Evans, the farmer who owned Barneby Boy, had already arrived, but he was a very unobtrusive owner. His horse was the first of Jan's three to go, due to run at one-thirty in the second race, which was the restricted hunts, open to horses qualified only with certain hunts in the area, the Radnor and West Hereford among them. He sidled up to Jan as she came out of the secretary's tent, looking around for her jockey. 'I've got the colours here,' he said proudly because his wife had made them. 'Has he come yet?'

'I hope so,' Jan said. 'He'll be bloody angry if he's

driven a hundred and twenty miles then misses his first ride.'

Gwillam looked alarmed at the prospect of having no jockey.

'Oh, don't worry,' Jan said. 'He always gets here in the nick of time. I think it adds to the excitement for him.'

Billy did arrive – within an ace of the deadline to declare jockeys.

He reappeared from the tented changing room in a matter of minutes in Gwillam's colours and walked into the raw-timber-railed paddock, where Annabel was already leading Barney around with the other runners.

Jan stood in the middle and watched the opposition. There were several horses she had never seen before on which the form guide was able to shed little light; there were four or five with respectable form. Not one of them looked as fit as Barney. She caught Billy's eye and he sauntered over, watched eagerly by those in the crowd round the rail who knew that he was the leading point-to-point rider in the region.

'There's a bit of sticky ground by the rails in the bottom left-hand corner,' Jan said quietly, 'just before the fourth, so go a bit wide and take it on the outside. Otherwise, I should think it'll ride pretty well. It should suit him, but don't forget he's a bit like Rear Gunner. Don't show him too much daylight until you have to.'

Billy nodded absently and, as always, Jan had the

impression he hadn't been listening to a word she said. But since he always followed her instructions as closely as he could, she had to assume he heard something.

'They don't look much,' he replied, still studying the other horses circling round them.

'Don't forget,' Jan said. 'There's always some potty farmer round here who thinks he can pull off a coup and once in while it happens.'

But Barneby Boy's performance, with Billy obeying his instructions to the letter, was almost an anticlimax. In a copybook piece of race-riding, Billy brought him alongside the leader coming to the last. They jumped it together as if they'd been synchronized, and it was only when they had taken another stride or two that Billy crouched down, leaned forward and urged his horse to get on with the job.

Barney stretched his neck and earned an extra yard with every stride right up to the winning post.

He passed it running on so strongly that it took Billy a hundred yards to pull him up. He turned and met Annabel running out onto the track to lead them in with his usual broad grin.

Gale Bird, in the maidens' race, didn't give Billy such a comfortable ride. Two from home she hit the top of the fence so hard that Jan had to shut her eyes, and found herself clutching her binoculars so tightly that her fingers hurt. But when she looked again the mare had recovered and seemed to have found fresh energy coming to the last. Billy was the first to take off and Gale Bird put down neatly with the fluid grace that had so impressed Jan when she'd first seen the mare.

To a roar from the crowd that had backed her, Gale Bird galloped home to give Jan and her team two wins in a row.

Back in the makeshift winners' enclosure, Billy rode in to a great reception. He looked almost as happy at his double as he'd been after winning on Rear Gunner. He jumped off, grinning and sweating. Jan threw her arms around him and once again felt a surge of feeling and tears welling up, just as she had at Ludlow. This time, she didn't succeed in holding them back and, shaking her head with a hopeless, apologetic grin, she helped Billy to unsaddle the horse and led the mare back to the lorry herself.

Annabel and an ecstatic Phil followed her and helped her to put the horse away before they took Lazy Dove from the box, with an hour to prepare him for his race, which was the last on the card.

The eight runners in the men's Open had completed one and a half circuits of the three they were set to run. They were approaching a big plain fence halfway along the back straight on the left-handed course. Lazy Dove had taken a strong hold as he always did. Jan had told Billy to not to fight him. He always seemed less troubled when he was in front and it was sensible to leave him there, provided, of course, it wasn't taking too much out of him.

Jan had watched the horse in trepidation as he approached each fence. So far, though, he'd done nothing wrong. Lazy Dove was a naturally athletic horse who, once he'd decided he was going to jump, did it with stylish poise.

She could tell even from the distance of three hundred yards that Billy was beginning to enjoy his ride until completely without warning, as they came up to the next fence, the horse veered sharply to one side, went up on his hocks for a moment before dropping down and careering off the course outside the wing.

A split second later Jan, gazing in horror through her binoculars, saw the reason for the horse's fright. A hare, which must have been quivering in the long grass and scrub inside the track since before racing had started, had flashed off across the meadow and disappeared into a hedge at the far end. Despite everything else going through her mind, Jan was deeply relieved that the problem had been caused by another animal, rather than some crazy fantasy in the horse's head.

Turning her glasses back to Lazy Dove, she saw that he hadn't decided to give up and was carting his jockey at a relentless gallop straight towards a large spreading sycamore tree. A second later he was under the lower branches, which swept over his head and took the jockey clean off his back.

The St John's ambulance was already in motion,

bouncing its way across the ancient pasture while Jan ran as fast as she could across the middle of the course, worried equally about her jockey and horse.

As she ran, she saw Lazy Dove at the far end of the field being flapped into a corner by the few spectators who had chosen to watch from that part of the course, while one of the hunt whips, in his pink coat for the occasion, cantered with a determined air along the edge of the meadow to take charge.

Jan carried on towards the sycamore and the small group of people now clustered under it beside the ambulance. She arrived out of breath to find Billy sitting up, at least, while a black-uniformed woman with a very large chest held a slab of bloody lint to his forehead beneath his floppy blond hair.

He looked up, saw Jan and grinned. 'It's all right, I'm not dead. I was only out for a few seconds. I reckon the tree came off worse than me!' He nodded up at the smaller splintered branches above him. 'What's the horse doing?'

Jan glanced across the meadow. 'They've just caught him. He looks OK – thank God!'

'Did you see what happened?' Billy asked eagerly, earning a frown from the stocky St John's Ambulance woman.

'That bloody hare?' Jan nodded. 'Yeah, I saw it. I only hope it hasn't set Lazy back. It's just the sort of thing he takes to heart.'

'And it knackered our treble.' The jockey grinned ruefully.

'Was he going that well?'

'Didn't you see? He was going ever so sweetly and jumping like a gazelle.'

'Ah well,' Jan said sounding more philosophical than she felt. 'He's not dead, you're not dead and you can't win them all.'

Billy, bandaged and banned from driving his car by the doctor on the race course, was driven back to Stonewall by Jan, while Philip drove the lorry with Annabel for company. On the journey home Jan experienced a mix of emotions – elation at their double, frustration at Billy's injury and relief that Lazy Dove was still in one piece. She was reminded of what her father had said a few days before – racing was an unpredictable business and, on the whole, they'd been very lucky that day.

When they got back to the farm, Jan stopped off at Olwen's bungalow to pick up the children. Olwen, ambivalent though she was about keeping the kids for any length of time, was looking explosive.

'A firm of estate agents in Evesham phoned this morning, after you'd gone; they thought they was talking to you, not me, and they said if you was to increase your offer for Edge Farm by ten thousand, their clients would accept it.'

Jan, in the process of picking up Matthew and checking his nappy, stopped, frozen. She hadn't said a word about Edge Farm to Olwen, aware that it would achieve nothing but conflict. She closed her eyes. 'What did you say?' she asked quietly.

'I said they'd got the wrong Mrs Hardy, but I'd pass on the message. If the firm's in Evesham,' she went on with more grit in her voice, 'where's Edge Farm?'

Jan accepted the inevitable. 'If you come up later, once we've got the horses done and the kids in bed, I'll show you.'

Up in the farmhouse Jan tried the agents' number as soon as she got through the door, but it was already after six. She hadn't expected a reply so soon and she didn't know how she would contain herself until the office reopened the following week. At the price they were asking, she knew she had the deal she needed.

Unable to keep the news to herself, she phoned her father, who chuckled gleefully and urged her to go ahead. She put the phone down, sharply aware that a whole new chapter in her life was about to begin.

By ten past nine on Monday morning the deal was done and the process of transferring ownership of Edge Farm, Stanfield, Gloucestershire to Mrs Jan Hardy had been set in motion.

5

Jan was standing in the grass parade ring at Doncaster Spring Sales. She leaned forward slightly and rested her hands on her knees while she focused all her attention on the dark bay gelding being trotted down the centre of the ring towards her.

From his breeding, the way he was built and his brief career on the flat, she reckoned the horse could have a bright future; but any weakness in his action or conformation could mean all the difference between a successful career as a hunter chaser, or a few miserable years of disappointment and a lot of vets' bills.

Harold Powell had found the excitement of winning a hunter chase on a National Hunt course so superior to winning a point-to-point that he had now set his sights even higher. He had asked Jan to look for another horse and insisted that she find him something capable of running with a good chance in the Christie's Foxhunters' at the Cheltenham Festival.

If Jan bought this horse for Harold, he would be easily the most expensive she'd ever had in her yard. In the next few minutes she'd have to decide if she was going to bid up to the ten thousand guineas Harold had given her to spend or sit on her hands. She was completely oblivious to anyone or anything else in the grass arena and quite unaware of the copper-coloured gelding being led in behind her.

The horse's lad was about to bring him in through the entrance when he stopped dead, straightened his forelegs and dug in his toes. Throwing his head in the air with ears lying flat down an arched neck, the gelding stared wildly over flared nostrils at the people lining the rails around the edge of the ring.

The groom swore and viciously jerked the lead rein down to tug the leery animal into the ring. He turned left to lead him clockwise along the tarmac path that ran just inside the perimeter rail, where most of the lookers leaned.

One of them waved his catalogue to a friend on the far side as the big chestnut trotted nervously by.

The horse reacted at once.

He reared and yanked the rope with burning speed through his minder's fist to the knot at the end. Howling with pain, the groom hung on, but the horse, still back on his hocks, now had space to veer sharply towards the middle of the ring. As his front feet came down, his quarters swivelled in again, with muscles bunched to buck and lash out in fear and anger at being dragged into a place where he didn't want to be.

Right in the line of fire of the animal's rear hooves

a small girl stood, rigid with terror as she saw what was about to happen to her.

A man standing near Jan saw her. With lightning instinctive reactions, he dived at the child, wrapped her in his arms and rolled away a split second before the iron-capped hooves whistled through the air onto where she had been standing.

The lad trotting the horse down the grass in the ring towards Jan pulled up short just as she became aware of the commotion behind her and heard hooves crashing to the ground.

Jan whipped round. Where Megan should have been standing, she saw only two long scars of brown earth gouged in the turf. Beyond it, everyone had scattered from the careering horse, with its groom still hanging on, grimly determined to bring it under control.

Jan searched around in panic. She couldn't focus through the mist that was suddenly clouding her eyes. 'Megan! Megan!' she shrieked.

'It's OK.'

Subconsciously Jan registered the deep, confident voice behind her. She didn't realize the man was talking to her until he spoke again, louder and more urgently.

'It's OK! She's here!'

Jan spun round. At the sight of her daughter safe, although in the arms of a complete stranger, she collapsed with relief. 'Megan, thank God!' She tried not to weep, but she was overcome by a surge of guilt at bringing her child here, then neglecting her.

By now the lad trotting the horse she'd been appraising had reached her side.

'Jaysus! That was so lucky.' He nodded at the man holding Megan. 'He grabbed the little lass in the nick of time! Right from under that animal's feet!'

Jan glanced at her child's saviour. 'Thank you! Thank you so much!' She saw the grass stains on his pale-lemon cord trousers where he'd dived across the turf to save her daughter and she thought how inadequate the words sounded.

'No problem,' he said with a smile.

'God, I feel terrible. It's my fault, I was so busy . . . I took my eye off her.'

'Well, don't worry. She's absolutely fine – aren't you?' he asked the little girl.

Megan, somehow diminished by the terror of what had happened and still utterly drained of her normal high colour, nodded uncertainly.

The man cocked a thick black brow at her. 'You'd be even finer if I got you an ice cream, wouldn't you?'

Now Megan's hazel-green eyes – just like her mother's – lit up and colour began to seep back into her cheeks.

The man glanced at Jan. 'If you want to carry on looking at that horse, I'll get her an ice cream and bring her back when he's been through the sales ring.'

He didn't seem surprised by her relief.

'That would be such a big help,' she said. 'I'm here

on my own, I'm afraid.' She shrugged her regret at not coming to the sales with an entourage, like real trainers. 'But haven't you got a horse to buy?'

'I *was* going to have a closer look at that one.' He nodded at the frenzied chestnut, now being led round by two anxious lads, and laughed wryly. 'But I've decided he's not really for me.'

Jan looked at him for a moment. She hoped she could judge people as well as she could horses. 'Well, if you wouldn't mind looking after Megan for a few minutes, that would be a real help.'

'I'll see you in front of the agents' boxes afterwards,' he grinned. 'Best of luck.'

The bidding rose above ten thousand guineas, then fifteen thousand, until finally the horse Jan wanted was knocked down for nearly twenty thousand guineas to a name which meant nothing to her.

She tried to be philosophical; she'd had plenty of practice over the last few months, but she clattered down the steps of the sales arena with a despondent look on her normally vivacious face.

'It's OK. There'll be others,' a voice behind her shoulder said lightly.

She wheeled round ready to deliver a pithy retort, until she saw it was the man who had saved Megan. The little girl was still clinging onto his large tanned fist.

'I know.' She managed to grin. 'But it's not often I

get the chance to spend that kind of money and I went way beyond my limit before I lost him.'

'Was the horse that good, then?'

'He'll win races', she said confidently, 'unless he goes to some plonker who couldn't train his own granny.'

'I should think some grannies take a bit of training,' he teased.

Jan laughed. 'Not so much as kids – they're much harder than horses.'

They'd reached the metal rail around the parade ring and leaned against it to watch the continuous stream of horses being shown off and presented in the best possible light by their vendors.

'This kid's not so bad.' The man nodded down at Megan, who was standing between them, finishing her ice cream. 'I saw her carrying your catalogue for you earlier this morning, when you were round at the stables looking at that big black horse from Wexford.'

Jan nodded guardedly. For the first time, she looked properly at the man to whom she had entrusted her daughter. Still in his twenties, she thought, nice lips, lazy chocolate brown eyes under a big flat cap of mustard checks. She didn't know him, but he looked familiar – one of those faces you saw around the races; better looking than most. As far she knew, he wasn't a trainer or an agent. Besides, he had the voice, the clothes and easy self-confidence of a typical horse-owning toff. But there was none of that snotty, aren't-I-close-to-God-Almighty arrogance about him.

'Who are you then?' she asked.

'I suppose it's time I introduced myself.' He held out a hand. 'Eddie Sullivan.'

'I'm Jan . . .'

'I know who you are,' he interrupted her with another gleaming smile while he took her hand for a second. 'I saw you leading in Rear Gunner after he won at Ludlow.' Eddie laughed. 'Actually, I thought you were the owner's wife, until I asked around.' He nodded at a light chestnut gelding on the far side of the ring, now prancing diagonally along the perimeter path. 'So, as a winning hunter chase trainer, I wonder if you'd mind telling me what you think of him?'

As it happened, she thought quite a lot.

She'd spotted the horse as soon as he was led into the ring and noticed he was thin, with a rough coat which obscured some of his finer qualities. She'd already decided that if he went cheaply enough, she'd buy him. 'That wouldn't be an easy horse to handle.'

As if to confirm her opinion, the horse suddenly got up on his toes and performed a lively, uncontrolled pirouette around his lad, before tossing his head in the air and trying to snatch the rope from his hands.

'Do you think you could teach him some manners?'

'I haven't found a horse yet that didn't respond to a bit of TLC.'

'Is that your secret?'

'It works better than bullying them.'

'Mm.' Eddie nodded thoughtfully. 'I don't know if he'd be right for the job I have in mind.'

'What job's that, then?'

'I'm looking for something to ride in the Foxhunters' at Aintree next year.'

She didn't miss the sudden glimmer of determination in Eddie's strong features. She took in the furrowed chin, tanned cheeks and crooked nose, acquired, she guessed, in some schoolboy skirmish on the rugby field. 'What, with you on board?' she asked, slightly amused.

He heard the hint of disbelief, but didn't resent it.

'I can do twelve stone,' he said, shaking his head to deny her implication.

'Have you ridden many hunter chases?'

'No, but I've ridden a few point-to-points.'

'Well,' she said, and looked at him. She wondered if he was flirting with her, or just probing her for whatever information she could give him. The knowledge she'd gathered from years of loving and handling horses didn't come easily, and she wouldn't normally have dished it out free, just for the sake of a pair of dark, sexy eyes. 'That horse definitely isn't the one for you,' she said, glad to be telling the truth, 'but I hope you find what you're looking for. And thanks a lot for what you did for Megan.' She flashed Eddie a sudden smile. 'I expect I'll see you later.'

Jan walked away, towing Megan. She tried to look as if she wasn't in a hurry, but the horse she and Eddie had been discussing was already being led towards the sale ring. She wanted to get there in time to put in a bid, and she didn't think there'd be many for such a scatty-looking animal.

Fifteen minutes later and fifteen hundred guineas poorer, Jan was telling her local horse transport company where to deliver her purchase.

She walked away from the stables feeling pleased with herself. After another look at the animal, she was sure that she was right, that his unpromising demeanour was a superficial problem, due to lack of confidence, and if there was one talent in which Jan was willing to take pride, it was her ability to restore a horse's self-esteem. This horse was definitely an improver, she thought.

In the seven tough but happy years she'd spent with John Hardy on the thin-soiled hills beyond Offa's Dyke, nearly all the horses she'd been asked to train and run in the local point-to-points had come to the job after blowing their earlier chances under rules; all of them had one dodge or another. If it was physical, she'd learned from her father as much as any vet about repairing horses; if it was a psychological problem, she was prepared to lavish as much time, understanding and patience as it took. Where others wouldn't have seen the problem, or invested the time, she'd found it was an investment that nearly always paid off.

Giving Megan her catalogue to carry, and clutching her hand very tightly this time, she walked back to the parade ring. She wanted a second look at another horse she'd already seen in the stable yard earlier in the day.

It was due to be sold in about half an hour and she knew that its vendor liked to give his lots a good long show before they went through the sale ring.

She'd been standing on the rail in her usual spot, with her back to the agents' boxes, when she felt another body ease into the small gap beside her. She turned from her inspection of the half-dozen horses in the ring and found Eddie beside her again, thumbing through his catalogue. 'Hello, you back, then?'

Eddie didn't answer for a moment. He was looking at the black horse from Wexford he'd been considering when he'd first seen Jan that morning.

He glanced at her and saw that she was assessing it too. They both knew that they were small players in this market, having automatically filtered out any entries with heavy swathes of black type which indicated large numbers of illustrious forebears or proven form. They could only afford to get interested in animals that came with nothing to recommend them but their physique. 'He's rather handsome, isn't he?'

'Huh,' Jan grunted. 'That's a typical mug's eyeful.'

'But you like the look of him.'

'Yes, he's pretty all right, but not enough bone – especially not for the job you want him for.'

'How do you mean?'

'If you want something that'll carry twelve stone for three or four miles, there's no point looking at anything that's got the slightest question mark in that department. You need a rugby player not a ballet dancer.'

'All right. What sort of horse would you recommend for me rather than that one, which I must say,' he added pointedly, 'I like very much?'

Jan couldn't help a grin. He'd neatly offered to back off the horse they both liked if she dispensed her advice for nothing.

'As it happens, when you told me what you were after, there was one which caught my eye, and he's just coming in the ring now.' She nodded at the opening. 'That dark bay, looks like a sort of Ploughman's Pickle horse. He's no oil painting,' she admitted, 'but he looks as honest as the day is long and he's bred to stay.'

Eddie looked doubtfully at the big-boned horse. 'He's got an arse the size of a barn door. Maybe he'd keep going, but would he be fast enough to win?'

Jan nodded. 'He'll win all right. I'd say by next spring that horse'll be well ready to run in a hunter chase. He's the right sort and he'd look after you.'

'What makes you think I need looking after?'

'Because I've never heard of you winning a race and at your age you should have done by now if you were any good.'

'I'm a late starter,' Eddie retorted.

'Then you'll certainly need looking after.'

Eddie thumbed through the catalogue resting on the rail in front of him.

'"Russian Eagle"', he read, '"won his first point-to-point in Ireland last year. He has been given time to mature." What the hell's that supposed to mean?'

Jan looked at him, and allowed the side of her mouth to turn up. 'If you don't already know and you're a serious buyer, you should get yourself a good agent.' She nodded over her shoulders at the row of small blue and white boxes that the bloodstock agents used as offices.

'Oh, come on,' Eddie cajoled her.

Jan relented. 'He's probably genuine enough. Looking at his breeding and his conformation; he'd be a bit slow maturing, that's all. His sire usually gets late developers so he's never been really fashionable. I wouldn't think he'd make a lot of money,' she went on, dropping any pretence that she wouldn't help Eddie. 'And if you do get him, I'd say he'd give a bloke like you as a good a chance of winning the Foxhunters' as any horse in this sale. In fact, you seem made for each other.'

Eddie was beginning to get caught up in her enthusiasm, when they both heard a soft, deep-throated chuckle behind them. They turned round together, and found themselves staring into the intense blue eyes of a racing legend.

A.D. O'Hagan, builder's mate from Killarney turned global currency speculator, owned at least fifty horses in training in Ireland and England. Now he was surrounded by a gaggle of hangers on. He had no need to attend the sales himself, but although A.D. – as he was universally known – could have bought every lot on offer without making much of a hole in his bank balance, Jan guessed he still liked the smell of a horse and a bargain, and had come just to relax.

Eddie's jaw dropped at the sudden ghastly thought that A.D. might like the same big horse that he was beginning to fancy himself.

Jan didn't seem to share that worry; but she found she couldn't help grinning under the powerful but benign gaze of this fabled owner.

'D'you like the look of him, then?' the Irishman asked Jan, nodding at Russian Eagle.

'Yes,' she nodded emphatically, not prepared to have her view swayed by an owner, even of A.D.'s magnificent scale. 'He'd take a bit of training, mind.'

'I tell you what, if anyone ever trained that great yoke to get round and win a half-decent race, I'd send 'em half a dozen horses of my own.'

The big Irishman gave her a patronizing but not unfriendly pat on the shoulder, and continued his promenade around the ring, trailing his entourage of agents, minders, aspiring young trainers, members of his racing staff and drinking partners from his humbler days.

'He's talking bollocks,' Eddie said. 'I bet he just fancies the animal for himself.'

'No, he doesn't,' Jan said, 'but don't let that put you off.'

'No.' Eddie laughed. 'What does he know, anyway? He only had a hundred and twenty winners last season.'

'So would you if you owned as many horses as he does.'

'You're right,' Eddie said, with his mind made up. 'When's this Ploughman's Pickle horse being sold, then?'

'Don't you want to see him have a trot first?'

'You have, haven't you?'

'Yes.'

'Then that's good enough for me.'

The auctioneer, sleek as a well-fed black cat, gazed around his audience with a hurt and slightly puzzled expression on his face. 'You don't buy good horses like this sitting on your hands, you know,' he admonished. 'Come on now, if you want to buy it you've got to bid for it. This would be a proper trainer's horse. Masses of potential in him. He's already got off the mark at a quality point-to-point in Ireland. Come on, somebody put me in at five thousand.'

He swept the sea of faces with his eyes, in unison with the spotters behind him. 'All right, three, then. Who'll give me three to get us started?'

Jan found herself thinking about the auction in Hay-on-Wye a month ago when Stonewall Farm had been sold for not a penny more than her reserve price. Without warning, out of nowhere, a disturbing new thought began to creep into her mind. But she was distracted when, across the ring, she spotted to her horror that Eddie was about to raise his hand. She concentrated on him and, when she had caught his eye, shook her head very faintly. Relieved, she saw him allow his hand, already level with his waist, to drop back, while they watched the auctioneer still struggle for his opening bid.

'Come on now, ladies and gentlemen. He may not be Twiggy; at least he's got plenty of bone . . . Two thousand? All right, thank you, sir, a thousand guineas I'm bid.' And now that he was off, his voice cranked up a gear and his whole bearing became optimistic once again as he took another bid for twelve hundred.

Eddie gave Jan a big smile. He looked very grateful that she had nodded at him to stay his hand earlier. The auctioneer was already stuck at seventeen hundred, looking for the next bid of eighteen hundred. His gavel was in the air, hovering reluctantly above the top of his pulpit, when Eddie gave a slight nod. The auctioneer's eye, sharp as a buzzard's, picked it up at once and he pounced.

'New bidder,' he crowed. 'It's with you, sir, at the back.' He turned to the last bidder. 'Don't lose him now. You don't often get a chance to buy a horse this size.' He ignored the ripple of titters that ran through the crowd.

A moment later his hardwood hammer hit the top of the desk and Russian Eagle was knocked down to Edward Sullivan for one thousand, eight hundred guineas.

Outside, Jan saw Eddie following his new possession back to the stable, where the horse had spent two nights since he had arrived from Ireland to be sold. Jan didn't think the people who'd brought him all that way would be at all happy with the price they'd got, especially after the auctioneers took their five per cent. But the groom smiled affably enough. 'You'll have a lot of fun with him; sure he's a great horse, wonderful nature and a real Christian. Where's he to go?'

'Back to my place in Gloucestershire for now,' Eddie said.

'Do you have transport?'

'I haven't organized it yet.'

'We'll drop him off for you, on our way back to Fishguard. What's the address?'

'Hang on,' Jan interrupted. 'Now you've got him, who's going to train him for you?'

Eddie grinned. 'I don't know. I haven't decided yet.'

'You're not very good at making decisions, are you?'

'I'm all right at decisions,' Eddie protested. 'It's the choosing that's the hard part.'

'Well, I chose the horse for you, so I may as well choose the trainer – no extra charge.'

'Fine,' Eddie laughed. 'Where shall I send him?'

With a smile, Jan turned to the Irish lad who was waiting to be told. 'Stonewall Farm, Painscastle, near Hay-on-Wye.'

Jan drove home with Megan. For the first half-hour of the journey, the little girl chatted away about everything she'd seen and heard. To Jan's relief, she seemed fully recovered from her scare in the parade ring.

'Mum, why didn't you buy a horse?'

'I did, that skinny one,' Jan said, thinking of her fifteen hundred guinea purchase. 'A man with a lorry's bringing him back for us. I was supposed to find a good one for Mr Powell as well, but they were all too expensive.' She wondered what Harold would say when she told him she hadn't found him a horse. 'But the kind man who saved you from being kicked has bought a nice big horse and he's sending it to us, then we'll take it with us to the new farm.'

Megan's eyes lit up at the thought of the new farm. 'I can't wait to live in a caravan!' she said.

Jan smiled as Megan's eyelids fluttered down and a few moments later she was fast asleep.

In the evening, as Jan was putting Megan to bed, Eddie Sullivan's horse arrived at Stonewall. Through the window she saw a lorry creeping up the farm drive.

Outside the sun was still above the purple ridges in the west and the old stone buildings glowed in its oblique rays. Jan hurried downstairs and out of the house as the lorry pulled up just inside the gate. The young driver jumped down: it was the man who had handled the horse at the sale. He seemed happy to be on his way home as he dropped the ramp and led out the horse. Jan continued down the steps, towards the big bay, wondering, for a moment, if her judgement had been right. The man saw her and grinned.

'Hello there! Here's your new tenant.' He looked around at Jan's tidy yard and nodded with approval. He glanced up at the horse's head and gave its lower lip an affectionate tug. 'You'll be happy here, Eagle,' he said. 'A lovely yard and a beautiful lady to make a fuss of you. I'm quite envious, actually.'

Jan couldn't help grinning. She thought she didn't mind whether the man was fond of the horse, or just using him for some unsubtle flirting.

'Do you work in the yard that sold him?' she asked.

'Oh yes. I'm what you might call the general dogsbody.'

'Do you know this horse?'

'I do.'

'And—?'

'He's as good as gold. I told yer man, he's real Christian. And he'll gallop faster than you'd think, though he can take a bit of a hold.'

Jan nodded as she stroked the horse's broad snout. She wondered how strong a rider Eddie Sullivan was. He was certainly a well-built, athletic sort, she thought, and not carrying any surplus weight. 'I think young Mr Sullivan could have some fun with him.'

The Irishman shrugged. 'He seemed a touch green to me, but he must know something about the job; he's Ron Sullivan's boy. Right,' he went on with unexpected decisiveness, 'I've got a ferry to catch.' He handed the head-collar rope to Jan. 'Best of luck with him. And if ever you're over in Killarney lookin' at horses, be sure to call by and see us.'

Jan led Russian Eagle into a box on the front that she'd had vacated for him.

The stocky Irishman whistled as he raised the tail ramp on his now empty lorry and shot the bolts home. 'Goodbye to you, Mrs Hardy,' he called while she was still unbuckling the horse's head-collar in his box. 'And don't forget, a woman with a good eye like yours will always be welcome at Castlefort Stables.'

The horse headed for the rack full of fresh hay at the back of the box and Jan let herself out as the driver was already swinging up into his cab.

'Don't we owe you something for transport?' she called.

'No. It was on my way. Light a little candle for me if you want. God bless.'

He banged the door shut, fired up a noisy engine and manoeuvred the lorry out of the yard and down the drive.

As he went, Jan watched him. She was beginning to learn that people in the horse world were no more subject to stereotyping or prejudiced reputation than those in any other human activity. She'd already met with real kindness, and blunt ruthlessness, when she'd been least expecting them. These anomalies didn't surprise her so much now, but it hadn't even remotely occurred to her that Eddie Sullivan might be Ron Sullivan's son.

Now she realized why Eddie had seemed vaguely

familiar. She was barely ten when she'd heard people talking about Ron Sullivan, who had come to the Cotswolds and bought one of the biggest houses in the area. Now Jan guessed she must have come across Eddie since then, perhaps around the local point-to-points, though it must have been when he was still a teenager.

But she had never met Ron in Gloucestershire or at the races. She'd seen him once or twice a few years before, when he'd been on a high and owned a lot of good horses in one of the big Lambourn yards, though not so much had been seen of him recently. She'd never had a conversation with him, but she'd read about him in the racing papers, she'd seen him interviewed on the television and she couldn't begin to match him to a son like Eddie.

As she watched the Irish lorry rumble out of sight down the lane, her thoughts were interrupted as another one appeared and turned up towards the house. A few minutes later, she was leading her fifteen hundred guineas' worth of scatty chestnut gelding into his new home beside Russian Eagle.

'He's lovely,' Annabel laughed. 'But he's so big!'

She and Jan were in Russian Eagle's stable next morning. It was nine o'clock and the children were already down at their grandmother's bungalow. When Annabel arrived, Jan had been about to take Lazy Dove out for a little work on his own. He was one of only two horses in her yard still entered to run before the end of the season in two weeks' time.

With the rest of the horses turned out or at home for the summer, Jan had laid off her lads a fortnight before, to keep costs down during the lean time. But Annabel hadn't come to work that morning; she simply wanted to see what new horses Jan had bought.

'He is big, but I still like the look of him,' Jan said. 'And the little bloke who dropped him off said he could certainly gallop. Mind you, he said he took a bit of holding as well, and I don't think this chap who's bought him knows what he's doing.'

'Who is he?'

Jan laughed. 'It's funny really. I met him in the most extraordinary way.' She told Annabel about the manic horse that had gone on the rampage and lashed out at Megan. 'I was terrified when I turned round and couldn't see her, but this man had just dived in and lifted her out of the way. I was so relieved, I even let him take her off to get an ice cream before I knew who he was.'

'Well, who was he, for God's sake?' Annabel laughed impatiently as she stroked Russian Eagle's nose.

'Oh, nobody you'd know.' Jan stopped. 'Though, come to think of it, you might. Have you ever heard of Ron Sullivan?'

'What?' Annabel sounded shocked. 'A big, flashy property tycoon covered in gold rings and bracelets? *He* dived and saved Meg?' she asked with disbelief.

'No, no! Not him. His son, Eddie.'

'Eddie?' Annabel gasped and suddenly took her hand off the horse's nose as if it were red hot.

'A-ha! I thought you'd know him.' Jan started to laugh, but stopped when she saw Annabel's face. 'Do you really know him?'

Annabel nodded. 'You could say so. He was at school with Charley, my brother. They were in the same year and the same house, and Eddie Sullivan was always a bit of a hero – you know, a rugger star, played in a rock band.' Annabel gave a rueful laugh. 'It was a rotten band, looking back on it, but at the time I thought it was just the best and Eddie was very popular. I must have been about thirteen when I first met him. I suppose I built him up into a sort of fantasy figure and I was absolutely besotted with him for a long time after that.'

'So, how well did you know him?' Jan asked, intrigued, as well as amused by the coincidence.

Annabel sighed. 'He was my first boyfriend.'

'Good Lord! Was he your first lover too?'

Annabel walked to the stable door and leaned over the bottom half with her back to Jan. 'Yes,' she nodded.

'Oh dear,' Jan murmured. 'What went wrong? Was he a bastard?'

'No, not really. It wasn't his fault, but it caused some massive rows in my family, I can tell you. My father didn't like him at all – he particularly didn't like the fact that Ron Sullivan is his father. It was awful. I'll tell you about it some time, but not now. And I'd rather you didn't mention what I've said to Eddie. I mean, he was only twenty-three at the time, though I think he'd already had a lot of girlfriends.'

'None of the men I went out with were ever that popular – in fact I don't think John had really been serious about anybody before me,' Jan said. 'Still, I think I know why you're worried, but if you decide to come with me to Edge Farm I should warn you that I think Eddie'll be around quite a bit. He wants to ride his horse in the Foxhunters' at Aintree.'

'I was going to tell you today. I *do* want to come! It's just the excuse I need to get away from home without being too far from Mum, and I'm bloody well not going to let something that happened five years ago spoil it for me!'

'That's great! You can live in the caravan with me and the kids.'

'No, don't worry. You'll need some space for yourself. I'll rent somewhere in the village, but I'll come and help you with the move and sort things out over the summer – as a friend, I mean. You won't have to pay me or anything, not till you get the horses back in.'

Jan looked at her friend in amazement. It seemed almost incredible that someone should offer to be so helpful without any obvious benefit to herself. 'Bel, if you come, that would be great, but I'd have to pay you, especially if you're going to look after the kids and everything. I was going to see if I could get an au pair anyway.'

'All right,' Annabel said, understanding Jan's embarrassment at the offer of free help. 'Pay me what you would have had to pay the au pair.'

'It'll be so nice to have a familiar face around, especially when I first move.'

'Have you got a date yet?'

'I've got to be out of here by June the twelfth. That's three weeks tomorrow. The removal people are coming next week and Philip's dad is helping me with all the hay and other horse stuff.'

'What are you doing now?'

'I was just about to take Lazy Dove out.'

'Can I come with you?'

'There's only Gale Bird left who needs exercise. You could ride her and save me doing it later.'

'Great! I'll go and tack her up.'

They took their time, hacking the horses across the hills. With the larks trilling upwards in a soft breeze under a sky of patchy blue and white, Jan began to think for the first time about what it would be like to move away.

'You're right,' she admitted to Annabel. 'I will miss the summer mornings up here. I don't really know where I'm going to ride out from Edge Farm for long exercise, but there won't be anything like the freedom I have here.'

'It's too late to change your mind now.' Annabel laughed.

'I haven't. I'm just admitting that I'll miss the hills a little.'

They chatted about Jan's plans for Edge Farm and how she hoped to attract a few ailing or problem horses into the yard to keep her busy during the summer. 'When you think about it, I only have the pointers from September through to May, if I'm lucky, and I'll still need some income from June to August.'

'Then you'll definitely need help. Phil's not coming over is he?'

'No. I'm fond of Phil, but in this new yard I don't intend to carry any passengers. Anyone I employ is going to have to do their job when they're supposed to and in the way I tell them. With horses, you can't keep taking your eye off the ball because you're looking over your shoulder at your staff all the time.'

'Does that include me, then?' Annabel asked with a grin.

'For God's sake, I'd never have to worry about you!'

As they reached the brow of the hill above Stonewall Farm, they could see right the way to the bottom of the valley, where the lane joined the Kington road. A car had just turned off the main road and was speeding between the hedges faster than any local car would have done.

'I wonder who that is,' Jan murmured.

'It's some kind of flashy convertible; must be a lost tourist.'

As they dropped down the track from the common land to the farm, they glimpsed the car again.

'It's coming to see you, Jan!' Annabel laughed as the car stopped at the bottom of the drive for a few seconds, before turning in and making its way much more slowly up the deeply rutted track towards Jan's yard. 'Do you know who it is?'

'I haven't a clue.'

'It's one of those new drop-head Mercedes,' Annabel said with a hint of disapproval. 'What on earth's it doing up here?'

They lost sight of the car behind the buildings, but they heard it stop, and the engine turn off. Jan and Annabel almost held their breaths as they clattered down the last few yards of the track, round the back of the barn and into the yard.

A man in a dark-brown leather flying jacket was sitting on the stone mounting block with his back to them. A thin plume of smoke drifted above his head.

Both feeling a little fazed by this unlikely looking visitor, Jan and Annabel slid off their horses. Annabel hung back as he turned to greet them.

It was Eddie Sullivan.

'Good morning,' he said with a big, lazy smile at Jan.

Jan nodded and smiled back.

Annabel stepped forward and drew in a quick breath. 'Hi, Eddie.'

He looked at her more sharply and took a moment to recognize her under her helmet. 'Bel! What on earth are you doing here?'

'Bel's my head groom,' Jan said, 'the backbone of my yard.'

'How extraordinary! I picked the right yard, then,' Eddie said, betraying nothing of what Annabel had told Jan earlier that morning. He stood up, brushing dust and moss from his jeans, and stubbed out a small cigar on the cobbles. 'I hope you don't mind me turning up like this, but I'm on my way to Brecon and I couldn't wait to see my new horse. I wanted to make sure I hadn't just got carried away bidding for him yesterday. He is here, isn't he?'

'Yes. The groom who was looking after him at the sales dropped him off last night. He's in the end box.' Jan nodded at Russian Eagle's stable and Eddie walked over to it.

'Go on in, if you want,' Jan called. 'We're just going to put these horses away, then we'll have a look at yours.'

'God, the world's a small place sometimes,' Annabel muttered.

'I'm not complaining,' Jan answered under her breath. 'He's not my type, but he seems a nice guy. Now he's one of my clients you'll just have to try and get on with him.'

'I will, once I've got used to the idea. But you go and deal with him, Jan. I'll put these two in their stables.' She took Lazy Dove's head and walked both horses round to the back yard.

Jan looked over Eagle's door and found Eddie with his arm around the horse's neck.

He glanced at her with a grin. 'He may be as fat as Billy Bunter, but he's sure as hell got a placid temperament.'

'I haven't had a chance to look at him properly since he got here. I'll pull him out so we can get a better look at him.'

Eddie stepped aside while Jan buckled on a head-collar and led the horse out.

'He doesn't look quite so vast outside the stable,' he said.

'Don't worry about his size. I've seen bigger horses win races and he's carrying plenty of condition. He must have been on some really good grass over in Ireland before they sent him to the sales. He's obviously a good doer. He'd finished every bit of hay when I went in earlier this morning.'

'When do you think I could ride him?' Eddie asked.

Jan looked at him and couldn't help smiling. There was an unexpected, engaging naivety about him. She still found it hard to see how he could be the son of the notorious Ron, about whom rumours of commercial wizardry and anecdotes of skulduggery circulated in equal quantities. She was well aware, though, that among thoroughbred horses, for example, stallions often didn't stamp their stock, while the mare's qualities were more likely to be passed on.

'I'd leave him for a bit. Let him settle and get used to us. Then in two weeks' time, we're all moving to my new yard in Gloucestershire.'

'Are you? Where exactly?'

'Edge Farm, Stanfield.'

'Great! That's much nearer me.'

'Where do you live then?' Jan asked innocently.

'In Nether Swell, near Stow.'

'I thought you might. That's near my mum and dad, at Riscombe.'

'I heard you came from there.'

'Been doing your homework, then?' Jan asked, pleased that he had.

Eddie nodded. 'So, why are you moving back?'

'My husband died in January. This was his farm and I didn't want to stay here without him. Besides, I've got to make a living. I've got two young kids.'

'I've already met one of them,' Eddie reminded her.

'I never thanked you properly for that,' Jan said. 'It all happened in such a rush. It was being at the sales, I suppose. It always gets me wound up.'

'It's meant to, that's part of the whole thing – to give the auction as much sense of drama as possible; it makes people excited and clouds their judgement. It happens to me all the time at picture sales.'

'Is that what you do?' Jan didn't hide her surprise. 'I thought people who dealt in art were usually—'. Her voice petered out in embarrassment.

'Gay?' Eddie grinned. 'How do you know I'm not? Would you mind if I were?'

'No. It wouldn't matter one iota to me. My dad used to call a horse "gay" if he was a playful and lively character, but with all this political correctness you can't say it now. And – you might have gathered – I'm not very good at being PC. But anyway, you're not gay,' she added with a laugh. 'I know that.'

'How do you know?'

'From the way you look at women.'

Eddie looked at her and raised an eyebrow. 'Is that so?'

Neither of them spoke for a moment and Jan suddenly felt she'd gone too far. She'd been determined, since she'd suggested he sent his horse to her, that she would treat Eddie in a thoroughly professional manner, and now here she was, as soon as she saw him again, flirting with him, as good as telling him that she fancied him – which she did, but only in an arms' length, academic sort of way. The memory of John was still too fresh for her to contemplate any kind of physical relationship.

'Anyway,' she hurried on, 'I think you should leave riding Russian Eagle for a bit. Once he's settled in at Edge Farm, we could bring him in early and I'll take him out and exercise him a little to see how he behaves, then I could start schooling you both.'

She looked up and saw Eddie smiling at her slightly flustered delivery, and, perhaps, at the idea of her schooling him.

'Whatever you say. I'll allow you to be the boss in our relationship in all matters equine. I won't attempt to ride the horse until you say so, and I promise to obey all your commands. In the meantime, I wouldn't mind taking another look at him.'

'It's a bit late for that, isn't it? He's already here, but I'll trot him up, just for you, so you haven't had a wasted journey.'

Jan tugged the horse's rope and, setting off at a brisk jog, she gee'd him into a surprisingly elegant trot. Going a little faster, she extended it until she got to the gate, where she turned and jogged back.

'He does look lighter when he's moving,' Eddie said.

Jan nodded. 'That's what I thought yesterday. Let's hope he can jump and gallop, too. Now, have you seen enough?'

'Yes thanks.'

'Then I'll put him away. Would you like a cup of coffee up at the house?'

Eddie looked a his watch. 'No, thanks. I've got a date to look at some pictures in a house the other side of Brecon and I'm late already.' He took his car keys from the pocket of his leather jacket. 'Would you send me details of your charges? Here's my address.' He handed her a card with 'The Sullivan Gallery' and an address in Stow-on-the-Wold printed on it. 'And say goodbye to Annabel for me. Tell her I'm looking forward to seeing her again when you move to Gloucestershire. Is she coming with you, by the way?'

Jan, still holding Russian Eagle, tilted her head to one side. 'To tell you the truth, I'm not sure now.'

'I hope she does,' Eddie said. He walked to his car, opened the door and dropped into the driver's seat.

By the time Annabel came round the corner from the back yard, he was already passing the bungalow at the bottom of the drive.

6

In the weeks following the Doncaster Sales, Jan had to put most of her energy into moving. Olwen Hardy seemed to have accepted at last that her daughter-in-law and grandchildren were leaving Stonewall – at least, she was co-operative about having the children while Jan was busy.

Jan had not foreseen how harrowing the process of dismantling a household could be. Stonewall had been first occupied by John's parents in 1948, and in a large house with a lot of storage space very little had been thrown out since then. There were piles of musty books and linen, old domestic appliances, crockery, cutlery, kitchen utensils, farm accounts and records, innumerable household knick-knacks, lamps, ornaments – a seemingly endless catalogue of modest, serviceable objects.

Sorting it all and trying to decide what to keep, what to sell, what to give away and what to take to the tip involved some difficult decisions, but Jan was determined to be methodical and logical about the job. She had been given a lot of tea chests and cardboard boxes by the firm in Hereford who were going to do the main move for her. Besides these, she had found a pile of empty trunks and suitcases in one of the attics. Everything she thought she shouldn't discard until she'd had a proper look at it she packed into them and then labelled them to be stored in the Dutch barn at Edge Farm. For the time being all these items, and the furniture she wanted to keep for the house which she hoped one day would appear at Edge Farm, were to be kept in the barn, raised off the ground and covered by tarpaulins.

Dealing with John's personal possessions upset her far more than she could have imagined. Going through his chests of drawers and his cupboards, seeing the selection of clothes passed on from his father and in some instances, she suspected, from his grandfather, and his own practical purchases, as well as a few more colourful items she had bought for him, was like having him back in the room with her.

She picked up a Fair Isle sweater he'd always liked, buried her face in it and was instantly transported back by the evocative odours trapped in its fibres. When she found the shirt he had worn on the day they were married, which he had never worn again, she couldn't hold back the tears any longer.

Surrounded by a heap of unassuming, well-worn workaday clothing, she sat on the floor and cried helplessly.

Matthew, she thought, *is never going to want any of this, not even in twenty years' time*.

She went downstairs and brought up a roll of black plastic bags she had bought for the purpose and stuffed all the clothes into them, until she had ten full sacks which she labelled 'Oxfam'. One by one she carried them all down to the back hall, ready to take with her next time she went to Hay. She felt better after that. She was sure that was what John would have wanted her to do.

That night, to her surprise, she slept a little better.

When she woke, she lay in bed thinking about John and his mother.

She tried to imagine how she would feel if she lost one of her children before she died and realized she could think of nothing worse. Whatever Olwen might think of her, she had have loved her son very much.

With a sudden rush of guilt, she went down and carried all the plastic bags back up, emptied them and arranged the contents in neat piles around the room.

For the rest of the morning she carried on sorting and tidying John's possessions. When she came across a beautifully crafted eighteenth-century gold fob watch, engraved with the initials of some former Hardy, complete with its chain and crude letter seal, she picked it out to give to Olwen.

Later, after she'd checked the horses, she walked down to the bungalow with Tigger and knocked on the door.

Olwen opened it and stared at her as if she were a total stranger.

'Good morning, Olwen,' she said, fishing in a carrier

bag she'd brought with her. 'I've brought down something of John's that I thought you might like to have.'

She took out the watch, which she had polished and wrapped in tissue paper, and passed it to the old woman.

Olwen took the package suspiciously and unwrapped it. She looked at the watch, turned it over and handed it back to Jan. 'I can't have this,' she said. 'It should go to his son. It's always been passed down from father to son.'

'Oh,' Jan said, feeling foolish. 'I'm sorry. Is there something else more personal you'd like instead? Maybe some of his clothes . . .?'

Olwen looked at her disdainfully. 'What would I want with any of his clothes?'

'I meant, as a sort of memento.'

'I'll come up, later, before tea, and select some items,' Olwen said firmly.

'Oh,' Jan said, taken by surprise. Olwen had declined every invitation to come up to the house since she had moved out of it. 'Fine. I'll try and have everything out for you to look at.'

Jan went back to prepare for Olwen's visit and wondered what she would choose. She decided that before she came she had better go through John's bureau, which stood against one wall of the sitting room and had always been locked except when John had been working at it.

Jan hadn't wanted to open it since he had gone, although she'd had to a few times to find bank statements and correspondence with MAFF, which John kept in there. Now she emptied all the drawers and pigeon-holes and spread out the contents.

Sitting on the floor in the middle of the room, she found several packets of photographs, for the most part grainy, monochrome shots taken with a rudimentary camera, but clear enough. One showed John when he was a boy of eight or nine, standing with his father, who was shearing a sheep in what was just recognizable as the yard outside. There was another of John when he was even younger, perhaps five, with a huge smile, sitting in front of his father on the pony old Mr Hardy had used to shepherd his flock out on the mountain.

In a small folder of its own, she found a more recent, good-quality colour photograph, taken six years before. She stared at it for a few moments, took it from its folder and turned it over. When she read the inscription, she sat back on her haunches and cried again.

'Jan? Are you all right?'

Jan looked up and saw Annabel, standing in the doorway with a sympathetic expression on her face.

Jan sniffed and nodded. 'I just found this,' she said. 'I've never seen it before and I never even knew he had it.' She held out the photograph for Annabel to see. It was a shot of a horse, obviously soon after winning a race, with Billy Hanks up, and grinning all over his face. On either side of the horse stood John, tall, dark, healthy and smiling shyly, and Jan, twenty-three years old, fresh, vital and beaming as if she would burst.

On the reverse, in John's old-fashioned writing were the words:

Jan's first winner – a Proud Moment!

Jan saw a few tears glisten in Annabel's eyes, too, and she felt better for having shared a little of her grief.

Annabel handed back the photo. 'Isn't it wonderful that he never told you he had it?'

Jan nodded. 'I can just about remember someone taking a picture. But John wasn't much of a one for photographs and I would never have expected him to get a copy.'

'Look, Jan, as I was coming up the drive I saw Olwen on her way here. I thought you might want to be ready for her.'

Jan got to her feet. 'Yes, thanks. I wonder if she's expecting tea. Probably not, but I'll get it all ready anyway, just to give her the satisfaction of saying she doesn't want it.'

As it turned out, Jan was wrong. Olwen spent half an hour wandering around the house and rummaging through all the things that Jan had sorted out.

Jan left her to it and sat in the kitchen with the children, giving them their tea, until the white-haired old woman walked in.

'I'll have some tea', she said, 'in the parlour.'

Jan took a tray of the best cups and saucers through into the sitting room, where she found Olwen sitting upright on one of the old sofas, looking intently at the picture over the mantelpiece.

She said nothing. Jan poured some tea and waited.

'I'll have the clock in the hall', Olwen said eventually, without preamble, 'and that picture.' She nodded in the direction of the mantelpiece.

The painting, though probably not of great quality, was, Jan thought, the most interesting thing in the house. In a crude version of Herring's style, it depicted a sporting horse being held by a scruffy groom against a background of an unmistakably Welsh hill, which John had identified. He had always said the picture had almost certainly been painted for one of the big land-owning families of the Usk valley, who had historically kept horses to race in harness. He had had no idea how the family had acquired it.

Jan winced. She knew Olwen had asked for it precisely because she herself liked it. And more particularly because it depicted a horse.

Jan bit her lip and nodded. 'That'll be nice for you, Olwen, but I'm worried about the clock. Do you have a room high enough to put it in?'

'Yes,' Olwen said, prepared for the objection. 'It can go in the hall, where the ceiling goes into the gable.'

'Fine,' Jan said. 'I'll ask the removal men to drop it in to you when they go past.'

'Can you bring the picture down before?'

Jan sighed. 'Yes, Olwen, of course.'

Olwen's visit did a lot to bring Jan back to earth. Once she had taken the picture down to the bungalow, she found she could throw herself into finishing the packing with all her usual energy, until, on the second Saturday after Doncaster, between finally clearing up and organizing the removal firm, she went to the races for the last point-to-point of the season in the area.

She took Gale Bird and Lazy Dove with Philip, who had volunteered to come for the day and help.

It was the first time Lazy Dove had run since he'd been chased off the course by a hare at Llandeilo, but Jan was confident from the work he'd been doing at home that he'd recovered from the experience.

She was right. The tough little gelding battled hard to finish third, within two lengths of the winner.

But the highlight of the day and, as far as Jan was concerned, a fitting finale to her fourth year's training at Stonewall was seeing her own mare, Gale Bird, romp home in the adjacent hunts' race, despite Billy Hanks being unable to take advantage of her five-pound mare's allowance. This was the mare's second consecutive win, giving Jan a final score for the season of fourteen wins between the flags, and the hunter chase at Ludlow – enough to make her champion trainer for the region.

But she had failed to keep a check on Phil's celebrations after the race and, tired as she was, she had to drive the lorry home herself while he slumped across the bench seat beside her and snored. She was glad this was the last time she would have to worry about him, but even so she was going to miss him.

Jan's mind wandered and she found herself thinking of other things she would miss in the valley that had been her home for the last seven years and, without warning, the idea of leaving the place where she'd been happy with John moved her to tears. She blinked, and glanced through blurred eyes at Philip, grateful now that he was sound asleep. But somehow she managed to work her way through the conflicting emotions of the day and she arrived home satisfied with what she'd achieved so far.

She was also pleased when, the week before she finally moved, she was given a strong indication of her success as a trainer. A journalist from *Horse & Hound* came to Stonewall to interview her, which gave her the chance to announce to the racing world that the next season she would be at a much more accessible yard in Gloucestershire.

Since her offer for Edge Farm had been accepted at the beginning of May, Jan had been searching for a good-sized mobile home that she and the children could live in while she earned enough money to build a new house there. She had found a serviceable second-hand one on a holiday site down by the River Wye.

The owner recognized Jan from his days at the races. He knew her circumstances and insisted that she pay only for its transport to Gloucestershire. In return, he suggested, she might like to give him a call some time when she had a runner she fancied. Jan was deeply impressed by such generosity and couldn't think what she'd done to deserve it from a complete stranger.

The caravan arrived at the new yard a few days before she was due to move. Leaving the children with Olwen, she drove over right away to prepare it and organize the electricity supply. Towards the end of the afternoon she found herself standing in the cramped living area, wondering if, after the rambling space of Stonewall, she'd been rather too optimistic in thinking she could live there with two small children and all their clutter. It was at this low moment that Annabel arrived, bringing with her a bottle of wine and a bunch of flowers to cheer Jan up. She had also brought a present for Megan – an exquisite doll's house, eighteen inches high and filled with miniature furniture and tiny Persian rugs.

'I hope you don't mind,' she said, putting it on the table and opening it up to show Jan. 'I know you're pushed for space, but I thought Megan might be really upset about leaving Stonewall and this could be a little house of her own.'

'Annabel!' Jan said, moved by her kindness. 'It's wonderful and she'll love it, but you can't give it to her. It must be worth a fortune.'

Annabel shrugged her slender shoulders with a smile. 'That doesn't matter. I haven't played with it for yonks and I want her to have it.'

'But you should keep it for when you've got a daughter of your own.'

Annabel, who had been rearranging some of the tiny furniture, paused and said nothing for a moment before closing the front of the house.

Jan looked at her closely. 'What's the matter? Don't you want to keep it for your own family?'

Annabel glanced up at her. 'No, it's OK,' she said quietly. 'I'll worry about that when the time comes and it would make me so happy to give it to Megan.'

Once Jan and Annabel had spruced up the caravan, they went out to take a look at the buildings. As they strolled around the farm, it came home to Jan just how much she was going to have to do to make the place work.

'It's all very well Dad saying I just need to knock up a few partitions and sling a tarpaulin over the roof, but how the hell am I going to find a builder I can trust to do it before all the horses arrive? What are the owners going to think, seeing their horses housed like that?'

Annabel put a hand on her forearm. 'Jan, stop fretting. There are no more races this season. There's no reason why all the horses can't go straight out. There's masses of grass in the paddocks.'

Jan nodded. 'I suppose so, but looking at this—', she waved a hand at the derelict barn, 'it suddenly all seems a bit much – the idea of living in a caravan with the children among all these ruins.'

'It'll be great, Jan! You know you can do it. I tell you what – why don't we go to the pub in the village now and start asking around for someone to come up and do the work for you?'

As they drove down the deeply rutted track to the road, Jan spotted several pieces of broken fencing. 'They'd better start with replacing some of these knackered rails,' she said gloomily.

The Fox & Pheasant had been a pub since the seventeenth century and hadn't changed much since that time. When she saw the people in there – healthy Gloucestershire faces like her own – she guessed that most of them were descended from the men who'd used the inn for the last few hundred years.

A tall girl in her twenties with chubby cheeks, big breasts and spiky black hair was behind the bar when Jan and Annabel walked in. She gave Jan a quick, shrewd glance with her chocolate brown eyes. 'Hello, I'm Julie,' she said. 'You're the people moving into Edge Farm, aren't you?'

'She is,' Annabel disclaimed. 'I'm not, but I'll be

helping out there and I'm looking for a cottage to rent in the village.'

'Oh well, you want to talk to him, then,' the barmaid nodded at a well-dressed, somewhat forbidding man sitting alone with his pewter mug on a settle in a dark corner of the pub.

'Thanks, I will.'

While Annabel walked over to talk to the unlikely looking landlord, Jan perched on a stool and told Julie that she needed a builder. A few minutes later she was being introduced to Gerry.

A local lad of twenty-five, Gerry was six foot three with a red face and hands like shovels, one of which he thrust forward shyly for Jan to shake.

'You're a builder, are you?' she asked.

'Joiner,' he mumbled. 'But I can do pretty much anything.'

'And you wouldn't try to stitch me up, just because I'm a woman?'

Gerry looked shocked at the thought. 'No – just the opposite, I should think, for someone as . . . someone like you.'

Jan smiled and wondered how he had been going to describe her. 'That's good, because once I've got my stables up, there's a whole house to build.'

She told him what had to be done first and he didn't need much persuading to come up and price the job. Doing his best to overcome his embarrassment, he was still thanking her for the opportunity when Annabel came back from her discussion with the old man on the settle.

'I think I might have found a cottage already,' she said. 'Mr Carey seems to own half the village.'

Julie, earwigging beside them, nodded. 'He does, and Stanfield Court. He's a miserable old git, though,' she added under her breath.

'Well, he's very kindly offered me', she glanced at the piece of paper where she'd written the address, 'Number Two, Glebe Cottages.'

'That's a nice little place,' Julie said, 'but he'll want an arm and a leg.'

'Judging by the way he was looking at her,' Jan said, 'it's not her arms he's interested in.'

'Oh, he's all right like that,' the barmaid said. 'Just bloody stingy.'

'Will you come and look at it with me?' Annabel asked Jan. 'He says he'll go and get the key now if I want.'

A quarter of an hour later they were inspecting the cottage, which was freshly painted but hadn't been modernized in the previous twenty years. 'I expect I can manage without a Poggenpohl kitchen.' Annabel laughed and turned to Jan. 'Do you know, this is the first time in my life that I'll be living on my own? Apart from school, I've only been away from home for a short time when I went to London, and for a few months in a hall of residence at Bristol, before that all went wrong too,' she murmured.

'You've never told me what happened there,' Jan said quietly.

'I was on the rebound – a lecherous don. I was so gullible—' Annabel shook her head. 'I suppose I was trying to get back at my father.' With an effort, she smiled. 'I don't want to start banging on about it now. I love this place.'

And within ten minutes she'd made up her mind to take the cottage.

They had decided to go back to Stonewall that evening, where Annabel would stay the night. Annabel drove them in her Golf, promising they'd get back half an hour quicker than they would in the Land Rover.

On the way home Jan laughed at the ease with which Annabel had been accommodated. 'It's just not fair the way men fall over backwards to do favours for tall, skinny, beautiful women, when people like me have to work so hard at it.'

'What are you talking about?' Annabel grinned back. 'You had that lumbering great builder eating out of your hands and you know it. He looked besotted the minute he clapped eyes on you.'

'That's just because he thought I might be a good punter,' Jan said with a cynical grunt.

Jan wondered, though, if that was the only reason, when she and Annabel arrived back at the farm next morning and found Gerry had already been up and repaired all the broken fencing he could find.

'Least you'll be able to keep your horses in when

they gets here. I thought that was the most important thing,' he said gruffly.

'It was, Gerry. Thanks very much. Now, have you had a look at the barn? I've drawn up a sort of a plan for what I want. I've got it in the caravan.'

By 12 June, Jan's moving day, Gerry had already made a good start on a run of solid stables within the stone walls of the barn and every square inch of the roof had been covered in old-fashioned khaki canvas tarpaulins. They didn't stand out too harshly against the hillside and the puddles in the barn had already disappeared. Reg had been over with his chain harrow to breathe some new life into the pasture, and with his billhook to repair the hedges. He was delighted to be useful and he was as excited as Jan at the imminent arrival of the horses.

At Stonewall in the morning Matthew was too young to understand the significance of the journey they were making that day, but Megan knew she was leaving the only home she'd ever known. Jan was aware that she still hadn't got used to losing her Dad and guessed that she didn't want to lose her home as well. Until then, Megan had never even spent so much as a single night away from Stonewall.

'Mum,' she said, as she refused to eat her cereal in the empty, echoing kitchen, 'how can I sleep if I'm not in my own room?'

'Meg, don't worry. You'll be fine after all the excitement of moving and seeing our new home. It'll be really nice to go to bed in our caravan, just you wait.'

Megan's face puckered, and the slits of her eyes filled with tears. 'I don't want to live in a stupid caravan! I want my dad! I want my friends. I want to stay here – this is my house!' she wailed.

Jan picked her up and hugged her. 'You'll soon find new friends, I promise, and you'll like the caravan after a few days. Please try, for Mummy?'

'There's another house over there, too,' Annabel said. 'And it's only this high.' She put her hand a foot and a half above the ground.

Megan stopped crying as her little mind absorbed the tantalizing prospect of a miniature home. 'Whose is it?' she sniffed.

'It's yours,' Annabel said. 'I hope you like it.'

'I think I will,' the little girl said, looking more confident.

By the time they dropped in at Olwen Hardy's bungalow on their way out with the children and the first load of horses, Megan was already looking forward to being at Edge Farm, if only to take possession of her own new household.

Olwen was less happy. 'Do you know what you're doing?' the old woman asked, with her dark eyes flaming. 'There's been Hardys at Stonewall for a hundred and fifty years.'

'I'm sorry, Olwen. I know you're going to miss the children and I will bring them over as often as I can, but I'm doing what's best for them. I've told you why.

I don't know how to make a living up here – so I have to go where I can.'

'It's terrible to think of Hardys living like tinkers in a caravan!'

Jan sighed. 'It won't be for ever. We'll build a beautiful house there, just you wait and see.'

At midday Jan followed the removal lorry up the track to Edge Farm. While her furniture and boxes were being stacked in the Dutch barn, she and Annabel unloaded the first four horses and loosed them into the paddock beside the barn. Then Jan climbed back into the lorry and headed straight back to pick up the last four of her charges. Harold Powell had decided it would make sense for his horses to summer with her where she could keep an eye on them, though he'd driven a hard bargain for their keep.

Gerry the carpenter had already recruited a stable hand to help Jan and Annabel. Roz Stoddard was Gerry's cousin and lived in the village. She was a large, loud, laughing girl, whom Jan liked on sight. She had worked in her mother's livery yard and had hunted since she was eight. She said she didn't mind what she had to ride or how many hours she worked in the yard, she just loved horses.

Annabel, Roz and Gerry were still in the yard with Reg as the sun dropped down behind the Malverns and Jan arrived with the three dogs and the remaining horses. When these were settled and quietly grazing in their new surroundings, Jan felt that now the move was complete; her new life was about to begin.

Understanding this, Annabel had gone down to the village with Roz and made a large casserole, which they brought up to the caravan for Jan's first dinner at Edge Farm. Gerry came back with a couple of bottles of wine and the four of them sat with Reg, crammed around the table in the mobile home, while the children dozed in their beds at the other end.

'Here's to you, Jan,' Gerry said, holding up his glass, 'and all the winners that are gonna come out of this place.'

Within a week of moving, Jan was already feeling at home. The dogs had helped by quickly finding their way around their new territory. Fly and Fred had been allocated the main barn as their dormitory, while Tigger, the terrier, had been favoured with a basket in the caravan. Fred, the lurcher, and Tigger had soon discovered that there was sport to be had in the warrens at the top of the farm, and old Fly had found the best way to pick up a titbit was to hang around the tack room when the humans were having their tea breaks.

Although she had eight useful horses in her paddocks, Jan hoped fervently she would have at least double that number by the start of the next point-to-point season. Besides Harold Powell's four geldings – Mister Mack, Lenny's Lad, Lazy Dove and Rear Gunner – she had Eddie Sullivan's horse, her own mare, Gale Bird, a horse called Derring Duke, who belonged to Owen Tollard, an electrical contractor in Brecon, and the skinny chestnut she'd bought at Doncaster but hadn't yet named.

Jan didn't intend that any of the horses would start work again until August at the earliest, and until she had recruited a few ailing or wayward animals for treatment she was going to devote all her attention to cleaning up her yard.

Despite haggling over the move and his disappointment that Jan hadn't yet found him another high-quality hunter-chaser, Harold had lost none of his enthusiasm. He came to see his horses at Edge Farm twice in the first week, which was more than when they'd been on his doorstep. Jan was very glad he'd chosen to send them with her, for she was now beginning to wonder whether she'd been kidding herself to think she would start picking up new owners in the first few months.

A week after the horses had arrived at Jan's farm, Colonel Gilbert, her father's landlord, phoned to ask if he could come and have a look at her set-up on Sunday morning.

When the day came, Jan was almost quivering with apprehension as she watched the colonel's Jeep bounce up her track. He had owned several good National Hunt horses and was a long-standing member of the Jockey Club, as well as a steward at several local race courses. When she'd been a small girl, she had met the colonel often with her father. Then he had always seemed a distant, somewhat unreal figure to have such a strong influence over the life of a small tenant farmer on his large estate. Later, she had seen much more of him when he'd sent horses to the big racing yard where she'd worked and, as a result, she'd ridden River Rocket for him to win the ladies' Open at the Heythrop point-to-point.

He parked outside the gate of a stable yard that was unrecognizable from the mess it had been when Jan and Reg first came to look at it. Gerry had painted every stick of timber and Annabel and Roz had swept the yard with so much gusto that there wasn't a wisp of straw out of place.

The colonel climbed out of his car and limped across the yard with a rigid leg which Jan had forgotten about. Following him was a tall, thin girl in her late twenties; Jan clearly remembered her angular frame, sharp elbows and pointed nose, but she hadn't seen her in the flesh since the day of River Rocket's win.

'Good morning, Colonel.' Jan flashed her impish smile.

'Hello, Jan,' he grinned back. 'It must be five years since we've seen you round here.'

Jan nodded. It was nearer eight.

'I was very sorry to hear the sad news about your husband.'

'I got your letter. Thank you, Colonel Gilbert.'

'Sorry it was just a couple of lines. Always so difficult on these occasions. Look, I hope you don't mind, I've brought Virginia along. She's decided that she's going to take up training too.'

Probably after her miserable performance as a jockey, Jan thought, and immediately chastised herself for a knee-jerk reaction to someone who happened to be younger and more privileged.

'Not at all,' Jan said. 'Hello, Virginia.'

Virginia was gazing around the yard with an expression of incredulity on her bony face. 'Are you really able to train from here?'

'I think so,' Jan said.

'Mrs Hardy won fourteen point-to-points and a good hunter chase last season,' the colonel said, although it was clear that Virginia knew all about Jan's record.

'I couldn't train from a yard like this; I've just applied for a public licence and I'm damn sure the Jockey Club wouldn't issue one for here.'

You snotty bitch, Jan thought, as she tried to smile. 'Best of luck. That's a bit out of my league, I'm afraid.'

'I don't see why it should be,' Colonel Gilbert grunted, 'but I'll gladly send you a useful old pointer for next season.'

Jan saw Virginia stiffen; she wondered if there was a subtext to this visit which had nothing to do with her. But she was grateful for the promise of the horse, and ecstatic at the thought that this eminent and knowledgeable man believed she was capable of getting a public licence. Up until now, she hadn't even dared consider it.

She decided to defuse her instinctive resentment of Virginia. She had always known that there was no such thing as a level playing field in racing – especially as a trainer, where a talentless man from an old racing family, with a big house, money, strong connections and a public school background stood a far higher chance of attracting well-bred horses with real potential than a gifted but skint, comprehensive-educated, widowed mother of two who lived in a caravan. But, even if she had to start this competition with both hands tied behind her back, she was determined that in the end the talent that she knew she had would show through. And at least Virginia shared the disadvantage of being female.

Jan showed Colonel Gilbert and his daughter everything that she had done to make her small plot of sloping land and its dilapidated buildings function as a place to keep and train racehorses.

The colonel was full of admiration.

'Your father told me how busy you'd been up here. I gather you've been working him pretty hard, too.'

'He volunteered,' Jan replied. The colonel had been so encouraging that she thought of asking him and Virginia into the caravan for coffee, but remembered in time that she hadn't cleared up after the kids' breakfast. Annabel was just walking back up the hill with Megan and Matthew and she could hear the baby grizzling already. 'Here are the kids now, so unless you want to stop and help me change Matty's nappy, you'll have to excuse me.'

'I think we'll leave you to it, Jan,' Colonel Gilbert laughed. 'Thanks for showing us everything you've done. We'll be back – at least, I will be.'

A few minutes later, Jan glanced up from the table where she was dealing with her son's disposable and watched the colonel's Jeep being driven cautiously down the hill. She still thrilled at his throwaway words.

He didn't see why a licence to train should be out of her league.

Until that morning the pinnacle of her ambitions had been to win one of the big hunter chases – either of the Foxhunters' or the Horse and Hound Cup. But now the idea had been planted in her mind, she felt sure that if she wanted a serious chance of a secure future for her children, she would have to get herself a licence to train under rules. Suddenly, her uncertain future looked bigger, brighter – and more daunting – than ever.

7

By the end of her second week, Jan was already feeling settled and happy at Edge Farm and ready to look beyond her immediate horizons. On a warm evening, at the end of a perfect summer's day, she decided to walk with the children down to Stanfield. Tigger came with them, hunting in and out of the hedgerows, while Jan pushed Matthew's buggy and sang songs with Megan. In the quiet village, the air was fragrant with the scent of flowers and privet blossom in the gardens as they made their way slowly up the main street to Glebe Cottages.

Annabel had moved in a few days before, after staying at the Fox & Pheasant while various small jobs were being done at the cottage. Jan hadn't asked how much rent Mr Carey was charging, but she suspected it was rather more than Annabel was earning as an au pair.

The cottage was a simple semi in the middle of the quiet village, built as a worker's home two or three centuries before. Ancient rambling roses and rampant honeysuckle clambered all over its rough-hewn golden stone walls. Inside, there was a sense of peace and contentment which seemed to reflect past happy lives that had once been lived there.

Annabel had already installed some curtains and good old furniture plundered from her indulgent parents' house. Jan felt a twinge of envy that she had been able to make everything look comfortable with such ease.

Annabel had made a tasty pasta salad and welcomed them warmly. When they had finished eating and the children were sleeping in the tiny spare room upstairs, the two friends settled down over a bottle of wine to talk about their plans for the yard.

Annabel had been told about a vet from Chipping Campden called James McNeill, recommended to her by a horse-owning friend of her father's.

'He sounds the sort you might get on with,' she said. 'He does everything – from racehorses to shires and gypsy ponies. Apparently he's quite a character.' She suggested Jan should contact him, and all the other vets in the area, to promote Edge Farm Stables as a recuperation home for injured horses, and a centre for schooling young or wayward ones.

The next morning Jan was being ushered into a drab, boxy little office in James McNeill's surgery on the edge of the Cotswold market town six miles away.

The vet was a large man, who made an unforgettable impression on anyone he met. His bright emerald eyes sparkled beneath a thick fringe of curly brown hair and he seemed able to look right into the mind of the person he was talking to. For a big man he had a surprisingly busy manner. He spoke so fast in his faint Scottish accent that Jan thought he would have been more at home behind a market stall than a desk in a surgery.

'I've heard a lot about you,' he said, nodding his head.

'Oh?' Jan was genuinely surprised.

'Colonel Gilbert seems to think a lot of you, but then that could just be compared to his daughter.'

'What do you mean?' Jan asked sharply.

James put a finger on the side of his nose. 'Sorry, I can't say more. A vet's surgery is like a priest's confessional.' It would be some time before Jan realized that James was in the habit of offering and withholding knowledge as a weapon. 'But I'm told we should expect great things and I saw that fine win you had at Ludlow in March.'

Jan couldn't help swelling with pride at this appreciation of what, to date, had been her greatest moment in racing. 'He's a super horse, Rear Gunner, and I'm fairly sure he'll still go on improving next season.'

James looked at her sharply. 'Take my advice, if that's true. Keep it to yourself, or you'll just inflate the owner's hopes and shorten the odds when the horse runs.'

Jan winced. He was right, she knew, but she wasn't sure she liked being picked up quite so assertively.

'Anyway,' the vet went on, 'tell me more about

what you're doing at Edge Farm – what a terrible old place, by the way. I hope you've managed to tidy it up.'

'Yeah, well,' Jan said, a little put out, 'it did look pretty awful, but like my dad said, it was bound to be a bit of a bargain because of it. Anyway, it was all I could afford. I only had a hill farm in Wales to sell and that just made its reserve.'

'I heard about that, too,' James said.

'What did you hear?' Jan asked sharply.

'Just that – it only made its reserve.' James shrugged. 'Still, that's better than not selling at all.'

Jan looked at him and tried to ignore a tremor of uneasiness. After all, she told herself, it was perfectly possible, even likely, that someone from this part of the world might have gone up to the sale in Hay to see if they could buy a cheap farm in Wales to run sheep on in the summer, and an experienced buyer could often tell from an auctioneer's body language when a lot had reached its reserve.

'It left me quite short of cash, though,' she answered, 'and I need some lodgers in my yard for the summer. I'm pretty good at repairing injured horses and I was hoping you might know of some that needed a bit of tender loving care.'

James opened his eyes a little wider. 'Were you now? Well, I expect we might be able to find a few tenants for you, but I'd better come over, hadn't I, to look at what facilities you can offer.' He gave Jan a completely unexpected beaming smile which seemed to light up the dingy little room.

Jan found herself glowing with gratitude at this optimistic response. 'Yes, please do. Come and have a meal,' she heard herself say before she'd considered the difficulty of entertaining guests in her caravan. Oh *God*, she thought, as she tried to hold her smile, *I'll have to borrow Annabel's microwave and park the kids somewhere for the evening.*

'Nonsense,' James laughed. 'I'll come and look at the place. Then I'd be delighted to take you out to dinner.'

Jan was filled with absurd relief at not being held to her rash invitation. 'Oh, thanks so much,' she gushed. 'That would be wonderful.'

James raised a ginger eyebrow. 'Let's hope so.'

Jan drove home rejecting a faint question mark over James McNeill's motives in offering her help. It was quite likely that, if he did send her any customers, he would want a cut. She would have to take that into consideration when she was working out her charges. Perhaps there was no reason why she shouldn't take him at his word and, anyway, there was nothing phoney about that lovely smile of his.

As she rumbled up the track to Edge Farm in her Land Rover, she thought that now she was inviting outsiders to the yard she really must do something about the ruts. As she neared the top, the sun flashed a sharp reflection off the sleek, silver bodywork of a convertible Mercedes. She recognized the number plate at once and felt a quick flutter of pleasure at the thought of seeing Eddie Sullivan again.

She parked beside his car and found him, evidently only just arrived, outside her caravan waiting for someone to answer his impatient knocking.

'Hi,' she said. 'You won't find anyone in there. The kids are down in the village with Annabel and I've been visiting the vet.'

'No problems with Russian Eagle, I hope?'

'No, thank goodness,' Jan laughed. 'He's not the sort of horse that has too many problems. I've just been drumming up a bit of business for the yard.'

'How's it all going? I'm sorry I haven't been before.'

'I was wondering what had happened to you,' Jan said sternly.

'I've been in Italy for three weeks, trying to buy paintings.'

'I bet!' Jan snorted. 'Chasing those little Italian *signorinas* all over the place, I should think.'

Eddie drew himself up. 'Now look here, Mrs Hardy, I never chase women—'

'Yeah, I know. They chase you,' she finished for him.

'I wasn't going to say that.'

'Maybe, but you were thinking it.'

Eddie laughed and shook his head. 'Look, I've come

here to be schooled over fences, not to be psychoanalysed.'

'Not today you haven't,' Jan said. 'All the horse were roughed off three weeks ago and I won't be bringing them back in till August at the earliest.'

'Oh,' Eddie said. 'Of course, I wasn't expecting you to be able to do anything today, but I had hoped, you know—?'

Jan couldn't help smiling at his disappointment. 'I suppose we *could* ride yours from the field to do a bit of schooling. But no galloping or anything like that until he's as fit as a flea.'

'You're the boss, Jan. By the way, I haven't had a bill yet.'

'It's the last day of the month, so you will tomorrow. I like to pride myself on the fact that mine is the first letter that pops through an owner's letter-box on the first day of the month. In the meantime, would you like a cup of coffee?'

'I'd love one.'

Sitting on the padded benches in the caravan, with a cafetière on the small table between them, they talked about Russian Eagle.

'Are you serious about wanting to ride him in the Foxhunters' at Aintree?' Jan asked.

'Deadly.'

'And it could be – if you didn't know what you were doing. Don't forget it's one and a bit circuits of the actual Grand National course.'

'I know,' Eddie nodded. 'That's why I want to do it.'

Jan shook her head. 'How many point-to-points did you say you'd won?' she asked sarcastically.

'Now, don't let's be defeatist about this. That's why I'm here. You're going to teach me how to do it properly.'

'You do realize that you – or at least the horse – has to win at least one open point-to-point to qualify to run in the Liverpool Foxhunters,' and you'll have to get an amateur rider's permit from the Jockey Club to ride under rules?'

Eddie nodded. 'I looked up the race he won in Ireland and he beat a couple of good horses. I did wonder why they hadn't hung on to him a bit longer.'

Jan shrugged. 'That's not what they do. They like to turn them into cash.'

Jan and Eddie went to inspect Russian Eagle and the other horses grazing in the sloping fields. He was intrigued by the past performance and prospects of each one.

'I'd love to see round the whole place, if you've got time?' he asked as they left the paddock.

'Sure,' Jan agreed.

As they walked, in between telling him what she planned to do with the barns and the house, she took the opportunity to find out more about him.

'If you don't mind me asking,' she said, 'how come you seem so much posher than your dad?'

'What do you mean "seem"? I ought to be posher than my father. He spent a small fortune sending me to Harrow and supporting me through university.'

'Did you go to university?'

'I thought everyone did these days, now every college of further education seems to be called a university.'

'I didn't.'

'You obviously didn't need it. But I spent three years in Exeter playing tennis, learning seduction techniques and studying history of art with a lot of Sloane Rangers.'

'On whom you practised your seduction techniques, no doubt.'

'The lucky ones, yes,' Eddie nodded, his eyes twinkling as he struggled to keep a straight face.

Jan laughed. 'So your dad made his fortune building houses, but decided his son was going to be a toff?'

'That's about it.'

'Doesn't it embarrass you, being so different from him?'

'Not in the slightest. He and I get on really well, though our personalities are utterly dissimilar; he has a tendency to be a control freak – which, thankfully, he's given up with me – whereas I'm very relaxed about what anyone else does. He likes to work his bollocks off getting down to his office at seven o'clock every morning, whereas I couldn't look at a column of figures before ten. But it doesn't worry me in the slightest that he still talks and dresses like the boss of an East End mob. In fact, I used to love it at school when he came to see me. The other parents all gazed in horror as he clambered into his Turbo Bentley. I must admit, though, my mother's more of a lady. I think that's why Dad was so keen – to show her family that, whatever he might have been, his son was going to be a bloody sight smarter than they were.'

'Didn't you mind?' Jan asked, appalled at this apparent abuse of a son.

'No. There are still ridiculously unfair advantages in looking as though you come from some old land-owning family, and I don't suppose it does anyone any harm.' Eddie shrugged. 'But that's enough of me; I'd like to hear more about you.'

When Eddie had left, after driving very cautiously down the track in his low-slung car, Jan was surprised to see how long he had been there and how easy she had found it to be with him. But when Annabel appeared at the gate with Megan and Matthew, she realized that she hadn't asked him anything about his friendship with her and he hadn't mentioned it. She wondered how Annabel would take the news that he had finally come to see his horse.

Annabel's first visible reaction was a sharp wince.

'I thought you'd be pleased,' Jan said.

'Well, I'm not. I told you, I made a real fool of myself over Eddie. I don't really know why now, but I threw myself at him and the poor guy just didn't know how to cope with it. In a way, I wish he'd been older and more of bastard. But when my father got involved, with my mother turning up at his little flat, and going round to see his mother – it was all so bloody embarrassing. Besides, I'm not really Eddie's type and I never was; all he talks about is pictures and racing. I shouldn't think he's ever read a book in his life. I'm sure he's much more into trendy, glamorous It-girls. But listen, Jan, I promised I wouldn't let him spoil it here for me, and I'm not going to. Just don't talk about it and I expect I'll be fine, OK?'

'Annabel, haven't you ever dumped a man?'

'Eddie didn't dump me,' Annabel came back sharply.

'All right.' Jan could see her friend was getting twitchy as she sometimes did if one probed too far. 'Like I said, if he comes again when you're here, at least be civil to him.'

'Of course I will. Anyway, if you think he's so terrific, why don't you go out with him?'

'Firstly, because he hasn't asked and I'm certainly not going to ask him. And, secondly, I'm not sure he's my type either – his old man may sound like one of the Kray brothers, but Eddie's probably a bit posh for me; I like my men more earthy. And, thirdly, it's less than six months since John died and I certainly don't feel like starting a relationship with anyone at present.'

'Yes, I know, but you could still have fun teasing Eddie,' Annabel grinned.

'Don't be such a bitch,' Jan remonstrated. 'One of the rules of Edge Farm Stables is that we never tease the owners – OK?'

'All right. What shall I do with Matthew?' She nodded at the baby sleeping in the buggy.

Jan leaned down and sniffed. 'I'd better sort him out. Come on in and have something to eat.'

When Jan had dealt with Matty at the other end of the caravan, she came and sat down to eat the sandwiches Annabel had made.

'You are an ace butty maker,' she nodding, with her mouth full.

'Thanks. How did you get on with the vet, by the way?'

Jan swallowed her mouthful. 'Pretty well. He says he's happy to come over and have a look at our set-up, and he could certainly send a few patients here.'

'What's in it for him?' Annabel asked.

'I suppose if I said "Nothing", you'd say I was naive to think any man would do something for nothing?'

'It'd be rare, let's face it.'

'As it happens, although this guy puts on a salt-of-the-earth sort of image, I wouldn't be surprised if he thinks he could be in for a useful cut. Nice for him – just sends the horses along to us and takes his ten per cent for doing nothing, as well as charging his client for coming over to look at the animal from time to time.'

Annabel nodded. 'But then, at least you'd know what you were in for – and you'd know where you stood.'

The first of July was a sizzler. Jan spent most of the day helping Gerry, who was dripping with sweat as he tried to mend a pump designed to fill the water troughs from a spring at the top of the long field. She wouldn't have known where to start without him.

Roz and Annabel had gone already and Jan and Gerry were cooling down with a bottle of cider, when Eddie's car appeared at the gate for the second time in two days.

'Gosh, you must be keen to drive over here in this heat,' Jan called once he'd parked and was walking up the hill to where they sat on some upturned logs outside the caravan.

Eddie was carrying a large cardboard box. He shrugged his shoulders with a one-sided smile. 'Not with the roof off. Besides, I come bearing gifts, and I'm not Greek, so you needn't worry.'

Jan saw Gerry look disdainfully at this interloper, and she feared that he already resented Eddie as a rival. She wondered how she would break it to him that she wasn't interested in either of them.

Eddie put the box on the ground by Jan's feet.

'Cider?' Jan asked.

'Very rustic, but probably the last thing you need in heat like this.' He opened the box and took out a handsome antique brass and glass oil lamp, and a bottle of champagne wrapped in a cold sleeve. He felt the neck. 'Just about OK. Where can I find some glasses?'

Jan told him and a moment later he emerged from her temporary home with three full tumblers.

Some time later, after Roz had agreed to babysit, Eddie took Jan down to the Fox & Pheasant for supper, where Julie the barmaid greeted her warmly.

Eddie was impressed. 'You've only been here a month and they already treat you like a local.'

'Well, I *am* nearly a local. I was only born and brought up eight miles away. But everyone here's been really helpful.'

'Enjoy it while you can. Once you start getting successful, they'll find things wrong with you.'

'You're very cynical for a young man.'

Eddie laughed. 'Sorry, mother.'

Once they'd ordered and were sitting at a table with a bottle of wine between them, Jan looked Eddie straight in his innocent brown eyes. 'And just why, by the way, have you asked me out tonight?'

'You're my trainer, for God's sake!' Eddie affected surprise. 'Isn't it part of the deal to buy one's trainer dinner every so often?'

'As long as it's just that.'

'It is. Well, mainly. When I arrived with that champagne, I admit I was more interested in sharing it with you and the beautiful Annabel than the truculent Gerry.'

'Ah!' Jan said knowingly. 'Poor Gerry; you mustn't upset him.'

'I did and said nothing to upset him. But why not tell him I came looking for Bel? I'm sure that would mollify him a little.'

'I don't know that you'll get a better response from Annabel, to tell you the truth.'

Eddie leaned back in the small chair on which he was perched. 'I dare say you're right. There's a lot of work to do there.'

He smiled at spiky-haired Julie, who was bustling across the bar towards them with a fistful of cutlery, which she plonked down on the table.

Jan thought about asking Eddie what had gone on between him and Annabel when they'd first met, but decided that she didn't really want to know, and used the arrival of Julie with their food to change the subject.

'Talking of work to be done, you must promise me not to upset Gerry. He's been absolutely brilliant and he works like a slave. He's even offered to start work on the house, though God knows how I'm going to afford the materials.'

'What sort of things are you going to need?'

'Everything – oak timbers, floorboards, roof tiles, flagstones – and I want them all old. I couldn't bear to live in a place that was all shiny and new.'

'I know what you mean; maybe I can help. If you

give me a list of what you want, I'll keep my eyes open around the sales and scrapyards. I've often picked up stuff like that for myself.'

Jan didn't mind admitting that she was happy to make use of any help a man was prepared to offer; besides, she was still uncertain what Eddie's motives were. There were no hints in his body language that he was flirting with her and his eyes shone with warm-hearted friendliness rather than red-hot passion.

She was no wiser after dinner when he dropped her outside the caravan and lightly brushed his lips across her cheek before he left.

Jan let herself in, and was surprised to see it was only half-past ten. The children were asleep and Roz was quite happy to sit and gossip for a while before she went home.

Roz had already got herself wrapped up in the lives of all the animals at Edge Farm, as well as the people. 'I can't wait to start doing some work with the horses,' she said.

'Eddie's raring to ride his, too,' Jan laughed. 'I've told him he'll just have to wait until August. But I've got a vet coming round to inspect us in the next few days and I'm hoping he might send us a few animals for running repairs or a dose of TLC.'

'Which vet's that?'

'James McNeill.'

Roz's eyes shot open. 'He's got a terrible reputation. They say there's not many men'll leave their wives alone in the same room as him.'

'Oh, God!' Jan groaned. 'A randy vet – that's all I need!'

Two days later, waiting for James McNeill to come up after a brief, businesslike phone call, Jan couldn't rid herself of the trepidation she felt. But when he arrived, he shook her hand as if she were another man, said no to coffee and asked if she could show him round right away.

He looked at her boxes and paddocks, then questioned her closely about her knowledge of horse health and welfare.

'I'm no bloody shop egg!' Jan told him.

Finally, when he'd seen enough, Jan asked him into her caravan, under the alarmed gaze of Annabel; Roz had already told her about James McNeill's rumoured sexual antics. But Jan felt that he would expect her to discuss charges with him in private.

He studied the official-looking tariff Annabel had typed out for Jan and nodded his approval. 'That seems fair enough for the kind of care you're offering,' he glanced up at her with no hint of humour in his eyes for the moment, 'provided you really can deliver it.'

'If you use Edge Farm, you won't be disappointed, Mr McNeill, I can assure you.'

'James,' he corrected. 'Please call me James. Let's hope you're right. I'll certainly try you. In fact,' he suddenly treated her to one of his big, beaming smiles, 'I may have something to send you the day after tomorrow.'

'Great,' Jan said, excited to think she might start earning more than a little keep money. Now that the yard was just about shipshape, and all the horses happily turned out, she was concerned that Roz and Annabel were under-employed.

The first patient at Edge Farm Stables arrived as promised and was installed in one of the new boxes Gerry had built. It was the first time any of them had been occupied, and Jan couldn't help popping her head into the barn every so often to see the evidence that she really was in business at last.

The horse had pulled a muscle in his back and, though James had repaired most of the damage, he still needed a lot of rest and very gentle exercise, as well as regular manipulation.

Jan was delighted to see how well Roz handled the animal and she found herself increasingly confident about the kind of service they could provide. Despite Roz's deeply cynical view of James McNeill's ultimate aims, Jan hoped that if they did a good job on this patient, a lot more would follow from the same source and, besides, whatever the stories about the vet's behaviour, he hadn't tried anything on with her.

It was Matthew's first birthday on 7 July and Jan held a tiny party for him, consisting of her parents, her three staff and two toddlers from the village whom she'd met with their mothers.

'You can be really proud of him,' Mary said as they sat outside the caravan and watched Matthew play with the giant plastic tractor Reg had given him. 'He's already walking really well, isn't he?'

Matty had just staggered to his feet and was reeling around on his chubby legs, blowing raspberries back at Gerry.

Jan laughed. 'He'll probably be an Olympic runner, Mum.'

'We always knew you were going to be a rider,' Mary defended herself with a smile. 'Anyway, it's lovely to have a little party like this, specially as you didn't do anything for your own birthday last month.'

'What?' Gerry exploded. 'You never told us. What day was that?'

'June the eighteenth, just after we'd moved,' Jan said. 'Quite frankly, I had so much going on, I almost forgot about it myself.'

'We didn't, dear,' Mary said.

'I know, Mum. Thanks, but I really didn't feel like making a fuss. I mean – thirty-one! What sort of an age is that?'

'Thirty-one. Cor!' Gerry shook his head. 'You don't look it!'

'Thanks, Gerry. You sure know how to make a girl feel good.'

Later, towards eight, when everyone else had gone and Annabel had helped Jan to put the children to bed, they went out and sat at a picnic table in front of the caravan in the warmth of the sun, still high above the Malverns.

'It sounds as if you've been lucky James McNeill hasn't tried to seduce you yet,' Annabel said.

Earlier in the day, before the birthday party, the vet had been to check on his patient's progress.

'Not really.' Jan shook her head. 'I think he just doesn't fancy me. Who'd be interested in a widowed mother of two who smells of horse all day long and hasn't got two beans to rub together?'

'Well, Eddie took you out the other night for a start,' Annabel said encouragingly.

'Yes, but not for that. He never touched me.'

'Did you want him to?' Annabel asked.

Jan glanced at her friend. 'To be honest, I don't know. I haven't been near another man since I met John, and even the thought is a little scary. Besides, I told you, Eddie's not my type.' Jan grinned. 'But it would be nice to be offered the chance to say no.'

'I don't think Eddie takes those sort of chances. Oh, look.' Annabel was pointing at the bottom of the track. 'You've got a visitor.'

A car had just turned in from the lane and was creeping up the hill like a shiny black beetle. It was a new BMW, which stopped beside Jan's lorry, thirty yards from where they sat.

'Do you know who it is?' Annabel asked.

'I haven't got a clue.'

They watched the driver get out. He was a slim man, mid-forties, five feet ten, with wavy dark hair a little too long and a gold ring glinting in the lobe of his left ear. He stood looking around for a few seconds before he saw them and started to walk towards the caravan.

'Hello there,' he called. 'They said in the pub I should find Jan Hardy up here. Is that one of you two?'

Irish, Jan thought. They were never far away in the racing world.

'Hello? I'm Jan Hardy and this is Annabel.'

'Good, good,' the man nodded. 'I was going to ring, then I thought, what the hell? I was on my way from looking at a club in Cheltenham and here y'are.'

'And who are you?'

'Jesus, I'm sorry. Did I not say? Eamon Fallon.' He held out a hand and solemnly shook Jan's, then Annabel's.

'Sit down,' Jan invited and he slipped onto the bench beside Annabel, opposite Jan. 'Would you like a drink?'

'No, thanks. I didn't come here for drinkin'.'

'What did you come for, then?' Jan asked.

'I saw a horse of yours win at Ludlow.'

'Rear Gunner?'

'That's it. It was very impressive. I've a couple of

horses of my own in a little yard up by Droitwich, running in the point-to-points. Dingle Bay and Posy's Pride.'

Jan nodded. 'I've seen them both run. They look nice horses.'

'They are very good horses and they should have been winning for me, but I made the mistake of putting them with another Kerry man. I don't know what he's been doing, but sure as hell he's not been training 'em.'

'I was surprised they didn't do better,' Jan ventured, 'given their form in Ireland. They should be running under rules over here.'

'You may be right there, but I've always loved the points back home, and I wanted a good crack at it here.'

'Do you live in England?'

'I do – in Birmingham. I've a couple of little clubs, you know.'

Jan tried to imagine what kind of clubs, but she didn't want to clutter the conversation with irrelevancies at this stage.

'So what would you like me to do?'

'I'd like you to train my horses for me.'

'To go pointing?'

'Of course. You don't have a public licence, do you?'

Jan laughed. 'They don't give licences to penniless hill farmers' widows.'

'Well, maybe they should, but I want my two to

run between the flags – for the moment. So, would you have them?'

'I'd have to look at them first.'

'But you've seen them.'

'That was months ago. Anything could have happened to them since then. There's no point you sending me something with a leg that's never going to mend, then getting all hot and bothered when it doesn't run.'

Eamon's left eye and shoulder twitched in a fleeting display of impatience, which Jan didn't miss. 'All right, then. You'd better go and have a look at them. But would you ever slip in there without letting y'man know what you're doing?'

Jan decided that she might as well look at Eamon Fallon's horses the next day. She rang the trainer, Jim Partridge, to make sure he'd be there. Then she left Annabel in charge of the children and set off in the Land Rover on what was a fine summer's morning.

Just after midday she turned into a grassy lane off the Kidderminster road and drove a few miles down it until she found a collection of ramshackle barns and stables partly hidden by woods. Surrounding the unpromising buildings were two paddocks, thick with docks and thistles, and fenced with rusting pig-wire. The half-dozen horses standing in them seemed too busy flicking the flies off their faces to get their heads down to eat.

Jan parked in the yard and stepped out onto a surface of ruptured concrete that looked as if it hadn't seen a broom for years. She stood there for a moment, listening to a thrush and a flock of scavenging starlings that had fled the yard on her approach. There was no sign or sound of any human presence.

'Hello?' Jan called, already disapproving of Jim Partridge for keeping horses in such squalid surroundings. 'Is there anyone in?'

There was an answering cough from a shed wedged between two of the barns and a small wiry man, unshaved and wearing grimy jodhpurs, emerged and blinked watery eyes in the sun.

'Oh,' he said with surprise, 'it's yourself, is it?'

Jan attempted a friendly smile. It hadn't occurred to her that she might be recognized. 'I'm Jan Hardy. I rang earlier.'

'But you didn't say who you were.'

'I never say who I am when I'm coming out to buy.'

Jim Partridge stiffened his short back defensively. 'To buy is it? How d'you know I've anything to sell?'

'I've never known an Irishman with horses who didn't and you were running a few nice-looking animals from here last season.'

He glowered at her suspiciously. 'I've only six horses here at the present, and none of them's for sale.'

'Well, you never know. Why not show me what's here, anyway? I've got a couple of punters prepared to pay good money for something that'll win for them.'

Jim eyed her hesitantly. 'Oh, all right. You may as well have a look. I'll get a lead.'

He disappeared into the nearest building and came out a few seconds later with a length of plaited bailer twine. He led Jan out of the yard and through the gate to the first paddock, where five of his six charges were clustered under a vast horse chestnut tree, flicking their tails and stamping their feet. Jan walked among them and wondered why anyone would send a horse to a place like this. From a quick assessment of their qualities, Jan decided that she could plausibly be interested in two of them.

'Who's this?' she asked, stroking the nose of a small bay gelding with four black feet. She knew he was neither of the horses she had come to see.

'That'd be Carlton Breeze – a very talented animal.'

Jan looked blank. 'What's he won?'

'He didn't do much this season, owing to a bit of a leg. He struck into himself badly and it went septic, but he's as right as rain now.'

'Would you trot him up the yard for me?' Jan asked, wondering how helpful that would be on ground that looked like the surface of the moon.

'Sure.'

She watched the horse's action from front and back as Jim ran him back and forth along a strip of level ground at the back of the stables.

'You're right,' Jan said. 'He's sound now. What do you suppose his owner would let him go for?'

'As a matter of fact, this horse is my own and if I were to sell him I'd be looking at fifteen thousand for him.'

'Fifteen thousand?' Jan asked, with a hint of incredulity, but not enough to be offensive.

'That's right,' the little man said.

'Who's that in the other field?' Jan asked, seeing a big, gaunt chestnut mare on her own, standing on a patch of dried mud and shaded from the sun by a hedge of runaway thorn.

'That's Posy's Pride. She'd not be for sale.' He turned away to lead the bay back to the field.

Jan carried on studying the mare, noting her lack of condition and stary coat. 'She doesn't look well,' Jan said.

'Well, we've had one or two little problems with her.'

In the first paddock, Jan thought she had identified Dingle Bay, a big rangy bay, as his name suggested. He looked a great deal better than the chestnut in the other paddock.

'He's a nice individual. Could I have a look at him?'

Jim shook his head. 'No, he wouldn't be for sale either.'

'Why?' Jan asked lightly. 'Who does he belong to?'

'An old friend of mine up at King's Heath. I used to do the dogs with him. I'd bring them over and he ran them at Perry Barr, before they closed it.'

'You must have been young then.'

'We were, and wild,' Jim cackled.

'What's he called?'

Jim hesitated. 'Eamon Fallon, but he'd never sell a good horse. Even if he did, he'd not be an easy man to negotiate with.'

'Trot him up for me anyway, just in case,' Jan cajoled. 'Then I'll have another look at Carlton Breeze.'

Jan left Jim Partridge's yard confident that he didn't know why she'd been there.

When she got home, she dialled Eamon's number and was answered by a woman with a strong Birmingham accent, who was evasive until Jan explained exactly why she was calling, after which she was finally answered by Eamon's own soft Kerry vowels.

'I saw those horses,' Jan said, feeling that despite his own easily delivered charm, any flannel would be wasted on him. 'The chestnut mare, Posy's Pride, looks dreadful – like she's got red worm, ringworm and a few other worms besides. I don't think she'll be doing a lot next season. But the other horse, Dingle Bay, looks useful. He doesn't look as if he's been made to do much work for some time, though. I talked Jim into trotting him up for me and the horse moved nice and straight.'

'Do you think you could train him?'

'Oh yes.'

'To win?'

'You might be able to make those kind of predictions about greyhounds, but you must know there's always an element of uncertainty with racehorses – especially jumpers.'

'I'd prefer less chat about the dogs,' Eamon said quietly. 'But you go and pick up Dingle Bay as soon as you can. I'll ring Jim and tell him you're coming to collect him, OK?'

'Yes, that's all right. But if you want me to pick him up, I'll have to charge you for the transport.'

'That's fair enough,' Eamon said. 'And maybe you should tell me how much you'll charge for training him.'

When she'd told him her rates, he gave a satisfied grunt. 'That'll be fine.'

Jim Partridge was expecting Jan when she arrived back at his yard with her lorry two days later. Dingle Bay was already in a stable, looking well groomed and with a clean head-collar.

'I don't know what the hell you did to get him to part with the horse,' Jim muttered under whisky breath.

'What do you mean?' Jan asked as she led Dingle Bay towards the ramp of her lorry.

'How did you persuade him to sell him to you?'

'I didn't. He hasn't sold it. He's sending him to me to train.'

The little man's shoulders collapsed abruptly. 'To

train? The bastard!' he sniffed. He seemed already resigned to the loss.

Jan was almost sorry for him, but another glance across the paddocks quickly dispelled the feeling. She led Dingle Bay into the box and tied him up. She walked down the ramp and swung it up with a little half-hearted help from Jim Partridge.

'I'll get the papers,' he muttered, still smouldering with resentment and walked across to the shed, which was evidently his office. Jan followed him into the gloomy little cabin with dirt-smeared windows and piles of dusty papers everywhere.

'I'm sorry you're losing the horse, but at least Mr Fallon's leaving you with Posy's Pride,' she said.

He grunted. 'We both know she won't be doing a lot next season, but', he suddenly pleaded, 'don't for pity's sake tell Eamon.'

Jan winced with regret. 'I'm afraid I already told him I didn't think she'd be ready to run for some time. I'm sorry, but, look, is he all paid up and everything?'

Jim glanced at her quickly as he handed her the horse's passport and certificates. 'What do you mean?'

'I mean does Mr Fallon owe you any money on the horse's keep? I wouldn't want to take a horse from a yard before it was paid up – otherwise you've no collateral.'

'It's all right about the money; he owes nothing.' The little man dismissed the problem with a backward wave of his skinny hand and Jan had the impression that it was probably Jim who was owing.

She nodded. 'Well,' she held out a hand. 'Thanks for getting the horse ready for me.'

He heaved a shoulder as they went back out into the yard, where he stood and watched while she walked to the cab of her lorry.

Jan started the engine and glanced in the wing-mirror at the forlorn figure, who didn't move as she drove up the short track to the lane.

On the motorway, heading back for Gloucestershire, she caught sight of herself in the mirror – the light blonde hair flicking in the wind, the innocent blue eyes – and hoped she wasn't guilty of overloading Jim Partridge's burden of woes.

She talked to Annabel about it when she got back to Edge Farm.

'But surely,' Annabel said, 'if Eamon hadn't sent the horse to us, he'd certainly have sent it somewhere else. There's absolutely no reason why you should feel bad about it. In the end, Jim Partridge's failures are his problem, not yours.'

Jan sighed and tried to push aside the memory of the pathetic look in the man's face as the best horse in his yard had been driven away.

8

By the end of July James McNeill had sent three more patients to Jan. Another horse had come in from a local farmer's wife for some schooling and there were still nine healthy racehorses in the paddocks – in all, just enough to cover the wages of her two girls, but not enough to deal with the ongoing costs of Gerry's building work.

The only way that she could see of financing this would be to take out a large mortgage, but she had no intention of jeopardizing her fragile business in order to make the repayments. She made up her mind to bite on the bullet and on a Friday evening towards the end of July she asked Gerry in for a drink.

When she told him that she would have to put the building work on hold, at first he looked shocked and turned pale. He quickly recovered, though.

'It's OK, Jan, I'll just carry on, and you pay me when you can, when things pick up. As soon as you start getting them horses to the races, there'll be people knocking the door down to send theirs here.'

'Gerry, be realistic. It's six months before there's

any racing. I'm sure I'll pick up a few more owners before then, but let's face it, there aren't going to be many, and I'm not going to have much more money coming in than I've got now.'

'That don't matter. I've got a few other jobs I can fit in to keep me ticking over.'

'I've still got to buy the materials.'

'Eddie's been bringing in most of what you need and he won't mind waiting; he's got plenty of money.'

'Gerry, I'm not going to build this house on charity. I can't be owing money to you and everybody else – not until I know I'm going to be earning some. The house will just have to wait.'

'You can't spend a winter up here in this place.' Gerry waved a disparaging arm around the mobile home.

'Why not? We know it's waterproof after that awful storm last week, and we've got a couple of radiators to keep us warm.'

'But Jan,' Gerry urged, desperate at the thought of not working up at Edge Farm, 'what about them kids?'

'I promise they'll be all right,' Jan put a hand on Gerry's. 'And to be honest, if it did get really bad, Annabel's always said we can move into the cottage.'

'She would,' he said sulkily, knowing he was beaten. 'But I can still come up here and help out, can't I?'

'Of course you can, if you want to.'

Jan watched him walk back down to his van, sad to see him so despondent. He'd already started putting in the footings, working on his own with the help of a mini-digger he'd borrowed. He'd been a tower of strength since she'd arrived at Edge Farm, and she knew that he was more than just interested in helping her out, but it was hard not to encourage him; besides, she couldn't help being touched by his gentle infatuation.

The following Sunday Jan took Megan and Matthew back to Wales to see their grandmother for the first time in five weeks. Olwen had made it clear she was no more reconciled to the loss of Stonewall than she had been when Jan had sold it and, although she still drove her own small car, it was highly unlikely that she would condone Jan's decision by visiting Edge Farm. Despite that, Jan owed it to her children to maintain contact with their grandmother, who was, after all, the only remaining member of their father's family.

She wasn't looking forward to lunch with Olwen, but she couldn't suppress a few pangs of nostalgia as they drove up from the Wye valley over the hills to Stonewall. The sun appeared sporadically between piles of cumulus that had drifted in from the Irish Sea. It bathed the curvaceous heathered contours in a seductive glow and reminded Jan of the excitement she had felt the first time she had ridden across those ridges.

'That's where Dad is,' Megan sang out when she saw the tiny white church of St Barnabas tucked in a fold between two hills. She leaned forward from her child's seat in the back of the Land Rover to see her mother's face. 'Do you think he's happy there?'

Jan was cheered by the question, which seemed to confirm that the little girl had positively come to terms with her father's death. 'Yes, darling,' she said. 'I think he is. It's a really peaceful place.' She didn't suggest going to see the grave; she would do that on her own later.

The farmhouse which had been the centre of her universe for the seven years of her married life looked abandoned and forlorn, although it was only seven weeks since they'd moved out. Jan had been back several times to collect a few last items in the week following their move, but she hadn't ventured up the drive since then. She wondered why the Davieses who'd bought the farm hadn't moved in. Someone had taken a cut of hay off the lower meadow, and the higher fields of permanent pasture were full of big, lowland sheep. She found she didn't want to look. She began to have an inkling of how it must have been for Olwen and she felt a little more sympathy for her.

Olwen opened the door and, without glancing at Jan, held out her arms to greet her granddaughter. In one hand she held a bag of Megan's favourite sweets.

'How's my beautiful little Megan?' she asked in her strong Cambrian accent. 'Come to see your Nana at last?' Jan didn't miss the side-swipe of accusation in the old woman's voice, but she stifled her urge to defend herself.

When Olwen had finished making a fuss of Megan, she turned her attention to the baby boy in Jan's arms, pointedly avoiding eye-contact with his mother. 'And how's Master Matthew Hardy? My goodness, you look more and more like your dad! He looked just the same as you at your age.'

Jan sighed to herself and offered the boy for Olwen to hold. Olwen took him and turned to carry him into the bungalow.

In the spotless living room, two mats had been laid out on the floor with toys. Without being told, Megan rushed straight towards a selection of dolls and My Little Ponies. The old woman sat Matthew on his mat and watched with satisfaction as he started immediately to play with a big, bright plastic activity centre.

Jan was getting fed up with Olwen's self-satisfied smirk. 'You haven't got anything a little more advanced for him, have you? He's a bit past just making squeaks.'

'He's happy enough with it,' Olwen growled; and Jan knew he was.

'How have you been, Olwen?'

'As if you cared,' the old woman muttered.

'Of course I care. You're the only family the children have on John's side.'

'There's not a lot more on your side, is there, with your brother gone missing.'

'He hasn't gone missing,' Jan started, before she

remembered how many times Olwen had tried to provoke her with Ben's absence and the implicit flaw in her family. 'After he left California, he went to Australia.'

'That's as good as missing,' Olwen retorted.

'I think he might be making a bit of money out there.'

'Oh yes?' Olwen asked sceptically. 'Then perhaps he'll come and buy this place back.' She nodded her head with a circular motion to indicate the old family farm that surrounded them.

'Olwen, it's just been sold. The new people have already got stock on it.'

'No they haven't. That's Bryn Morris's sheep. He's just took the grazing till the end of August. Stonewall Farm's back on the market.'

Jan was in the process of taking Matthew's nappies from a carrier bag she'd brought in with her. She stopped abruptly. 'Are you sure?'

'Look, here, in the *Hereford Times*, if you don't believe me.' Olwen picked up the local weekly, already open at a page of farm sales, with a photograph of Jan's old home prominent, and in bold print at the bottom of the advertisement, an asking price nearly a hundred thousand pounds more than it had been sold for at auction in April.

Jan felt the blood drain from her face. 'My God!'

'It's a bit late asking him,' Olwen grunted. 'You've been took to the cleaners by them auctioneers.'

'Don't be daft,' Jan said, more forcefully than she

felt. 'They sold it for as much as they could get on the day; I was there. Harold Powell only just nudged it up to its reserve price. If there had been a buyer there, they'd have taken on the Davieses.' Jan knew she was trying to convince herself as much as Olwen. The almost invisible, niggling suspicions she had had from time to time seemed suddenly magnified into a major catastrophe.

If, by bad judgement or being too hasty, Jan had sold the one asset John had left her for nearly a third less than its value, she would never be able to forgive herself for depriving her children of what would ultimately be theirs. Or, so help her, she was going to have to work like hell to make up for it!

'It's just the way the market goes, Olwen. Who could have known it would pick up so much in three months?'

'The man that stole our farm most likely did.'

'Look, if anyone has done anything crooked, I can promise you I'll find out who, and have them sorted.'

Olwen, looking Jan straight in the eye now, lifted one, cynical eyebrow. 'And how would that be?'

The sweet Welsh lamb that her mother-in-law served for lunch tasted to Jan like mouthfuls of straw tainted with some bitter sauce. She couldn't fight off the nausea she felt at having been so easily duped and she was now convinced that she'd been deliberately misled. By whom, she hardly dared to guess.

Driving back, the beauty of the evening sun didn't move her at all as she tried to plan what she should do next. She was determined not to rush in and scare her adversary into a defensive position. The farm had been openly back on the market now for about ten days, and the fact that she hadn't already been in touch with the agents might suggest to them that she knew and simply thought she had been a victim of a surge in the market.

She was about to turn up the last hill before dropping down to the Wye valley, when, abruptly, she thought of John.

'I think we will go and see Daddy after all,' she told Megan, 'and make sure that he's got some nice flowers.'

There was only a small bunch of freesias in a tiny glass vase on the grassy tump which marked John Hardy's grave; Jan had been told she couldn't put up a headstone for another year, to allow the earth to settle.

Jan guessed the flowers were Olwen's and was grateful to her for leaving them, but she promised herself that she would come back as soon as she could to put her own there. She stood with Matthew in her arms and Megan, wide-eyed but composed, beside her, clutching her hand, and thought of the cold damp day they had laid John to rest. She gazed at the grave and tried to see him lying deep beneath the surface, calm and thoughtful as he'd always been.

Gritting her teeth, she closed her eyes.

Dear John, she said silently, *you wouldn't have let*

this happen with the farm. You would have been calm and sensible about it. I was too hasty, I know, because I just wanted to get the whole business over and done with. Now I've lost so much! Please help me. Tell me what to do, if you can.

Reg and Eddie were in the yard when Jan got back, sitting side by side on a small bale of wheat straw. It was one of a thousand that Colonel Gilbert had sent over from Riscombe Manor that week. He had phoned afterwards. 'They're fifty pence each, and you can knock the cost off your training fees when I send you Sorcerer's Boy.'

Jan had been more than grateful. Both for the straw, which she was already using for some of the ailing horses who couldn't be bedded on shavings, and for the commitment the colonel had made to sending her a horse – Sorcerer's Boy had chalked up two good wins the previous season.

When Jan saw a bottle of cider resting precariously on the straw between her father and Eddie, she detected Reg's influence. These days, there was nothing he liked more than to swig cider and have a good gossip, preferably in the open air within scenting distance of livestock.

'Can I get you some glasses?' she asked, walking across the yard towards them.

Eddie stood up. 'Don't be so fussy. We've done very well sharing the bottle up until now. Anyway,

I'm off. Did you have a good time at your mother-in-law's?'

Jan stared at him, wishing he knew the trauma she'd been going through since she'd heard how she'd been conned over Stonewall. She wanted to blurt it all out. She needed to tell someone, as soon as possible, but her dad was there and he would want to hear it on his own first. She pulled herself together. 'Not too bad, thanks. Olwen spoiled the kids as usual, but that's no bad thing now and again.'

'Good,' Eddie smiled down at Megan, who had trailed across the yard behind Jan. 'I love spoiling them myself; it makes me feel like a king. I was just telling your dad I was coming over next weekend. Any chance I might get my leg over—' he paused with a grin, before adding, 'my horse?'

Jan tried to focus. 'Yes. You could ride him from the field gently. He's got plenty of weight on him.'

'Great! I'm looking forward to it already. I'll see you then.' He turned to Jan's father, who was still sitting contentedly on his bale. ''Bye, Reg. See you soon.'

Jan waited for the Mercedes to set off before she sat down where Eddie had been beside Reg.

He looked at her. 'What's the trouble, Janine? You look all washed out.'

At the sound of his soft, sympathetic voice, Jan burst into tears. 'Oh, Dad. I feel terrible – such a fool.'

'Why? What's that mother-in-law of yours been up to now?'

'Only pointing out the truth.'

'What truth?'

'That I've been a bloody fool, Dad, a complete fool, and it's cost me a fortune.' She told him all about the new advertisement in the *Hereford Times* for Stonewall Farm.

'Oh dear,' he murmured when she'd finished. 'I can see why you're so upset.' He shook his head. 'But you know there's nothing you can do about it, don't you?'

'Dad, there must be, if someone's taken advantage of me.'

'Not legally. The place was sold at public auction,' he shrugged, 'and that's that.'

'But I'm sure it was kept cheap deliberately. It only just crept up to my reserve price.'

'Did anyone make a fuss when it was knocked down? Did anyone jump up and say he was still bidding?'

Jan looked at him, knowing he was right. 'No,' she said quietly.

'There it is then,' Reg said. 'Allus you'll do by worrying about it is get yourself wound up and fretting like a young heifer, and that won't do you no good at all.'

'But, Dad, if people have cheated me, it must be people I know and I don't think they should get away with it.'

'Revenge? Is that what you're after?'

'No,' Jan shook her head vigorously. 'No, but justice. I can't just stand by and do nothing.'

'Then you're going to need some help.'

'Oh, Dad, you're very kind, but what could you do?'

'I wasn't thinking of me. I was thinking of your chum who's just gone. Master Eddie.'

'Eddie? Why do you call him my "chum"? He's a client.'

'Maybe, but he'd do a lot for you. He thinks the world of you, I can tell.'

'I don't know about that, but what do you think he could do?'

'He's a clever boy, and bold. Take my advice – you tell him what's happened and he'll help you get to the bottom of it.'

'But don't you think it's a bad idea for me to tell my customers about my problems, especially when I've made such a prat of myself?'

'He'll understand and he certainly won't take his horse away because of it.'

When she had put the children to bed that evening, Jan sat on her own in the lounge of their mobile home and watched the sun dropping over the dinosaur's back of the Malverns in the west.

While she and Roz had got on with the evening tasks around the stables, she had thought about what her father had said. And she knew now for certain that it wasn't revenge she wanted. But if people she had trusted had abused her, she bloody well wanted them to know that she knew.

She also knew that Reg was a reliable judge of character: that he approved so strongly of Eddie came as a surprise to her. She wouldn't have thought that the younger man's charm would have made any impact on him. But Reg had taken to Eddie from the start and trusted him. And he wouldn't have recommended him lightly.

Her hand hovered over the telephone for what seemed like minutes, while she stared at Eddie's phone number in the book.

There were other things to take into consideration as well. She didn't want him to think that she was pursuing him, or asking him to help her as an excuse to bring him closer to her. He also had to know that she was asking a favour with no strings attached – either way. She wondered if he would understand.

Her finger dropped to the keypad and few seconds later she heard his lazy, deep voice.

'Hello?'

'Hello, Eddie. It's Jan here.'

'Hello!' He sounded pleased to hear her. 'You OK? Or has there been a disaster? Has Eagle dropped dead?'

'No, no.' Jan couldn't help laughing. 'Eagle's fine. I'm sorry to ring you so late, but I've got a favour to ask.'

'Great. I love doing women favours.'

'Look, I've got no right to ask this. There's nothing in it for you,' she added, trying not to sound too stern.

'A selfless favour? I don't often do those, but I could try. What is it?'

'I can't tell you over the phone. When could you come over? I'd come to your place now, only I can't leave the kids.'

'I can't come right now, either. But I could get over first thing in the morning, if you like.'

He arrived at the caravan just after seven, and a few minutes before Annabel on a grey Monday morning.

'What on earth are you doing here so early?' Annabel asked suspiciously, seeing him drinking coffee while Jan helped Megan to get dressed.

'I just popped in for a word with my trainer,' he answered blandly. Jan hadn't yet told him what she wanted to talk about.

'I was going to ask Eddie if he could do me a favour,' Jan said, not meeting Annabel's eye.

'Oh, do you want me to disappear? I could get on with the feeds for the three invalids if you like.'

'Yes, please. The list's above the feed bins.'

'I know,' Annabel said, disappearing through the door.

When Annabel was out of earshot, Jan wondered whether it would matter if she talked about her problem in front of Megan, who had developed a habit of absorbing almost everything she heard.

'Do you want to pop down and help Bel?' Jan asked her.

Megan's eyes lit up, and a few seconds later Jan was watching her trot down to the yard behind Annabel's slender figure.

She noticed Eddie was watching too.

'What is it between you and Annabel?' she asked before she could stop herself.

He turned back to look at her and smiled ruefully. 'It's not easy. I wasn't going to talk to you about it, but I suppose she's already told you. We had a bit of a scene, five or six years ago. She ran away from school and turned up at my flat. She wasn't under-age or anything, but her father sent the police round – God knows why. Frankly, I think his archaic attitude was the cause of her problems in the first place. And even now she still seems a bit in awe of him. Otherwise why did she carry on living at home so long?'

'I think that was more to do with her mother,' Jan said. 'And the fact that she didn't want to go back to London.'

'There's more to it than just her dad, though. I don't know what, but something's left her insecure and with very little self-esteem for someone as bright and beautiful as she is.'

'She is very beautiful, isn't she,' Jan said with only a hint of envy.

'Yes, I think she is,' Eddie mused. 'In fact, I'm sure she is, but somehow she's not very – I don't know – sexy, I suppose is the only way you could put it. I'm very fond of her, she's lovely to look at, but I just don't fancy her.'

'Well, be kind to her, won't you?' Jan sighed.

'I should think kindness is the last thing she wants from me. But I certainly wouldn't want to do anything unkind,' Eddie promised. 'I can see what an asset she is to the yard and I don't want anything to upset that.'

'Good, because I've got another favour to ask you.'

'What's that?'

Jan picked up the paper, folded open at the page which contained the advertisement for Stonewall Farm, and pushed it across the table to him.

He took a few seconds to absorb the details before he flicked a curl of black hair from his eye and looked up. 'Oh dear,' he said, in the much same tone Reg had used.

'"Oh dear"! Is that all you can say?' Jan asked more sharply than she meant.

'It's just my restrained way of saying, "Bloody hell",' Eddie replied mildly. 'Obviously I realize that something's gone wrong in a big way. It looks as though you're about a hundred grand out of pocket.'

'Actually, a bit more than that. They're offering twenty acres less than I sold – the ground next to the bungalow. I suppose they think it might be worth sitting on that until my mother-in-law dies and I sell the bungalow, so they can flog off the land to the new occupants at an inflated price.'

'You're probably right,' Eddie agreed. 'Do you know who's actually selling it now?'

'No. I only discovered the place was for sale yesterday when Olwen tried to rub my nose in it, so I haven't been in contact with the agents since it came back on the market.'

'These aren't the people that sold it for you, are they?'

'No, of course not! They wouldn't be that stupid.' Again, Jan regretted her brusqueness. 'I'm sorry, Eddie, I shouldn't take it out on you. It's just that I feel such a fool for trusting certain people.'

'I understand. So what do you want me to do?'

'I want to know who really owns it at the moment – who's going to make the profit on it.'

'If they do make a profit. One thing you've got to bear in mind is that they haven't actually sold it yet. They may have misjudged the market.'

'I wish they had, but I don't think so. If you look at prices round here, they've been going up all the time and that's going to ripple out towards Wales. I've been reading, there are more and more Londoners selling their houses for fortunes and thinking it might be nice to have some of the good life and take up a bit of hobby farming – so long as they've plenty stashed away to live on,' she added sourly.

'Jan, you can't blame people for being lucky, and I'm bloody sure you won't be living on a shoestring for ever. But I'll see what I can do. Don't tell me your theories about it now, though,' he nodded at the paper. 'I don't want to start with any preconceptions.'

'When can you start?' Jan asked eagerly.

'Hang on!' Eddie laughed. 'And remember, whatever I discover, the chance of you getting anything back out of it is very slim.' He stood up. 'I've got to go. Thanks for the coffee. I'll be in touch as soon as I hear anything.'

Jan watched Eddie walk back to his car, glad that at least she now had a committed ally, but she didn't get much reassurance from this as she walked to the paddock behind the caravan and leaned over the rails. Gloomily, she looked at Rear Gunner, strong and with a big grass belly on him. He'd be ready to come back in soon to start his preparation for one of the really prestigious hunter chases the following spring.

Eddie still hadn't rung by Thursday morning and Jan's frustration was almost at breaking point. She'd spent the last few days full of guilt about her mishandling of the sale of Stonewall. She wasn't naturally a greedy woman – maybe that was why she'd been so thoughtless in disposing of what was her biggest financial asset – but, living in the caravan, she was constantly reminded that she was the sole parent of two young children in a complicated, costly world with a very small income. Whether she liked it or not, money mattered, and her sense of grievance was so strong that, despite her father's pessimism, she was sure she should get her fair share of the profit if Stonewall were resold for more than she'd received.

She was also confused about whether she wanted to

hear from Eddie for news of any progress, or because she just wanted to hear from Eddie.

But while she was trying to deal with these problems in her head, and for the most part on her own, she and her two helpers were getting on well in the yard. The horses who had been sent to her to convalesce were already showing signs of improvement and Jan felt confident that she hadn't attracted them there under false pretences. Her confidence was confirmed when James McNeill turned up shortly after midday and inspected the three animals under his care.

'It certainly looks as though you women have got the magic touch. Mind you.' He grinned. 'If I was being massaged by you lot every day, I'd pretty soon perk up.' He looked around at the three of them, to be met with Roz's distrustful glower. 'I'll tell you what. As a treat, I'll take you all out to lunch at the Fox!'

'We can't all go, we're expecting a new patient, any time now,' Jan said.

'That's OK,' Roz said. 'I'll stay.'

'And I'm meeting my mother in Cheltenham for lunch,' Annabel added.

'I don't think Roz is very keen on me,' James said when he and Jan were sitting at a table in the pub.

Jan laughed. 'She thinks you've got a bit of a reputation.'

'Have I?' James looked surprised. 'What for?'

'Seducing clients' wives, apparently.'

'Well then, you lot haven't anything to worry about, have you? None of you has a husband. Anyway,' he said, changing his tone, 'I'm really glad you're doing so well. I see you've got three or four other patients in and a nice-looking new racehorse in the paddock.'

'Yes,' Jan nodded. 'He's called Dingle Bay.'

'I think I saw him run – a little disappointing, I seem to remember. Whose is he?'

'He belongs to a businessman from Birmingham.' Jan said, thinking that was a pretty inadequate description of the voluble Eamon Fallon.

'As it happens, I may have another Brummie businessman for you,' James said thoughtfully. 'A bloke called Bernie Sutcliffe. He'll need a bit of working on; he's got piles of loot but he's as tight as a duck's arse.'

'Why does he want a racehorse then?'

'He doesn't, but Sandy, his girlfriend does and poor old Bernie's looks don't match up to his bank balance. He's got the body of a toad and a head like a blighted spud,' James said with the smugness of a man who had complete faith in his own appeal.

Unjustifiably so, Jan thought to herself. 'What's that got to do with it?' she asked.

'Sometimes he has to spend money to keep her interested in him. Sandy's an old friend of mine; she introduced me to him, and he asked me what was the cheapest way to own a racehorse. I told him to start with pointing.' James shrugged. 'And I *could* tell him that the best young trainer round here is you.' He leaned back in his chair and smiled.

Jan wondered if she was expected to grovel with gratitude. She lifted her left shoulder an inch. 'You must tell him what you think best.'

And, whatever his motives, James didn't refer to the potential owner again. He and Jan spent the rest of the hour they were in the pub discussing remedies for the various horses they were treating.

It was only afterwards, when he dropped her back at the stables with a businesslike farewell, that he added, 'I'll tell Bernie Sutcliffe to get in touch, if that's OK?'

Jan hadn't been back long and was checking a poultice on a strained tendon when the phone in her pocket rang.

'Hi, Jan. It's Eddie.'

'Hello?' Jan said hoarsely, and held her breath.

'I've got a bit of news. Will you be there in half an hour?'

Jan stopped what she was doing as soon as she heard a car turn into the drive. She walked round the end of the barn and saw the Mercedes. She waited by the new parking place Gerry had made while Eddie drove in.

'What did you find out?' she asked, even before he got out of the car.

'The place is already under offer at the full asking price,' Eddie said, straightening himself and putting a hand on her shoulder in a way he hadn't done before.

Jan bit her lip. 'Oh bloody hell! I *knew* they would get the money for it. Do you know who's selling it?'

'Davies and Company – a small agricultural engineers in Talgarth. They don't turn over a lot, but they own a few freehold sites in the town. They bought Stonewall from a farmer called Terry Davies, who just happens to be Rhys Davies's brother. He'd bought it at the auction. In fact, I gather he simply passed his contract straight on to them. According to Companies House, there are two equal shareholders in the firm. Rhys Davies and Harold Powell.'

Jan felt the blood drain from her face. 'The bastard!' she hissed.

All her muscles tensed and she clenched her teeth at the thought of Harold sitting with her in the pub in Hay, acting like a kind old uncle when she'd gone to see him after hearing the will read, and then later when she'd specifically asked him about selling Stonewall. He must have felt like a spider catching a half-crippled fly. He'd even pretended to discourage her from selling so soon at auction. And after all she'd done for him with his horses!

'Take it easy, Jan,' Eddie was saying. 'Shall we go up to the caravan and talk about it there?'

Jan looked across at Roz and Annabel in the yard. She nodded and silently they walked up the bank.

Inside, Jan asked, 'Do you want a drink?'

Eddie nodded. 'A beer, if you've got one.'

Jan took two stubby bottles from the fridge and emptied them into glasses before she sat down opposite Eddie.

'I just don't believe it!' she sighed. 'How could he do something like that to me? He knew my circumstances.'

'I don't suppose he feels he's done anything particularly wrong – certainly not illegal. It would be hard to prove that he'd talked you into selling it through him.'

'He didn't,' Jan said. 'That's what makes me so sick. He just watched me walk into it. He even tried to talk me *out* of it. The way the auction was run was totally straight, too.'

'No, it wasn't, at least not entirely. I've checked back and found that it was very lightly advertised.'

'They certainly put an ad in the papers,' Jan said. 'I saw it.'

'One small, low-key advertisement with no photo in the *Brecon & Radnor Express*, which only circulates in mid-Wales, where people don't buy farms unless they're being knocked out with no reserve. Compare that with the massive colour ads they've done this time.'

'The bastard!' she said again. 'He pitched it just right, didn't he? No wonder he was sweating the day of the sale, worrying that a real buyer might turn up.'

'He'd have told his accomplice to bid quietly, and if the bidding dried up too far below the reserve, he could just go on taking bids off the wall until he got there. He had to take the chance that a real buyer wouldn't come and run him up, and he'll have had his own limit. If he wanted to do it legally, there had to be a certain amount of luck involved.'

'But surely it can't be legal for an auctioneer to buy things he's selling?'

'There's no reason why he shouldn't. Anyway, it wasn't Harold Powell who bought Stonewall, it was Terry Davies.'

Jan took a deep breath. 'Right, I'm going to ring him.'

'Why? What are you going to tell him?'

'I'm going to ask him to give me some of the profit he's made, or I'll take him to court.'

'What's the point of that? It'll cost you money and you won't win.'

'We'll see. I'll sue him for incompetence and the publicity in a place like that won't do him any good at all. People need to be able to trust their auctioneers.'

'Well, whatever you do, I wouldn't ring him. You'll do a much better job if he's totally unprepared when you confront him with it. If you can, just sit it out until the next time he comes over. Do you know when that'll be?'

'He said he was coming on Saturday morning, about ten.'

'Oh, good. I'll be here too, then.'

9

On Saturday morning Harold Powell bowled up the track to the stables in a new Range Rover. Jan and Eddie watched as he parked beside the Mercedes and climbed out. He looked around at the yard and the paddocks with a faintly proprietorial air, in the way owners sometimes did when visiting their trainer, Jan had noticed, as if, without their horses in the yard, none of it would be possible.

He sauntered up to the caravan. Jan opened the door when he was still a few paces from it.

'Hello, Harold. How are you?'

'Fine, couldn't be better! Full of the joys of spring. How are the horses?'

'You can see for yourself. Rear Gunner's as fat as a barrel and ready to come in to start some light work.'

'And so is that great big thing over there,' Harold, said, pointing at Russian Eagle.

'Yes, he's going to be ridden today for the first time this season. He belongs to Eddie.'

As Harold climbed into the caravan, she waved a hand in Eddie's direction, 'Eddie Sullivan, this is

Harold Powell, my major owner and benefactor.' She smiled at the irony.

Harold preened himself. 'It's been a real pleasure helping you, and watching you do so well,' he said: odious and patronizing, Jan thought. 'That your Merc, is it?' he asked Eddie.

''Fraid so,' Eddie admitted.

'Lovely car,' Harold said approvingly. 'And what sort of business are you in?'

'Pictures – eighteenth-century sporting. That sort of thing.'

'Really?' Harold pricked up his ears. 'I'm senior partner in a firm of auctioneers over in Hay-on-Wye. We have a few good sales of antiques and paintings each year – a lot of nice stuff, too. We had a Herring through a couple of months ago.'

Eddie nodded. 'Though that one turned out not to be right, if I remember correctly.'

'Well, as it turned out, it was a contemporary copy,' Harold blathered, 'but, of course, we could only go on the expert advice we'd been given.'

Eddie nodded and caught Jan's glance. 'And do you ever buy in any pictures on you own behalf?'

'Oh no. Neither buyers nor vendors like it much. They always think you're up to something.'

'But you do in property sales.'

'Excuse me?' Harold asked, as if he couldn't possibly have heard correctly.

'When you're selling property by auction, you do sometimes buy on your own account.'

'Certainly not,' Harold said sharply.

'No, of course not,' Eddie agreed smoothly. 'That would be terrible PR for a small-town auctioneer, but if you were instructed to sell a farm that you thought might be offered at a lowish reserve, and you could keep the sale as low-key as possible, and fill up the saleroom with any old cronies who could be bothered to come in for a bit of a drink afterwards, and you managed to knock it down to a farmer who could sell it on to a company with no overt connection with yourself, but in which you had a substantial equity, you might acquire it that way. If you'd done particularly well and the market was going your way, you might be tempted to make a quick return on it, sometimes making as much as a hundred grand without touching the place.'

As Eddie spoke, the colour in Harold's face increased and the veins on his temple began to stand out. He looked at Jan, trying to keep a lid on his panic, and still wondering if he might be able to bluff it out. 'What the hell are you talking about?' he blustered.

'What are you getting so excited about?' Eddie asked with a dry smile. 'I was speaking hypothetically.'

'Oh no he wasn't.' Jan spoke at last in a low even voice. 'He was talking about Stonewall.'

'Bloody hell, Jan!' Harold turned on her indignantly. 'You don't think I'd do a thing like that to you, do you?'

'I know you did it! The farm was bought by Terry

Davies, who sold it straight on to a company run by his brother Rhys, with fifty per cent owned by you!'

'I don't have anything to do with the running of that company,' Harold protested.

'So it was just a coincidence?' Jan laughed scornfully. 'Isn't that amazing? I ask you to sell my farm, a company you happen to own buys it and three months later puts it back on the market for a hundred thousand pounds more than I got? You must be bloody cocky to take a risk like that!'

'Listen, Jan, I'm telling you, it *was* a coincidence,' Harold stammered. 'I'd no idea Rhys had bought it until it came back on the market a fortnight ago.'

'And you didn't think of telling me? I know I was bloody stupid the way I sold that place, but I'm not that daft. I'm suing you for negligence and professional what's-it-called.'

Harold's normally affable features had hardened into an ugly mask. 'If you start anything like that, I'll be taking all my horses away from here, I warn you.'

Four horses – half her existing string, such as it was. But Jan was already prepared. 'You didn't think they were staying here, did you?'

Jan opened the door of the caravan, jumped down over the two wooden steps and almost ran down to the yard. 'Roz, Annabel,' she yelled, 'can you get head-collars for Rear Gunner, Lazy Dove, Mister Mack and Lenny's Lad? Catch them all, bandage their legs and load them into the lorry. Then collect up all tack that belongs to Mr Powell.' She put her hands on her hips and turned back to Harold, who had followed her down to the yard. 'All right, Harold,' she said before as he opened his mouth to speak, 'where would you like them to go?'

Five hours later, Jan watched her lorry turn off the lane and creep back towards the stables.

Eddie had insisted that he should drive Harold's horses back to Wales. She hadn't stopped him. She realized what a hell of a journey it would have been for her, disposing of four horses – including the best in her yard – and half her training income.

It had been bad enough staying behind and seeing the gaps on the tack-room wall where the head-collars had been and so few horses in the paddock. But she felt better just seeing Eddie draw up and jump down from the cab with his usual grin.

'That was fun,' he said. 'I've never driven a truck before. It gives you a great feeling of power, doesn't it, bearing down on some poor little car in a narrow lane.'

'Haven't you got an HGV licence, then?' Jan asked, appalled.

'Good God, no.'

'You're mad! You should never have driven it! It's totally illegal and you were uninsured.'

'It's lucky I didn't hit anything then, isn't it? Anyway, I'm back now and I promise I'll never drive it again.'

'When you said you'd drive, I never dreamed you

didn't have a licence!' Jan tried to moderate her exasperation at the unnecessary risk. 'But like you said, you're back, so thanks a lot. I think I'd have kept wanting to turn round and bring them back.'

'I guessed you might regret chucking them out.'

Jan shook her head. 'I'm not regretting it one iota, the twisting bastard! How could I have gone on training for someone who did what he's done to me? And I tell you, Eddie, I *am* going to sue him.'

'It'll cost you, Jan. If money was tight before this, it's going to be a hell of a lot tighter now.'

'Don't I know it,' Jan sighed. 'And I could have done brilliantly with Rear Gunner next year.'

'Poor Jan, there is a horrible irony to the fact that not only has Harold cost you a fair price for your farm, but he's cost you his horses as well.'

'I always knew it was bad thing to end up too dependent on any one person. It's always difficult in my situation, with all the bills to pay at the end of every month, but I'll never let one owner dominate my yard again.'

'Brave words,' Eddie murmured, 'though you may find them hard to stick to. Now,' he went on with a change of tone, 'I seem to remember arriving here hours ago to ride my horse for the first time.'

'Come on then,' Jan said. 'We'll get him in and I'll come and watch you. We'll use the bottom field, that's the flattest.'

Jan threw herself into the job of improving Eddie's riding to a level where he might be expected to win races. For a while, she even managed to forget Harold Powell's treachery and the fact that she was currently down to four horses for the following point-to-point season.

She saw right away that, despite his enthusiasm, Eddie was an inexperienced rider. He sat too far back in the saddle and didn't keep contact with the horse's mouth through the reins; but he was athletic and supple enough to be taught and he seemed to get on well with his horse.

Eddie was also a quick learner and after a while Jan felt more optimistic about his riding. At the same time, she was delighted with Russian Eagle. Despite having been on grass for at least two months, the horse showed a liking for work that was very encouraging, as well as a healthy wish to please. These might not mean he had the will to win, but he could be a surprisingly easy horse to train.

'OK, that'll do,' Jan called after an hour of flat work. 'I don't know who's more knackered – you or the horse.'

Walking back to the stables to untack, Eddie seemed quite bullish.

'I know it's early days, but given that we know the horse has won a good point-to-point in Ireland, what do you think about the Foxhunters'?'

Jan laughed. 'Ask me again in a couple of months and I might be able to give you an opinion.'

'OK, but what about my riding?'

'Right now, you couldn't win a donkey derby, but if you work at it, you might get there. At least you aren't carrying any surplus body weight.'

'Maybe, but I'm still over twelve stone. I'll have to lose at least seven pounds to get to the right weight.'

'Well, don't overdo it.'

When they'd rubbed the horse down and let him back into the paddock, Eddie said he had to go.

'It's been a hell of a day for you,' he said. 'Will you be OK?'

'I should be,' Jan said, more confidently than she felt.

'Don't do anything hasty about Harold Powell, will you? It's bad enough losing the horses.'

'No,' Jan agreed. 'I won't do anything until next week, when I've had a chance to mull it over.'

Eddie climbed into his car and drove off with a wave. Feeling very grateful for his support, a smiling Jan walked back up to her mobile home.

Annabel was ready to leave.

'I've got their tea ready,' she said, 'and I've read Megan the first half of *Charlie and the Chocolate Factory*. I promised her you'd read her the rest.'

'Thanks,' Jan said. 'Actually, that's probably just what I need after today.'

Annabel made a sympathetic face. 'Poor Jan. Are you going to be able to afford to carry on without those four horses?'

'Well, I was only getting keep money for them, but

if I don't get some replacements and a few more in by September, it could be tricky. In the meantime, we'll just have to try and build up the horse repair side of things.'

'Now I know what Harold did to you, I'm sure you did the right thing. It must have taken a lot of guts, though.'

Gerry came up on Sunday morning and carried on with various jobs he'd found for himself. Roz and Annabel weren't due in, so Jan brought Megan and Matty down to the yard while she dealt with the horses' feeds and treatments.

Her mother and father had arranged to come over for lunch, which Mary was bringing with her to save Jan cooking. Reg helped Mary up the hill to the caravan, where she happily got on with preparing the food she'd brought, while Reg came down to look at Jan's tenants.

He studied the animals in the paddocks for a few minutes before he turned to Jan with a worried face. 'What's happened to your Mr Powell's horses?' he asked.

She swallowed. Her dad would probably take it as hard as she had.

They sat down opposite each other on two straw bales, and she told him the whole story, up to the point where Eddie had driven the horses back to Wales.

'I knew Eddie would help you', he nodded, 'and I think you've done the right thing, but it must have been hard.'

'What else could I do?'

'I suppose you might have thought to yourself that you were never going to get any kind of compensation for what he did, and the thing to do was just pretend you didn't know what had happened. At least then you'd have kept the good horses and the training fees.'

Jan looked at him. 'Would you have done that?'

Reg smiled and shook his head. 'No, my little Jan, I'd have done exactly what you've done, and bugger the money.'

'You don't think it's irresponsible of me, then? After all, I've got hardly anything coming in as it is. I'm beginning to think I'd have been better off staying at Stonewall. I've worked out that even if I had a dozen decent horses to go racing, I couldn't make more than a couple of hundred quid a week after all the costs, and that's without trying to build a new house. It's lucky we're building up the convalescent side a bit.'

'Well, Jan, you're a hard-working girl; you know what you're doing, and you've got plenty of determination. Things may look pretty bad at the moment, but your mum and I aren't too worried; we know you'll be all right in the long run.'

Jan spent a comfortable afternoon with her parents. Her mother was sewing the initials '*JH*' onto half a dozen exercise sheets Reg had bought Jan as a birthday present. They talked about one of Ben's rare letters that had arrived that week, posted in Australia, where he said he was touring with a band, though he didn't say which.

'What I say is', Mary sighed, 'at least he's alive. He can't be too gone on them drugs or he wouldn't be able to write these letters, would he? And he's doing what he loves.'

Jan and the children waved goodbye as her parents disappeared down the lane in Reg's old green Daihatsu, and she went back in, feeling that whatever the world chucked at her she could take it. In the morning she would go into Broadway to ask her solicitor if she had any chance of successfully suing Harold Powell's firm for mishandling the sale of her property.

She put the children to bed and they were already asleep behind the flimsy partition which separated their makeshift bedroom from the rest of the mobile home when she heard a car drive onto the new hard standing. When she looked out she saw James McNeill's Volvo.

As soon as he got out, she could see that something wasn't right. He stopped twice, then almost fell over as he carried on up towards the caravan.

She didn't need the blast of wine-laden breath that met her when she opened the door to know that he was very drunk. Suddenly uneasy, she was alarmed that a man like James McNeill should have lost control of himself.

At first, although obviously drunk, he seemed fairly normal.

'Just been having lunch with some clients at a stud near Ford', he said, 'and thought I'd check my patients on the way home.'

He stepped back unsteadily from the caravan; Jan came out and closed the door behind her. She didn't like leaving the children for long in case they woke up and panicked, but she didn't want James wandering around her yard on his own in the state he was in.

She walked briskly down the hill in front of him and waited outside the barn for him to follow. When he'd caught up, they walked in. Jan tried to open the first stable door, but the foot latch was stiff and she couldn't budge it without leaning down to push the door in a little.

She was bending over thinking she would have to ask Gerry to look at it for her, when she felt a pair of hands clutch her behind and squeeze. She shot upright and spun round, almost tipping James over.

'What the hell do you think you're doing?' she asked sharply.

The vet shrugged his shoulders defensively and shook his big curly head. 'Don't be like that; I'm only giving you a cuddle. It must have been a long time for you.'

Jan gritted her teeth. She didn't want a second

showdown in two days. 'Oh, that's what you were doing was it? Well, thanks very much, but I really don't want a cuddle right now.'

'All right, I'm sorry,' James said without any visible remorse and pushed past her, through the stable door which was now open.

'How's this little bugger?' he turned to her.

'That's the mare,' Jan answered coldly. 'I don't think she's feeling a thing on that hock now. Frankly, she might just as well go home.'

'Oh, the owners won't mind if she stays here another week or so,' James said conspiratorially, 'especially if I tell them she must.'

'I don't want to keep any horses here under false pretences, James. That's not how I operate.'

James shrugged a shoulder and leaned against his patient's quarters. 'It's up to you, but I heard you lost a few horses yesterday.'

Jan was amazed, as she had been before, by how quickly news travelled in the racing world, even at her lowly level.

'I didn't lose them, I told the owner to shift them.'

'Why on earth did you do that?'

'Because he cheated me out of a lot of money over a property he sold for me.'

'Poor old Jan,' James slurred. He put out a hand to touch her arm, but she shrugged it off. 'May I suggest', he went on, 'in future you don't let your principles get in the way of making a profit, or you won't last long in this game.'

Jan could hardly believe that this was the same man who had been so businesslike in all their dealings up to now. She walked to the door of the stables. 'James, I'm sorry to say this, but you seem far too drunk to make any judgement about these horses. Why not come back in the morning or next time you're passing?'

James's eyes seemed to glaze for a moment, then a big, uncontrolled leer spread across his face, which was nothing like his usual charming smile. He pushed himself away from the mare and walked carefully from the stable. As Jan shut and bolted the door, she felt his arms wrap themselves right round her waist, meeting in front of her stomach.

She turned as far as she could, to be met with a waft of sour, winy breath as his face lurched towards hers.

'You're so good,' he muttered. 'You deserve a little kiss.'

Jan moved sharply to avoid his lowering mouth and banged her head hard on the angle of the door frame. For a few moments of semi-consciousness her world went dark, with flashes of brilliant light. When she came to, she found herself lying on the shallow stack of straw bales inside the door of the barn. James McNeill's face was just above hers. There was a lecherous gleam in his eyes.

'All right, Jan? God, you're lovely!'

His cold, damp mouth descended on hers, and she

gritted her teeth as he tried to jab his tongue against them. A sudden nausea welled up in her and she could hardly breathe from the pressure of his body on hers. Suddenly she was desperate; she wanted to scream, but she had no breath to do it.

She felt him shift his body over her. Taking the chance the movement gave her, she brought her knee up with all the force she could find and drove it straight into his genitals.

The effect was instant.

He howled and fell sideways away from her, slipping off the bales and crashing to the ground. She quickly rolled off the straw and ran to the door, where she stood, panting with fear and rage, and looked back as the dogs ran in and started barking at the commotion.

James was doubled up, foetus-like and groaning. Slowly, he unfurled himself and pulled himself up until he was sitting with his back against the bales.

He looked up and saw her. He seemed suddenly sober. His eyes were filled with anger and he breathed deeply through quivering nostrils as he tried to regain control of himself.

Neither he nor Jan spoke. Slowly he pulled himself to his feet and walked towards her. She stood rigid, determined not to show any fear, but shaking inside.

He walked straight past her, out into the yard. She didn't move as she heard him walk away towards the gate. His footsteps stopped.

'My lorry will be here in the morning to collect the four horses I consigned. Have my bill ready, give it to the driver and it'll be settled by return.'

Jan didn't reply or turn around. The footsteps resumed, echoing from the building opposite, until James reached the gate and his car.

Jan still hadn't moved from the stable door when she heard the car reverse and move off down the drive. Her shoulders heaved and large tears welled up to sting the corners of her eyes and trickle down her face as she thought of the two small children asleep in the caravan.

Jan leaned against the sturdy oak stanchion of the barn door frame. Her back slithered slowly down the smooth old timber until she was sitting on the ground with her legs hunched up in front of her. Fred came up, sniffed and licked her ear. She put a hand out to stroke his bony back and gazed around through blurred eyes at the buildings, the spotless ground between, the new half-barrels of her favourite orange-red geraniums, which Gerry had brought up in a show of devotion.

She thought of all the extravagant expectations she'd had for her yard until just a few days before. All her dreams of building up a busy racing stables, turning out a string of winners, perhaps one day – she had dared to think – going on to train National Hunt horses, had completely collapsed. Even her short-term aim of building up the best convalescent home for horses in the Cotswolds was looking dicey if James McNeill's patients were to be removed next day.

If she was going to make anything out of the place to support herself and her children, she might even have to abandon this ambition and revert to the unglamorous, low-paid drudgery of keeping hunters at livery.

She closed her eyes, thought of the kids and sighed. If that was what she had to do to survive, so be it. She pulled herself together, got to her feet and walked from the yard back up to the caravan. Letting herself in quietly, she checked that the children were asleep and put the kettle on to boil. She heaped two self-indulgent spoonsful of sugar into a mug of tea and sat down at the table. From the shelf above her head, she pulled out a dog-eared file she had kept since first planning her yard at Edge Farm. She opened it and ran through her list of outgoings for the twentieth time to see which of them could be cut.

As she considered the options, she felt her tears returning. She shook her head desolately and wished that John was there, standing behind her, to guide her with his quiet, unhurried advice. The only people she could turn to now were her parents and she had no intention of upsetting them with an account of what James McNeill had just tried to do. Even if she lied to them about his reasons for removing the horses and, presumably, not sending any more, they would worry about her. They would want to help out with money, when she knew they had little enough of their own.

A couple of times, though, her hand strayed to the telephone, wanting to hear her father's reassuring voice, but she resisted. She thought about ringing Eddie; she could have told him exactly what happened, knowing he wouldn't be too shocked and would understand her reactions. But she felt she had asked more of him than she'd intended over the Harold business. She had already used up her share of his good will, given their principal relationship was that of owner and trainer, whatever additional undercurrents she might sometimes have sensed between them.

In the end, she picked up her handset and dialled Annabel's number. She listened, imagining the phone ringing in Annabel's pretty cottage kitchen, until an answerphone clicked in.

'Sorry I'm not here. Please leave a message after the beep and I'll call you back.'

'Annabel, it's Jan. Where are you? Something's happened and I need to talk to you. Call me if you can, any time up till midnight. Otherwise, see you in the morning,' she added bravely.

Jan barely slept that night. Annabel didn't ring, and half a dozen times Jan came close to dialling Eddie's number. But she held back, even harbouring a nagging and illogical idea that Annabel was with Eddie, and feeling confusingly ambivalent about it.

Annabel came in next morning, fresh and keen as

always, but as soon as she saw Jan, a worried frown creased her brow.

'Jan, you look terrible! What's wrong? I've only just picked up your message. I'm sorry I wasn't there last night. I went to have dinner at my parents' and decided to stay the night.'

Jan tried to smile. 'I don't pay you enough for what you do as it is, let alone expecting you to be on call the whole time.'

'What's happened?' Annabel pressed.

Jan sat down and felt her face collapse as tears welled up in her eyes. 'I'm afraid we're losing four of our patients today.' She went on to describe James McNeill's drunken arrival the previous evening and what he had done to her. She concluded that, without Harold's horses and no immediate prospect of others to come, she would have to advertise for hunting liveries. Failing that, she would just have to let Roz go; she and Annabel could manage the children and the horses between them.

Annabel, sitting opposite, put a hand on Jan's and shook her head. 'Jan, I know what James did must have come as an awful shock, but I'm afraid it's something that some men do, isn't it – more than you'd think, actually. And at least you gave him a good kicking.'

Jan couldn't help smiling a little at the thought. 'I tell you what, I certainly made his eyes water!'

'Yes, and you got rid of him. It seems the rumours

Roz heard must have been true. But it'd be a terrible shame if he stopped sending us horses.' Annabel's mouth tightened in a regretful wince.

'He's stopped all right,' Jan said. 'Anyway, I wouldn't have them.'

'Jan, this is your business; you can't be like that or take these things personally. It's your livelihood, whatever you think about him. And he certainly won't try to molest you again.'

'Yes, well, it's a bit hypothetical, isn't it?'

'OK, but there are several other people who have talked about sending you horses – Colonel Gilbert, and even old skinflint Mr Carey was muttering something about maybe sending us a horse for a bit of interest next winter.'

'Your landlord? I'll believe that when I see it,' Jan snorted.

'Funnily enough, I think he might. He's really rather nice, once you get to know him.'

'Hmm,' Jan grunted. 'That's not surprising. Men always tend to be nice to slim, beautiful girls. Anyway, thanks for listening. I suppose we'd better get on with some work.'

'Here's Roz,' Annabel said, seeing her car juddering up the track. 'Don't say anything about letting her go just yet. See how things are for the next week or so and you needn't pay me for August. I've honestly got all the money I need for the moment.'

'Of course I'll pay you. But you're right about Roz. I won't make any hasty decisions; I've made enough of those already.' Jan spoke ruefully, thinking of what John or her father might have done. 'But I'm still going to see the solicitors this morning to see if there's anything I can do about Harold Powell.'

Morris, Jones & Co. was a small, old-fashioned firm of solicitors in Broadway who had looked after Reg Pritchard's uncomplicated affairs for the last thirty years. The senior partner, Mr Russell, had known Jan since she was born and had seen her ride in her first point-to-points when she was a teenager.

Jan sat in front of his big mahogany desk in an office that smelled of musty paper and pipe tobacco. After a brief chat about the horses in Jan's yard and her prospects for the next season, she handed over her dossier of correspondence with Harris & Powell regarding Stonewall Farm. The old solicitor leafed through the sheaf of papers until he came to a newspaper cutting of a small advertisement for the sale. He took off his gold-rimmed glasses and leaned back in his chair.

'I'm afraid it looks as if Mr Powell's firm fulfilled all the normal statutory and professional obligations in the way they offered your property for sale. You could argue that they didn't do it all that well, but this would be terribly hard to prove and, undoubtedly, the case would be fought by their professional indemnity insurers.' A look of regret on the lawyer's face, rusty and wrinkled like an old iron roof, expressed his view of the inevitable outcome. 'If you lost, you would have to pay all their costs and I'm afraid you would find that you'd spent a great deal of money for absolutely nothing. In my opinion, legally, there's no point in pursuing this matter. I'm sorry.'

Jan stared at his kindly face, feeling almost sick with frustration at his passive attitude, but grateful for his desire to avoid wasting money that she didn't have.

'But surely', she said, 'the publicity would be very bad for a firm like theirs in a small town?'

The solicitor looked unconvinced. 'I don't suppose it would worry them much.' He glanced at a letter from Harris & Powell. 'I expect they've got a monopoly in the town and people soon forget small legal cases, if they ever bother to read the reports in the first place.'

'Well, I know Harold Powell, and I reckon he *would* be worried at the thought of bad publicity. Couldn't we scare him a bit and see what happens – let him know that we intend to take the matter further?'

Mr Russell nodded. 'We could certainly write him a strong letter to that effect. That wouldn't do any harm and, once in a while, it can produce a result.'

'How much would it cost?'

'To send one letter? About fifty pounds, I should think.'

Jan repressed her instinctive reaction to what seemed an exorbitant charge for one letter. 'All right,' she said. 'Would you do that? And make it very strong – as aggressive as a solicitor's allowed to be.'

The lawyer smiled. 'All right, Mrs Hardy.' He leaned forward over his desk. 'We may look mild and docile, but we do know how to bark when we have to.'

As James McNeill had threatened when he left the night before, a lorry arrived for his patients soon after Jan arrived back from Broadway. She watched with mixed emotions as the horses were driven away. It was a real blow that such a useful source of income should have dried up after only five weeks, but she knew she could never again be comfortable dealing with a man who had tried to abuse her in the way McNeill had.

With only four horses left, the farm had a distinctly empty feel to it. Sounds seemed to echo more loudly around the buildings and Jan's depression began to infect her two helpers as well.

As the week wore on, Jan felt no better and nothing appeared to alleviate her gloom, besides receiving a copy of an unexpectedly blunt letter Mr Russell had written to Harold Powell on her behalf. She prayed, without much hope, that it might have some effect.

Looking at her list of possible owners, she wondered what she could do to conjure up more. Angrily she crossed off the name Bernie Sutcliffe, the man James McNeill had said he was going to send to visit her yard.

She wondered if Eamon Fallon might be persuaded to buy another good horse. He looked as if he had the money, but he hadn't been to the yard since Dingle Bay had arrived.

She was sure that Colonel Gilbert would stick to his word – after all, he'd paid in advance with the delivery of straw. And Gwillam Evans, the farmer who had bred Rear Gunner and still owned his half-brother, Barneby Boy, had rung the week before to say he would at least come and look at her set-up, although it was over seventy miles away. That was all very well, she told herself, but in the meantime she couldn't live on fresh air and promises.

On Saturday morning, Reg and Mary called in on their way back from a shopping expedition to Evesham. While Reg immediately spotted the absence of some of Jan's injured tenants, Mary had other concerns.

Sitting in the caravan, where Megan was showing her the doll's house, Mary turned to Jan with a worried face. 'What's happened to Megan's shoes, Jan? They're practically falling to bits!'

'Nothing's happened to them, Mum. Just normal wear and tear.'

'But they shouldn't be that worn out. Where did you get them?'

'I can't remember now,' Jan said, pretending she hadn't realized the child's shoes were as bad as they were. 'Oxfam in Tewkesbury, I think.'

'You mean they were second-hand to start with?' Mary asked, appalled.

'They'd hardly been worn.'

'Well it's time you got her some new ones.'

'Mum, they're all right. Do you know what kid's shoes cost these days? It's a total rip-off, when they only fit them for a few months.'

'A child's feet are very important, Jan. I made sure that whatever else you had to go without, you always had good, solid shoes, and you always had lovely feet.'

'All right, all right, Mum. I'll get her some more, but right now, you know, I've got a few other priorities.'

Mary suddenly realized she had pushed Jan too far. 'Oh, I'm sorry, my duck. I know it's been hard for you. Your father said it must be with losing those horses of Mr Powell's. Look, if money's a bit short, let *me* get her the shoes.'

'No! No, Mum, I can cope!' Jan tried to soften her indignation. 'I don't want you to be worrying about me when it's hard enough for you to look after yourselves.'

'Your father and me would rather see you and Megan and Matty well and happy. We want to help you.'

'I know you want to help', Jan said, trying to stay calm, 'and I'm really grateful, but I promise you, I can manage on my own.'

'It's not as though you've a man to help you now.'

'For God's sake, Mum! I can manage without a man, you know – I'm bloody determined to. I'll cut the grass verges with nail scissors if I have to!' Jan heard her voice rising and regretted it at once. 'I'm sorry,' she mumbled

'That's all right, love,' Mary said gently. 'I know what you're like, and you always have been, but don't be too proud. Don't forget that we're always there if you really need us.'

As she watched her father's Daihatsu trundle away, she was glad she had been strong enough to turn down their offer of help, and she felt almost strengthened by it in her determination to pull herself through this early crisis in her new life at Edge Farm.

When Eddie appeared later in the morning for another schooling session on Russian Eagle, Jan didn't want him to see how hard the week's events had hit her. But after they'd done a good two hours' work, they went up to sit outside her caravan with a drink and Eddie took a long, thoughtful slug of his beer. He looked at her with friendly concern in his eyes.

'Jan, it's no good you bottling things up and being all retentive, you know – not with me. What's been going on?'

Jan lifted one shoulder. 'It was a bit hard, losing Harold's horses, I admit, but—'

'You've lost more than Harold's,' Eddie interrupted. 'You had seven horses in for repair last week and I've noticed there are only three now.'

Jan grimaced and nodded. 'James McNeill came round last Sunday; when he left, he told me he was sending a lorry to collect them.' She sighed. 'They went on Monday.'

Eddie's eyes widened at what this must have meant to her. 'What on earth did you do to let that happen?'

'What did I do? It was more what I *didn't* do!' Jan said. She took a gulp of cider and started to describe the vet's drunken attempt to have sex with her the previous Sunday.

As he listened, Eddie's face wrinkled. 'The bastard! I have to say, on the one occasion I met him, I thought he was dodgy, specially after Roz told me how he puts it about all over the place.' He leaned forward and topped up Jan's glass from the bottle beside him. 'Anyway, you're better off without a two-faced shit like that for a client.'

'I shouldn't take it so personally, though.'

'I should think it's bloody impossible not to. Anyway, there are plenty of other vets around who are also decent human beings.'

'I know, but I wish they'd just send me a few horses.'

'Have you asked them, or told them what you can offer?'

'I phoned them all when I first came here,' Jan said defensively.

'They'll probably need reminding and you should get in touch with the big racing stables round here, too; it might suit them to send young and injured horses here, rather than have them clogging up their yards – especially now they're bringing horses back in from their summer break. What you need is a really good professional-looking brochure printed which you can mail to everyone you can think of who might be a potential customer.'

Jan sighed. 'I know; you're right, but, as always, it's a question of money. Which comes first, the chicken or the egg?'

'Don't worry about that. I'll get it done and you can knock it off my training fees at the end of the season. And I tell you what,' he went on as if he'd had a sudden inspiration, 'I happen to have a dollop of cash at the moment from a big picture I sold, so why don't I pay you now for Eagle's training fees up to the end of the year? It would suit me if I didn't have to think about bills again for a few months.'

Jan drew in a quick breath. 'Oh, Eddie, I don't know. What if something went wrong with the horse and I couldn't go on training him?'

'He'd still be here while he was convalescing, wouldn't he? And if, God forbid, he was so badly hurt he had to be put down, he's well insured and I'd want you to find a replacement for him right away. I don't know of anyone else who could do a better job than you.'

'Well, if you're sure . . .'

'I am,' Eddie urged. 'It really would suit me, I promise.'

'All right,' Jan nodded, praying that she wouldn't regret the subtle change in their relationship that this would make. 'Thanks a lot. It would be an enormous help right now.'

'Fine. I'll bring the cash round . . .', he paused, Jan guessed, for a mental scroll through his diary, 'tomorrow evening. I know it's a Sunday, but if you can find a babysitter, I'll take you out to dinner as well, if you like.'

'Now you're spoiling me. You mustn't make a habit of it!' Jan smiled, very relieved by the removal of her immediate cash-flow problems, as well as Eddie's vote of confidence in her. But she found it hard to believe that, although he was three years younger than her, Eddie was ready to offer so much support without a more physical motive, and she was concerned not to let her gratitude turn into any other kind of emotion.

'Does that mean yes or no?' he asked.

'Yes, please. I can always drop the kids at my mum's if I can't get Roz or Annabel to sit.'

'I'm sure Gerry would do it for you,' Eddie said with a twinkle in his eye.

Jan shook her head. 'He already does more than he should for me. It wouldn't be right to encourage him.'

'You could look on it as a way of rewarding him for all he's done – he'd probably love to hang around here for an evening, feeling close to you, even if you weren't here.'

'Don't be unkind, Eddie. He's just a bit shy.'

'I know. He's a lovely chap. Now,' he said, looking at his watch, 'I'll have to go soon, but if you give me an idea of what you want to say in this brochure, I'll take a few digital shots of the place and put together some layouts on the computer.'

When he'd left, Jan admitted to herself how much Eddie's visit had cheered her. Her pressing cash-flow problems were all but resolved and, suddenly, everything she'd dreamed of now seemed possible. But it wasn't just the money and the encouragement Eddie had given her. Quite against her will, she'd also found herself comparing him with John – until she realized it was an impossible comparison. As men, they were poles apart and their individual appeal for her couldn't have been more different.

Jan began to enjoy the rest of the day, massaging a horse's back, lunging Gale Bird and walking round the fields checking all her other tenants with Megan, while she gave Matty a ride on her shoulders, pretending to be a horse herself.

After tea with the children, she still felt optimistic enough to pull out the plans of her house which she'd had drawn up – the house which she hoped to see rise from the rubble-strewn patch where once the old Edge Farm house had stood.

Beside the outline, already dug by Gerry, stood piles of stone blocks and tiles. Under a tarpaulin were several old oak beams, recycled pine rafters and floorboards – all found and sent over by Eddie over the last few weeks.

After gazing at the plans for a while, Jan went out and walked around the site, imagining how each room would be – where Matty and Megan would sleep, and where her kitchen window would look out across the broad sweep of the Severn Valley to the Malvern ridge.

She sat on a big hunk of golden limestone to watch the setting sun, chuckled to herself then sighed. It was going to be a bloody long time before any of the house was real, but now, at least for this evening, it felt like it might actually happen one day.

10

On Sunday evening, Eddie arrived as promised with a bag full of cash to cover his bills for the next five months. He also produced the draft of a professional-looking brochure – *Edge Farm Stables, Equine Recovery Centre*. Jan was delighted with it, so Eddie confirmed that he would have it printed and sent to everyone they could think of who might be interested in Jan's expertise.

When they'd finished drawing up a comprehensive list of addresses, Eddie took Jan to a noisy Italian restaurant near Cheltenham. All the waiters there seemed to be his best friend and Jan didn't miss the nudging and winking that went on between them. She wondered how many women Eddie had taken there before. Looking at him laughing and smiling, with his eyes twinkling, she found herself thinking what he'd be like in bed, though she dismissed the thought almost as soon as it had entered her mind. Besides, she thought, nothing he said or did suggested he wanted any more from her than her company and the chance to talk about horses.

Later, he dropped her back at the caravan and said goodnight with his usual fleeting kiss on one cheek. He promised to be back in a few days with the finished brochure.

The following day Jan went to her bank in Broadway to pay in the cash Eddie had brought and drove back buoyed up with renewed confidence.

On Thursday, though, when Annabel had gone home after work, leaving Jan alone with the children in the caravan, her depression seeped back.

Around nine, the evening turned gloomy. Lights had started to twinkle across the valley and the sky was turning thick black when a car's headlights swept off the lane and two powerful beams lit up her drive. She couldn't see what kind of car it was and she waited curiously to see who had come to visit her this late. She was not averse to some company to take her mind off things. It was only when the driver had parked and walked halfway up to the caravan that Jan saw it was Harold Powell.

Instinctively she shrank back and thought about locking the door, but she detected a hesitancy in Harold's approach which suggested he hadn't come aggressively.

Nevertheless, she waited until he knocked on the door.

'Who is it?'

'Jan, it's Harold. I've driven all the way over from Hay to see you. Can I come in?'

Jan opened the door and looked at him without

displaying any emotion. 'How did you know I'd be here?'

'I phoned earlier and your girl, Roz, said you would be. Didn't she tell you?'

Jan thought back. 'No, but I was up in the top paddock when she left. Anyway, as you're here I suppose you'd better come in.' Jan pulled the door open a little wider and beckoned him up.

He climbed the two wooden steps and sidled into the caravan.

Jan closed the door behind him and waved him to one of the padded benches. He sat and slid his knees under the table.

Jan didn't join him. 'Well, why are you here?' she asked.

'Look, Jan. I can understand what you must have thought when you saw Stonewall on the market for so much more than you got, but the simple fact is the market's hardened a hell of a lot in the last few months, and I did warn you at the time not to sell in a hurry. Whatever your solicitor says, we did everything by the book when we were selling the place.' He looked up at Jan, who still hadn't sat down. She said nothing and didn't react. 'Believe me,' he went on with a hint of desperation, 'I had no idea Davies bought the place just to turn it for a profit; I thought he was expanding, but I can see why you think it looks a bit iffy, and obviously we don't want clients feeling they've been ill-treated. So, we thought we should talk to you about it.'

'I don't want to talk about it. I want the extra profit you made out of my property.'

'If you'd waited until the summer, like I said, you'd have had it. It was your decision to sell when you did, not mine.'

'And it was your decision to put just one ad in the *Brecon & Radnor Express* and nowhere else.'

'Any serious buyer for a Welsh hill farm would always check the *Brecon & Radnor* – you know that.'

'Don't bullshit me, Harold. I've known you too long. You know damn well you wanted as few people as possible to see that ad. I can't think why I didn't complain at the time, but John wasn't long dead; I had other things on my mind and you took advantage of that; you knew I wanted to get away from the farm as soon as I could.'

'Like I say, Jan, it was your decision, not mine.'

'All right, so because my solicitor's sent you a letter you've decided to talk to me about it. What exactly did you want to say?'

'After all our expenses, and assuming the new buyer doesn't back down, we will make a profit of about fifty grand—'

'Harold! Don't talk rubbish! You'll make closer to a hundred.'

'Jan, calm down,' Harold said mildly. 'Think about all the expenses and the opportunity cost.'

'More bullshit,' Jan reorted. 'I see you've let the grass keep already.'

'At a very low rent, just to keep the fields grazed off.'

Jan uttered a cynical grunt. 'All right, then. What are you suggesting?'

'We propose, and this is completely without prejudice, mind—'

'What's that?'

'Any offer I make to you this evening is no admission of liability and would have no bearing on any subsequent court proceedings.'

'Go on.'

'We'd like you to sign this letter.' Harold pulled a folded sheet of paper from the pocket of his tweed jacket, opened it and put it on the table facing Jan.

She picked it up. It was a typed letter, addressed from Edge Farm with her name at the end, confirming that, in handling the sale of Stonewall Farm, in her opinion, Harris & Powell had acted properly and with professional integrity throughout. Jan looked up at Harold. 'Why on earth would I sign this?'

'Because, to show our sincerity in not wanting you to feel aggrieved, we would make you an ex-gratia payment of ten thousand pounds.'

Jan felt herself flush with satisfaction that her lawyer's letter had produced a result, but she felt deeply indignant that Harold thought she could be bought off so cheaply.

To avoid eye-contact with Harold, she looked down at the letter again. 'To sign this letter, so that you can avoid all the hassle and embarrassment of being sued by me, I'd want half the profit – fifty grand and not a penny less!'

'I told you, Jan, that's about all we made, and we could easily prove in court that we'd behaved properly.'

'Really? Well, the bad publicity would kill your business stone dead.'

Harold shook his head with a supercilious smile. 'I don't think so, Jan. Not when it comes out that you wanted the place sold as quickly as possible. Your mother-in-law would testify to that.'

Jan gulped. She knew it was true that if Olwen took Harold's side, the local community would trust her more than an outsider like herself.

'No,' Harold went on. 'Our offer is based on our sense of fairness.'

'It's because you don't want the hassle, Harold, let's face it. Or the legal bills.'

'Look, Jan. You can think what you like, but the bottom line is, if you sign that letter, we'll give you ten grand – cash.'

'All right, Harold,' Jan said. Harold's eyes gleamed triumphantly before Jan went on. 'You leave me the letter and I'll think about it.'

The brightness in Harold's eyes dimmed. 'Look, Jan, we don't want this dragging on and on.'

'It won't; I'll let you know what I think by the end of the week, OK?'

Harold took a deep breath and scrutinized Jan's face in an attempt to read her mind. 'All right,' he said, sliding himself along the bench to stand up. 'But just remember it's a very generous offer, which we are under no professional obligation to make, but we *are* honourable men.'

'I'm sure you are,' Jan said, opening the door to let Harold out. 'Thank you for thinking of me,' she added deadpan.

Harold paused for a moment, apparently to say something, but he seemed to think better of it and dropped down the two wooden steps before disappearing into the darkness towards his car. 'G'night Jan,' he called back when he reached the Range Rover.

Jan closed the door and picked up the letter Harold had left. She folded it and, with steady hands, tore it slowly into a handful of tiny squares and dropped them into her swing bin.

Although Jan had grown close to Annabel, she didn't tell her everything that went on in her life. She sensed that it could be dangerous or, at least, leave her potentially vulnerable, to expose too much of herself to any one person.

She sometimes felt, though, that this was a wasted exercise with Annabel, who seemed to have an uncanny knack of identifying her problems even before she was aware of them herself. The morning after Harold had been round, Jan told her little more than he'd come to offer some kind of recompense for any grievance she might have felt over the sale of Stonewall Farm. Annabel was sitting with a cup of coffee, brewed from freshly ground beans she'd bought for Jan in Cheltenham. She looked up and nodded. 'I was at a dinner party near Hay last weekend,' she said. 'Someone asked me why Harold had taken his horses from you. They couldn't understand it. And a woman said she'd asked Harold about it. Apparently he was really cagey, so now everyone thinks you had some kind of row, and, seeing the price that's being asked for Stonewall, they've put two and two together. Not that they know Harold has any connection with the new vendor, but, you know—'

'Yes, I know,' Jan said. 'And the smarmy creep was trying to kid me he didn't know his partner in the engineering firm had bought the farm.'

'Is there any chance he'd offer to send his horses back?'

'I've no idea,' said Jan, and meant it. She hadn't even considered that Harold would want to after the way she'd sent them home to him. 'Anyway, I wouldn't have them.'

'But, Jan, you know you'd have more winners next season with Rear Gunner. He'll easily qualify for the Foxhunters'.'

'Harold Powell would need to crawl on his hands and knees across a bed of burning coals to this caravan before I'd even think about training for him again.'

'Jan,' Annabel said with sudden sharpness, 'I've told you before, you mustn't take these things so personally. You're not offering to be an owner's best friend, you're just agreeing to train whatever horses they send you, however useless they are.'

'Well, I'll just tell you something, I'm not interested in training useless horses. It's far easier to train good ones and miles easier to get winners from them. I don't intend to take on any old rubbish, just for the training fee, which barely covers my costs anyway.'

'But Harold's aren't useless,' Annabel pointed out quietly.

'Too bad,' Jan said.

On her own, Jan wondered how far she could carry these principles and how much they would cost her. They were bound to cost, either financially or emotionally, or both, but were they worth it?

In the last fortnight she'd lost seven horses whom she desperately needed to provide cash-flow for her business, and yet it was the same desire not to compromise that had made her tear up Harold's letter.

Later that day Jan felt gratified when, through an ironic twist of fate, a new owner arrived at Edge Farm – an owner with little apparent knowledge of horses and all the trappings of big money. He had phoned in the morning to ask if she would be there, saying no more than he wanted to see her yard.

He drove up Jan's track in a brand-new Jaguar, and seemed to hesitate before committing himself to parking it among the collection of untidy vehicles on the hard standing. As soon as Jan caught sight of him, she decided that he was a very unattractive individual.

She and Roz watched him from the yard as he got out, locked the car and picked his way gingerly towards them, as if wary of contact between his black Gucci shoes and the naked earth.

'Cor!' Roz said. 'He looks a right pleb.'

'Shh,' Jan said, grinning.

As he came closer, Jan saw that his shoes were the only thing about him that shone. Everything else was grey and lustreless, especially his skin. Although Jan guessed he was in his mid-forties, there was already a patina of age on his deeply furrowed face. He had a long, thin head, topped with a covering of scanty, dull grey hair. He was about five foot eight, slightly hunched and wearing a jacket of tiny black and white checks. Close to, though, he smelt expensively clean and his shirt looked as if it was new out of its packaging that morning.

'Hello,' she said, meeting him as he reached the gateway into the yard.

'Are you Jan Hardy?' he asked with a lack of charm which would, in time, become familiar to her.

Jan nodded.

He held out a bony, light grey hand. 'I'm Bernie Sutcliffe. James McNeill told me about you.'

'Did he?' Jan asked. 'I'm very surprised. He took all his horses away at the beginning of last week.'

'I know. He told me. And that was when he told me not to come near you, but I like people who stand up to big bastards like McNeill. He tried to get his dirty paws on my girlfriend last week – thinks just 'cos he introduced us it gives him some kind of rights.' He spoke with a nasal whine and a strong Black Country accent.

'Ah,' Jan nodded, thinking she was beginning to see what had happened. 'He did mention you to me a few weeks ago.'

Bernie wagged his head up and down with quick, jerky nods. 'Did he tell you what I want?'

'He just said you might be interested in owning a racehorse and he'd suggested you try pointing first.'

'Yeah, well. Sandy, my girlfriend, she fancies it. I know nothing about it, but I'm a quick learner,' he added sharply, 'and I can smell when people are trying to tuck me up.'

'You won't smell anything like that round here, Mr Sutcliffe, I can assure you,' Jan said and wished she hadn't sounded quite so haughty.

'We'll see,' Bernie said ambiguously, before changing his tone. 'What would you suggest if I want a horse to win a few races?'

'First of all, whatever I suggest or do for you, there's absolutely no guarantee you'll have a winner. We can do a lot to shorten the odds; we can go out and find you the right horse with the right pedigree; we can enter it in the right races and in the right company. We can make sure we've got the best pilot on board. But we never cheat and we only play with a straight bat.'

'I've been told there's a lot that don't,' Bernie said.

'I wouldn't have thought so, Mr Sutcliffe, not in pointing. There'd not be much purpose to it. The prize money's pretty pathetic and it's almost impossible to get a large bet on.'

'Call me Bernie,' he grunted. 'I meant on the proper race tracks.'

'I wouldn't know. I don't have a professional licence so I can't run on National Hunt courses, except hunter chases, which are open to point-to-pointers, but they take a lot of winning.'

Bernie glanced at Roz, who was hovering near them. 'Haven't you got an office or something, where we can talk business?' he asked Jan.

'Only the caravan where I live.' She nodded up the hill.

'You live in that?' Bernie asked, not even trying to disguise his horror.

'I take my job seriously, Mr Sutcliffe—'

'Bernie,' he interrupted more impatiently, and Jan noticed for the first time that he was looking at her closely. He seemed pleased with what he saw.

'There was no house with this place when I bought it, but I need to be near my horses as much as possible; there's always things that can go wrong and the earlier you can catch them the better.'

Bernie nodded appreciatively. 'Let's go up there, then.'

Jan led him from the yard and up the bank. As they walked, she turned to look at him and saw his eyes flashing all round the place, taking in everything that was there.

'What's your business?' she asked conversationally.

His eye shot back to hers. 'Investments,' he said with deliberate vagueness before evidently deciding that was too unspecific to satisfy anyone. 'Salvage and property,' he added.

'Developing?' Jan asked, out of curiosity.

'Developing a bit. Letting mostly and a few other things.'

'Where are you based, then?' she asked as if it weren't obvious from his accent that it could only be in the Black Country.

'Brierley Hill.'

'Oh, right,' Jan said, not knowing where that was. They'd reached the caravan and she led him up the two steps. Inside she offered him a seat and a cup of tea.

He sat down and squeezed his legs under the table. For the next half-hour he grilled Jan on what sort of horse and service he could expect for the amount of money he wanted to spend. It wasn't a big budget and Jan told him if he wanted a good chance of winning anything beyond a member's race, he'd probably have to spend more.

'And to give yourself a realistic chance beyond that, you would really need two or three horses because any horse can go wrong. The bones, ligaments and muscles of a horse's legs are amongst its most vital assets. They're highly specialized limbs and when a horse is racing fit and tuned right up, it doesn't take a lot to damage them – sometimes just in their stable they can give themselves a knock that'll put them off for a month or so. And, of course, their lungs and their heart are all sensitive, particularly when they're under pressure.'

'All right, all right. You'll put me off the whole thing if you go on. Say I told you to spend ten grand, then could you get me something?'

'I should be able to find you a horse capable of winning. Then it's a hundred and thirty quid a week, plus shoeing, vet's bills and transport.'

'You're not using that slimy bastard McNeill for a vet are you?'

'No.'

'Good. How come he took his horses away from you?'

Jan took a deep breath. 'They weren't his, they belonged to his clients; they were here to be nursed back to full health – backs, legs, coughs – stuff like that. And he took them because he turned up here drunk, about ten o'clock at night, two Sundays ago and molested me in the barn. I'm afraid I had to give him a serious kick in the balls.'

Bernie's eyes lit up, and he uttered a harsh cackle. 'The dirty bastard. Serve him bloody well right! Good on you, girl! Well, if you see him again, you tell him Bernie Sutcliffe's having a horse with you, and let's rub his bloody nose in it, right?'

Annabel told Jan she wanted to take her and the children to the pub for supper that night, using Bernie's promise of a new horse as an excuse.

'But, Bel,' Jan protested, 'I think we should wait till he's bought and paid for one before we celebrate. He looks the type that could mess me about before anything happens.'

'Oh well, come out anyway. You've had a bloody awful couple of weeks and it's about time things turned around for you.'

Jan didn't argue. Before they went, she fed Matthew, loaded him into a papoose and wondered how long it would be before he was too heavy for her to carry.

It was a sunny evening and the pub was packed. A lot of people there seemed to know Jan and greeted her warmly. Julie behind the bar coochicooed at Matthew, who looked at her spiky hair and howled.

When Annabel had bought the drinks, they sat at a table looking at the menu. Jan noticed that Annabel kept glancing around the room and guessed that she was expecting someone to join them. She wondered if it was a man, but after a few minutes, a young woman emerged from the crowd and came up to the table.

'Hi, Annabel.'

'Hello, Penny; have a glass of wine,' Annabel offered, as the girl hovered before sitting down to join them.

'This is Penny Price,' Annabel told Jan. 'She comes from near my parents' home up at Kington.' Penny was in her late twenties, short but heavily built with stout arms and big breasts that filled her shirt. Her straight black hair and big, forthright brown eyes were typical of the country girls Jan knew from the Welsh borders. 'This is Jan Hardy, and Megan and Matthew.'

The girl nodded at Jan and the children with a shy grin. 'Yes, I know.' She shook Jan's hand. 'I recognize you from the races. I saw Rear Gunner's win at Ludlow and Lazy Dove's. I never saw horses so well turned out at the point-to-points.'

'I don't like to take them looking like ragamuffins.' Jan laughed. 'Do you go racing much?'

'Every time I can, to the points, mostly, and the big hunter chases.'

'Do you ride, too?'

'Not in races.' Penny laughed with a shake of her long hair. 'I used to hunt, but it got so expensive I couldn't keep it up once I went out to work and had to rent a flat of my own. But I kept my mare; she's a thoroughbred, by Oats,' she added proudly.

'What do you do with her now?' Jan asked.

'I put her in foal to Gunner B six years ago, but only once since then. The first foal was a colt. I was really worried because he got so big; he's only just grown into himself. But I had him gelded as a yearling, broke him in and backed him myself. He's going really well now.'

'Well done,' Jan said, seeing how much the whole

process meant to Penny. 'It must be very satisfying. I've never bred a horse myself. My dad once had a foal from an old mare Colonel Gilbert gave him, but it had a bog spavin and was never quite right. What are you going to do with yours?'

Penny glanced at Annabel, as if for support, then back at Jan. 'Well, I was hoping you might train him for me if you thought he could go pointing.'

With a twinge of guilt, Jan wondered how she was planning to pay even her modest fees if she already found hunting too expensive. 'I'll certainly have a look for you. He's a five-year-old, is he?'

Penny nodded.

'And a bit backward?'

'He's more or less caught up with himself now. He's a big horse – about seventeen hands, but I've had him jumping some small hedges and tree trunks, and he loves it.'

They talked a little more about the horse, until a girl came to take their order and Annabel suggested Penny should eat with them.

'Oh, no thanks,' Penny said, suddenly embarrassed. 'I mustn't interrupt your meal. It was really kind of you to let me talk to you about my horse. And whenever you can come up and see him, just let me know. Annabel's got my number.'

'Yes, I will,' Jan smiled, appreciating the girl's enthusiasm.

'And you needn't worry about the money,' Penny

said. 'I'm taking a night job at Sun Valley Chickens to pay for his training.'

Jan shook her head. 'I wasn't worried about the money. I just hope I like the horse because I'd love to train for someone who cares so much.' She stood up to say goodbye to Penny, and watched as she squeezed her broad hips through the crowded bar.

'Thanks,' Annabel said when Jan had sat down. 'Her mother works for my parents and when Penny heard I was working for you, she came up to ask if I'd introduce her to you, but she was adamant that I shouldn't say anything first.'

'I really do hope I like the horse. I meant what I said – I'd like to train for someone like that – someone who really loves their horse.'

Three days after she'd met Penny Price, Jan drove the lorry over to west Herefordshire to look at the horse she wanted her to train. He was living with his mother and younger sister in a small, steeply sloping paddock which Penny rented, beside a river on the edge of Kington.

'He's called Arrow Star', Penny said proudly as she led Jan into the field, 'because he was born right beside the River Arrow.'

Arrow Star certainly was a big horse. Jan was concerned because horses of his age and size could still be too narrow and gangly. But as she walked up and examined him, she was relieved to see that he had already broadened and developed a good, deep chest to match his height, with fine sloping shoulders, big-boned, well-shaped hocks and a nicely rounded behind.

Jan also liked the look of him overall; he held himself well and had a big, kind eye. She turned to Penny who was waiting eagerly for her opinion.

'Without seeing him do some work,' she said, 'I'd say he's got all the makings of a useful horse. I'd be very happy to train him. The only thing is he's a big baby and we may find he just isn't ready to race this coming season. Alternatively you could leave him in the field for another year, carry on riding him out a bit and school him over some proper hurdles.'

'But I'd like you to start with him now,' Penny said. 'I think he's ready and I'm prepared to take the gamble.'

'Just as long as you know it is a gamble. Unfortunately, I'll have to charge you either way, until I can say for sure that there's any sense in racing him next season.' Jan saw Penny's disappointment and tried to steer a course between reality and the girl's ambitions. 'Look, it should be OK. He's got the rest of the summer and he'll be six in the new year. But, in the end, you're paying. You must decide.'

'Yes please,' Penny's eyes were shining now at the prospect of her pride and joy going away to be trained by a woman she admired and whose career she had followed avidly through every local point-to-point.

11

As the summer came to a close and September crept by, Jan allowed herself to think back to those two weeks in August when everything had seemed so against her. She had been at her lowest point and now she felt she was finally through it.

Eddie had gone to Italy for a fortnight – to buy paintings, he said – but before he'd gone, he and Jan had posted the glossy new Edge Farm brochures to every possible customer within a seventy-mile radius. Enquiries and visitors had started to flow in almost at once, to the point where Jan now had all eight of her boxes in the barn filled with invalids and a waiting list. As soon as she'd asked him, Gerry had rushed to finish another run of ten timber boxes along the northern side of the yard.

Gwillam Evans had finally got around to making the journey over from Wales. Once he'd seen Jan's new yard, he had decided it was worth sending his horse all the way over to Edge Farm for her to resume training him, so Barneby Boy was now back in her charge.

Jan had also found a horse for Bernie Sutcliffe.

Arctic Hay was a ten-year-old from the big racing stables near Stow where she'd worked as a teenager. Jim Hely, a larger-than-life character from Limerick was head lad there, an old friend, and a firm believer in her talents. The horse had won several respectable chases in his time, but had lost his form. In a new environment and the less competitive arena of pointing, it was likely he would regain his enthusiasm for the job and win more races.

Bernie was thrilled when Jan told him she'd only spent six thousand pounds, not the ten he had rather reluctantly promised, and as soon as the horse was installed at Edge Farm, he appeared with Sandy, his girlfriend, who had persuaded him to buy a horse in the first place.

Sandy was a tall, loud girl, with implausibly peach-coloured hair and doll-like make-up. Everything about her suggested she liked having money spent on her and she made it clear that she felt short-changed by Bernie only buying a point-to-pointer for her to lead in to the winner's enclosure. Nevertheless she seemed determined to indoctrinate Bernie thoroughly into the mysteries and joys of horse racing and saw this as a starting point. At the same time she didn't want to encourage him to get too interested in Jan or, more to the point, Annabel.

As soon as the new stables were ready, Sorcerer's Boy arrived from Colonel Gilbert and a few days after that Annabel's landlord, Mr Carey, rang to say that he had a mare he would like her to train. Jan went with

Annabel to look at her, alone in a field at the furthest point of Mr Carey's large estate. She hadn't been touched for two years, he said, but had shown some promise as a youngster. In her current wild and unruly condition, she didn't look much at all, but Jan agreed to tidy her up and see what she could do.

From having had just three owners at the start of the summer – Eddie, Owen Tollard and Harold, who'd left – Jan now found herself with six more, Colonel Gilbert, Eamon Fallon, Penny Price, Bernie Sutcliffe, Gwillam Evans and Mr Carey. Then, at the end of September, one of her old owners from Stonewall, Alan Preece, who originally hadn't wanted to have his horses so far away, rang her and asked her if he could buy the chestnut she'd bought at the sales in May. She had ten horses now, which wasn't as many as she wanted, but it was a start, and with the recuperating animals she had all the work she and her two helpers could manage.

So it was that she found herself in a more optimistic frame of mind when Colonel Gilbert next came to see his horse and, having planted the seed of the idea in the first place, sat down with her and seriously urged her to think again about applying for a public trainer's licence.

The following day she went to discuss this potential quantum leap with her father.

Reg was sitting outside his house on an old oil

drum, forking pet food from a tin into enamelled dishes for the tribe of semi-feral cats that now inhabited the old farm buildings.

Jan sat down beside him, as she had so many times in the past when she had things to discuss with him. She knew Reg found it easier to say what he was thinking if they weren't sitting face to face.

'Dad, Colonel Gilbert was round yesterday to see Sorcerer's Boy and have a look at the yard. He was really nice about it all and said he'd heard good reports about what we've been doing with the sick horses we've had in. But he said that now the season's starting I should concentrate on training, and he didn't see how I could ever make a living just training pointers; there's a limit to the amount of money involved. He thinks I should look at getting a licence, like Virginia.'

'Virginia!' Reg snorted with unusual cynicism. 'She don't know nothing and I reckon the colonel knows it too.'

'But why should he be encouraging me?'

Reg shrugged his shoulders. 'I dunno, but he's a good bloke is Frank Gilbert; he wouldn't want to tell you to do the wrong thing.'

'I'd love to train National Hunt horses, Dad. I just don't have a clue if I'd be any good at it.'

'I should think it's much the same as what you do already. Feed 'em right, get 'em fit; look after them; find the right races.'

'The trouble is the Jockey Club make you give them

a bank guarantee for thirty-five thousand quid before they'll give you a licence!'

'What's that for?'

'Just to make sure everybody gets paid – your staff, farriers, vets, feed merchants and everybody else – if it all goes wrong.'

'Thirty-five thousand!' Reg sighed. 'You may as well forget it, then. That's too much risk and, anyway, we've none of us got that kind of money.'

'Oh Dad, I wouldn't dream of asking you for it! But I might be able to find someone to put it up for me. I've also got to produce a CV to show what I've done; I've got to get pledges from twelve different people saying they'll keep horses with me, but I've only got eight owners at the moment.'

'You'll get more as the season gets going, I should think.'

'I need them now, though.'

'What's the rush, Jan? Why not get another season's pointing under your belt and get everything right before you go for this licence?'

'Oh, Dad! I've done five seasons already. Can't you see, if I *can* get a licence, I want to get on with it!'

Reg sighed again. 'You always did want to do everything in a hurry. I don't suppose you'll ever change. Still, good luck to you.'

Jan thought she was due a little luck, so on Monday morning she rang the Jockey Club and told them she would like to apply for a public trainer's licence. The forms arrived the next day and Jan spent a long time studying them, wondering what her best strategy for finding a suitable guarantor would be. She considered putting an advertisement in *Horse & Hound* or the *Racing Post*, but shied away from dealing with the unknown quantities it might produce.

Later, she found Eddie in the tack room cleaning his bridle and asked him what he thought. He stopped what he was doing for a minute and his dark brown eyes focused on Jan's for a little longer than usual. 'Why don't I put up the bank guarantee?'

It had vaguely occurred to Jan before then that Eddie could be a potential backer but, not believing he was rich enough, she hadn't seriously considered him. She stared back at him, trying to see what lay behind this unexpected and very generous offer. But, as always, she saw no more than friendliness. 'I wasn't asking you, Eddie. If I was going to ask an owner, I'd have tried Eamon or Bernie, or someone like that. After all, why should you?'

'I've got just as much reason as those two – more really. And, anyway, let's assume that I'll never have to cough up; the money can sit in a high-interest account as long as it needs to. I've seen how you operate, and people like you don't go bust. Quite apart from that, I believe in you as a trainer, just seeing how the horses have come on in the few weeks since you brought them in and the way you've schooled me and Eagle.'

'Even so, you could still lose the lot if I got ill or something – I mean, you just never know – and you shouldn't do it unless you're prepared for that. Can you spare thirty-five thousand quid?'

Eddie grinned and lifted a hand. 'I'll let you know when the time comes. You get the papers for me and I'll do the rest. When are they likely to come and inspect your stables?'

'If I send the application right away, they said about the middle of next month.'

'Then we'd better all pull our fingers out and have this place looking as beautiful as it can be. It's a pity about the barn roof, but there it is. We can't do anything about that in such a short time.'

'What's wrong with the barn roof?' Jan asked indignantly. 'It doesn't leak, which is more than you can say for some of the professional yards I've seen.'

Eddie smiled at her indignation. 'Don't be so defensive. They'll be much more interested in what your horses look like and the results you get.'

'And what other people say about me.'

'Why should anyone say anything bad about you?'

'Oh, I don't know,' Jan shrugged. 'I sometimes get the feeling that not everyone wants a woman on her own to make it in this business, especially if you don't bow to their wishes.'

'Who are you thinking of?'

'James McNeill for a start. I'm bloody sure he'd try and put the boot in if he got the chance once it leaks out that I've applied for a licence. Even if he writes in telling them total rubbish, he's an established vet and they'd take it seriously.'

'Then for God's sake get in first with a pre-emptive strike,' Eddie urged. 'I thought you should have done at the time.'

'But I didn't want to start causing hassle when I'd only been here five minutes.'

'Look, Jan. The man's a bloody menace. If you hadn't been strong and quick enough to kick him in the balls, he'd have raped you. I think you should put in a formal complaint to the Royal College of Veterinary Surgeons and do it right away.'

'But it happened six weeks ago.'

'Just do it, Jan.' Eddie frowned angrily at the injustice.

Jan looked at him, and nodded. 'You're right. I will.'

The evening before the Jockey Club inspector was due to visit Edge Farm, Jan looked around her yard, hoping that she and her team had done all they could to make her premises acceptable. The children were in the tack room, watching a fuzzy old television Roz had brought in to keep them amused while Jan worked in the yard.

Jan had checked everything she could think of, making sure the horses and their stables were all looking their best, when Julie from the Fox & Pheasant drove up in her old pick-up.

'Hi, Jan,' she called, climbing out and banging the driver's door. 'How's it going?'

Jan walked across the yard to the parking place. 'OK, but I've got a bloke from the Jockey Club coming round tomorrow and I'm dead nervous about everything he'll find wrong.'

'Gerry told me you were having your inspection. He's even more worried about it than you are, I think.' Julie grinned. 'Poor Gerry, he's obsessed with everything up here.'

Jan felt a twinge of guilt that she might have been taking advantage of the young builder's obvious crush on her. 'He's been brilliant. I couldn't have done it without him.'

'That's why I came up. We've had a bit of a disaster down in the cellars and we need him urgently to sort out the drains. I can't find him anywhere and he's not answering his mobile. I thought he might be up here.'

'No,' Jan said. 'He went about an hour ago.'

'Yeah,' Julie nodded. 'I saw his car wasn't here. Oh,' she said, reacting to another car creeping up the track in the dark, 'perhaps this is him.'

Jan looked at the headlights until the car was close enough to see. Her heart pounded angrily when she recognized Harold Powell's Range Rover.

She hadn't contacted him since his last visit, although several times she'd thought about asking her solicitors to write to him to demand point-blank the money she considered she was owed. She'd held off only because she thought it wouldn't do Harold any harm to stew for a while, and she would rather apply the energy needed to pursue him and his partners after she'd dealt with her licence application.

Jan saw that Julie, who was naturally curious, was watching to see who would get out of the vehicle and she realized that she couldn't have any kind of conversation with Harold in front of her.

'It's Harold Powell, one of my owners,' she said quietly to her. 'He'll want to talk privately.'

Harold climbed down from the Range Rover and walked towards them. It was clear that, outwardly at least, he was trying to appear conciliatory.

'Hello, Jan. How are you?' he said in his warm, silky voice.

Jan raised an eyebrow. 'All right, thanks. Julie, this is Harold.'

'Hello,' Julie said. 'I'm just off. I'll see you Jan, and if you see Gerry before I do, tell him we need him, like now!'

'OK, Julie. 'Bye.'

Jan and Harold watched as the girl jumped into her pick-up and spun it noisily across the loose, gritty surface of the parking space. As her headlights bounced down the track and swept out onto the lane below, Jan turned to Harold. 'Well, what do you want?'

'To talk,' Harold shrugged. 'I hadn't heard from you, so I assume you're still feeling aggrieved. I was wondering if there was anything I could do to help.'

'You've got a nerve. I've told you what I want, and when I've got it I'll sign your letter.' She thought of the letter, in a hundred shreds as she'd tipped it into her bin.

'Jan, don't be unreasonable. Fifty thousand? That's crazy. But I have thought of something that might sway you to accept the offer we've already put on the table. I see you've got plenty of boxes here now, and very good it all looks too. So how about if I send those four horses back to you, right away, on full fees? That'd bring you in another six hundred a week.'

'Huh!' Jan snorted. 'You must be joking! The profit margin on my fees is tiny, and anyway, right now, I've got all the horses I can take. What I suggest you do is go back home and empty your piggy bank. If I haven't heard from you soon, my solicitors will be in touch and this time they'll mean business. And as you're driving home now, I want you to think of three things, Harold. First, how much I did for you with your horses over the years. Second, how much money you made out of me just because I trusted you. And third, how much harm the bad publicity would do your firm if I have to take you to court. Now, I've got things to do,' she said curtly and, turning her back on him, walked into the tack room.

Inside, she leaned tensely against a saddle rack and listened. For a few seconds there was no sound of movement outside, and Jan wondered what Harold was thinking of doing, until, abruptly and telegraphing his anger through his footsteps, he marched back across the yard, got into his vehicle, banged the door and skidded off the parking place.

Jan let out the breath she'd been holding in. She didn't care how long it took; she would get there in the end.

Damn it! she thought. She was still offering to let them keep half the profit they'd made on her farm! What she was dealing with now was pure, unadulterated greed. And if Harold thought she was just going to give up simply because she was an impecunious widow, he should know better.

When he came the following day the Jockey Club inspector looked at everything in Jan's yard, inside and out, carrying out his duties with a quiet, uncommunicative smile. He looked at the horses, the stables, the bedding, the condition of the tack, the feed room and veterinary supplies, the gallops, the accident records and the wages books.

Before he left, Jan asked him what his conclusions were, but he said no more than that he would write and let her know in due course.

That evening, bursting with frustration, she sat down with Gerry, Roz and Annabel and held a post-mortem.

'They can't turn you down, not on the stables,' Gerry shook his head. 'They look bloody tidy, perfect actually.'

'Thank God the gallop doesn't look too muddy at the moment,' Annabel added.

'Yes, but supposing he comes back next month when they're all cut up?' Roz asked.

'Colonel Gilbert said I could tell the Jockey Club I can use his big field that runs up the side of Barton Wood and always drains well – the one Virginia sometimes uses.'

'Wouldn't Virginia make a fuss about that?' Annabel suggested.

'Too bad,' Jan said. 'It's not *her* field.'

They were all still there when Eddie arrived to hear how the inspection had gone. As usual when he was around, Annabel sank into the background while Jan told him what their impressions had been.

'It sounds as if you've done all right. Anyway, I've filled in all these papers for you and I've asked the bank to endorse the guarantee form.'

In the week that followed three invalids went home, fully recovered, and two new horses arrived to be trained. They'd been sent by Frank Jellard, a wealthy fruit farmer from Evesham. Both horses, Supercrack and Cambrian Lad, had had promising form, and Jan was hopeful of improving on it. This increased her string of horses to twelve, including her own Gale Bird and the unnamed chestnut gelding.

Jan had to decide now how many more convalescing

horses she was prepared to take in, for although they brought in almost as much in fees as the racehorses, they tended to get in the way of the training schedules. She also had to take on another girl and a lad from the village to help with riding out. That hadn't been difficult; there was a waiting list of eager young kids wanting to work in her yard, and it was mainly a matter of judging which ones were serious and useful and which weren't. Emma Collins was a friend of Roz Stoddard's, with similar experience. Joe Paley was a traveller who was lodging with the Stoddards and, though he was a little too relaxed about his time-keeping for Jan's comfort, he was an excellent rider.

The yard was settling into a businesslike routine and Jan was beginning to enjoy being greeted in the lanes around Edge Farm as she headed up her small string of five or six. She liked to give her horses plenty of road work early on, to harden their legs before they started any serious work.

A week after the Jockey Club inspector had been, there was still no sign of his report. Jan tried not to think about it, but she knew that if he demanded any substantial changes she had no way of paying for them. However, she thought, as long as they hadn't turned her down, there was still hope.

But on the third Monday in October Jan's future plans were hit by a hammer blow.

It was a foul, grey-black morning, with wind howling down the broad sweep of the Severn plain from the north-west, spitting and blasting bursts of needle-sharp rain.

Megan had recently started at the primary school in the next village and Jan set off to take her there. She drove down the track, now gushing like a brook, and peered through the rain bucketing onto the windscreen. As she reached the bottom, she was startled to see that the gate to the lower paddock on the right was hanging open. The previous evening she had left three recovered horses there in New Zealand rugs.

She stopped the Land Rover and jumped out into the deluge. She ran into the field, praying that she would find the horses standing in a corner on the far side, in the lee of a tall hedge. But even as she ran, squinting through the downpour, she knew they wouldn't be there.

It took her less than thirty seconds to be certain and the fresh hoof prints in the mud around the gateway confirmed her worst fears. She ran back to the Land Rover with rainwater pouring off the brim of her hat and coursing down the folds of her waxed coat. She tried to grin at the little girl strapped wide-eyed in the passenger seat. 'I'm afraid you'll be late for school today, Meggy.'

'What's happened, Mum?'

'Someone's left the gate open and the horses have got out. They haven't come up to the farm, so they must have got onto the road, but I don't think they've been gone long.'

Jan hesitated at the bottom of the track. After an instant's thought, she decided to turn right towards the main road, where they would have got into the most trouble. Half a mile up the lane, at the junction with the Evesham road, she didn't know which way to turn until she spotted a blue light, blinking through the rain four hundred yards to her left. She spun out into the main road and raced up to where a small queue of cars had formed. Beyond the cars were two police vehicles and an articulated lorry, which had slewed off the road from the opposite direction. It was resting in the ditch at a forty-degree angle, while most of the three hundred sacks of potatoes it was carrying were scattered all around, ruptured and spilling their contents over the road.

A moment later, Jan saw one of the horses, with its New Zealand rug all twisted, tugging nervously at the end of a makeshift rope. It was being held by an anxious man who looked as if he was wondering what on earth to do with it. She drove on past the stationary cars until a policeman in a Day-Glo yellow jacket flagged her down fiercely. Jan lowered her window. 'That's my horse,' she bellowed over the wind.

'What about the others?' the policeman asked, nodding beyond the squad car.

Jan's heart almost stopped. She closed her eyes and grasped the steering wheel, trying to get to grips with what had happened. Taking a deep breath, she opened her eyes again and turned to Megan. 'I won't be a minute, Meg. Don't worry and don't move, all right?'

'I'll keep an eye on her, madam,' the policeman said, opening the door for her.

Jan ran down the road as fast as she could in wellingtons and knelt down by the first horse. There was a slight movement in the animal's ribcage and his eyelids flickered as Jan leaned down to find if he was still breathing.

With a faint whinny, he tried to raise a leg that twisted grotesquely, unmistakably broken in at least two places. Feeling suddenly weak, Jan looked up at the nearest of the two policemen. 'Have you called the vet?'

'There's one on his way from Chipping Campden. Should be here in about ten minutes. Are these all your horses?'

'Not actually mine, but I'm looking after them,' she gasped and felt sick as the full horror of what had happened began to overwhelm her.

'I'm afraid the other one was hit full on by the artic; he's in a terrible mess,' the patrolman said. 'I think he's already gone.'

Jan staggered to her feet. She felt strangely light-headed and had to force her legs to carry her to the other horse. She took one look at his mangled chest and head before she closed her eyes to fight the nausea welling up in her, but she made herself crouch down beside the animal.

One horse dead; another so badly damaged he would have to be put down. Jan squeezed her eyes tight shut, as she tried to make the stark horror of it go away, while she searched her mind over and over for a reason why the gate should have been open.

She knew she hadn't done it. She and Roz had led the three horses down to the field and she'd closed the gate behind them herself; she was absolutely certain.

Besides, the animals must only have escaped within the last hour or so and it was very likely they would have left soon after the gate had been opened. A dozen different reasons for it happening, with or without human assistance, spun around her head.

The sound of a plaintive whinny above the continuous howling of the wind reminded her that the third horse was still standing. The man holding him had led him away from the scene of the crash, maybe hoping he might pick grass on the verge, fifty yards beyond the articulated truck, past the queue of traffic that had built up behind it.

Jan walked briskly towards them. The man nodded. She didn't know him, but his face was familiar from the Fox & Pheasant.

'Thanks so much for catching him,' she said, seeing that the horse was being held by a piece of twisted orange binder twine lopped through his head-collar.

'He didn't take much catching. He was just standing there quivering with fright, but at least he wasn't hit.'

Jan nodded, quickly running her hands up and down the animal's legs and along his back, then soothing him with a steady flow of comforting words, before she turned back to the man holding him. 'There should be a vet here any minute to deal with the other two horses and I'll call the hunt kennels to take them away. I've got to ring my yard too and ask someone to come and collect this one. Would you mind hanging on to him for a few more moments while I go back and use the phone in my Land Rover?'

'No, that's fine,' he said.

When Jan opened the door of the Land Rover and leaned in, Megan was sitting quietly, not distressed but well aware that something serious was going on.

'What's happened, Mummy?'

'Some of the horses have been a bit hurt and I've just got to phone someone to come and take them home,' Jan said, plucking the phone from its cradle. 'I'll do it outside,' she smiled at Megan, closed the driver's door and walked round behind the vehicle, out of the wind.

First she dialled her yard. Annabel answered.

'Bel, it's Jan.'

'Hi, Jan. Everything all right? We thought you'd be back from school by now.'

'We never got there,' Jan said, bracing herself. 'There's been a major disaster.'

'Oh no! Is Megan all right?'

'Yes, she's fine. It's not her. Somehow the gate to the bottom paddock was opened. The three horses in it got out and ran up to the main road and I'm afraid there's been an almighty accident.' She shut her eyes, and suddenly all the strength which she'd summoned up to deliver the news without getting hysterical deserted her. Her shoulders collapsed as she sobbed into the phone. 'One's dead,' she choked. 'The other's so badly damaged it'll have to be put down.'

'My God!' Annabel gasped. 'How horrible!'

'Yes,' Jan tried to get herself together. 'Someone's got to get down here and collect the one that's OK. Bel, can you bring the trailer? I'll ring the kennels for the other two and there's a vet coming from—' Abruptly, Jan put a hand to her mouth. 'Oh God, the police said the vet's coming from Chipping Campden. I've only just thought – I bet it's James McNeill! Oh God, that's all I bloody need. He'll tell the whole world what's happened – especially now I've lodged that complaint about him!'

'No, no,' Annabel said urgently. 'He doesn't have to know they've got out from here. Roz can go down and ask Gill, her mother, to collect the horse in her lorry and say they're all hers. He doesn't know who she is.'

'What about the forms and everything? For the insurance and things?'

'We can worry about that afterwards,' Annabel said. 'Tell me where you are, and I'll tell Roz.'

'Turn left on the main road, about four hundred yards.'

Two hours later Jan was still shivering as she sat in the caravan with a large mug of tea.

When the vet – a man she'd never met before – had reached the scene of the crash, she had almost collapsed with relief that it wasn't James McNeill or his partner, and she'd stood in the rain while he'd despatched one horse and confirmed the other dead. Feeling sick and helpless, she'd watched the Evesham Vale huntsman winch the carcasses into his trailer.

Mrs Stoddard had arrived with her lorry only minutes after the vet and told him the horses had escaped from one of her fields, before she loaded the one remaining horse and brought it back to the yard, where it was now in a stable being pampered by Roz.

'What do you think happened?' Annabel asked.

Jan shook her head. 'God knows. I'm thinking maybe the latch was faulty and the wind did it. It was gusting like hell last night – the whole caravan was shaking.'

'Let's go down and have a look,' Annabel urged.

Jan nodded, and gulped down the rest of her mug. 'Come on, Meg,' she said to the wide-eyed little girl. 'We'll look at this gate, then I'll take you on to school.'

At least the rain had eased for a bit as they walked down to the Land Rover. They climbed in and drove down to the gate, which was still hanging out towards the track.

It was made of galvanized iron with a corrugated zinc panel fixed over the bottom three bars to stop horses putting their feet through and getting them stuck. It was normally opened inwards, into the field, but it could be secured only with a bolt which shot through a large staple on the outside of the eight-by-eight timber post, which made it easier to secure.

Where the staple should have been, there were two rusty slits in the wooden post. Jan looked down. The big black wrought-iron loop was lying, half hidden by long grass, a couple of feet in front of the post. She picked it up and tried to fix it back in the holes in which it had been lodged, but they had been enlarged when the staple had been torn out and it would have taken a hefty hit with a hammer to refix it.

'It looks like you were right,' Annabel said.

'I don't know. It really must have been blowing hard to have dislodged this thing. Look at the spikes on it.'

'But that wrinkly tin would have really caught the wind.'

'Oh hell!' Jan groaned. 'People will say it's my fault because I didn't check the bloody staple, or I should have had it fixed on the other side or something.'

'Jan, it was an accident, for God's sake! Real accidents do happen. Just because all these lawyers are always trying to persuade people to blame someone else. There's no way you could have known that a strong wind would blow hard enough to yank the bloody thing out.'

Jan looked at her, grateful for her support. 'Let's hope the owners and the insurers take it like that.

After all those brochures Eddie and I sent out – if everyone starts saying we can't even keep a horse in a paddock, it'll have been a total waste of time!'

'Relax, Jan; you're getting paranoid. I'm sure the insurance will be OK.'

'I don't think we'll get away with it.' Jan shook her head and put the big staple in her coat pocket. 'I'll get Gerry to replace this with an eye that bolts right through the post.' She looked at the rain which had started to pour heavily again. 'I'd better drop you up at the yard before I take Megan on to school.' She started walking towards the car.

'Hang on, Jan!' Annabel said sharply.

Jan turned. Annabel was staring at the ground in front of her. 'When did you last drive up to this gate?' she asked.

Jan looked down at a distinct set of tyre tracks, which showed that someone had driven up onto the broad, muddy verge, as if they'd been going to carry on into the field, but had stopped a couple of yards short of the gate. 'Not for weeks,' she answered. 'I've only walked horses down here.'

'Me too. And Gerry hasn't worked here recently has he?'

'No,' Jan said. 'Those tyre marks are very fresh anyway, or the rain would have washed them away more.' She glanced at Annabel. 'Are you thinking someone's given the wind a bit of a hand to push that staple out?'

'Well, why else would anyone turn here? Look, you can see, they've driven up, then they must have reversed up the track to drive back down again.'

'Someone might have been lost?' Jan suggested, without much conviction.

'I don't think so. And, anyway, I just don't see how the wind could have shoved that bloody great staple out. It looks to me as if someone's been having a go at you.'

'Oh God.' Jan didn't want to believe it, but she knelt down and gazed closely at the zigzag tread pattern in the soft earth, which she was sure couldn't be more than a few hours old. And she thought how absurdly vulnerable she was – simply by opening a gate someone had caused the death of two of the horses in her care. She turned her head and looked bleakly up at Annabel. 'I'm afraid you might be right.' She straightened her legs and gazed at the track, wondering whose malice had led to this.

'Who do you think it was?' Annabel prompted her.

Jan sighed. 'I don't know; perhaps it was James McNeill.'

'Because you complained about him to the RCVS?'

Jan nodded. 'I had a letter from them a few days ago asking for more details. He probably got a copy of it, too. I wish I hadn't done it now, but Eddie suggested I should, to stop McNeill saying anything negative about me to the Jockey Club.'

'He was right,' Annabel insisted. 'And anyway, why

should the disgusting bastard get away with it? He would have raped you if he could.'

'That's what Eddie said.'

'But there's not a lot you can do about this,' Annabel went on. 'You'll simply have to see if he follows it up. If it was McNeill, he'll show it in some way or other, I'm sure of that. In the meantime the best thing to do is carry on and treat it as an accident, like we first thought.'

'But I was going to get the police up.'

'Don't bother, Jan. It'd be a complete waste of time. Even if they could match this tyre tread to McNeill's car – and he probably didn't come in his own – there's no way anyone could prove he'd broken the fixing.'

'I suppose you're right, but it's bloody frustrating. I don't know how I'll contain myself, doing nothing.'

'Just carry on as normal and get it repaired. That's what I suggest.'

'OK, but I'll put a bloody great padlock on here in future, though that wouldn't have stopped this happening,' Jan added ruefully.

Jan apologized to the head teacher for dropping Megan off late, though she didn't tell her why, then she raced back to Gerry's house in the village. His mother told her he was working on an extension at the pub. She found him there and told him what had happened, without telling him about the tyre tracks and the possibility that James McNeill or someone else had done it deliberately, and then explained what was needed to repair the gate.

He nodded gravely, patently glad to be in Jan's confidence. 'There's some old iron eyes like that at Mr Carey's; they'll be a bit rusty, though.'

'That's fine, as long as it's sound, but when you've got time, buy a new one on my account to replace the one you take. I don't want to be pinching stuff from Mr Carey.'

Without asking why the job had to be done so urgently, Gerry immediately abandoned what he was doing. He went off to find the ironmongery he needed and Jan went back to the yard.

Annabel was waiting for her in the tack room.

'You never told me who the vet was,' Annabel said.

'I don't know, but it wasn't James McNeill or his partner. Gill's got his details.'

'What about the police?'

'Oh hell! I wasn't thinking; I told one of them they were my horses!' Jan punched a bag of nuts in frustration. 'What a bloody mess!'

Annabel sat down beside her and put an arm around her shoulder. 'Don't worry about it, Jan. It was an accident, pure and simple. Just calm down first, then you can decide what to do, and how to tell the owners.'

'But, Bel, I haven't even had the Jockey Club inspector's report. They haven't turned me down yet, but there's still a long way to go, and if they get to hear about this, it really could go against me. That must be why McNeill did it.'

'Jan, I know that – if it really was him. But you're not going to solve anything by panicking.'

'You're right,' Jan sighed. She knew she was lucky to have Bel with her at a time like this.

During the days following the accident and the death of the two horses, Jan couldn't believe that she wouldn't be blamed or penalized in some way for what had happened, despite the fact that she and Roz's mother, Gill, had not yet encountered any problems handling the formalities with the vet. So far, no official had been to ask Jan how the horses had got onto the road.

Nor had James McNeill, until four days after the event.

He arrived in the middle of the morning. Jan was in the yard on her own, mucking out and keeping an eye on Matthew while the others were out exercising. It was the first time she'd seen James in two months. She fought back her fear and walked up to him, still holding a muck fork, though she felt a sudden contraction in her guts at the thought that he might have been responsible for the death of the two horses.

Whether he was or not, she was sure he'd come to gloat.

'Hello,' she said. 'What do you want?' She made no move to invite him into the yard.

He stopped and looked at her as if nothing unusual had happened the last time they'd seen each other. 'I'd been thinking about sending a few horses here again, but I heard some got out the other day – and there was a bit of a disaster.'

Jan tried not to let her complexion change, nor to allow McNeill to see her urgent swallowing. 'From here?'

'I know exactly where they were,' James said quietly. 'And, of course, I realize these things happen. Gates wear out in time and without warning. No one should blame you. But then, not everyone is so understanding. Bernie Sutcliffe, for instance, might be a little pissed off to know that sort of thing goes on here.'

Without stopping to think about it, Jan came off the defensive and squared up to him. 'Oh, so this is what it's all about, is it? You've finally heard that I've bought a horse for Bernie and you're annoyed about it.'

'It would have been normal to let me know, since I recommended you to him in the first place.'

'You told him not to touch my yard and you know it. It's pathetic – because I wouldn't let you screw me!'

McNeill raised one of his thick, ginger eyebrows. 'I gather you've shared your thoughts on that incident with my professional body,' he said, as if it were a matter of complete indifference to him. 'I can't imagine what you think you're going to achieve. I also hear you've applied for a licence to train.' He allowed himself a brief, cynical smile. 'I don't suppose the Jockey Club inspector will be too impressed if he hears what happened to those horses and how you tried to cover it up.'

Looking at his big round face and the bland, false smile he was wearing, she felt like ramming the muck fork into it.

'Look, James, I've been asked to write a report on what you tried to do to me last time you came here. There were two witnesses to back it up,' she bluffed, 'and if you don't want me to send it back to the RCVS, I suggest you get yourself out of this yard – right now!' She didn't wait for his reaction, but turned and walked straight back to the stable she'd been mucking out when he'd arrived.

It seemed like an eternity before she heard the door of his car slam, the engine start, and the car rumble off down the track.

Once she was sure he'd gone, she found she was shaking at the thought that the Jockey Club might hear about the three horses who had got out. She'd been only too aware, since the day it had happened, that it would be a simple matter to confirm that two of them, both registered at Weatherby's, had died while technically in the charge of Edge Farm Stables. And it seemed unlikely now that her official complaint to the Royal College of Veterinary Surgeons would be any deterrent to James McNeill.

Jan was also conscious of the fact that it was she who had first rung the kennels, and it was possible that someone had mentioned this to McNeill. What chilled her most, though, was that the vet seemed to know how the horses had escaped and, as far as she was aware, apart from herself, only Annabel and Gerry knew the precise details. Nevertheless, his manner had left her with the strong impression that he had come to gloat: that he had heard about what had happened after the event, not that he had caused it himself.

After this encounter, the shadow of the accident hung over Jan like a dark cloud. Annabel and the others did what they could to cheer her up and tried to reassure her that no lasting damage had been done. At the same time Jan didn't want to worry them more by telling them about James McNeill's threat to draw the Jockey Club's attention to the incident.

12

Unexpectedly, and at short notice, Annabel received an invitation from Virginia Gilbert's brother, George, to a dinner party the following Saturday at Riscombe Manor. The next morning, when they were exercising Gale Bird and Russian Eagle, Jan asked her if she would be going.

'I don't particularly want to. I know who'll be there. George has got a whole lot of his friends coming down from London to shoot. One or two will bring girlfriends, but he needs some women to balance the numbers. Half the men will be drunk before dinner starts and they'll all talk about nothing but shooting.' She sighed. 'I suppose I'll have to go, though; it's just one of those evenings you have to put up with unless you want to be thought of as a complete outcast.' Annabel gave a short laugh. 'Sometimes I think I wouldn't mind that much if I was, by that lot.'

'I don't understand you, Bel,' Jan said. 'You're very attractive; there's no shortage of men after you. You could pick and choose as much as you liked.'

'That'd be fine if there were ever any men around who were the sort I wanted.'

'Well, what sort is that?' Jan asked, a little impatiently.

'Someone thoughtful; someone whose ego isn't bursting out all the time like most men's. Not an academic type necessarily, but not one of these air-head friends of George's who work in the City and just talk about money, cars and shooting, and who they slept with last night.'

'Definitely not Eddie any more, then?' Jan glanced at Annabel, who looked away.

'Jan, I told you, I got Eddie out of my system a long time ago. You know what I think of him now. Besides, I'm sure he's more interested in you.'

Jan laughed before she could stop herself. 'In me? You must be joking. For a start, I'm hardly his type, am I? I mean he's a sort of deb's delight, even if his old man *is* a cockney builder.'

'Funnily enough, Eddie was always quite clever about that – not making any attempt to disguise his parents makes him, like, a bit of rough you could take anywhere.'

'You think he does that deliberately?' Jan was disappointed.

'No,' Annabel said. 'Not really. He's far too genuine for that. But I still think he's interested in you.'

'A bit of rough for a bit of rough, eh?' Jan laughed. 'Well, for a start, he's a bit young for me; besides, I haven't been anywhere near another man since I met John. The very thought of it makes me feel quite odd. I must admit, though, Eddie's been a great friend. He always seems to turn up just when I need him with some plan to solve one of my problems.'

Annabel nodded. 'Yeah, I know that, but he and I . . . well, it ended more or less in disaster, but I'm not going to let that get in the way of my work for you, especially as he comes here so often.'

When Annabel arrived at Edge Farm the morning after the dinner party, she picked Megan up and gave her a quick squeeze before flopping down onto the bench. 'God, I need more sleep!'

'What on earth's happened to you? Did you give in to one of the City slickers?'

Annabel made a face. 'No, I did not, but I did sit around far too long talking with quite a nice, rather tubby man who's interested in horses, and I think I may have got you a new owner. That's why I've come up. He said he'd be over here about twelve. The only trouble is . . .' Annabel seemed reluctant to say whatever was on her mind.

'The only trouble is what?' Jan pressed.

'Virginia was at dinner last night, too, trying to put him off – telling him it was a waste of time and money owning pointers.'

'Well, that's for him to decide. We've been through all that before with owners.'

'Yes, but when I told him you've already applied for a licence, Virginia looked furious and said they don't just hand them out to anyone, and you wouldn't find it easy because the Jockey Club would take a dim view of the fact that some of your horses had got out, two had been killed and you'd been a bit evasive about them coming from your yard.'

Jan felt the blood drain from her face. 'Virginia said that?' she whispered. 'The bitch! And how the hell does she know?'

'She said her vet told her, and her vet—'

'Don't tell me – James McNeill,' Jan finished for her.

Annabel nodded. 'Did you know he's been talking about it?'

'I sort of did. He came round here last week and said he'd tell the Jockey Club, but I told him I was sending a report to the RCVS about him trying to rape me; I thought that might put him off.'

'It looks like he's found an indirect route then, doesn't it.'

'Do you think Virginia will tell the Jockey Club?' Jan asked, already sure of the answer.

'She's very jealous of you and not just because you've already got more horses than her. I've a horrible feeling she might.'

The potential new owner, Toby Waller, was as affable and rotund as Annabel had described him. He came, expressed his enthusiasm for Jan's yard and left with a promise to be in touch.

'I think he was just being polite,' Jan told her father when she arrived with Matthew at her parents' the following morning.

'Why should he be?' Mary asked.

'Because Virginia Gilbert was trying to put him off at a dinner party on Saturday night, Bel said.'

'Was Bel having dinner up at the Manor?' Mary asked, impressed.

'Yes; she knows George, poor girl, and he was having the first shoot of the season.'

'I know,' Reg nodded. 'Bloody useless most of them, the keeper said.'

'But why was Virginia trying to run you down?' Mary asked.

'That's easy,' Reg answered. 'She's worried our Jan might turn out a bloody sight better at training horses than she'll ever be, and she doesn't want to be shown up in front of all her posh friends round here. D'you remember what a fuss she made when Jan won that race on Rocket?'

'Why do people have to be like that?' Mary asked and shook her head in puzzlement, before bustling off with Matthew to pick apples in the small orchard behind the house.

'What's the matter, Jan?' her father asked when they were alone. 'I can see summat's up.'

Jan sat down in the deep moquette armchair that had been in the front room of the house for as long as she could remember. She nodded and bit her lip, trying to stop the tears that wanted to flow.

'I got the Jockey Club inspector's report at last. It arrived this morning.'

'Bloody hell, they took their time, didn't they?' Reg said, already defending her because he'd guessed what was coming. He sat down in an old rocking chair opposite her and pulled his pipe from a pocket of his battered tweed jacket.

'They say the stables are no good as they stand – at least, the stables in the barn aren't because the old asbestos sheets are flaking and causing dust. On top of that, because it's got a canvas roof over the asbestos and we keep hay and straw there, they say it would be too great a fire hazard if I wanted to stable horses for the public!'

'What do they expect you to do, then?'

'Keep the hay and straw somewhere else, I suppose, and reroof the barn – which is cobblers as it's all made of timber anyway. Dad, there's no way I can afford to do that and build a new hay store. I mean, they make it virtually impossible for someone like me, who doesn't have a lot of money or rich friends to sponsor the yard.' Jan sniffed. 'And there's worse: they said they'd heard about the two horses getting killed on the main road and that puts a "question mark" over my competence. They don't say who told them, but I bet it was Virginia, who got it from James McNeill.'

Reg nodded. Jan had told him at the time, without going into too much detail, about the vet's attack on her before he'd taken away all his horses back in August. 'Oh Jan, I'm really sorry – just as things were looking up for you.'

'I know. I've had loads of enquiries recently, too. I've turned away some of the repair work because we haven't got enough time to do them all and keep the other horses fit as well.'

'Well, my little pet, you're just going to have to be patient, aren't you, and write to them with what happened over the horses that got out. They'll understand if you tell it to 'em straight. And if you have a good season next time, you'll be able to do that roof to their satisfaction, I'm sure, so don't go getting yourself into a state. At least that Eddie Sullivan's agreed to put up the bond for you.'

'Yes, he's been great, but I haven't seen him for a week or so. I tried to phone him this morning to tell him about the inspector's report, but I couldn't get hold of him and the dopey girl at his shop in Stow said she hadn't heard from him herself since last Thursday.'

'Oh well, you know what they're like, these young chaps – all over the place they are. Look at our Ben.'

'That's a bit different, Dad. Eddie's supposed to be running a business.'

'Well, it don't matter too much at the moment, does it? You can't go ahead, anyway, till you can afford the work that needs to be done. Don't worry. Eddie's not going to go away.'

'No, he's not,' Jan agreed confidently and smiled at her father's attempts to cheer her up.

Jan had arranged to leave Matthew with her mother for the rest of the morning so that she could drive over to Lambourn to look at a couple of horses Frank Jellard had been offered. As she drove across the Cotswolds, over the Vale of the White Horse and the Berkshire Downs, Jan tried to come to terms with the idea that she would have to put her dreams of training under rules on hold for some considerable time. Her father's advice, as always, was level-headed and practical. Besides, she admitted, she didn't have any choice.

She tried to convince herself that she'd just have to do the best she could with the horses she had and make enough of a mark on the point-to-point scene to ease her transition to National Hunt racing the following year.

The trouble was, all her instincts were screaming at her to get on with it now, telling her that every season spent outside the world of 'real' racing was a season wasted. Driving for the first time into the Lambourn valley, lying comfortably among rolling green hills, which was home to several hundred racehorses, only increased her ambitions. The sight of strings of top-class animals being ridden through a village dedicated to horse racing, making their way to the gallops on the downs, made her mouth water.

But she wasn't going to let the authority of the place affect her judgement. She told herself that she might only be a point-to-point trainer from the back end of nowhere, but she wouldn't let anyone talk down to her or bully her into taking any horses she didn't want. Nor, when she arrived at the stables, did she let herself be blinded by the displays of affluence in the pristine stone yard, the immaculate lawns and massive troughs planted with geraniums. And when the head lad, barely glancing at her down his long nose, led out the two horses on offer and trotted them up for her, she didn't have to look long to realize that someone was trying to offload their rubbish onto her owner. She politely but firmly rejected both horses and drove away from the Mecca of National Hunt racing empty-handed, but knowing she'd done her job well.

As she reached the top of the hill on the road north, she glanced back at the village of Lambourn and vowed to herself that one day she'd be back, leading her own string up onto those broad, white-railed gallops.

That evening Jan phoned Frank Jellard and told him the horses in Lambourn he'd been offered were unlikely ever to see a race course again, but if he was serious about wanting more, she would carry on looking for a couple that might give him some fun around the points. Jan had already recognized that Jellard was one of those difficult owners who thought he knew a lot more about horses than he did, and she put her views as tactfully as she knew how. In the end, after a nerve-racking, twenty-minute conversation, he agreed.

She put the phone down, delighted, and glanced

outside, where the wet, black night was being pierced by a pair of flickering headlamps. She couldn't see what type of vehicle had just pulled up, but a few moments later there was a knock on the door of the caravan. Jan opened it and found Eddie standing at the bottom of the steps with rain dripping from a shapeless waxed hat.

'Hi!' She smiled, pleased to see him. 'You look a little damp.'

Eddie stepped up and through the door. 'I'm more than a little damp,' he said.

Jan looked at him sharply. She'd never heard him so gloomy.

'Why, what's happened?'

'Have you still got any of that Bushmills the Irishman gave you?'

'Yes,' Jan said, closing the door behind him and taking his wet hat and coat. 'I'll get a glass.'

Eddie slipped onto the bench and pulled a packet of cigarettes from his pocket. 'Smoking?' Jan asked. 'Since when did you take up smoking?'

'Since this weekend,' Eddie said stonily.

Jan put the glass of whiskey on the table in front of him. 'For God's sake, Eddie. Has someone died or what?'

'Not quite. My father—', Eddie glanced at Jan with large, apologetic brown eyes, 'my father has just been made totally, comprehensively, balls-achingly bankrupt. He went down so fast, he didn't even touch the sides. And it looks like he's taken me with him.'

Jan felt her jaw sag as she suddenly realized how much she had been relying on Eddie; his disaster seemed to affect her almost as much as him. Slowly she sat down opposite him.

'How come he's taken you with him?' she asked huskily.

'Any assets I had were all tied up in his various companies. I just used them as security for any funding I needed, for the business and so on. The banks called in my overdrafts. My cottage is part of the estate and my father's bankers have already foreclosed on the lot. I've got to be out at the end of the week. And the Merc's had to go back.'

'Oh, Eddie. That's awful!' Jan wailed, loud enough to bring Megan sleepily from her end of the caravan.

'What's the matter, Mummy?' she asked.

'Sorry, darling. Did I wake you? Mummy's just had a bit of a surprise, that's all. Do you want a drink?'

Jan felt there was something surreal about the sense of normality which she was trying to convey to her daughter, knowing the little girl's antennae were finely tuned to calamity. But she managed to keep up the charade until Megan was back in bed and the door closed between them again.

'God, I'm sorry to drop a bomb like this when you've already got all the problems you need,' Eddie grunted.

'Don't worry.' Jan tried to laugh. 'I haven't even told you the latest news here.' She gave him the salient points of the Jockey Club inspector's report and its various implications. 'I'm going to have to wait until I've had quite a lot of work done before I reapply,' she said.

'I'll find someone else to put up your bond,' Eddie said.

'God, don't worry about that now! At least you've still got your business.'

'What there is left of it,' Eddie groaned.

'Why, what's the problem there?' Jan couldn't help wondering who would be paying for Russian Eagle once the advance Eddie had given her had been used up.

'No money; too much stock, not enough sales. Business has been lousy – anyway for the last couple of months; there's the staff wages and the ridiculous rent I'm paying. I'm locked into a terrible seven-year lease which I'll never shift, and I've got a massive VAT bill to deal with at the end of November from that big sale I made in the summer.'

Jan was finding it hard to handle a deflated, despairing Eddie. Until now in their relationship it had always been he who had been the solid, immovable rock. Now that he needed support, she was conscious that she had little to offer in return.

'Well, at least Eagle's keep is paid up to the end of the year, I'll school you for nothing and you should have some fun on him when the season gets going.'

She was glad to see how much this made Eddie perk up.

'Do you really think I might win on him?'

'I'd say there was a good chance, though you've got a lot more work to do on yourself. You'll need to lose that last half stone and get into a gym to tone up your muscles. You'll never race three and half miles if you're not as fit as a flea.'

'What about the Aintree Foxhunters'? Do you think I might get somewhere in that?'

Jan laughed. 'Anything's possible, I suppose; he could even win it, but we've got to get you and him to win at least one open point-to-point, just to qualify to run in it.'

'But you do think he could do it?'

'I couldn't be sure, not till I've seen him doing more fast work. But he's won over that distance in Ireland, so he must stay. The trip wouldn't be a problem for him.'

Eddie took another slug of whiskey and grinned at her. 'I'll bloody well do it!' he laughed. 'They can take what they like, the thieving bastards, but they're not having my horse!'

Eamon Fallon stood beside Jan in the middle of Colonel Gilbert's big field. A broad strip of well-kept turf curved along the edge of a dense wood of mature oaks on two sides of the field, making a gentle rising gallop of five furlongs. He lowered his binoculars, turned to Jan and shook a long skein of wavy black hair from his forehead. His blue eyes shone with delight.

'Dingle looks brilliant. I'd barely recognize him from the horse in Jim's yard last winter. You've done a grand job.'

'So far,' Jan warned. It was really too soon for a horse to be doing much fast work and she didn't encourage over-optimism in her owners.

'And that big horse, behind,' Eamon nodded. 'He looks useful, too. Who's he?'

'He came over from Ireland for the Doncaster sales. Eddie Sullivan bought him. He wants to ride him in the Foxhunters' at Liverpool next April.'

'Eddie Sullivan? Would that be Ron Sullivan's boy?'

'Yes,' Jan said guardedly. She was already wary of telling one owner anything about another.

'Does he have any money left?'

'Why do you ask?' Jan said, as if she didn't know what he was talking about.

'Did you not hear? Ron Sullivan went bust last month in some order. It was in all the Sunday papers. He made a load of money from building houses, but he must have got greedy or careless. For the last few years he's been piling money into one of those software companies making video games, then they got sued in the States for a few hundred million for causing some juvenile to turn on his family. The whole lot's crashed, leaving Ron holding the baby for over thirty million.'

Jan hadn't asked Eddie any of the details of his father's downfall, mainly because it wasn't any of her business and she hadn't really wanted to know. She'd heard a little about Ron himself and his colourful history from Toby Waller, Annabel's friend, who had come again to talk to Jan about training a horse he had found himself.

Toby had been at Harrow with Eddie and had seen the succession of Bentleys and Ferraris with which Ron had tried to impress the other parents at the school. But, Toby had added, there had always been something engaging about Ron's naive flamboyance and most people thought Eddie was a perfectly presentable human being, despite his outrageous father.

'I don't train horses for his dad, so I wouldn't know,' Jan said. 'And Eddie's prepaid his bill up to the end of the year,' she added, scotching any ideas Eamon might have had that Eddie was getting a free ride from her.

'I wonder if that's the horse A.D. was talking about,' Eamon said thoughtfully.

'Do you mean A.D. O'Hagan?'

'I do.'

With a jolt, Jan remembered the Irish tycoon's comments when she'd given Eddie her first appraisal of Russian Eagle. 'In which case, it could be,' Jan said. 'He was standing behind me when we were talking about it. I'm amazed he remembered, though.'

'A.D. remembers everything. That's one of the secrets of his genius. As a matter of fact, I think it's inherited from his forefathers. They were big horse dealers, and illiterate, so they couldn't write anything down. A.D. says his father could remember the size, age, colour and price of every horse he ever sold.'

'How do you know him, then?' Jan asked.

'Oh, I used to do a little work for him some years ago,' Eamon said with a vagueness that Jan realized marked a dead end. 'So,' he went on with a change of tone, 'do you think we might win a few with Dingle?'

'I hope so.'

'I heard you're thinking of training National Hunt horses.'

Jan wondered who he'd heard it from, although she was getting used to the way information and, more often, misinformation flew around the racing world. 'I might apply next year,' she said.

'Get me a winner at the points and I'll put a couple with you when you get a licence.' Eamon turned to her with a grin and the morning sun glinted on the big gold hoop that dangled from his left ear.

Since she'd started training, Jan had been struck by the extraordinary variety and shapes in which owners came, and the range of motives which attracted them to keep racehorses, even at her modest level of the game. People like Colonel Gilbert and Eamon, despite their different approaches, were both in it for the sport and nothing else. At first she thought Eamon was a gambler, but it was obvious that if he did want a serious bet he wouldn't bother with the restrictions of the point-to-point betting market.

Frank Jellard liked horses, but he also liked impressing his friends, whereas Bernie Sutcliffe seemed to have no affinity whatever with the animals, although he liked telling people about his racehorse, too, and had already brought a few of them to see Arctic Hay.

At first, Jan had been concerned that for him horse-owning was just a weapon in his campaign to keep his girlfriend, Sandy, compliant, but in the last few visits Sandy hadn't been with him and his interest seemed to be more concentrated on Annabel and, to some extent, Jan herself, than on his horse.

She was fairly sure that Annabel was also the reason Toby Waller came back for a third visit. But Jan didn't feel any resentment, especially when he asked her if she could find him a horse. The one he'd told her he was going to look at had turned out to be sold already.

He appeared on foot at the Saturday meet of the Evesham Vale Hunt, where Jan and the others had taken five horses for one of their qualifying days, and followed by car for most of the time they were out. When they all got back to the yard, he was waiting for them.

While they were sitting in the tack room discussing his budget, Jan noticed that he couldn't take his eyes off Annabel, who was busy cleaning tack. Later, when she and Toby had gone up to the caravan, Jan took the opportunity to ask if he knew anything about Annabel and Eddie.

'No,' Toby shook his head vigorously. 'I wouldn't have thought he was her type at all. Eddie's a nice enough guy, but he's a total playboy really. That picture business of his is just a front for pottering about Europe and staying in big country houses. At least, it was,' he added wryly. 'I fear that now Dad has gone belly up, Master Eddie is going to have to be a little more serious.'

Jan couldn't square this view of Eddie with the good advice and commitment he'd given her over the last few months, but she said nothing. Instead, she suggested that Toby might be interested in buying Gale Bird, who was already beginning to look like a useful racehorse. 'If you bought her from me, I'd be able to redo the roof of the barn and get rid of those horrible old tarpaulins.'

'But what about your house?' Toby asked, looking at the undisturbed stacks of stone and timber beside the footings.

'That'll have to wait,' Jan laughed. 'Even if I had the money to crack on with it now, it wouldn't be ready until March or April, so the kids and I might as well get through the winter first. We'll think about the house next year.'

Toby phoned two days later and said he'd decided to buy Gale Bird. He told Jan he was still in Gloucestershire and suggested that he should come round for a drink to complete the formalities. At midday he arrived with Eddie, who was at the wheel of a much-dented Land Rover, already well into its teens and a stark contrast to the Mercedes.

Jan watched curiously as he drove up towards the

caravan and parked on the slope outside. Then he and Toby started to manhandle a bulky, black object out from the back.

As they staggered towards the caravan with it, Gerry arrived in his van and climbed out with a tool bag and a heavy-duty welding torch.

'Morning, Jan,' Eddie called as they got closer to the door.

She opened it to find the three men grinning up at her.

'If you're going to live in this bloody tin can all winter,' Eddie said, 'we've decided you've got to have some heat.'

On the ground between them was a small wood-burning stove.

Eddie had done his homework. Jan realized he must surreptitiously have taken dimensions and worked out how the stove would fit in. Within minutes Gerry had cut a hole for the flue in the roof of the caravan, and the other two were bolting the stove to the floor. Within an hour the new fire was functional, and in a small ceremony accompanied by a bottle of champagne they lit some kindling and filled the fire box from a load of split oak logs they'd brought, storing the remainder under the caravan where Jan could easily get at them.

She was delighted, not just with the heat, which filled the small space almost at once, but also with the combined generosity of three men, who owed her no more allegiance than pure friendship. After they had christened the stove, Toby produced another bottle to celebrate his formal acquisition of Gale Bird.

While they were drinking his champagne, they talked about what they might expect Gale Bird to do when the point-to-point season started in two months' time. Toby glanced out of the window just as Julie was driving up to the yard in her pick-up. She parked and climbed out.

'Good God! Who on earth's this?' Toby asked, unfamiliar with the sight of Julie and her hair, more outlandish than ever since she'd had it dyed bright purple a few weeks before.

Eddie laughed. 'That's our village barmaid. Now you're an owner at this yard, you'll have to get used to seeing her down at the Fox & Pheasant.'

'Impressive shape,' Toby said, seeing her unashamedly large breasts as she walked up towards the caravan.

Jan got up and opened the door. 'Morning, Julie. What brings you up here at this time of day?'

'Nothing really. Monday's my day off, so I thought I'd look in and see how it's all going.'

'You're just in time for a glass of champagne to celebrate a new owner,' Jan said, standing back as Julie climbed into the cramped space around the stove. 'This is Julie,' she introduced. 'And this is Toby Waller, who's just bought my mare Gale Bird from me.'

Toby got to his feet with an old-fashioned display of good manners which had Julie tittering.

'He only wanted to come round today to see Annabel,' Jan went on with a grin, 'but I didn't tell him she'd gone to her parents for the day.'

'I did not,' Toby protested unconvincingly.

Julie sat down and the conversation reverted, as it usually did, to horses. Seeing a large framed photograph that Jan had recently found space to hang on the wall, she asked which horse it was.

'That was my first hunter chase winner, at Ludlow last March – Rear Gunner. I haven't got him any more,' said Jan with a pained face.

'What happened to him, then?'

'He was one of Harold Powell's.'

Toby glanced at her. 'Was that the chap Eddie was telling me about – the auctioneer who bought your old farm and sold it a few months later for nearly a hundred grand more?'

'That's the man. Bloody crook. He pretended to be a friend of mine. I'd trained his horses and done well with them for four or five years. Then he took complete advantage of me just after my husband died.'

Toby nodded and turned to Eddie. 'Were those his horses you had to drive back to Wales?'

'That's right.' Eddie grinned at the memory of it and told the others about Jan's rage at his not having an HGV licence.

'But,' Toby looked at Jan, 'aren't you trying to sue this chap?'

'The solicitors in Broadway wrote to him; then he turned up here with a pathetic offer and I told him to get stuffed. He came back again last month, wouldn't up his offer, and not a lot's happened since. Mr Russell, the solicitor, doesn't think I've got much of a chance because technically they did it all by the book. But I still reckon they might not want the publicity of a court case, even if they didn't lose.'

'I'm sure they wouldn't, but the trouble is no lawyer is going to work that hard for you because they'd know there's a limit to what you can spend, and they'd be up against some big firm acting for this chap's professional indemnity insurers, who'd want to fight it all the way.'

'Yes,' Jan nodded ruefully. 'That's what I thought.'

'I'll put you on to my London solicitors. They're real heavyweights. They'll get the ball rolling for you again.'

'Harold Powell?' Julie asked. 'Wasn't he the bloke who turned up when I was up here one evening about four weeks ago?'

'Yes, that was him. That was the second time he came to persuade me to take a few thousand in settlement for what he'd done to me. I told him to get lost and I haven't heard a squeak from him since.'

'I saw him again,' Julie said, 'a few days after that. Where did you say he lives?'

'In Wales, between Hay and Brecon. Were you up there?'

'No way. I was at the pub in the next village, the Star. The girl there's a friend of mine and she does my hair. She's done this colour for me.' Julie proudly shook her head of purple spikes. 'I was up in her room while she was doing it and I saw that bloke in the car park. He'd just come out of the pub and he stopped to have a chat with one of them pikey boys – a cousin of that kid Joe Paley that works for you.'

Jan stiffened. 'How long after you'd seen him here?'

'No more than a couple of days. Why?'

'It doesn't matter, but what was he called, the boy he was talking to?'

'I don't know.'

'Would Joe know?'

'I should think so.'

'Jan,' Toby asked, 'what do you think he was doing?'

'I don't know. Maybe it's just me being paranoid,' Jan said quickly, not wanting to air her suspicions.

'OK, but if you think there's the remotest chance it could have something to do with your dispute with him, you've got to tell your lawyers. Would you like me to sort out this London firm for you?'

Jan dithered for a moment. London lawyers, insurance companies with bottomless coffers – it all sounded way out of her league. And yet there was no way she wanted to see Harold get away with what he'd done to her.

'Yes, all right,' she said. 'That would be a great help.'

When Toby, Eddie and Julie had gone, Jan settled down to give Matthew his lunch. While she watched him eat, she thought about what Julie had told her, and before she went back down to the yard to get on with her afternoon chores she rang Gerry on his mobile. She asked him if he could drop in that evening.

Gerry arrived early, ready, as always, to do whatever she asked.

Discreetly, during the afternoon she'd asked Joe Paley if he had a cousin who used the pub in the next village.

Joe admitted that he knew Amos Smith, the boy whom Julie had described, but he claimed to be only a distant blood connection with the sixteen-year-old, who came from one of the more disreputable families in the area.

Jan confided in Gerry – with a stern warning it mustn't go any further – that she thought Harold Powell had recruited Amos Smith to let the horses out of the bottom field, which had resulted in them being killed on the main road.

'What do you want me to do about it?' Gerry asked, twitching with eagerness to see justice done.

'See if you can find him, on his own, and ask him how much Harold Powell paid him to open that gate.'

It was two days before she saw Gerry again; he arrived late in the evening and put his head around the door of the caravan with a shamefaced smile.

'Sorry, Jan,' he said right away. 'It looks like I've blown it.'

'Come in out of the rain, Gerry; I won't eat you.'

Gerry squeezed his large frame into the confined space.

'Sit down, for God's sake,' Jan smiled. 'You make the place untidy standing around like that.'

Gerry sat on one of the small benches, while Jan got him a can of Stella, which she knew he liked.

'OK, so how did you blow it?' she asked.

'I found him easily enough in the Star, but he wouldn't come out and talk to me. I couldn't get him on his own, so I just had to say in front of his mates I wanted to talk about a bloke he'd met in the car park there a few weeks ago. I could see he knew what I was talking about, like, but he said he didn't. He said he hadn't met a bloke in the car park, any time. I told him he'd been seen, but I didn't say who by; then he and his mates just told me to piss off.'

'Did they threaten you at all?'

'No, but they would have done if I'd pushed it any more. Anyway, I went back there tonight and some of the same blokes are there, playing pool and drinking like hell – I reckon they pulled off some scam – but this young lad, Amos, he wasn't with them and they said he'd gone.'

'Gone? Gone where?' Jan said in frustration.

'They said they didn't know – maybe apple-picking over in Herefordshire; but they sure as hell weren't going to tell me. So it looks like I scared him off before I got anything out of him.'

Jan sighed. 'It does, but never mind. Maybe we should have done it some other way. I suppose I should have got the police to check those tyre marks when they were there.'

'I doubt that would have helped. He probably came in a stolen vehicle anyway. I'm sorry I blew it, Jan.'

'You did what you could, Gerry. Thanks. I may be barking up completely the wrong tree, but I've got a hunch that Harold was involved in letting the horses out – if anyone did. Could you keep your eyes and ears open and tell me when Amos turns up again?'

13

As autumn crept inevitably towards winter, Jan began to feel that her first half year at Edge Farm had been some sort of psychological trial, as if God had decided to test her skill and stamina.

She'd had to face Harold's treachery over Stonewall and, maybe, his attempt to undermine her reputation by organizing the escape and death of two of her horses; James McNeill's sexual forays; the Jockey Club inspector's damning verdict on her premises, and her principal backer's financial collapse. But she recognized that the route to a Jockey Club licence might well be a two-circuit race and she was now better prepared for any more obstacles that might crop up.

At least it now looked as if McNeill's threat to report her to the Jockey Club for the lost horses had been neutralized by her own warning that she would follow up her complaint with his professional body. She was sure that, otherwise, she would have heard something by now, which gave her more time to establish who the real culprit was.

At the same time, despite all the disasters and

setbacks, the underlying strength of her yard had been growing. Every one of her staff – the girls and the lads – had committed themselves to Edge Farm Stables, backed up by people like her mum and dad, Billy Hanks and Gerry. Even Darren and Tom, the two boys from the village who came up every Saturday to earn a little money cutting docks and thistles in the paddocks, had developed a fierce loyalty to Jan. They both dreamed of being jockeys and swore that as soon as they were big enough they'd be up and riding out for her every day.

Jan's owners, although very different, all seemed to have become devoted to the cause. Hardly a day went by without one or other of them dropping in to see their horse and chat about their prospects. And they had each promised to support Jan's application for a public licence by pledging to keep a horse in training with her when she turned professional.

With the caravan now permanently warm, even the thought of spending the rest of the winter there was bearable, and Jan felt less guilty about her shortcomings as a mother in using the money from the sale of Gale Bird to pay Gerry to put a new roof on the barn instead of building the house.

Also, in a subtle reversal of roles, she'd found time to give Eddie some support in his unfamiliar state of penury.

He told Jan that he'd managed to keep his small shop going in Stow with the help of a couple of part-time pensioners who didn't need so much money. The sale of a large picture would cheer him up for a few days, but it was obvious that he was fighting a losing battle. He had, though, found somewhere to live after he'd been evicted from his cottage in the grounds of Windrush Grange, his father's old house.

Jan had never been to the cottage, by all accounts pure Cotswold chocolate box and, given the change in Eddie's circumstances, she was glad she hadn't, but he had asked Jan round to see his new home a few days after he'd moved in.

She rang him and said she could drop in on her way to the saddler's at Stow one Saturday morning. He sounded pleased and more cheerful than he had for quite some time, but when she arrived there, although he'd warned her that Old Ford Mill was fairly dilapidated, she wasn't prepared for what she found.

It was hidden behind a long, high wall and ancient gates of paint-peeled timber. When she pushed them open and drove onto a weed-covered circle of broken cobbles, she found the mill house was built of the local sandstone, like every other house in the village, and three hundred years on marshy ground beside its mill-pond had given the stone a faint coating of green moss. A massive wisteria, which must have been clambering up the building for over a hundred years, covered most of the front and dangled like a curtain over the small windows. Although undeniably picturesque, the place looked as if it had been uninhabited for years. Wild creepers and saplings seemed to have taken root in every available crack in the side walls and a lot of the stone roof tiles showed signs of slippage.

Jan parked her Land Rover beside Eddie's much older model and was relieved that she'd decided to leave Megan and Matthew with Roz for the morning – Eddie's mill house looked like a death trap for inquisitive children.

As she climbed down from the Land Rover, the big oak front door opened and Eddie came out.

'Morning,' he called, 'and welcome to Old Ford Mill. What do you think of it?' He had reached Jan and leaned down to kiss her cheek. 'Isn't it beautiful?'

Jan laughed. 'It's like something out of an old painting by Constable. Is there any electricity?'

'God, no. This is seriously archaic living, and very green.'

'I can see that,' Jan nodded at the weed-infested walls. 'What about water?'

'There's a hand pump in the kitchen and a range that must be a hundred years old. I've also got a few lodgers,' Eddie grinned, 'of the furry variety.'

Jan shook her head in disbelief as he led her through a dark, low-beamed hall into a kitchen where nothing appeared to have changed in the previous century. 'Eddie, how can you live in a place like this?'

'That's what my dad said when he stayed last night,' Eddie laughed. 'As a matter of fact, he's only just popped out to get the papers. He won't be long. I told him you were coming round and he's looking forward to meeting you, so you must stay until he gets back.'

Ron Sullivan was a legendary character, one of the most colourful racehorse owners in recent years, and ever since she had met Eddie Jan had wondered about the relationship between father and son. It would be strange finally to meet Ron in these bizarre circumstances, but she thought she'd enjoy it more than if he'd still been living up at Windrush Grange, surrounded by flunkeys, limousines and all the trappings of big, new money.

'What's he like, your dad?' she asked.

Eddie had taken a big iron kettle off the range and was pouring boiling water into a cafetière. 'We'll have some coffee and I'll tell you.'

When Eddie had filled the two mugs, he sat down with Jan at a large scrubbed table and leaned back in his chair.

'When you meet Dad, you'll find he's an out-and-out Londoner, born in the East End and never pretended he wasn't. He left school at sixteen back in the fifties without a qualification to his name, but he went out and became an apprentice brickie. And though he never passed an exam in his life, he's a clever old bastard, always a very quick learner. I should think he soon knew every dodge in the book and found he could make a lot more money handling men than bricks. He did really well in the building boom in the sixties and by the early seventies he'd moved away from East Ham and was employing a couple of dozen men as a subcontractor on the big new housing estates going up around Dagenham. It was then he discovered what he likes to call his natural sense of style.' Eddie grinned. 'You'll see what I mean, but he started getting a few bigger jobs out in Essex. The size and the price of the houses he was building began to rise, and he managed to get a lot of very good guys onto his payroll. Some of them were still working for him until a fortnight ago and that's really upset him.

'Anyway, when there was that big property crash in the early seventies, he was still in his thirties, but he was already running a big building company and he'd made an awful lot of money. That gave him a fantastic chance to snap up some bargain sites after the crash in seventy-four, when most of the big property companies got buried under massive stocks of land. Then he just took his time and developed them as prices slowly recovered.'

'But when did he marry your mum?' Jan asked, not so concerned with the business history of Eddie's family.

'That was back in sixty-two. He always says it was a great time then. The Beatles had just released "Love Me Do", and all the girls were starting to take the pill. I think Dad enjoyed himself, but not my mother. Still, she managed to persuade him to build their first big house, a great lump of a place on the edge of Harold Hill. That's where I was born, but I can hardly remember it because when I was about four Mum made my father buy a place on St George's Hill, the smart side of London. And that's when one of his posh chums persuaded him to put me down for Harrow.' Eddie laughed. 'I'm not sure he doesn't regret it, though we still get on really well.' He cocked an ear at the sound of a car coming through the gate. 'That'll be him now, so you can see for yourself.'

Ron Sullivan made his presence felt with a bellow at Eddie as soon as he walked through the front door. When he came into the kitchen, Jan saw he was a big man in his early sixties. There was something about him that seemed to announce the fact that he'd made his first million back in the seventies and, like an old institution clinging to tradition in the hope of averting change, he still wore his silver grey hair, which framed his large tanned face, in a short-topped, long-tailed style, like a footballer of the period. To complete the statement, he was wearing chunky gold rings with a neck chain to match, a lime green jacket and canary yellow trousers.

'Dad,' Eddie said with what sounded to Jan like genuine affection, 'I want you to meet Jan Hardy, my trainer. Jan, this is my dad, Ron Sullivan.'

Jan took the big hand extended to her and sensed a latent power in Ron that wasn't present in his son.

'Pleased to meet you,' Ron growled. 'Though I don't know how the bloody hell Eddie thinks he's going to pay your wages now. I mean, look at this place!' He raised his brows as his eyes swept the ancient room.

Jan shrugged a shoulder. 'He's already paid his

training fees up to the end of the year and I'm schooling him for nothing.'

'He'll need some bloody schooling,' Ron laughed. 'They taught him bugger all at that toffs' school. After all that wonga I spent, he's still only a bleedin' shopkeeper!'

'Now then, Dad. Don't get too excited. There's not a lot you can do about it now and at least I know something about pictures. You never know, I may yet restore the Sullivan millions.'

Ron looked at his son, not without affection, but with no illusions about his money-making talents. 'Listen, son, for all you'll earn in that little shop of yours, you might as well urinate into a hurricane. Just try and scratch a living, Ed, that's all I ask. I was worth thirty million a couple of years ago.' He laughed bitterly and shook his head. 'And now,' he glanced at the Rolex Oyster on his wrist, 'at midday precisely my beautiful house, Windrush Grange, five hundred acres and half a dozen cottages, becomes the property of Mr Cyril Goldstone.'

He sat down and for a few moments, his whole face collapsed, which gave Jan an inkling of how it must feel to have fallen so far, so fast.

Eddie filled a mug with coffee and pushed it to his father across the old deal table. 'Cyril Goldstone, the bookie? You lost that much to him?'

'No, of course I didn't, but the official receiver accepted his offer for the house, the land and everything in it.' Ron heaved a shoulder. 'I'm sorry, son.'

'That's OK, Dad. I've had a good run with your money and I think I'm going to like this place anyway.'

Ron scowled around the dilapidated kitchen. 'Dump, more like. How much are you paying for it?'

'Nothing, I've just got to do it up slowly and in return I have it for ten years.'

Ron shook his head. 'It's hard to tell who's conning who, isn't it?' He turned to Jan and smiled. 'What do you think?'

'I'll tell you in ten years,' Jan replied.

'Well done! Spoken like a true trainer,' Ron laughed. 'I used to have a few horses in training myself, you know.'

'Yes, I remember,' Jan said. 'Have you any more?'

'No, Jan, I haven't. When I tell you I'm boracic lint, I mean totally bloody skint.' His face clouded again.

'But how could someone like you, who's made so much and knows so much, end up like that?'

For a moment Ron looked up, his eyes blazing and Jan thought he was going to chew her out for her cheek; but, with a visible effort, he eased the tension. 'Yeah, well, it must look bloody odd, I know. I suppose you could say I got seduced. They said I'd turn twenty million into half a billion.' He shrugged a shoulder to emphasize his own gullibility. 'Of course, I didn't believe the numbers. I'd have been quite happy to turn twenty mill into a hundred, and I thought there was a good chance of that.'

'What were you punting on?' Eddie asked.

'A bunch of villains, as it turned out – slimy little

City slickers I could have eaten for breakfast if we'd been dealing in property. They knew they were cruising for a bruising in the States, they wanted their money out and they saw me coming. But I'm not blaming anyone except me. I can barely switch on my own computer, so what the hell was I doing getting into software when the whole world was already in for the ride? But that's not the point. It don't really matter why it happened, does it? That's history. The banks have gone for everything, I haven't an effing shred of a counterclaim, not without spending a bleedin' pile on briefs who won't get out of bed for less than ten grand. And there's another bunch of villains that wants the half a mill off of me I borrowed to keep things goin' a bit longer. They were round a couple of days ago – said they wanted to remind me that health's important.'

'What other bunch of villains?' Eddie asked shakily.

Hearing the worry in his voice, Jan could tell he was dreading the worst.

'They call themselves a bank.' Ron shrugged. 'I knew what they were when I dealt with them, but I was sure I'd be out of the shit in time to settle up.'

'But they can't go after you now, can they, if you've been made bankrupt?'

'As it happens, I haven't yet. It's not till tomorrow I'm formally declared totally and utterly boracic! Don't you think the hacks would have got onto it by now if it'd already happened? Anyway, they couldn't give a monkey's about the laws of bankruptcy, or any other laws for that matter.'

'Jesus, Dad! What are you going to do about it?'

Ron managed to pull a grin across his broad face. 'I'll think of something – I always have. And your lovely little trainer doesn't want to hear all my personal problems, does she?' he said, giving Jan a big grin. 'Don't get excited about it, son.' He stood up and shook his yellow trousers back into shape. 'Right, I've got to go. I'll see you in a couple of weeks when I've got it sorted.'

Ron said a brief goodbye to them both and gave Jan a farewell kiss on the cheek.

She and Eddie watched him walk from the house to a small Ford, which she guessed was hired.

Jan looked at Eddie. 'He's a hell of a bloke, isn't he, your dad?'

Eddie nodded; she saw that there was the hint of a tear in his eye. 'He's a rogue, though. He doesn't want anyone's sympathy; and, frankly, he doesn't deserve it. He was always the winner in everything he did and for a man like Dad who's made it all himself this is the ultimate humiliation. He hates the fact that he got so comprehensively shafted when he really should have known better.'

'But you're worried about him, what he said about that loan, aren't you?'

Eddie bit his lip and nodded again. 'It's not just him I'm worried about. My mother's house in London is still technically half his, and if anyone cottons on to that she'd end up getting booted out too and that would break her heart – on top of everything else that's happened. And she's still very fond of my dad.'

'Why did they split up then?'

'Well, it's hard to understand your own parents' relationship, but I think she'd just lost interest in sex and, in a funny sort of way, he was too honest just to go out and get a mistress. She wasn't too bitter about it when he said he wanted a divorce and he found her this beautiful little Georgian house in St John's Wood ten or eleven years ago. She gets on with loads of charity stuff that keeps her busy and nags me about why I don't take any girls back to meet her,' Eddie grinned.

'Why don't you?'

'I don't think that's the sort of thing a trainer should be discussing with her client, do you? I asked you over to look at my historic residence, so let me show you round.'

After Eddie had proudly shown Jan the full extent and dilapidated condition of the mill house, he suggested lunch at the White Horse, his village local. Jan arranged for Roz to stay with the children a little longer and tried not to feel guilty about having a few hours to herself without the children.

The landlord and regulars in the White Horse were

intrigued to meet Jan. They'd heard a lot about her – not only from Eddie, but also from Billy Hanks, who lived in the village. They were encouraging, but Jan couldn't help feeling some resentment at always being compared to Virginia Gilbert; as far as Jan was concerned, all she had in common with Colonel Gilbert's daughter was her gender.

When they had their drinks and a plateful of sandwiches on the table in front of them, Eddie asked Jan what progress she'd made with Harold.

'Gerry went to find this lad that Julie saw him talking to,' Jan said, 'but he wouldn't admit to anything. He had a crowd of his mates with him so there wasn't a lot poor Gerry could do. Then, when he went back the next day, Gerry was really mortified because this kid, Amos Smith, had done a runner – at least, his mates said he'd gone off apple-picking somewhere and wouldn't be back.'

'I'm not surprised, but if we can't talk to him, maybe we should go and ask Harold Powell what he was up to in that car park.'

Jan nodded. 'That's what I was thinking.'

'Then let's do it,' Eddie said. 'There's no point hanging about while the trail goes cold. We could go over there this afternoon.'

'No.' Jan shook her head doubtfully. 'I must pick up the kids.'

'Bring them with you. You could always drop them at their grandmother's.'

'OK,' Jan said, making her mind up. 'We're bound to find him somewhere and it would be better if he had no warning we were coming.'

Eddie insisted on going in his Land Rover, which added to the journey time. But it was a bright autumn day and Olwen had sounded pleased when Jan had phoned to ask if she could bring Megan and Matty over for tea.

'What are you doing over here?' Olwen asked, eyeing Eddie suspiciously when they arrived.

Jan couldn't see any benefit in discussing her mission with her mother-in-law. 'We've come to see about a horse,' she said, with a vague grain of truth. 'We'll be a couple of hours. I hope that's all right?'

'You know I'm always very happy to have my son's children,' Olwen said stiffly.

Harold lived in a handsome Edwardian stone house about fifteen minutes from Stonewall Farm, in a small village just above the River Wye, north of Hay.

A long drive approached the house between iron-railed paddocks. Jan recognized a few of the horses grazing in them.

'He must be trying to train them himself,' she remarked.

'That's what he said he was going to do, with a couple of girls,' Eddie confirmed. 'I thought it was just sour grapes.'

'There's no reason why he shouldn't try, though I don't think he has a prayer of getting the feed and the exercise right. I can't see Rear Gunner here, though.'

'I wonder if Harold is.'

'It looks like it,' Jan said as they turned into a sweep of gravel in front of the house, where Harold's new Range Rover stood, sparkling clean in front of a handsome weeping ash.

Eddie parked beside it, switched off the engine and turned to Jan. 'Here we go then.'

'How are we going to play this?' Jan asked, suddenly scared now they were here.

'Keep cool. He'll be worried too. We'll hit him head on, as if we had positive proof that he did it.'

They climbed out and crunched with confident strides across the gravel towards a light oak front door.

They mounted two broad, smooth stone steps and Eddie pressed a large china bell push.

The door was opened by Sheila Powell. Her eyes narrowed at once, though Jan wasn't sure if it was from the sunlight or at the sight of her.

'I didn't know you were coming round,' she said, revealing that she was used to her husband not telling her what was going on.

'Nor does Harold,' Jan said. 'We just dropped in on the off-chance. It looks as though we're in luck,' she added, nodding over her shoulder at the Range Rover.

'He's watching the rugby – Llanelli–Bath,' Sheila said.

'I'm sure he'd like to talk to us, though. I just heard on the radio Llanelli is taking a bit of a drubbing,' Eddie said, putting on a convincing smile.

Sheila shrugged, in the certain knowledge that whatever she did would be wrong, and opened the door to let them in. 'You'd better wait in there,' she said, pushing open the door of a small formal drawing room off the dark front hall.

Jan and Eddie looked at each other, both slightly nervous in the cold, anonymous room. A few moments later Harold came in. He was wearing a bland, inquisitive smile as he walked through the door.

'Hello, Jan, and Mr Sullivan, isn't it?'

'That's right,' Eddie nodded.

'Sorry to interrupt your rugby, Harold.'

'No problem,' Harold said, affably. 'What can I do for you?'

Jan looked at him, sensing that his friendliness was a sure sign of insecurity. 'I've already told you that, Harold, but I haven't heard from you lately.'

Harold's lips straightened and the flesh round his jaw became firmer. 'I've told you what we can offer, bearing in mind that we're not obliged to offer anything at all. But as you're an old friend I persuaded my partners that we should, in the interests of good will. Are you sure you want to discuss this in front of Mr Sullivan?'

'Certainly,' Jan said. 'He knows what's been going on. In fact he can tell you a little more about what we know already.'

'Oh, really?' Harold said, looking coldly at Eddie, but Jan didn't miss his Adam's apple jerk as he swallowed.

'There's one thing Amos Smith didn't tell us before he went missing,' Eddie said, impressing Jan with his calm delivery, 'and that's how much you paid him to open the gate and let out Jan's horses, two of which, as you'll have heard by now, were killed.'

Harold didn't answer at once, but his face seemed to darken in colour as his eyes darted from Eddie's to Jan's. 'What the hell are you talking about?' he spluttered suddenly. 'Why would I want to kill Jan's horses? How would that help me?'

'I expect you thought it would put her off pursuing you through the courts for the money you robbed her of.'

'I think, Mr Sullivan, you should keep your nose out of other people's business.'

'I asked Eddie to help,' Jan interjected. 'And I trust him completely.'

'Let's hope he's a bit more trustworthy than his father, then,' Harold sneered.

Jan saw Eddie wince. She glared at Harold. 'I hope you could say the same about your own kids,' she snapped.

'Look, if you've just come here to insult me with fairy stories, you may as well leave. I don't know what the hell you're talking about, or any Amos Smith.'

'You don't remember the young man you talked to

in a pub car park on October the sixteenth, less than four miles from Edge Farm?'

'I remember some young bloke – a right chancer, by the look of things – asking if he could clean my car. I had some good tack in the back and I told him to clear off, but I didn't ask his name.'

Jan looked away, at a gold carriage clock ticking quietly on the mantel-shelf. Harold's indignation and explanation seemed totally plausible.

'What were you doing in that part of Gloucestershire, anyway?' Eddie pressed, ignoring Harold's denial.

'I'd had a bit of business in Oxford on behalf of some clients. I was on my way back and I thought of visiting Jan, to see if we could work out her grievance over the sale of Stonewall, and I stopped for a bit of lunch to think about what we could do. Then, given the reception I had last time, I thought better of it and carried on home.'

Eddie stared at Harold, without saying anything for a moment. 'You had that answer all nicely worked out, didn't you? But, unfortunately for you, Amos told us about your conversation with him and what you asked him to do.' Eddie shrugged his shoulders, to convey the futility of Harold denying it.

But Harold was smiling now. 'Look, Mr Sullivan,' he said soothingly, 'I don't know where on earth you got your information from, but I can assure you this lad never told you anything like that, or, if he did, he was making it up because he thought there might be a few bob in it. And, believe me, I understand that Jan feels unhappy that the farm fetched a great deal more money a few months after we sold it for her, but anyone will confirm that the market hardened a hell of a lot last spring. We'd like to help: we've made an offer and I don't see how we could be expected to do more.'

'You could have offered more, to make up for my loss through your bad advice alone, never mind deliberately keeping the price down so you could buy it cheaply and make a nice turn for yourself.'

'Look, Jan, I've said I can understand you grievance, but we're just going round in circles now. I had nothing to do with your horses getting out and I take great exception to you coming here with Mr Sullivan to accuse me of it. I think we may as well bring this meeting to a close. Our original offer still stands. All you have to do is sign the simple document I left you and that'll be that.'

Jan glanced at Eddie. 'Let's go.'

Eddie raised a shoulder. 'Mr Powell, we know what you did, and when Amos Smith reappears the police will be talking to him about it.'

Harold said nothing; he just waited for them to leave the room. Jan went first, but as she reached the door she couldn't stop herself from turning back once more. 'There's something else I'd like to know, as I put a hell of a lot of work into him. What have you done with Rear Gunner?'

Harold raised his eyebrows. 'You did well with him,

I've always said so,' he agreed, 'but to see him achieve his true potential I've sent him to a professional yard. He's with Virginia Gilbert now; she wants to run him in a few good hunter chases.'

'The bastard!' Jan gasped as soon as they were back in the Land Rover and Eddie had started the noisy diesel engine. 'He's done exactly what he knew would really annoy me.'

'Then don't give him the satisfaction of seeing it,' Eddie said quietly as he swung the car round in front of the house and headed back down the drive towards the main road.

'As for that cock-and-bull story about Amos wanting to clean his car—'

'I think he's seen Amos since Gerry did.'

'Yes,' Jan nodded. 'He was so confident that we didn't really know anything, and his mates said Amos had gone to pick apples in Herefordshire. He could easily be somewhere out this way; there's loads of orchards still being picked.'

'He knows there's nothing we can do, I'm afraid.'

'But do you really think he did it?'

'Frankly, I just don't know.'

'Oh God!' Jan groaned. 'It's horrible, being so sure you know one minute and then having to accept you may have got it all wrong.'

'Have you been in touch with those solicitors Toby Waller suggested?' Eddie asked.

'No, not yet. But I will, first thing Monday morning. I'll get them to send Harold a final warning that we're going to go after him for the difference between what I got for Stonewall and what he got for it.'

14

'You've done what!?' Jan's shoulders collapsed and her mouth fell open.

Three days after they'd been to see Harold in Wales, Eddie was sitting opposite her at the small wooden table in her caravan. Between them were the remains of a Chinese takeaway, a vase of flowers and a bottle of wine, most of which had been drunk by Eddie. The light from a pair of fat, flickering candles on wrought-iron brackets gleamed off a few silver trophies and framed photographs of winning horses squeezed onto the tiny shelves.

'What happened was,' he said, 'I went back to the Grange to see Cyril Goldstone, to sort of welcome him into our old home. He didn't take it too well, but as he's a bookie and I had to make conversation, I asked him what price he'd give me on Russian Eagle to win the Aintree Foxhunters' with me riding. He just laughed at first, but when he offered me a hundred to one I had to go for it.'

Jan shook her head. 'But five thousand quid? Eddie, you're barking mad.'

'Look Jan, my father owes this dodgy Italian bank half a million. If he can keep them off his back somehow until next spring and we can win this race, I can get him off the hook and Mum can keep her house.'

'But where did you find five grand?'

'Ah, well,' Eddie winced. 'That's the tricky bit. I'd been keeping it on deposit at the bank to pay my VAT next week.'

'For God's sake – how are you going to pay it now?'

Eddie shrugged. 'I don't know – pray, I suppose.'

Jan couldn't believe anyone could do anything so utterly foolish. She had been thinking what a good evening they were having until then.

'You must be out of your head having a ridiculous bet like that.'

'But, Jan,' he said with a puzzled smile, 'you said you thought Eagle could do it.'

'For Christ's sake, Eddie! Where have you been all your life? There's a mile of difference between "could" win and "will" win.'

Eddie refused to be shaken. 'Do you still think he could win?'

'Like I've said before, all we've got to go on is his form, which says he can do the distance; so far his jumping looks reliable, though I don't think he's got a lot of speed. In a poor contest, with the right conditions and a competent jockey – yes, it's just *possible* he *could* win.'

'That'll do for me.' Eddie grinned and topped up their glasses.

Jan pushed hers away. 'No. That's enough for me – and for you, if you seriously think you're going to come in and ride work at seven tomorrow – especially if you want to nudge your chances below a hundred to one.'

Eddie looked at her steadily for a moment, as if he were trying to spot a chink of softness or invitation in her firm blue eyes.

'It's no good looking at me like a dog at a bone,' Jan said, suppressing a smile. 'You're going home to bed.'

Eddie nodded with a grin and stood up. 'Goodnight Jan.' He leaned across the narrow table top and lightly kissed her forehead. 'Do you know, I do believe you're the best-looking trainer in Gloucestershire.'

'That's not saying much, Eddie. You've had far too much to drink, you're looking at me by candlelight, and the only other female trainer in Gloucestershire is Virginia Gilbert. Get on home, you berk, and leave me alone.'

As he stepped down from the caravan, she flashed a smile at his back. He turned, just in time to catch it lingering on her lips. 'Eddie,' she said more gently.

'Yes?' He put a foot back on the first step.

She put her hands on his shoulders and gently pushed him back. 'Promise me you won't ever have any more big bets on horses in my yard without talking to me first?'

Eddie was more muted the next few times he came to Edge Farm to be schooled on Eagle. But Jan also noticed a new determination in his efforts and she realized that, crazy as it seemed, he was completely serious about winning the Aintree race.

One morning, after he'd gone, she talked about it with Annabel, without telling her just how dire Ron Sullivan's predicament was.

'The trouble is,' Annabel said, 'whenever Eddie got into trouble in the past, he would just go to Ron, who bailed him out, or the bank would lend him what he needed against his shares in Sullivan Homes. Now Ron's in trouble, Eddie wants to help him, but he actually hasn't got a clue how to deal with the pressure. I don't suppose he's ever been seriously tested in his life.'

'I wish I could do more to help,' Jan said. 'I never told him he had a *good* chance of winning, just that he *could* win if he's very lucky and he gets a good run. That's one of the dangers of training. If someone's pestering you about whether their horse might win such and such a race, you say it could be possible and they take it you're predicting a win. I mean, Eddie's horse is coming together all right and he's really worked on his riding – I'm pretty confident he'll win a few point-to-points if we enter him in the right ones, but,' Jan sighed, 'we'll be very lucky to do more than that.'

'Are you OK, Jan?' Annabel was looking more closely at her. 'You seem a bit wiped out.'

'I am. Matty was up half the night coughing, and I was thinking that we shouldn't still be living in a caravan, though I don't think that's what's causing it. But then there's everything else. We all work our backsides off here; you do it for half what you should, Gerry never sends in all the bills he should, and I still can't really get ahead of the game enough to start building a proper house or anything. I need that licence badly, but what with the Jockey Club turning me down and everything else—' Jan shook her head, 'I sometimes feel like giving up. OK, I think we might be passed on the fire risk next time, but they weren't that happy about the gallops either. Then Virginia's complained about those horses getting out and now I don't even have anyone to put up the guarantee.'

'You could always ask Bernie,' Annabel said. 'He'd do anything for you.'

'I think it's you he comes to see, actually.'

'Oh no, it's not; you should try him.'

'Frankly, I'd rather not be in hock to someone like Bernie, when you look how he uses his money to keep Sandy interested.'

'That's all she's interested in, anyway,' Annabel said.

'I don't think he'd do it,' Jan said. 'The fact of the matter is there aren't that many people prepared to stick their necks out for people like me, especially being a woman.'

'Oh, Jan,' Annabel gave her arm a squeeze, 'don't sell yourself short. You've got a lot of support. Of course, I know it's been tough this last few months and you're still getting over John; there's been James McNeill and Harold and all that to deal with, but at least all the horses in the yard look great.'

'Thanks, Bel.' Jan smiled wanly. 'I suppose you're right, but sometimes I wonder if it's worth all the worry and the stress, and spiteful people ganging up against you, when all you're trying to do is make a living.'

'By the way, I forgot to tell you, Mr Carey came round last night and invited me and you and anyone to do with the stables to a bonfire party tonight. Apparently he does it every year on December the first for all the village. Julie says it's something to do with him being Catholic and not believing in Guy Fawkes Night. He provides most of the fireworks and the pub lays on some booze.'

Victor Carey, Jan was learning, was a man with two distinct sides. Since she'd had his horse, August Moon, in the yard, he'd been up a few times. He'd shown a good knowledge of horses and racing and he was looking forward to seeing his mare run. Mr Carey had never married, no one knew why, and there was no obvious reason. Jan concluded it was because, under his curt manner, he was very shy. But despite regular displays of astounding meanness, there were occasional flashes of great generosity, of which the firework party was a good example.

Jan decided to take her children; all the people who worked for her were coming and she told a few of the owners whom she'd spoken to that day about it. So, as darkness fell, she arrived at the paddock, which was surrounded on three sides by woodland and facing the heavy stone features of Stanfield Court, where a massive bonfire had just been lit.

Julie from the pub was standing behind a trestle table, serving mulled wine in plastic mugs and pop for the children.

Eddie Sullivan was already standing at the temporary bar.

'Hello, Jan. Have a drink.' He handed her one and got another for Megan. 'Is Matthew up for anything?' he asked.

Matthew was gurgling from a sling on Jan's back. 'He's quite happy at the moment, but I shouldn't think that'll last long once the fireworks start. I may have to make a hasty exit. Anyway, what brings you here?'

'I thought I might find you. The thing is, I've got a major problem. I sent off my VAT return with a cheque for just over five grand and, unless there's a miracle, when it hits my bank next week it's going to bounce like a *Baywatch* boob and I'll be in deep manure. They'll start sending in the bailiffs.'

It was obvious to Jan that Eddie had already had a few drinks. 'Look, there's not a lot I can do about it, I wish there were, but—'

'Good God, I'm not expecting you to lend me the money or anything, but there is something else you could do; I may have to sell Eagle in a hurry to raise the cash. He'd be worth five grand, wouldn't he?'

'More, probably, but not if you want to sell him quickly.'

'As long as I can get enough to cover this bloody cheque, but the trouble is I've got to sell him to someone who'll let me ride him in the Foxhunters'.'

'That would narrow the field considerably. A lot of people want that sort of horse to ride themselves.'

'But can you try to think of someone, maybe someone who's told you to look for a horse?'

'All right, Eddie, but if you're serious about wanting to keep the ride, it's going to be bloody hard to find someone who'll commit themselves into letting you do it.'

'Look Jan, I've *got* to keep that ride. I've told my father that I think I can pull something out of the hat for him. He doesn't believe me, and of course, I didn't tell him what it was, but I really want to do this for him.'

Jan looked at him with fondness and frustration. 'Eddie, for God's sake, how many times have I told you, even if you keep this ride, your chances of winning the race aren't a lot better than Cyril Goldstone's given you.'

'But I've got a really good feeling about it so, please, do what you can.'

She looked at him and sighed. 'All right, Eddie. But I wish you could think of some other way of finding this money.'

'I'm looking, believe me, I'm looking,' he said gloomily.

Annabel had just arrived. Eddie spotted her and, Jan noticed, managed to transform himself in an instant into the carefree, life and soul of the party he liked to seem. Jan watched curiously as he walked over, planted a kiss on Annabel's cheek and greeted her with his usual joking banter.

Her thoughts were interrupted by Victor Carey, who came up and greeted her with a quick, tight-lipped smile.

'It's very kind of you to ask us all, Mr Carey,' Jan said, seeing how the firelight deepened the furrows in his pasty, wrinkled face. 'Though I'm not sure what he's going to do when the fireworks start.' She nodded over her shoulder at Matthew, slumbering on her back.

'There'll be quite a show, but you could always take him into the house. You could still see them from in there.'

'Thanks.'

'By the way, I wanted to tell you; I've seen how dedicated you are up at that yard and I'd very much like to see you get your licence. I just hope the incident with the loose horses hasn't gone against you.'

Jan was surprised that Victor Carey knew about the accident and its repercussions, but she was touched by his evident wish to see her succeed.

She wondered if this might be a time to talk to him about the other problem she had, of finding a suitable backer to pledge the thirty-five thousand pounds the Jockey Club demanded. But her instincts warned her that this was probably beyond the limits of his generosity.

When Mr Carey leaned down to light the first of the fireworks ten minutes later, it was not Matthew but Megan who hated the flashes and bangs and howled loudly. Jan thought of taking up Mr Carey's offer and retreating to the house, but she decided it would be easier just to take her daughter home and calm her there. She slipped away while everyone was still gasping at a series of monster set pieces, which must have cost a small fortune, defying the popular view of Mr Carey's stinginess.

Bernie Sutcliffe rang in the morning to say he was passing and could he drop in around midday.

The dogs announced his arrival. They always seemed to bark more at Bernie than at anyone else. Roz used to joke about it: 'It's like he's got a particular smell to a dog and I don't mean all that pongy after-shave he wears.'

Jan was thinking of it as she went out to greet him.

'Hello, darling, what are you smiling about?' he asked when he saw her, and a big grin distorted his long, bony face. 'Or are you just pleased to see me?'

'Always pleased to see owners,' Jan replied. 'Sorry about the dogs, though.'

'Oh that's all right. I expect they can just smell my new one.'

'I didn't know you were a dog lover, Bernie.'

'I'm not. But I've got a warehouse where I keep all sorts of good stuff, down by the canal in Brierley Hill and the alarms there are always packing up, or the villains know how to get round them. I thought the best thing would be to get a really fierce dog, so I went along to this place where they take in strays, and give 'em away if you want them and there was this great big sort of Dobermann thing. If you just walked near him, he growled like a lion. So I said, like, I'll have him, and they put him in the back of me car. But when I got home I was a bit worried because when I opened the door, he didn't bloody growl at all. And when I get him into the warehouse he turns out to be a pussy cat.'

Jan tried to keep a straight face as she listened to Bernie's whingeing tale of disappointment.

'Still,' she said, 'at least he'll bark when anyone turns up.'

'Oh, no. He doesn't bark!' Bernie said resentfully.

'What does he do then?'

'He just sort of sniffs. He's bloody useless; the trouble is I've got quite fond of him and I can't send him back, and he eats about twenty quid's worth of meat every week.'

At that Jan couldn't stop herself from grinning. She

already knew Bernie hated to see money spent unnecessarily. He'd been through the first two bills she'd sent him with a magnifying glass, suspiciously demanding an explanation for every item. Jan had got herself in the habit of keeping a record card for each horse in her care, so that she could keep a check on any medication and treatment they'd had. As a result, she'd been delighted to provide documentary evidence of every single item she'd charged for.

'Anyway,' he went on, 'I wanted a word with you.'

Jan wondered what was coming as they walked across the yard to the tack room, where she tended to conduct most of her business.

'So, what is it you want?' Jan asked.

'I thought I might treat myself to another horse. I like the way the other one you got for me is coming along.'

'What sort of horse?'

'You know, something that'll win a few good races, maybe one of these hunter chases or whatever they call them when point-to-point horses run on proper tracks; that's what Sandy really wants to see.'

For her own sake and Annabel's, Jan was relieved to hear that Sandy's opinion was still a factor. She thought for a moment and took a deep breath. 'What about Russian Eagle?'

'You mean Eddie Sullivan's bloody great horse?'

'I do.'

'Huh,' Bernie grunted. 'I thought he might be feeling the pinch a bit after old Ron hit the skids,' he said, as if he were thinking, *There, but for the Grace of God* . . . 'How much is the horse worth?'

'If we entered him at Doncaster Sales, he'd probably make six or seven, the way he looks now and on his Irish form. But I should tell you, there's one proviso: Eddie's determined to win the Aintree Foxhunters' on him. I think he's had a bit of a bet, but he *must* be riding the horse himself, so whoever buys him would have to agree to that.'

'That's not a problem. I'm not going to bloody well ride him, am I? And if he thinks he can win . . . Do you think he can win?'

'Like I told Eddie, if all the conditions suit him, he could.'

'What do you mean all the conditions? You mean if all the other horses fall over?'

'No. He's quite capable of jumping round and as long as he doesn't have to quicken too much at the finish, he really does stand a chance.'

'Will he win anything else?'

'He ought to win a few points,' Jan said with complete confidence, 'and some smaller hunter chases. He's not the sort of horse that's likely to go wrong and I should think he'll stay three and a half miles, no trouble.'

'OK. I'll give him four grand for it.'

Jan shook her head. 'No you won't. He needs five and he won't take less.'

'Well it may not be his choice. Tell him I'm offering

four and he can ride the horse. If he wants it, tell him to ring my office.'

At midday the next day Jan sat opposite Eddie in the caravan and watched him dial Bernie Sutcliffe's office number. She felt almost as jittery as she had before Rear Gunner had run in the Shropshire Gold Cup at Ludlow.

Although Eddie's chances of winning his bet were pretty slim, it might just be possible; she also knew it meant everything to him and she really cared. For Eddie, she guessed, it was a way not only of helping his father and showing his appreciation for all he'd been given over the years, it was also a means of proving to Ron that he, too, could pull off a spectacular coup.

It followed inevitably that Eagle winning the Foxhunters', hazy prospect that it was, had become all-important to Jan as well.

'Hello,' Eddie said in his deep, comfortable voice. 'Can I speak to Mr Sutcliffe, please?'

He looked up, put his hand over the mouthpiece and grinned at Jan. 'What on earth is Sutcliffe Industries?'

'I don't know,' Jan said. 'Eamon Fallon says he's into scrap metal and recycling paper and makes a packet out of it. Four or five grand would be absolute peanuts to him.'

'Yeah, well, some people get very possessive about their peanuts. Hello?' he said, turning his attention back to the phone while he fiddled with a pen and doodled on the note pad on the table in front of him.

'Bernie! Good morning. It's Edward Sullivan . . . No, no, I haven't got the bailiffs in yet, but thanks for asking . . . I was just ringing to thank you for your offer for Russian Eagle, but I'm afraid I've accepted a higher one . . . Good Lord, no. I just wanted to let you know, out of politeness . . . Not at all . . . Where am I now? I'm at Edge Farm, in Jan's caravan . . . Yes, of course I've got all my clothes on.' Eddie tried to laugh while screwing up his face and shaking his head at Jan. 'Fine, if you want. I'll be here for a while I expect . . . OK. Goodbye, Bernie.'

Eddie put down the phone. 'Good God, he's a dirty-minded little sod. For some reason, he seemed really excited at the idea that I might have been in here naked with you.'

'Urgh,' Jan grunted. 'Anyway, what did he say?'

'He said he would call me back.'

Jan grinned. 'He'll take it then. Well done; you're acting is very good – which makes me a bit worried, actually. I've noticed: you can turn on the charm more or less at will, can't you?'

'Not all the time,' Eddie said seriously, 'and I think you know that too.'

'Why don't you ever show your real side to Annabel?'

'If by that you're saying I'm only real when I'm

feeling gloomy and sorry for myself, you're wrong. I'm lucky; most of the time I really enjoy life, though I admit it's been a little tough recently. And anyway, look what a brave face you put on things when they've all been going wrong for you. I don't jump on you and accuse you of being bogus, do I?'

Jan held up a mollifying hand. 'All right, I'm sorry. But, even so, you did a great job on Bernie. If he'd thought you were just trying to talk him into having the horse, he'd have backed off. Now he just thinks he's lost a bargain.'

'I know. I may not be the deal king like Dad, but I wasn't born yesterday.'

'If you shut up, I'll get you a drink,' Jan said, 'because there's something else you might be able to do for me.'

'You can always ask. Is there any of that Irish left?'

'Not much.' Jan reached behind her and took a bottle from a shelf. From a cupboard, she took a glass tumbler, poured half a finger of whiskey into it and slid it across the table like a barmaid in a Western saloon.

Eddie eyed the paltry measure with disdain. 'Never mind. So, what can I do for you?'

'I would do it myself, but I wondered if there was any way you might be able to sound out Victor Carey about my bond. He was talking to me at the firework party; he's very pleased with the way August Moon's coming on and he seemed quite interested in what I'm trying to do here. He said he'd like to see me with a licence.'

'I think he'd be far more likely to consider a request for a guarantee if it came from you directly,' Eddie commented.

'I will ask him myself but, before I do, I wouldn't mind if you sounded him out first. It would be just as embarrassing for me as for him if he wanted to turn me down.'

'Isn't there anyone else who you think might be easier and more committed?'

'Possibly, but the truth is I don't want anyone who's going to interfere all the time and feel, because their money's on the line, they've got the right to tell me how to do my job or to put their oar into my accounts and things.'

'You mean, someone like Bernie?'

'Yes, or Frank Jellard or Eamon Fallon, for that matter. And, of course, I can hardly ask Colonel Gilbert; Virginia would go bananas.'

'You're right there. OK, I'll find some excuse to talk to Carey and, if it leads into it easily enough, I'll bring the conversation round to your licence application and how difficult everything is because you just can't raise the guarantee. Frankly, I should think he'll smell it's a put-up job, but I'll do my best.'

'Thanks, Eddie. You're a good mate. You can have the rest of this whiskey; there's only a tiddly bit.' Jan poured the last few drops of the spirit into Eddie's glass. He downed it in one slug and stood up.

'OK, Mrs H. I'm off.'

'Hang on, what about Bernie?'

'Tell him I've gone, but he can ring me at home later.' Eddie thought for a moment. 'I think I'll leave the answerphone on.'

'Don't push your luck,' Jan said and gave him a grateful smile.

The following day was a Tuesday and Jan had to take a lorryload of horses hunting to catch up on their qualifying days in time for racing in the New Year. She arrived back at the stables fully expecting to have heard something from either Eddie or Bernie about Russian Eagle. But although there were five messages from Bernie, there was nothing from Eddie.

On Wednesday Jan rang Eddie's home number. She smiled as she listened to the message on his answerphone before leaving her own: 'Listen, Eddie, I hope you return this call, even if you're not returning Bernie's. He's going mad; says he can't get hold of you anywhere. He's so desperate he even asked me if I knew how much you'd got for the horse. I said I didn't know, but I thought six, and he said he'd match that if I could talk you into it. So, call me back to confirm what you want to do, though I expect I know already.'

The third week before Christmas was a much better week for Eddie, and for Jan.

Ownership of Russian Eagle was transferred to Bernie, and Eddie paid into the bank five of the six thousand pounds Bernie had given him, just in time to cover his VAT payment. He also told Jan to keep the three weeks' training fees he had already paid for Eagle, saying that she deserved it as commission on the sale.

Jan had also found two more suitable horses for Frank Jellard. One, Nuthatch, came from the same yard as Arctic Hay and the other, a small horse called Rhythm Stick, Jan bought from a local farmer's widow who had no interest in racing. Both were animals Jan considered very trainable. They had cost a little more than Frank had said he wanted to pay, but he didn't grumble and wrote out a cheque as soon as he'd seen them.

Fortunately, during a dry spell over the preceding ten days, Gerry had abandoned his current customers and rushed up to Edge to finish the barn roof in green, galvanized iron before the prevailing wet weather returned. With Frank Jellard's two new horses and two invalids still in, the yard was now at its full capacity of sixteen.

At the end of the week, Eddie arrived for a schooling session as Billy Hanks came back from riding out a couple of Jan's horses. The amateur jockey, who had a day job in Gloucester market, was in demand from several trainers in the area, but he had taken to coming to Jan's more than the others. He stood by her to watch Eddie for the first time as she was schooling him over the steeplechase fences.

Jan knew Eddie had improved but she found it hard to be objective about his performance.

'What do you think of him?' she asked Billy.

'I tell you what, I've known Eddie Sullivan for a long time and if you'd told me a year ago he was going to try and ride in races himself, I wouldn't have believed you. Not that he isn't a fit-looking bloke, it's just that he was always on the piss and chasing women.'

'Eddie? Chasing?'

'Well, maybe not; he's too bloody lazy for that; but he was definitely screwing them.'

'Oh, Billy, I don't want to hear about that.'

Billy laughed. 'All right, all right, but what I'm saying is I didn't think he had it in him to stick at it, but fair play, he's lost a bit of weight and you've taught him well. He's definitely seeing a stride into his fences and helping his horse.'

'What about the horse?' Jan asked.

'He's a good sort, isn't he – quite athletic for his size. What distance do you reckon he needs?'

'No less than three miles, I should have thought, probably three and a half. I suspect in the shake-up he could be a bit one paced.'

'He jumps nicely, though, and he'll make ground in the air. What does Eddie want to do with him?'

'Unfortunately, it's not up to him; he sold the horse

to Bernie Sutcliffe, but I'm pretty sure Bernie'll let him ride it in the Fox-hunters' at Liverpool.'

'Why the hell did he sell him?'

'You'd have to ask him that.'

'I think I know,' Billy said. 'I see he's had to get himself a rich girlfriend, too.'

Jan turned sharply to look at him, wondering if, finally, Eddie and Annabel had got it together and been too coy to tell her. She hesitated before she asked, as casually as she could, 'Oh? Who's that? Annabel?'

'God, no! I said rich, not posh. Sharon Goldstone.'

For a moment, Jan couldn't make the connection. 'Who's she when she's at home?'

'Cyril's daughter – you know, that bookie who bought the Grange from Ron. They were saying in the White Horse she's really gone after him, and she's only eighteen.'

Jan felt slightly sick, although she was well aware she had no right to resent the fact that Eddie didn't tell her everything about his private life. 'Oh well,' she tried to say lightly, 'so long as it doesn't affect his riding.'

Later, when Billy had gone to work and Eddie was drinking coffee with Jan in the tack room, she restrained her immediate impulse to ask him about Sharon Goldstone. As they talked about the day's work, she began to open the bundle of envelopes the postman had left. Most contained bills, but there was also a cheque from Bernie and a letter from Toby's lawyers in London. She read it twice before handing it to Eddie.

With Eddie's help, a few days after they had seen Harold Powell at his home, she had sent the solicitors a full account of what had happened, with copies of her correspondence and the advertisements that had been published each time Stonewall had been sold, and asked them to approach Harold.

They had immediately fired off a letter informing Harold's solicitors of their intention to recover the fraudulent profit gained by their client and his associates. Now they were writing to say that they had received a reply to the effect that Mr Powell denied any liability, with details of how his firm had followed rigorously all the statutory procedures for selling property by auction. Any public suggestion that their client had acted in any way dishonestly or unprofessionally would be treated as a serious libel.

Toby's lawyers added that it was unfortunate that Mrs Hardy no longer had the letter, or a copy, in which Mr Powell had proposed an ex gratia payment of ten thousand pounds. They took the view, however, that it was still possible that Mr Powell's firm would rather avoid the publicity of a messy case, with a possible reference to the DPP's office.

Eddie read the letter and looked up at Jan. 'At least they'll run with it a little further.'

'As long as they think I can pay. I dread to think how much even these first two letters have cost.'

'I'd say it was worth pushing it a bit further before you settle for Harold's ten thousand.'

'There's no way I'm going to settle for that. I'd rather have nothing,' Jan said fiercely.

'That's all very well, and highly principled, but you can't feed Megan and Matty on nothing.'

'All right. I'll risk another letter,' Jan said, more firmly than she felt. 'Oh, by the way, did you have a chance to go and see Mr Carey?'

'Yes, I did, yesterday. I said I'd come to see him about some of your owners getting together to give you a decent Christmas present.'

'Oh, Eddie, you shouldn't have done.'

'Don't get excited; we didn't come to any decision about that, but at least it meant we could talk about you, so it was comparatively easy for me to mention that you were determined to get a licence as soon as you could but a lot of things were getting in the way. I left the thirty-five grand bond until last. He may have smelt a rat, I don't know, but he didn't seem too put off by it.'

'What did he say?'

'He didn't say anything; he just nodded.'

'He nodded?'

'Yes.'

'That means "yes",' Jan said excitedly.

'Take it easy, Jan; it could just mean he was listening to what I was saying. I know I said I'd help you find another backer, but frankly, with Victor Carey, it's up to you to talk him into it. I've sown the seed, though; I don't imagine he'll be that surprised and I'm sure he'll listen.'

The day turned more wet and blustery and by the evening, when everyone else had gone home, and Jan was giving the children their tea, the prospect of venturing out to ask a man she hardly knew to put up a considerable amount of money as a guarantee for her business was not inviting. But she felt that if she allowed anything to stop her now, all momentum in her pursuit of a career as a National Hunt trainer would dissipate. Time would move on, another year would pass, and she would still just be training pointers for peanuts, with no money to pay for a house or the growing needs of her two children.

She picked up the phone and dialled Victor Carey's number. When he answered, her throat went dry and her words came out in a croak.

'Hello, Mr Carey. It's Jan Hardy here. I was wondering, if you were in, whether I could pop over and have a quick chat with you about something?'

'What would that be?' he answered dryly.

'It's to do with the running of the yard.'

'I see. And what exactly do you want to talk to me about?'

'Well, as you know, I've been applying for a full licence to train, and one of the things the Jockey Club want is—' she paused, 'a dozen people to give pledges that they'll send me horses to train.'

'There's no need to come and see me about that. I'd be quite happy to confirm that I would go on using your services, even though, of course, my horse hasn't run from your yard yet.'

'Oh, thanks.' Jan desperately cast around in her head for a way of broaching the real topic. 'But there was something else—'

'And what is that?'

God, Jan thought, *this man is not making it easy*.

'D'you know, I think I'd prefer to come and talk to you about it face to face, if you don't mind, rather than over the phone.'

'I see. When do you want to come?'

'I thought, perhaps, this evening? About half-six? If you're not busy?'

Mr Carey didn't answer for a moment, then with what sounded to Jan like a sigh, he said, 'Come round by all means. I'll expect you at six-thirty, then.'

Jan phoned Annabel next, to ask if she could leave the children with her. Annabel agreed, but Jan thought she sounded subdued, much quieter than normal. Her impression was confirmed when she arrived with Megan and Matthew. Once the children were happily crawling all over Annabel's small drawing room, she had time to ask her about it.

'I'm going to have to take a day or two off next week,' Annabel said, 'if that's OK?'

'Of course it is. You never take time off and I

sometimes think you should – better now than when racing starts. What are you going to do?'

'I have to go to London.'

'What for? Shopping? A man?' Jan grinned.

'No. I've got to go into hospital for a few tests.'

'Oh Bel, no! What for? What's the trouble?' Jan gazed at her friend with concern.

'It's OK, Jan. It's not what you think, or anything remotely life-threatening. It's just something I have to do.'

Jan could tell that Annabel didn't want to tell her more at this stage and curbed her usual thirst for detail. 'Of course you must have the time off, though I'll miss you, even for a couple of days.'

Annabel nodded. 'Why are you going up to see Mr Carey? He's not worried about August Moon is he?'

'No, not at all. In fact, I think he's quite excited about seeing her run again – not that he likes to show it much. I was going to talk to him about my licence application.'

'Ah.' Annabel looked doubtful. 'Best of luck and thanks for being so good about the time off. I'll see you later.'

Jan parked the Land Rover by the back door of Stanfield Court. Before she got out of the vehicle, she sat for a moment listening to the rain drumming on the roof.

Why? she thought. *Why am I having to go through*

this humiliating performance, going round with a begging bowl, just so that a bunch of pompous stuffed shirts in a big office in Portman Square will allow me to do what I already know I can do perfectly well?

She hated having to depend on others to achieve her aims. But she had to accept that in the career she had chosen, and in her circumstances, she had absolutely no option. She took a deep breath, let herself out into the rain, and ran across to shelter under the big stone arch of the back door, while she tugged at the old iron bell pull beside it.

Jan had no idea if anyone else lived in the rambling Victorian mansion with Mr Carey, but she wasn't expecting him to open the door himself. However, he did, and greeted her crisply.

'Evening, Jan. Come on in. Foul night.' He showed her along a corridor to a musty library, where a few coals glowed in a small iron fireplace. He waved her into an armchair by the fire and walked across the room to a sideboard in front of the heavily curtained windows, where a single bottle of sherry stood with two glasses.

'Sherry all right?' he asked over his shoulder.

'Yes, thank you.'

He filled both glasses carefully and carried them back, placing one on a small table beside Jan's chair.

Still standing, he took a sip and appeared to savour the sherry for a few moments, while Jan tried to decide how she was going to present her case.

'So,' he said suddenly, 'the Jockey Club, in its

wisdom, thinks you should lodge a guarantee of thirty-odd thousand pounds before they'll let you have a public licence?'

Jan felt slightly breathless, as if all the wind had been taken from her sail. 'Well. Yes, actually, I was going to—'

'I guessed as much. And I have looked into this particular requirement. I understand it's to provide a fund from which any workers or suppliers would be paid if you were to cease trading.'

'Yes, that sort of thing,' Jan said.

'Hmm.' Carey took another swig of his sherry. 'Presumably you don't have liquid assets of that amount?'

Jan shook her head.

'Nor your family?'

'No, Dad doesn't even own his own place and their total savings wouldn't be half that, I shouldn't think.'

'Yes, well, it has been hard recently.' He lifted his eyes. 'I haven't made a profit on this farm for five years now.'

Jan felt her stomach sink.

Carey sat down in a chair opposite and looked hard at her. 'Tell me, what horses do you have at the moment and how many do you think you might be able to train next year?'

Jan took a few minutes to describe each horse in the yard, what she thought she might be able to do with them in the coming season and which could, possibly, go on to run under rules, including Mr Carey's own August Moon.

He listened carefully, nodding as she spoke.

When she had finished, he downed the rest of his sherry and stood up again. 'Right. I think I've got the picture. I realize you are hoping I might put up an appropriate guarantee to support your licence application. I've heard what you have to say and I'll let you know in due course if I can help.'

Jan got up too, with her knees shaking. She had no idea whether or not he was interested in helping her. He would let her know 'in due course'! 'When?' she wanted to scream.

'Thank you,' she said, as mildly as she could. 'If you do decide to, I'd be ever so grateful.' She noticed her hand was shaking as she reached down to pick up her glass and finish her drink.

Jan went to bed that night feeling more alone than she had done since the day John Hardy had died.

Annabel was away for three days. Jan felt her absence more acutely than she'd expected, even though Roz, Emma and Joe rallied round to take over the extra work. They were helped by Billy Hanks, who, by now, was coming up two or three times a week. Jan took Billy's frequent visits to be a direct reflection of his opinion of the horses in her yard, most of which he would be riding when the season started in five weeks' time.

Mid-December was always a tricky period in a pointing yard. The animals were fit and nearly ready for the job, but bringing them to their peak too soon would have them wiped out before the season was half over. Jan was convinced that, despite the absence of Rear Gunner, she had a better string than she'd ever had. At least, as her father had suggested, she might make an impression on the point-to-point world while her next licence application went in, but her pleasure at seeing the horses coming on so well with so few problems was soured by a complete silence from Mr Carey. He had called in a couple of times, and only once broached the subject, as if it were something trivial that he was looking into.

Her equilibrium wasn't helped the evening before Annabel was due back. She was reading *The BFG* to Megan when the phone rang. Still with a smile on her face, she answered.

'Hi, Edge Farm Stables.'

'It's Harold here.' There was none of the old friendliness in his voice.

Jan cleared her throat. 'What do you want?'

'I just want to tell you that if you see that young chap around – the one we talked about when you came to see me with your friend – and I hear there's been any suggestion I was in any way responsible or knew anything about those horses of yours getting out, I'd have to protect my reputation.'

'I should think it needs protecting,' Jan returned sharply.

'I mean it. If anyone suggests I was involved in deliberately causing the death of those horses, I'll have no alternative but to do you for slander.'

'What do you mean "do" me?'

'I mean take you to court. I've been very reasonable with you, Jan. I've made you a fair offer for the sake of our former friendship, but I'm just warning you, don't go asking questions or making allegations, or you'll find yourself in court and my offer will be withdrawn.'

'You can withdraw what you like, Harold, but I still want the money you helped yourself to from Stonewall.'

'I expect you do, but I wouldn't count on anything from that particular source if you're planning your budget.'

After this conversation, Jan wondered if Joe Paley's cousin, Amos Smith, would ever reappear in the district. Twelve days before Christmas, the next time Eddie came to ride out, she told him about her conversation with Harold and Eddie suggested that he and Gerry keep an eye out for the boy. He was also keen to tell Jan about his plan for an impromptu Edge Farm Christmas party at his house. Although Jan was grateful to him for the idea, she found she couldn't work up much enthusiasm for it.

'What's the matter, Jan? Things aren't that bad, are they?'

'They aren't that good either.'

'Haven't you heard anything from Carey yet?'

'No.' Jan was deliberately non-committal.

Eddie didn't press her.

'OK, so you don't feel like holding a Christmas party yourself; then I'll have one anyway and invite everyone who's got anything to do with the yard.'

'What? All the owners? Even Bernie?'

'Even Bernie and his sniffing Dobermann, if he likes.'

'What about Cyril Goldstone?'

Eddie raised a quizzical eyebrow. 'Cyril? Does he have a horse in this yard now?'

'No, but I hear you're pretty chummy with his family.'

A smile spread slowly across Eddie's face. 'Jan, are you a bit jealous, or what?'

'No, of course I'm not; but I wouldn't mind being told about things.'

'If we sat down and I told you about all the women who come chasing after me, you'd soon get very bored.'

Jan couldn't help laughing. 'You arrogant bastard! You've got such a big head! I heard she'd made most of the running, mind,' she conceded.

'Sharon Goldstone may look like a slightly fleshed-out version of Barbie, but she also wears pink fluffy slippers, leopard-skin leggings and drives a Japanese convertible; she and I are hardly likely to be soul-mates. Besides, she's only eighteen and frankly she doesn't know a lot.'

'But you might be charitable and teach her?'

'Look, the only reason I went out with Sharon was to keep her old man happy. If she'd gone running back to him saying I'd stood her up or turned her down or whatever, he might have got nasty.'

'So what? Why should you care if some horrible old bookmaker doesn't like you?'

'Jan,' Eddie said with a rare display of honest self-analysis, 'I should have thought you knew me well enough by now to know that I don't like being disliked by anyone. Some may consider this a weakness; I consider it a strategy for life.'

'In other words, you can't say "no" to anyone.'

'That's about it,' Eddie laughed.

'Well, I have to say I think that's pretty pathetic.'

'And as I want you to go on liking me too, I won't say what I think of what you're thinking.' He gave her a big, bland smile. 'Anyway, I'd rather you didn't mention Sharon to Annabel.'

'Why on earth not? Annabel's not interested in you.'

'Maybe not, but I still crave her approval.'

'I *will* enjoy this party,' Jan said, 'seeing which of the women you end up with in a dark corner.'

'Dark corner? The whole of my house is dark. I've only got lamps and candles to light the place, remember.'

Jan relaxed. 'I'm sorry, Eddie; I was just teasing.

Thanks for suggesting the party. I'll tell everyone, if that's what you want. What day?'

'Friday, the twenty-first. I expect a lot of people will already be doing something, but that's too bad. By the way, where's Annabel?'

'She went to London for a few days.'

'What for?'

'I don't know.' Jan shrugged. 'She said she needed to go and I wasn't going to stop her.'

'Oh.' Eddie looked surprised. 'When's she due back?'

'Tonight.'

'I'll give her a ring later, then.'

That evening, Jan thought that if Eddie had tried to ring her, he was out of luck because Annabel had driven straight to Edge Farm on her way back from London and stayed to have supper in the caravan.

Jan had seen that she was feeling very sorry for herself as soon as she'd walked through the door.

'Let's have a bottle of wine,' she suggested and Annabel, not normally a drinker, nodded keenly.

When they each had a glass in their hand, and the place was lit only by a small lamp and the glow of the wood-burner, Jan asked her what had happened.

'I'm afraid this is going to sound pretty pathetic from a girl of twenty-three, but the fact is for some time I've been pretty sure I'll never be able to have children.'

Jan closed her eyes, suddenly understanding, knowing that this answered a lot of questions about Annabel and her behaviour.

'Oh, Bel,' she said and reached out to take the girl's slender hand in hers. 'It's not a bit pathetic to feel bad about it at your age. For God's sake, in the old days you'd already be well into child-bearing and all that. And I know bloody well how I'd feel if I hadn't or couldn't have any. But what did the hospital actually say?'

'They said my tubes and my uterus malfunction so badly that I'll never ovulate properly or be able to retain a foetus.'

'So even *in vitro* wouldn't work?'

Annabel shook her head. Her pale chestnut hair shimmered in the lamplight and for the first time since she'd known her, Jan saw she was crying. Jan leaned over and put an arm around her shoulders.

'Believe me, Bel, I *do* understand. I see now why you gave that beautiful doll's house to Meg and why you seem so distant with men you like. It explains why you love the horses so much and are so good with them.'

'That's not the only reason why I'm wary of men. The fact is the two relationships I've had so far both went wrong pretty quickly, and my father's always treated me and Charley like a couple of junior squaddies. Charley's gone, and I've made up my mind I'm not going to take any more stick from Dad, even though Mum didn't want me to leave. I've known for ages I had problems, but to be told point-blank that I'll always be infertile was devastating.'

'Oh God,' Jan groaned, her own eyes damp with sympathy, 'why is life so bloody unfair?'

15

Annabel was in a completely different mood when she arrived at Jan's caravan an hour before they'd planned to set off for Eddie's party.

During the week since Annabel had been back from London, Jan had tried to help her come to terms with the devastating diagnosis. 'There are other ways of having a family,' she'd told her, 'and being able to have babies isn't the only thing men are looking for in a woman. You've got masses to offer and you should make the most of it if you want to meet the kind of man who'll appreciate you for your intelligence and kindness, as well as for being a stunning woman.'

'Being stunning, as you call it, isn't much of an advantage really,' Annabel answered morosely. 'So many men are just interested in you for sex, it takes a lot of wading through the dross to identify the ones who see you as a person.'

'Hm,' Jan grunted. 'I don't know too many women who'd complain.'

On the evening of the party Annabel arrived early, keen to help Jan with her hair and make-up.

'I'm a bit scared about this,' Jan admitted. 'John and I were never asked to parties, if they even had them in mid-Wales.' It must be at least eight or nine years since she'd been in a room full of young stags, all drinking and dancing in an atmosphere charged with testosterone. 'I don't think I'm ready for it yet,' she said. 'I really don't want to go.'

'Look, I don't want to go much, either,' Annabel said, 'but you never know, there might be a few interesting people and Eddie must have gone to an awful lot of trouble.'

'No, he hasn't. Believe it or not, he's had his mum down helping him.'

'Gosh, I can hardly imagine Eddie's mother,' Annabel said. 'I've never met her, but she's probably rather sweet. And she must have a bit of character to have married someone like Ron Sullivan in the first place.'

'Eddie told me the break-up was fairly amicable. He thinks she'd just gone off the physical side of their relationship, and of course men can't seem to understand that it's not particularly unusual for some women to lose their sex drive once they've had a few babies.'

'Oh,' Annabel asked with a grin, 'have you?'

'That's unfair. I suppose it depends who's offering but, frankly, I haven't felt like being close to anyone since John died.'

'There are plenty of men interested in you, though.'

'It's just as well I'm not interested in them; I simply

haven't got the time for a relationship while I'm trying to build up this yard.'

'Even so, tonight I'm going to make you look absolutely fabulous.'

'You'll be lucky!' Jan laughed. 'Still, Eddie did once say I was the best-looking trainer in Gloucestershire.'

'Compared to who – Virginia Gilbert?' Annabel said, screwing up her face.

'That's what I said. Not saying much for me, was it? Mind you, Eddie *was* pretty drunk at the time!'

They stopped off to drop Jan's children at their grandparents in Riscombe and Mary asked them in for a cup of tea. She wasn't sure how to handle Annabel – a friend of their landlord's son, but also their daughter's employee. But Annabel made it easy for her, and agreed that Jan was looking 'like a little angel'. They left Riscombe late deliberately, so they would arrive an hour after the party had started. When they were nearly there, Jan was more grateful than she would admit that Annabel was with her.

It was all very well for Eddie, she thought, and, for that matter, Roz and Emma, who were off at parties or discos every weekend. For a thirty-one-year-old widowed mother of two, it was bound to be a different experience.

There were cars parked up the banks and all over the verges for twenty or thirty yards on either side of the gates to Old Ford Mill.

'Gosh,' Annabel said. 'Eddie seems to have invited the whole of Gloucestershire.'

'Billy Hanks said he was coming with a lot of his racing friends.'

'And he's sure to have asked the Gilberts,' Annabel said, 'and a few from the other big houses round here.'

It was a clear, starry night, and Annabel parked her Golf down the lane, out of harm's way. As they walked towards the house, she and Jan heard music and laughter drifting through the crisp, still air and the drone of a petrol generator Eddie had hired to power the disco. Jan struggled to control another dose of panic as they walked between the high stone gateposts and across the cobbles towards the open front door. Once inside the hall, though, they were met with welcoming smiles by a group of friendly faces and she felt herself relax a little.

'Let's find Eddie first and tell him we're here,' she said.

Annabel nodded. They made their way to the kitchen and walked into a freshly painted room, lit entirely with candles and oil lamps. To give him his due, Jan thought, Eddie had made the large room very inviting. Clusters of holly, ivy and mistletoe and a few traditional decorations made it look as it might have done at Christmas a hundred years before. There were a couple of dozen people in the room, picking at canapés, but there was no sign of Eddie. On the pine table in the middle stood a capacious terracotta bowl full of spicy wine cup, being ladled out by a tall, handsome woman, aged about sixty.

Jan guessed at once from her firm features, wavy dark hair and chocolate brown eyes that this must be Eddie's mother.

As she took a glass, she asked, 'Are you Mrs Sullivan?'

The woman nodded with a smile. 'I'm afraid so. Eddie needed someone to come and clear up after this is over.'

'I'm Jan Hardy. I . . .'

'I know exactly who you are,' Mrs Sullivan said. 'Edward's told me all about you.'

Annabel leaned over Jan's shoulder. 'Would you like me to take over, serving that drink?' she asked Mrs Sullivan. 'You might like a chat with Jan.'

'I'm sure I would. Thank you, dear.'

Jan followed Eddie's mother, squeezing through the crowd back into the hall. Mrs Sullivan looked over her shoulder and almost had to shout over the sound system, 'There's a quiet place – a sort of study at the back of the house.'

Last time Jan had seen the small room it had been full of packing cases and dust. Now there was a big kilim rug on the polished floorboards and fat candles burned in wall sconces, flickering off the oak linen-fold panelling. Two small sofas had been placed on either side of a big log fire. Otherwise, the room was empty.

'This is a big improvement since I last saw it,' Jan said.

'I sent him up a bit of furniture. What he had in the cottage only filled a couple of rooms here. Of course, the whole place has got to be practically rebuilt before he can decorate or furnish it properly.'

Jan detected Mrs Sullivan's London background in her voice, but it was much less obvious than Ron's. And from her manner and her clothes it was clear that she'd put her origins behind her long ago.

'I told him I thought he was mad to take this place on,' Jan said, as they sat down opposite each other in front of the fire, 'but he just laughed. He's been really good about getting materials for the house I'm building, though. I'm sure he'll make something of this place and at least he's not paying any rent.'

'Poor Edward. He's not used to poverty. He's never known it, not like me and his father.'

'Don't worry, Mrs Sullivan, he's tougher than you might think.'

'Do call me Sue, please. But you're right, he is quite tough. He was a big support to me when his father and I split up and he comes to see me whenever he's in London. But I've never felt he was achieving much. He's just been playing with this gallery. In a way, what's happened to Ron could be the making of Edward. His father spoiled him really, at least financially. Edward told me he had to sell the horse he was keeping with you. I think he was quite upset about it, but he says he's still going to ride it.'

'I hope so.' Jan assumed that Eddie hadn't told his mother about his ridiculous bet with Cyril Goldstone. 'His riding's improved a lot and I think he's really determined to win because of what's happened recently.'

Eddie's mother looked at her. Jan took in her strong features and gentle, intelligent eyes.

'But I'm still worried about him,' Mrs Sullivan said. 'He's quite capable of going off and doing something stupid if he thinks it will get him out of trouble in a hurry.'

Jan nodded. 'I know what you mean,' she said, truthfully, 'but he talks to me quite a bit, so I usually know what's going on.'

'He thinks a lot of you.' Mrs Sullivan looked at Jan thoughtfully. 'And he listens to what you say, which is more than he does with most people, including me.'

'I haven't got much advice to give him about anything, except racehorses, but at least he's really committed to getting a result with Eagle – we both are. I just hope he gets the chance.'

'You realize, I suppose, that he was quite involved with Annabel Halstead a few years ago, when she was still very young.'

'I thought she was seventeen then,' Jan said.

'That's young enough, especially coming from the kind of rigid discipline her father seems to dish out.'

'Poor Bel. She's over it now and she's getting on fine.'

'What about Edward, though?'

'You mean his love life?'

'Yes.'

Jan shrugged her shoulders. 'I don't know. He never says.'

'Well, whatever you do with him, keep him focused.' Mrs Sullivan gave Jan a warning look. 'He's always had a tendency to lose interest quite quickly once he's achieved anything,' Mrs Sullivan said. 'His father's just the same, that's why he's ended up bankrupt.'

Jan wondered if the fact that Sue Sullivan's home was still partly owned by Ron was causing her any nightmares, or if she even knew about the existence of the Italian bank Ron owed money to. She didn't think she could ask, so she changed the subject back to Eddie.

'If he loses interest in his riding, that's his problem, not mine. But I hope he doesn't; at least it gives him some kind of discipline.'

Susan leaned forward confidentially, although there was still no one else in the room. 'You will keep an eye on him for me, won't you? I can see you've got your feet firmly on the ground. If I give you my number in London, you could always phone me if you felt like it.' She fished a card from her small handbag and handed it to Jan.

'Thank you,' Jan said. 'I think he'll be fine, but if he seems to need a mother's guiding hand, I'll give you a ring.'

Susan stood up. 'Now, you ought to go and mix

with the young things. I've monopolized you long enough.'

Eddie was holding court in the hall at the bottom of the stairs and greeted Jan with a lot of fuss and a kiss on the cheek.

'If you want a laugh, have a look in there.' He nodded towards the music. 'Bernie's dancing with Sandy, but I'm not sure he's too happy.'

Before Jan had a chance to go and watch, the drama spilled out into the hall when Sandy walked out with her peach-coloured hair flying round her head like stuffing from a burst cushion. She was followed by Bernie, dressed in an absurdly baggy Armani suit.

'You nasty little bastard!' she was shouting in her sharp Birmingham voice. 'Spying on me like some dirty old pervert!'

'And finding you with your knickers round your ankles and your skirt over your head being shagged by some penniless little jockey,' Bernie shouted back at her as she stormed towards the front door.

Billy Hanks emerged from the dance room behind Bernie with a look of sheepish triumph on his face.

Sandy, who was taller than Bernie, spun round and glared at him. 'He may be penniless, but he's a bloody sight better at it than you, so you can stuff all your money up your arse!' She flounced out of the front door with her turquoise and gold chiffon skirt swirling round the top of her long brown legs.

After a moment's hesitation, Billy went too, with Bernie's eyes blazing after him.

'Oh dear,' Jan murmured to Eddie. 'Do you think that's the end of Bernie's horse-owning career as well?'

To Jan's surprise, Annabel wanted to leave first.

'There's nobody left who's sober enough to talk to,' she said.

'There's more to life than conversation,' Jan said with a grin.

'Don't start that; you know I'm not a party girl. Though I have enjoyed seeing some of these people, and watching Jimmy Hely dance with Virginia Gilbert was a real laugh.'

'She's not very sexy, is she.'

'It's hard to say if you're not a man, but I doubt it.'

'Did you talk to Eddie's mother at all?' Jan asked as they crunched along the icy lane to the car.

'A little. I though she was very charismatic. Extraordinary to think that her parents were first-generation Italian immigrants selling ice cream around London before the war. She said she loved it when she and Ron first moved out here with Eddie – the pure Englishness of the houses and the landscape. I think she misses it, poor thing, but when she and Ron divorced she decided to throw herself into two big charities in London. Now she's such a successful fund-raiser everyone wants her on their committees. It's strange because I'm sure she didn't deliberately turn her back on her family, but somehow she's turned into a real English lady.'

Jan nodded. 'I was always a bit puzzled how someone like Ron had produced Eddie, but meeting Sue explains it. Anyway, he's lucky to have a mother who'll come and help out at a do like this.'

'It was a good party, you must admit,' Annabel said.

'And nearly everyone who has anything to do with Edge Farm was there, weren't they, except for Allan Preece and old Gwillam Evans.'

'And Mr Carey,' Annabel added.

'Well, I didn't expect him to come. It's two weeks since I saw him about putting up the guarantee for my licence. He said he'd think about it, but he still hasn't let me know and he must realize I'm waiting every day to hear. My whole career's at stake.'

'I'm sure he's not doing it on purpose, he's very shy.'

'I know he's interested in my getting a licence and at least he's agreed to pledge a horse, but I don't think he understands what it's like to be a mother on your own, trying to make a living with two small children.'

'Well, I'm sure he'll be up before Christmas to see his horse; ask him again then.'

Victor Carey did come up – the next morning. Jan was tacking up Eagle, Dingle Bay and Colonel Gilbert's horse, Sorcerer's Boy, when he arrived.

He walked across the yard to look into the paddock, where most of the horses had been turned out in their

New Zealand rugs for a few hours of freedom. Having inspected them, he came over to the box where Jan was putting a saddle on Eagle. 'My mare's looking well. How's she working?'

Jan looked up from the girth she was buckling. 'Fine. She gave me a good feel this morning when we did a bit of fast work up at Colonel Gilbert's.'

'How often do you use his gallops?'

'Once or twice a week, to give the horses a change and so our own gallop can have a rest.'

'Will the Jockey Club be happy with that arrangement when you apply for your licence?'

'I think so. Colonel Gilbert said they would be.'

Mr Carey nodded. 'He ought to know.'

Jan closed her eyes, and prayed for him to get on with it, to put her out of her misery.

'I've been thinking about that guarantee you asked me to put up.'

Jan nodded, but didn't trust herself to say anything.

'I'll do it—', he paused, 'when I've seen how you get on this season. It seems to me that if you're asking me to take this risk, I should have a good idea of how well, or not, you are likely to do.'

Jan quivered at the prospect of another delay. 'But Mr Carey,' she said, trying not to sound wheedling, 'I *do* have a track record. I was champion point-to-point trainer in my region last year.'

'But this is a new area and a different yard. It simply may not work as well for you.'

Jan took a deep breath. 'So when do you think you might be in a position to make a definite decision?' she asked.

'Oh, I should think towards the end of February. You will have had a fair few runners by then, weather permitting.'

'OK, fine. Thank you,' Jan said, casting around in her mind for other options, although she realized that there was some justification for Mr Carey's attitude. And he probably had no idea how much it mattered to her. She let herself out of the stable and walked back to his car with him, making polite conversation as best she could, whilst trying to hide her bitter disappointment.

As Mr Carey drove out, Eddie's old Land Rover turned into the drive and the two vehicles crossed. Eddie parked and jumped out, wearing jeans and jodhpur boots. He was carrying a pair of suede chaps. Billy Hanks emerged from the passenger door.

'Morning, boys,' Jan called. 'I've tacked up the horses, though I didn't really think you'd make it after last night.'

'I wasn't up too late,' Billy said.

'No? I bet that Sandy kept you awake, though.'

'No she didn't.' Billy laughed. 'She realized she couldn't get back to Brum without Bernie, so she went back to the party and made him drive her home.'

'And my mother woke me up with a cup of tea this morning,' Eddie groaned. 'Thank God I was on my own.'

'Hmm,' Jan grunted. 'I don't think she has any illusions about your activities.'

'I'm glad you've met her,' Eddie said, 'as you're my sort of surrogate mother up here.'

'Shut up, you cheeky brat,' Jan said, 'and go and get your horse out of his stable. We're late enough as it is.'

Eddie was on Russian Eagle, Billy on Dingle Bay, and Jan rode Sorcerer's Boy. The colonel's horse was a big rangy twelve-year-old bay and a very experienced chaser; Dingle Bay at nine had a couple of point-to-point seasons behind him and two years' hurdling in Ireland. Jan wanted Eagle and Eddie to get used to jumping in company and planned to school them all together after they'd ridden to the top field and had a good half-speed gallop up to the ridge.

On the way out, in bright winter sunshine, they talked about the party, the incidents, the accidents and the damage, emotional and physical.

'Fortunately,' Eddie said, 'there's very little to break in the house and as far as I can see, apart from a bit of wax on the carpets, according to Mother no real harm's been done, though I don't suppose she knows about Sandy, Bernie and matey, here.'

'It seemed like a really good party,' Jan said. 'I didn't think I was going to enjoy it at all, but I had a good laugh with a lot of people.'

'They all liked meeting you, too,' Eddie nodded.

'Especially the ones who hadn't seen you since you first rode pointers round here ten years ago. You might find you've got yourself a few more owners.'

'I could only take horses that were almost fit, though,' Jan said, 'or we'd have no chance of getting them ready in time to do much this season.'

'I tell you one person who wasn't pleased to see you,' Billy laughed, 'Virginia Gilbert.'

Jan shook her head. 'I don't know what her problem is. You'd have thought she'd be quite happy getting Rear Gunner, who was my best horse last year. Never mind her, though. Let's give these horses a bit of a blow.'

She rousted Sorcerer's Boy into a canter until they reached the broad strip of well-seasoned turf that swept up to the top of the field for just under four hundred yards. She squeezed hard with her legs and gave him more rein until he was really stretching his neck. To her great satisfaction, Dingle Bay soon cruised past her, and Russian Eagle kept right up on her horse's tail.

At the top, she called over to Billy. 'How did he feel?'

'Bloody great! He's got plenty more in the tank.'

'How did Eagle feel?'

'In my very amateur experience, absolutely brilliant,' Eddie called back, 'and I still had a good hold of him.'

'We'll work him with Gale Bird at Colonel Gilbert's after the New Year and that'll give us a better idea of his pace. Now let's get back to the schooling fences and see how your jumping is coming on.'

Later, when they were hacking back to the yard, Billy turned to Jan. 'D'you know, if you'd bet me last spring that you were going to get young lover boy here to jump horses like that over fences, I'd have taken as much dosh as you wanted; but now he's doing a great job – as good as anyone riding pointers and better than most.' He turned to grin his approval at Eddie, too.

'You'd better watch out then, Billy,' Eddie said. 'I might nick the championship off you this season.'

'There's more to it than schooling at home,' Billy laughed, 'and I ain't going to tell you what that is.'

16

Christmas Day started like any other for Jan, mucking out and feeding, but only two horses were going to be exercised that day.

Roz and Emma had volunteered to come up and help. The three women got through the jobs in a cheerful mood despite a heavy grey sky hanging over the top of the ridge.

After she'd given the children their breakfast, she put on their warmest coats and piled them into the Land Rover with a collection of hastily wrapped presents. First, she drove down to the village, where she joined the congregation in the big, fifteenth-century church of honeyed stone. Within its quiet, reassuring walls, she tried to pray. Although she was uncertain about the value of prayer, deep down she sometimes felt a need to communicate with a supreme being whom she understood to be God. She was also glad to be there to show her children that there was a side to Christmas which did not involve presents and material things.

Seeing Mr Carey sitting in the front pew like an

old-time squire, she tried to quell her bitter disappointment at his procrastination over her guarantee, and prayed that it would be all right in the end. After the service, touched by the friendship shown to her and the children by other churchgoers, she drove on to her parents' house in Riscombe.

This would be the first Christmas for years that Jan had not spent with John and Mary had wanted to make it as special as she possibly could. The house was a riot of bright tinsel, with a massive Christmas tree and piles of beautifully beribboned gifts for Jan and the children.

Mary was a good, simple cook and she had made a great effort to create a traditional Christmas Day for them all. The sense of celebration was enhanced by a card which had arrived from Jan's brother on Christmas Eve.

Without actually saying so, Ben hinted that he might be returning to England during the coming year; he really was getting somewhere in the music business at last. He didn't say exactly what he was doing, or why he would be coming back, but the thought of seeing him again three years after he'd left had made Mary look ten years younger and, as Megan observed bluntly, she didn't seem to hobble as much as she had.

Inevitably, most of the conversation at lunch was taken up with Jan's progress at Edge Farm and her frustration at trying to put together everything she needed for a successful licence application. Mary admitted that she didn't really see why it was so important. Reg understood, though, but he repeated his advice that Jan should be patient, that if she was as good at the job as he knew she was, it would only be a matter of time.

After lunch they played games with the children, and Reg volunteered to act the horse for little Matthew. 'By God,' he exclaimed to Jan as Matthew urged him on, 'I can tell you've already taught the little fella to use his legs and heels.'

And it was true that, where Megan had always been rather uninterested in the idea of sitting on a horse, tiny Matthew had already demonstrated a healthy fascination with them.

'You'll have to get him a little pony, like we got you,' Mary said. 'You can see now he's going to be keen.'

'He's going to have to be bloody keen before I start filling up my yard with ponies, I can tell you.' Jan laughed, disguising her fervent hope that at least one of her two children had inherited her enthusiasm.

Back in the caravan that night, tucked up under her duvet with the stove still glowing, and content to be on her own, Jan thought about the year that had just passed. Despite the obstacles in her way, her disastrous mishandling of the sale of Stonewall and the subsequent deadlock with Harold, she felt that she had made some good decisions and had achieved a little measurable success. She had established a presence in her new yard, albeit unproven, as Mr Carey had so bluntly pointed out. But whether her horses were good enough to win, when push came to shove, she would only know once they'd raced the opposition.

Most of her owners were new and had lodged their horses with her entirely on trust. She still found it amazing that they had shown such loyalty before the season had even started. They had, as Eddie had hinted, clubbed together to buy her a new set of exercise tack and sheets to add to the half-dozen Reg had given her for her birthday.

But after six months of running a point-to-point yard, she was certain that if she was ever going to make any kind of living, and a life for her children, she had to get a professional licence and get it pretty damn soon.

Before she slept, her mind drifted from happy anticipation at maybe seeing her brother again to less comfortable thoughts about the trip she and the children would be making to Olwen Hardy at Stonewall in two days' time, which led on inevitably to Harold Powell and his excessive greed. Despite Gerry's vigilance, with some help from Eddie, no one had seen Amos Smith, so there'd still been no chance of hearing his version of the conversation with Harold. His cousin claimed that Amos hadn't been seen since Gerry had first spoken to him. Jan knew the loose ends of the incident were a potential time bomb unless they could be tied up, especially before her next licence application came up for review should Victor agree to back her. The thought that, in the meantime, Harold had deliberately sent Rear Gunner to Virginia Gilbert to compete against her, made her blood boil.

Thinking of Virginia, James McNeill and Harold, she found it extraordinary how easy it was to make enemies she felt she'd done nothing to deserve, and before a single runner had been sent out from her new yard.

On a brighter Boxing Day morning four horses from Edge Farm were going to the meet of the Evesham Vale Hunt on the wide, grassy margins of Broadway's main street in front of the Amberley Arms.

Jan had fond memories of the event from the years before she'd gone to live in Wales; she'd always enjoyed being part of a profoundly English tradition in such a pretty setting, and she was really looking forward to putting in an appearance again.

Edge Farm had been sending out horses to hunt regularly since the start of the season because each horse had to have a card signed by the Master of the Hunt to confirm that it had been out with them at least seven times before it was allowed to run in point-to-point races the following season. And Jan had always felt that hunting provided horses with such a natural environment in which to jump, plus all the excitement of being with others, that it went a long way to preparing them for the more artificial circumstances of the steeplechase course.

She was up at seven to give the horses a small feed before plaiting their manes and tails. Edward, Annabel and Roz came in soon after nine to tack the horses and get them loaded onto the lorry. They were all looking forward to the day's hunting and bantered competitively about who was going to do what if the hunt really took off. Jan felt a surge of pride, seeing fit and obviously well-kept animals being so beautifully turned out from her yard.

Reg and Mary arrived in their Land Rover to take the children to the meet. Afterwards they were going to follow the progress of the hounds as best they could from the road. Reg had always enjoyed doing this; although he'd never followed a hunt on horseback, he had been following 'on foot' nearly all his life. Now, in retirement, it provided most of his social life for the winter months.

Since Jan had come back to Gloucestershire, it hadn't taken her long to become a recognized member of the hunt. There were still a number of followers who'd been hunting ten years before, whom she'd known since she'd last been a regular. There was also a big contingent of newcomers, mostly from London, who believed the best way to integrate with their new rural environment was to hunt across it.

A lot of the locals suffered from a knee-jerk prejudice against these rich townies who could afford all the best horses, but Jan took them as they came. She had soon concluded that, if they were genuine with her, she was ready to reciprocate. As a result, she'd already had some enquiries about training their pointers the following season. When she told them she was hoping to train National Hunt horses, most people had still been interested, mainly because her horses always stood out anywhere as the fittest and the best turned out.

Virginia Gilbert didn't hunt often; she didn't have to qualify her horses and she was nearly always racing on a Saturday. But on Boxing Day she was there with an entourage of friends and hangers on, and making it very clear that, in the pecking order of racing people out with the hunt that day, she ruled the roost.

Jan refused to be intimidated and smiled at her as she rode past from the lorry to the meet.

Scattered among the large crowd of people on foot who had come to enjoy the traditional spectacle, hotel staff were handing round glasses of mulled wine, ginger cup and port, with trays of small sausage rolls that flaked all over the horses' plaits and the riders' coats as they ate them.

Jan looked at Eddie and smiled at the splendid picture he made in a gleaming top hat he was wearing specially for the occasion. He was obviously planning to make the most of the day and walked Russian Eagle around the gathering. A lot of people there seemed pleased to see him, although, Jan was amused to see, some kept their distance, presumably not willing to be tarred by association with the recent demise of the Sullivans. Jan was well aware that there would always be a few old-fashioned snobs who resented a man with

Ron Sullivan's working-class origins buying a house like Windrush Grange, and living there for twenty years without making any effort to blend with his neighbours. As far as they were concerned, Ron's son was no better, however popular he might be with the girls in the area.

Reg walked Megan among the horses to where Jan and Annabel stood side by side, as quietly as they could on horses who were now stamping their feet and rattling the bits in their mouths, impatient to move off. He lifted the little girl up to Jan, who straddled her across the front of her saddle for a few moments. But Megan didn't enjoy it, and wriggled vigorously until Jan handed her back down.

'I'm afraid she's not going to take to it, Dad,' Jan laughed.

'Don't you believe it. We'll get her hunting soon as she's big enough – so long as they don't ban it,' he added with a disparaging cough.

At that moment the huntsman tootled his horn at the hounds, who gathered around him as he moved off up the main street among a sea of waving tails. When the master followed, Jan and her party tucked in close behind. If hounds started to hunt early on, they had no intention of getting caught behind a field of people whose horses wouldn't jump. Unlike a lot of other point-to-point trainers, Jan truly believed in hunting her horses properly, not just putting in an appearance at the meet then lurking out of harm's way until one o'clock when the master would sign their cards. She also believed that a horse who was nervous in company or who had gone a little stale could be very effectively cured with a season's hunting.

It was only as they were moving away that Jan first noticed Bernie Sutcliffe among the onlookers. She heard him shout across the road to Eddie. 'You look after my horse, mind.'

Jan wondered how Eddie would take it, or how many people knew he'd had to sell the horse, but, to his credit, she thought, he shouted back cheerfully. 'I'll make sure he has a great day. I'll bring him back safe and sound, don't you worry.'

A moment later, both she and Eddie spotted a young blonde girl standing just behind Bernie, who turned to her and pointed at Russian Eagle as they rode past.

'I see Bernie's got himself a replacement for Sandy. That's lucky.'

'I'm not sure it is, as a matter of fact,' Eddie said, more quietly. 'That's Sharon Goldstone and I really don't think she can see much in Bernie to attract her. After all, she's got lots of money of her own.'

'And she's already sampled the charms of Eddie Sullivan,' Jan added with a grin.

Eddie was about to answer when a terrier on a long lead shot out and snapped ferociously at Russian Eagle's legs. The big horse, normally reluctant to make a fuss, half reared and covered the next fifty yards in a high-stepping, fretful canter with Eddie trying to sit still and keep his dignity.

Jan laughed. 'If you fall off, that topper won't be much help to you.'

'Of course I'm not going to fall off,' he hissed back in embarrassment.

Russian Eagle behaved beautifully for the rest of the morning. Eddie kept him near the front with Roz and Annabel, and Jan was delighted to see that the horse didn't look twice at any of the hedges or post and rail fences they came across over the next few hours.

At a long break outside a dense covert, Jan and her team gathered to eat the sandwiches they had brought and chat about the morning's hunting. But the moment was spoiled for Jan, when Annabel suddenly exclaimed, 'Oh, God! Jan, you're not going to like this. Look!'

Annabel nodded towards the gate of the field the hunt was standing in. A group of three horses and riders had just trotted through, led by Virginia Gilbert.

Eddie didn't understand what the fuss was about. 'Virginia's been out all morning,' he said. 'She was at the meet. I've been chatting to her a bit, winding her up that I might move this chap to her yard.'

'She probably believed you,' Jan said. 'She's really rubbing my nose in it today. She's just gone and changed horses, though we haven't done nearly enough to justify it.'

'So?' Eddie said. 'Maybe she's qualified one and wants a bit of fun now.'

'I don't think so. The horse she's on now is Harold Powell's. That's Rear Gunner.'

The week between Christmas and New Year was a busy one at Edge Farm. Jan had a lot of work to do with horses who were getting close to full fitness. She was pleased to find that seeing Virginia out on Rear Gunner had simply sharpened her determination. Furthermore, Eddie had come back at the end of the day and announced that he had found himself next to Virginia late in the afternoon. He had asked her point-blank if she was planning to run the horse in the Foxhunters'; she had said she was.

That's it, Jan thought. *The gauntlet's been thrown down.*

After a couple of busy days, Jan managed to squeeze in a trip to Stonewall with the children to see Olwen.

Over a strained lunch, her mother-in-law questioned Jan sharply on what she was doing about Harold Powell. Jan didn't intend to tell her what she and Eddie suspected and the confrontation they'd had at Harold's house the last time she'd brought the children over. It took all her patience to explain that solicitors had been instructed and she didn't want to rush matters. She also kept off the subject of her licence application, knowing this would be treated with barbed scepticism.

However, she recognized that Olwen had made a

great effort for the children and had bought them some beautiful presents. Jan tried to keep their normal antagonism to a minimum and, as they left, she promised they would come again soon.

Jan didn't see Bernie again until the end of the week, when she saw at once that Sharon Goldstone wasn't with him, nor was any other candidate to replace the flighty Sandy. Jan prayed that he wouldn't decide to home in on her.

Most of the people involved with Edge Farm had gone in a minibus to a New Year's Eve party at one of the clubs Eamon Fallon ran on the outskirts of Cheltenham. For the first time, Jan began to get an idea of Eamon's business. The club was more sophisticated than Jan had expected and it was clear that he was held in awe by some of the people who worked for him.

After they'd eaten dinner, which she found surprisingly good, Jan still didn't feel comfortable and was unable to relax. She wasn't enjoying herself much when Bernie Sutcliffe, who'd been hovering all evening, finally sat down in an empty chair beside her and draped his arm around her. 'It's time you and I got better acquainted,' he said.

Jan's heart sank.

'I feel I know you pretty well already, Bernie,' she said lightly. 'You come down to the yard often enough.'

Bernie stiffened. 'And why shouldn't I? I'm paying you to look after my two horses.'

'It's OK, Bernie, I wasn't complaining. Of course I like owners to take an interest in their horses and I know you'll have great fun with yours.'

'Do you think it's safe to let Eddie go hunting on Russian Eagle, though?'

'As safe as anyone else and the horse has to be hunted to qualify him to run. Anyway, Boxing Day was his last day, so from now on we'll be concentrating on serious work. He'll probably run for the first time on the nineteenth.'

'As soon as that? Will he be ready?'

'He's not far off being ready now.'

'And you're happy about Eddie riding him?'

Jan looked Bernie straight in the eyes. 'Completely. You ask Billy Hanks what he thinks of Eddie's riding.'

Bernie looked back. 'I will. I will.'

Jan felt a nervous twinge. She had promised Eddie he would keep the ride on Eagle, but in truth, if Bernie felt like it, he could have anyone on the horse and he had to be convinced that Eddie had a better chance than any other amateur jockey.

Bernie stood up abruptly. 'Right. It's time you and I had a dance,' he said with a leer that Jan couldn't believe he thought was attractive.

Trying not to show her reluctance, she got to her feet and tried to smile compliantly. At least the disco wasn't playing anything slow and smoochy.

Bernie's dancing looked very uncomfortable. He

contorted himself into a series of bony, angular shapes, grimacing and clicking his fingers randomly and out of time with the music. Jan was fit and lithe from her regular riding and in good shape for dancing. When she'd danced with Eddie at his party she'd really enjoyed it. But tonight, with Bernie, she couldn't. She was almost certain that Bernie was going to make a move on her and she dreaded having to fend him off.

When the record came to an end, she flashed him a big smile. 'That was great! I'm just going to the loo. See you in a minute.' She walked off the dance floor and headed for the ladies' without looking back. When she emerged, she saw Eddie and some of the others sitting round their table. She caught a glimpse of Bernie's back at the bar so she went and sat down next to Eddie. 'Look, I don't want you to take this the wrong way, but would you mind dancing with me if Bernie looks like he's going to ask me again?'

'Sure,' Eddie grinned. 'It would be a pleasure, but you could try Billy, as well, otherwise Bernie might think I'm your favourite.'

From then on, each time Bernie came up Jan made sure she was dancing with either Billy or Eddie. In between, Bernie was drinking from two magnums of champagne he'd insisted on buying and sat hunched sulkily in his chair, staring at the dancers. It was after one o'clock, and his fifth failure to get Jan to dance, that he finally lost it.

He marched across the floor and pushed himself between Jan and Billy. 'You can't do this,' he shouted.

'You're taking the piss, aren't you? I can see you all laughing. How the hell would you pay the bloody bills on your place if I wasn't paying you all that money? I've had enough of you lot, all thinking you know so bloody much. Well, if you do, why haven't you got more money?' He was spitting as his voice rose and everyone had stopped dancing to watch the row unfold.

'Calm down, Bernie,' Jan said. 'I'm only having a dance.'

'Having a dance? With that randy young sod? He's not interested in dancing.'

'Well that's all he's getting. You're out of order, Bernie. This is meant to be a celebration. Nobody's laughing at you.'

'They won't now, not now I'm taking both my horses out of your yard.'

Eddie was standing behind Bernie. He'd been looking apprehensive, signalling to Jan to ease off. Now his face fell and he paled.

'Hang on, Bernie,' he said, coming round to face him. 'You'd be crazy to move them now, just before the season starts. I promise you, I wasn't laughing either.'

'You, you toffee-nosed, potless prat!' Bernie turned on him and snarled. 'Do you think I'm going to take any advice from you?' Shaking with rage and, it seemed, with fright at his own anger, he looked back at Jan. 'I'm telling you, them horses are going. You'll be hearing from me.'

He continued to glare at her for a few moments with his jaw quivering, before he turned abruptly and walked off the dance floor, to a ripple of applause from some of the drunken revellers.

Jan hardly slept. The party had broken up as soon as Bernie left and the journey back in the minibus had passed in almost total silence. When her alarm clock finally woke her at seven-thirty, she reckoned she'd been asleep for no more than twenty minutes.

Feeling sick and weak, she made herself a cup of tea before the children woke up and sat at her table in the caravan, looking out at a grey dawn trying to seep through the blanket of clouds draped over the Cotswolds' edge.

Somehow, she knew, she had mismanaged the whole affair yesterday. She was beginning to realize that if she had to rely entirely on the whims of people who sent their horses to her, she must learn to handle them with kid gloves.

It wasn't as if Bernie was one of those owners who was going to tell her what to do, or when she should or shouldn't run their horses. Up until now, he'd been prepared to let her guide him, accepting his own lack of knowledge. But because she hadn't given enough thought to the party at Eamon's club, which she hadn't even enjoyed, it looked as if she'd lost one owner and badly upset another. Eamon had looked extremely annoyed about the fracas, although no damage had been done. For the next two days, every time the telephone rang, Jan picked it up expecting Bernie to tell her that a lorry was on its way to collect his horses.

The call came eventually on 3 January.

'Hello, Jan? It's Bernie here.'

Jan held her breath for a moment. She could detect no aggression in the five words, only a hint of self-effacement.

'Hi, Bernie. Still got a headache?'

'Not now. But I did have. I don't usually drink a lot.'

Jan waited. She didn't trust herself to say the right thing next.

'Look,' Bernie went on. 'I made a bit of fool of myself, I realize that. And I know it would be daft to take the horses away before you've even had a chance to run them.'

Jan expelled a long breath. 'Well, it would really,' she tried to say calmly.

'So,' Bernie sighed. 'I'll leave them where they are. I'll be down some time to see them.'

'Whenever you like, Bernie,' Jan said. 'You're always welcome,' she added and, at that moment, she meant it.

For the next two weeks only a few mild frosts upset the rhythm of Jan's training regime. The horses were working so consistently that she found herself almost waiting for the next setback. In the meantime, she had qualified them all with the Evesham Vale and could concentrate on bringing each one to the boil, ready for their first race.

The earliest point-to-point Jan planned to go to was on 19 January, a Saturday meeting in Wiltshire where she'd entered four horses, including Russian Eagle in the men's Open race. When she rang Eddie at his shop to tell him he was overjoyed.

He came round that evening. 'Thank God, we're going to be under orders at last!'

Jan knew what his priorities were. 'How's your dad getting on with his cash-flow problems?'

'He's managed to keep the Italians at bay with a little bit of dough. He says he's convinced them that there's more to come. As long as they believe him, they won't go over the top and, thank God, they haven't sussed his connection with my mother's house.'

'Why don't the other banks he owed money to know about it?'

'There's no reason why they should. Even if they did, the proper banks couldn't do anything about it because she owns half the house and never gave her consent for it to be mortgaged.'

Jan knew that, for Eddie, Russian Eagle's race was the first step in his campaign to save his father from unscrupulous creditors. She also knew he was placing unjustifiable hope on winning the Foxhunters' at

Liverpool, but she'd made up her mind that her best strategy, as a friend, was to support him. She couldn't see that any good would be done by constantly reminding him that it was, at best, a very long shot. After all, every once in a while, long shots did win, if not always for the right reasons.

17

The night before her first race of the season was one of Jan's worst since the weeks immediately after John's death. She was conscious that it was just over a year since then, and she had vivid memories of his last, horrendous weeks and of watching his coffin being lowered into the black peaty soil of St Barnabas's churchyard.

She was woken by her alarm after she'd barely slept and she felt horrible for the first half-hour of the morning. Somehow, though, as she always did and with the help of a few cups of strong tea, she managed to kick herself into action and every time her jitters returned she quashed them.

The anxiety of knowing that, if she was to get her licence, she had first to prove to Victor Carey she hadn't lost her touch as a trainer, combined with all the other trials she had endured over her first seven months at Edge Farm, had brought her close to paranoia, she thought. Showing not just Victor Carey but the world that Edge Farm Stables was a fully functioning racehorse training establishment had become almost an obsession, far more than it had ever been at Stonewall. Now so much seemed to hang on its success.

But she made sure she didn't let her fear show to Emma, Roz and Joe, who were coming with her to the races.

Having set off with an hour to spare, they arrived early and Jan drove her lorry into an empty field reserved for horseboxes beside the race course of ten fences. The track was laid out between flags below a crest of beech trees on a gentle, south-facing chalk down near Devizes.

She looked around at a scene that made her heart beat faster and felt at once the familiar pre-race tightening of the guts, that dread of the start mixed with a yearning for her horses to come home safely.

The cloud cover was high and only a mild wind stroked the top of the winter corn in the surrounding fields. There was already a large turnout of point-to-point fans, keen to see in the new season. An hour before the first race the car park was filling up with picnic parties equipped for all weather conditions and a crowd of people ebbed and flowed between the marquees and trade stands.

Stepping down from the cab, Jan breathed in the air, knowing that she truly was a part of this scene. Even when she moved on to the grown-up world of National Hunt racing, she knew she would never forget all she had learned and the joy she had known in the amateur game.

'Morning, guv'nor!' The deep, familiar voice floated among the cluster of lorries, and Jan turned to see Eddie and Billy walking towards her with broad smiles on their faces. Eddie was carrying a soft tan leather bag and Billy a black nylon Umbro, which, Jan thought, neatly summed up the differences between them.

'Morning, boys. I hope you've been behaving yourselves.'

'I can't speak for him,' Billy nodded at Eddie, 'but I was tucked up in bed well before ten last night, on my own with the *Racing Post*.'

'Give us a hand with the ramp, then,' Jan said, and shot down the long bolts that secured the tailgate to the back of the box. 'I had to put Eagle on last,' she said, 'so we'll get him off and let him have a stroll for twenty minutes while I get the others ready.'

They lowered the ramp. Jan jumped up and untied Eagle's rope. She led him down with his head held high, his nostrils flared as he lifted his knees in short, bouncy steps, looking around with quick, jerky movements. He knew something unusual was going to happen and that things were expected of him.

'Crikey!' Eddie said with a hint of uneasiness. 'He looks a bit full of himself.'

'You didn't want me to bring him half-asleep, did you?'

'But he looks like he's been on wacky baccy.'

Jan led the horse in a short circle behind the lorry.

'He's fine! What do you want in a race – a Morris Minor or a Ferrari?'

Eddie laughed nervously. 'All right, all right. It's just that I've never seen him like this; he's absolutely bursting.'

'He knows what he's here for. And I tell you what – I think he'll give you a bloody good run. What about you, though? You look a bit peaky.'

Eddie made a face. 'I didn't sleep a wink last night.'

'Oh Gawd!' Roz said with a loud groan. 'Who were you with?'

Eddie looked hurt. 'I was on my own,' he protested. 'I was staying with my mother in London and drove down this morning.'

'Were you really that nervous?' Jan asked more sympathetically. 'I didn't think anything ever worried you.'

'I'm all right now,' Eddie answered, 'but do you think I can do it?'

Billy laughed. 'You look like you're about to fill your nappy.'

'Shut up, Billy,' Jan said. 'I need to build his confidence and I won't have you destroying it. Eddie, I know you can do it.' She handed Eagle to Joe Paley, who walked away, talking to the big horse.

Billy was due to ride in the first race and headed for the jockeys' changing room while Jan and Roz led out the other two horses – Arrow Star and Supercrack, one of Frank Jellard's – who were running in different divisions of the maiden race.

While they were grooming, Penny Price arrived with her mother – a small, nervous woman, who hung back, evidently overawed by the idea of being involved with racehorses.

Penny flung her arms around her big gelding's neck. 'Hello, Arrow boy! How are you? Cor, you look well. Doesn't he look well, Jan?'

'He's been doing really nicely, as I told you, and his jumping's been brilliant. I know we thought he might need more time, but I'm not a bit worried about it now.'

'What does Billy think?' Penny asked anxiously.

'He's happy.'

Jan saw tears of excitement in Penny's eyes as she gazed at her pride and joy. 'Gosh,' she said. 'I can hardly believe that at last my baby's going racing and you've made him look so like a racehorse!'

'Thanks,' said Jan. 'I've done my best and it's what he's bred for.'

Penny looked at her watch. 'Oh, my God, there's a whole hour still to go. I don't know what I'm going to do with myself.'

'Come back to the car and have a cup of tea,' her mother suggested tentatively.

Penny nodded. 'OK, Mum.' She walked away with frequent glances back over her shoulder at her horse.

'She worships you. You'd better do bloody well,' Jan murmured into the horse's ear.

About an hour later Penny Price was hugging Arrow Star with tears running down her face as he stood in a makeshift winner's slot at the edge of the timber-railed paddock.

'I just can't believe it! I can't believe it.' She shook her head and sobbed, as her mother stood by, wondering what she should do. Penny turned to Jan with her face as white as a ghost, streaked with her tears and the horse's sweat. 'Thank you, Jan, so very, very much!'

'Just doing my job,' Jan said, more lightly than she felt, as she tried to keep her emotions under control. Of all the people who had entrusted horses to her care, she had most wanted to see Penny have a winner, and that it should be her first of the new season as well as the first she'd sent out from Edge Farm only increased her pleasure.

But the big buzz for Jan was that Arrow Star's win confirmed the state of all her other horses and her judgement as to which were ready to race.

Billy Hanks was also rather pleased with himself for getting off the mark on the first day as he bounced out of the changing room ten minutes later for his next ride on Frank Jellard's horse, Supercrack.

The brown gelding could only deliver a third in his division of the maiden, but Jan wasn't complaining. She knew he had room to improve. She and Roz led him back to the lorry and were just about to load him, when Bernie Sutcliffe strutted up.

Jan had been dreading meeting Bernie. Since his

drunken threat on New Year's Eve to remove the horses and his subsequent climbdown, Bernie had been to the yard only once, a week before, to see his two horses. Then, despite his experience at Eamon's club, he had tried to persuade Jan to have dinner with him. Jan genuinely couldn't find a babysitter that evening; at least, she would have had to look further than she was prepared to for the sake of an evening with Bernie. He'd gone off with all the smouldering resentment of a thwarted teenager.

Of course Bernie had already heard about Jan's win in the second race, which he seemed to accept as normal, so he couldn't understand why she hadn't repeated the achievement in the third race.

'Bernie, there were fifteen horses in each division; one of ours beat fourteen of them, and the other beat twelve. I'm quite happy about that.'

'Well, what about this open race, then? Are we going to win that?'

'As I'm not a prophet and I don't have a crystal ball, I wouldn't like to say, but, as you can see the horse is fit and ready to run; he's schooled well at home; I've really got him lifting his feet over the tops of the fences because some of these are very solid.'

'What about him?' Bernie nodded towards Eddie, who had just walked into view.

'Eddie's well up to the job. And he's giving the horse plenty of help – they make a good combination.'

Bernie turned to Eddie, and shouted at him as he approached. ''Ere, you're not overweight, are you? We don't want him carting round a load of stuff he doesn't need to.'

'Don't you worry, Bernie,' Eddie said, trying a little too hard to sound confident, Jan thought. 'I'm right on the mark, so I won't be carrying any dead weight and I've got a decent-sized saddle.'

To see Eagle's race, Jan and her team wanted to watch from the bonnet of Eddie's Land Rover, which was parked well up the hill, giving them a view of the whole course. Bernie wanted them all to watch from his Jaguar, right on the rails by the finish, from where half the course was invisible. But, outvoted, he puffed up the hill with the others, where he perched on the bonnet of the Land Rover and grumbled about the disgusting state of the vehicle.

In the paddock before the race, Jan had taken Eddie's arm and given it a quick squeeze. 'Don't try to start winning until the second half of the final circuit,' she'd said. 'But don't lose touch with the others on the way round. Just jump him off quietly and let him keep his place, gaining a length or so each jump. Ease him back if you get too near the front. He won't need a lot of asking when you want to quicken; take a tighter grip and he'll fly. Just look at him now!'

Jan was right. Russian Eagle looked superb, striding round beside Roz as if the rest of the runners didn't exist. Bernie, unfamiliar with the scene, had wandered away across the ring to have a closer look at his horse.

'I just hope I don't let him down,' Eddie said quietly, so only Jan could hear.

She detected a faint tremor in his voice. She looked at him again and took in the pale greyness of his face. 'Don't worry! I've told you, I wouldn't let you go if I didn't think you could do a proper job. It's my reputation too, you know.'

He smiled weakly. 'You'd better be right for both our sakes, then.'

'Aren't I always?'

'Yes, Jan,' Eddie grinned. 'Without exception.'

Just then the 'Get mounted' signal was given. Roz turned the horse to face inwards and Jan legged her jockey into the saddle, squeezing his leg and giving him a last encouraging smile. 'Go for it, Eddie.'

Now, up on the bank watching Russian Eagle circle with the twelve other runners before the starter tried to get them into some sort of straight line, she could easily understand the tension Eddie must have been feeling. She gazed at the pair through her binoculars. Eagle still seemed to be on his toes, but at least compliant; he was going where Eddie was asking him to go and he wasn't throwing any silly tantrums at the short delay.

A moment later they were off.

Eddie quickly settled Eagle in tenth place as they came up to the first fence. He eased him back and gave himself time to place the horse right. He took off in a trajectory a foot higher than any of the horses beside him and flew past them in the air. It was as good a jump as any Jan had seen him do at home.

What really excited Jan, though, was that Eddie was managing to sit on the horse and stay in perfect harmony with him. He wasn't fussing him or pestering him, but keeping his hands steady, moving them forward only with the animal's neck each time he stretched for a jump. As the field passed the winning post for the first time with a circuit to race, Eddie was lying in the middle of the field. Behind him two of the runners, seemingly brought out too early in the season, were showing signs of tiredness. Pointlessly, their jockeys had already pulled their whips out.

On the bottom straight there was a row of three plain fences, handily spaced. The two leading horses took them well, a couple more fiddled and made mistakes at the first and hadn't recovered by the time they were turning the long, right-handed bend heading towards home. Eagle had taken the fences in his stride with easy grace, earning an admiring remark from the course commentator.

Jan, gazing transfixed through her glasses, waited for Eddie to pick up his horse and ask him for more.

But Eddie sat still, cruising past two more until he was lying third and just five lengths off the leaders.

'Come on, Eddie. For God's sake, pick him up!' she grunted through clenched teeth.

Bernie looked up at her sharply. 'What's wrong?'

'Nothing's wrong; it's just that he's leaving it a bit

late.' But they all gasped together as Eagle stood right off the penultimate fence, flew it again with a spectacular leap into second place and started to close the gap on the leader.

Jan, Roz and Joe were all screaming their heads off; Jan felt as if her lungs would burst. She was sure the horse could hear her. Even Bernie allowed himself one discreet, plaintive, 'Come on, my son!'

Eagle reached the last fence a stride behind, made a length in the air and landed with his nose at the other's girth. The leader's jockey looked over his shoulder, lifted his stick for the first time and brought it down hard on his horse's rump. Eddie leaned forward, working his legs and starting to pump his fists over Eagle's withers. The big horse kept on, inching forward until his nose was at the other's shoulder. Two strides more and he reached his neck. And the finishing post.

Jan wanted to yell, *Eddie, you fucking idiot, why didn't you bloody well ask him when I told you to?* But she knew Bernie was beside her and she had no intention of blaming Eddie in front of him.

Jan watched for a few more seconds as Eddie tried to pull up Russian Eagle, to make sure the horse was still sound, but they galloped for another quarter of a mile before Eddie finally managed to stop him. When they had turned and were trotting back to the paddock, Jan lowered her glasses and looked at Bernie with a grin as big as she could muster.

'There you are! A brilliant race! Another hundred yards and he'd have made it!'

'But he didn't, did he.'

'For God's sake, Bernie! He ran a blinder. I'm sure he'll be winning next time out.'

'Maybe next time the jockey will know what to do.'

'Bernie, he rode him beautifully! Frankly, I'm amazed how well he did; he hardly moved on him.'

'Well, maybe he should have got his whip out like the other bloke, then he'd have got up there and won.'

'Not every horse responds to the whip, you know. It positively stops some of them. I certainly wouldn't have wanted the horse hit.'

Bernie looked at her. 'All right,' he said. 'At least we got placed, so it's not a complete donkey I've bought.'

'He certainly isn't,' Jan insisted. 'That was a very competitive race; several horses in it have won races. Did you look at the form?' She pulled out the printed yellow guide, which gave the ratings and past performances of each runner, and waved it under his nose.

''Course I did, but you always said this was a good horse. I paid six grand for it, remember.'

'At least you now know you've got good value for your money.'

'Not till he's won, I haven't,' Bernie snapped and set off down the hill towards the marquees.

Jan watched him go.

'What an ungrateful little shit!' Roz burst out indignantly, almost before he was out of earshot.

'Right, we've got to get down there,' Jan said. 'You

run on, Roz – you're faster than me. Go and lead Eagle in. Do you know where to put him?'

'Next to where we put Arrow Star?'

'That's it,' Jan laughed, quite happy, despite the initial disappointment of Eagle's race, to have had a good win and a very strong second on her first day's pointing for over seven months.

On her way to the paddock, she bumped into Billy, who was carrying his saddle from the no-hoper he'd had to pull up.

'Eddie should have got up there,' he grunted.

'I know, Billy, I know, but if you'd ridden your first race as well as that, you'd be entitled to be proud of yourself.'

'That's not the point, though, is it? Like you always say, what you need is winners and lots of them.'

'Listen, I know what I need, and it's not advice from you right now,' Jan said sharply and carried on towards the paddock, where she could see Roz leading Russian Eagle into the second slot. As they reached it, Eddie jumped off with his legs buckling slightly. Jan regretted her sharpness with Billy almost at once, but she had to sustain her loyalty to Eddie. She told herself that he really had ridden a cracking race for his first time out, and she wanted nothing to detract from that for his sake. She also wanted nothing to diminish his chances of riding Russian Eagle when he finally ran in the Aintree Foxhunters'.

By the time Bernie had seen his horse clapped into the ring and half a dozen complete strangers had come up to tell him how well his horse had run, and how he was bound to win soon, he seemed mollified. 'When you've got back and put the horse to bed, I'll get you all a meal at that steakhouse by the motorway at Tewkesbury,' he offered, including everyone except Billy in the invitation. Jan guessed he still hadn't forgiven Billy for going off with Sandy. That, at least, would deter him from suggesting or, worse still, insisting that Billy should ride Eagle next time.

'Great!' Jan said, and turned to Eddie, who had just come back from the weighing room. 'Do you want to come and have a steak with all of us later? Bernie's treat.'

'Yes, please. I could do with a steak after that.'

'You could have had two steaks if you'd have won,' Bernie said.

'Next time, Bernie. Next time.'

They walked back to the lorry with Russian Eagle, patting him and telling him what a magnificent animal he was. Jan had to admit, she couldn't have asked more from him, under the circumstances.

'Well?' she asked Eddie. 'How does it feel?'

Eddie grinned. 'So bloody good – and that's just coming second! Winning must be better than sex.'

'Let's hope you get there next time, then,' Jan said with a laugh.

Once Eagle had been washed down and scraped dry, he had a long drink and was allowed a few minutes' grazing before they loaded him with the others and heaved up the ramp of the lorry.

It was a two-hour haul home. Putting the horses away, getting themselves showered and changed took Jan and her team another hour, so it was nearly nine before they arrived at the steakhouse, where Bernie was waiting for them impatiently. They were all so tired that the dinner wasn't a great success.

Bernie sent back his steak twice, first because it was overdone and, again, when its replacement was underdone. Eddie seemed too exhausted to say much, and nobody really wanted to talk to Bernie.

Afterwards, when they'd said their thank yous and goodbyes to Bernie, Roz and Joe went off to the loos and Eddie walked back to the Land Rover with Jan, talking about the race. It was the first time they had been alone.

'Look, Eddie, you rode a great race and I don't want to take anything away from you because it was your first ride, but I really think you could have won if you'd pushed him along coming into the final bend, like I told you.'

'I know,' Eddie admitted. 'I suppose I thought that at the time. It was just that the horse was going so well, and I was so chuffed with the way he was jumping, I didn't want to do anything to upset his rhythm.'

'That's what I thought,' Jan said, 'but you did start

to ride him out right at the end, didn't you, and it worked. Next time, start a lot earlier. And it wouldn't do any harm just to wave the whip, even if you don't want to use it. I did notice, too, that you looked fairly knackered when you came into the unsaddling enclosure.'

'Next time,' Eddie said, 'I'll be fitter and we'll win.'

They had reached the Land Rover, which was in a dark corner of the car park. Eddie shrugged his shoulders. 'I'm sorry I let you down,' he said.

Without thinking, Jan reached up a hand and put it behind his neck. 'Don't be so stupid. You rode a great race and I'm proud of you. You've been a good pupil.'

'Thanks,' Eddie grinned. He wrapped his long arms around Jan and gave her a quick squeeze. 'And you've been a brilliant mistress.'

'What's that!?' Bernie Sutcliffe's voice cut through the air like a knife.

Jan almost jumped out of her skin. Eddie released her and spun round to see Bernie, dimly visible in the glow of a distant light, glaring at them.

'I don't believe it!' Bernie said. 'What's all that about a brilliant mistress? Are you two having some kind of relationship or what? I mean – what's going on?'

'Good God, Bernie! Don't come creeping up like that. Of course we're not having a scene. He said I was a good mistress in the sense of *teaching*, you know, as in race riding.'

'And having a good snog too, by the look of things,' Bernie snapped.

'Look,' Eddie said coldly, 'if Jan and I wanted a snog, as you put it, that would be our business and none of yours, but as it happens, we don't. I just gave Jan a thank-you hug for all she's done for me, OK? It's not such a difficult idea to grasp is it? Or do you only hug people when you're having sex with them?'

'You'd better watch it,' Bernie glared at him sharply. He turned back to Jan. 'I'll be in touch, all right?'

He spun round and walked quickly across the car park to his Jaguar.

Jan and Eddie didn't speak for a moment.

'What a horrible little toad,' Eddie said eventually. 'He deserves a good thumping.'

'Yes, Eddie, but I'm afraid he owns that bloody horse of yours, so whatever you do, don't do anything else to upset him. Right?'

'Jan! Jan! Come and look at Eagle!' Roz's voice wasn't normally short on volume, but in the tack room Jan could hardly hear it over the whine of the wind and the rattle of rain on the iron roof.

The morning after the glory of Arrow Star's win, and Russian Eagle's impressive second, life had returned rudely to the cold, wet and inglorious mood of an English winter. Jan had slept very little in her caravan the night before; even her wood-burner hadn't been enough to stop the cold wind forcing its way through cracks in the walls she hadn't known existed until then.

She was already thinking the worst as she pulled her waxed hat down over her head and wrapped John's old mac tightly around her to run across the open space to Eagle's box.

She shook most of the rain from her coat and let herself into the stable, where Roz was holding Eagle in a head-collar and rope.

'Look!' Roz groaned. 'I'll just walk him in the barn.' She started to lead the horse out. Before he had even left the stable, Jan could see he was as lame as a cat on his off-foreleg.

'OK, Roz, don't bother to take him out. I can see.' Jan walked over to the horse and ran her hand gently down the hurting leg, right to the crown of his hoof. She swore to herself. The lower shin and fetlock joint were severely swollen and positively hot to the touch. 'I wonder what the hell he's done. He's given himself a knock somehow, but it wasn't showing yesterday.'

'Poor Eddie,' Roz gasped.

'Never mind poor Eddie! What about poor Russian Eagle?'

'Well, of course I'm sorry for him too, but he'll mend and Eddie hasn't got much time to win a race to qualify the horse for the Foxhunters'.'

Jan sighed. 'Yeah; well, there's not much I can do about that.'

When Annabel came up for lunch in the caravan with Jan and the children, she brought a video of *The Sound of Music* for Megan and a bottle of wine for her and Jan.

After Roz had left that morning, Jan finally got round to opening the previous day's post. If Eagle's lameness had depressed her, one of the bills she received completely extinguished the lingering glow of victory from the day before. She showed it to Annabel.

'My God,' Annabel gasped. 'Six hundred pounds! Is this from the solicitors Toby recommended?'

Jan nodded. 'I suppose if we eventually take Harold to court and win, he'll have to reimburse me for all these charges, but if we lose or decide we haven't got a case, I'll have to pay them myself and there'll be more before we even get to that stage.'

'I'm sure Toby can't have been expecting them to charge so much. If I were you, I'd ring them and check it's right.'

'I will. The trouble is that, however bullish these lawyers are, they've got nothing to lose, have they?'

'That's right. My father always says that preachers and lawyers are the only tradesmen in the world who can tell their clients how much of their services they need.'

'Well, I think just for the moment I've had as much as I can afford. I'll let things stew for a while and see what crops up.'

The next two weeks seemed destined to go on as they had started. When Jan's new vet, Chris Roberts, had come out for his weekly visit, he'd declared that the horse must have hit a guard rail and told her to go on poulticing and hosing the leg gently with cold water to bring the swelling down as soon as possible. 'But I wouldn't do any work on it for at least ten days,' he advised forcefully.

Jan paled as she saw all those months she'd thought she had to qualify the horse for Aintree vanishing until there would be no time left to win the necessary Open race.

She also had two horses entered to run on the Wednesday. When she had them groomed and ready to go, she rang the secretary for a final check, only to be told that the course in Herefordshire was waterlogged on the bottom bend and they'd had to call it off. She banged down the phone in frustration.

After the elation of Saturday, Eddie's reaction caused her more concern. She discovered that he was by no means as sanguine as she'd always thought. He became almost morose when he saw Eagle's leg and was convinced it would take twice as long as the vet had said to recover.

'No, it won't,' Jan told him while they drank tea in the tack room amid the smell of well-cleaned leather. 'It's not that serious. It was obviously a hard knock and he's bruised the bone, which will take a while to settle down.'

'But he'll lose fitness, too, won't he?'

'A little,' Jan conceded, 'but if all goes well, we'll soon get him back on song.'

Eddie looked at Jan, as bleak and serious as she'd ever seen him. 'We've *got* to do this, Jan. I can't tell you how much it matters to me. It's not only winning the money; it's . . .' Eddie closed his eyes for a moment, Jan thought like a small boy having a dream. '. . . It's the first time I've ever set myself a real, hard challenge.' He blinked and looked at her. 'Life's always been a bit of a breeze for me, you know. At my age – quite intelligent, just about good-looking enough and fairly rich until a couple of months ago – I've never had to try too hard at anything. But now I've got to, I'll do whatever it takes.'

'I do understand,' Jan said quietly, moved that he'd chosen to reveal this side of himself to her, 'and I'll do whatever I can to help.' She shook her head. 'But don't you think you should have gone for something easier?'

'I could have done, I suppose, but this presented itself and it's all about risk and return; the bigger the risk, the bigger the reward, they say.'

Jan was thinking about Eddie's challenge and his previously hidden reserves of determination as she drove back from the races with a lorry load of runners the following Saturday. Of the four horses on the lorry, there was a single winner – Gale Bird in the adjacent hunts' race – and she was finding her own resolve severely tested.

As the following week went on, the going got heavier.

The gallops were too wet to use because of the

constant downpour and she had to accept the fact that Nuthatch, whom she had entered for a very competitive Open the following Saturday, simply wasn't ready to run.

She phoned Frank Jellard to tell him.

'But, Jan,' he replied, 'I saw him work two weeks ago and you said he would easily be ready.'

'I didn't know it was going to rain continually since then and, anyway, as it turned out, I was wrong. I'm sorry, Mr Jellard.'

'I've got four horses with you now, Jan, and I've been completely supportive. I've written to the Jockey Club recommending you, but so far this season I've had one runner who's come a miserable third.'

'Actually it was a very good third, considering what he was up against. And I'm not a wizard: if the horses aren't ready, they aren't ready, and there's nothing any human being can do about the weather; we can only do our best.'

'I want that horse to run, Jan, on Saturday. I'm sure he's ready; I saw he was with my own eyes two weeks ago, so, if you don't mind, please go ahead, and remember – I own the horse and I pay the bills.'

'I don't know if you pay your doctor's bills, but if you do, I bet you still follow his instructions when he tells you what to do.'

'Jan, you're not a doctor. You're not even a professional trainer in the real sense of the word, and I'm the customer, so the horse runs. Let that be the end of the matter.'

The morning after their phone call, Jan rode Jellard's horse out in the torrential rain to satisfy herself that she was right.

Later, drying off in the caravan before a midday snack with Annabel and Roz, she took a deep breath and rang him at the office of his big fruit-growing business.

'Mr Jellard,' she said when she'd been put through to him, 'it's Jan Hardy here. I've had another look at Nuthatch. I rode him myself to be sure, and I have to say that I strongly advise you not to run him on Saturday.'

'You've already given me your very strong advice in this matter,' Jellard answered coldly, 'and I've told you what I want. If you won't do it, you can expect my lorry round to collect all four horses next week. Is that clear?'

Jan started to mumble a reply, then stopped. 'Yes it bloody well is clear, and if the horse comes back injured, be it on your head.'

'Be it on yours, Jan,' she heard, before the line went dead.

Jan looked at Annabel and wanted to burst into tears. 'For God's sake,' she sniffed, 'what the hell am I supposed to do? I tell him he might do his horse serious damage if he insists I run it, and he just says he'll take them all away if I don't.'

'Then you'll just have to run it, Jan,' Annabel said. 'You can always tell Billy to pull up if he feels the horse is wrong. You certainly can't afford to lose four horses right now and two of them will do really well, once they're ready.'

'That's the point – once they're ready! Why the hell can't people understand that horses aren't machines? And you know I've always said that if I send a horse out to race it's ready to do its job.'

18

Reg Pritchard lowered a pair of well-worn binoculars and shook his tweed-capped head.

'You shouldn't be running that horse.'

Jan wished he hadn't insisted on coming, but they were only twenty-five miles from Riscombe and Reg had driven himself.

She was also worried it was so obvious that Nuthatch wasn't ready to run. He hadn't even looked right in the paddock. Jellard, standing beside her, was all smiles. In his ignorance, he hadn't noticed the horse's condition. Jan had told Billy earlier what to do, but there, in the owner's hearing, she'd said, 'This is a very competitive race, Billy, with two strong front runners. Don't take them on; wait till they come back to you, then have a go at them.'

Jellard had been satisfied.

Jan had been mortified. She hated the lying and the subterfuge; she hated the compromise.

Now her father was looking at her accusingly.

'Dad, I didn't want him to run. He needed at least another two weeks; he's a difficult horse to get fit anyway. But Frank Jellard said he would take all his horses away if I didn't run him.'

'What a bloody idiot!' Reg exploded. 'You should have told him where to shove 'em!'

'Dad, how could I? He's paying me a lot of money at the moment.'

Reg turned his attention back to the race, which had reached the halfway stage. 'Young Billy's pulling him up.'

'Good. I told him to.'

'That's not going to please your owner then, is it?'

'It's better than the horse breaking down,' Jan murmured through teeth clenched in anticipation at the row she was going to have with Jellard after the race.

'You're right, Jan,' Reg sighed. 'It's not an easy game, is it, this training? I don't think I'd want to try it, knowing there's always problems, with some people wanting one thing, and some another, and they've always got you over a barrel.'

'No, Dad,' Jan agreed. 'It isn't easy. If it was, everybody would be doing it, wouldn't they?'

'Still, at least you're going home with another winner,' Reg grunted with satisfaction.

'Yes, Eamon will be pleased, and he's the sort of owner who wouldn't dream of telling me what to do.'

'Hey, Jan,' Reg said suddenly, tugging at her sleeve, 'isn't that the bloke you used to train for? The one who had that good horse?'

Jan followed her father's gaze.

'Yeah, that's Harold Powell,' she said, refusing to

be put out by the sight of him. 'He owns Rear Gunner. I saw he had a runner here – not one I know and it did nothing. I didn't think he'd be here, though; it's quite a long way for him.'

'Oh,' Reg said warily. 'It looks like he's seen you. He's coming over.'

'Don't worry, Dad. He's not going to attack me here.'

'And don't you have a go at him either, mind.'

'Hello, Jan,' Harold greeted her loudly with no hint of animosity as he approached. 'Sorry that last horse of yours didn't make it round.'

Jan shrugged a shoulder. 'As you know, it happens.'

'Still, that was a nice win you had,' he went on grudgingly. 'But I was hoping I might have seen that good horse of yours that came from Ireland. Russian Eagle, isn't he?'

'Yes,' Jan sighed, wondering what was coming next.

'I heard a rumour you're going to run him in the Foxhunters' at Aintree, if you can qualify him in time.'

'The owner would like to,' Jan nodded.

'Well, best of luck to him. Virginia's entered Gunner for it and he's going brilliantly now; he'll take all the beating.' He stretched his mouth into a quick, false smile, turned on his heels and walked off without waiting for her reaction.

Reg gazed after him, furious. 'What an arrogant pillock! Who the hell does he think he is?'

'Don't worry about it, Dad. It's his problem, not ours,' Jan said, wishing she meant it.

She was painfully conscious that the London solicitors, despite their large bills, hadn't achieved any more than Mr Russell from Broadway and no one had seen Amos Smith since he had moved on the previous autumn. But while she'd been focusing on training her horses and getting them to the races as well prepared as she could, she'd been forced to put the whole business on the back burner, until the boy came back or something else turned up.

She tried not to let Harold spoil her day and was delighted when Eamon rang that evening, full of praise.

'I'm just sorry I wasn't there to see it,' he said. 'I knew you'd get a win out of him sometime. I didn't know it would be so soon. I'll try and make sure I'm there next time, but I've got a few little problems to deal with.'

'He's a super horse and he really ran his socks off. Eamon, look, I've got a little problem, too. I've just sent you out a bill for January and I haven't had December's money yet.'

'Jaysus! Have you not? What the hell has that accountant of mine been up to? You take your eye off the ball for a second—'

'I do need it, Eamon. I can't feed these horses on thin air.'

'Jan, I know that. Don't say another word. It'll be dealt with.'

As Jan put the phone down, she thought about what her father had said at the races that day. She agreed that anyone going into this job needed a strong constitution to expose themselves to the frustrations and vagaries of other people's behaviour, when a lot of people who supported your business considered themselves your friends when it suited them and not when it didn't.

She was beginning to develop insights that went well beyond the basic requirements of training horses. And one of these was telling her not to hold her breath while she waited for Eamon Fallon's cheque.

She sighed and got ready for bed. At least Jellard had accepted Billy Hanks's explanation for pulling up Nuthatch in the end, and his four horses were still in her yard.

Jan helped Annabel to carry Sunday lunch into the small dining room of her cottage. Toby Waller and Megan were already sitting at the table, with Matthew beside them in a high chair, specially brought in by Annabel.

Toby bustled to his feet. 'At the risk of appearing to demean women, may I offer my services as a carver?'

'As Bel's cooked it,' Jan said with a grin, 'and Meg and I did the spuds, you might as well do something to help. I don't feel a bit demeaned. Do you, Bel?'

'No,' Annabel laughed. 'There's a knife and steel on the top in the kitchen, Toby, so go to it.'

Jan watched unashamedly to see how Annabel and

Toby were getting on. Although, physically, Toby wasn't very attractive, he was thoroughly considerate, and, she knew from her dealings with him, highly intelligent. Jan could see how his solid dependability and also, maybe, the fact that he was less attractive than Annabel might boost her confidence.

She thought back over a conversation she'd had with Annabel while they'd been riding out together soon after Toby had appeared on the scene. She had asked, 'What do you want in a man, then – a small tummy or a big brain?'

'Both, I suppose,' Annabel had answered.

Looking at Toby now, seeing him doing his able best to be charming and entertaining, Jan wondered how much his physical appearance mattered, and found herself thinking about what she was really looking for. She came, as she'd often done, to the worrying conclusion that she wasn't looking for anyone at all – worrying because she hadn't set out to make herself totally independent, she had simply found that as a woman doing the job she'd chosen an autonomous mindset was essential, and if it was this that stopped her taking men seriously, she thought, that was just too bad.

Whatever Annabel thought of Toby, as far as Jan was concerned he had turned out to be an ideal owner. Although he liked detailed reports, he left all the decisions about Gale Bird's training and running to her. He wasn't proprietorial or condescending when he came to the yard; he always paid his bills on time, and Jan knew that, unlike Penny Price, he could easily afford to. The day after Gale Bird had won, when he'd come up to Edge Farm, he had said, 'I'm sure all of you have helped to produce my mare so well,' and had left a present for everyone in the yard.

At lunch he fed Matthew, told Megan jokes and gently teased Annabel. He topped off the day by announcing that he would like to have a second horse at Edge Farm.

'By the way,' he said later, as he was showing Jan to the door, 'I've told my lawyers that I'm picking up the tab for any work they've done for you on this Harold Powell case.'

'But, Toby—' Jan started to protest.

He held up a hand. 'No, it's OK. I suggested them; I'll handle them. I think in due course they'll get a result for you. If they do, you can pay me back. And I don't want to hear another word about it,' he grinned.

After a perfect winter Sunday lunch and Toby's generosity, which she didn't think she'd done anything to deserve, Jan drove her children back to the caravan feeling more able to cope with the endless daily challenges in running a small yard. Even Bernie Sutcliffe's unannounced arrival just as she was putting Matthew to bed didn't spoil the day for her.

Bernie had brought a bottle of wine, and a bunch of

surprisingly tasteful flowers – definitely not the sort that men often buy from garage forecourts as an afterthought.

'Bernie, I'm sorry,' she said, 'but if you want to look at the horse now, you can't. I'm on my own. Anyway, I don't usually have owners coming at this time of night.'

'Come on, Jan. That doesn't apply to me does it? I mean we're friends, aren't we?'

'Yes, of course. Come in, then, and thank you for the flowers.'

'Do you like 'em? My mum chose them, she said you would.'

Jan was struck by this unexpected aspect of Bernie's private life. 'They're lovely, but I still can't go down to the yard. I won't leave the children on their own at night.'

'Never mind. Just tell me how he is.'

'Who? Russian Eagle?'

'Who else?'

'He's getting there. We should be able to start light work with him again this week. Then there's a good race for him on the twenty-third; we'll try and get him ready for that.'

'Is he still entered for that big race you said, at Aintree, just before the Grand National?'

'The Foxhunters' – yes,' Jan answered carefully. 'It's two days before the National, actually, over the same course, but just one and a bit circuits.'

'Do you think he'll be able to go?'

'I told you when you bought him, he's got to win an open point-to-point to qualify. He nearly won last time and there's a good chance he will next time.'

'I wouldn't mind having a horse go up there, but only if I don't make a complete prat of myself. I thought I might ask up some of my family and friends to watch. What do you think?'

'I think, if he qualifies, he'll be as good as some of the others and a great deal better than most, but, you know, it's still a long way off and a lot can change.'

'What do you mean? He's still the same horse.'

'A horse's performance only has to vary by a fraction of a per cent to make the difference between winning and not.'

'What about the jockey?'

Jan hoped her reaction didn't show. 'Eddie's riding him very well; I've got no worries on that score.'

'I wouldn't want that cocky little bastard Billy Hanks riding him. Are there others we could ask?'

'Not really,' Jan said, 'and when you bought the horse from Eddie, you agreed he would go on having the ride as part of the deal.'

'I don't remember signing anything about that.'

Jan felt herself go pale and she hoped Bernie hadn't noticed. 'No, you don't sign that sort of thing. In racing your word should be enough. My dad always said your word is your bond.'

'Is that right?' Bernie asked, disingenuously. 'Anyway,

another reason I came round was to ask you out to dinner, Tuesday week, to give you plenty of time to find a babysitter. All right?'

Jan, caught on a back foot, didn't have time to think of a plausible reason why she couldn't go at ten days' notice, but with luck something might crop up to stop her. 'That should be fine,' she said. 'Thanks very much.'

It was only when Jan looked in the stable diary that she realized the day Bernie had asked her to dinner was Valentine's Day.

From time to time, during the busy days after he turned up with the flowers, she'd tried to think of a reason not to go out with him, but she hadn't got it in her to be so cruel as to offer him a transparent excuse for not going, and now it was almost too late. Finally she resigned herself, and hoped Bernie wasn't going to take her to some tackily romantic venue. At least she would have good news to report on Russian Eagle, who had started work again and was going well.

Eddie came that afternoon to carry on schooling. Jan was glad to see that both horse and rider were improving all the time. Although they had yet to win even their one qualifying race, Jan didn't feel it injudicious to tell Eddie that she certainly hadn't written him off in the Foxhunters'.

Before he went, Jan asked him if he was doing anything special for Valentine's Day.

'Good God, is it today? I never take any notice of it,' he said brusquely. 'It's a load of rubbish invented by flower sellers for men who haven't the imagination to be romantic without a bit of help.'

'But you have?' Jan asked cynically.

'Play your cards right and one day you might find out,' he grinned.

Roz came in the evening to look after the children and watched as Jan got ready for Bernie's arrival.

'Cor, bloody hell, Jan, you don't want to look too sexy or that little prat'll be all over you.'

'Come on, Roz; you can hardly call this outfit sexy.'

'It bloody well is, with that slit up the side. You shouldn't do yourself down, Jan. There's a lot of blokes round here as fancies you.'

Jan didn't feel inclined to believe her; at the same time, she agreed that the wrap-around skirt she had borrowed from Annabel – the only garment from her wardrobe that fitted Jan – might be seen as deliberately seductive. 'Oh, bugger,' she said. 'You're right. I'd better wear that dress I got for Eamon's party.'

She went back to her small section of the caravan and came out in a modest but not unflattering silk dress that had been a Christmas present from Annabel.

'He'll still fancy yer,' Roz said, 'but least it's not like deliberate temptation. He was right brassed off, wasn't he, when you kept dancing with Eddie and Billy at Eamon's.'

'I had a dance with him too, remember?'

'I don't remember a lot, to tell the truth. That Eamon got me so drunk.'

'Eamon did?' It was the first Jan had heard of it.

'Yeah, course he did, but he didn't try anything, like; not much anyway.'

'Have you seen him since?'

'Only when he's been here. He told me he's got to sell his share in that club already; he says they've squeezed him out.'

'Who's squeezed him out?'

'The other people that owns it, he said. It's not all his, you know, but he found the place and put it all together.'

'Oh, I thought it was his, the way he was going on.'

'Probably he wanted you to think he had plenty of money to pay his bills,' Roz said candidly.

'He's left that a bit late, now, I'm afraid.'

'Why?' Roz was shocked. 'Hasn't he been paying yer?'

'Not for the last two months.'

'Cor!' Roz gasped with a shake of her unruly black curls. 'Aren't people bastards? Oh well,' she said, immediately brightening, 'it might mean you get to have his horse and he's lovely, Dingle Bay.'

Valentine's Day dinner with Bernie was as awful as Jan had feared.

He had booked them into a large, second-rate restaurant near Gloucester that specialized in 'events' and had a cabaret of unconvincing sixties and seventies tribute acts, climaxing with a Tom Jones, who Jan thought looked more like Del Boy from *Only Fools and Horses*.

Jan thought about fools and horses while she tried to look as if she was having a good evening, without yawning and looking at her watch too often. She wondered why some men were incapable of reading the signs women gave out that clearly displayed their lack of interest; she supposed their egos were to blame.

When the cabaret had finished and a disco took over, Jan danced with Bernie a few times. To her relief, he didn't force himself on her and, when they sat down for what she hoped might be a last drink, she was beginning to be grateful for his restraint.

'I was talking to your jockey the other day,' Bernie said, as if he were making a bit of light conversation.

'Eddie?'

'No, Billy.'

'I didn't think you two were on speaking terms,' Jan said with a slight smile.

'Because of Sandy? No, well, he did me a big favour really. I mean, it showed me what a right little tart she was, so I came round to thinking I was grateful to him. I mean, when there's women like you around, who needs a Sandy?'

Jan cringed, but couldn't think of an answer which wouldn't sound conceited or rude, so kept silent.

'Anyway,' Bernie went on. 'I took him out for a

drink in the White Horse, and we got chatting about him riding Russian Eagle.'

Jan looked down and fumbled for something in her bag to hide her panic. 'What about him riding Eagle?' she asked, as evenly as she could.

'Well, Billy's virtually a pro, isn't he? After all, he rides all your other horses, so I got to thinking. I know there was talk of Eddie Sullivan riding my horse when I bought it, but he's had his ride; you might say he's had his chance. Billy reckons he would have won on Eagle last time.'

Jan shook her head vigorously. 'I doubt it. The thing is Eagle's not a horse to put under pressure any more than you have to. That's why I asked Eddie to ride him like that.'

'But you didn't. I heard you say, "Start going for it halfway round the last circuit", and he didn't, did he?'

'Eddie understands that horse better than anyone in the yard,' Jan hurried on. 'He's ridden him and schooled him more than anyone else and I know he'll win on him next time out.'

'Look, why's he so keen to ride the horse anyway, now he doesn't own it?'

Jan looked hard at Bernie. He didn't know that Eddie stood to win half a million if he rode and won on Russian Eagle at Aintree.

'I suppose because he chose and bought the horse,' Jan tried to say casually. 'He's put a lot into it and he wants to be part of the result. He told me,' she went on truthfully, 'he's set himself this Aintree race as a sort of challenge, perhaps to get back a bit of self-esteem after what happened to him last year.'

'You mean what happened to that old bastard, Ron,' Bernie interjected.

'I suppose he's trying to show that he can stand on his own two feet and be something.'

'Well, he'll have to find another horse to do it on because from now on I want Billy Hanks to ride both the horses I keep with you and he's agreed.'

Sitting beside Bernie in the Jaguar as he drove her home, Jan couldn't speak. Her mind was in complete turmoil about what she would say to Eddie. After all, it had been her idea that Bernie should buy the horse. She'd also said to Eddie there'd be no problem over him keeping the ride.

Now she felt like a traitor for letting this happen.

She wasn't pleased with Billy, either.

In some ways she couldn't blame him. If Bernie had asked him point-blank whether he would have won the race in which Eddie came second, Jan, for one, would have had to agree if he'd said 'yes'. She'd thought it herself at the time. Billy knew nothing about Eddie's bet or how important the Foxhunters' was to him so there was, Jan had to admit, no ethical reason why Billy shouldn't have accepted the offer to ride Russian Eagle when the owner asked him.

When Jan wanted to talk to Eddie on the phone next day, she couldn't get him on any of his usual numbers. By midday she was desperate, but determined that she should tell him what Bernie had said before he heard it from someone else.

She convinced herself eventually that she had to go into Stow to see the saddler, but she finished her business there in less than five minutes and hurried round the corner to Eddie's shop. She pushed open the door underneath a sign that read, *THE SULLIVAN GALLERY* and, underneath, *E. R. Sullivan – Sporting Pictures* and walked into the small showroom. It smelled of coir carpeting and pot-pourri. The only sounds were the ticking of a carriage clock over the unused fireplace and the rustle of paper as an old man behind the desk folded up his copy of the *Daily Telegraph*. It was the first time Jan had been in the shop since the previous October and she hadn't taken much in then. It seemed to her, though, that the walls were a lot emptier.

The old man – well into his eighties, Jan guessed – smiled over the top of his gold half-moon glasses as he rose from his chair.

'Good afternoon. What can I do for you?'

'I'm looking for Eddie Sullivan.'

'Mr Sullivan's been called away to London on business, I'm afraid,' the man answered, a little cagily, Jan thought.

'You didn't tell me he was going to London when I rang earlier, you just said he'd popped out.'

'Who are you, madam?'

'Jan Hardy. I've got the racing stables over at Stanfield.'

The old man looked relieved. 'Of course. I should have recognized you. I know exactly who you are. I'm Jack Singleton, a sort of part-time manager. I'm sorry, but there are one or two people who want to talk to Eddie whom he's not very keen to see himself.'

'Do you know where he is, then?'

'Not exactly. But I know he'll be back at his house at eight this evening; he's arranged to meet his father there.'

'I tried to leave a message at the house,' Jan said, 'but I just got a funny sound on the phone.'

'I think he may have forgotten to pay the bill.'

Jan winced. If Eddie was so hard up that he was having trouble paying his phone bill, Bernie's decision would hit him even harder.

She looked more closely at the elderly shop assistant and guessed that he was on Eddie's side. 'Tell me,' she said. 'How's business here?'

Jack Singleton raised a bushy white eyebrow a few centimetres. 'I'm afraid the stock's rather low, and what there is isn't all that good.'

Jan glanced at the few pictures on the wall – a fishing scene, a group of implausible men shooting duck, and an oddly shaped racehorse being held by an even less convincing eighteenth-century groom – and began to understand why Eddie had been so pessimistic about his business future. She looked back at Jack

Singleton. 'I don't know anything about pictures,' she said, 'but I think I see what you mean.'

'I fear we won't be here much longer.' He shrugged his shoulders regretfully.

'That's a shame,' Jan said, thinking this was a bit of an understatement.

'But I hear great things of his racing.'

Jan nodded. 'He's done really well. I hope it keeps going well for him,' she said, trying not to reveal she thought this was now a fairly bleak prospect. 'If you're talking to him, can you tell him I'll come round to the Mill at about eight?'

'Certainly,' Jack Singleton said. 'May I say that I think he's very lucky to have someone like you to inspire him at a time like this?'

As Jan drove to Old Ford Mill that evening, she wondered what Eddie had told Jack and if she really was an inspiration to him. He wouldn't be too inspired, she thought, when she told him Bernie was adamant that Billy Hanks should ride Russian Eagle from now on. It seemed to her that with all his other problems Eddie had been clinging to his hopes of winning the big bet like a bankrupt clutching a lottery ticket.

She drove in through the open gates and saw Eddie's battered vehicle parked outside the front door.

She took a few deep breaths and climbed out of her

own Land Rover, which wasn't in much better shape, then walked up to knock on the door.

It was opened by Ron Sullivan. 'Well, well, well!' he said with a smile spreading across his big, tanned face. 'If it isn't Little Miss Donkey Walloper.' He opened the door wider and with a wave of his big hand beckoned Jan into the gloomy hall, lit only by a glimmer from Eddie's oil lamps in the kitchen.

'Hello, Mr Sullivan,' Jan replied, rather coldly. She thought that, of all the names she'd been called over the years, she liked Little Miss Donkey Walloper the least. 'Most of my friends call me Jan.'

'I'm sorry, Jan,' Ron laughed. 'It's only because I fancy you. Gawd knows what you see in that bent-nosed son of mine, though.'

'Thanks, Dad,' Eddie said coming up behind Ron. 'Hi, Jan. Jack told me you were coming. What's up?'

'Actually,' Jan said, 'I've got some bad news.'

'You'd better come into the kitchen and have a drink first.' Jan didn't miss the slight quake in Eddie's voice.

'Is this something you don't want me to hear?' Ron asked.

'I'm sure it's OK, Dad,' Eddie said, as he took down a bottle of wine from a big pine dresser that stretched along one wall. He filled three glasses and put them on the table. 'What's happened?' he asked Jan.

Jan sat down and took a gulp from her glass. 'Bernie—' Jan started, then sighed. 'Bernie asked me out to dinner last night,' she said slowly. 'It was pretty awful, but he told me he'd been speaking to Billy Hanks; he asked him if he would ride Eagle for him in future and Billy said yes.'

Eddie's jaw slackened; he screwed up his face for a moment. 'Oh, God,' he grunted. 'Still, at least you haven't come to tell me Eagle's dead, which was what I thought first.'

'No, Eagle's fine; I'd been planning for you to ride him Saturday week at the Warwick; he stands a good chance. But now Billy will have to. I'm really sorry, but there's nothing I can do about it.'

'What's the problem?' Ron joined in. 'Ed's been jocked off, so what? There's always other horses to ride.'

Jan realized that Ron didn't know anything about Eddie's great plan to get him out of trouble. She left Eddie to answer for himself.

'I'd rather set my heart on riding this particular horse in the Aintree Foxhunters', Dad.'

'Had you, by 'eck? Well, that's what I'd call a triumph of fantasy over sanity. Since when did you think you could jump round the National course?'

'He can do it OK, Mr Sullivan,' Jan said, impressed that Eddie had kept his considerable progress a secret from his father.

'Call me Ron,' he boomed.

'He can do it, Ron. He's worked really hard at it and he's doing brilliantly. Didn't he tell you he nearly won last month?'

Ron turned to his son, visibly impressed. 'Ed, my boy! What's the point of hiding your talents from your old man?'

Eddie shrugged. 'I'm not that great yet, but I thought if I did get anywhere at Aintree, it would come as a nice surprise for you.'

'And it bloody well would have. But is this right?' He turned back to Jan. 'The geezer that owns this 'orse – he's robbed Eddie of the ride?'

Jan nodded.

'Why's that?' Ron asked.

'He thought Eddie should have won last time out.'

'The time he come second?'

'That's right.'

'What a berk! Who is he?'

'A businessman from the Black Country called Bernie Sutcliffe.'

Ron raised a shoulder. 'Never 'eard of him.'

'He's a big scrap merchant of some sort,' Eddie said.

'I'm sorry, Ed,' Ron said, shaking his head. 'In the old days, I could have done something for you, called in a couple of favours. But,' he sighed, 'as it is—'

Suddenly, it seemed to Jan, Ron looked smaller.

But Eddie was putting a brave face on the problem. 'Presumably,' he said, 'the only way I'd get the ride back would be if someone else bought him from Bernie and they agreed to let me?'

'Yes,' Jan said, 'but knowing Bernie, the only time to buy from him would be when he's already decided to sell.'

'That's easy,' Ron said, pulling up a kitchen chair and sitting down. Jan guessed he still enjoyed cooking up a plan. 'The only time I wanted to sell a horse was when it couldn't win. So, don't let this one win. Simple.'

Jan looked at him and shook her head. 'Firstly, I'd never deliberately send out a horse to lose; secondly, we have to win with him to qualify for the Aintree race; and, thirdly, Billy Hanks would go straight back to Bernie even if I did tell him not to try.'

'You don't need to tell him to do anything; you could just not train the horse well enough. That shouldn't be too hard,' Ron chuckled. 'It's what most of the racehorse trainers in this country do anyway!'

'That would still leave my first two reasons for not doing it,' Jan said.

'All right, then, the only other option's to offer this geezer a pile of dough for the animal.'

Eddie shook his head this time. 'Bernie's one of those people who, the more you offered him, the more he'd want, and you'd have to go way beyond any sensible price before he'd sell. Besides, none of us have got that sort of money.'

'No,' agreed Ron. 'Specially not me.' He stood up to mark the finality of this statement. 'But, as there doesn't seem to be much you can do about your little problem, I can tell you I have got just about enough wonga in my pocket to take us all out for a meal at that nice boozer in the village. Come to think of it, they probably owe me a few drinks in there from when I let them shoot across the Manor last winter.'

Jan thought Ron was right: there was no more to be said about Russian Eagle, and so they didn't discuss him any further in the White Horse. Despite all the frustrations and disappointment caused by Bernie's Valentine's Day announcement, and the parlous state in which Ron and his son now found themselves, Jan had a very enjoyable evening.

She was surprised how much interest her horses had generated in the pub, though she guessed that, as it was the local Eddie and Billy used, it was inevitable that her runners were widely discussed there.

But with Ron and Eddie she didn't only talk about the horses and Ron seemed to know something about any topic that cropped up. Out of curiosity, Jan asked him what he was going to do with himself – if he had any plans to rise one day, Phoenix-like, from the smouldering ruins of his old business empire. But he wouldn't be drawn.

'Let's just say I've got plans,' he said, and added more quietly, 'where the gum tree grows.'

When the conversation came back to racing, Ron was happy to talk about his past experiences. 'I owned jumpers for twenty-five years,' he told Jan. 'I've had some of the best trainers in the country look after horses for me and some of the worst – they were often the dearest. The ones I always admired most were them who didn't allow owners to run their lives. They trained on their terms and nobody else's. If you tried to tell 'em what to do, they just told you to eff off and take your horses with you. Of course, some of them smarmy, Old Etonian brown-nosers just oiled around, agreeing with everything you said provided you had enough money – bloody terrific at the old gin and tonic, but effing useless at training horses. This bloke Jellard you was telling me about, who wanted you to run a horse that wasn't ready; next time, tell him to get stuffed and take his horses with him. When it comes to it, he won't. Mark my words, there's very few serious people who don't respect a person – specially a woman – who stands up for their principles.'

Jan nodded ruefully. Next time she would take that risk with Jellard. 'What about the nice owners who don't tell me what to do, but don't pay their bills?'

'They're no good to you either. You can't run your yard on wind and three-fifths of sod all, however bloody charming they are. Put an interest charge on their bills and if they haven't coughed up halfway through the next month send a couple of reminders. If that don't work, issue a writ through the small claims court. It doesn't take five minutes and it don't cost much. That's a sort of training for them. Once they know they're going to get a writ every couple of months if they're late paying, they'll soon learn to send a cheque on time. Whatever happens, never let them owe you more than their horse is worth and never let them take a horse away if they still owe you.'

Driving home on her own after the meal in the pub, paid for by some past debt to Ron which the landlord remembered, Jan thought of all the advice Eddie's dad had given her, and she knew on the whole it was right, albeit hard-nosed and pragmatic. With Eamon and his financial problems, for instance, she came to the conclusion that much as she liked the man, she would need to follow Ron's advice.

But she still didn't know what to do about Eddie and Russian Eagle.

Although she knew Eddie was a lot more upset by the news than he'd let on, he had assured her that he realized it wasn't her fault and there was nothing she could do about it. It was always a problem, he'd said, when irrational human pettiness got in the way of one's plans and he'd admitted that if he'd handled his own business affairs properly in the first place, he would never have had to sell the horse to Bernie.

Jan was worried, though, that she hadn't seen Eddie at Edge Farm or heard from him during the week before the Warwickshire point-to-point. She wished there was something she could have done. Nevertheless, she still had her job to do and the three horses to get ready to run. The first four days of the week were bright, icy and hard as rock and without an all-weather gallop she couldn't get the work into the horses that she knew they needed. By Friday, however, the cold front had retreated and the meeting went ahead the next day.

Joe was off sick and it was Roz's turn to mind the children and the horses at home while Jan and Annabel went racing. Normally, however depressed Jan became – about being without John, or without a house, or cold and broke – she could put it all out of her mind when she had horses to run. This time, though, she found it impossible.

She was doubtful that Eddie would turn up to watch Russian Eagle being ridden by Billy, so it was a great surprise when she saw him in the distance shortly after she'd arrived with Annabel. He was as bright and breezy as he'd always been and even offered to help as a supplementary groom.

Jan held her breath for a moment when Billy Hanks appeared for his ride on the first of her three runners. He obviously wasn't expecting to see Eddie.

'Morning, Billy,' Eddie greeted him affably.

Billy nodded back warily. 'Hello, Eddie.'

'Jan's got three good rides for you today; I thought I might see if anyone will give me a price on the treble.'

Billy beckoned Eddie to him. 'Look, mate,' Jan heard him say, 'I'm sorry about Russian Eagle, but the bloke had made his mind up he didn't want you to ride it; he just doesn't like you for some reason; sounds ridiculous but he thinks you're too posh to be riding for him.'

Eddie laughed. 'That's a joke, if he'd ever met my old man.'

'If I hadn't said I'd take the ride,' Billy went on, 'he'd have found someone else anyway.'

'I'm sure you're right, Billy. Don't worry about it; no hard feelings. Anyway,' Eddie added lightly, 'it's not the end of the world and you'll probably get him round Aintree much better than me.'

Jan listened while she and Annabel were getting Derring Duke ready for his first run of the season in the adjacent hunts' race. She had to admire Eddie for the front he was putting on. She would never have guessed how much it mattered to him if he hadn't already told her. She was also fairly sure that the main reason Bernie didn't want Eddie to ride Eagle was that, despite their denials, he thought she and Eddie were in some sort of a relationship.

The rest of the afternoon went particularly well for Jan. Derring Duke won his race and Gwillam Evans's gelding, Barneby Boy, won the restricted race.

Eddie came back to the lorry beaming with vicarious pride. 'Jan, you're a little genius to produce two winners in fields like that. If Eagle goes out and wins now, I'll take the thick end of a monkey off the bookies.'

'Don't count on it,' Jan said. 'He needed more work

than I could safely give him this week with all the frost, and it took him a little time to come right after that leg injury he got when we last ran him.'

'God, I'm sorry about that.'

'Don't be daft, it wasn't your fault. I don't even know if he did it racing. He could have done it in his stable that night. It does happen occasionally.'

'Maybe I just didn't make him pick his feet up high enough.'

'It wasn't your fault, all right?' Jan repeated.

'Well I hope he wins today because I'll put all my winnings on him for the Foxhunters', whoever rides him.'

But Jan had a strong feeling in her innards that Russian Eagle wasn't going to win that day. She thought he really had needed that little bit of extra work to tone up his muscles.

When Bernie Sutcliffe arrived to watch his horse run, with three men who looked very out of place on a point-to-point course, Jan tried to warn him that Eagle might not be back to peak fitness yet.

But Bernie was too busy showing off to his friends to hear a word she said.

'I've changed his jockey since he last ran, and I've told him how I want the horse ridden,' he was saying importantly, as if he knew what he was talking about.

As the horses were going down to the start, the friends went off smugly to place their bets, confident that they were privy to inside knowledge.

When they came back, Jan stayed with Bernie to watch the race.

Russian Eagle jumped round perfectly, but on the last half circuit he lost touch and finished halfway down the field.

Jan wasn't too disappointed. She knew he could have done a lot better if he'd been a little fitter but, as she glanced at Bernie, she was shocked by the expression of bitter bafflement on his face. His upper lip was quivering and he wouldn't look at his friends, who, in turn, seemed totally crestfallen.

Jan didn't dare think how much they must have lost on the strength of Bernie's boundless confidence.

'The little bastard,' Bernie was muttering.

'Who?' Jan asked. 'Billy?'

'Yes,' Bernie hissed. 'He never rode him out, like he said he would, after that other idiot of yours never got after him properly.'

'Billy rode a perfect race; the horse just wasn't fit enough.'

'Why the hell didn't you tell me?'

'Bernie, don't start shouting at me. I did tell you before you all went off to have a bet. I said he took some time to get over that bad leg and I wasn't sure he was there yet. All being well, he'll be spot on next time.'

'Oh, great,' Bernie said cynically. 'That's what you said last time – the old trainer's lament – people have told me about it. You know, "He's bound to win, sooner or later." Just so long as you go on paying the bills. And when he never wins, it's a bit too late to ask for your money back, isn't it?'

'That's totally unfair, but if that's how you feel Bernie, maybe you should take the horse to another yard because I won't put up with that kind of talk.'

Bernie glanced for the first time at his companions before he turned back decisively to Jan. 'No, I won't do that. But next time we run him, I'm choosing the jockey.'

'Bernie, you chose the jockey this time.'

'Out of two? I don't call that much of a choice. No, I've got someone in mind who'll make sure he bloody well pulls his finger out.'

'We'll see about that,' Jan said, as she went down to the course to help Annabel bring Eagle back.

For the next few days, Jan wanted to pick up the phone and tell Bernie to take his horses away, rather than be dictated to about who should or shouldn't ride them.

On the other hand, the only chance she had of retrieving the ride on Eagle for Eddie was to keep the horse in the yard.

19

When Arctic Hay won for Bernie at a midweek meeting of the Radnorshire Hunt, she thought she might be able to bring him back on side, but he rang that evening and told her he'd got the man he wanted to ride Eagle next time, a well-known amateur jockey from the south-west who didn't usually venture up to the Midlands.

Jan hadn't often seen Roger Williams race, but she knew he had a reputation for hard, aggressive riding. Although she didn't particularly want him to ride Eagle, he did get a good number of winners and under point-to-point rules he couldn't use his whip excessively.

She tried to ring Eddie at his shop to tell him about it. He wasn't there, but Jack Singleton told her Eddie had managed to assign the lease on the premises and they were closing at the end of the week.

Poor Eddie, Jan thought. When she'd first met him, he had plenty of money and obviously enjoyed the illusion that he made a living from buying and selling pictures. Maybe he did have an eye for them, but it seemed to her that he'd never got to grips with the fundamentals of the business. Possibly, as his mother had hinted, his attention span was just too short.

Yet he'd shown a lot of determination in his riding, and though he'd lost the ride on Russian Eagle, there was no reason why he shouldn't carry on with other horses. If by some chance he was ever able to ride Eagle again, at least he'd then be schooled, fit and ready.

Without much hope, she dialled the Mill. To her surprise, it rang and Eddie answered.

'I'm glad you've got the phone back on,' she said.

'Yes,' Eddie laughed. 'But I haven't got a kitchen dresser any more.'

'For God's sake, Eddie. You can't just flog off everything around you.'

'It's OK. I've got a few thing coming together,' Eddie said vaguely.

Jan wasn't convinced, but she didn't say so. 'Good, but do you still have time to do a little schooling? I've got some horses here I wouldn't mind you riding in a few races.'

'Are you sure?' Eddie asked doubtfully.

Jan was touched by his lack of vanity, in this department at least. 'Yes, of course I'm sure. I wouldn't ask otherwise. I've got to win races you know.'

'I'd love to ride some more. I thought after Bernie had put the mockers on Eagle I'd be a bit superfluous around the yard.'

'Well, you won't be, so when can you come for another session?'

Eddie had always liked Victor Carey's dappled grey mare, August Moon, and Jan had him riding work and schooling her that week. After the horses were all put away and fed late on Thursday morning, she asked him up to the caravan for a coffee.

'I think I'll ring Mr Carey,' she said, 'and ask him if he minds you riding his horse this Saturday, if you'd like me to.'

'Yes.' Eddie looked pleased. 'I'd love you to, if you think I'm up to it, but won't Billy expect the ride?'

'Maybe, but even he can't ride two horses at once; Sorcerer's Boy goes in the same race.'

'Are you running Eagle in the Open, too?'

'No, not this time. He's still not quite right and Bernie's insisted on giving this bloke Roger Williams the ride next time. He's a hard jockey, so I don't want him riding Eagle until he's ready – next week, I hope.'

Eddie flipped through the list of entries lying on Jan's table. 'I see Virginia's running one of her pointers in that race – looks like a bit of a superstar.'

Jan shrugged. 'I don't know why she bothers when she made such a thing about getting her licence and running under rules, but it's too bad. If Eagle's right, I've got to send him. We're getting very short of time to qualify him otherwise.'

'Bernie's never going to sell that horse,' Eddie said

gloomily. 'I've been trying to work out some other way of dealing with the mess Dad's in, but I'm not getting anywhere. He's managed to buy a little more time again, but . . .' Eddie shook his head and Jan glimpsed the despair he felt.

'Look,' she said with a deal of false optimism, 'something'll turn up. It's amazing how often it does. You never know, Bernie just might give up the horse and you just might win the race. It's not all over until the fat lady sings.'

'Thanks, Jan,' Eddie said wryly. 'A little shot of bullshit goes a long way with me at the moment.'

Over the next few days Jan was concerned that Eddie's gloom might affect his riding; she knew from her own experience that for a jockey to set off with a defeatist attitude was the worst possible way to start a race, irrespective of the horse's abilities.

Although August Moon hadn't run in a race for over three years, she had been a surprisingly easy horse to train, and Jan felt that she stood a good chance, even beside an experienced old-timer like Sorcerer's Boy.

On the first Saturday in March she drove her lorry to a big, busy race meeting on the wealthy fringes of the Home Counties. There was a massive crowd on whom the sun smiled as the threatened rain was kept at bay. Jan found to her surprise that Victor Carey and

Colonel Gilbert had both come to watch their horses, which were running in the same race. They were too well-mannered to show anything but friendly rivalry towards each other as they stood on either side of Jan.

'I've never seen Eddie Sullivan ride before,' the colonel remarked. 'Does he know what he's doing?'

Jan laughed. She knew he was having a good-humoured poke at Victor Carey. 'He's only ridden one race before, but he nearly won on Russian Eagle.'

'Is that the horse he was hoping to ride in the Foxhunters'?'

'Yes, but unfortunately he sold it to another of my owners, who doesn't want him to ride it now.'

'That's a bit tough on him.'

'Yes, but as he was doing so well I asked him if he'd come and ride some others for me.'

'You've certainly turned my mare out very well,' Victor Carey said, evidently not wanting to discuss Eddie's riding ability right now. Jan had told him all he wanted to know when she'd first asked him if Eddie could have the ride.

'Thanks,' Jan nodded. 'She enjoys her work and it didn't take long to get the grass belly off.'

The lightly framed, athletic horse had undoubtedly caught people's eye in the paddock. As an unknown quantity, having been off the course for so long, the odds the bookies were offering started long. But punters who thought they could tell a fit and talented animal when they saw one, especially with Jan Hardy's name beside it, had been quick to get their money on and the odds had shortened dramatically, though Sorcerer's Boy remained favourite.

In the final stages of the race, with the massive crowd roaring the two favourites home, Billy and Eddie swapped places twice at the front of the field, until August Moon's longer stride carried her a neck in front of Colonel Gilbert's old chaser on the run to the line.

The owners shook hands warmly and congratulated each other. Jan was almost boiling with excitement. It wasn't the first time she'd sent out the winner and the runner-up in a race like this, but she was ecstatic about Eddie's riding. He'd ridden a well-judged, intelligent race and made the best possible use of the mare. Coming to the finish, he'd barely used his whip, but squeezed her right up to the winning line with only hands and heels in the way he knew she liked best.

The result completely justified her professional judgement and she knew it must have gone a long way to restoring Eddie's morale. But the real prize for the day's victory arrived the next morning, a warm, damp Sunday, in the form of an invitation from Mr Carey asking Jan to go round for a drink at six that evening.

The day before he had given the lie to his reputation for parsimony by handing her grooms a hundred pounds – as a thank you, he said, for the most enjoyable race he had ever watched. Jan couldn't stop herself from thinking that maybe, at last, the pernickety old man had decided that she was worthy of his thirty-five-thousand-pound guarantee.

But she did not believe it was truly going to happen until he sat her down at a table in his library with a glass of dry sherry and placed in front of her a letter, neatly typed and already signed by him. It was addressed to the stewards of the Jockey Club, and informed them that he was prepared to act as guarantor to Mrs Jan Hardy of Edge Farm, who was applying for a professional licence to train racehorses.

Jan drove home in the Land Rover as if she were sitting on a magic carpet. All the months of uncertainty and waiting made his decision seem quite unreal now it had finally come. At home she hugged the wonderful news to herself, reluctant to tell anyone else, in case, by some crazy mischance, she had misunderstood what Mr Carey had said, or the implications of the letter he had written. Or in case he changed his mind.

She didn't let her hand stray near the telephone until eight o'clock next morning, when, having kept the news from Annabel, Roz and Joe for an hour, she was at last prepared to believe it was true.

She came back from riding out first lot and went straight up to the caravan to phone her father, determined that he should be the first to know.

By noon that day Jan's second formal application to the Jockey Club was in the post. Gerry arrived at lunchtime, following a call from Jan, who had tracked him down to where he was working in the next village. He had run out of things to do at Edge Farm over the past few weeks, when Jan had called a halt to any more work on the house until the spring. Now he was delighted to be asked back.

'Hi, Gerry,' Jan bubbled and gave the young builder a quick peck on the cheek.

'Cor!' he gasped at her news. 'That's brilliant. You'll be on the telly and all.'

'Never mind the telly. One day I'll be able to run horses in the biggest races in the country! The Gold Cup, the Grand National, the Hennessy, the King George! It's a whole different ball game!'

'Don't get too excited, Jan. You'll need the horses first.'

'Oh, I'll find them all right, don't you worry about that,' Jan laughed, not admitting that she'd lain awake half the night wondering how she would find owners prepared to buy the sort of horse capable of winning top-class races. 'Here's the list of things the inspector complained about last time. I'm pretty sure we've done them all, but could you go round and make certain? Repaint anything that looks a bit tatty. Then check every inch of fencing and double-check all the gates and their catches. They might take a special interest in that after Virginia took it upon herself to tell them about the horses that got out.'

Eddie came round later with some bottles of Spanish champagne. 'If you hold your nose while you drink it, it doesn't taste too bad,' he said.

'I wouldn't want the real thing anyway,' Jan said. 'It might be unlucky before the old fogeys at the Jockey Club have actually given me the green light.'

Reg and Mary arrived soon after Eddie.

Like Jan, Reg had reservations about premature celebration, but he was still prepared to knock back a few glasses of Spanish fizz. They sat around in the cramped little mobile home, with the wood-burner glowing and Jan's favourite candles on the table, and talked about everything they would like to see at Edge Farm Stables.

'A swimming pool for the horses,' Gerry said.

'And a horse walker,' Roz interjected; she hated all the walking that had to be done early in the training cycle.

'An all-weather gallop is what I need most,' Jan said, thinking of the few critical weeks of training that had been lost through frost.

'Steady on,' Reg said with an indulgent smile. 'What you need before any of that is owners, so you can pay for it all, and so you have the right type of horses. Winning point-to-points is all very well, but it's a big step up to National Hunt racing.'

'Well,' Eddie said, raising a glass. 'Here's to Jan. Twelve winners so far this season; let's make it twenty and the championship.'

'And I owe you one too, Eddie,' Jan replied. 'It was

the win on August Moon that made up old Carey's mind. He was thrilled to bits with the way you rode him.'

Annabel laughed. 'You're not kidding. I've never seen him so cheerful. I think if I'd asked him there and then to let me off a month's rent, he would have done.'

The party carried on until Reg and Mary got up to leave at ten.

'It's another day tomorrow, Jan,' her father said.

'Yes,' Jan nodded. 'And, Eddie, if you're coming up at seven to ride out, you'd better get off home to bed, too.'

When Jan woke in the morning, her head was still buzzing. She wondered why she was so much more excited about her licence application this time than she had been when she'd applied for it back in the autumn.

Of course, now she'd sent out a good number of winners from Edge Farm and she knew that she'd dealt with all the Jockey Club's practical objections to the stables. She also had a strong guarantor and more than a dozen owners pledged. This time round a professional licence looked a far more likely prospect.

On her way down to the yard, as the sun broke out over the hill behind her, she stopped by her building site. She looked at the two-dimensional skeleton of her new house and indulged in a few minutes' fantasy.

'Soon,' she said to herself. 'Soon we'll have a yard full of quality horses and a house to live in.'

Eddie arrived just before seven, looking lean, fit and, Jan thought to herself, really quite handsome. She was still pleased that she'd been proved right in giving him the chance to ride the previous Saturday, but as much as she wanted to help him, she couldn't see the beginning of a strategy to get him back on Russian Eagle.

She talked to him about it while they were hosing the mud off the horses' legs in the yard after their work.

'You know, I can't do what your father suggested. I can't kid Bernie that Eagle's a turkey,' she said.

Eddie laughed. 'Obviously: if he's an eagle, he can't be a turkey.'

'Shut up and listen. I mean it. I'd love to do something, but I've racked my brains and so far I can't find a way.'

'Is Bernie still all right otherwise?'

'Apart from the fact that he's started making moves on Annabel.' Jan shook her head. 'I ask you, as if he had a chance!'

'I suppose someone like Bernie, who has an awful lot of money, now and again finds a tart like Sandy who'll put up with him for a bit, so he thinks that all women are susceptible to a fat wallet. But apart from everything else, Annabel's got plenty of her own dough, anyway.'

'I sometimes wonder why you haven't tried a bit harder there yourself,' Jan said.

'Listen, although I'm not mercenary, do you think I haven't? I promise you, whatever she's interested in, it's not me. A lot of man hours have been spent trying to figure out what turns her on.'

Jan thought about Annabel's chronic insecurity and wondered how Eddie would react if he knew the cause. But it was up to Annabel, and no one else, to decide who should know about it. As far as Jan knew, she was the only person Annabel had told.

'Anyway,' she said, 'I think she's managed to let Bernie know that she's not interested without being too brutal about it.'

'Hmm, I doubt it. I get the impression Bernie's not a very subtle chap. Still, I suppose Annabel's old enough to look after herself now.'

After they'd had a mug of coffee in the tack room, Eddie left for a sale, where the last of his pictures from the shop were due to be auctioned.

He hadn't been gone more than a minute when a small blue BMW purred up the track to the yard and stopped. Susan Sullivan got out and stood looking around.

'I saw Eddie's old rattle-trap up here,' she said, as Jan walked up to her, 'and thought I'd let him get out of the way first. He didn't stay the night here by any chance, did he?'

'No, he didn't,' Jan said firmly. 'He came at seven and rode out first lot.'

'I'm sorry,' Susan said. 'I can't help wanting to know

about his love life, however much I tell myself it's none of my business.'

'Well, I'm afraid I can't help you there.'

'I'm glad he's so keen on this racing business, though. I hear he won a good race last week. I could hardly believe it.'

'He did very well.'

'Good. The reason I've come out here to see you is that I'm rather worried about him. I know he's found it difficult to handle what happened to his father. He wants to help and so do I, but there's a limit to what I can do. Has he told you anything about his plans?'

Jan shook her head. 'No. I don't think he wants to talk about it. I know he's been selling off the few bits he's still got, just to clear old debts as far as I can tell. And poor Ed – he sold his horse, which he was hoping to win a big race on, to a man who won't even let him ride it.'

'He told me about that. He seemed very put out.' Susan looked sharply at Jan. 'Do you know why?'

Jan gazed steadily back at Eddie's mother for a few moments, not giving anything away, until, slowly, she nodded. 'If you want to come up and have a cup of coffee with me in the caravan, I'll tell you. It's a long and frustrating story, I'm afraid.'

In the mobile home, Susan Sullivan gazed around her, clearly puzzled that a mother and two small children could squeeze into such a tiny space.

Jan made her promise that she wouldn't tell anyone else what she was about to say. Susan agreed and Jan felt she could trust her.

She was surprised to find that Susan had no idea about Ron's final, imprudent loan and the threat this now represented to him, and possibly to her own home, should they discover Ron owned half of it.

When Susan heard about Eddie's plan to deal with the debt by placing a massive bet, she laughed. 'What were his chances of winning?'

Jan felt oddly hurt by Susan's reaction to her son's heroic solution to the problem. 'He could have done it,' she said defensively. 'The horse could be good enough and he's improving generally. And Eddie's just about up to the job. Actually, after last Saturday, I'd say well up to the job.'

Susan shook her head. 'Poor Eddie.'

'It wasn't just to win the money he was doing it,' Jan went on. 'I think he really wants to prove that he can pull off some amazing deal, like his dad used to. OK, you could say he's trying to do it the easy way by gambling, but at least he was backing himself. And he knew he'd get much bigger odds out of Cyril Goldstone if he rode the horse himself.'

Susan nodded. 'I understand what you're saying. Is there no way you can get the horse back from this Bernie chap, or at least talk him into letting Eddie ride it?'

'There probably is.' Jan made a face. 'What you might call the old-fashioned way.'

'But you're obviously not prepared to do that.'

'No. I'm very fond of Eddie, but there are limits to my loyalty. And Bernie's turned his attentions to Annabel now.'

'Annabel Halstead?'

'Yes.'

'I'm not surprised, she's very attractive. She was one of the few girls Eddie ever took out that I liked, if only she hadn't been so young. Of course, I've never met most of the others, but her parents made a real fuss – at least, her father did and sent her mother round to speak to me – as if I could tell Eddie who to see and who not to see. He was already twenty-three. But, that said, I think maybe Bel was a bit too negative for him.'

'I don't know about that,' Jan said. 'She's been a brilliant friend to me. Don't ask me why, but she's always loved working with me and the horses, and she's a really intelligent girl. I'm sure she could have done almost anything she wanted.'

'Not everyone wants the glamorous life, though, especially if they've already had a taste and know they can have it any time. Where's she living now?'

'She rents a cottage in the village from Mr Carey, who owns a lot of property down there. Eddie won on his mare last week and Mr Carey's standing guarantor for my application for a professional licence.'

'You're going into the big time, are you?' Susan smiled, impressed.

'I hope so,' Jan said. 'I've got two kids to bring up on my own and I'll never do it satisfactorily by winning a few point-to-point races.'

'Well, best of luck. And thank you for telling me about Eddie's bet. I won't tell a soul.'

'If any of the girls notice you've been here, I'll ask them not to say anything,' Jan said.

Annabel's Golf skidded to a halt on the hard standing. She climbed out and banged the door shut.

'Bloody Bernie!' she snapped.

Jan had never seen her so angry. 'What's he done now?' she asked, walking down from the caravan towards her.

'That man's got a hide like a rhino! He's asked me out again tonight! He just doesn't know when to take no for an answer.'

'Oh God, is he still pestering you?'

'You can say that again! He keeps phoning and sending me flowers. I mean, I don't want to sound snotty, but he must realize that we hardly speak the same language. Yet he thinks because he's made a lot of money and I come from a wealthy family we must have something in common. It's pathetic!'

'Calm down, Bel. I'll have a word with him.'

'No, don't. There's no reason why you should do my dirty work for me.'

The two women walked into the yard. Darren

and Tom, as keen as ever to learn everything they could about racehorses and earn Brownie points from Jan, had come in early to help prepare the three horses who were running at the Banbury point-to-point that afternoon. They were busy grooming Russian Eagle.

'Is Bernie coming this afternoon to watch Eagle run?' Jan asked.

'Yes, of course,' Annabel groaned.

'I wonder if he'll bring any of his dodgy-looking mates,' Jan said, 'though they were probably so disillusioned by losing all their money last time that they won't be back.'

'He didn't say if he was bringing anyone, but he's sure Eagle will win with this other jockey; I think he's promised him a huge present. It's crazy,' Annabel sighed. 'As if getting a jockey with a reputation for whacking horses was the answer! I don't think he understands the first thing about racing. He only ever wanted a horse in the first place because of that ghastly girlfriend of his and to snub James McNeill for making a pass at her. Now, unfortunately, he seems to have got a taste for it.'

'I know,' Jan sighed. 'He reads the racing papers from cover to cover every day, but he still knows nothing. I just hope Roger Williams doesn't ride Eagle too hard today. It won't suit him.'

'Does Eagle have much of chance anyway, against this superstar of Virginia's?'

'Against Treble Up? That partly depends on who's

riding him. If it's her younger brother, Harry, that'll help. He's an even worse rider than she was.'

'Actually, I think he is,' Annabel said. 'He was talking about it last time I was over there.'

'How long ago was that?'

'A week or so. Toby Waller came up and George asked me over to dinner again.'

'How's it going with Toby?'

'He's a good friend.'

'That's all?'

Annabel nodded ruefully. 'I find I can't overlook the aesthetic considerations.'

'I don't know,' Jan said with a grin. 'Compared with Bernie, he's quite attractive.'

Bernie's was one of the first faces they saw as they drove into the lorry park just before midday. He was evidently on his own and hopping impatiently from foot to foot.

'How is he?' he asked breathlessly before Jan's feet had even touched the ground.

'He's in good order,' Jan said, and watched his face change as Annabel climbed out of the other side of the cab. For a few seconds, his confidence seemed to desert him; his mouth slackened into a damp, unattractive 'O'. Jan shook her head in amazement that he had allowed himself to become so obviously besotted, and climbed up to let herself in through the groom's door into the back of the lorry. Joe and Darren had travelled in there with the horses, communicating with Jan when they had to via a baby alarm that Gerry had rigged up.

Inside, she was glad to see that the three horses were relaxed. None of them had sweated up and they all looked comparatively docile.

'Well done, boys,' she said, giving each of them a quick rub on the nose. She lingered for a moment with Russian Eagle, fondling his big, floppy lower lip while she stroked his neck. 'Do your best today, boy. I'll tell that cocky jockey not to use his stick at all, then with luck he won't use it much.'

Eagle nodded, as if he approved of the plan.

Jan let herself out and jumped down. 'He's looking fine, Bernie. If you stick around for a while, I'll get him off and you can help groom him,' she teased.

'I wouldn't know how to do that,' Bernie protested.

'Don't you worry, I'll teach you; it's part of my new scheme for owner participation.'

'I've got a couple of other things to do,' Bernie snapped and turned sharply to walk off towards the trade stands before Jan could push him into staying and getting his hands dirty.

'How did you get on with the other horses?' Bernie asked later, after the first two had both finished their races.

'Didn't you see?' Jan asked.

'No, I hadn't got a horse running; I wasn't interested. I was in the car, watching the football on telly.'

'Neither of them troubled the judges today, I'm afraid.'

'Who was riding them.'

'Billy Hanks, of course.'

'Oh well. There you are. That little bugger doesn't know how to ride a finish.'

'You think so, do you? Well, he managed to ride the most winners in the whole Midlands area last season, so he must have got something right.'

'This bloke I've got today,' Bernie said excitedly, 'I went to watch him ride before I asked him, obviously, and he lent me some videos so I could see more. He really understands a horse and how to get the best out of it.'

'By knocking seven bells out of it, I hear. If I see him use his stick too much, I'll draw it to the attention of the stewards. I don't like having my horses bullied.'

'Jan,' Bernie said as if he were talking to a child, 'he's not your horse; he's mine.'

'Listen, Bernie; any horse in my charge I treat as my own, and I'll be mightily pissed off if this jockey of yours does any kind of damage to Eagle, OK?'

Not trusting herself to say more, Jan turned and walked as briskly as she could towards the parade ring, where Annabel had taken Russian Eagle.

Several horses were already striding around the small ring and Jan stopped for a moment to lean against the rail and look at them. There was one long-stepping, rangy individual with the yellow initials VG appliquéd on his navy sheet. Jan assumed this was

Treble Up, though she'd never seen the horse before. She waited for the groom to walk by and checked the number on her arm. He was definitely Virginia's superstar, but there was no sign of the trainer. Jan guessed she was saddling other horses for more important races at a National Hunt course somewhere.

Looking round, she saw Annabel approaching with Eagle and made her way round to walk into the ring with them. While Annabel carried on leading the horse round the perimeter, Treble Up's groom whipped off his sheet and gave Jan her first proper view of the horse. Jan stood in the centre of the ring and tried to make an unbiased comparison between Eagle and Virginia's runner.

From their conformation, they were very different animals. Undoubtedly, over two miles, Treble Up would have had the advantage, although Eagle's sound jumping would be a big help. On a three-mile course like today's, she thought Eagle probably had the edge, but the records confirmed that Virginia's horse stayed as well. In truth, Jan knew that it was too hard to call here in the paddock and the question could only be answered out on the track.

She was joined now by a somewhat subdued Bernie, who had come strutting into the ring with his ungainly, unbalanced stride, and stood six feet away from her. He didn't speak until the jockeys began to spill into the ring, a sudden flurry of colour among the drab olive and khaki waxed jackets of the race goers.

Roger Williams walked over to them and placed himself tactfully between herself and Bernie. He was fairly tall and very skinny, with a thin, beaky nose and useful long arms. He turned to Jan and lifted both eyebrows for his instructions.

Jan knew Bernie had already briefed him and she took in the jockey's self-satisfied smirk. She fixed him with her steeliest glare and was glad to see him quail a bit.

'This horse stands right off and jumps big, so don't fiddle with him at the fences. Keep in touch with the leaders, but don't produce him until you've jumped the third last. Ride him out with hands and heels because if he comes back with a single welt on his arse I'll have your guts for garters. All right?' She gave him a quick cold smile.

'Sure,' the jockey said.

'You do as I said,' Bernie chipped in from the other side, 'and I've told you what happens.' He nodded meaningfully.

'OK, Mr Sutcliffe.'

'Go and mount up,' Jan said. She didn't want a stand-up row in the paddock about how the race should be ridden.

Annabel drew up with Eagle and Jan legged the lanky jockey up into the saddle. The last jockey to mount – typically, Jan thought – was Harry Gilbert, an arrogant nineteen-year-old with long blond curls that dangled from under his helmet.

Jan drew in a deep breath. It would feel very good

indeed, she thought, to beat him and Virginia Gilbert's hotpot.

Jan couldn't face watching the race with Bernie. She managed to slip away into the crowd as he walked down towards the winning post. She would just have to think up an excuse after the race was over.

As the runners reached the start, at the most distant point on the course, she found herself standing beside Colonel Gilbert.

'Hello, Jan,' he nodded while a smile creased his red cheeks. 'Your chap's looking nice.'

'Thanks. So's yours. The bookies seem to think a lot of him, too; hardly any of them will take money for him. Ours is only fives.'

'I know; I've just had a tenner's worth.'

'Gosh, didn't you back yours?'

'Not mine, Jan. I can assure you. Ginny runs an autonomous operation.'

'She's not here today, though?'

'No. She's got a couple of runners at Sandown.'

'Bit more important than here, then.'

'Who's to say?' Colonel Gilbert looked at her with a warm smile in his bright blue eyes. 'How's the licence application coming on?'

'I've just sent in a fresh one,' Jan said. 'I've got everything sorted in the yard now, though I had a bit a trouble finding a backer until Mr Carey very kindly said he would do it.'

'He'll be a good chap to have behind you. He's very careful, I know, but once he's committed, he won't let you down. Ah, I see they're off,' he said, raising his binoculars.

Taking a deep breath, Jan did the same.

For the first mile of the race, Treble Up took the lead; Jan knew he was a front runner and she'd been expecting him to go on. Roger and Russian Eagle lay towards the back of a closely bunched field. As they thundered past the post for the first time, with two full circuits to go, Eagle looked perfectly comfortable.

Out in the country on the far side the field began to get strung out, leaving a cluster of six horses at the front; Eagle was the last of this bunch and Jan felt quite happy about his position.

They came round a long, left-handed bend and passed the post for the second time. Treble Up was still leading, but two others had moved up beside him. Jan noticed that Harry Gilbert was beginning to bounce around on his saddle. Heading for the fence going away from the crowd, she saw his elbows come up like a pair of duck's wings and his hand reach for the sky as they cleared it.

'Oh dear,' Colonel Gilbert murmured beside Jan. 'Harry must be getting tired. I didn't think he was fit enough to ride a race, but he insisted.'

'The horse is going all right, though,' Jan said politely.

'He's not getting a lot of help, I'm afraid. Your horse looks cool as a cucumber. Why have you got that man from Devon riding him?'

'The owner wanted him and was a bit definite about it.'

'Oh, well; so far so good.'

They carried on watching in silence as the order at the front end of the field changed half a mile from home. The two horses who had been tracking Treble Up passed him and ran on strongly to the fence before the long, left-handed curve that would bring them back again to the home straight. Five lengths behind them, Russian Eagle overtook Treble Up. He put in a magnificent jump that left him in third place, two lengths ahead of Virginia's hot shot, but still behind another bay and a well-backed grey called Melon Tree.

Coming round the curve, with a jump on the apex, Eagle was beginning to close the gap to the two leaders. Jan clutched her binoculars like a vice, clenched her teeth and was scarcely aware of breathing as her horse gained ground inch by inch. Behind him, Treble Up was flagging and beginning to look like an also ran.

Roger Williams, old hand that he was, knew perfectly well how to ride a finish without using his stick, but he couldn't help waving it like a bandmaster beating time behind his back, and the horse was responding to the driving rhythm of his body.

At the penultimate fence, Eagle landed a length behind the leaders.

At the last, he was in the air as the two in front touched down. Jan thanked God that he was on the outside, where the ground was slightly higher and the going faster.

Two strides after the fence, Roger Williams cracked his whip down on Eagle's quarters. The big horse stretched his neck and visibly quickened.

The crowd roared; Jan screamed.

Eagle surged past the other bay and crossed the line nose to nose with Melon Tree.

'Russian Eagle and Melon Tree have gone past together,' the commentator said with irritating calmness, while Jan seethed with frustration. From where she was standing, twenty yards from the post, she just couldn't see which horse had clinched it.

She closed her eyes and waited for the announcement of the judges' decision.

'First, Melon Tree; second, Russian Eagle. The third horse . . .'

Jan clenched her fists.

Didn't these people know how much it mattered for Eagle to win?

She sighed. They didn't. Why should they? And, anyway, he hadn't.

But even if Eddie wasn't going to ride the horse at Aintree, Jan was determined to get Eagle there, if only to show that she could keep her part of the bargain.

She felt a moment's anxiety when she wondered what Bernie would say, coming second again by such a tiny margin. She had no complaints about Roger Williams's riding, though she didn't doubt that Bernie would find something to grumble about.

She decided she didn't give a damn. The horse had run superbly; perhaps he could have done with a couple more furlongs, but considering Melon Tree's form she was happy enough.

She wasn't sorry that Treble Up's connections had the ignominy of seeing their hotpot favourite coming home a distant fifth. At least the colonel had had the good sense not to back a horse ridden by his younger son.

'Bad luck, Jan,' he said with genuine feeling.

'Thanks.' Jan smiled wryly with a philosophical shrug of her shoulders, before setting off through the crowds to the course. She ducked under the rope which edged the track and, to her surprise, saw Bernie was already out there, walking with short angry strides towards his horse.

Eagle and Roger had just pulled up and turned to come back. Jan caught up with Bernie.

'That was a shame,' she said. 'We ran him bloody close.'

Bernie turned with his small eyes blazing. 'Jan, I'm sick of him coming sodding second!'

'Bernie, he ran a superb race and beat a lot of nice horses!'

'Next time, I want him to win, so just you make sure you find the right race.'

Jan sighed, though she knew it wasn't worth arguing. 'Bernie, I don't have that much choice. There are good horses in all these Opens.'

Eagle and Roger had reached them. Before Jan could stop him, Bernie caught hold of the reins. 'What the hell were you doing? I thought you said you'd make sure you'd get him there.'

'Mr Sutcliffe, I said I'd do everything I knew to get him there and I did, but that Melon Tree is a hell of a good horse.'

'You're all full of crap, you people!' Bernie said disgustedly and, to Jan's relief, let go of the reins. He took a last look at the jockey, glared at Jan and marched off the course.

Jan took a deep breath and reached up to take Eagle's rein.

'Well done, boy,' she said giving the big horse a vigorous pat on the neck. It was damp with sweat and his flanks were still heaving, but, although he'd had a hard race, he didn't seem at all distressed.

As she led him back towards the paddock, she looked up at Roger Williams. 'By the way, I saw that last crack you gave him, but as it was only one I'll let you off.'

The jockey grinned at her. 'I had to focus his mind on the job.'

'You did well. Never mind Bernie.'

Annabel and the two boys joined them. She led Eagle into the paddock and the slot marked 'Second'.

Roger Williams jumped down and Jan quickly untacked the horse, while Darren flung a sweat rug over his back.

When they reached the lorry, Jan handed the rope to Darren and filled a bucket with warm water from an old milk churn in the box. She put it in front of Russian Eagle, who lowered his head and thirstily sucked up a few pints in as many seconds.

'Oh my God!' Bernie suddenly wailed behind her.

Jan hadn't realized he was there. She looked round and saw him gazing in horror at the horse's head, where a tiny drop of blood had appeared in one of his nostrils.

Jan refused to panic. She'd had several horses who bled a little after a hard race, when the exertion and the consequent blood pressure caused a small vein in the upper nostril to burst. Sometimes it didn't mean anything and until now she'd never seen a sign of it in Eagle.

She was about to reassure Bernie that a small show of blood was probably nothing to worry about, when it suddenly occurred to her that it might be useful to let him worry.

'Oh, hell,' she said, sucking her teeth as she leaned down to take a closer look. 'He must have burst a vessel.'

'I knew it!' Bernie groaned. 'I knew there was something the matter with him! I've been told about this bleeding. One of my friends – he had a horse that did this. It ended up totally knackered; he had to give it away for nothing,' he said, and his former pride in the horse turned instantly to disparagement.

'Relax, Bernie,' Jan said, sensing that Bernie's horse-owning friend, whoever he was, had already done what she was trying to do. 'Lots of horses occasionally bleed a little; it may not mean a thing, so don't do anything hasty.'

'Oh, I know you'd like me to keep the horse and carry on coughing up a hundred and fifty quid a week for a dodgy animal that'll break down any minute. No thanks.'

'Just wait and let the vet have a look at him,' Jan pleaded, while the others looked on silently.

'He's just come a strong second in a very good race, too,' Annabel said.

To Jan's dismay, Bernie seemed to waver a minute at Annabel's intervention. She shot her a quick glance, and Annabel made a guilty face, realizing she'd over-egged the pudding.

Bernie straightened his back and turned away for a moment. 'All right. We'll see what the vet says,' he said, breathing deeply.

He took one last disgusted look at his horse. The thin trickle of blood had reached the end of the animal's nose. He shook his head hopelessly before he turned to Annabel. 'Am I seeing you later, or what?'

Jan watched Annabel's reaction.

'Of course,' Annabel said brightly. 'That'd be great.'

Bernie looked stunned for a moment. Jan guessed

that, despite his thick skin, he'd been prepared for Annabel's rejection.

'Oh, right then. I'll pick you up from your place, about half-seven.' Bernie smirked triumphantly. He took a last look at his horse and walked from the lorry park to get his car.

Jan turned to Annabel. 'Well, that's your evening sorted,' she said sarcastically.

When the vet came in two days later, Jan told him about the slight bleed in Russian Eagle's nose and asked him to take a look at the horse.

He agreed with Jan's view that there was probably nothing much to worry about, but said that in the circumstances he would come again at the end of the week and talk to Bernie.

As they watched him drive away, Jan asked Annabel how Saturday evening with Bernie had gone.

'Pretty awful, but I think I may have made a bit of progress.'

'About what?'

'Wait and see.'

20

Over the next few days Jan had no runners, but on Saturday she had three going to a point-to-point on a picturesque meadow fringed with spiky topped willows on the far bank of the River Severn, near Tewkesbury.

Her best hope for the day was Dingle Bay, with Billy Hanks riding, while Eddie was on board Rhythm Stick, one of Frank Jellard's horses. On the way there, she felt that any one of the horses could win.

By the end of the afternoon, although one had pulled up, Eddie had come a respectable third and Dingle Bay had won for the second time that season.

Eamon Fallon had turned up unexpectedly a minute before the 'off' was called for Dingle Bay's race and he'd yelled himself hoarse beside Jan.

At the end of it, he hugged her, went off to the bookies and came back with two hundred pounds in a bundle of notes, which he handed to Jan.

'I'm sorry, but that's all I've got for you. You'll have to sell the horse now, take out what I owe you and let me have whatever's left.'

'Oh, no!' Jan groaned. 'You said you were having problems, but I didn't know they were as bad as that.'

'Yes, well, nor did I until recently. But it seems I'm a little too trusting of people who don't merit it.'

'I'm really sorry, Eamon. I can't say I wasn't getting worried about the situation, but I've enjoyed training Dingle Bay for you.'

'Don't worry about me; I just don't want you to suffer because of it. You've done a grand job with the horse and you should be able to get a good price for him.'

'Wouldn't you rather I sent him to the spring sales?'

'I'd rather the job was done privately, if you don't mind. I'd want my share of it in cash.'

'It's funny how sometimes your judgement can be completely wrong,' Jan remarked to Annabel as they were going home in the lorry. 'Look at Eamon; the minute I saw him, I thought, "I'll have to watch him." You know what he's like – all talk, flash cars and leather jackets – and when he stopped paying me, I thought, "Right, wait for it, girl. There'll be a lorry up here any minute to collect the horse," and of course I wouldn't have let him leave the yard until the account was settled. But he really doesn't want me to lose out, and he's trusting me completely to sell the horse and give him what's left. It's made me feel quite guilty for doubting him.'

'No wonder the poor chap got so seriously fleeced by these other people, then, if he's that trusting.'

'He knows I've got the horse, so I suppose he thinks he hasn't got much choice. Even so, he won't get fleeced by me,' Jan said firmly. 'We'll find a really good buyer for him; all they've got to do is promise to keep him at Edge Farm,' she grinned.

'Toby might buy him. He's really been enjoying his pointing since he bought Gale Bird.'

'You mean he's been enjoying coming to the races to ogle you.'

'No,' Annabel said mildly. 'He's not like that. He understands.'

Jan wondered, but said nothing more on the subject for the moment.

'Or,' Annabel went on thoughtfully, 'maybe I could persuade Bernie to buy Dingle Bay.'

When Jan got back to Edge Farm, Mary Pritchard was waiting for her in the caravan. Roz had reluctantly taken the day off to be a bridesmaid at the wedding of one of her many cousins, and Jan's mother had volunteered to come over and look after the children.

'Thanks, Mum,' Jan said, picking up Matthew to give him a hug. 'How have they been?'

'They've been as good as gold. Ate all their dinner, and Megan helped me make a cake for their tea. But your young builder chap, Gerry, came up here in a bit of state. He said to tell you Mr Carey's had a heart attack and they've took him in an ambulance to the Nuffield in Cheltenham.'

'Oh my God!' Jan gasped. She was shocked. It had never occurred to her that Victor Carey was getting on in years. 'How bad is he?'

'Oh, he's not too bad, Gerry said. But they had to take him in to be sure.'

'So he's not dying?'

'No. Maybe you should telephone the hospital and find out.'

'I'll go and see him now,' Annabel said decisively. She phoned the hospital for directions and within five minutes her Golf was spurting down the drive.

Jan watched her go with mixed emotions, all negative.

Since she'd begun to have more dealings with Mr Carey, Jan had become fond of him. He didn't laugh very much, if ever, and he could be frustratingly pedantic, but in his quiet way he was enthusiastic, loyal and consistent, and Jan realized she would be very upset if an untimely illness suddenly removed him.

Annabel didn't come to see Jan on her way back from the hospital, but she phoned to say that Mr Carey seemed comfortable enough and he sent his warm regards to Jan and congratulations on Dingle Bay's win. He was also anxious to know if August Moon would be running the next Saturday, as planned.

'If he wants her to run, we'll make bloody sure she does,' Jan said. 'Actually, I think she's in with a good chance.'

For the next few days Jan prayed for Mr Carey and concentrated most of her attention on August Moon, Russian Eagle, Arrow Star and Derring Duke, who were all due to run the following weekend. But all the time at the back of her mind was the thought that poor old Mr Carey had suddenly proved to be as vulnerable as anyone else. The talk in the village was that no close family had come to see him and she felt sad that, rich as he was, he should be so alone in the world.

She found she couldn't even produce much enthusiasm when Toby's lawyers wrote to say that a local investigation agency had unearthed two more cases in which Harold and the Davieses appeared to have acted wrongly and that, once they had enough evidence, they would consider taking further action against him.

In the meantime, in the wider world and a mere ten miles away, the Cheltenham Festival was being held. For the first two days Jan brought a television down to the tack room, and both afternoons she and her staff were glued to it.

'Next year we'll be running horses there, just you wait!' Roz said.

Although Jan knew this was pie in the sky, she couldn't keep her own dreams in check. Watching some of the world's best steeplechasers in action, she was more impatient than ever to be granted her own licence.

At the beginning of the week she'd had a letter from the Jockey Club to confirm that the stewards would like to interview her on Monday, 15 April. That was nearly four weeks away! She didn't know how she would keep sane until then, but, at least the news from the hospital about Mr Carey was good; he was expected home by the weekend, albeit with a full-time nurse.

On Thursday, Gold Cup Day, Jan took herself off to Cheltenham and didn't allow herself to feel one iota of guilt.

As well as her vast estate, Annabel's great-aunt had left Major Halstead a large box at Cheltenham race course. But the major wasn't particularly interested in racing and allowed Annabel to use it for this one day's racing.

She had made a great effort to cater for all the staff from Edge Farm as well as a few other friends. Jan was very appreciative, but after lunch in the box and watching the unpredictable cavalry charge of the Triumph Hurdle, she wasn't sure that she liked this way of watching the races. She felt cocooned in the private dining room with a small band of friends, when she should have been out mixing with the eclectic band of racing nuts, many from Ireland, who made the pilgrimage to Cheltenham every year and gave the festival its unique atmosphere.

The difficulty for Jan had been finding someone to look after the yard while they were all away. Eddie, with an air of great martyrdom, had offered to, so that everyone else could go. But Annabel was adamant that he must come too. In the end, once the morning work was over, Gerry and Jan's father had been press-ganged into minding the shop until Jan got back around six-thirty to do the feeding.

As the afternoon went on, Jan found herself spending more time looking down on the saddling boxes and the pre-parade ring. She watched one race on tiptoes on the lawn in front of the stands. She watched another from the box, but her favourite spot was alongside the railed enclosure reserved for owners and trainers. She was unashamedly fascinated by the famous faces she saw in there.

She couldn't deny that she longed to be there herself one day, chatting to an eager owner who had bought the kind of horse that could win a race like this. But she hardly dared to indulge her fantasies about what she might one day achieve at this, the supreme National Hunt meeting. She found herself looking at the highest quality jumping bloodstock in the world in a different light now that she felt she was within sight of competing with them herself.

Although she immersed herself in the run-up to the highlight of the festival, the Gold Cup, it was inevitable that she should relate more to the big amateur chase that was run later in the afternoon on the same course. The Christie's Foxhunters', though worth more and slightly more competitive, was run under similar conditions to the Aintree race Eddie had been so keen to win – until Bernie had jocked him off.

Eddie and Jan watched the race together, with Annabel and Roz.

'It's so sad you can't ride Eagle at Aintree,' Jan said. 'Look at this lot.' She nodded at the riders coming out onto the course to canter down to the start. Most of them looked very inexperienced compared to the professionals who rode six or more races every day.

'Good Lord!' Eddie said. 'Do *I* look that bad?'

'Not any more, you don't. You did when you first came out to ride last August, but there's not too much wrong with you now except your lack of experience.'

Eddie sighed. 'Well, I'm grateful to you for the few rides you've given me – I loved August Moon last week, but unless I get this ride back on Eagle by some bloody miracle, I don't think I'll be doing much next season.'

'Oh, Ed,' Annabel said, sounding disappointed, 'you can't give up after Jan's spent so much time on you; it wouldn't be fair to her. Anyway, maybe a miracle will turn up.'

'Yeah,' Eddie said gloomily, 'sure it will. I suppose Roger's riding him this Saturday?'

'We'll see,' Jan said. 'I haven't talked to Bernie about it yet. He hasn't even told me what he wants to do with the horse since we saw the vet last week.'

'What did the vet tell him?'

'Much the same as I had said. It might never happen again, or every so often, or it could get worse.'

'How did Bernie take it?' Eddie asked.

'He looked as if he'd just bought a car off me and found it hadn't got an engine.'

'Well,' Annabel said, 'you can ask him in a minute. I saw him earlier and invited him up to the box for a drink after this race.'

'Is he here, then? I wonder why he didn't tell me he was coming,' Jan said. 'It was nice of you to ask him up, though; you didn't have to on my account.'

'I didn't. I felt a bit sorry for him, actually; he's so pathetic, but at least he's behaved himself. I've been out twice with him now and at least he hasn't tried to pounce on me.'

'I'd knee him straight in the goolies if he tried it on me,' Jan said.

Eddie laughed. 'He's probably sussed that already.'

When he arrived, Bernie seemed subdued and somewhat overawed by Major Halstead's box.

'I asked if I could buy one of these,' he said wistfully. 'They just looked at me as if I was the poor relation and said they'd put my name on a waiting list, but they didn't foresee any coming vacant for a very long time. Someone usually has to die first, I'm told.'

'People do hang on to them,' Annabel said. 'My great-aunt took this one over from her father; it's one of the original boxes.'

Jan guessed that Eddie didn't want to talk to Bernie, given the grief Bernie's decision had caused him, so she decided to tackle Bernie head on.

'Look, Bernie, as you're here, I need to know if you definitely want Russian Eagle to run on Sunday.'

'I don't know. That vet of yours said he could easily burst another blood vessel.'

'Well, it's up to you. If you want him to run at Aintree, we need a win and we haven't got much time left. I could only get him entered for one more race after that.'

'I'll let you know tomorrow definitely.'

'And who's going to ride him?'

'It'll have to be your Billy Hanks, if I decide to run him.'

Jan looked at him. She would happily have throttled him, but she tried not to let it show. 'Make sure you ring me tomorrow then.'

Bernie went off to have a bet on the next race at the Tote counter along the corridor and Jan turned to Annabel, who was chatting to Eddie. 'Why do people have to be so bloody difficult!'

'Don't worry,' Annabel said. 'I'll talk to him about it tonight. I'm having dinner with him.'

'What?' Jan remonstrated. 'Again?'

'This'll be the very last time,' Annabel said enigmatically. 'I intend to make that clear.'

Eddie and Jan walked down to the paddock to look at the runners in the County Hurdle.

'What the hell do you think Annabel's up to? I'm sure she doesn't like Bernie, but she never wants to come out to dinner with me.'

Jan glanced at him. He looked hurt and mystified.

'I don't know,' she said truthfully, although she was forming a pretty good idea. 'Maybe she's doing it out of kindness.'

'It'd be kinder to tell him to get stuffed rather than build up his hopes. Mind you, he deserves it; he's a little shit the way he's messing around with Eagle!' Eddie shook his head in despair.

'I don't blame you for being miffed,' Jan said compassionately. 'I know you're fond of Annabel, but remember, she was quite hurt last time round even if it wasn't your fault. And she thinks you're into It-girls, whatever they are. Give her time.'

'I don't think I've got much hope there, really. I know she's not impressed by a chubby wallet like Bernie's, but I don't suppose she's interested in a total bankrupt either.'

'For a start, you're not a total bankrupt and, to be fair to her,' Jan said as they joined the crowd around the parade ring, 'I don't think she gives a damn about that sort of thing. Anyway, let's have a look at these horses if you want to win back some of the money you've lost.'

On their way back from the paddock, Jan ran almost face first into Virginia Gilbert. Unless she wanted to appear inexcusably rude in front of other people, Virginia had no choice but to say something, although the words had to be forced out between a pair of tight lips.

'Oh, hello, Jan. I gather we're going to meet at Aintree.'

'I'm looking forward to it,' Jan replied, with the most convincing smile she could muster.

Virginia glanced at Eddie, not without a gleam of interest, Jan noted. 'Are you riding?' she asked.

'If Jan thinks I'm good enough.' He gave a non-committal grin.

'I'm sure you'll be good enough for Jan,' Virginia said, lifting her beaky nose.

'Thanks,' Eddie laughed.

Virginia hurried on to catch up with the owners she was accompanying.

'Snotty cow,' Jan murmured.

'Now then, Jan. Don't sink to her level. Let's just hope Bernie doesn't screw it up.'

'He still won't let you ride, Eddie. You may as well accept it.' She glanced at him and caught him off guard. The bleakness in his eyes at the thought of losing his chance to win on Russian Eagle told her just how much it mattered to him, whatever the odds against him.

With Mr Carey's agreement, Jan asked Eddie if he would ride August Moon again at the following Sunday's point-to-point at a parkland course west of Hereford.

On the morning after Gold Cup Day, he was up at the yard early to ride out.

'Where's Annabel?' he asked, looking round as they tacked up.

'She phoned just now and asked me if she could come in late for once. After all she did for us yesterday, I couldn't say no, could I?'

'But,' Eddie said, looking baffled, 'she never comes in late. What the hell has she been doing?'

'Relax, Eddie. I'm sure there's a good reason.'

'I dare say there is, but it's such a horrible thought.'

Jan smiled to herself; she guessed Eddie hated the idea that anyone, especially Bernie, might have made more progress with Annabel than he had.

When they came back with the first lot, Eddie offered to ride a second and help with the mucking out to make up for Annabel's absence. Later, after they'd all had breakfast, he still showed no signs of leaving.

'Look, Eddie,' Jan said, 'if you're going to hang around here all morning, you might as well do something useful. The bales in the hay store need restacking. You can use these.' She threw a pair of leather gloves at him.

He caught them with a grin. 'I suppose they are a bit heavy for you girls.'

Over the next hour Jan saw Eddie glance several times down the track towards the lane. She was as intrigued as Eddie to know why Annabel was late, but, unlike him, she was absolutely certain that a night of passion with Bernie Sutcliffe was not the reason.

When at last the black Golf turned off the road,

Eddie was the first to look up and start walking towards the car park.

Jan enjoyed a drama and didn't want to miss anything. She followed quickly and was standing beside Eddie as Annabel pulled up. They waited while she got out and leaned back in to the car to pick up a folder. She closed the door and stood looking at them for a moment with a small, triumphant smile on her face.

'Annabel?' Jan said suspiciously. 'What have you done?'

'I've done the dirty deed with Bernie,' she said.

'What?' Eddie and Jan yelled together.

Annabel laughed, then put on a face of affronted disgust. 'God, no; not that! As if I could!'

'Well then,' Eddie asked with a tremble in his voice, 'what dirty deed have you done?'

'I've persuaded him to buy Dingle Bay!' Annabel resumed her victorious look and started walking towards the yard, while Eddie and Jan followed.

'Oh,' said Jan, feeling a little let down. 'That's great, but why did it take all night?'

'It didn't, but I arranged to meet him this morning at my solicitors in Cheltenham to get it all agreed in writing.' She patted the folder she was carrying.

Jan looked quizzically at her. 'You didn't have to do that. That's my job. Eamon only gave me the authority to deal with it.'

'Yes, of course, you'll have to sign your side of things and you'll get the money for Dingle, but it was the other half of the deal that I really wanted to tie up.'

'What other half of the deal?' Jan asked, impatient at Annabel's deliberate vagueness.

'Basically, I've bought Dingle Bay, so I'll be laying for him, and I've passed him on to Bernie in a straight swap for Russian Eagle.'

Eddie and Jan both stopped dead in their tracks. Annabel turned to see their reaction.

Eddie looked at her in puzzled astonishment, with his chest heaving. 'Jesus! That's fantastic!' he laughed.

Jan smiled and shook her head. 'But where did you get the money?'

'Do you remember, I told you, I've always had that trust my great-aunt set up for me and Charley when she left the estate to Dad? I'll have to persuade the trustees to cough up. I've made very few demands on it, though, and I don't think I'll have too much trouble but, so you don't have to wait for the money, I've organized a loan from my bank. And you can take his training fees out of my wages.'

'Are you sure you want to do this, though?'

'Of course I am. Eagle's been my favourite since he arrived at Stonewall. I know he'll win more races and I think he'll be a bloody good investment – at least, that's what I'll tell the trustees,' she added with a grin. 'So you'd better make sure he does.'

'Bel, you devious little cow! I thought you might be up to something like that,' Jan said. 'But to persuade him to swap Eagle for Dingle Bay – that was brilliant!'

'I suddenly thought of it yesterday when he came up to the box at Cheltenham, and I was pretty sure he'd go for it. He wouldn't have to part with any money and he would save face. I knew he was terrified of hanging on to Eagle, thinking he might burst another blood vessel any minute, but he didn't want to seem too wimpish about it. This way, he's got a winning horse without any question mark over it.'

'Bel,' Eddie asked carefully, 'if what you're now saying is that you own Eagle, what are your plans for him?'

'I thought, if he qualifies, I'd ask Roger Williams to ride him in the Foxhunters' for me,' she said, deadpan.

Eddie stared at her. A muscle in his jaw twitched. He looked as of he were about to say something very angry, changed his mind and walked on past Annabel, towards the tack room.

Annabel looked after him, waiting until he had almost disappeared through the door. 'Eddie,' she laughed. 'I've changed my mind. I want you to ride him.'

'For fuck's sake!' Eddie spun round. 'Don't do that to me!' He laughed. 'I didn't think you had it in you to be that nasty.'

'Of course I wouldn't have bought the horse if I hadn't known how desperate you were to ride him, though, as a matter of fact, it was your mother's idea.'

'My mother's?' Eddie said in astonishment.

'She was up here a few weeks ago,' Jan said. 'I promised not to tell you, but I didn't know she'd been to see Bel, too. Anyway, you'd better get your act together, now you've got two rides on Sunday. I just hope you're bloody well up to it.'

Jan rang Mr Carey's house next morning. Julie's mother, who cleaned for him, answered the phone and told her that Mr Carey was home from hospital. She went off for a few minutes before coming back to tell Jan that he would like to see her if she could call round early that evening.

Jan took a couple of her maidens to run at a local meeting in the afternoon. Although she came back empty-handed, both had run as well as she could have hoped and she wasn't too disappointed. When she went to Mr Carey's, she was shown up to his bedroom by an efficient but taciturn nurse. It was the first time Jan had seen him since his heart attack and she was shocked by the change in him. He was propped up against a bank of white pillows on a large, Victorian mahogany bed. His face seemed to have collapsed into a waxy mask of pale, sagging folds. His voice was thin and breathy, but his pale blue eyes were as sharp as ever beneath their hooded brows.

He brushed aside her enquiries about his health. 'Tell me how you got on today.'

She gave him a short account of both horses' performance.

He knew which horses she was talking about and, although they weren't his, he understood exactly what she was saying. 'You're right not to be too put out,' he said. 'As a National Hunt trainer, you'd be doing very well to get one in five of your runners first past the post. Of course, you must always go out to win, but take the losers in your stride.'

'August Moon's definitely going tomorrow in the confined race, with Eddie Sullivan on board, as you agreed. He's riding Russian Eagle in the Open, too.'

'Good,' Mr Carey nodded faintly. 'I'm so pleased with the way the mare's going, I wonder if we mightn't try racing her under rules again next season?'

Jan was doubtful. 'She hasn't won an Open yet and she's getting a bit long in the tooth, though I suppose we might find a race that suits her. If she were mine, I think I'd run her between the flags for another year and then maybe send her to stud.'

'You could be right. Anyway, I'm looking forward very much to hearing how she runs tomorrow. Would you be kind enough to come in and tell me afterwards? Bring the children if you can't find a minder. The nurse will give them some tea and cake if I ask her.'

'I'll do that, Mr Carey. Would you like me to put something on August Moon for you tomorrow, if the odds aren't too bad?'

'Oh no, I never bet. For me, the sport is between the horses, not the bookmakers and the punters.'

The grey stone mansion and its ancient parkland, where the West Hereford Harriers' meeting was being held, lay under a clear, blue sky. It was a bright day, recalling the recent passing of winter with a nip in the breeze, which ruffled the budding branches of the trees around the course.

Jan responded to the change in the weather like a lark on the wing. Everything was on course with her licence application; she had recovered the debt she was owed by Eamon. Annabel was now an owner, as well as head groom, and had persuaded one of her brothers to pay for half of Russian Eagle and split the training fees. Eddie once again had the ride on him and they still had two more chances to win an open point-to-point to qualify the horse for the big race at Aintree.

Jan drove into the area roped off for lorries and managed to park beneath the broad spreading branches of a massive old oak. They had four runners on board and Billy Hanks was riding the two that Eddie wasn't.

Jan walked the course with both of them. She knew it well and it was one of her favourites. It was all on permanent pasture, but the ground could sometimes be a little boggy just before the fence on one of the bottom corners. Jan and her jockeys inspected the ground there carefully and decided the only route to take was on the inside.

Walking back to the lorry, they looked up between the parkland oaks and across the sweep of sheep-grazed turf, broken only by the white timber running rails and the big, solid birch fences, to where a large crowd was gathering below the high terraces in front of the house.

'This is such a beautiful course. I'd love to win here,' Eddie said.

Billy laughed. 'You soppy bugger! It don't matter what the bloody course looks like so long as you win.'

But Jan understood. 'I know what you mean, Eddie. So you go for it!'

Jan thought it was perfectly possible for Eddie to score a double that day. She hadn't said so and, to her surprise, Eddie hadn't mentioned it either, although everyone else in the yard had been talking about the possibility.

An hour later she legged him up on August Moon wearing Mr Carey's colours of pink and grey stripes. Watching them leave the parade ring, she thought he had just the right balance of fear and confidence to ride at his best. As the runners were going down to the start, Jan and Annabel walked across to the other side of the track, from where they could see every fence.

She was glad Annabel was with her and watched calmly as the race started. She felt very proud of Eddie and a little pleased with herself at the way he rode the mare. He was presenting her correctly at every fence and letting her travel quietly between them. He was lying comfortably within the front half of the field of twelve and cruising when they came past the post at the start of the final circuit.

The runners dropped down the slope towards the far corner, all still in contention, in a fast moving splash of colour against a backdrop of green and brown.

Jan peered through her binoculars, hoping Eddie had room to take the short way across the corner again. There were five horses abreast and Jan saw with a sudden jerk in her guts that Eddie was cutting the corner too tightly coming to the fence. As they got to it, the horse nearest him wasn't leaving him room to get a line on the obstacle. A second later, August Moon's head popped up, above the side of the wing. The mare's front legs came over, leaving her back end stranded. Eddie shot from the saddle and landed four or five yards outside the wing.

Jan gasped and trained her glasses on the pink and grey bundle until it moved and slowly stood up. She flicked her attention back to the horse, which had scrambled backwards off the wing and was trotting around aimlessly behind the fence.

The St John's ambulance was already bouncing down the far side of the track to where Eddie was limping towards them.

Jan looked at Annabel. 'What a cock up! Eh? At least they're both still standing. If I get the horse, can you check Eddie?'

'He'll be all right. They'll look after him. I'll come with you.'

The two women set of at a run diagonally across the course. As they ran, they saw a public-spirited spectator had already caught hold of the mare's reins and walked her off the course. August Moon seemed to have calmed down after the first confusion of hitting the wing and losing her jockey and had put her head down to sample some of the lush grass that grew in that part of the park.

'Get her head up!' Jan panted pointlessly into the breeze, too far away to be heard.

'At least someone's caught her,' Annabel puffed back. 'In fact, I think I'm going to walk.'

Jan slowed as well and they carried on at a brisk stride down to the corner of the track. As they reached it, the ambulance drove up and stopped. Eddie climbed out.

'How is she?' he asked, peering at August Moon.

'I haven't had a look at her yet,' Jan said. 'But she seems OK.' She turned to the man who had caught the horse. 'Thanks very much; that's saved us a lot of running about.'

'No problem,' he answered with a touch of self-importance. 'She didn't mind being caught. She's a lovely animal.' He looked at Eddie. 'You should talk to the stewards about that fella who didn't let you back in.'

Eddie shook his head wearily. 'No. It was my fault; I went too far inside to get off that patch of soft ground. He just carried on on his own line.'

Jan nodded. 'I wish he wasn't right, but I'm afraid he is. OK, Eddie, you might as well get a lift in the ambulance and get checked over. Does anything hurt?'

'Only my pride.'

'Better get checked anyway. Bel and I will walk the horse up. See you back at the lorry.'

There was one more race before the Open. Jan didn't have a runner in it and as Eddie had returned from the St John's ambulance, having been thoroughly checked over, he sat with her in the cab of the lorry, silent for the most part, chewing gum and trying to keep up his resolve.

Jan had brought some tea in a flask and poured a cup for him.

'Relax, Eddie. Just remember, though I want you to win very much, in the end it's only a horse race and, whatever happens, it isn't a matter of life and death.'

'Maybe,' he grunted, 'but it could make the difference between a comfortable life and a pretty uncertain one.'

'Eddie, the last thing I want to do is sound negative but, while I really think you could win today, the Foxhunters' is a much bigger challenge. I know it means a hell of a lot to you to win it, but you've got to be prepared for the fact that you might not.'

'I've made contingency plans in case I don't, but the last thing I want to do is to carry them out.'

'Why, what are they?'

'As I have no intention of losing today or on Thursday week, there's no point in telling you. I shouldn't even have mentioned there was another option.'

Jan sighed. It had occurred to her that she'd been trying to persuade a jockey that he might not win, when she'd always believed that going out with total self-belief was an essential tool in a jockey's armoury. 'OK. Have it your own way. Go out and win! You know you can do it.'

And she pointed out to Eddie that he had the psychological advantage: of the nine runners, three had already been beaten by Eagle that season and he hadn't met the others before.

Russian Eagle looked magnificent in the paddock and caught a lot of eyes. As a result of his performance against Melon Tree at Banbury, he was a strong favourite with the bookies.

Jan legged Eddie up into the saddle, where he sat limply, pale and nervous in Annabel's colours of blue and green hoops.

'Pull yourself together, Eddie, for God's sake,' Jan said quietly. She didn't want to show him up in front of the other jockeys.

'I'll be all right, Jan. Once we're off.'

'Just ride him like you rode Moon until you fell off. Keep in touch, watch that corner this time and start pushing him along three from home.'

Eddie nodded, squeezed Eagle's flanks and steered him towards the gate out onto the course.

Jan turned to Annabel. 'I suppose I'll have to watch this race with you too, now you're the owner.'

'I think you should,' Annabel grinned. 'Poor Eddie looks pretty ghastly, doesn't he?'

'He'll be OK.'

'But Eagle looks great!' Annabel said proudly.

'That's because his groom won't leave him alone and stop fussing over him.' Jan laughed.

They walked across the course to the same spot where they had watched August Moon's race and Darren tagged along too.

'My God,' Annabel said, 'now I own this horse, I'm beginning to realize how terrifying it is. I'm shaking like a leaf!'

Jan, too, found her heart thumping more than normal before a race, simply because it meant so much to Eddie. She gazed through her binoculars at Eagle standing quietly on one side, having his girth checked. While the others milled around, he looked as if he held their fidgeting in disdain. When the starter called them in, Eddie moved him forward and they set off from an ideal spot in the middle of the track. The nine runners went off at a good crack and took the first fence in a bunch, but by the third they'd begun to get strung out as the pace had its effect.

'What d'you think, boss?' Darren squeaked with excitement, as the field came past the winning post for the first time.

'I think there's another circuit to go, but Eagle looks happy enough.'

'Can I take him to Aintree if he wins today?'

Annabel laughed. 'Do you think he'll win, then?'

'Course I do! I've put twenty quid on.'

Jan's instincts were to give him a good rollocking there and then. Fourteen-year-old boys putting on bets like that could be habit forming, but for the moment she decided to defer the lecture. 'Then he'd bloody well better win, hadn't he?' she muttered.

Two minutes later Eagle flew over the last fence. Jan held her breath until she saw just how far he was in front of the next horse. She let it out again with a rush when she saw they had a clear five-length advantage. She had no doubts about Eagle's ability to hold on and fight off any challenge that might be launched.

Annabel grabbed her by the arm when they saw Eddie give the horse one quick slap across its quarters, just as Roger Williams had done two weeks before, and Eagle stretched a little more. By the time he reached the post he was seven lengths clear of the second and Darren, who'd shouted himself voiceless on the run in, was trembling so much Jan thought he would do himself damage.

'Darren,' she said, a little hoarse from her own vocal exertions, 'pull yourself together, lad. You've got to get down and lead that horse in for Bel.'

He looked at her, puzzled, as if he'd just come out of a dream, then his face broke into a huge smile as he turned to Annabel. 'Bloody hell, Bel! He's done it!'

'He sure has,' Annabel agreed joyfully. 'Now go and get him, you silly little monkey.'

She and Jan followed closely behind as he ran to the course, ducked under the rails and raced up the track to where Eddie had finally pulled up and was trotting back towards the paddock.

They reached him just before Darren led the horse off the course.

Jan dabbed a small tear from the corner of her eye and gave Eddie the biggest smile her face could muster. 'Eddie! I'm so proud of you! And you too, old boy,' she added, giving Eagle a hug. 'I told you you could do it!'

Eddie was breathless and beaming so broadly he could hardly speak. 'Thanks, Jan,' he managed. 'You're a star.' He turned to Annabel, who like Jan was trying to fight back the tears. 'Bel, I don't know what made you buy this horse, but thank God you did! I'm really, really grateful.'

'Don't thank me, Eddie,' she replied through her laughter. 'You were pretty bloody brilliant yourself!'

Jan persuaded everyone to postpone any celebration and merry-making until after they'd got back with the horses. She let Darren run off and find the bookie, who now owed him sixty pounds for his two-to-one bet, while she washed Eagle down, and checked for any signs of bleeding.

'He's clear,' she told Annabel, who was holding her horse's head.

'Thank God!' she said. 'You were worried he mightn't be, weren't you?'

'It was always possible that it could happen again.'

'But you thought he might, didn't you?' Eddie asked.

'I was worried,' Jan admitted. 'I've been around horses long enough to know that it doesn't take much to make them go wrong. If you've had a warning like that, you've got to take it seriously. In a way, Bernie was half-right to get so panicky – thank God he did, though,' she added with a laugh.

'And thank God for Bel. It's just too bloody fantastic. Thanks to her I got the ride back.' He shook his head. 'And there I was, thinking she'd gone off to bed with Bernie on Gold Cup Day!'

'As if I could!' Annabel protested.

'I did tell you at the time it was absolutely out of the question,' Jan reminded him. 'But don't forget I can see Bernie through a woman's eyes and I can tell you, it's not a pretty sight!'

On the way home, Jan decided that one of the first people she should see was Victor Carey. She hoped he would be well enough to appreciate the yard's success that day and as soon as she was happy that Eagle and the other horses were settled in for the night, she asked Roz to keep an eye on the children for twenty minutes while she drove down to Stanfield Court.

When she walked into his large bedroom, Mr Carey's wrinkled features were lit by a single forty-watt bulb that shone beneath a tasselled lampshade on the far side of the room. Jan strained to see him as he listened intently to her description of the day's races.

'I can't tell you how thrilled I am you've had a win with Russian Eagle,' he said between stertorous breaths. 'And what a disappointment for Edward with Moony.'

'At least he wasn't hurt, nor was the horse. They'll have another race next week.'

'I'll look forward to that,' Mr Carey wheezed. 'And thank you so much.'

He closed his eyes and appeared to sink a little deeper into his pillows.

'Thanks, Mr Carey. Goodnight, then,' Jan said and tiptoed from the room.

The champagne was already chilled and waiting when Jan arrived back at Edge Farm. No cheap substitutes for Annabel, Jan thought with a smile. In an hour of celebration, Jan was surprised to see just how much everyone in the yard had wanted Eddie to win this race and go on to Aintree with Eagle. When Eddie suggested they go out to dinner, Jan wanted to say no, but Roz leaped in.

'You've *gotta* go, Jan. Don't worry, I'll look after the kids. You and Eddie really deserve it, and Annabel's the owner, so she's gotta go too!'

Jan would happily have stayed at home. For her, seeing the horse cross the line first was enough celebration in its own right, but she recognized that having a party with owners and jockeys was part of the job and she'd better get used to it.

News of Russian Eagle's success had already reached the Fox & Pheasant, so there was much rejoicing over Jan's win by the regulars who liked to follow local horses. Eddie had become a popular person in the pub and the pair of them were congratulated with genuine warmth.

Jan felt that, whatever difficulties she had yet to conquer to get her licence, she had the great comfort of knowing she'd been accepted here in the village. But at midnight she asked Eddie if he would drop her back at the caravan.

'It's been a great day, Eddie, but I'm absolutely cream-crackered. I started at six and I'm up again at six tomorrow.'

'Of course,' he said. 'I shouldn't have made you come.'

'I'm glad I did, though,' Jan said as they were driving up the lane back to the yard. 'And I hope it will be the first of many for you on Eagle.'

Eddie inclined his head. 'So do I and the next one's the big one! Do you know, I still find it extraordinary that all this started from my seeing a little girl about to be kicked by a mad horse at Doncaster Sales last May.'

'I sometimes think all our lives are shaped by a

chain of coincidence and chance which we can't control, however much we think we're in command.'

'Do you?' Eddie said, surprised. 'So do I, as it happens, but I had the firm impression that you were very much a believer in being master of one's own destiny.'

'An individual can only do so much. Of course, you mustn't ignore the chances you're offered, but in the end you need a bit of luck, or help from God, depending on your point of view.'

'He was on our side today, eh, Jan?'

'Yeah,' she smiled. 'It looked like it.'

Eddie dropped her at the hard standing and waited there for a moment while she walked up to the caravan.

21

Three weeks after Jan had sent in her second application, the same Jockey Club inspector came to check her premises again. This time he arrived knowing that she had already sent out a flurry of winning pointers from the yard.

But, as Jan had anticipated, he first made a beeline for the gates and fences. Satisfied with these, he turned his attention to the buildings, approved the new treatment Gerry had given them and complimented Jan on the state of her grass gallop.

'We're lucky with that,' she said. 'The soil's pretty shallow here and water runs off down the hill without really soaking in, so provided we don't go on it straight after rain, it doesn't get cut up too much.'

'Good. Well, I don't think I need detain you any longer. I'm glad to be able to tell you that I will be sending in a positive report on all aspects of your establishment. I hope everything goes well for you at Portman Square next month. And I see you've got Russian Eagle entered for the Foxhunters' at Liverpool. Will he run, do you think?'

'Now he's qualified, I very much hope so,' Jan said.

'Good, and the best of luck.'

Jan didn't see Eddie all day. He'd rung in the morning to say he had to go to London early and couldn't come in to ride. He rang again on his way back and asked if she could meet him for a drink at the White Horse.

Although it was a Monday, there was a large crowd in the pub when Jan arrived just after eight, and several people had been over to Herefordshire the day before to see her horses run. Eddie had arrived before her and was on the receiving end of a lot of jokes about which part of the fence to jump. To Jan's relief, with Eagle's win under his belt, he seemed to be taking them in good part.

'Why did you want me to come for a drink, then?' she asked when she could talk to him alone.

'Just to say thanks for yesterday and sorry for mucking up on Moon, and because I thought you would bring Annabel with you.'

'Eddie, you creep! Why didn't you say so? I'd have brought her.'

'No,' Eddie retracted. 'It was you I wanted to see, I promise. I was going to ask: now I'm definitely riding in the Foxhunters', do you really think I'm up to it?'

'Hello, hello. If it isn't young Mr Sullivan,' said a voice directly behind Jan's shoulder.

She turned and saw a short, balding man in a bright green tweed suit. Standing behind him was Sharon

Goldstone. *This man,* Jan thought, *is either Sharon's latest conquest or her father*.

'Hello, Cyril,' Eddie said. 'I've never seen you down here before, fraternizing with the enemy.'

'I don't consider this lot the enemy,' Cyril said, looking around him with undisguised scorn.

'That must be because you haven't got a betting shop near here. There are some formidable punters among this lot, I can assure you.'

'Hmm,' Cyril grunted cynically. 'They don't look very rich on it.'

'Shut up, Dad,' Sharon whined over his shoulder. 'They're all right. Don't be so bloody rude.'

Cyril appeared abruptly to realize that he'd been indiscreet. 'I'm sorry,' he said, looking around the room in general, though nobody seemed to have heard, or taken offence. 'But I'm glad I've seen you, Edward. I hear you had a fall yesterday.'

Eddie shrugged his shoulders as if it couldn't have mattered less. 'I'm afraid I'm a bit of a beginner.'

'But you qualified that horse for Aintree, didn't you?' Cyril's eyes hardened. 'So don't give me the old bullshit. I wasn't born yesterday, son.'

Eddie looked at him steadily. 'No I would say there was nothing of the newborn babe about you, Cyril, apart perhaps from your lack of hair.'

'You lippy young toe-rag!' Cyril's eyes blazed for a moment. 'It's no wonder you've gone bloody skint is it, chucking your money around on silly bets!'

Eddie shrugged his shoulders again. 'Oh well. I had

money then. Won some, lost some. But Cyril, how rude of me! I haven't introduced you to—'

'I know who she is.'

'But she may not know who you are, Cyril.'

The little man attempted to smile through clenched teeth.

'This is Cyril Goldstone,' Eddie said to Jan. 'He owns about fifty betting shops.'

'Now you're a jockey,' Jan said with a grin, 'I'm not sure you should be talking to him, then.'

'All right. I'll stop,' Eddie answered, as if Cyril wasn't there. 'I'll just get him a drink first. What would you like, Cyril?'

'Nothing. I don't want a drink with you.'

'OK. Sharon?'

'White wine, please.'

'I'll get it, Sharon,' Cyril said. He grasped her by the upper arm and started to lead her to another part of the bar.

Sharon shook herself free. 'Piss off, Dad!'

Jan saw the back of Cyril's ears go plum red as he changed direction and headed for the door.

Sharon was looking at Eddie with bright, laughing eyes. 'God, it kills me the way you do that to him,' she tittered, covering her mouth with one hand. 'He gets so wound up 'cos he knows you don't give a shit.'

'As it happens, I do give a shit,' Eddie said. 'I just don't like him knowing.'

Eddie went up to Edge Farm two mornings later to ride out with Jan, Roz and Joe.

'I don't think you should trust Sharon Goldstone,' Jan said to him as they hacked up to the gallop under a choppy March sky.

'I don't.'

'But you admitted to her the other day at the pub, after her dad had gone, that this bet matters to you. I'm sure she'll tell him.'

'Jan, Cyril's a very wily old fox. He knows perfectly well it matters to me. Astonishingly enough, I think he just came down to find out how confident I was.' Eddie grinned. 'Even someone as rich as Cyril doesn't like to lose half a million if they can help it.'

'I don't suppose he's that worried,' Jan said. 'After all, you've only won that single race with Eagle.'

'True,' Eddie agreed. 'But he'll be thinking about it, and it might come in handy if Sharon thinks I don't know she goes back and tells him everything.'

'It made me laugh the way that tart was all over you when you gave him such a hard time. She obviously fancies you.'

'And,' Eddie said ruefully, 'as you might have noticed from what she was wearing, she hasn't got much taste.'

Jan chuckled and turned round to Roz and Joe, who were following. 'OK, let's do a bit of work!'

The four horses turned into the bottom of the grass gallop and did a half-speed in pairs. It was a steep climb for the last fifty yards, but Eagle was scarcely blowing at the top.

'Good,' Jan shouted across at Eddie. 'He's as fit as I've seen him. We mustn't overdo it if we want him spot on in eight days' time. And the fitter he is, the less chance of him bleeding again.'

When they got back to the yard, the phone in the tack room was ringing.

Jan looked at her watch. It was ten to eight; too early for most owners.

She picked up the phone. 'Hello, Edge Farm Stables.'

'Jan? It's Julie here, from the pub. My mum's just rung; she works up at Mr Carey's. She found him—'

Jan's heart missed a beat. She knew what she was going to hear.

Julie sniffed. 'She found him . . . dead.'

'Oh no! How terrible!'

'Yes, she's phoned for an ambulance and told the police; but it was probably another heart attack.'

'Oh, God!' Jan groaned. When he'd said he was on the mend, she'd believed him because she had wanted to. She suddenly realized that she cared very much, and not because she would have to find someone else to put up the bond.

Instantly she felt guilty for even allowing herself to think of this aspect of the old man's death.

'I thought you'd want to know,' Julie was saying.

'You know, him having a horse with you and everything.'

'Yes, thanks. I saw quite a bit of him recently.'

'Mum said he liked you and he was very interested in what you were doing up there.'

'Well, thanks for telling me, Julie.'

'That's all right. See you soon. 'Bye.'

Jan put down the phone and looked at it. The others had all come in, filling the tack room, and saw her face.

'Mr Carey?' Annabel asked.

Jan nodded. Annabel looked away. 'Oh. The poor old chap,' she said. 'Was it a heart attack?'

'I don't know,' Jan answered. 'Julie's mother found him and called an ambulance – a bit late really, I suppose.'

'Oh dear,' Eddie sighed. 'I was worried this might happen.'

After all the exhilarating events of the previous few weeks, with Annabel buying Eagle, Eddie getting back the ride on him, Eagle's win and the inspector's good report on Edge Farm, Jan was hit very hard by Victor Carey's death.

Now, once again, it seemed that the forces of nature were determined to block her path, just when there was light at the end of the tunnel. She cried herself to sleep, not knowing if she was crying for her own loss or for Mr Carey. Nevertheless, she prayed to God that he would give her just one more chance to make a future for her children.

Jan was awake and up early the next morning. She looked across the broad Severn Vale to see the rays of a dawn sun hit the sharp, humped back of the Malverns, as isolated clusters of fat clouds were thrust over it by a fickle March wind.

She stepped outside and faced it, wanting the cool air to cleanse her mind and blow away the doubt and fears of the night. She took several deep breaths and told herself firmly whatever mountains came her way, she would climb them.

She didn't have John, but she had a yard full of nice horses; she had almost a score of winners to her name that season and her friends were as loyal as she could have wished.

She would miss old Mr Carey, for his wisdom and for himself. She was sure, though, that somehow another backer would appear eventually from somewhere to put up the guarantee she needed.

As if to dampen her revived spirits, however, the big rain-bearing clouds decided to empty their contents over the west of England for the next two days and every Saturday point-to-point meeting in the region was abandoned.

With the familiar contrariness of the English

weather, the rain stopped at midday and the sky began to clear. Philosophically Jan took the opportunity to have the afternoon off and went shopping with her children in Cheltenham.

When she got back, Annabel invited her to dinner at the cottage with Toby Waller and a few other friends interested in racing. Jan was exhausted. She couldn't get into the right mood and, feeling a little guilty at letting Annabel down, left at eleven to drive back to the caravan.

Roz, who had been babysitting again, was gathering up her things to leave as Jan walked through the door.

'Hi, Jan!' she greeted her. 'Nice evening?'

'Great, thanks, but I'm ready for bed. We've got most of the horses to take out tomorrow, I'm afraid.'

'That's OK. I'll be up at half-seven. Oh, by the way, I forgot to say, earlier this afternoon, when you were in Cheltenham, that tacky blonde girl who knows Eddie came up.'

'Which tacky blonde girl?' Jan asked.

'There's only one like this – I reckon she's called Sharon.'

Jan tensed at once and pricked her ears. 'Sharon? What did she want?'

'Well I didn't talk to her much. Joe did; he said she wanted to have a look around the yard because she was thinking of having a horse here.' Roz shrugged her shoulders. 'You've often said owners come in all shapes and sizes. Anyway, Joe spent a good hour showing her round and that, and apparently, when she went, she said she'd give you a ring about definitely sending a horse, so that's good isn't it?'

Jan didn't answer at once. 'Did she leave her number or give Joe her name?'

Roz thought for a moment. 'I don't know. I didn't ask.'

When Roz had gone, Jan told herself not to be paranoid. For a start, there wasn't much Sharon could have done, even if she'd had a good snoop. Besides, it was perfectly possible the girl did want to keep a pointer, and it was quite clear that she wouldn't mind an excuse to be hanging around Eddie a lot more. Jan smiled as she wondered what effect that might have on Annabel's attitude towards him.

She went through to look at the children, who were sleeping contentedly, and got into bed herself, where she lay awake thinking about the future.

She had no more idea than she'd had a week ago about who she could turn to for the guarantee she needed, but she was confident that if Eagle did win at Aintree in five days' time, a volunteer would appear.

22

The Martell Foxhunters' Chase took place at Aintree on the Thursday of the Grand National meeting – two days before the world-famous race was run over the same course, although it was nearly two miles shorter. The fourth race on the card, it was due to start at three forty-five.

As Jan had only a sketchy idea of the course's layout and what she was supposed to do when she got there, she decided to arrive at least four hours before the 'off'. She'd never been to Liverpool or its suburb, Aintree, but she estimated the journey time in her elderly lorry at three and a half hours and added another hour to allow for traffic jams and breakdowns.

At five-thirty she slipped out of bed, being careful not to wake the children on the other side of the flimsy partition, and walked in chilly darkness down to the yard. She let herself into Eagle's box and gave him a small feed and fresh water. Then she checked his tack, his passport and everything else she needed or might need to get him to the start of the biggest race of her career.

In the still, pre-dawn silence, with the momentous day in front of her, she felt alone and vulnerable.

In the end, she thought, if it went wrong today, whatever happened, it would be her fault: for not preparing the horse properly; for letting the wrong jockey ride it; for entering a sub-standard horse in the first place.

If they won, she would share the credit equally with the horse and the jockey. That was the deal. That was the way it would be perceived.

As a hint of pink seeped into the eastern sky above the Cotswold edge and the birds began their spring morning chatter, the peace was shattered by Annabel driving up the track, followed closely by Joe in his unbaffled Ford Fiesta, bringing Darren with him.

In the tack room, they drank mugs of tea and talked with subdued voices in deference to the day ahead of them.

At six-fifteen Roz arrived and went with Jan up to the caravan. They checked that everything Megan and Matty would need for the day was ready. When the children woke, Roz was going to give them breakfast then drive them over to Jan's mother. It was Reg's idea that they should spend the day there, so Mary wouldn't get lonely while he was up at Aintree watching the race. He thought the children might take her mind off all the tension of the day.

When Jan was satisfied that she'd thought of everything they would need, she left Roz and went back down to the yard, where she switched on all the lights. Annabel came out of the tack room and they went to Eagle's stable. Annabel held the horse while Jan bandaged his legs and buckled on his travel rug.

She led him up the lowered ramp of the lorry, carefully secured his head-collar rope and shot down the bolts of the partitions. Everything that she had done before a thousand times she checked and double-checked today. Finally, she made sure the horse was settled and they closed the ramp.

On a list she'd made, she ticked off everything they had to take. Once she was completely satisfied, Joe and Darren clambered into the box, while she got up into the cab with Annabel and started the engine. She didn't speak for the first twenty minutes, as they trundled towards the motorway junction at Tewkesbury, but once they were on the M5, which was comparatively uncongested at that time of the morning, she relaxed.

She glanced at Annabel. 'Nervous?' she asked.

'Not yet. But this is about the most exciting thing I've ever done in my life. I think it's incredible, really – there I was riding out over the Welsh hills to get away from the crowds and hassle of London and, though I've always loved horses, I had absolutely no interest in racing and all the bull that goes with it.' Annabel laughed. 'But now here I am, an owner for heaven's sake, taking a horse to Aintree to race over the Grand National course!'

Jan smiled because she understood what Annabel

was saying. It had pleased her to see how her friend had blossomed and opened up since she'd moved to Stanfield and Edge Farm.

'I think it was fantastic, what you did for Eddie,' Jan said.

'I didn't do it for him; I did it for me.'

'In which case, lucky Eddie.'

'He's one of life's lucky men,' Annabel said enigmatically.

'Not if his business career is anything to go by,' Jan said realistically.

'There's a lot more to life than business. And I really, deeply hope he's lucky today.'

'Don't we all!' Jan agreed with a laugh.

At seven-thirty they hit a traffic jam on the motorway, where it ran through the Black Country. Jan looked out across the sprawl of factories, tower blocks and nineteenth-century industrial housing and thought of Bernie.

'I wonder if Eagle's former owner will come today,' she said.

'I don't know,' Annabel shrugged. 'Now my negotiations with Bernie are over, I haven't seen anything of him.'

'He hasn't phoned me for over a week,' Jan said. 'I wonder if he's fed up with racing.'

'He's still got two good horses, Dingle Bay and Arctic Hay,' Annabel said, 'but maybe he is. I don't think his heart was ever really in it. By the way, didn't your mother-in-law want to come with us too?'

'No way!' Jan raised her eyebrows. 'But she would have been the first to ring and moan if I hadn't asked her. My mum's not coming either; she's looking after the kids and, anyway, she felt she couldn't take the excitement. Mind you, I'm not sure *I* can, the way my gut's feeling. But at least Eddie's bringing Dad and Gerry.'

The two friends chatted sporadically as the lorry rumbled north past the Potteries, over the flat lands of Cheshire and was buffeted by wind on the high-backed bridge across the Manchester ship canal. At ten o'clock there was already a lot of traffic converging on Aintree racecourse, but there were no serious hold-ups and Jan was soon steering her old lorry into the parking area.

Russian Eagle had travelled well, although he had sweated a little under his rug. They lowered the ramp and Joe unbolted the partition. He swung it to one side to let Jan lead the horse off. Once in the stable yard, they washed the sticky sweat off his neck and shoulders with warm water and tidied up his mane and tail. When they'd finished, Darren walked him round for twenty minutes in a paddock by the stables to give his legs a stretch, while Annabel and Jan went off to find the loos and a cup of tea.

On this first morning of the National meeting, there was already a buzz about Aintree, though, Jan guessed, not as much as there would be on Saturday, when the world's greatest steeplechase would be run. She made her way to the stables, three blocks of brick-built boxes that had clearly seen better days and many generations of runners in the Grand National, some with the names of famous winners over the top door. She found which stable had been allocated to Russian Eagle and Darren led him in.

Afterwards she and Annabel went back to the lorry and sat in the cab. Annabel was reading the racing papers and trying to keep calm. She was thrilled to see her green and blue colours with her name printed alongside Eagle's on the day's card.

There were twenty-two runners declared and, below the list, a brief summary of their form and projected odds.

'Who's favourite?' Jan asked.

'The Irish horse – Supreme General. He belongs to A.D. O'Hagan with Mickey Flanagan on board. He's the Irish amateur champion, isn't he?'

'Yes,' Jan said. 'Though why A.D. O'Hagan's bothering with hunter chases when he owns the favourite for the Grand National, God only knows.'

'They've got Eagle at twenty to one!' Annabel said. 'And Rear Gunner at sixteens!'

There were seven horses listed at shorter odds. They were all animals with more experience than Russian

Eagle or Gunner and, she had to admit, ridden by far more experienced jockeys than Eddie.

'But you saw Eagle and Eddie going round last time they raced,' Jan said, 'so you shouldn't be feeling too nervous. The fences are much bigger, of course, but that won't be a problem for Eagle. If Gunner's fit, I'd say he'd be as much of a danger to us as Supreme General. In the end it's going to be a matter of stamina and finishing speed. And I think we might have enough of both.'

'Do you really believe we can do it?' Annabel asked doubtfully. 'I assumed you entered him for a bit of fun and because Eddie wanted it so badly.'

'I promise you, I wouldn't have entered him if I thought he had absolutely no chance. I've said all along, with luck in running, it's possible.'

'Don't worry,' Annabel laughed nervously. 'I'm not holding my breath.' She looked at her watch. 'Shall we wander up and see if we can find Eddie and your dad?'

Jan had arranged to meet Eddie, Reg and Gerry outside the weighing room at twelve o'clock, to make their final declarations before they walked the course.

Trying to keep a lid on their excitement, they walked up a little early to find the three men already waiting outside the old cream-painted timber building.

'Oh dear,' Annabel said into Jan's ear before they'd reached them, 'Eddie looks like a ghost.'

'Don't tell him,' Jan warned. 'Hello, Dad,' she said

more loudly. 'Morning, Eddie. Hi, Gerry! You didn't get lost then?'

'No,' said Eddie in a croaky voice.

'Great. Eagle's fine. He's had a bit of a walk and now he's in a tatty old stable having a good look at what's going on.'

'I think I'll go and have a look at him,' Eddie said.

'He's fine, Eddie. They won't allow you in anyway because you haven't got a stable pass. I'll just declare him and then we'll walk the course.'

Jan went inside and tried to keep herself from trembling as she filled in the declaration form, confirming to the clerk of the scales that her horse was there and would be running. It was a very different procedure from the point-to-points she was used to and the officials, who seemed to understand her nervousness, smiled and reassured her with a few words of encouragement.

As she went back out, she thought that, now they were utterly committed, she just wished they could get on with it.

'Right,' she said. 'Who's coming?'

The lads stayed with the horse while Jan set off towards the world-famous course with Eddie, Annabel, Reg and Gerry.

A light wind ruffled the dark green turf, blowing out the moisture from a slight fall of rain the night before. The sky above them was patchily blue, with high, mackerel clouds crossing slowly from the west.

'He'll like this ground,' Jan observed as they walked towards the first fence.

Eddie nodded, stopping to hack his heel into the earth. 'Just as long as there's a bit of a cut.'

'This'll be the fourth,' Jan said as they reached the plain fence. 'You start back over there,' she pointed across the angle of the course to a point on the far side of the stands, 'and before you turn for this one you'll already have jumped a plain fence, the Chair and the water, but we'll have a look at how to take them on the way back.'

Jan couldn't ignore a profound sense of history, walking the famous course she'd seen so many times on the television. She and Eddie had played dozens of videos of previous runnings of the Foxhunters' and of the Grand National itself. But nothing could have prepared them for actually being on the course and standing in front of the massive spruce-topped fences; they looked so much bigger in real life.

They walked in a line between each of the obstacles down the long straight, judging the best place to take them. 'I reckon there's always less traffic up the inside,' Jan said to Eddie. 'The fences are a little higher here, but that won't bother Eagle.'

Eddie nodded, but as they gazed at Becher's Brook she knew he was still very unsure of himself.

'He won't have any problems with this,' she said as lightly as she could. 'Try to take it on the inner; there'll be less chance of any fallers as you land.'

As they walked on to the Canal Turn and Valentine's, Jan didn't let Eddie see just how daunted she was by the reality of the notoriously demanding course. She also had to control her irritation at her father and Gerry, who didn't help by gasping at every fence and looking sorrowfully at Eddie.

They crossed the Melling Road and turned left-handed into the home straight, heading for the stands, which would soon start filling up, until they reached the point from which the Foxhunters' Chase would start.

'OK, Eddie.' Jan tried to sound businesslike. 'There are going to be twenty-two of you galloping up to the first plain fence, all on top of each other, and anyone at the back just isn't going to see it, so for God's sake, try to jump off quickly, go up the inside and give your horse a bit of light for the first few fences. Most of these hunters will be able to jump; but there'll be plenty of pilot errors to cause problems.'

As they carried on to the Chair and the Water, Jan looked at Eddie again. Where he had been pale before, he was now eau de Nil. She took a deep breath, relieved that she hadn't eaten any breakfast.

Bloody hell! What am I doing here? she thought. *There's no way this can work, not with Eddie. He's bound to bottle out – he just doesn't know enough!*

She stood beside him in front of the water jump. 'Whatever you do, Eddie, you've got to stay committed; you *mustn't* lose heart going into these fences.

Eagle can jump them all, big and tidily. You know that, so just don't forget it!'

*

They had a couple of hours to kill before they needed to think about getting ready, but nobody wanted to go to the public areas, where their nervousness would be seen. They went instead to the marquee that served as the lads' canteen, where they had endless cups of tea while they watched the racing on television. Jan noticed that, although Rear Gunner had been declared, there was no sign of Virginia or any of her staff.

Jan could see that Eddie was making a supreme effort to keep himself together. Although there was still a nervous tremble in his voice, he was trying to make a few jokes and talk about the race in a calm, workmanlike way. But she wasn't surprised that he didn't want anything to eat or drink. She insisted, though, that he swallow a small glass of water before he made his way back to the changing room.

Jan and Annabel began to prepare Eagle for his big day as soon as they arrived back in the stable yard. They gave the tack a final polish and sent him out with a plaited mane, gleaming oiled hooves and diamonds on his quarters. Eagle seemed to know something special was happening and bounced around the pre-parade ring while Jan went to collect his saddle from the weighing room.

She tacked him up carefully, running a surcingle over the tiny racing saddle and lifting each of his front legs in turn to make sure that no skin was being pinched under the girth.

Darren and Joe led him back to the parade ring, while Gerry and Reg leaned over the rails outside. Jan and Annabel followed Eagle.

'Well,' Jan said. 'This is it.'

'Don't worry,' Annabel said with a smile. 'You've got him here in wonderful shape; I know they'll do their best. All I care about is that they both come back safe and sound – and I mean that.'

'Thanks, Bel. D'you know, if I'd had any idea that it was going to be as stressful as this, I just don't think I'd have come.'

'You're going to have to get used to it, Jan, when you get your licence.'

'*If* I get my licence.'

'Of course you will. Now, you've done all you can for this race, so relax and try to enjoy it.'

As Eddie and the other twenty-one jockeys were walking into the ring, Jan caught sight of Harold Powell's colours as his jockey, Jimmy Marlow, marched up to his owner, who was standing with Virginia Gilbert. Virginia looked studiedly calm and a little aloof from the mostly amateur trainers who filled the arena.

Among the jockeys, Eddie was by no means the only one showing signs of nerves. She guessed it must be much tougher for these amateurs than for the pros who would be riding the same course – but twice round – in two days' time.

'You'll be OK, Eddie,' she said as he reached them. 'Usual instructions – keep in touch with the leaders all the way round and start pushing on when you turn for home with two left to jump. And don't forget what I said about the run in – the Chair will be fenced off and you have to cut across towards the elbow to pick up the running rail, so don't lose your way. Try to get there first and stay alongside it to help keep him balanced up to the line.'

They had rehearsed this on their walk round. Eddie nodded. 'Sure,' he managed to croak. 'Eagle looks great.'

'Thanks.' Jan forced a faint smile. 'He's fine and raring to go. He'll give you a great ride.'

As Jan legged him up onto the horse a few minutes later, she felt his knee quiver and gave it a quick squeeze. 'You can do it, Ed,' she smiled, and stood back to watch him rejoin the other runners circling the ring.

When the horse had left the paddock, Jan left Annabel to watch in the members' stand with Gerry and Reg, while she made her way up to the owners' and trainers' stand.

On her way to Aintree that morning, Jan had made up her mind that she didn't want anyone with her while she watched the race.

On the trainers' stand she was unknown and anonymous, alone but surrounded by an almost tangible buzz and the nervous fretting of people who didn't often run horses at meetings as big as this. She made her way to the front and took her binoculars from their case to watch Eddie and Russian Eagle canter down to the start.

For those few brief moments of limbo before the 'Off', Jan felt terribly exposed and vulnerable. She'd chosen to put herself in this position, but now she was finding it hard to cope on her own and once again she longed for John's quiet presence.

She closed her eyes and took several deep breaths. When she was ready she resumed her scrutiny of the field and tried to concentrate on the green and blue hoops as they circled round behind the starting tape. She couldn't help keeping half an eye on Jimmy Marlow on Rear Gunner. She had to admit that Jimmy gave his horse a useful advantage. He'd had a good season riding under rules for Virginia and must have been one of the most experienced amateurs on the circuit. She could only pray that Eagle's strong finish would make up for Eddie's greenness.

When they were finally called into line, Jan was glad to see that Eddie had managed to find a gap towards the inside. As the tape flew up, he was in the front line of runners, galloping in a ragged charge towards the first fence.

Eagle held his position and took it abreast of another five, gained a little ground and galloped on towards the Chair. Jan swallowed and closed her eyes for a few seconds. She opened them, to see her horse fly over the formidable obstacle behind three others and touch down fluidly.

She felt herself relax a little now they were running and the first major obstacle was out of the way. As far she could see, Eddie had a good hold of the horse and they cleared the Water comfortably.

The runners headed for the tight left-hand bend before the long straight, swung well wide and curved back to line themselves up for the first of the six fences down the back. Sensibly Eddie eased up a little before he reached it, lying sixth and still on the inside rail.

Jan glanced back quickly over the rest of the field to identify the horses that had fallen at the first two fences, reducing the field to nineteen. One fancied horse had gone, but Supreme General in A.D. O'Hagan's famous colours was still in the race, going easily near the front. Just behind Eagle, Rear Gunner was still cruising with his long easy stride.

They took one, then two plain fences on the straight with no fallers. The open ditch halfway down claimed two victims and the next two fences removed one more. As they approached Becher's, Jan prayed quietly. 'God, please let him jump this!' He did it with ease, but three other runners weren't so lucky.

At each fence Jan wasn't sure what to expect. Every time Eagle's head and Eddie's blue and green colours bobbed back into view she felt a surge of relief as he picked up and galloped on to the next fence.

Jan knew Eddie was dreading the sharp bend on the inside of the Canal Turn and she felt her body tense vicariously as he headed straight for the corner. She gasped with relief when he took off and cleared it as well as any of his rivals.

There were six fences and eleven horses left in the race, with the leaders still going strongly. Jan studied her horse for signs of fatigue, but Eddie seemed to have him on the bit as easily as he would have done at this distance in any of the point-to-points in which they'd run.

At Valentine's Brook before the Melling Road, Eagle passed a horse in the air on his inside and a loose horse on his outer. With a deft twist as he landed, he avoided a collision with the riderless animal and was in fourth place with only five lengths separating him from the leader, and Eddie still wasn't kicking.

'Well done, Eddie!' Jan whispered to herself, hardly able to believe what she was seeing, but when they'd turned the bend towards the stands, Eddie started to move on the horse, his hands and heels in unison, working like pistons. Eagle began to progress up the field towards the leaders. Jan dared not even think there'd be a problem with the last two fences: just to be in the first four would be triumph enough for her!

But her excitement almost boiled over when Russian Eagle put in a huge jump over the open ditch. Within two strides of landing he'd passed all bar one of his rivals. Only Supreme General was in front, urged on by howls of support from all the Irishmen in the stands.

Halfway between the last two fences Eddie lifted his stick and brought it down just once. Eagle knew what he had to do. He stood right off at the last plain fence and projected himself into a leap that drew an audible gasp from the crowd, and a groan from the Irish as he landed half a length ahead.

Jan gasped too, but with sudden shock.

When Eddie landed his right stirrup lifted a little as his saddle slipped to the left. He managed to jerk it straight again by stepping down hard on his offside iron. Jan felt a stab of guilt for sending the horse out in such a way that this could have happened. She thanked God there were no more fences to jump. She was sure, just as long as Eddie could keep balanced on the run in, he would get there.

Gripping her binoculars, her knuckles white, Jan watched as Eddie resolutely gathered Eagle up and tracked slightly right to cut across the elbow and pick up the rail at the far end. The Chair was now railed off, leaving a small gap on the left to encourage riderless horses to leave the course before the run in.

Jan saw the disaster that was about to happen seconds before Eddie.

The loose horse, ranging up on his outside, had made up his mind to head for the gap between the Chair and the inner rail. He veered sharply left, cannoning into Russian Eagle. The two animals hit each other with a thud that could be heard in the stands and the momentum of the crash seemed to tip Eddie's saddle halfway round the horse's side. There was a long, anguished 'Oooooh!' from the crowd as he crashed to the ground, leaving his left foot still in the stirrup. He was dragged, bouncing like a doll, for several strides before his boot slipped from the iron and he fell away.

Eagle galloped on in confusion, carried to the left by the loose horse who had caused all the mayhem, forcing him on the wrong side of the running rail, past the Water Jump and on towards the winning post.

Jan froze for a moment, rigid with disbelief. She trained her binoculars on Eddie's green and blue colours as she had a few weeks before, willing him to move.

This time he didn't.

Jan didn't know how long she waited, oblivious to all the sounds of jubilation around her as the Irish horse came home to tumultuous applause, followed by a hard-finishing Rear Gunner, who must have passed three horses since clearing the second from home.

At last, as if by a small miracle, she saw Eddie stir. Slowly he raised his head, then propped himself up on his elbow. By the time the ambulance reached him, he was sitting up and rubbing his shoulder.

'Thank God!' Jan gasped. 'He's alive! He can move!'

And it was only now that she started to think about what could have led to his crashing fall.

A loose horse had hit Russian Eagle, but for some inexplicable reason Eddie's girth had got loose and the collision had sent the saddle slithering round Eagle's belly and tipped his rider over the side.

She couldn't begin to think how, but for some reason she hadn't tacked the horse up properly. In the nervous excitement of the build-up to the race, she must have forgotten something.

Eddie and Eagle had been on their way to win! They had been pulling away from the Irish horse with no sign of weakening.

She had to get to them.

She turned and was confronted by a sea of people heading for the narrow spiral staircase that was the only way down from the trainers' stand.

She pushed between the backs that blocked her way. 'Sorry!' she gasped, thrusting wildly towards the vortex at the top of the stairs. She could think of nothing but getting out of this place, out onto the course, and everywhere there were people stopping her. It seemed like hours before she got to the stairs and plunged down them, banging her wrists against the rails as she went, and shoved on through the crowds on the lower levels until she reached the ground. She burst out into the open with an impenetrable mass of people still cheering home the heavily backed winner. She dived headlong into the melee and pushed her way through blindly until she reached the rails and clambered over them, not giving a damn what anyone thought. She ran wildly down the course until she met the ambulance creeping gingerly towards her.

She stood in front of it, waving until the driver realized she wanted him to stop.

'I'm the trainer!' she gasped between searing breaths. 'How's Eddie?'

'He's your jockey, is he?' the driver asked.

'Yes. Yes. I need to know how he is.'

The driver opened his door and let Jan lean in to see Eddie sitting on a bench in the back of the vehicle with another paramedic beside him.

'Eddie! Are you all right?'

To her intense relief, he managed a weak grin. 'I'm alive; I think I've bust my collarbone.'

'Oh, thank God!'

Jan almost collapsed onto the driver's lap. She pulled herself up. She didn't care if her eyes were streaming with tears. 'I've got to see about Eagle. I'm so sorry, Eddie. I just don't know what happened – why it slipped!'

'It's OK, Jan. Go and see the horse. I'll see you later.'

Darren had reached Russian Eagle before Jan. He was still on the course, holding the horse's reins, up by the far end of the stands in front of a large, watching crowd. He and Eagle were walking quietly back to a gate at the corner of the track. The horse seemed no more than a little indignant about what had happened and perfectly sound.

'Thank God!' Jan heard herself say again.

Darren looked over to see her running towards them. There were tears in his eyes too.

'He's all right, Jan. He's fine,' he stuttered. 'How's Eddie?'

'Broken collarbone.'

Darren looked relieved. 'It was a hell of crash. And the bugger was going to win!' He winced.

Jan didn't dare think how much money he had put on Eagle.

Then, with savage abruptness, she was reminded how much Eddie had been going to win from Cyril Goldstone.

'Oh my God,' she groaned. Everything, the whole disaster, Eagle losing the race, Eddie losing his money and nearly being killed – it was all her fault because she'd insisted on doing everything herself and she'd got it wrong!

Somehow, somewhere, she'd totally screwed the whole thing up.

'Didn't his saddle slip?' she asked.

'Yes, I just slid it back over again, so I could lead him in.'

'Just stop a moment, for God's sake!'

In a few short strides, she was beside the horse on his near side, unbuckling the surcingle, which she pulled off, and she watched as the girth, unrestrained now, flopped off and dangled beneath the horse's belly.

'What the hell—?'

She reached down and lifted the end, to find there was no buckle. A few ends of thread where it had been attached, projected randomly from the heavy nylon web.

She lifted the saddle flap and found the metal buckle in its leather sleeve still fixed to the girth straps. There was nothing random about the threads on the inner side – they had all been neatly cut.

The relief of knowing that she wasn't to blame, intense as it was, didn't sustain her for long. It didn't change the fact that her dream of winning this premier race, when it had come so close to reality, had collapsed, and all the hopes she'd pinned on it, however unreasonable they might have seemed, had been justified as Eagle jumped the last in front.

Somehow, to reorient her mind, she concentrated on the immediate problem. 'I'll take the horse,' she said to Darren. 'Thanks.'

Darren handed her the reins.

'You take the saddle back to the weighing room,' she told him, 'but give me that girth and buckle.'

Gingerly, clearly aware of the significance of the severed stitching, the boy unbuckled both ends and passed them to Jan, who shoved them into a pocket of her sheepskin.

With Darren trailing unhappily behind, she led Eagle through the gate and around the back of the stands to the stables. Her father, Annabel and Gerry were waiting at the entrance, looking like the chief mourners at a funeral.

Jan clenched her teeth and resolved not to break down again. She led the horse into his stable and took his bridle off while the others watched in silence. She threw a sweat rug over him and let herself out.

She looked around at all the other trainers and lads getting their horses ready to race, or washing down others who had just run. 'We'll leave him there for a minute. Darren, you stop with him. Give him a wash and then a small drink – and make sure it's lukewarm.' She turned to the others. 'Let's go to the lorry.'

When they were all crammed into the cab, Jan looked at them. She pulled the girth and the severed buckle from her pocket and put them on Annabel's lap. 'We were sabotaged,' she said simply.

Annabel picked up the buckle and webbing strap and examined the uniformly, cleanly severed threads.

'But who, who on earth would do it?' she asked, in a state of shock.

'Did any of you know, except Bel, that Eddie had five grand at a hundred to one for Eagle to win with him on board?'

'Jesus,' Gerry said. 'He was going to win half a million?' he whispered.

'You told me he'd had a big bet, but you didn't say how much or who with,' Annabel corrected her.

'Cyril Goldstone.'

The three of them gazed at Jan in stunned silence.

'My God, Jan,' Reg said at last. 'What have you let yourself in for?'

'I haven't let myself in for anything, Dad. Eddie had a bet. I told him at the time I thought he was crazy, but he had every right to try and win.' Jan had been watching Annabel. 'You knew about the bet, didn't you?' she said to her.

'Yes. Mrs Sullivan told me.'

'Because I told her,' Jan sighed. 'Was that why you bought Eagle from Bernie?'

'Partly. I knew no one else was going to help Eddie; and, besides, I thought it was a good deal. I loved seeing him run today, and, as far as I'm concerned, he was the winner.'

'Too right,' Gerry agreed. 'He ran an absolute blinder and never put a foot wrong. I just couldn't believe it when he took off for home after the last. He was never going to get caught.'

'OK, OK,' Jan said impatiently. 'What am I going to do about it?'

'You'll never prove a thing,' Reg said.

'That depends on who actually cut the stitching,' Gerry said.

'Hold on! Has anyone seen Joe?' Jan asked.

'Not since before the race and he was already half-cut by then.'

'If it was him,' Annabel said, 'the only way you'll get anywhere is not to let him think you remotely suspect him – perhaps not even to mention that you know it was done at all. If he thinks he's in the clear, sooner or later he's bound to do or say something that'll incriminate him.'

Jan thought for a moment. No action was always better than a knee jerk. 'OK. We're just going to pretend the saddle slipped without any outside help – agreed. I'd better get straight back and tell Darren not to say anything to Joe. I just hope he hasn't seen him already.'

'OK,' Annabel nodded calmly.

'We'll go and find Eddie and tell him what happened and what we're going to do about it. We'll aim to get back here in half an hour. Just make damn sure no one else hears a word about this,' Jan warned.

Jan hurried back to the stables and found Darren sitting morosely on a straw bale in front of Eagle's box.

'Darren, come in the box with me,' she said.

He looked at her, puzzled, but followed her.

Inside Jan closed the door and beckoned him into the far corner, beyond Eagle. 'Have you seen Joe?'

'Nope. He was getting well pissed before the race and I didn't want to go round with him.'

'If you see him, I don't want you to say a word about the broken girth. Do you understand?'

Comprehension flickered slowly in the boy's eyes. 'Yeah, I think I do.'

'Just tell him we think the saddle slipped with all

the sweat and stretching the horse had to do over those jumps, and that I couldn't have tightened the girth properly.'

'I get you.' Darren nodded with a complicit grin. 'The bastard!'

'Darren.' Jan gave him her steeliest look. 'You promise me you'll say and do nothing to let him or anyone else know we suspect him. Just treat him absolutely as normal, otherwise I'll skin you alive.'

'Don't you worry, Jan, I won't tell him nothing!'

'Good. Now, put all the tack in the bag as normal in case he comes back and let Eagle have a bit of hay. I'm just going for a pee, then we'll put him in the lorry.'

Jan stayed in the ladies' for a few minutes, needing the chance to sit down on her own. She stared at the back of the door and wondered if there was anything she could have done to stop this happening.

She could honestly say it had never occurred to her that Cyril Goldstone would try to save his money with blatant skulduggery, and yet it had been so easy for him!

From where she looked at the moment, there was very little to prove he'd been responsible, other than purely circumstantial evidence, and anyway, in the end, in full view of twenty thousand spectators, Eddie had still been on his way to win the race until the loose horse had collided with him, which even Cyril couldn't have organized.

There was no way they could ever pin it on him, or even point the finger at him, unless Joe Paley confessed.

Jan made her way back through the stands, hoping that she might see Joe. Most people were preoccupied with the next race and were either heading outside, jostling to get money on at the Tote or gazing up at the television view of the horses going down to the start of the Mildmay course.

Outside there was a rush of people coming from the paddock and the Tote windows. Jan, standing indecisive for a moment, felt herself jostled and then, distinctly, a hand on the small of her back. She spun round, eyes blazing, ready to rebuke the groper and found herself staring into Harold Powell's opaque blue eyes.

'What bad luck!' he said, so insincerely that the thought flashed through her mind that he might have been responsible for what had been done to Eagle's girth. But she did everything she could to disguise her suspicion.

'Yes, wasn't it? Comes of using an amateur, I suppose,' she said, keeping up the charade by half-blaming herself. 'But he did insist.'

'It's not his horse, though.'

'No, but he has a lot of influence with the owner. Listen, Harold, he's hurt now and I've got to go and see how he is.'

'Well, I can't say I was sorry to see him fall. There's

a nice lot of money for the runner-up.' Harold gave her a freezing smile before pushing his way past her back into the stands.

She gazed at him for a moment, enraged by all he'd put her through. By God, she thought, if there was any justice in the world, she'd see him pay dearly.

As she turned to carry on back to the stables, she saw Eamon Fallon a little apart from the main flow of people and just about to head up the stairs to the private boxes. She hadn't seen him for weeks, not since the day he'd told her she would have to sell Dingle Bay to settle his account with her.

Since then, and Annabel buying the horse to swap it for Russian Eagle, Jan had rung him to say that she had the cash he wanted and he'd sent a tall, taciturn Irishman to collect it. She had made the courier sign for the money, but she'd had no further acknowledgement from Eamon, and felt a little resentful, in view of all the trouble she'd taken. She was considering whether she really wanted to talk to him right then, when he happened to turn and see her.

He smiled broadly and beckoned her over with a friendly wave.

A little guardedly, she walked to the bottom of the steps. 'Hello Eamon. Did you get that money?'

His eyes slid to one side for a minute and he frowned. 'I did,' he said. 'Thanks. But Jan, what terrible bad luck with your horse! It was a really fine run and I'd have backed it myself but I'm here with the man who owns the winner.' He nodded over his shoulder to where, a few steps above him, another man stood. Although in the periphery of her vision Jan had been conscious of a compelling presence, only when she raised her eyes did she realize it was none other than A.D. O'Hagan. 'He'd like to congratulate you,' Eamon said and stepped aside deferentially.

O'Hagan nodded and a quick uplift at the corner of his mouth registered her existence while his intense blue eyes seemed to burn into her. Jan felt almost mesmerized by the legendary man, whom she'd met just once before at the Doncaster Sales, the day Eddie had bought Russian Eagle.

'Well done,' he said. 'you had my fella beat and that other one you used to train. It was an impressive performance.' His mouth widened a little and his eyes glittered in appreciation. 'We'll meet again for sure when you have another crack at us. Even before that, maybe.' He turned and his immaculate brown brogues clicked up the concrete steps.

Eamon winked at her. 'Take care now,' he said and turned to follow O'Hagan.

She stared after them, her speculation over the connection between these two enigmatic Irishmen replacing for a moment the horrible aftermath of Eagle's race. But her preoccupation was disturbed by another familiar voice behind her shoulder.

''Ello, Jan,' a deep voice said, which despite its strong cockney vowels, had more than a little in common with Eddie's. 'You're keepin' illustrious company.'

Jan turned round to find Ron Sullivan standing languidly in the loudest check suit of pink and green tweed she'd ever seen. There was a smile on his face as he looked at her and A.D. O'Hagan's disappearing back.

'Hello, Ron,' she smiled. 'I didn't know you were here. Have you seen your son?' she went on quickly, suddenly reminded of Eddie's condition.

'I have now,' Ron said. 'I found him in the hospital they've got here having his collarbone strapped.'

'I haven't even seen him since he was carted off in the ambulance,' Jan said. 'I've been rushing around trying to sort Eagle and find out . . .'

'What the hell happened?' Ron finished for her.

She nodded, biting her lip with a fresh rush of frustration.

'But how's Eddie?' she asked.

'He's fine,' Ron smiled. 'He'll be a little sore and, as you can imagine, he's more than a bit pissed off at losing the race.'

He still doesn't know about the bet, Jan thought. 'He did well,' she said, thinking how lame that sounded.

'Well?' Ron guffawed. 'He was absolutely effing fantastic! I couldn't believe the way he rode round that course, and you, my girl, are a little genius. Because if he can keep clear of them loose horses, he'll beat Superior General next time!'

'That's what O'Hagan just said.'

'Anyway,' Ron said. 'I'd get you a drink, darlin', but I've got to make tracks a bit sharpish. I shouldn't have come today, but I didn't want to miss my boy,' he chuckled. 'And I'm bloody glad I didn't!'

'Are you seeing Eddie again?'

'Not just now,' Ron answered.

'See you soon, then, I hope,' Jan said.

He leaned down and kissed her on both cheeks.

'Maybe,' he said before he spun round and marched off, straight into the oncoming flow of people surging out to watch the race that was about to start.

Jan stood for a moment, trying to fathom out what it was about their brief meeting that she found disturbing. She was sorry he'd gone so quickly, too, because she thought he could have given her some useful advice about how to deal with what had happened to Eagle's tack.

But by now Annabel and the others would be wondering where she'd got to. They'd be waiting to get Eagle into the lorry and go home. She turned and walked briskly towards the stables.

Darren was still outside Eagle's box.

'Any sign of Joe?'

'Yeh,' Darren nodded. 'He comes back looking dead rough, like he's been in a fight. He goes, "Where's the boss?" and I go, "I don't know," and he says, "Tell her not to wait for me. I'll be getting a lift back."'

'What!' Jan exploded.

'It's not my fault, Jan,' Darren said, alarmed by her outburst.

'I know,' she said quickly. 'I'm not blaming you, but I'm bloody angry at Joe. But if he's gone, he's gone,' she said more calmly. 'Let's get Eagle out of here and take him home.'

The long journey back to Gloucestershire from Aintree was one of the most miserable Jan had ever made.

Darren was in the back with Eagle and Annabel was in the cab beside her, trying hard to cheer her up, but nothing could shift the black cloud of depression that enveloped Jan.

Having come so close to winning, watching Eddie do exactly what they had set out to achieve when he'd bought Russian Eagle, then seeing it all crumble, whether through accident or malicious intent, was devastating and had left her almost choking with rage.

Jan couldn't bear the inane music and chatter on the radio, and the journey passed in almost total silence. It persisted back at the yard, four hours after leaving Aintree race course when, in the gusty drizzle falling on the Cotswold edge, they unloaded Eagle and bedded him down for the night.

Roz was waiting for them and had done all the other horses with Emma. She had already picked up the children from Riscombe and put them to bed. She was almost as gloomy as the others, having watched the race on television. She told Jan that Gerry had phoned an hour before to say that Eddie had been taken to the Fazakerley Hospital, which he'd been allowed to leave once his shoulder had been rebandaged. Gerry was now driving him home with Reg in the Land Rover.

*

At half-past nine Darren and Roz finally went home. Jan asked Annabel if she would stay with her for a while and they made their way back up to the caravan.

'Do you think we'll ever see Joe Paley again?' Annabel asked.

Jan shrugged. 'It must have been him who did it – there's no one else. I don't see how he could come back here and face us.'

'He hasn't really got any roots in the village, has he?'

'None at all – his family are travellers. I think they happened to be in the area last year when I was looking for more lads; he probably heard from Roz and just showed up. I always felt he was a bit dodgy, but I put up with him because he's a bloody good work rider.'

'So he could go anywhere now and find a job in a yard, just on the strength of his riding?'

'Well, I certainly won't be giving him a reference,' Jan said wryly.

Annabel smiled at this sign that Jan was starting to see beyond the immediate catastrophe.

Jan was also beginning to accept that what had happened would have happened anyway, even if someone hadn't nicked the stitching on the girth. The loose horse had hit Eagle so hard that if the saddle hadn't slipped and dumped Eddie on terra firma, he would certainly never have recovered and got straight again in time to challenge Supreme General. It was just possible that a really experienced professional jockey might have seen the loose horse ranging up on him and managed to take avoiding action, but professional jockeys didn't ride in hunter chases.

They talked for a while longer, until Jan yawned. 'I expect you want to go to bed, Bel,' she said. 'It's a long time since five o'clock this morning.'

Annabel yawned too and stood up. 'Yes, I'll have to go or I'll end up on the floor in here. I wonder how the others are getting on.'

'No doubt they'll be up here in the morning like larks. We'll start a bit later, at eight, OK?'

'Sure,' Annabel nodded. 'I'm sorry you've had such a hell of a day. I'm sure it won't look so bad in the morning and at least we know Eagle's a winner.'

'There's no doubt about that. Thanks, Bel.' Jan managed another weary smile. 'Goodnight.'

At midnight, when Jan had already fallen into a deep sleep, she was woken by a furious shrieking.

She came to in a panic, wondering what all the commotion was, when she realized it was only the phone beside her bed.

She picked it up.

'Hello,' she murmured.

'Hi, Jan! I've woken you, I'm sorry. It's Eddie.'

Jan shrugged and tried to focus. 'What do you want, Eddie?'

'Just to let you know that the bloody Land Rover's broken down; none of us know what the hell's wrong with it, but it won't start again and we've booked into a little motel somewhere near Stoke-on-Trent. Your dad says he doesn't want to wake your mother now, but could you ring her first thing in the morning and tell her?'

'Sure. The poor old thing will be worried as hell when she wakes without him.'

'Thanks. Sorry to have woken you.'

'That's OK. How are you, by the way? I'm sorry I never got back to see you again.'

'Not too bad,' Eddie said, with a hint of understatement. 'At least I didn't get kicked in the head or anything.'

'Did the others tell you what happened?'

'Yes, it's OK, Jan. I know it wasn't your fault.'

'I don't know who I'm bloody angrier with, Joe or that loose horse.'

'It may not have been Joe,' Eddie said.

'We won't talk about it now,' Jan said. 'Are you coming here tomorrow?'

'That depends how long they take to repair the Land Rover. But I'll be in Saturday morning, for sure.'

'See you then, and if I forgot to tell you before – you rode brilliantly!'

She could hear Eddie's pleased laugh. 'Thanks Jan; it was all down to you.'

'No it wasn't, but I'll see you tomorrow. G'night.'

'Night Jan.'

23

By Friday evening Eddie hadn't appeared, but Reg had phoned to say he was home. Edge Farm had more or less settled back into its usual routine. Although the Grand National was being held the next day, Jan had four runners to send out to point-to-points.

She was up at six-thirty on Saturday morning and was joined by Emma, Roz and Darren, who had taken a day to recover from the Aintree trip. As Jan had predicted, they hadn't seen or heard anything from Joe Paley; she guessed they never would and there seemed to be a tacit understanding that his name would not even be mentioned in the yard from now on, in the faint hope that it would help erase the awful memory of the race.

Around ten o'clock Eddie, pasty-faced and with his arm in a sling, limped quietly into the yard to see Eagle. Jan noticed how his status had altered as a result of his heroic ride. She found herself regarding him in a new light, too, as someone who, having identified an impossible target, had gone out and all but achieved it.

He hadn't stayed long, though, and she hadn't had a chance – if she was honest she had avoided it – to talk to him about Ron's Italian bankers. However, he said he'd be up again that evening to watch a replay of the Grand National on her video.

Even a successful day at the races, with a win and two seconds, didn't do a lot to improve Jan's frame of mind. She couldn't shift the dark cloud that still hung over her. She was pleased to see Eddie, though, when he arrived with a bottle of wine just as she'd finished putting the children to bed.

Eddie poured the wine and Jan turned on her video. During the preamble that led up to the Grand National, when they'd just settled themselves down on the bench, there was a knock at the door. Jan got up and opened it and was astonished to see Joe Paley standing outside.

She looked at him in amazement.

His thin, bony white face was bruised and haggard, and his eyes looked as if all the fluid his body contained had drained through them.

'Joe? What the hell do you want?' Jan asked.

'Can I come in?'

Jan nodded, and stepped back to allow the skinny young man in grimy black jeans and leather jacket into the caravan.

Eddie switched off the video and leaned back on

the bench, while Jan stared at the prodigal lad, waiting for an explanation.

'Can I have a drink?' he said in a small voice.

'Tea?' Jan asked.

He nodded, and Jan put a kettle on the top of the wood-burner.

'Joe, you'd better sit down.'

The lad perched on a small wooden chair at the end of the table, put his hands down and stared at his filthy fingernails in silence. Finally, he mumbled, 'I'm sorry, Jan.'

'It's Eddie you nearly killed. It's him you'd better say sorry to.'

Joe raised his eyes and allowed them to rest for a few moments on Eddie's, before he looked down again with his lower jaw working quietly on a piece of gum. 'It was that Sharon's fault,' he said. 'When she come here, she said after I was to meet her up by the big wood at the Manor – you know, where she lives. And when I gets there, she's not there, but her dad's waiting. He's done it deliberate, like, to get me where no one's going to see us.' Joe took a deep, sobbing breath and shook his head.

Jan poured some boiling water over the tea bag in a mug, topped it with milk, heaped in the three spoonsful of sugar, which she knew he liked, and put it on the table in front of him. No one spoke while he picked it up and took a long gulp.

'Shit, I'm sorry!' he muttered jerkily. 'But that

fuckin' Goldstone – he pulls a wedge of twenties from his pocket and waves it under my nose. He goes, "I hear you like a bit of a bet." "So?" I says, and he goes, "You can have plenty of bets with this; this is a grand, and it's all yours if you do me a very small favour. It won't take you more than ten seconds." And he pulls a girth like one of ours from his pocket and shows me how it's been nicked only on the back side of the buckle, so's you'd never see it unless you was looking for it. He goes, "You do that on Thursday with Russian Eagle's girth, and this grand is yours, all right?" And he puts it away. "Is that all?" I says.'

Joe lifted his head and looked at them both, the lids of his small brown eyes twitching. 'Well, it was a grand, like. I didn't want to do you no harm, Eddie, but I never seen so much dosh!' His shoulders shook.

Jan looked at Eddie. His eyebrows lifted. 'Poor little sod. Did you get the money?' he asked Joe directly.

'Nah! The fat bastard! I was watching him during the race. He was on the rail and when he saw you jump the last in front, he goes effing mad, all red and screaming until that loose horse come out of nowhere and knocked you off. After the race, when he's calmed down a bit, I goes up to him and says, "Can I have my grand?" like, and he just says to fuck off 'cos I never done what he said, and Eddie's fallen off 'cos of the other horse, which were nothing to do with me.'

Joe took another breath and leaned back in his chair. 'I was already a bit pissed and I felt real bad about what had happened to Eddie, so I went mad, telling him what a bloody crook he was, and two of his geezers got hold of me, carted me round the back of the stables and gave me a right duffing.' Joe's nasal voice was working up to a crescendo. 'They says if I ever say anything like that again, or tell anyone Mr Goldstone said he'd give me some money to do what I done, he'd fucking have me topped!' Joe's shoulders began to heave again and he flopped forward on to the table, shaking his head and sobbing.

Jan and Eddie looked at him and at each other. Eddie stretched out a hand and put it on the lad's quivering shoulder. 'Joe, it's OK. Just tell me why you came back and told us all this.'

Slowly the heaving subsided. Joe raised his thin torso in his scuffed leather jacket and looked warily at Eddie. 'I come back because I never should have done it, not to you, not to Eagle, not to her.' He indicated Jan with a backward nod of his head. 'She's been good to me here, bailed me out when I've needed it; treated me with a bit of respect.'

'And what do you expect us to do about it?'

'Please, Eddie, don't do nuffin'! You'll never prove Goldstone done it, even if I stands up and points the finger. He never gave me no money, no one saw us talking. He'll just say it's a load of bollocks and then he'll fuckin' do me!' Joe's voice cracked again.

'Jesus!' Jan said, looking at Eddie. 'What do we do?'

Eddie leaned his back against the wall of the caravan.

He winced as he twisted his shoulder, then smiled ruefully. 'Nothing, for the moment. There's no point. But at least we know for sure who did it and who ordered it. But I swear to you one day, when the dust has settled and he's least expecting it, I'll get Cyril Goldstone. I'm in no hurry, but when I do I'll make him sweat and I'll get every penny out of him I should have won.'

Jan looked at him in a way she wouldn't have done a few days before. Now that she knew what he was capable of once he was resolved, with a guilty tingle of excitement, she believed him.

'OK, Joe,' she said. 'Sit up and pull yourself together.'

The lad shuffled himself upright in the chair.

'Have you got somewhere to go tonight?' Jan asked.

'Yeh,' he nodded. 'I still got my room at Mrs Stoddard's.'

'And you've got your bike outside?'

Joe nodded. 'Yeh.'

'Well, get off home, then, and I'm very glad you came back and told me what happened. It must have taken a lot of guts. But there's one more thing I've got to ask you.'

Joe cocked an eyebrow, unused to telling people any more than was absolutely necessary. 'What's that?' he grunted.

'That cousin of yours, Amos Smith – did he ever come back?'

'Maybe – I dunno.'

'But it's possible he's back, or might still come back?'

'Yeh. He's been gone all winter. He'll want to get back to see his family for the summer.'

'We really want to talk to him still,' Eddie said. 'If you see him, could you tell him that if I come and look for him again and he can answer a couple of questions, we won't do anything that'll get him into trouble.'

Joe shrugged his skinny shoulders. 'I can tell him, I s'pose, if I see him.'

'Would you do that, Joe – try and convince him that it'll be OK?' Jan said gently. 'Please, for me?'

'Maybe,' said Joe, 'but I ain't promising.'

'All right.' Jan thought it better not to press him. 'In the meantime, take the day off tomorrow and get some sleep. Then come in sharp Monday morning. All right?'

Joe nodded, pushed back his chair and got to his feet. There was the ghost of a smile on his face, hurriedly banished, in case Jan thought he'd got off too lightly.

'It's OK, Joe, you can smile. But if you ever do anything like this again, you've had it; there'll be no second chance. Understood?'

He bit his lip and wriggled his feet. 'Yeh. Thanks, Jan. Thanks, Eddie.'

He turned abruptly and let himself out of the caravan.

Eddie looked at Jan. 'Do you feel better now?'

She nodded with a smile. 'Much.'

'Good. I'm pleased about that.'

Eddie switched the video back on and they settled down to watch the Grand National. When they'd seen it all, they played the race over twice, gazing at the running rail and the elbow, where, in their race, Eagle had been forced off the track.

'So, what a week, eh?' Eddie said when Jan had turned off the television. 'How do you feel about it all now?'

'Horrible. Knowing that someone deliberately tried to sabotage us, without giving a damn who got hurt!' Jan shook her head, as if she still couldn't believe it. 'And I haven't cancelled my appointment with the Jockey Club yet.'

'When is it?'

'Monday week, nine days' time.'

'You'll have to,' Eddie grimaced. 'You can't just turn up and tell them your backer's dead.'

'No,' Jan said, resigned. 'I'll ring them first thing this Monday and tell them.'

They talked a little more before Eddie yawned unstoppably and announced that he would have to go home.

'Eddie, is it really safe for you to drive with your arm in a sling?'

'It's OK; I can use my elbow to steer when I'm changing gear,' he grinned.

'Don't get caught and take care, all right?' Jan said gently. 'You're lucky to be alive as it is.'

After he'd gone, Jan tidied up and went in to settle Megan, who had woken up and called for her. She was still reading her a story when there was another burst of knocking on the door.

She put the book down and went warily to see who was there. She found Eddie standing outside again.

Just for a moment it crossed her mind that he had come back to spend more time with her, and she wasn't sure if she was pleased or not about this.

'Sorry, Jan,' he said. 'I know this sounds crazy, but could I doss down in your hay barn?'

'Why on earth do you want to do that? Has your Land Rover broken down again?'

'No. When I got home, I found the gates open and I'm pretty sure I left them closed. Being just a little cautious at the moment, I drove on past and parked up the lane. I walked back and let myself into the garden at the far end. I crept back round the side of the house and saw a great silver Cadillac parked behind the gate so I wouldn't have seen it until I'd driven in. There was a couple of blokes sitting in it, smoking and talking – too quietly for me to hear anything. Then one of them got out; he was absolutely massive. I know one thing: whatever they were doing, they weren't there for the good of my health, so I didn't hang about.'

'But why would they be after you?'

'I don't know, but I bet they've somehow clocked the connection between me and my old man, perhaps after that race was on telly. It's possible they knew Dad was up at Aintree. Anyway, right now,' Eddie said ruefully, patting his bandaged arm, 'I'm not in a position to help them and, call me a coward if you like, but I'm in no condition to deal with a pair of professional heavies.'

'But, Eddie, if they saw you racing, it wouldn't be hard for them to connect you with this place, either,' Jan said nervously.

'I know, I know. I'll go tomorrow, but just for tonight they're not going to come here. If anyone does turn up out of the blue, I'll lie low. Tell them you haven't seen me since Thursday and you think I've gone to Italy to buy pictures or something – yes, that'll do, Italy.'

Jan sighed. She thought she had enough on her plate without trying to fob off a pair of oversized debt collectors, but, on the other hand, she felt she owed Eddie and he had a right to ask a favour, at least, just for a night.

'OK, if you think you'll be all right in the barn.'

'I'll be fine. It won't be the first time I've crashed out among the hay bales.'

'But I bet you weren't on your own last time.'

Eddie grinned. 'I can't remember.' He gave her a wave and headed back down the hill into the darkness.

'We're not starting till late tomorrow, with everyone so knackered and it being Sunday,' she called after him. 'So nobody'll be in to wake you too early.'

'OK, thanks. Goodnight.'

She stood in the doorway, wondering if she was being a little cruel by making him sleep in the barn. Still, she thought, it was his idea, not hers.

Jan enjoyed the luxury of a lie-in once in a while. And after a busy but successful day at the point-to-point the day before and Eddie's late visit, she didn't stir until after nine.

She had to wake the children, too, and walked through into the living area of the caravan and drew back the skimpy curtains to reveal a pleasing view across the broad river valley to the Malverns, with Bredon Hill on the right, basking in the morning glow.

A flash of reflected sunlight from a car windscreen on the lane below caught her eye and she saw a large, black Mercedes cruising along the narrow road. She was wondering idly who was driving around in such a flashy car at this time of the morning, when it slowed and turned in at the bottom of her drive.

Jan gasped. Maybe this was something to do with the heavies in the Cadillac who'd called on Eddie the night before. The men he'd seen must have tracked him down after all and called up their boss to deal with him.

By now the Mercedes was progressing slowly but

smoothly up the rough track. She thought about running down to the barn to warn Eddie, but there was no way she could get there before the car reached the top. Determined not to show any fear, Jan hurriedly pulled on some jeans, a T-shirt and a fleece, poked her feet into a pair of boots and dragged a brush through her hair before she went out and walked down to greet her visitors. As she walked she glanced nervously at the yard and the open door of the hay barn, and prayed that Eddie had heard the car and checked it out before he showed himself.

The black limousine pulled up and a chauffeur in a cap got out to open the rear door. It occurred to Jan briefly that this was a very extravagant way to collect debts, but she guessed if these people had lent Ron half a million there must be substantial resources behind the organization. Then, with a sudden, horrified spasm, Jan realized that the Mercedes was parked right next to Eddie's battered old Land Rover. These people must surely know the number of his car!

On legs like rubber, she watched as a man in a light tan cashmere coat stepped from the car, putting on dark glasses as he did so.

There was, extraordinarily, something familiar about him and Jan struggled through her memory banks to pinpoint it.

'Good morning.' His voice floated up through the still air and Jan recognized it instantly. She had heard it just three days before at Aintree. Even with his piercing blue eyes obscured, there was an unmistakable aura about A.D. O'Hagan.

Jan tried to smile. She couldn't believe it. How on earth could Ron be in hock to someone like O'Hagan? The crazy coincidence was just too horrible.

'Hello,' she murmured, hearing the words come out thin and croaky. 'What can I do for you?'

'Plenty, I hope,' O'Hagan said with one of his disappearing smiles. 'I apologize for coming like this, so early and unannounced, but Eamon Fallon convinced me a trainer of your skill wouldn't be far from her horses at this time of day.'

Jan wondered why he was being so affable if he'd come looking for Eddie, but she saw no point in not playing along for the moment.

'I'd business in Cheltenham after the National yesterday,' he went on. 'I won't fly, so now we're on our way to catch the Fishguard ferry back to Waterford, so I felt it was too good an opportunity to miss.'

Jan was daring to believe, just faintly, that maybe A.D. O'Hagan wasn't here on a debt-collecting mission, and she was beginning to think that, whatever his business was, he was far too big a wheel to be doing that kind of thing himself.

'That's fine, Mr O'Hagan,' Jan said. 'How can I help you?'

'Is there anywhere we could sit and have a cup of coffee for a moment?'

'Yes, of course, if you don't mind my caravan. It's a bit of a mess because I was up late with a friend watching a replay of the National. I expect you were too,' she added, remembering that O'Hagan's horse had come third.

'I did watch it a couple of times,' he agreed lightly. 'And don't worry about the mess.'

In fact the caravan was as spick and span as Jan always liked to keep it, and a good glow was coming from the wood-burner. O'Hagan stepped up and looked around appreciatively. 'This caravan's a bit more upmarket than the one my dad was born in,' he said with a smile.

Jan waved him to one of the benches and he slid in while she spooned some coffee into a cafetière. When it was made, she filled two cups and put them on the table between herself and her visitor.

'Now, Jan – if I may call you that? – you remember what I said to you when we first met at Doncaster?'

Jan gulped and nodded. Did she remember! She could have repeated it word for word.

'As I recall, I told you that if you could train that yoke to win a good hunter chase, I'd send you half a dozen horses of my own.'

Jan felt herself trembling. The abrupt switch from rank fear five minutes earlier to the unspeakable joy she was now experiencing was almost too much to bear.

'I remember very well,' she said. 'I thought you were joking.'

'I was, but I still meant it. And what you've achieved in ten months with that animal is little short of a miracle. I hear you'd not an easy task with the pilot, either.'

Jan was grinning so widely now she could hardly speak. 'When I saw the horse, I thought he might be easy to train and I was lucky.'

'T'wasn't luck. You just have a very good eye and there's no doubt that you're an exceptional trainer. But Eamon tells me you've set your heart on taking out a professional licence.'

Jan nodded and smiled painfully. 'I've got my interview a week tomorrow.'

'I also hear you can't put up the funds the Jockey Club need and the fella who was going to do it for you has just rather inconsiderately gone to meet his maker.'

'You could say that,' Jan admitted.

'Well, no problem. If you write down all your details for me now, one of my people will be up to look through your books – that is, if you don't mind?'

'No, that's fine,' Jan said faintly.

'We'll get that all sorted and the paperwork done by the end of the week. I'll also tell the Jockey Club that I'll be sending you six good horses. You could come over to Ireland next month and pick some you like. Now, how would that suit you, Mrs Hardy?'

Jan tried to control her delight. She managed a cheeky grin. 'How do you think it would suit me, Mr O'Hagan? I can't thank you enough.'

A.D. O'Hagan was already on his way, with the Mercedes crunching quietly down Jan's drive, when she went into the barn.

'Eddie? Where are you?'

A moment later, a dishevelled figure appeared at the top of the stack of hay bales, and Eddie slithered down. He arrived at the bottom, blinking in the sun and trying to get rid of some of the hay clinging to his clothing.

'Who just drove off?'

'You're not going to believe this!' Jan said and spent the next ten minutes convincing him.

'Bloody hell!' Eddie laughed. 'What a story! That makes up for everything that's gone wrong and a whole lot more besides. Are you sure he means it?'

'Oh, he means it all right. A man as rich as him doesn't bother to go around bullshitting. After all, when you think about it, everything he said about what I've done with Eagle is perfectly true.'

'Now then, I don't want you getting all big-headed, especially if I'm not going to be around to keep you in your place.'

'Well, why wouldn't you be around?' Jan asked.

'I'm afraid I'm going to have to disappear for a bit. I won't be much of a loss, though, will I, if I've only got one useful arm.'

'How long are you going for?' Jan frowned.

'I'm not sure. Not long, I shouldn't think. You know, there's quite a mess to sort out, then we'll see.'

Jan knew Eddie well enough to know that when he didn't want to be pressed, he wouldn't be. 'Don't go for too long,' she said, a little plaintively. 'You're part of the furniture round here now.'

Eddie brushed the last bits of hay off his jersey. 'I'll be back, I promise.' He leaned down and kissed her on each cheek, perhaps a little longer than a goodbye required. ''Bye Jan,' he said. He turned and walked briskly across the yard to his Land Rover.

Jan felt a few tears fall as he had to turn over the engine of the old vehicle several times before it would fire, and then he was off, bouncing wildly down the track.

I'll have to get that drive seen to if A.D. O'Hagan's going to be coming here, she thought, trying to displace what she was thinking about Eddie.

Joe Paley drove his motorbike up the track in the early gloom of Monday morning before anyone else had arrived. Jan was delighted but surprised to see a passenger hunched on the small pillion seat. She wondered if Joe had brought a new recruit; she hoped not, because, just now, she had no plans to take on any more staff.

Joe stopped his bike and they both jumped off. While he wheeled it into an old shed where he liked to keep it out of the weather, his passenger walked up to meet Jan as she was on her way down to the yard.

'Hello?' Jan said, not recognizing the young man, though he looked as if he came from a similar mould to Joe.

He nodded back curtly. He was small, in his late teens with dark, unwashed hair and a row of rings down the edge of one ear.

'I'm Amos,' he announced in a thin, throaty voice. 'A bloke called Gerry says you been looking for me.'

Jan was stunned. She'd given up any hope of ever seeing Amos Smith, but here he was, offering himself up.

'Good Lord,' she said before she could stop herself. 'Yes, I did want to see you for a chat. I'll just tell Joe what to do. Go on up to the caravan. It's a bit warmer in there.'

'A'right,' he grunted.

She almost ran down to the yard, suddenly reluctant to leave such a dodgy character in her home without supervision. But when she got back he was sitting at the table, looking at the pictures in a TV magazine.

'Thanks for coming,' Jan said, thinking this sounded a bit lame. 'Would you like some tea?'

'A'right.'

Jan put a kettle on the wood-burner, which was still roasting hot. 'Did Gerry tell you why we wanted to see you?'

'Nope, but Joe reckoned he knew why.'

'What did Joe say?'

'Said you wanted to know if a bloke in a black

Range Rover talked to me at the Star, in the car park, back in the autumn.'

'Yes,' Jan said. 'That's right. Did you talk to him?'

The boy nodded.

Jan waited, but he didn't offer any more.

'Well,' she prompted impatiently. 'What did he want?'

Amos Smith lifted one shoulder, as if his answer was utterly inconsequential. 'He said if I loosed open a gate to one of your fields, he'd drop me a hundred quid.'

Jan stared at him, hardly able to believe his admission, and the confirmation at last of Harold Powell's guilt.

'So, you did it,' she added, unnecessarily, she thought.

'Nope.' He shook his head.

'But you must have done,' Jan said sharply. 'After the horses got out we went and found that someone had pulled out the staple that holds the gate bolt.'

'Maybe they did, but it weren't me. When I got there, at half-past six in the morning, like he told me, the gate was open like, swinging into the lane down there.'

Jan shuddered. She didn't want him to be telling the truth, but her every instinct said he was. She didn't want him to see her dilemma, though, and walked through to the other end of the caravan, wishing Eddie was around to give his advice.

She screwed up her eyes. 'Bloody hell!' she hissed.

'Mumma?' Megan asked.

'Oh sorry, Meg. Go back to sleep for a bit, will you?'

Then Jan thought of Toby. He sometimes stayed at the Fox & Pheasant at weekends, not returning to London until midday on Monday.

She went back into the living room and smiled at Amos. 'I never made your tea,' she said, quickly pouring boiling water onto a tea bag in a mug and shoving a bowl of sugar across the table. 'Would you mind hanging on for a friend of mine to come up and hear what you've told me?'

'Not the police, or nuffink?'

'No, of course not. No one wants to incriminate you when you haven't done anything.'

Amos lifted one eyebrow. 'A'right,' he shrugged. 'I'll want something for my time.'

Jan looked away and picked up her phone. She punched Toby's mobile number, praying that he was still down in the village.

He answered in a thick, sleepy voice. Jan had obviously woken him. She glanced guiltily at her watch; it was still only five to seven.

'Toby, I'm really sorry to ring you so early, but it's important. There's a chap up here I need you to come and see. Where are you now?'

Toby was still in the Fox and wanted to know who was with Jan.

'I can't tell you, not over the phone. But please, will you come?'

A few moments later, when she put the phone down, Toby was on his way.

Jan and Amos had a stilted conversation while they waited until Toby arrived, freshly shaved, in a little over fifteen minutes.

'Thanks for coming,' Jan said as she opened the door of the caravan. She waved a hand at the surly boy, still sucking tea from his mug. 'This is Amos Smith.'

Toby raised his eyebrows, impressed, while Jan told him what the boy had said. He nodded as he listened and, when Jan had stopped, sat down at the table opposite Amos.

'Now, Amos, if you can give me good straight, clear answers to what I'm going to ask you, I'll give you a hundred quid. And if you come back later and say the same to a gentleman from my solicitors', I'll give you another. OK?'

Amos nodded. It was clear he understood. Jan, uncomfortable about paying for the information, stifled her reservations. Toby was a practical man; he knew what he was doing.

'You told Jan that the man in the Range Rover offered you a hundred pounds to open the gate at the bottom of her lane, right?'

'Yeh.'

'Do you know what the man was called?'

'Harold Powell.'

'How do you know?'

''Cos he give me his address to come and get the money when I done the job.'

'And did you go and get the money?'

'Yeh,' Amos said. 'He heard the horses got out. I never told him the gate was already open.'

Toby smiled. 'Good. That's very helpful and, as far as I can tell, you haven't committed a crime apart from fraudulently extracting a hundred quid from Harold Powell and I don't suppose he'll be reporting you for that. And now you've earned another hundred,' Toby said smoothly, taking a wallet from his jacket and pulling five twenty-pound notes from it. 'Come here tomorrow, at the same time, and say exactly what you've just said to me, and there'll be five more twenties.'

'I'll want two hundred,' Amos said quickly. 'If it's another bloke.'

After that, the rest of the week was one of wary optimism for Jan. She didn't tell any of the staff about O'Hagan until, on Wednesday, an accountant from his organization phoned and asked if he could come up the following day to go over Jan's records.

Then, she felt, it was safe to announce that A.D. O'Hagan was putting up the guarantee she needed and would be sending six top-class horses to Edge Farm.

Roz, Emma, Joe and even Annabel were stunned,

then ecstatic that their loyalty and effort had been so impressively recognized. They immediately went about their work in the warming spring sunshine with smiles to match and a lightness that had been noticeably missing since Eddie's fall.

24

Five days later Jan walked out of the main door of a plain, post-war office building in a big, leafy London square. She looked with distaste at the constant stream of traffic that swirled around it – noisy, smelly, mechanical and a hundred miles from the scent of spring grass, the tang of horse sweat and the soft creak of leather that characterized her world.

She turned left and walked along a wide pavement, thronged with strangers who couldn't give a damn whether she lived or died before she reached the end of the square.

I agree with Annabel, Jan thought, *I don't like London. I don't ever want to come up here again.*

She paused at the side of the road, waited for a green flashing pedestrian and crossed over. She turned right and carried on walking, bemused by the vast diversity of people milling around the entrance of the big modern hotel which filled one side of the square.

She stopped outside, beneath the hotel's oriental-looking canopy. She took a tentative step towards the entrance and changed her mind. She wasn't ready yet.

She wanted more time on her own to allow the Jockey Club's decision to sink in.

She carried on; she would walk right round the square first before she went back into the hotel. As she walked, she thought back to the beginning of the previous year, when she'd seen John dead and she'd finally had to accept that she was on her own.

She thought about her decision to move from Stonewall, to start a new life and to make a living by doing the only thing she knew. As she crossed the road and remembered Harold Powell's deceit, she grimaced.

With a smile, she acknowledged the advice and wisdom of her father. She also understood her mother's timid reaction to her plans, all the sewing and support with the children that Mary had given freely despite her misgivings. She wondered, too, how far she could have got without Annabel's quiet loyalty.

Loyalty, she thought, was an underrated virtue. Mr Carey, once he had made up his mind, had shown her great loyalty. At his funeral the week before, she'd seen how many people he had shown generosity to under the cloak of his shyness. Most of the owners at Edge Farm, appreciating what he had done for Jan, had been there: Penny Price, solidly respectful; Gwillam Evans, all the way from Brecon, and Colonel Gilbert, standing rigidly to attention at the graveside in Stanfield churchyard as a mark of his regard.

That morning, before Annabel had come to collect Jan, a letter had arrived from Mr Carey's solicitors to say in dry, legal terms that he had left a mare, August

Moon, to Mrs Janine Hardy. Whatever else happened to her that day, she felt, Mr Carey's kind legacy would at least make it bearable.

She'd had another letter, too, from Toby's solicitors in Lincoln's Inn.

They were pleased to inform her that Harold Powell, having taken into consideration all the facts as presented by them, had agreed that he would reimburse to Mrs Hardy the full difference between the original sales price achieved by his firm at auction and the subsequent private treaty sale price of Stonewall Farm, less, of course, their normal agent's commission on that difference, plus expenses.

Jan had thought the agent's fee was a bit of a nerve, but, in the end, the eighty thousand pounds she would be left with after paying the solicitors' bill would go a long way to paying for the improvements she needed at Edge Farm, without going cap in hand to A.D. O'Hagan.

She crossed another broad street, clogged with panting cars and stinking diesel taxis, and wished Eddie could have been with her today.

She thought how much he would have enjoyed seeing her in action, inside the hallowed doors of the Jockey Club. She smiled and even laughed a little to herself at the memory.

She'd been shaking as she walked through the grand, forbidding doors. Inside, her throat had dried up as she asked where to go.

In the soundless stuffiness of the lift she'd been alone, staring at the doors when it stopped. She waited for them to open and panicked when she thought they never would – until she saw that another pair of doors had silently slid back behind her to reveal a reception area. Some people were there grinning at her as she reddened, and stepped out feeling a complete fool.

What a way to start the most important interview of my life, she'd thought. *I can't even find my way out of the lift.*

It was worse, much worse, than going to see the bank manager.

The receptionist greeted her with no more than a faint raising of the eyebrows.

I bet she did more than raise her eyebrows to Virginia High and Mighty Gilbert, Jan thought, while she sat for what seemed like an age in reception, bursting to go to the loo, but not daring to ask in case her moment came and she wasn't there.

Eventually a minion, a dapper, tight-lipped young man, appeared and ushered her into the stark committee room.

God, Jan panicked, *what the hell am I doing here? They'll never accept me.*

She felt as if she was up on a charge of murder.

But at least she was invited to sit down at one end of a highly polished, antique mahogany table, which looked the length of a cricket pitch. At the far end sat three Jockey Club stewards, traditional, old-school representatives of the governing body of British horse racing, talking in whispers so that she wouldn't hear what they were saying, and passing little notes to each other as she answered their queries.

How rude, she thought.

Now, less than half an hour later, she could barely remember any of the questions they'd asked.

Some, she recalled, seemed quite irrelevant, and a darned cheek: like how much money had her husband left her in his will.

She'd become indignant. 'What's that got to do with anything?'

They hadn't liked that and, for a while, she wondered if she'd blown it.

Finally, they released her and told her to wait in reception.

She'd sat there in a trance, hardly daring to move, in case it jeopardized her chances of being granted her licence.

The same minion had reappeared, still po-faced, and asked her to come back in front of the committee to hear their verdict.

Jan saw three sombre faces at the distant end of the table.

Oh shit! she thought. *This is it.*

As she walked round the square, her self-confidence grew. By the time she'd done a complete circuit and arrived back once more beneath the hotel's deep canopy, she knew she was ready and she could handle anything the future could throw at her.

She took a deep breath, straightened the skirt of the suit which Annabel had chosen with her and walked through the wide doors into the lobby where she'd left her parents an hour earlier.

Annabel was with them. She had said she would take Mary and Reg through to the coffee shop and keep them calm until Jan returned. But evidently they hadn't made it that far; they were still in the lobby, sitting in deep, slightly awkward tub chairs around a coffee table. Reg had a pint of bitter in front of him, half full, Mary had a sweet sherry, hardly touched, and Annabel a glass of sparkling Perrier water.

Jan saw them first.

'Hi,' she said, more loudly than she meant to, and they turned together to look at her.

At first, mischievously, she didn't allow any expression on her face and the few seconds of uncertainty seemed to linger on theirs for several moments, until she clenched her fist, raised her arm and punched the air above her head. She didn't care who saw or who heard.

'Mum, Dad, Bel!' she shouted triumphantly as the tears began to flow. 'Guess what? I got it! I've got my licence. At last . . .' She tried to stifle her sobs. '. . . It's real! I'm a proper racehorse trainer!'

Epilogue

Two days later, when Annabel was on her way up to have breakfast with Jan, the postman arrived and handed her the mail. As she stepped into the caravan, she was idly flipping through it, out of habit, when she stopped and extracted a postcard. She turned it over. 'It's not really rude to read other people's postcards, is it?' she grinned naughtily. 'After all, the postman could, if he felt like it.'

'Where's it from?' Jan asked.

'Australia.'

'Oh, great!' Jan said. 'It'll be from Ben! I wonder when he's coming home?'

'It's not from Ben,' Annabel said, passing the card to Jan. 'And I feel there's something you haven't been telling me.'

Jan looked at the photo on the card briefly, as part of a guessing game she liked to play – trying to think who would have chosen a particular card. This one was a slightly dull, inactive shot of the empty stands at Melbourne race course, which looked as if it had been given away for nothing. But that was enough of a hint and she was ready for the surprisingly arty, italic hand on the other side.

> *Hi Jan,*
> *Up to my knees in horse shit still, but in another world.*
> *See you, and thanks for everything.*
> *Love, E.*

Jan sniffed and didn't look at her friend for a moment. When she did, she gave her a sheepish grin. 'Sorry, Bel. I don't think I really wanted to believe it.'

'You and Eddie?' Annabel put her head on one side and shook it. 'I don't think so.'

'No, I know, but I miss him, Bel. I wish he'd told me why he was going.'

'I think they've all gone,' Annabel said thoughtfully. 'I mean Ron, Eddie and Susan. I saw an advert for her house in *Country Life* last month. I think they just decided to sell up, get back together and go away. Susan hinted at it when she came to see me, though she would have liked Eddie to win his bet as well.'

'It's ridiculous, isn't it,' Jan mused. 'When you think how much was hanging on that one race and what the outcome of it has been.'

'Maybe you're right when you say life's just a game of chance and a chain of coincidence which we can't control.'

'God knows, but right now I don't care!'

and she was ready to ride something [illegible] hand on the other side.

'Hi, Jim,

[illegible] in your [illegible] to [illegible] world.

See your [illegible] for everything.

Lucy.'

[illegible] smiled and [illegible] look at [illegible] the [illegible] when [illegible] [illegible] [illegible] Lucy [illegible] really wanted to [illegible].

'You [illegible]?' [illegible] her hand on [illegible] and [illegible]. 'I don't think so.'

'No. I know but I [illegible] her. [illegible] had told me [illegible] was going.'

'I think they've all gone,' [illegible] said thoughtfully. 'I mean [illegible] and [illegible]. I saw an advert for the house in Country Life last month. I think they just decided to sell the [illegible] together and go away. [illegible] even [illegible] the [illegible] to see me, though she would have asked Eddie to [illegible] herself.'

'It's [illegible]. When you think how much was hanging [illegible] and [illegible].'

'Maybe [illegible] when you say the [illegible] of [illegible] a chain of [illegible] which we can't control.'

'God knows [illegible].'

The Vendetta

Prologue

'Why the hell're you so late with this?' the voice of Tim Farr's boss, Jim Tree, rasped. 'We've already got the story off the wires. This accident happened, what – six hours ago?'

'Yes, I know, but I followed the recovery vehicle that carted the wrecks away. Then I went to the hospital. I did phone in to keep you in the picture, so to speak.'

Jimmy snorted.

'Well, you should've spoken to me. OK, I'll tell you what I want. A colour piece, five hundred words, faxed over to me by midnight. That's in thirty-five minutes' time, so you'd better move your arse, son. And don't make this story too poncy.'

The reporter's fingers paused, reached for a styrofoam cup of coffee, raised it to his lips. He looked at his watch. Eleven twenty-five. He hurriedly put down the cup and pounded on, trying to summon up a mental picture of the drama he had watched unfolding on Cleeve Hill earlier that evening.

> Jan Hardy was the National Hunt heroine from the unconsidered Edge Farm yard, who burst onto the racing scene only a couple of seasons ago and

> whose horse Magic Maestro had just sensationally won the Cathcart Chase. I had seen her face radiant in the winners' enclosure, and her broad smile lighting up the presentation ceremony. Now, as they carefully shuttled her on a stretcher to the waiting ambulance, the pretty features were obscured by the oxygen mask. And lodged in that bell of blonde hair were tiny granules of shattered glass, which shone under the lights like glitter dust. The knot of lookers-on, marshalled behind the police barrier, uttered a collective sigh as the crew hoisted her through the ambulance doors and we saw her, unmistakably, move her arm, then her head. At least she was alive.
>
> But from a distance I couldn't be sure about her companion, apparently the driver of the car. They took another forty-five minutes to get the young man out. He was covered in blood and appeared lifeless. I asked a policeman who he was. He just shook his head, but later I learned it was Eddie Sullivan. He's a close friend of Mrs Hardy and many fans of the jumping game will remember the race he rode as an amateur rider in the Foxhunters' Chase at Aintree's Grand National meeting two years ago on a horse she trained. The name of Jan Hardy was then virtually unknown, but in a sensational race Sullivan, on Russian Eagle, approached the last of the great fences certain to win, until under bizarre circumstances he came to grief when his saddle slipped on landing . . .

Ten minutes later Tim had finished the story. He had included almost everything he knew about the accident except for one small fact, something he had noticed about Eddie's smashed car. It was a small detail, which indicated there was something about the accident that was not quite straightforward. It might lead nowhere or, on the other hand, it might lead to a terrific story. But that would have to wait until tomorrow.

He scrolled back to the top of the piece and thought about the headline. It was always worth putting one in, though the sub-editors usually considered they knew better. He rejigged it:

JAN HARDY: FATAL TRAGEDY MARS DAY OF TRIUMPH

Then he added his byline:

By Tim Farr

1

Numb from shock, drowsy from drugs, Jan drifted in and out of consciousness. She understood she was in bed. But there was a background of buzzing and occasional cheeps, like a hedgerow in summer. Periodically her mind came into focus and the hedgerow dissolved into the hospital. She was besieged by medical paraphernalia – drip stands, tubes, wires, bleeping monitors. She shut her eyes. Her body felt as if it was bobbing weightlessly in warm water. Opening her eyelids again, she knew she was staring at the ceiling, where the strip light seemed to her as sharp and real as anything she had ever seen in her life. She understood for a moment it was the source of the buzzing. Her hearing seemed selectively amplified. She heard a voice in some other room or corridor call out the word, 'Doctor!'

Much less clear were the figures in white and blue flitting around the blurred periphery of her vision. She tried to move her head. Someone touched her arm. A needle went in and she returned to semi-consciousness. Now she was at the same time in a hospital ward *and* in the corner of a ripe June hayfield. Something rattled and she heard the harness of a horse, smelled the leather. A door hinge whinnied, a trolley clattered exactly like her pony's hooves on the cobbled surface of the yard when she was a girl. Somewhere down the ward a shaken pillow snorted like a horse going to exercise in the early morning.

A little later images of the previous day began to form in her brain, messages she could not read properly. They floated past her like a surreal landscape viewed from a ghostly train. Eddie insisted he would drive her home. She picked up a race card. She stood in the centre of the paddock, giving Finbar Howlett, the jockey, his instructions. She placed a two pound bet on the Tote for the kids. The crowd shouted at the start of the Gold Cup – the Cheltenham roar. She handed Magic Maestro's passport across the counter to the declarations clerk. Leading the horse from the pre-parade ring, Joe Paley looked as grave as a chess player. Finbar got a leg up into the saddle and Magic Maestro skittered for a moment before walking on. Drumming hooves. Virginia Gilbert queening it in the trainers' bar. Eddie insisted he would drive her home. The last fence. Excitement. Whoops of joy. The winners' enclosure. The trophy presentation, with cheers and clapping. The face of Harold Powell snarling at her by the weighing room. A.D. O'Hagan in the hospitality box, beckoning the waiter to pour more champagne. Eddie insisting he would drive her home . . .

These impressions seemed unconnected, like a randomly shuffled pack of picture cards. Her mind fumbled with them for a while, and then she fell back into a deep sleep.

A woman in a white coat and with glossy dark hair was beside her bed. It was early morning.

'Nurse, what's happened?' Jan asked. 'Why am I in hospital?'

He throat and mouth were dry. She could manage no more than a creaky whisper. The woman leaned nearer.

'It's Dr Pierson, Jan. Penny Pierson.'

'Are you a doctor?'

Jan found she could shift her head, and it didn't hurt. She looked sideways and saw the folded earpieces of a stethoscope protruding from a pocket of the white coat.

'Oh, yes, so you are. Sorry.'

'Are you feeling better?'

'Better? I don't know. Can you tell me what happened? I don't . . . I can't remember.'

Dr Pierson perched herself on the bed beside Jan.

'Well, you've been in a road accident. Coming away from the racecourse, so I've been told.'

'An accident? Did I smash up the Shogun?'

'No, it wasn't you driving.'

'Oh.'

Then her brain sparked a connection. *Eddie insisting he would drive her home.*

'Eddie. Eddie was driving,' Jan said. 'Something . . . some car hit us.'

'Is it coming back to you?'

'Bits of it.'

'Good. You'll remember it all in time. Bit by bit.'

In her mind, fog still swirled around the previous night, but it was true that more and more was coming back to her. It was dark. They were in Eddie's old two-seater Morgan. Its throaty engine was coughing bronchitically as he accelerated up the hill.

'Some other car was there, going fast,' she said as a whole chunk of memory cleared the mist. 'Eddie went off the road and we crashed . . . Then, nothing, until I woke up – *When? – Last night? This morning?* – and the car was a complete wreck. Eddie was knocked out. At least, I thought he was. I was talking to him, and he didn't reply. And then I thought maybe he wasn't knocked out. I mean, I thought . . .'

She felt a sudden panic and began shaking. She snapped her head sideways to look at Dr Pierson and this time the suddenness of her movement caused pain in her neck and the side of her face, which she now realized was bandaged. Her voice was little more than a parched croak.

'He *is* OK? He wasn't moving. I think I thought he was dead.'

The doctor smiled again.

'No, Jan, it's all right. Eddie's still with us. But he's very poorly. He's in the intensive care unit.'

'Thank God.'

Jan raised her hands, still trembling violently, to her face. Dressings covered her cheeks and temples. Her hands too were bandaged. She let them fall back to the covers and suddenly the tears came.

'Thank God. Oh, thank God . . .'

Physically, Jan had come off lightly, with superficial face wounds, a throbbing bump just above her right temple, and bruises where the car's impact had thrown her body against the seat belt. There were also cuts to her hands, caused when she had tried to brush away the crumbs of window glass that had showered down on her. Otherwise, incredibly, she seemed unhurt.

No longer needed, the drips and monitors were wheeled away and one of the nurses, a sympathetic Scottish girl, gave Jan a mirror.

'See?' she said. 'It's no so bad.'

Jan saw that dressings wrapped her head from the crown to beneath her chin, making a square white frame for her even whiter features, the eyes hollow and sunken from shock.

'I look like a nun in a horror film,' she commented disapprovingly.

At half-past nine her parents were the first visitors to arrive, her father holding a big bunch of bananas and her mother, practical as ever, carried a holdall with a change of clothes and Jan's toilet bag.

'We stopped at Edge on the way to pick them up,' she said. 'Fran will be down with the children in a few minutes.'

'But what about school?' Jan asked.

'Oh, they can miss the first hour. It's more important they see you – they wouldn't be able to concentrate anyway.'

Perched on the bedside chair, Mary Pritchard looked pale and strained, though she would not have admitted it. Reg made a more convincing show of cheerfulness.

'You look fantastic, girl.'

His daughter knew it was a well-meaning lie, though

she could tell also that Reg was mightily relieved to see things were not a great deal worse.

'Don't be daft. How can I look fantastic, Dad? I'm a bloody mess.'

'A few cuts. You did worse trying to gallop your pony through that copse as a child, remember?'

'Well, I'm not a child now. And what's the news about Eddie? They won't tell me anything.'

'Eddie'll be all right. He's young and strong.'

'Then why's he in intensive care?'

She caught Reg and Mary exchanging a doubtful glance.

'Mum? Dad? Please, I need to know. I'm sure he wasn't wearing his seat belt. I thought he was dead. Dad, can't you try and find out how he is? I can't stand the way they're not telling me anything.'

Reg said he would ask about Eddie if the chance came up. But Jan knew her father too well and it was obvious he already had more information than he was letting on. She did not pursue the matter, for now Fran, the woman who acted as her nanny and general helper around the house, arrived with Megan and Matty. The children approached their mother with serious faces. The sight of the bandages and the dark blue bruises frightened them. After a few moments' consideration, Megan turned to her grandad.

'Mummy looks like a mummy. She's frightening me.'

Jan blinked back her tears.

After three-quarters of an hour, during which Reg reassured Jan that all was well in the yard, and that he'd been told by Annabel how well Magic Maestro had come out of his race and eaten up his feed, Mary Pritchard saw that her daughter was exhausted and began to shoo the family out.

'These children are due at school,' she told her daughter, 'and you need to rest.'

'No, I don't. I have to go home. I thought I would get out today, but now they're telling me not until tomorrow at the earliest. It's the bump on my head they're concerned about, though of course it's nothing.'

Mary placed the palm of her hand across her daughter's forehead, in a gesture she had always used to soothe Jan as a small child.

'Nothing is important after an accident like that, child. You need to look after yourself. Get your strength. Annabel will be all right at the yard for a day or two, I'll have the little ones and your dad can drive them to school.'

Jan lay back on the pillows and closed her eyes.

'All right, Mum, don't go on. I'll try. I just wish I knew something about Eddie.'

Later in the day, after Jan had been moved out of the A and E department and into a room off a general ward 'for observation', she awoke from what was probably the deepest sleep of her life. Her bandages were now removed and replaced by smaller dressings, and she was beginning to feel more herself. Her face, although it was swollen, was otherwise surprisingly lightly damaged with, as Penny Pierson told her, no danger of any permanent scarring.

'Your skin will be pristine again in a few days,' the

doctor said. 'The bruises will last a little longer, but I'd say you'll be at least presentable by the end of next week. It's just that bump on your head that we want to keep an eye on.'

'Please tell me how Eddie is. Is he bad?'

Dr Pierson studied her patient for a few moments, weighing up how much to divulge.

'Mr Sullivan's got problems,' she said judiciously. 'We're doing all we can for him.'

'What do you mean – problems? What problems? Is he conscious? Can I see him?'

The doctor shook her head.

'I'm afraid not. He's not fully conscious yet.'

'But I could *see* him, couldn't I? Just for a moment?'

'I don't think it's advisable, Jan. Not just yet.'

Jan knew it was pointless to continue the argument. Instead she broached the subject that had been nagging at her ever since she'd woken up in the morning.

'I vaguely remember there was another car – in the accident, I mean. Was it overtaking us? Or coming the other way? I'm still a bit muddled. Was there another car?'

'Jan, I'm just the doctor. But I can tell you someone else was brought in.'

'The driver of the other car?'

'He was apparently driving another car, yes.'

'And? How is he?'

Dr Pierson laid a hand on Jan's briefly, and said in a soft voice, 'I'm really sorry to say this, Jan, but he didn't make it. He was pronounced dead on arrival.'

'Dead on arrival,' Jan repeated dully.

'In fact, I believe he was killed instantly.'

'I see.'

Closing her eyes, Jan breathed deeply in and out, feeling the seat-belt bruises around her left collarbone. The life of a stranger cut off in an instant, and she had been there.

'Do you know his name?'

'No,' said Penny Pierson, 'and I don't think it's a good idea for you to worry about it. Don't make me regret that I told you, hey? You've got to be strong. Your family needs you at home, so don't go and make yourself worse.'

She stood up and bustled towards the door, but then spun round, reminded of something.

'Oh, yes, I forgot, there's a Detective Inspector Hadfield who's been wanting to see you. He called in this morning and said he'd be back this afternoon. Shall we stall him? I can get the consultant to tell him to go away if you like.'

Jan waved her hand, dismissing the idea.

'No, no, it's OK. Let him come in. I'd like to see him.'

And find out what he knows, she added to herself.

DI Brian Hadfield, of the plain-clothes branch, turned up within the hour. He tiptoed into the room, as if afraid to waken the occupant, though he could see Jan was awake and expecting him. He was of medium height, with a thatch of grey hair and blue eyes twinkling out of a ruddy complexion. A small uniformed woman constable was in attendance.

'Mrs Hardy, may I say what a fan I am of yours? That Irish National with Russian Eagle, what a finish. Great win.'

'Thank you,' Jan said mechanically. 'Would you like to sit down? How can I help?'

Jan tried to assess the policeman as he shifted the bedside chair into a position closer to her. He looked innocuous enough. But that 'what a fan I am' stuff was a warning sign. Maybe he really was a racing enthusiast. On the other hand, maybe he'd done a spot of research just so he could butter her up. Jan had never had anything against the police, but she was instinctively wary about a complete stranger paying her compliments, particularly a policeman.

'We're investigating the serious road traffic accident on Cleeve Hill last night – as you've probably guessed . . .'

He gave a slight hiccup of a laugh. Was he nervous?

'And obviously we want to know exactly what happened, so at some point we're going to need to take your statement about the incident.'

'My statement?'

She hadn't visualized this. She'd thought it would be DI Hadfield briefing *her* on what had happened.

'Yes,' he said. 'There's nothing to worry about. It's just your version of events.'

Jan hauled herself into a slightly more upright position in the bed.

'My *version*? I thought you'd come to tell me what happened. Now you're making it sound as if there's something suspicious, as if I did something wrong.'

Hadfield's cheerful face wilted slightly. He held up his hand.

'Oh, don't get me wrong, Mrs Hardy. You see,

unfortunately a man has died: the driver of the other car.'

'I heard just before you arrived. I'm sorry.'

'You were in Mr Sullivan's car, the Morgan?'

Jan nodded.

'So the thing is – obviously – there now has to be a full police investigation, and as Mr Sullivan's in no state to speak to us, you're the only one who can throw any light on the situation at the moment.'

Jan frowned. Alarm bells were ringing. The truth was that she had not yet fully constructed her memory of the previous night. In fact, subconsciously, she'd probably been avoiding doing so. Her memory was still only jumbled fragments. And she was quite sure she shouldn't give Hadfield a statement consisting of fragments. She would have to be certain of the truth before she could tell it.

'I guess I'm still shocked – I did have a nasty blow on the head, you know. I can't really remember what happened fully. Not yet anyway.'

'Can't you tell me *anything*?'

He spoke gently, regretfully.

'Sorry, Inspector. I've got lots of rather fuzzy impressions, nothing concrete. It'll all come back eventually though, I'm told. The doctor will explain . . .'

The policeman had to accept Jan's polite refusal to give a statement, and he withdrew, tiptoeing out of the room in the same bizarre way he had come in.

Later that afternoon there seemed to be a lull in ward activity. Jan was hardly breathing as she slipped out of bed and put on her dressing gown. She opened the door of her room and looked out: the corridor was deserted. She quietly crept out and headed for the stairwell. Holding the banister tightly, she went down one flight. Her legs felt weak and wobbly but they held her.

On the next floor she saw a sign with an arrow pointing to the intensive care unit. She padded in its direction, and after what seemed like an age came to the unit, which was entered by a pair of swing doors. Amazingly nobody challenged her as she eased her way through. Now she was in a corridor which ran past a suite of dimly lit rooms, furnished with beds that looked more like operating tables, each surrounded by batteries of high-tech equipment. Each interior could be seen from the corridor through a double-glazed window, although the rooms had slatted blinds. Some had been drawn shut on the inside. The patients' names were written on small cards posted on the doors.

She counted six rooms before the corridor was broken by the nurses' station. The first room was empty. The second housed a patient who was, as she could see through the slats, encased in bandages. She checked the name on the door, but it meant nothing. The third room was occupied by a female, but on the door of the fourth she found what she was looking for: 'Edward Sullivan'.

The blinds were lowered but not fully shut, so Jan could peer between them. The lighting was dim, but sufficient to give a view of the bed and the patient. He lay there, heavily bandaged around the head, arms and midriff, encircled by the latest electronic machinery and drip stands. His bare chest, rising and falling as he breathed, was the only movement he made. She could see the electrodes that fed the cardiograph machines and other monitoring devices. The black hair sprouting above the head dressing seemed like Eddie's. But this man had a huge head and face, a bulbous nose, bloated jowls and lips like frankfurter sausages. This man was not Eddie. Had they moved him and forgotten to change the name card? If so, where was he?

'Can I help you?'

A blue-uniformed nursing sister had bustled up without Jan noticing.

'Er, I don't know,' said Jan, startled. She instantly collected herself and indicated the intensive care room. 'Actually I'm wondering about Eddie Sullivan. I'm Jan Hardy and I was with him, you see, in the car.'

'Oh?'

'Well, see it's his name here on the door, but this isn't him. Can you tell me what's happened? Where is he? Have you moved him? Has he come round? Is he able to see anyone?'

The sister gave a faint smile.

'Oh, this is him all right.'

Jan jabbed a finger in the direction of the patient.

'*That's* Eddie?' she asked in disbelief.

'Large as life.'

'But it can't be.'

'Oh, no doubt his face looks a bit different from when you last saw him. It often happens after car accidents. I've had mothers in here unable to recognize their own sons. Don't worry too much, I can assure you his face will return to normal.'

Shocked, Jan studied the supine patient again, and now realized that it was indeed Eddie, his features so grossly distorted by swellings and a large haematoma as to be unrecognizable.

'He came off much worse than me, didn't he?' she said quietly. 'Is he unconscious?'

'Yes, I'm afraid so.'

'In a coma?'

'That's just a term for it, but don't be too worried. It's amazing how quickly young people can recover.'

'When will he wake up?'

The sister shrugged.

'You can never be sure. He's quite heavily sedated, but we think the signs are good.'

'So he'll make a full recovery?'

The nurse smiled again, a professional and practised smile, but comforting all the same.

'We take one step at a time around here, Mrs Hardy. The first thing is for him to be fully conscious. The doctor thinks he might, just might, come round in a day or so. Then we can reassess him.'

On her way back to her own bed, Jan began to have thoughts of a kind she had not entertained before. What if Eddie didn't come round? What if he stayed in a coma for years? What if he died?

As she climbed the stairs, Eddie's voice suddenly came back to her, as he gunned the spluttering engine of the Morgan. *I bloody love you, Jan Hardy*. Yes, he really had said that last night. And what was more, she'd said the same thing back to him, the only time she'd said those words since the death of her husband, John.

Oh, Eddie, you stupid, stupid, irresponsible idiot! You didn't wear your seat belt and now look at you. Silently she wept.

2

'God, I feel shit,' Jan whispered to herself early on Saturday morning. At eight-thirty the trauma specialist appeared in her room on his rounds. His manner was reassuringly decisive.

'Did you sleep well?'

'Not very. I feel like I've been run over by a steamroller.'

'But the headache's eased?'

Jan nodded.

'Good. How's your memory of the accident?'

'I've got most of what happened, I think, though not necessarily in the correct order.'

'That's quite a usual pattern. The pieces will slot into place sooner rather than later. In the meantime . . .'

He looked at the medical notes, asked a few more questions as to how she felt generally. Then he spoke to the nursing sister and scribbled something on the notes.

'Well, Mrs Hardy, I see no reason to keep you in. Go home. But you need to rest for a few more days. That can be done as easily there as here – more easily, maybe.'

'What about riding?' she asked.

'Riding? I wouldn't consider that resting, myself.'

Jan took him to mean that if *she* thought riding was resting, then she could go ahead and do it.

'Please could you tell me about my friend, Eddie? Yesterday he was still unconscious. Has there been any change?'

The doctor shook his head regretfully.

'No change overnight, I'm afraid. These things can be unpredictable, but I think we can say his condition has stabilized. We are still monitoring him closely and that's all I can say at the moment.'

It was one of Jan's stable lads, Joe Paley, Magic Maestro's work rider, who drove down in the Shogun to collect her. Despite a shaky start, Joe had proved to be one of Jan's most loyal members of staff.

''Lo, Mrs H,' he mumbled when she met him in the hospital lobby. 'I'm sorry for your trouble.'

It was the only mention he made of the accident. Joe was not a garrulous young man except when talking to, or about, horses. So on the way back to Edge Farm he let himself be questioned about the yard: how Maestro had come out of his race, the trouble they were having with Russian Eagle's foot, and the well-being of a possible future star hurdler, A.D. O'Hagan's Wexford Lad, who'd had sore shins. They were just coming to the prospects for today's racing and Jan's two runners at Uttoxeter when Joe turned off the road and up the track that led to Edge Farm Stables.

As they drove up the tarmac drive to the house, passing the newly completed stable yard, her heart lightened as she saw her three dogs, Fred, Tigger and Fly, come pelting out of the office to greet her. They were followed a split second later by the slender figure of her assistant trainer, Annabel.

'I can't tell you what a shock it was,' said Annabel. They were sitting at the big kitchen table with mugs of tea.

'We didn't know anything until the police called, about nine-thirty, tenish. When you and Eddie didn't come home, we thought maybe you'd gone off to a hotel for a celebration dinner or something. You know, an impulse thing.'

'Dinner, *or something*? Bel, as if I would without phoning.'

Annabel giggled. Relief at the early return of her friend and boss had made her effervescent.

'Eddie would. I thought maybe he'd talked you into it.'

But the thought of Eddie quickly dampened their spirits.

'How is he?' Bel continued, sensing Jan's gloom.

'I saw him in the ICU. He's completely unrecognizable. Bel, *never* drive without wearing a seat belt. He's a complete mess: his nose is broken and his jaw. Everything in his face is huge; even his bruises have bruises. He's still out of it. I don't think they really know how badly he's hurt, I mean the extent of his internal injuries. I guess they'll wait until he wakes up . . .'

She let the sentence hang, but the unspoken words

if he ever wakes up were understood between them. Suddenly Jan felt a welling up in her chest and her eyes prickled. Annabel reached for her hand.

'Are you OK? Come on, I'm sure he'll be fine. You know Eddie.'

Jan nodded, swallowing the emotion and taking a deep breath. She was not going to cry now. At least she was alive. Eddie was alive. That was all that mattered at this precise moment. The future was the future and she would climb whatever mountains came her way – she knew that also.

Jan rose briskly, ripped off a sheet of kitchen paper and blew her nose. 'Have you spoken to the Sullivans?'

'Yesterday morning. I couldn't tell them much because I didn't know much. So I just said Eddie's in hospital and we'd call them with an update later today.'

'OK, I'll do that in a minute. Now, what about Uttoxeter? I don't think I'm quite up to going racing, not with this face anyway. Can you cope?'

Annabel nodded.

'No problem. It's already sorted. I'm taking Roz and Con. The rest of the crew will be here, so there's no need for you to roll up your sleeves.'

Annabel had made a list of the well-wishers who'd called to ask how Jan was. Most of her owners had rung yesterday, after reading about the crash in their morning papers – Johnny Carlton-Brown, Bernie Sutcliffe, Lady Fairford, Colonel Gilbert and, of course, Toby Waller the banker, who was Jan's most constant loyal friend and adviser.

'What about A.D.?' Jan asked.

'Phoned last night from Switzerland. Wants you to call him as soon as you're well enough. If you can't get him, he says can you talk to Jimmy O'Driscoll at Aigmont.'

Jan wrinkled her nose. She didn't much care for A.D.'s racing manager, who ostensibly oversaw the huge equine operation that was centred on the billionaire's estate in County Wicklow.

'I'll call the owners later and reassure them,' she promised, 'when things are quiet. They're entitled to know what's going on.'

'Oh, and Tony Robertson called this morning. He said he'd be over to see you about four-thirty.'

Jan smiled. As her family doctor, Tony paid her rather more attention than might be expected of a busy GP. But then, he was also her most persistent suitor; he had asked her to marry him as recently as last Christmas. She liked the man. She even rather fancied him. But could she persuade herself to think of him as anything other than a friend?

On that question might hang her whole future.

Jan waved the horsebox off to Uttoxeter, then curled up on the sofa with the phone. First she called Eddie's parents in Queensland. His father Ron came on the line first.

'Wotcher, Jan,' he barked. 'You OK?'

'I'm all right, thanks, Ron. I just had a couple of nights in hospital, nothing too serious.'

'Good girl. Now what about my boy? Smashed himself up, has he?'

'I'm afraid he's not too well. He's still unconscious and it's impossible to say any more until he comes round. Hello?'

Muffled fragments of a tearful argument could be heard at the Sullivan end and then Sue Sullivan was speaking.

'Jan, Jan are you still there? Oh, good. Where exactly is Edward?'

'Cheltenham General, in the intensive care unit. Shall I give you the number?'

She rummaged in her bag and pulled out a bit of paper.

After Jan had recited the number, Sue continued, 'I'll be getting a flight over, but I don't know exactly how soon that will be. But be sure to tell Edward I'm on my way.'

Jan spent the rest of the morning working her way through the list of other callers. She spoke to Lady Fairford and Colonel Gilbert, assuring them of her basic well-being, and left messages for Johnny, Toby and Bernie. At last she dialled the Swiss number that, so she had been told, would connect her with A.D. O'Hagan.

O'Hagan was a phenomenon. Thirty years before he had been a mere building-site hod carrier from Killarney. Now he was a big-time currency dealer, international poker player, and the owner of a string of more than fifty (mostly very expensive) racehorses, as well as the proprietor of a renowned stud. At first he had been a complete enigma to Jan, originally taking an interest in her after they'd met at the Doncaster Sales nearly four years ago, when she was an unknown trainer of point-to-pointers. Her early fears that A.D. might be just another chequebook Romeo had disappeared when she saw him with his beautiful opera-singer wife Siobhan, to whom A.D. was single-mindedly devoted. In fact, as Jan had gradually come to understand, single-mindedness was A.D.'s outstanding trait, and it had made him what he was today. He had made several fortunes by spotting opportunities that no one else could see, and then by watching them with all the concentration of a falcon on a field mouse. But oddly, though he had a raptor's eye, he did not have the manners of a predator. He was, in fact, unfailingly courteous and could on occasion be extremely generous.

But A.D. never relaxed his grip on his business interests, which included his racing operation. Although nominally the racing manager, Jimmy O'Driscoll was in reality not much more than an office boy, a glorified gofer. Leaving as little as possible to chance, A.D. gave his personal attention to the career of each and every one of his horses just as meticulously as he timed the trades he made on the world's financial markets. He also moved quickly once his mind was made up. With little evidence to go on but Jan's feat in successfully training one difficult hunter-chaser, Russian Eagle, he had decided to act as the guarantor in her application for a public trainer's licence. He had then got Edge Farm off to a flying start by sending her half a dozen good National Hunt horses.

Of course A.D. was a tough man to please. Jan knew that the Irishman had, at times, been more than a little disappointed by her yard's record with his horses during most of the current season. Apart from Galway Fox winning a two-mile hurdle in January, and Magic Maestro's fantastic performance two days before at Cheltenham, there had been little to put out the bunting for. As she dialled his number, she wondered what he would think of her capping their hard-earned victory at Cheltenham by almost getting herself killed in a car with Eddie Sullivan.

'Hello Jan. I'm on the golf course, so I hope you'll excuse me if I'm brief. You're all right?'

'Yes, I'm fine. I've probably suffered more damage falling off horses. I got away with a few scratches and a bump on the head. Eddie's badly smashed up, though.'

'Eddie again, is it? I'm beginning to regret I ever gave that young man the means to get back from Australia. When will you be back at work yourself?'

'I only got home a few hours ago, but I'm fifty per cent back already. It'll be a hundred per cent by next week. And as you know I've got the best team working for me, so you have no need to worry.'

'I never worry, Jan. Are my horses all right? What about Maestro after Thursday?'

'Never better, A.D. He's been demolishing his feed.'

'And Wexford Lad's shins?'

'On the mend.'

'Grand. Look after yourself, I'll be in touch soon.'

In the afternoon Jan dozed off and on and watched television in between. It was the Saturday after the

Cheltenham Festival, and she reckoned racing was still suffering from a monumental collective hangover, which meant it was a perfect time to nick a couple of races when nobody was looking. She watched as her first runner, a strong, intelligent horse called Blue Boar, named after the owner's cordon bleu restaurant in Bath, ran well into third place. Two races later, after she had watched one of Virginia Gilbert's hurdlers prevail in a tight three-way finish, an old-timer whom Jan trained for Virginia's father, Colonel Gilbert, Wolf's Rock, ran the race of his life to take the two-mile chase.

Jan was well aware that Virginia Gilbert did not like her, so she appreciated the colonel's gesture of friendship in keeping Wolf's Rock with her instead of transferring the horse to his daughter's yard. Wolf had originally been regarded as a staying chaser in the making, but a breathing problem had restricted him to the shorter distances. He couldn't quite compete at top level with the two-mile specialists, but here, in a modest race run to suit him and on ground that had been softened by overnight rain, he was able to dictate the pace. Under young Luke Lacy, he powered over the last with four lengths in hand and held on to defeat the favourite's late thrust. Jan smiled at the cheering she heard emanating from the office, where her staff always gathered to watch the TV races: somebody had had a bet. She was pretty sure she'd seen the colonel and Annabel in the background during the televised paddock preview and, though she knew he was no heavy gambler, she hoped the old man had had at least a small bet himself. At twelve to one, it had not been a bad touch.

But Jan's mood of elation evaporated when, five minutes later, she opened the front door to be confronted by the smiling face of Detective Inspector Brian Hadfield. At his right shoulder was the small, thick-legged woman police officer she had seen before.

'Mrs Hardy,' said Hadfield with apologetic formality, 'may I say how very pleased I was when I telephoned the hospital to learn you had been discharged?'

He swayed around and gestured a little theatrically with his arm towards the stable block. 'And may I add what a delightful and impressive place you have here?'

'Thank you, Inspector.'

She decided it was best to be polite, though, if Hadfield's remarks had been intended to charm, they had had the opposite effect. 'What can I do for you?' she asked rather more sarcastically than she had intended.

'It's that little matter of your statement again, I'm afraid. I was wondering if the events of Thursday evening are a little clearer to you now.'

Jan suddenly felt weak and very confused. She put a hand against the door frame to steady herself, looking from Hadfield to his companion.

'I don't know . . . it's a bit of a surprise, you just pitching up. You didn't phone to say you were coming.'

'You see we were passing the end of your road and we thought: might as well drop in on the off-chance. You know how it is. My job's a bit like yours

Mrs Hardy – a policeman's work is never done, as they say.'

She suddenly felt drained and light headed. She would not be able to make much of a statement, but she felt unable to fight Hadfield's smiling persistence.

'You'd better come in. Go right through.'

She stepped back and gestured them inside. As they filed past and disappeared into the kitchen, she realized that now a second car had drawn up outside the house, and bounding from it was Tony Robertson with his medical bag.

'Jan! For goodness sake, you're as white as a ghost. What's going on? Who are those guys?'

'Police,' she hissed. 'They've come to take a statement. They just turned up out of the blue.'

'About the accident? I don't think you look up to it, old girl. Want me to have a word?'

She hesitated, then gave a fractional nod of the head. Tony strode ahead of her into the kitchen.

'Look, I'm Mrs Hardy's GP.'

Hadfield, with his hands stuck in his trouser pockets, was deep in contemplation of Jan's pinboard, stuck with postcards, photographs of her horses in action, and the children's pony club rosettes. He swivelled round.

'Oh! How d'you do, Dr . . .?'

He pulled his right hand from his pocket as if to hold it out, but realized just in time that there was a chance Tony would refuse to shake it.

'Dr Robertson, Anthony Robertson, from Winchcombe. Now you know perfectly well, although I understand why you're here, that Mrs Hardy has been through a very traumatic experience—'

Hadfield tried to interrupt, but Tony held up his hand.

'Please let me finish. A very traumatic accident *less* than forty-eight hours ago, and furthermore she has just returned from a stay in hospital. So I really think it's inappropriate for the police to be pressuring her to make a statement before she has fully recovered her senses and strength.'

Jan stood there, with her back to the Aga and her fingers gripping the towel rail, worried at the aggressive tenor of Tony's speech. Nothing Hadfield had done really justified it. On the other hand he bloody should have phoned to say that he was calling. Just for a moment, he bristled with indignation. Then his shoulders dropped and the smile returned.

'Fine, fine,' he said. 'I merely thought it might be easier for Mrs Hardy here in her own home, you know.'

'It would be. But not now, not today, and not until I say she's medically fit to talk to you. All right?'

Hadfield glanced at the constable and tipped his head towards the door.

'We'll make ourselves scarce then, Doctor. Mrs Hardy, I'm so sorry if you think we've been heavy-handed. That was not my intention, I assure you.'

Was there the faintest insinuation in his voice, the merest hint that he thought he had sensed something suspect about this patient–doctor relationship? For a moment Jan thought there was, then she told herself she'd imagined it.

'That saw them off,' said Tony in triumph as he closed the door on the two officers.

How very like a man, thought Jan, as Tony took her blood pressure, and questioned her about her sleeping and appetite. Everything had to be win or lose, biff or be biffed. But she was very grateful for the way he'd kicked Hadfield into touch, knowing she would not have been able to do it on her own with such effect.

'Thanks, Tony, but you were a bit hard on the poor sod. He was doing his job, if a bit clumsily.'

The doctor smiled as he folded away his blood-pressure monitor.

'I know. But I feel a compulsion to protect you, Jan. I feel so . . .'

Jan cut him off.

'Tony, please don't. Not now, this is a professional visit.'

He closed his bag of tricks.

'OK, you're right. But it's difficult. I'm wondering if I should go on being your GP, actually. Medical ethics and all that.'

Jan did not respond, but as she watched him drive away a few minutes later she was thinking about the problem that faced her. She didn't want to encourage Tony, but she couldn't decide which course of action was preferable. If she agreed to register with another doctor, would that tacitly acknowledge Tony's idea of their relationship? On the other hand, if she remained his patient, that might give him the same message. The rule-of-thumb formula, *if in doubt do nothing,* was not generally Jan's preferred way. But in this case she thought it was best.

Jan lay down on the sofa and dozed off, waking only when she heard cheering coming from the yard and somebody clapping. The horsebox had returned in triumph. She hurried as best she could out into the yard to congratulate everybody, but most of all the horses. Back in his stable, Wolf's Rock snorted and shook his head as she gave him a Polo mint. As he crunched appreciatively, she ran her hands up and down each of his legs to feel for any heat that would indicate he had taken a knock or somehow jarred himself up – though the latter was unlikely on the soft ground he had raced on today. He was sound, and there was nothing amiss with Blue Boar either. Relieved, Jan gave the horses one last kiss on the nose before bolting the doors.

'I saw Virginia Gilbert at the races,' said Annabel casually as they walked back to the office after evening stables. 'She was looking nauseatingly pleased with her hurdles winner.'

'She had two winners as a matter of fact,' said Jan gloomily. 'Another at Warwick. It's been quite a day for the Gilbert family.'

'Well, she couldn't resist making a snide remark aimed at you.'

'Oh? What?'

'Asked how you were, of course, in all sincerity, apparently – I don't think. Then she said: "And how's Eddie 'accident-prone' Sullivan?", making the apostrophes with her fingers in the air. So insensitive, so stupid. I wanted to spit.'

'That woman!' said Jan, patting Annabel's shoulder. 'She loves to gloat, but we mustn't let it upset us. We must rise above it. We've the dear old colonel to think of. He's been a very good friend to me unlike his daughter, and he's a fantastic landlord to my parents as well, you know.'

Jan knew this was an important point, and a paramount reason not to let the rivalry between herself and Virginia get out of hand. The cottage in which the Pritchards were tenants, and the few acres on which Reg ran some sheep ('Just to keep my hand in,' he insisted) were part of the Riscombe Manor estate.

'How *is* Eddie, though? Any news?' Annabel asked.

'I don't know, but I suppose he's holding his own as nobody's phoned me to say otherwise. I'll ring the hospital right now and get an update.'

When they reached the office Jan made the call, speaking to the ICU nurse's station.

'No change,' she told Annabel, as she disconnected. 'He's still out of it, I'm afraid.'

'Oh, the poor thing,' said Annabel, shaking her head slowly. 'Do you think he's going to be all right?'

Suddenly Jan, for the first time since the crash, felt brisk and strong. Something about the way Wolf had churned his way to victory inspired her.

'Bel, do you know? I'm going to stop being worried about him. I think he leads a charmed existence. Any day now he's going to wake up and ask for a glass of champagne. I just feel it – in fact, I *know* it.'

3

Jan had slept deeply enough with the help of some pills which Tony had prescribed for her, but she woke early, feeling a rush of anxiety that drove her out of bed and into her clothes before she realized she ought to be lying in and trying to rest. There were no 'days off' at Edge Farm, any more than at other racing stables, but even in normal times – and how she wished they could get back to those – Sunday was a more leisurely day. The staff clocked on two hours later than in the rest of the week and even the boss had a luxurious extra hour in bed.

On Sundays, only the horses due to run the next day or on a Tuesday would be given a canter. The rest generally stood in their boxes. The only other exceptions this morning were horses like Wolf's Rock and Blue Boar, who had raced the previous day. These would be led out to stretch their legs and ease their weary muscles, followed by a small trot to double-check that they'd come through their races in good shape. Jan had felt the two horses' legs yesterday, but she knew that problems could also develop overnight and it was this thought that had been nagging at her. No horse could tell you how it felt, but experienced horse people read the animal's state from numerous signs, often instinctively. Sometimes Jan surprised herself by being utterly certain that this or that horse was not right without being able to say exactly why she thought so, except that there was something about the animal. As often as not her intuition was based on little more than the look of the horse's eye, or the feel of its coat, but she was almost invariably right. Sometimes her hand picked up one of these early warnings even before her brain did.

It was twenty-past-six by the kitchen clock when Jan laced her boots and pulled on her coat. She took a last swig of tea from her mug and set off down the yard, with the dogs gambolling ahead of her. When she had first arrived at Edge Farm, almost three years before, the site was desolate. She had lived in a mobile home while her house was built on the foundations of the old demolished farmhouse. Her handful of point-to-point horses had been stabled in the semi-ruined stone barn. Now she had a roomy new house faced in golden Cotswold stone. The horses had new quarters too – a timber-built stable yard, with the walls faced with creosoted weather-boarding, arranged on the conventional pattern that had been used in racing for two hundred years and more: thirty-eight boxes, the tack room, feed store and office ranged on four sides of a square to form an enclosed, inward-looking quadrangle. Each box had the traditional door to allow the horses to look out as they wished. Jan's devoted builder Gerry had finished the last side of the square less than a year ago, topping off the building with a stately, centrally placed arched gateway surmounted by a weathercock facing towards the house, which stood in a slightly more elevated position on the hill.

Edge could not have been an easy holding to farm. Most of the fields sloped, rising in steepness to the top of a west-facing Cotswold escarpment, which was exposed to the weather but had a panoramic view across the valley. Beyond the stables, out on the hill-side, were Jan's gallops. A good turf strip began in the top field and ran away just beneath the top of the ridge with another short strip of turf for Jan's run of schooling fences. She had recently added a new four-furlong all-weather gallop. Nearer to the house were half a dozen fenced paddocks, one of which contained a mini show-jumping ring with jumps of various coloured poles for Megan's use.

In two half-barrels, positioned on either side of the archway, the daffodils planted by Edge Farm's self-appointed gardener, Reg, shook and rolled with the wind. The weathercock swivelled on its axis, squeaking, as Jan unlocked the gate and walked to the centre of the yard. The stable doors had all been closed and securely bolted the previous night, but she could hear the horses nickering and pawing their bedding in anticipation as they sensed her presence. She was still some way short of a full complement. There were twenty-four boxes occupied, twenty-two by horses in training and the others by Monarch and Smarty, Megan's ponies. Jan knew that when she did fill the yard she would need more staff, but the whole enterprise had grown so naturally from its unpromising beginnings that she suddenly felt it was really good to be alive. This was her world. Apart from the love of her family and, if she was lucky one day, that of a good man, what more could she ask for?

It was around mid-morning when Jan rang the hospital. Eddie had not woken up calling for a champagne breakfast as she had predicted. In fact, Eddie had done nothing. He still lay there, 'out of danger', but not yet back in the land of the living.

Jan had seen Eddie's condition, and it was obvious he would not be coming out of hospital soon even after he woke up. And when he did, he would need a lot of aftercare.

'I think I'll go over to Stow, to Eddie's pub,' she told Annabel, who had arrived for work at nine. 'He's still paying for the room, which is a waste of money that he probably hasn't got in any case. I thought I'd settle the account and bring his stuff back here for the time being.'

Annabel looked at her friend doubtfully.

'Are you sure you're all right to drive? Why don't you let me take you?'

It hadn't occurred to Jan that driving might be a problem. She thought about it, then shook her head. Of course she was all right, she had to be. It was only like getting straight back on the horse that had thrown you.

'No, no, Bel. I'm fine, and you've got plenty of stuff to do here.'

A few minutes later Jan sat behind the wheel of the Shogun and turned the ignition key. The engine fired first flick, setting up a thunderous smoky roar and judder as she revved the engine hard to warm it up. She slipped it into gear and cautiously set off down the lane. There was no problem turning onto the deserted public road, where she confidently began to pick up speed.

After about three-quarters of a mile the road passed through a small wood and climbed steeply. Jan had still not seen another vehicle, but now, as she accelerated, she realized one was approaching fast from the other side of the summit. It came into sight, breasting the rise with the chrome of the radiator grille flashing, bearing down on her like a giant bird.

'Christ!'

Jan was suddenly seized by inexplicable panic. She braked and the tyres yelped as the Mitsubishi swerved to the right. The other car swished up to her and powered past, just missing Jan's wayward bonnet as she over-corrected and veered to the left. For a few seconds, just as she was breasting the summit, she was all over the road frantically wrestling with the steering wheel, until finally the Shogun came to rest on the grass verge, its nearside wheels a couple of feet short of a roadside drainage ditch.

She was breathing hard and her heart pounded so loudly it shook her whole body. The spot over her temple, where the bump had now almost subsided, was throbbing again. She sat in silence and thought about what had just happened. Both her vehicle and the other had been safely on their own sides of the road. There had been no danger whatsoever, except in her mind. But the sudden appearance of another vehicle had been so like the accident on Cleeve Hill that it had been shocking enough to make her lose control. Weak and trembling, she stayed in the driver's seat – she did not know for how long – her eyes shut but visualizing again the wreckage of the cars on Thursday night and Eddie's battered face covered in blood. After a while she opened the door and slid out. She walked up and down for a few paces, sucking in the cool spring air until her heartbeat returned to normal and the trembling stopped. Eventually she got back into the driver's seat, and with a determined effort to dismiss all her morbid thoughts, she drove on to the King's Head pub in Stow, where Eddie had been living.

When Jan arrived, she was invited into the manager Mr Whiteside's office. He was a trimly dressed man in his forties. When she explained her intentions, he replied, 'Yes, of course, Mrs Hardy, that will be perfectly all right. I had heard about the accident and was expecting someone to call.'

Reaching down beside his desk he yanked a rolled copy of the *Wessex Daily News* from his wastebasket and unfolded it to show Jan the headline: JAN HARDY: FATAL TRAGEDY MARS DAY OF TRIUMPH.

'It's Friday's edition,' he went on. 'Everybody was very upset. Eddie's been rather a favourite around here, as a matter of fact. I do hope he's making good progress.'

Jan was too dumbfounded to reply immediately. She looked numbly at the bold-type letters. She had not foreseen that there would be publicity. Why had no one mentioned this article before now?

'Oh,' she said, as Whiteside's enquiry penetrated the fog she looked through. 'No, he's not really. I mean he's still unconscious, so from that point of view he's still not too well.'

'Oh dear. I'm so sorry, Mrs Hardy. It must have been a terrible ordeal for you. What a mercy you weren't badly hurt yourself.'

'Yes, thank you. I was very lucky, very lucky indeed. With Eddie, it's just a question of waiting till he comes round, you see.'

'Well, when he does, give him our best, will you? Now, here's the key to his room, and while you're packing his things I'll get his bill made up. He's paid up to the beginning of last week, so it's not a horrendous amount.'

Jan stood up and took the key.

'Do you mind if I keep the newspaper?' she asked.

Eddie's room was not one of the pub's four-poster suites, much vaunted in the publicity literature that she'd seen in the lobby, but a cramped, budget-priced single room with a low, sloping ceiling right under the eaves. The space had been carefully cleaned and tidied by the chambermaid, giving the illusion that Eddie was an organized, orderly person.

'Like hell you are, Eddie Sullivan,' Jan muttered under her breath.

She sat on the bed and opened the *Wessex Daily News* at Tim Farr's story. She read it, then read it again. Oddly enough, it did not torment her. It was like reading about something that had happened to someone else, not her and Eddie. But one detail did have a dramatic effect. The name of the other driver –

the dead man – was William Moorhouse. Until this moment she had been able to think of the man's death as something abstract, even though it had happened so close to her and so violently. But now she actually knew his name she thought about him differently, as a person with family, workmates and neighbours. William Moorhouse was a real person; now he was dead.

Slowly she refolded the newspaper and put it down, remembering why she was there. A large leather holdall was pushed into the narrow space between the top of the wardrobe and the ceiling. She stretched up and pulled it down, then set it open on the bed. She quickly packed Eddie's shoes and clothes, tucking in the alarm clock and the half a dozen paperbacks from the bedside table. Crossing to the basin, she swept Eddie's toothbrush, toothpaste, shampoo and shaving gear into his washbag, which she dropped into the holdall on top of the clothes, alongside a half-empty bottle of malt whisky she found on the window ledge. She could not help thinking about the physical associations of every object – the clothing that had touched his skin and still smelt of his aftershave, the brush his teeth, the bottle his hand – but she didn't linger over these thoughts. She worked swiftly and efficiently until the holdall was crammed full.

Jan looked about her once more. It was odd she'd found no personal papers, no chequebook or passport. She slid open the drawer of the bedside table, but saw only a few coins, a penknife and a packet of mints. She dropped these into the side pocket of the holdall and zipped the bag up. A final thought made her kneel to peer under the bed, where she immediately noticed a

Louise – 'the slapper' as Jan thought of her – was notorious for sleeping around, and that the baby might not be his daughter after all. In the weeks before the accident, it had been decided that only a DNA test would resolve the matter. The result of this was anxiously awaited.

Edge Farm came into sight from the road, perched on its hillside and surrounded by green fields and white-painted railings. At the same moment, another fragment of Thursday night's jigsaw dropped jarringly into place. Moments before the accident Jan had taken a call on Eddie's mobile, a message left by Sue Sullivan, his mother, in Australia. 'I've got some very important news,' she'd said. 'Give me a ring as soon as you get a chance.' What news? Was it to tell Eddie the test result? If so, it hadn't happened as he'd had no chance to return the call before the crash.

Suddenly, Jan needed her children with her. She drove straight on past the end of the Edge Farm drive to Riscombe, where she picked them up and took them home.

The blue airmail letter was still in Jan's pocket as she settled herself in the chair beside Eddie's bed shortly after three o'clock that afternoon. A few minutes earlier the sister had greeted her with a serene smile.

'Eddie's doing well. He's been making noises.'

'Has he been *talking*?'

The sister shook her head.

'Oh no, not yet. But we do think he's turned the corner. He can hear you if you speak loudly enough.'

Now, as Jan watched Eddie's chest rise and fall in unison with his breathing, she wished she knew what, if anything at all, was going on in his head. None of the high-tech monitoring equipment stacked around him on trolleys, winking and humming, could tell her that.

'Eddie!' Jan said leaning forward to put her mouth close to his ear. 'It's Jan. Can you hear me? Your mum's coming over from Oz. She could even be here tomorrow.'

Jan straightened and studied his face, but saw no reaction. He lay still, eyes closed, bandaged hands lying outside the covers. She leaned down again, but spoke louder this time.

'Everyone at Edge has been asking for you. I got your stuff from Stow, from the pub. Your friend Mr Whiteside sends his best wishes. He said you were their favourite guest.'

There was still no discernible response.

'They obviously don't know you like I do. I even paid your room bill.'

Had his lips moved? She thought she'd seen the faintest twitch; perhaps it was her imagination.

'So that's a little matter of a hundred and seventy-five quid you owe me, Eddie Sullivan.'

This time she wasn't mistaken, she was sure. Eddie's lips were moving. They were forming words.

'What was that? Eddie? I didn't hear.'

She leaned right over him to catch what he was saying. It was the thinnest murmur, carried on the faintest breath.

'Try again, Eddie. I didn't get it.'

This time he put in more effort, though the words still seemed to be coming from another room.

'Tough luck, Jan Hardy,' he was saying. 'I'm skint.'

'Eddie. Oh, Eddie, you're awake!'

4

'Dec! What the *bloody hell* are you doing? Catch up!'

On Monday mornings the majority of the horses took light exercise, just walking or trotting. Relief about Eddie had at least given Jan a night of deep, satisfying sleep and she had awoken determined to ride out with her first lot. It felt wonderful to be out there on such a bright morning, with boisterous cotton-wool clouds chasing across the watery sun. She sat high on Supercall's broad back and had told Dec to trot Magic Maestro alongside so she could have a look at his action, but they kept lagging behind.

'Sorry, Mrs H,' said Dec as he came alongside. He had a grin across his face that would grate a carrot. 'I'll tell you what, it's just grand to have you back on form.'

Jan couldn't help smiling too.

'Don't be so cheeky, you little sod. Concentrate.'

Later, after the staff had scoffed their bacon and eggs in the kitchen, Jan scrubbed Matty's face for school and sent him off in the car with Megan and Fran. She gave a huge sigh and decided to go down to the office to tackle the heap of paperwork that had built up since last week. It was a job she disliked intensely, but it had to be done. She was half an hour into it when the phone rang.

'Mrs Hardy? Good morning, it's Brian Hadfield. How are you feeling today? Much better, I hope.'

This wasn't just the conventional greeting. It sounded like Hadfield really wanted to know how Jan was.

'I'm pretty well, thank you, Inspector. I'm back in harness now. Trying to forget about last week, and doing my best to get on with my life, you know?'

'Well, I hope you haven't literally forgotten about last week. I mean, I still need that statement from you – remember?'

'No, of course I haven't forgotten that.'

'Have you seen Dr Robertson today by any chance?'

'He said he'd drop round tomorrow morning sometime.'

'I fully understand his concern for you as his patient, Mrs Hardy, but could you discuss the urgency of this matter with him and call me back? It seems to me, if you *are* back at work, this might be a good moment for me to get the business of the statement out of the way and to let you concentrate on your horses, bearing in mind what Dr Robertson said on Saturday . . .'

Jan could see no point in delaying any further. Everything had become so much clearer and more positive to her now that she decided it was time to get on with it. Hadfield would have his statement eventually, so why not today? It was as good a time as any.

'I agree completely, Mr Hadfield. And as I feel so much better now, I don't think the doctor would have any objection. Why don't you come over later today?'

They agreed that Hadfield would visit the stables at two that afternoon.

Later in the morning Jan and Fran drove to the hypermarket four miles away, a weekly fridge-stocking expedition that they always made together. Jan particularly enjoyed the company of the housekeeper-nanny because she was the only person, apart from Reg and Mary, whom she could talk to about the children to her heart's content. Fran was a down-to-earth woman in her forties who took a keen interest in Megan and Matty's development.

'Matty got such a fright when he saw me in hospital on Friday,' Jan told her. 'Did he say anything to you on the way to school?'

'Oh, he's right as rain now, bless him. He and Meg were chatting about it quite normally, like it was an everyday event almost. You know how kids are – they soon recover. And you're hardly marked, you know, Jan, physically anyway.'

'I know, I was so lucky.'

The rest of the journey was spent chatting about the school as Fran reminded her of the social events in its calendar. Jan cringed and hoped she would be able to attend them all.

While Fran was queuing at the fresh-meat counter Jan was going round the tinned foods shelves. They needed sweetcorn, tuna and baked beans. She was hesitating between four or eight tins of beans when she heard a voice behind her.

'Hello, Mrs Hardy.'

The young man pushing the shopping trolley was familiar, but Jan couldn't quite place him. She glanced down at his shopping. Lager, frozen dinners, bacon, chocolate cereals – young bachelor stuff.

'Sorry, do I know you?'

'We met at your open day the year before last. Tim Farr, *Wessex Daily News*.'

The penny dropped instantly. Jan held her breath. She wanted to bollock him, but decided to temper her inclination.

'You . . . it was you who wrote that piece. Last week.'

'About your accident? Yes, that was me. How's Mr Sullivan?'

'He's better, thank you. Far from well, but certainly better than he was.'

'I'm glad.'

'Are you? Isn't it better news, from your point of view, if he's worse – and worse news if he's better?'

Farr looked uncomfortable.

'Mrs Hardy, there's a difference between what the paper reports and what I feel. Not all journalists are vultures, you know. At least, I try not to be.'

'I'm glad to hear it,' said Jan a little less sceptically. 'So you were there, on Cleeve Hill?'

'I was about twenty-five cars behind you.'

Jan turned back to the shelves and took down a four-tin pack.

'You got an exclusive then. Lucky you.'

'I wouldn't quite put it that way.'

'Well, you needn't look so hangdog and ashamed of yourself. It wasn't such a bad article.'

'The thing is, Mrs Hardy, I was going to call you, so it's quite a coincidence bumping into you here. I was wondering if you were aware of something. It's just that on Thursday night I had a chance to look at Mr Sullivan's Morgan at the garage they took it to, and I noticed the tax disc.'

He paused, as if to add more significance to what he had just said. But Jan couldn't imagine what this might be.

'Tax disc?' she enquired. 'So? All cars have them, you know. It's the law.'

'Um, I'm aware of that, but they're supposed to be fully paid up. Mr Sullivan's expired in December.'

Jan scowled at him.

'It must have been the old one you saw,' she spat out before she could regain her composure.

'But there wasn't another one, I'm positive. I looked. I was wondering if you knew whether he had in fact recently renewed his road fund licence.'

'Look, what are you trying to make out of this? I really don't think it's any of your bloody business, anyway.'

'Well, if Mr Sullivan was driving the car illegally—'

Jan snorted.

'Don't talk such damned rubbish. Of course he wasn't. Now, if you'll excuse me, I've got my shopping to do.'

She snatched another pack of baked beans, gave a sharp forward shove to her trolley, and left him in the aisle gaping after her.

It was a few minutes after two as Jan spooned instant coffee into three mugs before adding hot water and milk. She shook half a packet of digestives onto a plate and carried the tray through to the living room, where a smug Detective Inspector Hadfield and his uniformed companion awaited her.

She was going to slide the tray onto the low coffee table, which was partly surrounded by the sofa and chairs, but it was already in use. DI Hadfield had placed a small battery-driven recorder there.

'I hope you don't mind this,' he said matter of factly. 'It's usual procedure nowadays, and it will help us put together an accurate statement for you to sign. I assume you prefer to do it this way. You do, of course, have the option of writing out your own statement of the events that took place on Thursday evening.'

Jan shook her head hastily and put the tray down on a chair.

'No, no, it's OK. I'd much prefer it this way.'

'That's good. It'll probably save time in the long run.'

As she handed round the coffees, she sensed it was obvious that the inspector also preferred to use the recorder since it allowed him to ask Jan questions. Jan sat opposite Hadfield, and he quickly got down to business.

'Now, let's just cover what happened prior to your leaving the racecourse. One of your horses had just won, I believe.'

'Yes, the Cathcart. Apart from the Irish National last year, it was the biggest win of my career.'

Jan told him about the success of Magic Maestro, and the celebrations in A.D.'s box afterwards. It was clear Hadfield was more interested in the latter.

'And you and Mr Sullivan were there in Mr O'Hagan's party?'

'Yes.'

'I imagine there was a fair amount of drink consumed. Champagne, was it?'

Jan could obviously see where this line of questioning was going.

'Yes, but Eddie didn't have any, well, hardly any. "A gnat's bladderful" was his exact expression, I think, when he offered to drive me home.'

'He offered?'

'Yes, it was his idea. He said it was my day and I should be able to celebrate it.'

'How long were you at the party?'

'Well, it didn't finish till some time after six, maybe six-thirty. I was popping in and out of the box. I had various things to do with the horse, getting him bandaged up before packing him off home with my assistant trainer and travelling head lad.'

'And they were?'

'Annabel Halstead is my assistant. The lad was Joe Paley.'

Hadfield asked Jan to describe the drive from the trainers' car park towards Cleeve Hill.

'It was dark. We were in Eddie's Morgan. It kept misfiring slightly, nothing serious, but I remember that quite clearly.'

'What age is the car?'

Jan shrugged.

'I wouldn't know. Old. But it is, or rather it *was*, his pride and joy. He tried to keep it in good nick.'

'What was the traffic like?'

'Most of the race traffic had dispersed by then, so the road seemed just about normal. Eddie was accelerating up the hill when a car appeared out of the blue coming the other way and going really fast. At the same time another car was overtaking us, going at a mad speed. That's when the crash happened.'

'I see. So you're saying there was a *third* car?'

'Yes. It was just passing us.'

'And are you saying then that this third car caused the accident?'

'I don't know, not for sure; but yes, I think so. It all happened so quickly, but I was aware of another car coming up behind, making the oncoming one swerve to avoid it. And at the same time Eddie's car was being bumped off the road.'

'He was *bumped*?'

'Yes, I reckon so. I think the overtaking car must have barged us in some way. Trying to make room to get through, I imagine.'

'What happened to the overtaking car after it barged you?'

'I really don't know. We were a little too distracted to notice.'

The woman police officer reached for a digestive while Hadfield scratched his head.

'So just to get this straight, you're saying that there was a *third* car, overtaking you very fast at the same time as the oncoming vehicle bore down on you from higher up the hill, but on its proper side of the road. And it was the overtaking car which forced the oncoming car to swerve and hit the tree. And at the same time you and Mr Sullivan were pushed off the road by this overtaking car barging into you.'

'Yes. That's how I remember it. You sound surprised.'

'Well, it's just that no one's mentioned this other car before, Mrs Hardy. It does sound like an extremely important detail – I'll look into it. Do you have any idea of the make of this third car?'

'A big car. Some kind of four-wheel drive, maybe?'

'Not a van or a small lorry?'

'No, definitely a car, but much bigger, I mean much taller, than us.'

Hadfield was taking notes energetically, the smile coming and going on his face as he concentrated.

'I think that's really all I can tell you,' Jan added, after watching him for a few moments. 'I was dazed for a while after that.'

Hadfield sipped his coffee and turned his ambiguous smile on her once again.

'There's just one more thing, Mrs Hardy. You say Mr Sullivan kept his Morgan in as good nick as possible, yes?'

'Yes, I would say so. Although the Morgan's not a cheap car to maintain and Eddie isn't that well off. He's only just come back from Australia and he hasn't a regular job or anything.'

'Did you know he hadn't paid his road tax, Mrs Hardy?'

Jan's heart thumped.

'No. No, I didn't.'

'And that his tyres were badly worn, well below the legal limit?'

'No, I certainly didn't know that.'

Holding the silence for a few seconds, Hadfield looked at what he had written, then snapped shut his notebook. He reached over and pressed the OFF button on the recorder, then stood up. Hurriedly the constable crammed the rest of the biscuit into her mouth, drained her mug and followed suit.

'We won't detain you any further now,' said Hadfield, still smiling as he picked up the recorder and handed it to the constable. 'Do call us if anything else occurs to you. In the meanwhile I'll have the interview typed up as a statement for you to sign.'

After Jan had shut the door on the two police officers, she turned and flopped back against it with her eyes tight shut. She felt as if she had been interrogated. Those last two questions had shaken her. On Thursday night Eddie was driving an illegal car and the tyres were bald. She could easily guess the thoughts behind *that* particular fact. What if the Morgan had had a blowout? What if Eddie was actually responsible for the crash and the death of the other driver?

The door bell rang nerve-janglingly above her head and she jumped. Opening the door again, she found Hadfield's constable standing on the step, carrying a plastic bin bag. She held it out to Jan.

'Sorry, Mrs Hardy. We almost forgot this. It's Mr Sullivan's effects – we recovered them from the car.'

Jan took the bin bag through to the kitchen and

emptied it on the table. There was a small tartan travelling rug, the Morgan's service log, a battered road atlas, Eddie's cloth cap, an umbrella, a tin of toffees and his mobile phone. She shook the plastic bag and one last thing dropped out, a key ring with the Morgan's ignition key, among various others.

Jan picked them up and weighed them in her hand, wondering.

A few minutes later Eddie's attaché case lay open on the kitchen table beside the heap of stuff from the car. It had not been hard to identify the small key which would open it. Jan felt that she was prying, but the need to know was stronger than her integrity at that precise moment. Had Eddie renewed his road tax? Was he even insured? She needed to know, for God's sake. She hunted through the old envelopes and scruffy papers, finding a few unopened bills, Eddie's passport, and a book of travellers' cheques in Australian dollars. At last she came to a brown envelope containing Eddie's motoring documents. The car registration was there, but there was no hint of a tax disc, and the MOT was hopelessly out of date. At last, she turned over the insurance document.

It confirmed her worst fears. Unless Eddie had fixed something up verbally in the last few days, it did not look as if he had renewed the policy when it expired five months earlier. Jan knew that it was a criminal offence to be driving uninsured, and obviously you were in dire straits if you got involved in a fatal accident. Would this lead the police to prosecute Eddie for the death of the other driver? Would they prejudge his guilt?

Something else about the way Hadfield had behaved was bugging her. When he questioned her about the third car overtaking, he had almost seemed to disbelieve her. Now it occurred to her for the first time how much they needed to identify that third car. Without it Eddie was going to have to take the whole blame for the accident full on the chin, for the wrecked cars, the injuries and, far worse, the death of an innocent man.

5

'I didn't know why I'm here,' said Eddie in a low, faraway voice. 'They had to tell me. The last thing I remember is that Magic Maestro won the Cathc—, the race. Unless I dreamt it.'

It was the middle of the morning, which had begun with Jan riding out first thing. She had then driven the children to school and kept on driving to Cheltenham General Hospital, where she found that Eddie had been brought out of the ICU to an observation ward. There were five other beds, three of which were occupied by immobile, heavily bandaged patients.

'No, you didn't dream it,' she said. 'A lot's happened since then so it does seem a bit like a dream, even to me. But he won the race all right.'

'Is he OK?'

'Yes, Eddie, he's fine. It's you we're concerned about at the moment.'

'Well, I do seem to have smashed myself up a bit. You look OK, though.'

'I had a couple of nights in here. A few cuts and bruises. But I was luckier than you.'

'I suppose the car's gone for a Brighton?'

'Gone to Brighton? What on earth for, Eddie?'

'No, the car, is it . . . smashed up?'

'Did you mean "gone for a burton"?'

'That's what I said.'

'No you didn't. You said "gone for a Brighton".'

'If you say so. But what about my *Morgan*?'

There was impatience in Eddie's voice. He looked at her quizzically.

Jan shook her head. 'I don't know. I'll try and find out.'

Eddie rolled his heavily bandaged head from side to side on the pillow. He grimaced.

'You all right?' Jan asked, concerned.

'No, my bloody head aches like a bastard.'

'I'll ask the nurse for some painkillers.'

'Forget that . . . the thing is I want to know the store. They're not . . . *telling* me anything, you see.'

'What are they not telling you, Eddie?'

'What's really wrong with me, how badly I'm messed up. I know I can't talk properly, keep making mishaps, misshapes . . .'

'Mistakes?'

'Yes. And I've got this permanent blinding headache and there's more . . .'

'Yes, Eddie, what more?'

'I can't move.'

'Of course you can't. They've got you immobilized.'

'Yes, I know. But, Jan, I can't even waggle my toes.'

'At first I thought he was all right,' said Jan half an hour later to Dr Matthews, the trauma specialist.

'But later he seemed worse?' he prompted. 'He

probably got tired. That's normal. He will tire very quickly for the time being.'

'Talking to him's peculiar. He makes weird mistakes with words. Just now he said "gone for a Brighton" instead of "gone for a burton". Oh, and another one, "I want to know the *store*." He doesn't even know he's doing it. It's surreal. But what's more worrying is that he says he can't move his toes. He's afraid he's paralysed.'

Dr Matthews had a file open in front of him containing Eddie's medical notes. He consulted it for a moment, turning over two or three pages before unhooking his half-moon spectacles. He gave Jan an understanding smile, though his eyes were serious.

'Eddie has a fractured skull, Mrs Hardy, which will heal. But he also has a brain injury, which may take a little more time. If you want me to get technical, it's likely to be an acceleration-deceleration trauma, which is when the head is moving rapidly and then is stopped by something.'

He demonstrated by punching his right fist into the palm of his left hand.

'It's typical of a car accident. The brain whacks against the front of the skull, then recoils to hit the back. There'll certainly be bruising to the cerebral cortex. And a part of the brain called the temporal lobe, below the cerebral cortex, can be actually punctured by slamming into bony projections on the inside of the skull. There could be some particular areas of bleeding. So I'm not surprised he has a "bloody headache", as he put it and we would expect some degree of cognitive, behavioural and even motor dysfunction.'

'Which translated means?'

'Oh, sorry. What I mean is dysfunction of his mental processes, for instance, when memory and word selection are impaired. There could be some noticeable behavioural changes too. And motor dysfunction means that certain movements could become difficult, or restricted, as in the case of Eddie's toes.'

'So he *could* be paralysed?'

'It's much too early to say anything like that, Mrs Hardy. But the symptoms of traumatic brain injury can indeed mimic those of a stroke, including some degree of paralysis. On the other hand, Eddie also has a number of broken bones and other problems, which might include spinal injury. Obviously that could affect his lack of movement, so it's all going to have to be fully investigated.'

'How do you mean, investigated?'

'We'll have to arrange for scans and some other tests in a day or two. In the meantime the best thing we can do is to reassure him.'

Jan did some essential shopping in Cheltenham and had a quick sandwich for lunch at a coffee shop. Then, at Hadfield's invitation, she called at the police station to view her typed-up statement. It accurately reflected what she had told Hadfield on Sunday and she signed it. By two in the afternoon she was back in the hospital and at Eddie's bedside with magazines and fruit. But she could say nothing reassuring about the car. She had been to the garage and seen the wreck for herself.

'I'm afraid the Morgan's going to need completely

rebuilding, at least the front end. New engine, the lot. I've been to the garage and that's what they told me.'

Eddie seemed unworried by the news.

'Oh well. Ins— in-sur-ance will pay up.'

He spoke the long word carefully, picking his way through the syllables.

'Will it?' Jan said. 'I'm not sure you had any.'

'Of course I did.'

'You may have had once, but I can't find anything that says you were covered last week. In which case the Morgan was uninsured and, what's more, the road tax and MOT were out of date and the tyres were nearly bald.'

'Nothing but problems!' Eddie groaned.

'Yes, problems. It seems the whole car was illegal, Eddie, and shouldn't have been on the road at all.'

'What about the in— the insurance?'

'Eddie, I've just told you. You didn't *have* any insurance.'

Eddie worked on the puzzle for a few moments, but eventually gave up the struggle. He shut his eyes and let his mind drift.

'I can't wait . . . to get back behind the wheel of the old car,' he said dreamily. 'Lower the top, wings in my hair.'

'Wind.'

'Sorry?'

'The usual phrase for when you're driving an open car: "wind in my hair".'

Eddie frowned and opened his eyes to stare at her, as if he suspected she was having him on.

'Yes, I know that Jan. What are you talk— talking about?'

She took his hand and stroked it.

'Nothing, Eddie. Wings are more poetic, anyway.'

Now he was looking back at her completely nonplussed.

'Never mind, Eddie, it's not important. You were talking about your beloved car.'

His bewilderment dissolved into a contented smile as he languidly closed his eyes again.

'My lovely Morgan, yes, the love of my life,' he whispered.

Jan leaned forward.

'Do you know something, Eddie Sullivan? You said I was that.'

'What?'

'You said you loved *me*. Just before the accident. But you don't remember, do you?'

Jan kissed his forehead and got up to leave. If she hurried she could be back at Edge in time for evening stables.

Jan's tour of the yard was an important part of the daily schedule at Edge Farm. Once all the boxes had been mucked out, the horses would be thoroughly groomed and their feet greased by the lad or girl whose job it was to look after them. The bedding would be refreshed and carefully spread around the stable floor, with the walls banked about two foot higher. Jan and Annabel would go from box to box, where the horses were 'stood up' wearing just a head collar, their bodies stripped for a thorough inspection, to decide on the exercise they would be doing the following day and discuss their food rations.

Jan was particularly keen to have a look at Russian Eagle, who held an entry in the Aintree Grand National, which was due to be run in eleven days. After winning the Irish National at Fairyhouse last spring, he was Jan's most prominent horse, and the obvious stable pick of the big race. More than that, he was in with a big chance.

In assessing her horses' condition Jan relied on her eyes and, equally as much, her hands. She looked into Eagle's eyes and nostrils, then squeezed the top of his neck. She moved around him, rubbing her hand along his ribcage and the top of his back and loins – it was always her left hand, which she held loosely – gliding up and down each of his legs, feeling for the slightest bump and any sign of heat or tenderness. Over time, her hand seemed to form a memory. Imprinted with information, it swept over each horse. She was accomplished at detecting anomalies, or a slight variation from what was normal for that animal.

Eagle had eaten up all his feed and was in pretty good all-round shape. Jan's hand detected nothing wrong with his legs.

'He's still a bit burly, we'll give him a good gallop in the morning. Finbar's coming over to ride out.'

Annabel made a note on her clipboard. Finbar Howlett would be partnering the horse at Liverpool and, since he had not ridden him before, this would give the two of them a chance to get acquainted. Jan rubbed Eagle's nose and broke a large carrot in two halves, which he crunched appreciatively. With a final pat on the neck, she left his box and moved on to the next.

The yard, in fact, had two Grand National entries. The second was Arctic Hay, who was one of the longest-standing residents of Jan's yard, although never one of its stars. His owner, the Brummie scrap-metal dealer Bernie Sutcliffe, had insisted Jan enter him, even though she told him the horse would have little chance.

'The National's a bloody lottery anyway, ain't it?' he had argued back in January. 'Or so I am led to believe.'

'Bernie, that's bollocks. Most years the race is won by one of the better horses. We all know that jump racing has an element of chance, and the National has more of it than most because it's four and a half miles with a lot of runners and huge fences. It's not easy to be sure in advance if a horse will be suited to it or not. Of course, the chance is lessened if you have a good jumper.'

'So take the chance. I've got a feeling he might go well.'

Jan sighed with indignation.

'Bernie, the National's a uniquely demanding test. We'd be throwing Arctic Hay in at the deep end; he's an old horse and he might not appreciate it, quite frankly.'

'He *might*. As you said, we won't know till we've tried. And, remember, I'd still be the owner of that Russian Eagle if I hadn't kindly sold him to young

Annabel – now he's one of the ante-post favourites. It bloody hurts when I think about that. Having my own runner will make me feel a bit better.'

Bernie had been determined to have his day out at Aintree – so Jan had no choice but to indulge him. She would never have agreed if it meant putting the horse at risk, but Arctic Hay was a wily old campaigner and a sound jumper. If he could keep out of trouble in the cavalry charge to the first fence, Jan thought he had a reasonable chance of getting twice round the Aintree track safely. Slowly, but safely.

Jan gave as much attention to Arctic Hay as she had to Russian Eagle, and she could find nothing amiss.

'You deserve your chance,' she told him, rubbing his muzzle before giving him a carrot.

Toby Waller, an old school friend of Eddie's, had for long been one of Jan's confidants, and had helped her out of more than one difficulty. He was a rich young man, not super-rich, but well used to handling large sums of money, both as the son of a wealthy family and as a successful merchant banker in his own right. He also happened to have a very cool, shrewd head on his shoulders, at least in matters of finance and the law. So when he rang later to enquire how both Jan and Eddie were, she realized he was just the person to unburden herself to.

'Toby, you're not free tonight, by any chance?'

'Well, yes, I could very easily be,' he said. 'And, if it's for you, I already am. Are you coming to town?'

'God, no. Don't be silly, you know how I hate it. I was wondering if I could tempt you down here and we could have dinner. I desperately need a sympathetic ear.'

It was rather a naked appeal, but Toby understood perfectly.

'Into which you will pour your woes?' he said. 'I'd love to and what's more . . .'

She heard him turning the pages of his diary.

'I don't have any meetings tomorrow morning, at least nothing that can't be postponed. So, that's settled. I am inveigled. Shall we say eight-thirty in the Fox?'

Toby was single and did not have a girlfriend, or at least not one he owned up to. He was tangle-haired and tubby and held not a shred of sex appeal either for Jan or Annabel. Jan welcomed this because it made his loyalty and friendship even more valuable, something solid and uncomplicated. For Annabel, the matter was slightly different. Toby had been distantly and pessimistically in love with her for years, but Annabel was well used to the type of man who blushed like a postbox and lost the power of speech when he came into her presence. But she treated Toby as he was – one of the nicest of the breed she had ever met.

The village of Stanfield, a brisk twenty minutes' walk from Edge Farm, was lucky in its pub. The Fox & Pheasant had long practice in hospitality, having provided beer to thirsty travellers and farm workers since the reign of Charles II. It had a few clean, comfortable rooms for overnight accommodation and provided proper country fare.

When Jan arrived, Toby was already perched on a bar stool, in heated discussion with a group of locals about football. He leapt down and greeted her with a big hug.

'What shall we have?' he asked, as he ushered her into the dining area. 'A bottle of the bubbly stuff, I think, to celebrate your good fortune.'

'Good fortune? Is that what you call it?'

'Yes, Jan, I do. You're unscathed, thank heaven. By all accounts it was a dreadful crash.'

'Yes, it was. But Eddie—'

Toby held up his hand.

'We'll talk about Eddie later. Let's deal with you first. Are you really all right?'

'Yes, I'm fine. I was wearing the seat belt, so I didn't hit anything and, miraculously, nothing hit me except broken glass. Mind you, my boobs are rather bruised.'

'So no breakages?'

'Only to my peace of mind. But then racehorse trainers don't get much of that at the best of times.'

'Well, for someone who's had windscreen glass showering into them, you look wonderful. Now, that drink.'

Toby went back to the bar, ordered a bottle of Dom Pérignon, and returned with two menus.

'A big steak for me, I think. I'm starving. What about you?'

Jan chose poached salmon with a side salad. While they waited for the food they sipped the chilled champagne, as Toby told her about his recent week's fishing on a stretch of the river Tay in Scotland.

'It never ceases to amaze me how some blokes just have to spit in the water and a bloody great salmon rises to it.'

'Did you catch anything?'

He shrugged.

'A grayling or two. But who cares? What I really like is standing in my waders in the gurgling stream, hundreds of miles from debentures, corporate bonds and scrip issues. It's pure therapy. Talking of which, how are my horses?'

Jan looked vague and didn't answer. It was obvious to Toby that her mind was only half engaged, when normally she was completely focused on her work.

'OK, Jan,' he said after a few moments. 'Tell me what's on your mind. It's about Eddie, isn't it?'

'Yes. I think he's in real trouble, Toby.'

'So I gather. But at least he's awake.'

'Yes, thank God for that.'

'I can just imagine him lying there, wrapped up like Rameses II, with tubes going in and out and a face like a half-eaten sherry trifle.'

The image made Jan snigger.

'Stop it, Toby. Don't mock the afflicted. The poor chap's badly hurt, with head injuries and God knows what further down.'

'Further down?'

'I mean his spine, idiot. At the moment they don't know how bad it is.'

'But bad on what scale?'

'On a scale from making a full recovery, and being

able to ride a horse with all his old panache, to being stuck in a wheelchair for the rest of his life.'

Toby became more serious.

'I see,' he continued. 'That bad. I'm really sorry.'

'Anyway, when I say he's in trouble, I'm not just talking about his health.'

She told Toby about the conversations with Tim Farr, Hadfield's reference to the Morgan's bald tyres and her own researches in Eddie's attaché case.

'I felt awful poking around amongst his private things, but I had to. He had motor insurance documents all right, but they expired some time last summer.'

'I see. And there was no sign that he'd paid the road tax or had the MOT done?'

'None whatsoever. In the meantime, the police are investigating the accident further.'

'I think you'd better tell me about what happened that night, and I mean every little detail you can remember.'

She described it as fully as she could, beginning with A.D. O'Hagan's celebration party and ending with her waking up in hospital the next morning. Then she handed him a copy of the statement she had signed for Inspector Hadfield, which Toby read carefully.

'Given what you've told me,' he said, handing back the sheet of paper, 'this statement seems reasonable. Anyway, the important thing is that you're in the clear. You were a passenger and in no way responsible for anything that happened. I imagine the police are interested in Eddie, though, and they may prosecute him for driving an untaxed, uninsured and perhaps unroadworthy car. I don't know how bad that can be in legal terms, but it's certainly made far worse by the fact that there was an accident and that a man died. They will also have been very interested as to how much he had to drink at A.D.'s party.'

'But Eddie wasn't responsible. It was the driver of the other car, the one that overtook us – it caused all the mayhem. It's him they should be looking for.'

'Oh, they will be. You can be sure of that. But it all happened very quickly in the dark. Do you know if there are any independent witnesses who saw this other car, the four-wheel drive?'

'Which I'm now pretty sure was a Range Rover.'

'The Range Rover, then?'

'No, I don't. But the journalist I mentioned – Tim Farr – he might, I suppose. He was behind us on the road and it may have passed him. Or he may have spoken to other witnesses who saw. Apparently he stayed around at the scene for quite some time.'

'Right. I think it might be worth having a word or two with Mr Farr. Can you face it? I would do it, but you already know him, so—'

'Yes, I'll be all right doing that.'

'Has Inspector Hadfield said anything about an inquest?'

Jan hadn't thought of an inquest. She shook her head, new panicky thoughts whizzing through her mind.

'No, no, he never mentioned it. Will I have to give evidence?'

'Possibly. When you next speak to Hadfield, I suggest you ask him. Or you could contact the coroner's office directly, if you prefer. In the meantime I'll have a word with my solicitor. The drink thing may not arise because, as Eddie was unconscious for three days, he can't have given a blood sample for testing. But it's best we know the worst they can fling at him.'

'Eddie's mother's due to arrive from Australia any time now and . . .'

She was on the verge of telling Toby about Louise and her baby daughter, but she held back. This was Eddie's secret, not hers.

'Well, it's just that I'd like to be able to put her in the picture if I can.'

Toby smiled, creasing his fleshy, well-fed jowls. His eyes had the sparkle of a supreme optimist.

'Look, don't worry, Jan, I promise I won't hang around. I'll make that call tomorrow. Now drink up your champers and let's order pudding. I thought we might have a nice dessert wine to go with it.'

Getting ready for bed, Jan felt intensely grateful that she had friends like Toby. There had been many moments since John's death when she had been isolated, a woman in a man's game, a pauper in the world of the rich. But she had never actually felt lonely – with such good friends and family behind her, how could she?

A while later, as she was lying in the dark drifting off to sleep, the bedside phone rang sharply. Jan jerked awake and fumbled for the light, squinting as the room came to life. It was eleven o'clock. Instead of letting the answering machine take the call, she grabbed the phone, thinking the caller might be Sue Sullivan arriving from Australia.

'Hello?' she said.

There was silence, no one answered.

'Hello, hello . . .'

Still no one spoke. Jan tried a third time.

'Who's there? Hello, who is it?'

Getting no response, she hung up, turned off the light and lay staring into the darkness. It was extremely unsettling: either the caller wanted to speak to her but for some reason couldn't get through, which was tantalizing enough at this hour; or it was a wrong number. Or perhaps there was someone who deliberately wanted to frighten her. If so, they had been successful.

She waited for the phone to ring again. She was awake now, her senses and nerves fully alert. She gulped water from the bedside glass, composed herself and fifteen minutes later she was convinced the call was a wrong number.

Until it happened again.

'Hello, who is this?' she gasped, her throat so tight she almost choked.

This time she was positive she could hear background noises, a car sweeping past, or wind in trees, or maybe just someone breathing. Whatever it was, there was definitely someone on the other end of the line now, she was certain.

'Look, speak now or I'll hang up. And I won't pick up the phone again.'

6

As a faint ribbon of light appeared along the heights above Edge Farm and the morning routine of the racing stable began to unfold, Jan's common sense reasserted itself. The anonymous phone calls must have been a wrong number, she told herself. There had been no heavy breather. Just a hiss on the line.

At five to six the staff began arriving to muck out. Roz Stoddard and her sister Karen had already been in since five-thirty, going round the boxes with a small morning feed, checking the manger and water pots and that the occupants had come through the night without mishap. Annabel had driven up, looking her usual stylish self, and giving a lift to Emma, one of Jan's local stable lasses. Declan and Connor, having moved from the old caravan into a room in the village, arrived on a pair of violently rattling old bikes that they had persuaded Jan to buy for them. The two Irish lads rarely communicated with anyone first thing in the morning except in grunts. It was not until they got up on a horse's back that their good humour returned and the banter started. They were followed by the local boys Darren and Tom, rider and pillion on Darren's scooter, and finally on foot by Joe Paley, who was his usual five or ten minutes late.

Wednesdays and Saturdays were work days, when those horses in full training were given a serious gallop to test their wind and stretch their muscles to the limit. The amount of work Jan gave her horses depended to some extent on their physique but also on their temperament. Some horses were grafters and soaked up as much exercise as she cared to give them. Others would sulk if she galloped them a single furlong further than they liked. This did not apply to either of her Grand National horses, and she had planned to work them together this morning, with Arctic Hay's rider weighing a stone less than Russian Eagle's, just to even things up.

With minutes to spare before seven, the time Jan's first lot always pulled out, Finbar Howlett drove up to ride out the big horse.

'He gave me a great feel, Mrs Hardy,' said Finbar, as they walked back into the yard, where the jockey slipped off the horse's back. 'Fantastic long stride he's got. He should fly the big Aintree fences.'

'He already has,' said Jan. 'I want you to look at the video of his Foxhunters' before you go. He jumped Valentine's like a pole-vaulter that day.'

In a more modest way Arctic Hay had done his stuff, too, but had been predictably unable to match Eagle's loping stride and finished ten lengths behind.

After breakfast Jan settled Finbar down with the videotape showing the Foxhunters' Chase of two years earlier, when Russian Eagle had been ridden by Eddie and damn near won the race. Then she phoned the hospital. Eddie, it seemed, was feeling better. His headache had eased and he was speaking more coherently. She decided to drive down to visit him at midday, and then go straight on to Chepstow, where Teenage Red, owned by the rock group Band of Brothers, was to run in a bumper and Penny Price's Arrow Star had an engagement in the three-mile chase.

She decided to take the Australian letter with her. She would have to judge whether Eddie was in a fit state to talk about his possible child in Australia; at some point he would have to face up to this. But when she arrived on the ward any thoughts of solving the problem vanished. Sitting beside Eddie's bed was the slim, upright figure of a woman in her early sixties: Sue Sullivan.

The greeting Eddie's mother gave Jan was poised perfectly between the kiss of near strangers and the enthusiastic hug you might give to a family member.

'I flew into Heathrow early this morning and hired a car,' Sue Sullivan said. 'I was just going to phone you. I can't tell you how grateful we are to you for looking after Edward so brilliantly.'

Her tone was bright, but there was an edge to it that revealed the strain she was obviously feeling.

'It's not a problem. I know he would have done the same for me. But you must be very tired, Sue.'

'I must confess I am a bit. It's such a long flight. But I was desperate to see my boy.'

'Well, look, I've got to go on from here to Chepstow racecourse. We've got a couple of runners there. But, please, go back to Edge and rest. I'll phone my housekeeper, Fran, to let her know you're coming, and she'll make up a bed for you. That is, if you don't mind Megan's room. I haven't got a spare.'

'Jan, you have plenty to deal with, don't mind me. I can stay in town – there must be a hotel that's reasonable.'

'Sue, I wouldn't hear of it. You're staying with us.'

'Well, that is really kind of you.'

Jan dragged up a chair on the other side of the bed and gave Eddie the latest news from the yard, what little there was. He questioned her about a few things, still speaking deliberately, but already hitting fewer wrong words. Amongst other things, she mentioned Russian Eagle's good work earlier in the morning.

'Yes, Russian Eagle,' said Eddie, giving the impression that a particle of memory had just dropped into place. 'I'm riding . . . riding him in the National, aren't I?'

'What, you? Don't be silly. Finbar's on him.'

'No, I am. I'm his jock, his . . . jockey. And I'll be up and about in a couple of days. I won't have any . . . problem doing the weight. I've hardly eaten a thing, it's such crap they feed us here.'

'Eddie, you're *not* riding him. Not this time.'

Jan and Sue exchanged a rueful smile at Eddie's wind-up.

'Jan! *I'm* riding him, OK? That's . . . my . . . bloody horse and I'm bloody riding him.'

Jan was shaken. She now realized this was not meant to be a wind-up, Eddie was genuinely agitated.

Sue took his hand and stroked it in a motherly way. 'Darling, you're too badly hurt. You can't ride in any races at the moment, Edward. You've been in a car crash.'

'Yes, I know I've been in a *sodding* car crash, Mother. I *know* what happened. All right?'

Sue Sullivan was astounded by her son's vehemence, and even more startled when she saw tears welling up in his eyes.

'Hey, Eddie,' said Jan, 'it's OK. It's OK. You're going to be fine, though it may take a little longer than a couple of days. You will just have to be patient.'

Eddie was breathing hard and looking in turn from Jan to his mother, swivelling his glistening brown eyes from side to side, as if it was too painful to move his head.

On a sudden impulse, Jan added, 'Tell you what, though. You can ride Eagle in next year's National. I promise you'll be fit enough by then. What do you say to that?'

Eddie looked at her to gauge whether she could be trusted. Jan didn't particularly like or understand the look. Distrust did not become Eddie. It was not in his nature, any more than he was given to sudden outbursts of irrational rage.

'All right,' he mumbled. 'It's a deal. You've given your word.'

'Jan! It's great to see you back racing again. And so soon.'

The ruddy-faced Captain Freckle, the clerk of the course at Chepstow, beamed at her as she handed in the passports of her runners at the declarations office.

'Yes, I was very lucky.'

She clung to this phrase throughout the afternoon. Everywhere she went, when people said how wonderful it was to see her, how well she looked, she replied how lucky she had been. Was all this just passing bonhomie, she wondered. Of course, much of it was, but although the bonhomie was fleeting it didn't stop it being true. The numerous handshakes, pats on the back and pecks on the cheek were signs of the racing tribe welcoming back one of their own, one who had been through an ordeal and survived and Jan took genuine pleasure from it. Hers was a small, out-of-the-way yard, only three years in business and still struggling to establish itself. But she felt she had been accepted into the tribe now, well, by most of them at least.

Arrow Star was owned by one of Jan's nicest and most enthusiastic owners. Penny Price was a local woman, of about thirty, who worked in the daytime as a secretary and at a chicken factory during the night to help meet the training fees. She had bred Arrow Star herself and he was her only pride and joy. Things had become a little easier for Penny after her parents had signed up as joint owners. They were small, uncomplicated farmers, people like Reg and Mary, not well off but the salt of the earth.

Jan felt the least she could do was to try her damnedest to make the big horse pay his way. He was huge – 'a bit of a hippo' was how one jockey had described him. Nevertheless, he had landed third place in the unconventional cross-country race at Cheltenham back in November. Even though he faced more conventional steeplechase fences today, it was not beyond the bounds of possibility that Willy Summers, the experienced jockey Jan had engaged to ride him, could repeat the success and bring in another few hundred pounds in place money.

To the delight of the Price family, Arrow Star did even better. The horse plugged around the circuit at a moderate pace, putting in mighty leaps at every obstacle, which kept him on terms with the slicker, faster animals. Then, unexpectedly after the turn for home, there was a pile up. The runners were approaching the penultimate fence halfway along Chepstow's demanding home run, with Arrow Star racing on his own a few lengths off the field. Suddenly, out of the blue, a loose horse appeared alongside the bunch. Instead of running round the fence, as most do, he swerved left and right like a world-class rugby player before jumping the fence diagonally across the leaders. He cannoned into the front two, bringing them down, which in turn hampered the other horses and left their jockeys clinging round their necks. Arrow Star, travelling behind with a wet sail, pricked his ears in amazement and pinged the fence. He didn't shirk his responsibility and galloped to the last; hurling himself over it, he churned his way to the line, passing it a length and a half clear.

The famous gap-toothed grin of Willy Summers was a joy to behold, though it was the delight of Arrow Star's owner as she led her horse into the unsaddling enclosure that lit the whole place. For Jan this was one of her best moments in racing, to win for owners who were also good friends. She knew Arrow Star was never going to set the world on fire, but there would never be a more genuine horse in training. Now there was definitely not a happier or more deserving owner than Penny Price anywhere in the world.

Jan and Annabel were drinking coffee in the crowded owners' and trainers' bar when Jan noticed Virginia Gilbert come in with a wiry sort of man, just above average height and dressed in a tailored tweed suit and check cap. He removed the headgear as he stalked through the door to reveal a sleek head of black hair. Jan's heart sank – it was Harold Powell. She quickly turned her back and, tapping Annabel on the arm, indicated the new arrivals with a movement of her head.

Jan's dealings with Harold Powell had developed over the previous four years and every new turn in them had been unpleasant.

'He's obviously got plenty of money still,' commented Annabel.

'I know. It seems people like him always have lots hidden away somewhere.'

'But what's he doing here with Virginia?'

'Plotting my downfall probably,' said Jan gloomily.

'You mean, after what he said to you at Cheltenham?'

Jan looked at Annabel blankly.

'What? He was at Cheltenham?'

'Don't you remember? You said he confronted you near the saddling boxes. He told you that you'd ruined his life.'

Jan narrowed her eyes and strained to get the memory. *Near the saddling boxes.* Yes, that was it. Harold quivering with rage. Harold actually believed Jan had deliberately done him down, that she'd waged a personal campaign against him. Harold snarling his contempt and promising her, 'You'll get what's coming to you.'

She flicked an anxious glance across at Harold and Virginia. They were sitting at a table on the far side of the room, deep in conversation, and did not appear to have registered Jan's presence in the bar.

'Come, on, Bel,' she said. 'We're getting out of here. I'm not staying in the same room as that man.'

Teenage Red did not give Jan a double that day. He had been a little short of work, but Jan and Annabel agreed on the way home that he would be a live contender next time out.

After the ritual of evening stables Jan had started making supper for the children, when Sue Sullivan appeared, looking surprisingly alert for a woman with jet-lag.

'I didn't want to sleep too long. Ron says you've got to reset the body clock after a long flight and you can't do that by giving in to sleep at the wrong time of day.'

They sat at the kitchen table and ate beans on toast, while Megan entertained Sue at great length with an account of her riding exploits in the world of junior eventing with Monarch, the pony that Colonel Gilbert had lent her.

'One day I'm going to be the new Lucinda Green and Matty's going to be the new Murty McGrath,' she announced, with the blind certainty that only a child can have.

'That's good,' said Sue. 'You must always aim for the top.'

An hour later the children went off to bed while the two women settled down with a bottle of wine in front of the fire.

'Were you shocked to see Eddie?' Jan enquired.

'Yes, a little. Even though I'd spent the whole journey imagining he'd be even worse.'

'Yes, I know.' Jan sighed. 'That's the curse of motherhood, imagining the worst.'

'It's odd, but he seems different. I know he's all bandaged up and in pain, but the Edward I knew always laughed off his hurts – always.'

'Yes, making light of things was his way, wasn't it?'

'But what I want to say is, he's so lucky to have you, Jan. I couldn't wish for better. In fact I am very much hoping that—'

'There's precious little I can do for him at the moment,' Jan interrupted, fearful of hearing what Sue Sullivan was hoping for. 'He won't be up and about for weeks, so the doctors are saying.'

'But there's so *much* you can do, Jan. Don't you see? I mean, after he's had all the hospital treatment? And even during it he's going to need lots of support if he's ever to get back to his old cheery self. He's going to need a good woman by his side. I know Ron agrees. You two are made for each other.'

Suddenly Jan felt wildly nervous about where this was going to head. She tried to steer the conversation into another channel.

'Is he like Ron? In character, I mean.'

'In some ways very. Ron's hopeless on his own, too. I mean, he doesn't look after himself.'

Sue laughed.

'I should think right now he's sitting down to a boiled egg for breakfast. Then he'll have more of the same for his tea. Terribly bad for his cholesterol, but that's all he ever eats if I'm not there. Either that or cheese, possibly a few beans.'

Jan smiled, thinking of the meal they'd had earlier.

'Anyway,' Sue went on, 'that is why I said what I said, about you and Edward. I just can't hang around in England for too long. Ron needs me. That's why I went back, you see, back to the marriage. You knew we'd separated shortly before Ron's business went for six?'

Jan nodded.

'Well, when that Mafia gang or whoever they were went after him and he had to scarper to Australia, I knew I couldn't let him go on his own. Even though we'd been living apart for eighteen months, I was still doing his *laundry*, for goodness sake. We'd been married for thirty-five years. I suppose we couldn't manage apart, either of us.'

'You too?'

'Yes, me too. I guess I must still be hooked on him. He really is a good man, Jan – not always the most reliable, I know, not always the most sensible either, but good underneath all that.'

Jan understood that Sue wasn't only talking about her husband, but about her son. She was appealing to Jan on Eddie's behalf, an appeal that Eddie would rather die than make for himself.

'Yes,' said Jan as brightly as she could, 'of course he is. Now, I haven't told you about how we got on at Chepstow, yet, have I?'

Jan told Sue about the runs of Arrow Star and Teenage Red, and promised to take her down the yard to see the horses in the morning. Suddenly she was suppressing yawns. It was time to tidy up before going to bed.

Jan had just switched off the light and was settling down to sleep when the phone at her bedside gave a loud shrill. She reached out, without turning on the light, and picked up the receiver.

'Yes?'

Was it that fluctuating hiss again, or breathing?

'Who is this, please?'

She was doing her best to sound authoritative, in control. But this had no apparent effect. Whoever had dialled her number had either not got through or was deliberately keeping silent.

After twenty seconds Jan put down the receiver, switched on the light and swung her legs out of the bed so she was sitting. Suddenly she felt almost sick with anger. Who the hell was it? How dare they disturb her like this? She felt along the lead of the phone and pulled the plug out of the Telecom socket. Then she went downstairs to the hall and did the same.

Back in bed, she breathed deeply and tried to quieten her pounding heart. Of course, she had heard of people being plagued by anonymous malicious phone calls, but it had never happened to her. Sometimes the calls meant nothing at all because they were done by harmless nutters. *That must be it,* she thought. Some prat who had lost money on one of her horses. They'd soon give up, or bet on another horse and start bothering the trainer of that one.

The thought, and the knowledge that the phone could not ring again until she reconnected it, calmed her and she eventually fell asleep.

7

'Hello, Jan. It's Toby. Are you busy?'

'I'm doing my entries, but it can wait.'

It was mid-morning as Jan took the call in the office, where she had been dealing with a fistful of paperwork which she'd generated as she searched for suitable races for her horses.

'It's about the discussion we had on Tuesday night. I have talked off the record to a lawyer friend about Eddie's little problem.'

'I hope you're going to tell me it *is* a little problem.'

'Well, not exactly, I'm afraid.'

'Not good news, then?'

'Mixed, I'd say. The first thing is that, because someone died in the accident, a thorough police investigation is inevitable, which we more or less predicted. Have you found out anything else?'

Jan had called the coroner's office the previous afternoon.

'Yes, the coroner's already opened the inquest but adjourned it. Apparently if there's a proper trial, the inquest might not be needed as all the evidence will be presented in court and they won't want to prejudge it.'

'Which is as I thought. What about the post-mortem?'

'By all accounts they've done one already. What do you think that means?'

'Obviously the family will want the body released for burial. But first the coroner needs to establish if the guy was drunk, had taken drugs or had a heart attack whilst driving.'

'I see. So where does this leave Eddie?'

'Right. Eddie has several relatively minor driving offences to face, namely driving without valid documentation, which he is obviously guilty of, and driving an unfit vehicle, which he may well be guilty of. Normally they would attract fines and might mean he's disqualified from driving.'

'But *was* the Morgan unfit?'

'I can only go on what you've told me, but my friend says that if the car's tyres were as you described them then it was demonstrably unfit for the road and that's an offence. But having discovered this, and knowing that Eddie didn't have a current MOT certificate, the police will take a closer look at the whole car, or what's left of it, especially at the things checked in an MOT test, such as the brake pads. If they find these were badly worn, or there were any other dangerous defects, they can say the accident was a result of these faults, and that it was his responsibility. Then if the police thought they could make it stick, they'd charge him.'

'But what with, Toby? I'm really scared. What if they try to implicate me?'

'They won't, Jan, but Eddie could be accused of death by reckless driving, that's my best guess.'

'The best? You're joking.'

'Sorry, Jan, not the right word. Anyway, here's the serious bit. If he's found guilty, he could be looking at a custodial sentence, anything from a few months to five years.'

'*Five years, for Christ's sake,*' Jan gasped as she clutched the desk to steady herself.

'That's reserved for extreme cases. The average is two to three years.'

'Two to three *years*? Dear God, Toby, please tell me this isn't real.'

Toby's voice, usually so humorous, remained low and serious.

'Jan, please don't be so upset. It hasn't happened, not yet. And it may never. My friend agrees with what I told you on Tuesday night and the circumstances of the accident mean that the police will find it extremely difficult to establish exactly what happened for sure.'

'Toby, for fuck's sake, I *know* what happened. Why won't anyone believe me? It had nothing to do with Eddie's brakes, or his tyres. The Range Rover forced both of us off the road – *that's what happened.*'

'Jan, it's going to serve no useful purpose getting angry and losing control. I know what you said in your statement and that you were with Eddie and saw it all. But the police will definitely want an independent witness, or some other kind of evidence.'

'You mean they will never believe me?'

'I don't know. They may, they should. But don't

forget we pay them to be suspicious about things like this. Anyway, the positive point is, if they really can't be sure how the accident happened, they are hardly likely to prosecute Eddie, except on the minor charges.'

'And if they find the car that barged us off the road while making the other poor sod hit a tree, they'll go after him,' Jan continued weakly.

'Exactly. But there's something else my friend mentioned.'

'Go on. I might as well have it all.'

'Have you thought about the dead man? Or rather, have you considered his family and his insurers? Theoretically Eddie shouldn't have been on the road in that car, should he? So what are they going to make of his liability?'

Jan suddenly saw what Toby was getting at.

'Oh my God, the insurance!'

'Yes, the insurance. There will undoubtedly be a claim, which Eddie almost certainly wasn't covered for. In which case the family might feel entitled to damages. So Eddie could be sued for everything he's got. And more.'

'I suppose that's all right, then. He hasn't got a pot to piss in.'

After putting down the receiver, Jan went up to the house, to find Sue sitting in the kitchen writing postcards. While she made a mug of tea, Jan very gently gave an edited version of her conversation with Toby, leaving out the mention of prison and of the possible claim by relations of the deceased.

Sue took it all calmly. 'I think it's far more important to get him better than to worry him about all this legal stuff.'

'Do you know if he's seen Hadfield yet?' Jan asked, handing Sue a mug.

'The policeman? No, I don't think so.'

'He'll want Eddie's statement about the accident.'

Sue waved her hand dismissively and smiled.

'Waste of time, dear. Edward can't remember a thing about it. And he's got memory blanks going back weeks. He says that the whole time since he came back from Australia's a complete fog.'

'What about before he came back?'

'What do you mean?'

Jan took a deep breath and fetched the airmail letter which she had still not delivered.

'This arrived for him at the King's Head on Saturday. I haven't given it to him because I thought it might be something to do with that girl, her baby and the DNA test.'

Sue looked at her sharply.

'You know about the test?'

'Yes, Eddie told me.'

Taking the envelope Sue looked at it casually.

'And you were worried it would upset him, you mean? It's OK, the letter's from me. It's mostly about what his father and I'd been up to, but there *is* news about Alice, the child, in it. And I've been wondering when you'd ask about her.'

'I've been wondering if I should.'

'That's funny. We've both been skating around the subject, haven't we? It's like something that shouldn't be mentioned.'

'Nevertheless, it's still been on my mind.'

'Mine too. But with Edward being so badly hurt, I've not had the heart to mention it to him. I'm not sure he'd remember it, anyway.'

Jan sat down opposite Eddie's mother. 'What's going on? I think I've got a right to know if Eddie really is a father.'

'Jan, I agree with you entirely.'

Sue laid the letter on the table in front of her, looking fixedly at it as she spoke.

'The fact is we still don't know. We're waiting for the result of the test to come through, or we were when I left. As it is at the moment, Alice might be our granddaughter, or she might not be.'

She tapped the envelope on the table with a fore-finger capped by crimson nail varnish.

'I wrote that she's in foster care. I suppose it's for the best, for the time being. The mother doesn't want her now, probably never did.'

Sue's last remark was loaded with contempt.

'Well, Eddie does,' said Jan. 'I mean, if he's the father, he does. He told me as much.'

'Yes. And if the little mite's his, then we'll have to take her, won't we?'

By Sunday, ten days after the accident, Jan had begun to count the reasons to be cheerful. She was feeling and looking more like her old self. There had been no more weird phone calls. And the stable had a winner for A.D. O'Hagan at Newbury on Saturday. When she visited Eddie on Sunday she realized how much he had improved, at least physically. He could sit up in bed and the head dressings had been simplified to a white cap of crêpe bandaging around his cranium. His bare face was decorated with the dark little knots of his stitches, which weren't pretty, but it seemed like progress. The bruising, though, still looked like the colours of a sherry trifle, but the puffiness in his face had mostly subsided.

However, Eddie himself was anything but cheerful.

It was late afternoon and Jan was alone with him.

'How are you feeling?' she asked.

'Not very clever,' Eddie answered in a grumpy manner. 'Still, at least I can talk properly even if I can't bloody walk.'

'You're starting physiotherapy next week, aren't you? That'll help, I'm sure.'

'Not if I'm paralysed it sodding won't. That'll be me, for life.'

'Don't talk such rubbish, Eddie. You sound like someone who's given up, and that's not like you.'

There was a pause. Eddie was staring straight ahead.

'A policeman was here,' he said.

'Hadfield? Yes, I met him. He's investigating the accident. What did he want?'

'He wanted me to tell him all about it. Which I couldn't as it's a complete fucking blank. He kept going on about the poor state of the Morgan and accused me of not keeping up the insurance, MOT and the rest. I told him it wasn't true, it couldn't possibly be.'

Jan caught her breath.

'You mean you *did* renew them?'

'I've no idea.'

'Oh. It seems you didn't, Eddie. I can't find anything and I've searched everywhere.'

'Perhaps I forgot to. That's a laugh. Now I've forgotten that I forgot.'

'Look, stop worrying about it for now. It'll all come back, I'm sure, but it will take time. What's the last thing you do remember?'

'Sun, surf, Foster's lager. Australia. Everything after that's blurred. I do remember stuff, but none of it makes sense.'

Driving back to Edge, Jan suddenly found her eyes filling with tears. She pulled into a lay-by and tried to control the wave of emotion. Eddie's moroseness was like a pall of gloom hanging over them. Then, as she reflected, she realized her feelings were not so much pity for him, as self-pity. What could he remember about her? Could he recall the reason he'd come back to England? Did he remember they had been passionate lovers? And if he didn't, where did that leave her?

'Stop this right now,' Jan scolded herself.

Rummaging in her pocket, she found a screwed-up tissue; she blew her nose several times and drove on, determined she would overcome this problem, however big it was.

As she let herself into the house, Fran was in the hall holding the phone. She quickly put her hand over the mouthpiece.

'It's a reporter – Tim Farr?' she whispered.

Jan sighed and took the receiver.

'Hello, Mr Farr. How are you?' she asked.

'Tim, please.'

'What can I do for you?' Jan continued.

'It's in connection with the accident, I mean Cleeve Hill. Do you have a few moments to talk?'

'I might have. Go on, spit it out.'

'The police have put out an appeal for witnesses. They are particularly interested in the driver of a vehicle that may have left the scene before the police arrived.'

Jan sat down on the upright chair next to the small telephone table.

'What kind of car?'

'A big four-wheel drive evidently.'

'Like a Range Rover?'

'Yes. To quote the press release, "possibly resembling a Range Rover". Registration number, not known. Colour of car, ditto.'

Jan tried to sound matter of fact, but she was electrified. It seemed that Hadfield's interviews with other motorists at the scene might have corroborated her statement.

'Mr Farr, Tim, do you know how the police got hold of this?'

'No, they just call it "information received".'

'But you were driving behind us. Were you passed by a Range Rover going really fast, driven by a lunatic?'

'No, Mrs Hardy. But I was quite a long way behind you, remember. The police were already arriving when I turned up. What about you? Do you know anything positive about this other vehicle?'

Jan hesitated.

'No, Tim, I'm sorry I don't. I've really got nothing to add. I suppose your best bet is to get on to Hadfield.'

'I already have. He won't confirm if it's a positive or not.'

It was not yet six o'clock the next morning, with *Farming Today* still on the kitchen radio, when Jan heard the clatter of running feet outside, followed by a furious ringing on the front-door bell.

'Jan! Come quick!'

It was Roz, Jan's head girl, who always arrived for work first. She was jumping up and down on the doorstep and clearly agitated.

'Quick! It's Eagle!'

They ran like Steve Cram and Seb Coe, helter-skelter back down to the yard.

Russian Eagle was lying upside down, with his head towards the stable door and his legs fast against the right-hand wall. He was breathing noisily, the great barrel of his thorax heaving up and down. His big eyes were watery and bloodshot, rolling around with distress. Blood trickled from his nostrils and his mouth dribbled sticky saliva.

'He's cast,' said Jan in despair. 'We've got to get him up, *now*.'

Jan ran and unhooked a lunge rein from the tack-room wall. She knew this was something that happened from time to time, though it seemed inexplicable to anyone not close to horses. Eagle had got down for a roll and got wedged in a position he could not get free from. In a blind panic, he would have struck out with his hooves, desperate to release himself, and banged his head on the floor several times.

He might have lain there for several hours, occasionally renewing his struggle until he was completely exhausted. Jan knew he could have done himself untold damage.

'You'll have to come in with me,' she told Roz, whose face was frozen with fear. 'And for Christ's sake don't get crushed.'

Jan grabbed the head-collar from a hook by the stable door and went into the box. She immediately knelt beside Eagle's head, talking to the horse, soothing him like a hypnotist. She stroked his neck and he feebly lifted his head off the floor. Slowly she worked the collar over his nose before pulling the long leather strip behind his ears and buckling it.

Jan instructed Roz to hold Eagle's head tight to the floor while she fixed the lunge rein to his hind leg. She knew this was a precarious move – if Eagle renewed his fight for freedom both she and Roz could be seriously injured. Thankfully Con and Dec appeared at that moment and helped Jan give an almighty tug on the lunge rein, flipping Eagle back into his correct position. The battered horse lay quiet for a moment before staggering drunkenly to his feet.

Jan looked him over carefully and knew straight away they were in trouble, but, to confirm it, she asked Roz to walk him gently into the yard. Instantly, they could both detect the horse's lameness.

'Off-hind,' Roz said.

Jan carefully ran her hand down all his legs in turn and felt that somehow or other he had got off lightly. The problem in the off-hind leg was obvious by the extra heat and swelling, but she would need the vet to diagnose the underlying injury. Miraculously, the other three seemed normal. Jan felt sure Eagle's injured leg wasn't fractured.

'It's bad enough, though,' she said as the big horse stood swishing his tail, feeling as subdued as she did.

At that moment Annabel, Eagle's co-owner with A.D. O'Hagan, appeared out of the gloom. As Jan told her what had happened, Bel stood looking at her horse in disbelief, then burst into floods of tears. Jan handed her a tissue and felt like joining her.

'I suppose that's his chance in the National gone,' said Annabel. 'Give him to me, I'll take him, Roz. He needs washing down and a drink of warm water. You can give me a hand, if you like.'

'I'll phone the vet,' said Jan, already heading for the office.

Later, in the kitchen after the first lot had come in from the gallops, Megan was unusually quiet over her bowl of cereal. 'What does it mean, cast in his box?' she asked.

Jan dropped some sliced bread into the toaster.

'It means they lie down in their box and they can't get up.'

'Why can't they get up? I've seen Smarty roll and he always gets up.'

'Well, it depends on the position they're in. Horses have rather stiff spines. Much stiffer than dogs or cats. So they're less flexible and if they're in certain positions, like, for instance, getting too close to the wall of the box or having their bottom wedged in the corner, they can't bend their backs far enough to twist over onto the other side.'

'Why don't they just get up, though?'

'It's by rolling over that they get their hind legs under them, which is the only way they can get up again.'

'And if they're too close to the wall they can't roll?'

'Exactly.'

'Is Eagle going to be all right?'

'I hope so. We'll know when the vet gets here, which will be soon or I'll throttle her.'

The ebullient Shirley McGregor was in the yard by nine-thirty. She examined Eagle and confirmed that he had got off lightly.

'I've seen loads of them with their jawbones fractured, where they've bashed their heads on the concrete floor.'

'I always make sure the floor's covered all over with plenty of bedding,' said Jan.

'Good, it's probably saved us a lot of grief. And I'd say the leg's going to mend OK, but it'll take time. This one's in the National, isn't he?'

Jan shrugged and sighed at the same time.

'Yes, he was. Not any more, though. What's more, I'm going to have to ring A.D. O'Hagan and tell him. He isn't going to like it . . .'

'I'll take an X-ray just to be sure we know what we're dealing with. I've brought my portable with me. If we'e not happy in a day or two you may have to bring him to the surgery, but I really wouldn't want to travel him at the moment.'

Forty minutes later Shirley bounced into the office to give Jan her prognosis.

'I'm sure it'll mend completely, but you won't be able to do much with him for a while. So . . .'

She beamed at Jan.

'It's an enforced holiday for him.'

There was always a collective sense of loss when a fancied horse had to be taken out of a big race through injury. Shirley's noisy cheerfulness was normally popular around Edge Farm, but the young vet was not sensitive to atmosphere, and seemed oblivious to the sombre mood that had settled over the yard.

'Can you do me a written report as soon as possible? In simple language, please,' Jan asked. 'I'll need all the details. A.D.'s a stickler and with this particular horse I'm going to have to give him chapter and verse.'

'That's all right, no problem. Any other patients for me to look at while I'm here? How's that splint? Has it settled?'

On her regular Thursday visits Shirley had been treating Miller's Lodge, one of Johnny Carlton-Brown's horses.

'It's much better. We thought he'd be back doing a little light work next week.'

'Want me to have a look?'

Jan shook her head.

'No, it's OK. It'll wait till Thursday when you do your rounds.'

'By the way, how's Eddie?'

Shirley had asked casually enough, but Jan couldn't help remembering the previous year, when Shirley had made a play for Eddie.

'Eddie?' Jan said crisply. 'He's enjoying an enforced holiday too.'

8

As soon as Shirley McGregor had left, Annabel burst into the office. After her initial tears, she had been monosyllabic while riding work on the gallops and later back in the yard, doing her duties with grim-faced efficiency. But a forceful storm had been brewing inside her; now it was about to burst.

'I can't *believe* you let this happen to my beautiful Eagle,' she lashed out, choking with emotion.

Her outline was framed in the doorway, and Jan could clearly see that she was shaking.

'What on earth do you mean, Bel? I didn't "let this happen". It just did – all by its bloody self.'

'But Eagle was in the very best shape of his life in the biggest week of his life. You should've been more careful.'

Jan was astounded. Annabel had always been Jan's closest ally. She was an invaluable assistant. Was she now turning against her too?

'For Christ's sake, Bel. It wasn't a question of being more careful. How could it be? He was cast in his box. I wish to God it hadn't happened, but it did. It affects me as well, you know. It was just an awful random accident.'

'No, it's that bloody car crash!' Annabel's voice was quavering. 'It's taken your mind off the job.'

'Bel, no! That's unforgivable! I won't have that.'

Jan pushed back her chair. Getting to her feet, she faced Annabel, an entirely new, completely unexpected Annabel. Jan understood her friend's passionate regard for the animals in their care and her even more partisan love for, and pride in, Russian Eagle. But this need to blame someone for what was an unforeseen, unforeseeable even, disaster seemed so unlike her.

'I tell you what's really unforgivable, Jan. It's unforgivable that Russian Eagle can't run for the biggest honour there is for him. It's unforgivable that you didn't put a round-the-clock watch on his stable.'

'Now just wait a *minute*, Bel.' Jan couldn't help raising her voice. 'No one, but *no one* could have predicted this. You're not bloody thinking straight. You're pissed off, you're disappointed, but—'

'Disappointed?' Annabel's voice was shrill. 'Yes, I'm disappointed all right, Jan, in *you*. Eagle was going to win, I just know he was. And now he won't even get the chance.'

Jan felt her own temper surge up to the same level.

'Now *look*, you're right out of order, young lady, and you'd better get your head together, if you want to go on working here. Do you understand? I will not put up with the accusations you've made. Not from you, or anybody else for that matter.'

But Annabel had already turned and stalked out. Jan shot to the open door and watched her 'friend' cross the yard towards the main gate. The dogs, who had been lolling around under the archway, sprang to life, as if energized by Annabel's irrational anger. They scurried after her, leaping around her long striding legs. Through the arch, Jan could see Bel jerk open the rear door of her car to let the dogs pile in. With squealing tyres, she drove off as fast as she could, clattering the loose stones which edged the drive, and disappeared up the track leading to the top of the ridge and the gallops.

'That's all I bloody needed,' Jan muttered. She shook her head in disbelief and returned to her desk. She was aware that it was not unknown for the big yards to keep a round-the-clock watch on horses prior to an important race. There had been cases of Derby favourites being threatened by criminals, and consequently requiring that kind of protection. But Jan had only ever kept vigil for a mare about to foal, or for horses with a life-threatening illness. It was wholly unreasonable – and completely beyond her means – to mount a twenty-four-hour guard on a healthy horse just because he had a big race coming up. A.D. O'Hagan, Annabel's partner in the ownership of Russian Eagle, would agree, Jan was certain. Otherwise he would have insisted on the precaution himself. He had not, of course, because it was absurd.

With a swift intake of breath Jan remembered that A.D. still did not know Eagle was out of the National. As she lifted the phone, her hand still trembling at Annabel's reaction, she wondered what A.D.'s response would be like. If there was one thing as certain as sunrise, Jan knew that he never, under any circumstances, became hysterical.

She called his mobile, but an automatic voice

informed her politely that the number was at present unavailable. She joggled the phone cradle and dialled Aigmont, getting through immediately to A.D.'s secretary.

'Mr O'Hagan's away, Mrs Hardy. I can't reach him at the moment, I'm afraid. Is there a problem? Can I help?'

'It's about—'

Jan checked herself. She must be discreet. Almost anything connected with A.D.'s racing activities was potentially sensitive, but when it concerned a well-fancied runner just a few days before the Grand National thousands of pounds in ante-post bets could be at stake. And quite a lot of that would probably be A.D.'s. It would be best if no one at his end knew about Russian Eagle before he did.

'It's OK, but could you ask him to contact me as soon as possible, please? It is rather important.'

Three hours later Annabel returned. The yard had no runners today and Jan was in the house, arranging some of Reg's daffodils in a vase, when the blonde head of her assistant passed the kitchen window. Annabel let herself in through the front door and wandered quietly into the kitchen, where she headed straight for the electric kettle, which she shook to check if there was any water inside.

'I went for a walk along the ridge.' She spoke in a subdued, contrite voice. 'I needed to clear my head.'

'And have you?'

'Yes.'

'I'm very glad to hear it.'

Annabel switched the kettle on. She bit her lip as she concentrated on making two mugs of tea, while her eyes looked anywhere rather than meet Jan's gaze. She brought the steaming mugs to the table and placed her elbows on it, propping her chin on her hands.

'I'm really sorry, Jan,' she said at last. 'It was completely unprofessional of me to lose it like that. You're right, of course. No one could have foreseen what happened. I was just so disappointed that I let it get the better of me. I was thinking like an owner who knows nothing about the job, for God's sake!'

'Well, I'm sorry too that I raised my voice and yelled like I did, and I'm terribly sorry about Eagle. I do understand how personally you take everything about him. Of course you were thinking like an owner because you are one – well, half one. But, honestly, everyone's depressed about this. Don't you think I was desperate for him to run? Don't you think I could do with the ackers if he had won, or was placed even?'

'He must be feeling pretty sorry for himself, poor sod. All wound up to go and then nothing. What a let-down.'

It was not until the evening that Jan's phone rang and she heard A.D.'s even, measured tones.

'Jan, I'm sorry I couldn't get back to you earlier. I was involved in rather a long poker game.'

Jan took a deep breath. 'I've got some bad news, I'm afraid, A.D.'

'What's that, then?'

A.D. listened without interruption as she explained the morning's sequence of events.

'You've taken him out of the race?'

'No, I wanted to talk to you first. But I'll have to do it tomorrow. No choice. I'll send you a copy of the vet's report, of course.'

'Yes, do that. And you can refer any press enquiries to me, if you like. What a damnable thing. There'd be no chance of a crack at the Irish National again, I suppose?'

The Irish Grand National at Fairyhouse was two weeks after the Aintree event and Russian Eagle had a precautionary entry in the race he'd won the previous season.

'No, A.D. I think it'll take a bit longer than that. I really am sorry.'

'Would he be ready to run again before the summer? Uttoxeter maybe?'

'Oh yes, I hope so. He'll be as sound as a bell in a month, with any luck.'

'Oh well, these things happen to most horses. They're not machines you know, even if some people treat them as such.'

'Will you still be at Aintree?'

'Why wouldn't I be? I'll be there all three days for sure. 'Bye Jan.'

He hung up abruptly.

Sue had established her own routine. She drove down to Cheltenham to see Eddie each morning, always asking Jan whether she could get anything from the

shops on the way back. Jan had come to rely on her for odd loaves of bread, pints of milk, jars of coffee or a bottle of wine for their dinner in the evening.

On Wednesday morning Jan had asked if Sue would drop into the bank and pay in a few cheques, then gather some extra groceries from the supermarket, while Megan had requested a pony magazine from the village store. Sue always carried out her small commissions to the letter, so it was a complete surprise when she arrived back at lunchtime empty-handed, with a dazed expression on her face.

'Oh, Jan,' she said, slapping her forehead. 'I've completely forgotten Megan's magazine, and the tea and things. How stupid of me.'

'Never mind, they're not that important. What about the bank?'

Sue fished in her bag and drew out the bundle of cheques, neatly tucked into Jan's paying-in book. She handed them back to Jan.

'Sorry, I forgot those too.'

'Sue, is something the matter?'

'I had a row with Edward, you see, or rather he picked a fight with me. It was horrible. I could think about nothing else all the way back.'

'Why on earth did he do that?'

'Well, it's something I haven't told you yet, but you should know anyway. I was speaking to Ron last night and he told me about the DNA test on the child.'

Jan had been leafing through the cheques, making sure they were all there. Now she froze. The cheques had suddenly lost all interest for her.

'The DNA test? Why? What did Ron say?'

Sue took off her coat and went to hang it in the hall. Returning, she paused in front of the kitchen mirror to check her hair.

'Well, as you know, we've all been on tenterhooks, haven't we? And the result should have been through by now, according to what we were told earlier. So Ron telephoned the lab to ask what was going on and they said the certified sample Edward sent them, I think it was a few hairs off his head or something, got lost. They couldn't find them. Would you believe it?'

'Was this before or after they did the test?'

'Oh, before. Apparently the sample went missing more or less immediately on arrival at the lab. So now they say we have to get another one certified and sent over.'

'Did you tell Eddie?'

'That's what caused the ructions, I'm sad to say. Edward still can't remember deciding to go ahead with a paternity test or providing the original sample. He remembers all about the baby, and he remembers that good-for-nothing Louise, but he got quite worked up and cross about her – he called her a slut, which I wouldn't disagree with, by the way. I think he really hates the mention of her now.'

'Is that what you argued about?'

'No, it was about the replacement sample for the DNA test. He suddenly said he'd lost all interest and couldn't give a damn. He wasn't going to go ahead with it, didn't think he'd be able to look after a child in his condition, and he said she would be better off being adopted. Of course, I told him not to be silly and that Ron and I would have her, if that's what it came to, until Edward was ready to take her on. But he shouted at me that he thought he was *never* going to get better. He said, "I'm going to be an effing basket case, Mum, and you might as well get effing used to the idea." He was shouting at me so loudly that the nurse came in to ask what the matter was. I told him it was stuff and nonsense, of course he's going to make a complete recovery, even if it does take a little time. And then, of course, I went too far and said that, even if he doesn't get better, everything would be all right. He really didn't like hearing that – it seems all the negativity has to come from him. He doesn't want to hear the rest of us saying he might not recover. But the point I was trying to make was that Ron and I would be only too happy to raise our granddaughter, as best we could, if we have to.'

'I know you would and I'm sure Eddie will too, in time.'

Sue shrugged.

'Well, we may never know because he won't have the test now, not at any price.'

'Not at the moment,' Jan said gently, 'but he may some day.'

Sue's face was twisted with the pain only a mother feels at the thought of her son's distressing behaviour.

'I don't know. He's so very angry, Jan, it's frightening. He's never been like this before. He called me all sorts of names, said I was interfering in his life and I should eff off back to Australia and his dad, and he didn't want to hear another word about the sodding baby ever again. He's washed his hands of her. As far as he's concerned, she's history. He told me to get out and as I was leaving he shouted, "You're all history."'

Jan usually managed a visit to Eddie every second afternoon and found him quieter than before and oddly disengaged, except when he became irritable over trivial things – the nursing, he claimed, wasn't up to standard and the hospital food was total crap. Today, as she crossed the hospital car park, she wondered how he would be after his appalling row with Sue. He had raised the bar with that one. From being merely tetchy and depressed he had completely lost his self-control, shouting, swearing, not caring a single jot what he said. And what was even more puzzling he had changed his mind about the baby. Why?

As she pushed through the swing door of the reception area, she saw a familiar figure advancing towards her.

'Mrs Hardy!'

It was Brian Hadfield, evidently on his way out.

'Inspector. How are you?'

'Never better, thank you. I've been in to see Eddie. Afraid he wasn't too pleased to see me, though.'

'Was it about the accident?' Jan asked innocently, knowing perfectly well it could be about nothing else.

'Yes, as a matter of fact. And now that I've bumped into you, perhaps we could have a word. Cup of tea in the cafeteria?'

Jan followed Hadfield down a corridor, through another pair of doors and into a bright, pleasant room with a dozen or so tables. Hadfield bustled over to the counter and came back with tea in two styrofoam cups.

'I must say,' he remarked, with that trademark smile playing ever pleasantly over his lips, 'Eddie's looking very much better, isn't he?'

'Yes, I think he is.'

'But he's not feeling better, that's the trouble. When he thinks about the future he's only looking on the pessimistic side. But that's a no-win policy, in my opinion.'

'So what brought you here to see him, Mr Hadfield?'

'I needed to get the signature witnessed on his statement. Not that the statement gets us very far.'

'What do you mean?'

'He really hasn't got anything to say. I mean, for instance, he won't confirm your allegation that the accident was brought about by a third vehicle overtaking and forcing both his and Mr Moorhouse's cars off the road.'

'Inspector Hadfield, it's not an allegation. It's the truth. And of course Eddie won't confirm it. He doesn't remember anything. He's got post-traumatic amnesia.'

Hadfield sipped his tea before slowly lowering his cup.

'Has he now?'

'Of course he has. If he could remember, don't you think he'd tell you?'

'I'm sure he would if there *was* another car, Mrs Hardy.'

Jan felt herself growing hot around the neck and face. How dare Hadfield cast doubt on the truth of her statement?

'I told you, there was. I'll repeat it until I'm blue in the face, if you like. And I've read in the press that you've put out a call for any witnesses who saw a four-by-four driving away. So why are you continuing to doubt this? I'm sure one of the other drivers must have noticed it passing them, the way it was being driven before it caught up with us.'

Hadfield shook his head.

'Not necessarily. I've questioned all of them. No dice, I'm afraid. If the car exists—'

'Don't go there again. I've *told* you it exists!'

Hadfield held up a finger. 'What I was hoping for was a witness further up the road who saw this vehicle driving away from the accident. It could have been parked up and only come onto the road after you drove by.'

Jan considered this for the first time.

'I see, yes. I didn't think of that. Following us, you mean.'

'Following you in a manner of speaking, yes.'

'But presuming it was following us on purpose, suppose it was trying to get to us to run us off the road deliberately.'

Hadfield frowned.

'You've lost me, Mrs Hardy. Who would want to do that?'

'A man called Harold Powell, he might. He had already threatened me at Cheltenham racecourse a few hours before the crash. *And* he drives a Range Rover.'

Hadfield looked startled and the smile left his lips for a moment. He reached for his notebook.

'I think you'd better tell me a bit more about this, Mrs Hardy.'

Hadfield listened carefully to the saga of Stonewall Farm and the death of Olwen Hardy, making a few entries in the notebook. When Jan had finished, he asked if she knew Harold Powell's address. He jotted it down and drained the tea from his cup.

'I wish you'd told me all this before, Mrs Hardy.'

'I couldn't tell you about Harold threatening me because for a long time the five or six hours before the crash were a complete blank. I couldn't even remember my own horse had won. I had to look at the video to convince myself it was true.'

Hadfield's smile returned.

'Well, it can happen in these cases,' he conceded. 'And you say that, since then, you've been receiving anonymous phone calls?'

'Yes. Two.'

'When exactly?'

She told him the date and times.

'And did whoever it was say anything, anything at all?'

'No. I kept asking who it was. Then I hung up.'

'How long before you hung up?'

Jan shrugged.

'Twenty, thirty seconds.'

'But you heard breathing?'

'I thought I did. I presume the object of the exercise was to freak me out.'

'That's a possibility. Some men get a sexual thrill

out of doing just that, you know – particularly to a good-looking woman like yourself.'

Hadfield's clumsy gallantry seemed grossly out of place. Ignoring it, Jan pressed on.

'So you are saying the phone calls had nothing to do with the accident.'

'I'm saying neither. They may have or they may not. It might just be a case of a wrong number. But I'll certainly look into it. In the meantime I'll enquire into Mr Powell's movements on the day of the accident, and I'll have a quiet word with Dyfed and Powys Constabulary about your mother-in-law's death. Don't worry, Mrs Hardy, we'll get to the bottom of this and if Harold Powell's behind any of it, we'll have him sooner or later.'

Going into Eddie's room a few minutes later, Jan found him staring morosely into space.

'Here, I've brought you some reading to improve your taste.'

She dropped the latest *Country Life* on his bed, then leaned over and kissed him. Eddie's head did not move and his lips were unresponsive and cold.

'Well, aren't you even going to say hi?'

'Hi.'

'Did your mum tell you about Russian Eagle?'

'Yes.'

'Is that all you're going to say?'

'What is there to say?'

'Look, Eddie, what's the matter? I need to know.

What's happened to that "larky lad" I used to love so much?'

'He was in a car crash, remember? Not that I can. All I know is I'm completely fucked up. I can't walk. I'm never going to be able to walk. And the police think I'm a fucking criminal.'

'That's such a load of crap. I've just seen Hadfield and he confirmed he's looking for the third car, the Range Rover that shoved us off the road. You know what? I think it might have been driven by our old friend, Harold Powell. In fact I'm convinced it was.'

'Who's that?'

'Harold Powell – you know, he threatened me at the racecourse, said I'd get what's coming to me.'

'Never heard of him,' Eddie replied in an even more truculent manner.

With a sigh, Jan flopped down on a chair beside the bed and changed tack.

'Never mind. It'll all come back eventually, I know it. And as for this rubbish about being paralysed, I saw Dr Matthews in the corridor just now – you remember, your doctor? He said, when you're fit to travel they'll see if they can get you into Stoke Mandeville, the spinal injuries rehab centre. They're brilliant down there, they work wonders.'

'They'll have to.'

Jan wanted to shake him.

'Look, I just wish you'd snap out of this, Eddie. We've all had enough of it. You're going to be fine. So just stay focused and keep that thought in the front of your pea brain.'

Eddie didn't even muster the faintest smile. Before he would have risen to the bait immediately with a swift riposte, now he just scowled.

'Your mum said you had a bit of a row,' she went on, trying to speak more gently. 'Is that why you're so miserable? Are you thinking about the baby in Australia? Is that it?'

'No,' said Eddie. 'That's not it. I'm thinking about spending my life in a wheelchair. My whole life in a wheelchair – in *prison*.'

9

It was a fine spring day, with the daffodils in full bloom and a bright blue sky, as Jan breathed, with relish, the crisp air. No matter that her horse had little chance in the race, there was something magical about Grand National day. Jan entered the course at long last, after being in heavy traffic for what seemed like an eternity. Not that Dec and Con minded at all as most of the women on Merseyside were dolled up in skimpy fashion dresses. Jan noticed, much to her amusement, the lads' eyes swivelling round like fruit machines at the delights passing by.

One of the first people Jan met was Bernie Sutcliffe, the owner of her only runner, Arctic Hay. The Birmingham scrap dealer made no concession to the countryside way of life and was resplendent in his shiny grey suit, camel-hair coat and flashy grey shoes.

''Ullo, Jan. What'd yow think orr chances orr?' Bernie asked excitedly. 'Shall I back 'im?'

'Hang on, Bernie, I've only just arrived myself. Let's go and see Arctic first, then you can walk the course with me.' Jan thought this would get Bernie back down and also settle her nerves, as well as killing a bit of time before the famous race.

'Bloody 'ell,' said Bernie as they approached Becher's Brook, 'I feel as sick as a dog. I didn't realize the fences were this big.'

Jan smiled at Bernie's discomfort. 'I know,' she said. 'And remember we'll be safely in the stands when the horses are careering over these fences at about thirty miles per hour.'

As they continued their walk, Jan poked the ground with one of Reg's old walking sticks, paying particular attention to the take-off and landing sides at each fence. After two days of continuous rain earlier in the week, the going was still soft.

'This'll be fine for Arctic,' Jan panted, 'and there's less chance of the faster horses having their own way. It'll definitely favour the better jumpers.'

'Is 'e a better jumper?'

'He's a careful, steady old lad, Bernie, but don't get counting your chickens.' After the shock of Becher's they rounded the Canal Turn, when Jan noticed Bernie's stride had shortened dramatically as they approached the next fence, Valentine's Brook. Bernie reached for the running rail like a punch-drunk boxer would reach for the ropes and peeled off one of his shoes.

Jan stifled a giggle. 'Isn't it wet enough for those crocs, Bernie?'

''Ere, yow taking the piss out of my shoes, Jan? I might 'ave bought 'em on the market, but they still cost me a 'undred and fifty oles. They're ruined and me feet are soaking. Look, even the colour's run out of me socks. Can't we get a sodding taxi back to the stands?'

Now Jan laughed out loud at the sight of Bernie's foot. 'Never mind,' she giggled, 'a couple of stiff whiskies in the owners' and trainers' will soon anaesthetize them.'

'I bloody 'ope so, Jan. I'm crippled.'

The buzz in the trainers' bar was electric, with everyone excited and nervous at the same time. Several of Jan's owners were already there, to add their support, they said, whilst A.D. was ensconced in a private box which he had hired for the whole meeting. He had phoned Jan on the way to the races and asked if she would join him for a drink before racing started. After a quick drink, Jan left Bernie with the rest of the gang and made her way through the thronging crowd in search of A.D.'s suite.

Standing beside her husband, Siobhan O'Hagan beamed a welcoming smile.

'Come in, Jan. It's great to see you. You look fantastic considering the accident.'

'You mean the crash or the fact that Eagle didn't make it here? I don't know which hurts the most,' Jan said ruefully.

A.D. gave Jan a peck on each cheek.

'Ah well, I remember someone in racing wrote a book once called *The Glorious Uncertainty*, which describes this game to a tee – you should read it. Now, what will you have?'

As the afternoon unfolded and the first three races were run, the big one approached. As the tension in the crowd was rapidly reaching a crescendo, Jan looked at her watch. It was time for her to make her way to the weighing room to collect the saddle from Finbar Howlett, her jockey. This time she had insisted Finbar's valet provide them with brand-new leathers and irons and a new girth and surcingle to keep the saddle securely in place. She wasn't taking any chances, but still she was still racked with nerves at every stage of the saddling process as she remembered the time that Russian Eagle's tack was sabotaged when Eddie rode him in the Foxhunters'.

'Come on, get a grip on yourself,' she chided. 'You've done this hundreds of times before. What's the difference today?'

In the tense period between the emergence of the forty runners onto the course, to parade in front of the stands, and the moment when the starter would press the lever to launch them hurtling towards the first fence, Jan knew her job was over for now. She could do no more for Arctic Hay. She scanned the crowd and realized the entire mass were seized by a collective nervousness with calls and bursts of anxious laughter breaking out from various sections of the packed stands. The bookmakers shouted last-minute prices from the rails and out on the course the horses were jinking and jogging round in a disorganized circle behind the starting gate. Some of the jockeys dismounted, others had their girths checked one last time. Finally, as everyone's emotional temperature crept up towards the danger zone, the starter called the field into line. It was time for the off.

Arctic Hay was Jan's first-ever runner in the Grand National, but in her eyes he covered himself in glory. True, he finished in last place and was at least two furlongs behind the winner, but twenty-six of the runners had fallen by the wayside and he hadn't. Jan, who'd never hoped for anything better, was delighted, though she was a little worried about Bernie, thinking his self-esteem might be punctured by coming last. Yet Bernie seemed as close to contentment as his nature would allow.

'I never thought I'd actually enjoy watching an 'orse of mine bringing up the rear. Now 'e knows 'is way round we can come back next time and win it.'

'Steady on, Bernie, don't get your hopes up too high. I love your horse too, but he's still more of a Land Rover than a Ferrari, you know. The old boy will be rising fourteen and I wouldn't want to risk him at that age.'

'Uh, we'll see about that,' muttered Bernie.

A.D. O'Hagan had asked Jan to rejoin him in his box for a drink after the big race. Some of the hospitality boxes at Aintree overlook the course in a perfect place to watch the battle to the winning line. With Russian Eagle out of action, A.D. had no National runner this year, but his party turned into a celebration anyway as one of his Irish-trained stars had taken the highly prestigious Aintree Hurdle with irresistible authority.

When Jan returned, the box was in uproar.

Dermot O'Hare, A.D.'s Irish trainer, spotted her first, and raised his glass of Guinness.

'How's me girl?' he called out.

'I don't know how your girl is, Dermot – ' Jan smiled sweetly – 'but I'm very well, thanks.'

Jimmy O'Driscoll, who was standing beside Dermot, had just been taking a swig from his glass. He snorted with laughter and came up with his face splattered with creamy froth.

'Give it up, Der, you're wasting your time,' he said loudly. 'I don't think the lady's interested.'

A.D. crossed the room, beckoning to a waiter with a tray of drinks. Jan took a glass of wine and he guided her to a quiet corner.

'Don't mind those two chancers, Jan,' he murmured. 'Congratulations on the performance of your horse, by the way. Now, I'm afraid I didn't ask you back here just for social reasons. I was wanting a little word. But first, how's Russian Eagle?'

'Still a bit sore, but he's improving.'

'That's grand. Well, what I wanted to say was I've another horse for you. He's a four-year-old gelding that we picked up privately in the winter. Very good-looking, well-bred type which I paid a good price for, probably a bit too much as it's turned out. I was expecting him to be in all the top novice hurdles. In fact, I liked him so much I was thinking he'd be the successor to the horse that won today. So far it's not working out too well.'

'Why, what's the problem?' asked Jan.

'He's impressive enough on the gallops when he's got friends and relations around him, but he's a disaster at the races. Fights the bridle, won't settle in a race, only wants to run like the blazes.'

'Still, it's a bonus he wants to run. Not all of them do.'

'I know, I know, but flat out – that's all this fellow wants to do. He's no brakes. Treats the jockey like a passenger. We've had three runs out of him and in the first he blazed away in front for a mile, ten, twenty lengths clear. In fact, Murty thought he was going to be carted all the way to Cashel Rock, but he'd galloped himself into the ground, done too much too soon and finished tailed off, so in his next two races we put a citation bridle on him. This, as I'm sure you know already, is one of the most severe bits available for anchoring uncontrollable, headstrong horses.'

'Really – a citation? He's that bad?'

A.D. nodded. 'He is, but the fact is, it's not really helped. It's stopping him all right, but he fights it like the devil and, as you know, that hurts. So now he's refusing to race at all and on top of that he's jibbing at the horsebox and is difficult to travel. I'd say he needs a change of scene and some sympathetic handling.'

'It sounds like the kind of challenge I relish and I shouldn't turn it down,' said Jan.

'OK, that's great. I'll make the arrangements.'

Back at Edge Farm on Sunday, Jan walked up to the house after evening stables. The day before a beautifully packaged bottle of champagne had arrived by special delivery, with a note saying, *Dear Jan, This is so that you can toast Arctic Hay's homecoming. Well done. Love, Tony.* Jan had been touched by his thoughtfulness and she agreed the horse thoroughly deserved to have a glass raised to him.

The house was unusually quiet. Sue Sullivan had left the day before in a hire car to visit her sister in Cornwall, while Megan and Matty had been despatched to spent the weekend with their grandparents. As she passed through the hall, Jan noticed the light on the answering machine was blinking and pressed the play button. 'Hello, Jan, it's Tony. I've got news about Eddie. Give me a ring when you get a moment, I'm at home.'

She dialled Tony's number.

'Jan, what a great run from Arctic Hay. You must be delighted.'

'Thanks, Tony, we all are. And now I've got just the thing to celebrate with. That was just so thoughtful of you. As a matter of fact, I'm just about to get it out of the fridge and take it down to the yard. But what's this about Eddie?'

'I was over at the hospital this morning and bumped into Frank Matthews, Eddie's consultant. You know that they've been uncertain how much of his problem is spinal and how much is down to the head injury? Well, now the scans have confirmed it. He does have a degree of spinal damage.'

'Oh God, Tony. How bad?'

'Not as bad as it sounds. There's been a certain amount of what they call spinal shock, which is indicated by the swelling and bleeding in tissue around where the spine has been put under stress. That generally goes away. However, there may, just may, at this stage be some underlying damage to the spinal cord itself which can't be properly assessed until the effects of spinal shock have subsided. Either way, Eddie will have some hard work to do in the rehabilitation unit when they transfer him to Stoke Mandeville.'

'God, that's awful,' Jan gasped. 'When are they moving him?'

'They'll take him over there by ambulance next week. Apparently, the sooner his therapy gets started the less danger there is of some long-term or irreversible disability. I understand Mrs Sullivan's going in for a chat with the team at Cheltenham on Monday, but she won't have heard about the latest results. I thought you both might like to know in advance.'

'Thanks, Tony. I really appreciate it. Eddie's mother will too. She's away for the weekend, but I'll tell her the minute she returns.'

As Jan carried a fistful of assorted glasses and the champagne down to the yard, she wondered why Tony had called her. Was it really just the act of a friend? Or was it to make sure she knew he still cared for her? But he had already done that with the bottle of bubbly. On the other hand, Tony knew perfectly well that Eddie's reappearance in her life had been the immediate reason why she had said no to a close relationship with himself. She seriously hoped the phone call about Eddie's medical condition was not a disguised form of gloating.

On Tuesday, almost three weeks after the Cleeve Hill accident, Eddie was taken to the National Spinal

Injuries Centre at Stoke Mandeville Hospital. The next day, Sue and Jan made the sixty-plus-mile drive to see how he had settled in.

They found him propped up in a room on his own, not looking very different from how he'd been at Cheltenham – bandaged, bedridden and suspicious.

'This place is full of people in wheelchairs. They haven't fitted me for one yet.'

'Eddie, you're not going to need one,' Jan said, doing her best to reassure him.

'Or if you do it'll only be temporary,' added Sue cautiously.

'A guy came in and gave me a speech on spinal shock and something else. Anterior cord syndrome, I think that's what he said. I still don't know what it is. Why can't they give it out in words of one syllable? It was too much like hard work trying to follow what he meant.'

'Oh, Edward, you must at least try,' said his mother, doing her best to coax him.

'Anyway, it was all medical jargon,' Eddie said darkly. 'I don't think they want me to know the real facts. And they definitely know more than they are telling, that's for sure.'

The conversation was haphazard as Eddie seemed reluctant to join in and preferred to watch the television. Channel Four was showing the first races of the Newmarket flat season, the Craven meeting, in which the second race was a fairly low-grade mile-and-a-quarter handicap. Jan normally didn't pay particular attention to the rival racing code, but during the race build-up she was captivated by the sight of a handsome four-year-old bay gelding with a white blaze snaking down his nose called Velvet Dynasty, a name she thought she'd seen somewhere recently, though she couldn't recall where. He was in a muck sweat, almost pulling his lad's arm off with sharp jerks of his head, but she could see what a nice short-backed, deep-chested horse he was. During the race, which was easily won by the well-prepared favourite, Jan scrutinized the horse's every move. Velvet Dynasty ran a stinker, continually changing his legs and windmilling his tail like an animal out of sorts. His young jockey was obviously having a nightmare ride, which he made worse by trying to switch his mount from the inside of the field to the outside before veering back inside again, as if he'd lost his steering as well as his head.

Jan was musing on what a nice chaser the horse might make if he took to the jumping game. It might make a man of him, she considered – given the right handling he could be all right.

Suddenly the sister breezed in to announce that in ten minutes it would be time for Eddie's physiotherapy and made it abundantly clear that she wanted his visitors to make themselves scarce.

'Eddie,' Jan said as she and Sue got up to go, 'I'm afraid I'm not going to be able to come over to see you quite as often as I did when you were in Cheltenham. But I promise I'll come whenever I can.'

'But I'll be here,' said Sue brightly, glancing quickly at Jan. 'I thought I might put myself in a guest house in Aylesbury so as to be close at hand. You know, I can bring in some bits and pieces every day.'

Eddie's grunted acknowledgement and sour face made Jan reflect that that the old cheeky smile, which had been his most endearing feature, hadn't once lit up his face since the accident.

'Are you really going to stay in a B and B?' Jan asked Sue as they settled in the car a few minutes later. 'He won't be coming out for weeks, I shouldn't think.'

'Well, dear, I've got to head back to Australia before too long.' Sue sighed. 'Edward's out of danger now, and Ron needs me too, you know. Of course, I want to see as much of Edward as I can before I go, so I think a B and B's the only option, don't you?'

It took an hour and a half to get back to Edge. Jan parked the Shogun and Sue jumped out to greet Megan and Matty, who had pelted out of the house at the sound of the approaching car. Jan stayed in the driving seat for a while, pondering. Eddie still had a huge corner to turn. How could she possibly help him from this distance, with Sue going home and a tightly staffed racing stable to be kept going? Admittedly, things would get a little better in a month's time, when the horses were out to grass for six weeks and the staff began taking their holidays. But, even then, there was still loads to do around Edge Farm without having to make the long journey to see Eddie.

Four days later Jan took two horses to Worcester, A.D. O'Hagan's Erin's Jet and Toby's black gelding, Nero's Friend. Bordering the river Severn, Worcester is one of the most accessible courses in England and, on a day like this, with just a few clouds flying high and white across the undiluted blue of the sky, Jan felt it was the perfect place to go racing.

She had high hopes for both her runners. Erin's Jet was returning after winning at the course the previous year and, while Toby's big black horse was a newcomer, she was sure he would appreciate Worcester's flat, galloping track.

The double she had envisaged did not come off. Erin's Jet found a couple too good for him and finished third, but Nero at least confirmed the promise Jan had seen when she'd recommended Toby Waller to lay out £35,000 at the Derby Sale in Ireland the previous year. He cantered to the start as if he felt he owned the place, and came back in a style that suggested he really did, jumping rhythmically and beating his field by six lengths.

After she'd sent Nero back to the stables on the far side of the course, Jan doubled back for the presentation of the prize. Toby's podgy cheeks were pink with excitement as he collected his trophy and he beamed with all the pride of an owner accepting the Cheltenham Gold Cup.

Afterwards he quickly made his excuses. 'Jan, I've got to shoot off. Got a meeting with some important clients. But that was a great moment. I could get really used to this.'

He kissed Jan enthusiastically on both cheeks and headed for the car park. Jan wandered back to the paddock, where she stood watching the runners in the next race as they circled.

'Jan, how very nice to see you,' a male voice called out.

She spun round and saw that Colonel Gilbert was heading towards her, accompanied by his daughter Virginia. The latter's grim face was looking every bit as sharp as a well-honed hatchet. *She must have swallowed the lemon from her gin and tonic,* Jan thought.

10

'Hello, Colonel! Virginia.'

Jan's response to the colonel's greeting was genuinely warm. Her acknowledgement of his daughter was a little cooler. Virginia's pale green dress under a matching jacket was clearly the expensive product of some couturier. The jacket had the exaggerated puffed-up shoulders that were in fashion and which Jan thought were particularly unsuited to Virginia's bony figure.

'Hello, Jan,' Virginia said, with equally muted enthusiasm. 'Busy as ever, I see.'

Jan had no time to think of a response to this remark, whatever it was supposed to mean, as Virginia immediately turned to her father.

'Daddy, I've got to shoot off. I've arranged to have a drink with Patrick Lamberhurst. I'll see you later.'

'Yes, fine,' Colonel Gilbert said good-humouredly. 'I'll stay here and have a dekko at the runners for the next.'

He watched his only daughter skitter off on her unsuitable high heels, and then turned back to Jan, who said, 'I saw your runner in the long-distance race,

Colonel. I would be surprised if he didn't improve a lot for the run.'

'Which is exactly what Ginnie's hoping. He's a lazy old sod at home. But that's a bloody good-looking chap *you* won with.'

'Yes, he's special, isn't he?'

'You bought him yourself?'

Jan laughed.

'Not exactly. I don't have that kind of spare cash. But I told Toby Waller if he didn't stump up I'd have his guts for garters.'

The colonel sighed, but his eyes were twinkling.

'You have a good eye and a great natural touch with a horse, Jan. Somehow I don't think my Ginnie has quite the same talent. She needs to work at it a bit harder, I suspect.'

Jan found herself blushing. The colonel was a bony old boy with plum-coloured cheeks and a pronounced limp, but he had charm and knew how to deliver a compliment. He was also, as Jan knew, a staunch friend who, despite her rivalry with his daughter, had supported Jan's training career from the first.

'How's my old friend Wolf?' he asked.

Most of the colonel's horses – he owned half a dozen at least – were with his daughter these days, but Wolf's Rock, which the colonel had bred himself on his small stud at Riscombe, had always been trained by Jan. With his sporadic breathing problems, Wolf had been lightly raced this season.

'He's ready for a run. I've got a two-mile chase at Hereford in my sights.'

'Good. Fax me over the details, would you? Now,

what's your total strength at Edge Farm these days? I remember last year you were aiming for thirty horses. Have you got there yet?'

'No, I'm still a few short. I nearly made it, though, until I lost some after the Gary West fiasco.'

'Oh yes, an unfortunate business that. Still, at least it means you'd be able to squeeze in another horse of mine, I hope. Do you remember I said I might send you another one or two?'

Jan took a quick look at the route Virginia had taken, worried that she might suddenly reappear.

'Oh, yes of course. But what about—? Well, what about Virginia?'

'Ginnie's got about as many as she can reasonably cope with at the moment. But a maiden aunt of mine finally gave up the ghost in her nursing home and left me a bit of dosh on the understanding I must put it to good use, so I thought of you. How about helping me spend it on a new horse?'

'Colonel, I'd absolutely love to. I'll be going to the July sale at Newmarket, which is for horses in training, so I can have a look at what's on offer there if you like.'

'Ideally I want a youngster that might develop into a top-class three-mile chaser, after having a bit of fun over hurdles along the way. I should think with your eye you might spot one that's been running on the flat, but really has a secret yen to go jumping.'

'If only I could read their minds that easily – ' Jan laughed – 'it would simplify things enormously. But I'm sure there'll be some decent candidates at Tatts.'

'That's good. So do your homework with the catalogue and, if you find anything suitable, let me have the details in advance. If I like the look of them, I'll give you the OK to bid. Shall we say up to £20,000?'

'Fine, but you know I will have to see the horse in person, so to speak, before I can recommend bidding.'

The colonel nodded.

'Naturally, Jan. I might even come to the sale myself. Four eyes can often be better than two in that situation.'

He turned towards the paddock and waved an arm in the direction of the horses, who were now being mounted.

'So, what do we think of this little lot?'

Driving back down the M5 with Declan in the lorry, Jan felt exhilarated by the colonel's request. Apart from the thrill of racing itself, there was nothing quite like the buzz from getting a new horse. Every one was a different challenge. In her eyes every one was a champion until proved otherwise.

When they pulled into the yard, Jan found a visitor waiting for her. Tim Farr was leaning against the bonnet of his car, smoking a cigarette. He dropped it like a scalded cat and quickly ground it out with his foot as the horsebox drew near.

'Hello, Mrs Hardy,' he said as she jumped down from the cab.

'Mr Farr.'

'Tim,' he corrected. 'Did you have a successful day?'

'Yes, quite satisfactory, thanks. I hope you've not

come to be a nuisance. I've still got work to do, you know.'

Jan jerked her thumb towards the horsebox as Dec was busy lowering the ramp. Erin's Jet and Nero's Friend were shifting around expectantly – she could hear them nicker. *They are thinking about the warm mash in their mangers,* she thought and smiled.

'I was just wondering if I could put something to you,' Farr continued, oblivious to Jan's frustration. 'It's about the accident on Cleeve Hill.'

'You're not still worrying at that old bone? I'd have thought it's stale news by now.'

'The thing is, I've been wondering if maybe it wasn't an accident at all.'

Jan spun round and stared at him.

'How do you mean? Of course it was.'

'I'm thinking of that four-by-four, the Range Rover or whatever it was the police have been looking for. Maybe the driver is more than a potential witness. Maybe it was involved in the incident, but they drove away unscathed. Maybe it *caused* the accident.'

'Ye-es?'

'Is that what happened?'

Jan shook her head.

'No go, I'm afraid. Those are not my words. You're doing the talking, not me.'

'All right, I'll continue my train of thought. I know I'm flying by the seat of my pants here, so to speak, but suppose we go one step further and say maybe the four-by-four, the Range Rover, caused the accident *deliberately*.'

'Hang on a minute. Where on earth could you get that idea from?'

'I was looking at the cuttings file – you know, on you, Edge Farm, and all that. There wasn't much except bits and pieces from the sports pages, though a great deal more from the period after you won the Irish National, and there's also a couple of reports on the trial of some former owners of yours – the Sharps? It seemed to me that they could still have a pretty powerful grudge against you since you gave evidence at their trial.'

Jan relaxed a little. Farr was on completely the wrong tack now, she realized, and she rather preferred it that way.

'It's not possible. The Sharps are all in prison,' she said.

'But they could get someone on the outside to harass you. To make threatening phone calls, follow your car, things like that?'

Christ! Did he know about the phone calls? Just who had Farr been talking to?

'Look, I appreciate your concern, but this is really nothing whatever to do with you. I think it's best we leave it to the police.'

'But it would help Eddie, wouldn't it, if the responsibility was deflected away from him?'

'Look, he *wasn't* responsible—'

'That's what I'm saying and maybe I can help prove it. If this other vehicle was driven by a person whose registration is unknown, cloned even, then he or she will be almost impossible to trace. But if it was driven by someone who actively wanted to harm you, then it's not going to be too difficult to draw up a list of suspects. Look, here's my card in case you think of anything.'

Jan's heart sank again. Talk of a list of suspects was ominous and Tim Farr sounded gripped by the idea of playing the sleuth.

'I don't see how you can help or why I should want you to help. I've already said the police are investigating the whole kit and caboodle. It's their job, or hadn't you heard that? And the last thing I want is bad publicity for the yard.'

Farr shrugged. 'Sometimes, Mrs Hardy, publicity is inevitable. The trick is to make sure it's the right kind of publicity, and that it's honest. Come on, surely you must be interested in the whole truth emerging. I'm certain the family of William Moorhouse is.'

Jan looked him in the eyes, glaring. Then she pointed to the crushed butt end which lay on the ground between them.

'I hope you're going to pick that up and take it away with you,' she said. 'By the way, please don't ever smoke in my yard again, it's far too dangerous.'

She turned and joined Declan, who had already led Erin's Jet to his stable.

The wayward horse that A.D. was entrusting to Jan arrived a week later from Ireland, via the Holyhead ferry. Morning Glory was a rich chestnut with a star on his forehead, not a big horse by any means, but with enough size to impress the eye.

'He looks fit,' said Jan as Roz led him from the

lorry. She noted with approval the broad, sloping shoulders, good feet and knees, and his well-rounded quarters. 'He's carrying his head a bit low, though, isn't he?'

'He's had a Mickey Finn,' said the grizzled lad who had driven the transporter, 'or we'd never have got him loaded. He usually kicks out like a maniac, you know, and it's odds on he'd have hurt himself if we hadn't doped him. That feller's as mad as the devil's dog.'

Jan looked closely into the horse's eyes and could see the effects of the tranquillizer ACP. Morning Glory was regarding her with a dull, uncurious gaze that was quite alien to any horse in a strange new environment. It would be impossible to make an accurate assessment of him until the tranquillizer had worn off completely. Jan decided to allot him a stable away from the other horses on the west side of the yard, where all the boxes were empty and where he could acclimatize gradually. It would not be until Morning Glory felt completely at home that she would expect him to take a full part in the stable's daily routine; only then would she find out the true scale of the task that A.D. had set her.

The next weekend was Easter, one of the busiest times of the year for a racing stables. Jan's yard was no exception as there were eleven National Hunt race meetings distributed between the Saturday and the Monday of the bank holiday weekend. These were very popular with owners, since the extra day off made it easier for *them* to see their horses run. Edge Farm was due to send out six runners, all with different owners – two on the Saturday and four on the Monday. In the middle of all this came the Children's Easter Parade at Chiselcombe.

Most of Good Friday, which is traditionally a day without racing, was devoted to creating Megan's and Matty's costumes. Megan's sudden desire to go to the parade on her pony dressed as Joan of Arc had to be swiftly quashed.

'I don't think animals are allowed in the rules, darling,' said Jan. 'And, anyway, some children might be nervous if you turned up for the parade on Monarch, and I'm sure some of the others would be jealous, which we should avoid. What about going as the Easter Bunny?'

'Yuk, no! That's *so* boring. If I can't have Monarch with me, I'm going to go as a great white shark. I'm going to be Jaws.'

Matty was equally resistant to the idea that he might be anything as easily constructed as an Easter egg. Instead he had to be an Egyptian mummy or he would be nothing.

Reminded of Megan's remark to her at the hospital, Jan burst into laughter.

'So you're not frightened of mummies any more? That's good.'

While Jan worked out the best way to wrap Matty from head to foot in crêpe bandages, Megan, helped by Annabel, created the top half of a great white. The nose and jaws, made of cardboard pointing upwards and fashioned like a helmet, fitted over Megan's head, but extended considerably higher. They were covered in fabric from an old umbrella and vividly painted with eyes, grinning mouth and sharp teeth. A dorsal fin, a tailored black bin bag, and a pair of rubber frogman's flippers completed the unlikely transformation.

'I'm rising out of the sea to grab my prey, so it doesn't matter if you can't see my tail fins properly,' Megan announced in a muffled voice, peering out through tiny holes drilled in the fish's lower jaw.

The parade was held, under an overcast sky, in the neighbouring village of Chiselcombe, and consisted of several circuits of the village green to the accompaniment of the local silver band and a lot of laughter. Then the judges conferred and the vicar handed out prizes at the war memorial. About half the children were dressed as Easter bunnies or eggs, while the other half represented a motley crew of cartoon characters, pop stars, robots and a sugar plum fairy. Jan stood in the centre of the green and agreed with Annabel that Megan and Matty were by far the best and most imaginative entrants.

Annabel laughed and pointed at the other mothers. 'They all think that about their little darlings, too, you know.'

Nevertheless Jan couldn't help being disappointed when the prizes went to a Michael Jackson lookalike and a Catwoman, with the sugar plum fairy getting a special mention. But the children did not seem to mind in the slightest and, as light rain began to fall, the silver band led them in a long, capering crocodile to the vicarage, where tea was laid on in a marquee.

For half an hour Jan chatted to fellow parents from the village school. She knew several of the mothers quite well, yet for some reason their conversation seemed unnaturally stilted, as if they were nervous of saying something offensive to Jan about the accident. At first she put this down to the difficulty some people have discussing the misfortunes of others, although several did eventually ask about Eddie, giving Jan the impression that news of their relationship had percolated more deeply into the local community than she had suspected. Jan also had the feeling that people were looking at her, discussing her even, and this became so uncomfortable and disturbing she suddenly decided it was time to leave. By now the rain had intensified and was drumming even more loudly on the marquee as Jan looked around for the children. Unexpectedly, Viv Taylor-Jones, the vicar's wife, a tall, youngish woman in a printed dress, bare legs hairier than Russian Eagle's and Jesus-creeper sandals, approached.

'Jan, look, this is a bit awkward. Do you think you could pop over to the house for a moment?' she asked in her clipped Oxford accent.

'Certainly. What for?'

'Something's come up, which the vicar and I feel you should know about.'

Unable to imagine what might have come up, Jan instructed the children to find their friends and play a while longer, before following Viv across the soggy lawn, and through French windows, into a large, sombre drawing room.

'This came last week. I think you should read it.'

Rain lashed the windows, and the wind moaned in the huge chimney above the unlit fireplace, as Viv handed Jan a sheet of paper. It was headed: PRESS

RELEASE. EDGE FARM – A STABLE IN CRISIS? With growing disbelief, Jan read on.

> The fatal road crash which involved the National Hunt trainer Mrs Jan Hardy of Edge Farm, Stanfield, and her close friend Eddie Sullivan, who occasionally rides her horses, has been the subject of widespread speculation in the tightly knit equestrian community of the Cotswolds. The accident happened after racing on Gold Cup Day at the Cheltenham National Hunt Festival, when two cars were involved in a serious accident on Cleeve Hill.
>
> The driver of one of the cars involved, Mr William Moorhouse, died at the scene. Mrs Hardy sustained face and head injuries, and was detained in hospital overnight. Sullivan was more seriously injured and is now under treatment at the National Spinal Injuries Centre at Stoke Mandeville Hospital. Sullivan was at the wheel of a two-seater sports car, which neighbours say he was often seen driving at speed around the Gloucestershire and Oxfordshire countryside. He had earlier in the afternoon been celebrating the victory of Mrs Hardy's horse Magic Maestro in the Cathcart Chase. The death of Mr Moorhouse, and the serious injury to Sullivan, has cast a blanket of gloom over Mrs Hardy's racing operation, typified by her horse Arctic Hay's poor showing in the Grand National last weekend, where he finished in last place.
>
> Sullivan's father Ron, the former wealthy property tycoon who now lives 'quietly' in Australia, said of his son's condition that it was 'typical of the boy. He's always enjoyed life to

> the full and that means he sometimes has to pay the price, doesn't it?' Release ends.

At the bottom was some small print, including a phone and a fax number.

> This press release is issued by the Cotswold News Agency as a service to the community. It may be freely used whole or in part by news or broadcasting organizations, parish magazines and any other outlets giving news and information about the Cotswolds.

Jan had finished reading, but continued to stare at the sheet of paper. It was beyond belief. What was this news agency trying to achieve? Nothing here was actually untrue, nothing was libellous, though the insinuation was monstrous – that Eddie had been drinking heavily before the accident, that he was a well-known hell-raiser, that she and Eddie were being gossiped about throughout the countryside, that her yard was 'in crisis'.

'This is filthy rubbish. How did you get it?' Jan asked.

Viv was nervously smoothing her straight hair with the long bony fingers of both hands. Her wide mouth briefly twisted into an embarrassed smile.

'I'm the editor of the parish magazine. It just came in the post,' the vicar's wife answered nervously.

'Does that mean it's been sent everywhere in the area, to all the parish magazines?'

'I guess it must have been, probably the community freesheets and the local radio stations, and the established papers too.'

'And what the hell *is* this Cotswold News Service?'

Viv shrugged.

'It must be new. I've never had anything from them before, and I've been doing the mag three years now.'

Jan scanned the text of the press release again.

'This is bloody *outrageous*. Who the hell do they think they are? Why are they doing this?'

She sprang to her feet and folded the paper.

'Can I keep it?'

'Of course.'

'I'm going to find out who's behind this, Viv, and I'm not going to let this rest until somebody's issued an apology.'

The rain had cleared by the time the Shogun turned off the road, so the ribbon of tarmac leading up to Edge Farm gleamed as a few fresh rays of sunshine penetrated the cloud. Arriving at the house, the children pounded up the stairs to their rooms and Jan went straight to the kitchen, where she set about making supper. As she worked the insinuating words of the press release came back to her mind again.

'It's unbelievable,' she told herself, the anger charging her body once more. 'It's absolutely bloody *unreal*.'

Jan's back was turned to the kitchen door as she filled a saucepan with water, raised the cover on the Aga and slapped the pan down on the hot ring. A few spilled drops fizzled and spat as they made contact with the heat, but above the noise she was aware of a click behind her from the latch of the kitchen door.

'Is that you Megan? Matty?' she called out. 'Supper'll be ready in fifteen minutes, OK?'

'No, I'm afraid you're talking to someone else.'

Jan spun round and her mouth fell open. A woman of about her own age, a complete stranger, was standing in the doorway.

'Who the hell are you?' demanded Jan. 'And how did you get in?'

'The door was off the latch,' said the woman. 'I just pushed and it opened. Am I speaking to Mrs Jan Hardy?'

'Yes, you are. And who in blazes are you?'

The woman was as white as a ghost and very agitated, but obviously determined. She took another step forward into the kitchen.

'My name is Rachel Moorhouse,' she said. 'I'm the wife of William Moorhouse.'

11

'Can I offer you anything? Tea, coffee maybe?' Jan asked stumblingly, unnerved by the woman's sudden appearance.

Rachel Moorhouse shook her head and continued walking into the room. She pulled out a chair and sat at the kitchen table, placing her handbag in front of her like a defensive wall. She was a sturdily built woman, wearing jeans and a loose blue shirt, with an unkempt head of wiry black hair.

'Look,' said Jan, almost at a loss for words. 'I'm terribly sorry about what happened, I—'

'Well, don't be. I didn't come here for your sympathy.'

'Then why *did* you come?'

Rachel dug deep into her large shoulder bag and came up with a packet of gum. She folded a piece in half and shoved it into her mouth, then began chewing it with grim determination.

'It's difficult to say, really. To actually see someone who was there when he died, I suppose. And to find out what I'm up against.'

'Up against?'

'The police say it wasn't his fault. He'd never left

his side of the road, not until he swerved to the left and hit the tree. He was avoiding an oncoming car, they said, in the middle of the road. Your boyfriend's car, as I understand it, yes?'

Jan shook her head.

'No, no. You've got it all wrong. It wasn't like that, it wasn't like that at all.'

Rachel sighed.

'Yes, of course. You would say that.'

'Look, if you really want to know how it happened—'

'No, no, please. Don't bother,' Rachel said, holding up her hand.

It was as if she was excusing Jan from a chore. She sat chewing noisily and there was an awkward pause. Rather than stand there like a nincompoop, Jan went back to preparing the supper, chopping an onion and then dropping the pieces into the frying pan sizzling on the hob. Rachel watched her stonily.

'You're a widow too, so I hear.'

'Yes. My husband died four years ago. It was a form of cancer.'

'But look at you now, with no problems at all.' Rachel chided in a monotonous voice. 'You're young, good-looking enough, and you've got a nice business. Train horses, don't you?'

Jan suppressed her annoyance at the woman's supposition that running Edge Farm was a complete doddle.

'Yes, that's right.'

'I've never had a career. Too late now. I'll be forty-eight next time. Forty-eight, and going nowhere.'

She exhaled, a shaky self-pitying sigh.

'Hey, come on,' broke in Jan, momentarily provoked. 'That's not old at all. And I don't think it's ever too late, anyway.'

'Huh.'

Jan scissored the rind off some rashers of bacon and chopped them ready for the pan.

'I expect you loved your husband,' Rachel remarked at last.

'Yes I did, and I'm sure you loved William too,' Jan risked, crossing in front of her to the fridge, where she rooted around for mushrooms.

'Me? Oh yes, I was besotted. Loved him to distraction.'

She watched Jan at work, almost suspiciously.

'But that was a long time ago, then it was him who got distracted.'

'Really? What do you mean?'

'Oh, the obvious. Younger flesh. Totty.'

It was not just the words, but the way she said them, that made Jan suddenly realize the truth about Rachel Moorhouse. The woman was not mourning or grieving. She was not even sad. She was angry – deeply, bitterly, corrosively angry.

There was a further pause, only filled with the noise of sizzling onions and the bacon Jan had just added, and the sound of her slicing mushrooms. Then Rachel spoke again. 'He shouldn't have been anywhere near Cheltenham that night, you know. He told me he was going to Cirencester to a funeral. Ha, ha! That's funny, when you think about it. He was a solicitor, you see. A lot of his business was tied up with nursing and retirement homes, so there was an endless supply of old biddies among his clients. They adored him – he had charm, you see, charm to spare for everyone except me. So he'd draw up their wills, that sort of thing, and when they died he said the least he could do was turn up at their funeral. It took me years to find out this was all a sham.'

'He was seeing another woman?'

'Women. Dozens, probably, for all I know. I've no idea how many or where he found them over the years. He was a world-class, Olympic gold-medal bastard, I do know that.'

Jan dropped the sliced mushrooms into the frying pan and stirred them into the bacon and onions.

'So you'd *think*,' said Rachel, 'that I'd be glad to be rid of him. Well you couldn't be more wrong there. He died leaving me completely in the lurch. Negative equity on the house, nothing in his bank account, investments disappeared, life insurance virtually worthless. His pension fund's the same. As for his bloody stamp collection – or rather, to be absolutely precise, British and Commonwealth covers – there were five books of them and he used to go on and on and *on* about how cannily he had bought them, and how they were worth a mint.'

'Weren't they?'

'I got eighty-five quid for the lot. I was told it was pretty standard, a child's collection. And to top that, the icing on the cake even, is that I've still got to look after Wendy.'

'Is that your daughter?'

Again, a bitter laugh.

'No, the kids are all right. Two teenagers. But Wendy lives with us. She's my blind mother-in-law.'

Suddenly Rachel pushed the chair back and stood up. She ran her fingers through her hair, pushing it behind her ears. She bent forward to pick up her bag from the floor, then moved towards the door.

'Well, I won't impose on you any longer. William's partner in the firm is being very helpful, I will say that for him. He probably feels guilty as hell because he knew all along that my husband was a total shit. So he's offered to represent me in the court case. It will ease his conscience, I expect.'

Jan's heart thumped a warning.

'Oh really? What court case?' she enquired, following her visitor out into the hall.

Rachel had hold of the front door. She turned and pointed her index finger at Jan.

'The court case where we sue *you* and your sodding *boyfriend* for damages. It was because you killed that swine between you that we can't meet the mortgage payments, the school fees, or the heating and light bills and frankly not even the bloody food we eat. And I'm telling you, Jan Hardy, I'm not going to let you get away with it.'

It was Rachel's parting shot as she gave a sharp pull on the door knob and let herself out, hurrying to her car in an unexpectedly businesslike manner, which gave the distinct impression of an assignment successfully achieved. Jan watched until she had gone and returned with a hollow pit in the middle of her stomach to the kitchen. The frying pan was sending up billows of black smoke as its contents burned to a crisp.

'Jesus,' she said, picking up the red-hot pan and hurling it into the sink. 'What a crap day.'

With four runners to send out on Easter Monday, Jan had little time to form an opinion about the Cotswold News Agency or the threat posed by Rachel Moorhouse and her solicitor friend. Yet both niggled at the back of her mind and, to make matters worse, she had a bad time at the races, which to others, Jan concluded, would seem to give substance to the horrible idea, enshrined in the press release, that her stable was struggling. Annabel had been at Chepstow, overseeing two lacklustre performances by horses that never looked threatening, and finished in midfield, while Jan was at Hereford, where both of the Edge Farm runners had the misfortune to fall, fortunately without damaging themselves.

After the last race Jan found Toby Waller and Johnny Carlton-Brown, her respective owners, in the members' restaurant, consoling themselves with an early supper and a bottle of Chablis. While JCB was at the bar getting her a drink, she tapped Toby's arm.

'Are you going straight back to London?'

'No, I'm staying the night in Malvern. We've a client living there who wants to get involved in the issue of junk bonds on Wall Street, the crazy fool. I've got to go tomorrow morning and try and talk him out of it.'

'You couldn't drive back via Edge, could you?

There's something I want to show you, and I need a chat anyway. Things have been happening and I'm rather worried.'

Toby lifted his glass and winked.

'More developments, eh? Righty ho, m'dear. Will do. I'll be with you by teatime.'

Despite her sense of gloom, not to mention impending doom, Jan giggled.

'Toby, sometimes you sound ridiculously like Bertie Wooster. I hope you're not driving yourself, by the way.'

'No, no. The bank's laid on a driver so I can work while we are on the road. I'm very much their favourite son at the moment.'

On the Tuesday morning Jan decided to drive over before lunch to see Eddie. It was a month since the accident and he had only made limited progress. The temporary inflammation resulting from the shock to his spine was subsiding, but he still felt weakness in both legs and found walking extremely difficult. If there was any underlying damage to his spine, it had not revealed itself.

The injury to his brain gave him even more trouble: he had recurring headaches which were severe and he was generally despondent and uncooperative. Memories of the weeks preceding the accident had been returning in short bursts, though he said he still knew nothing at all about the event itself, or of anything else that happened during the ten-day period before it.

Jan found Sue Sullivan sitting with her son, working

with intense concentration on a piece of embroidery, which she quickly put aside as Jan came into the room.

'I had to have something to occupy me,' she said. 'It's great therapy, as I keep telling Edward. I think he should try it.'

'No way,' Eddie said sharply. 'You won't catch me stitching pictures. I'm not a poof. That's women's work.'

They talked about the weekend's racing. Eddie had seen the results in the racing paper that was delivered to him each day and was highly critical of the jockey and his tactics at Hereford.

'I don't know why you employ that clown, Jan,' he grumbled. 'He rides too short, and I bet he pushed Flamenco too hard approaching the hurdles. When I rode him on the gallops, what he hated most was being forced. He doesn't like the rider dictating to him. As a matter of fact, I bet he fell in protest.'

The idea that the horse fell deliberately was completely absurd, but even so Jan knew there was something useful in what Eddie was saying. Good horses are generally difficult customers or, at least, have minds of their own. Understanding them is half the success of training and riding can be, more often than not, a question of firm diplomacy.

The fact that Eddie had a point did not make it any easier to put up with, however.

'Eddie, Finbar is a good jockey and you know it. You're just being obnoxious,' Jan said, 'and I do mean that in a caring way.'

'If you say so,' he said, with a pout and a shrug.

This short outburst from Eddie was not typical of

the whole visit. Jan stayed three-quarters of an hour, during which he was largely silent and uncommunicative, though at times he seemed to be possessed by an inner tension, which he showed by biting his lip and drumming his fingers on the counterpane. Jan became increasingly tense. She tried hard to remain good-humoured, but two or three times found herself speaking more sharply to Eddie than she had intended. When it was time to leave, she felt, if she was honest with herself, relieved.

Sue accompanied Jan back to the car park. She said she had been very comfortable in the bed and breakfast, but now it was time to go home.

'I've got a reservation on a flight back to Australia,' she said. 'The day after tomorrow. Poor Ron is in dire straits. Or maybe I should say diet straits. He's so bored with boiled eggs and tinned spaghetti that he's taken to eating out every night. It's costing him a fortune and it's terrible for his cholesterol – he just loves rich sauces.'

Privately Jan thought: *How pathetic is that? A man's wife has to fly halfway around the world to save him from having too many restaurant meals? Excuse me while I throw up!*

Jan would never dream of saying this to Sue. So instead she asked her if she was worried about leaving Eddie behind.

'Yes, of course I am. He's changed, Jan. I mean, as his mother I can still see he's the same person inside. Of course, I have the advantage of remembering him as a little boy who had tantrums when he couldn't get his own way, but there's no excuse for that in a grown-up, though we mustn't forget what he's been through and still is going through. He'll get over it, I'm sure, with our help.'

Standing beside Jan's car, Sue kissed her on both cheeks.

'Jan, I thank the good Lord Edward's got you. I know you'll always be there for him. If I didn't, I would be rather afraid. He's so down about his prospects. He won't talk about little Alice or about the future in any shape or form. He hates the hospital and he's terribly rude to everybody who's there when they are being so kind to him. He won't even discuss what he's going to do when he leaves. It's like a closed book.'

Sue shook her head.

'So you will give him somewhere to live and look after him when he comes out, won't you, dear? You wouldn't leave him to cope on his own, would you?'

'Of course not, Sue,' Jan replied fearfully. 'I'd never do that, not if I thought for one minute he couldn't manage.'

'He can't. He really can't, Jan. More than anything, I want to see Edward settled in life and I am looking to you, you know that, don't you?'

Ten minutes later, as she turned on to the A40 just east of Oxford, Jan was still thinking about Sue's parting remarks – they came across as a mother's protective feelings, which Jan, being a mother herself, knew were perfectly natural, inevitable even. But at the same time they were infuriating. Sue actually thought Jan would marry Eddie – that was what she was getting at – just because he might struggle to survive on his own, as his father was struggling now out in Australia. But what about Jan's own happiness and that of her children? And what about Edge Farm and all the people who depended on its success?

Jan was beginning to appreciate in her heart that these things were more important to her than ministering to Eddie Sullivan and his existential problems – if that was the right word for them.

Toby arrived in his firm's chauffeur-driven car promptly, as promised, at four o'clock. He found Jan working on race entries in her office.

'So, how did you get on with the junk bonds?' she asked.

Toby wafted a hand in the air.

'Piece of cake. I told him they're only for high-rollers, he'd be putting his alimony payments at risk and showed him a safer alternative. He folded like a concertina.'

'It's the kind of thing A.D. O'Hagan's into, isn't it – junk bonds?'

'Exactly. He's a high-roller. But *he* can afford to get it wrong occasionally. Now, what was it you wanted to talk about?'

As Toby sat down Jan began in reverse order with the visit of Rachel Moorhouse, giving a detailed rundown of the previous day's conversation in her kitchen. Toby listened attentively.

'Well, it's rather as I feared,' he said when she had finished. 'Only maybe it's worse. This woman doesn't just think she may be entitled to compensation. She's desperate for it.'

'At first I was only thinking of her as a victim,' said Jan. 'I mean, that's how she played it. But then, at the end, she just turned on me, you know? Came right out and threatened me with this legal action. I couldn't believe it.'

Toby scratched his head and considered.

'It's rather odd behaviour, I must say. And I'm not sure if it does her case any good, if she's seen to be harassing you in any way.'

'OK, fine, but Rachel Moorhouse was only the half of it. Look at this, Toby.'

Jan handed across the press release, issued by the self-proclaimed Cotswold News Agency. Toby fished a pair of half-moon glasses from his breast pocket and read it through, pursing his lips, then frowning as he came to the end.

'Where did you get this?'

'The vicar's wife gave it to me, believe it or not, and she said more than likely it's gone to all the other parish magazines, and everywhere else dealing in local news.'

'But this is a gossip-column story, stuffed with innuendo, though nothing you could actually nail as a lie, or libel. *A parish magazine*? That's unlikely in the extreme. This is not the sort of thing to put alongside the vicar's rehash of his Sunday sermon, or reports from the bring-and-buy sale.'

'But that's what Viv Taylor-Jones does. She runs the parish mag.'

'Well, it's very curious.'

He thought for a moment, pinching his bulbous nose between finger and thumb.

'I rather suspect skulduggery, Jan.'

He waved the paper in the air.

'This is the equivalent of a poison-pen letter. I think someone's trying to blacken your name and Eddie's, it's as simple as that. May I keep it? I'll do a photocopy and send it back, if you like. I'll see if I can find out who these people are, and if what they're doing is legal.'

'Could it be Rachel Moorhouse, do you think? Or Harold Powell?'

'I have no idea, but maybe. It might be possible to make a complaint to the police, though I don't know if that's advisable because it would just give the story more legs, if you see what I mean. It may just be better to let the thing run out of steam by itself.'

'But will it?'

Toby shrugged.

'If it's just a passing interest of some journalist scraping the gossip off his shoe, it might. On the other hand, if it's some sort of vendetta against you and/or Eddie, it probably won't.'

'What about the threat of legal action by the Moorhouse woman against *me*? Surely that's a vendetta!'

'I don't know. She's obviously a bitter woman, she has reason to be, and who can blame her? But the threat does need to be taken seriously if, as seems to be the case, she's obtained good legal advice. We shall have to do the same. But remember, the threat of legal action is one thing. Actually bringing an action is something else.'

'But she seems to think she can get *me*, not just Eddie. And you said I was in the clear.'

'I meant with the police. I really don't know how it would play in a civil case. I don't know if they've got a case or just a prayer. I'll look into it and let you know. You just get on with the job of training your horses and leave the worrying to your Uncle Toby.'

'But I can't help worrying. I had that journalist Tim Farr here the other night. I thought he was fantasizing because he said he had a theory that the accident on Cleeve Hill wasn't an accident after all, and that the driver of the Range Rover was deliberately trying to run us off the road. But I must say I'm more concerned now if everything I've been telling you ties in.'

'Well, Tim Farr's theory can't tie in with Rachel Moorhouse, since she only fits into the equation as a *result* of the accident. I suppose it could point to Harold Powell. You did say he drove a Range Rover, didn't you?'

He stood up.

'Well, in my opinion, it's useless to speculate too much. We must wait till we've got some more facts. Now, Jan, I think I've just about got time to pop down and pay a visit to my three heroes in the yard.'

Determined to follow Toby's advice, Jan concentrated on the horses for the next few days. High amongst her priorities was the progress of A.D. O'Hagan's Morning

Glory, or MG as he was now known in the yard. She had let him get over the tranquillizer, and had spent as much time as she could with him, to enable them both to get used to one another's idiosyncrasies. Then she took him out on his own for some walking exercise along the quiet lanes surrounding Edge Farm, talking to him to reassure him. Each time MG got anxious Jan drew to a halt and patted him on the neck, encouraging him to pick grass from the banks. When she felt the horse relax she would walk on, and every time the horse 'boiled up' she repeated the process.

It was not until ten days later that Jan decided to give Morning Glory a canter. She was in the saddle, riding full jerk, as the horses left the yard that morning and walked in an orderly file up the track towards the gallop. Jan could feel MG's muscles begin to tighten, then his whole body stiffened as his head came higher.

'Christ, he's strong,' Jan called to Annabel as the horse made a loud snorting noise from his nostrils. Jan felt a huge surge of electricity run through MG's body as he fly jumped into the air, bounding forward like a crazed kangaroo. He veered to the left of the two horses in front of him, colliding with Roz on Arrow Star, then he was gone, accelerating like a Ferrari past the rest of the string. Jan shortened her reins, but with the bit firmly clenched between his teeth Morning Glory took not a blind bit of notice.

'Hang on, Jan, hang on.' Bel's voice could be heard in the distance. As the horse careered towards the gallop, Jan knew she was losing the battle. *We'll be safe when we get to the grass*, she thought. *He'll have run himself out by the time he reaches the top*. But MG had other ideas and a few seconds later he was bearing down on the railed fence which separated the gallop from the field next door.

'Shit,' Jan shouted as she realized she was about to find out what kind of jumper her new horse really was.

12

Morning Glory left the ground outrageously early. Jan felt he would certainly smash into the fence and launch her like a wayward missile, somersaulting over his ears. Instead he blasted off, tucking his forelegs tight up under his body, and threw himself to the other side of the fence in a beautiful arc, landing and resuming his gallop in one movement. It was a perfect exhibition of the art of hurdling.

The field where they landed was flat for about two hundred yards then rose steeply, which immediately took the fire out of the horse. As Jan steered him in a series of ever-decreasing circles, she was at last able to take control, slowly bringing him to a standstill. But the horse was still keyed up, his ears pricked to catch every nuance of sound in this strange new field.

'Christ, MG,' said Jan, patting his neck to calm him. 'You're quite something, you mad bastard.'

The horse snorted as if he understood and took displeasure in the comment, the vapour streaming from his nostrils in the cool morning air.

'Are you all right, Jan?' Bel called when she and the rest of the string reached the top of the gallop.

'Jesus, Mrs H, I was bricking it and I was only

watching,' shouted Roz. 'Are there any lumps in wind?'

'I'm not sure,' Jan gasped. 'I'll let you know when I get home.' She was blowing hard, her face as bright a Belisha beacon.

Later that morning Jan and Annabel were discussing Morning Glory's escapade and deciding what their plan of action should be.

'What made him charge off?' Bel asked.

'I'm not sure. I could feel his whole body start to tense the minute he set foot on the track,' replied Jan. 'And his head got higher and higher. I was talking to him, patting his neck the whole time, then he just exploded. It was bloody hairy, I can tell you. No brakes, no steering. I tried pulling the bit through his mouth from left to right, but it had no effect. I knew I was losing the fight well before we reached the gallop, so I decided to sit still until he ran out of steam. I've seen people jump off runaways, but I haven't the bottle to do that. I would sooner take my chances and stay on board. Mind you, I never expected him to jump that post-and-rail fence like he did; it must be at least four foot high. It was amazing, terrifying but amazing. If he jumps like that on the track he'll make a great chaser.'

They were a fortnight away from winding the stable down for the summer, when the horses would then be turned out into the fields to eat grass and grow fat in peace. It was their annual rest from the routine of stable life, and the development of the youngsters during that time was incredible.

Jan decided not to turn Morning Glory out with the others. Instead she would go on quietly working with him.

'I thought we'd take a few steps back and just walk him. Then every three or four days I can take him into the pony paddock and pop him over some of Megan's jumps. Hopefully the variety will keep him interested in life.'

'What about his tack?'

'I'll try a ring bit first, then a snaffle and hopefully, one day, we can move on to a nylon bit.'

'But they used a citation in Ireland, didn't they?'

Jan knew that a citation bridle would stop a runaway train, but the action of the bit inside the horse's mouth, which was to prise it open when the reins were pulled, was quite harsh and brought its own problems.

'Yes,' she agreed, 'I know they did and you've seen his mouth. Those big sores on the inside of the cheeks just add to his difficulties. The citation's only a last resort, if all else fails.'

Jan had put a call through to A.D. O'Hagan and, later that evening, he phoned back.

'He carted me good and proper into the next field, A.D., and I have to say he jumped the fence in between brilliantly. I had no choice. He stood off and sailed over as if he had been doing it all his life. If I hadn't been so petrified, I'd have cheered.'

'Would you say he's a fast horse, Jan?'

'Oh yes, he's fast all right. But I think he has a problem with other horses being alongside him. If we can cure him of that, we might have a hell of a racehorse.'

'Good. Well, I hope to see him out over hurdles in the autumn. I'm looking to recoup some of the punts I laid out to buy him, you know.'

'We'll have to wait and see if he's going to be ready.'

A.D. laughed. 'He'll be ready. I'm confident if anyone can get him sorted, you can.'

'I suppose,' Jan admitted warily, knowing it would not be a piece of cake.

'Keep up the good work. 'Bye.'

Toby called Jan from London a week after she had first shown him the press release.

'Right, I've got some information, but nothing positive yet.'

'And?'

'As you know, the press release provides no actual info, but it does gives a phone and a fax number. Unfortunately the phone isn't being answered, but it's a live number and the fax is receiving too. I've put a message on it asking them to contact me, but nothing's come back yet.'

'Do you think the numbers were just made up?'

'No, because I've found out they both belong to the same address.'

'How did you do that?'

'I talked to our friend Sandy Wilson.'

Sandy was a retired policeman and a member of a syndicate who had a horse with Jan.

Toby went on: 'Do you know what a reverse telephone directory is?'

'Not a clue.'

'It finds the names and addresses attached to every telephone number in the country. It's a restricted resource, not available to the general public, but of course the police find it very useful.'

'And?'

'Sandy got a friend to run these numbers through it and guess what? They both belong to the same subscriber in Evesham. It's in North Street.'

Jan wrote the address down. Evesham was only twenty minutes' drive away.

'Is there a name?'

'Strangway, initials G.S. That's it.'

'Look, Toby, leave that with me. I'll see if I can find out a bit more from this end. There's a limit to what you can do in London. And thanks. I can't tell you how grateful I am. Now, what about the business of Mrs Moorhouse?'

'It's rather complicated. The insurers, particularly Moorhouse's own vehicle insurers, are bound to become involved, and if it turns out Eddie had none, there's an industry scheme to cover victims of uninsured drivers. But the question of additional compensation may come on top of that. It would of course be in Mrs Moorhouse's interest to see a criminal conviction because she would then be able to prove liability; on top of that she could apply to the Criminal Injuries Compensation Board.'

'So it depends on what the police decide to do. Is that what you're saying?'

'Exactly.'

After Jan had hung up, she delved in her bag for Tim Farr's business card. She found it and dialled his number.

'Mrs Hardy,' cried Farr with welcoming gusto. 'How nice to hear from you.'

'I'm ringing you purely because I am hoping you can give me some information. I hope you don't mind.'

'Why should I mind? Information is my business.'

'Good. So tell me, is there such an outfit as the Cotswold News Agency?'

'The Cotswold News Agency? No. If there was, I'd definitely know about it. It doesn't exist.'

'Is there any agency covering this area, possibly located in Evesham?'

Farr thought for a moment.

'There's a local paper. But no news bureau. I'd say the area was too small to support such an operation.'

'Have you ever heard of any such agency or bureau, or whatever you want to call it, operating for the benefit of parish magazines, community news-sheets, things like that?'

Again there was a pause.

'No, in fact I think the idea's absurd,' he said. 'Outlets like parish mags don't pay for their copy. They haven't got the money, or even the desire, to subscribe to any kind of news agency. It just wouldn't happen, Mrs Hardy. Would you mind telling me what this is about?'

'Sorry, Mr Farr. I can't, not at the moment. Maybe at some point in the future I will enlighten you. 'Bye for now.'

The next day, with no runners to take to the races, Jan drove to the market town of Evesham, determined to discover who was trying to blacken her name with their bogus agency. North Street was a minor residential road, and the address was an old flat-fronted terraced cottage, opening directly onto the pavement. The place didn't look as if it had received any maintenance in living memory. The paint on the door and window frames was flaking off and the single ground-floor window was covered in grime. A lace curtain, brown with dirt, prevented any view of the interior. It looked an unlikely address for a thriving media business.

A stooped, skinny man in his fifties answered her long blast on the doorbell. He had thin grey hair combed over a mostly bald pate, and wore a baggy woollen cardigan.

'Mr Strangway?'

'Yes?'

'Morning. My name's Jan Hardy.'

She looked him directly in the eyes, but saw no sign that the name meant anything.

'Yes? How can I help?'

'Could I discuss a professional matter with you?'

Strangway stepped aside and ushered Jan into the house.

'Please, go through into the sitting room. It's on your right.'

The room was gloomy and unkempt, like its occupier. On the mantelpiece a smouldering cigarette was balanced on the rim of an ashtray. Next to it a glass-fronted mahogany case contained a dramatic little tableau – a stuffed kestrel seizing a vole in its talons. Jan looked around. Other cases were distributed around the room, each displaying stuffed birds, animals or fish. She saw a fox, a large brown trout, a pair of budgerigars and what looked like a domestic cat.

Strangway shuffled in behind her, his breath wheezing. Reclaiming his cigarette, he took a long drag.

'So, Mrs Hardy, how can I help you?' He exhaled and let out a brief bronchial cough. 'It is *Mrs* Hardy? I like to be correct, you know.'

'Yes, Mrs,' confirmed Jan,

'So, is it about a two-legged or a four-legged friend? Or maybe you're an angler bringing me a prize fish?'

'I'm sorry?'

'To preserve.'

Jan glanced again at the display cases all around them.

'I'm sorry . . . I don't understand.'

'You said it was a professional matter.'

Then it dawned on her.

'You're not . . .? You don't . . .?'

'Yes, that's right. Come with me, I'll show you around.'

Strangway beckoned to her as he went back to the hall. He led the way through the kitchen and out into a narrow, uncultivated garden, at the end of which was a large shed. He released the padlock on the door and showed her in.

'This, you might say, is the nerve centre of the operation,' he announced proudly, 'which I rather grandly call my studio.'

Under the shed window was a scrubbed wooden table, harshly illuminated by a bright overhanging spotlight. On it was the crucified corpse of a large white rabbit, with its body spread open from belly to throat, surrounded by an array of scalpels, clamps and syringes. Jars of chemicals stood on a rack to one side.

Jan put her hand to her mouth, suddenly feeling nauseous. The smell of formaldehyde was overpowering.

'Could we go outside, please?' she asked weakly.

Back in the garden, Strangway was looking quizzical. He dropped his cigarette and ground it out.

'So what is it you wish me to give immortality to? As a matter of fact I'm very busy at the moment, but I expect I can fit another job in, as long as it's not a rhino.'

His laugh turned into a fit of coughing.

Jan waited for this to subside before she continued. 'Mr Strangway, I'm sorry to disappoint you, but it wasn't taxidermy that brought me here.'

She handed him the paper issued by the 'Cotswold News Agency'. He read it through, then looked up bemused.

'Oh, you train horses, do you? It's not something I follow, the turf, so you'll excuse me for not recognizing you.'

'That's quite all right.'

Strangway pointed to the paper.

'I can see this is about you, but I don't understand what it has to do with me. I don't think we've met before – or have we?'

Jan shook her head.

'I don't think so, Mr Strangway. But look at the phone and fax numbers given there.'

He studied the page once more.

'Oh yes! How odd. They're my numbers!' he said in amazement.

She was sure he was genuinely surprised.

'I can only think,' he went on, 'that it's some misprint, a typographical error perhaps.'

Jan shook her head.

'No, it can't be. Look, both your lines are given. We tried phoning, but didn't get a reply, so we sent a fax . . .'

Strangway slapped his brow.

'Oh yes, the fax! I chucked it. Just thought it was a wrong number. It was from a Mr Waller, if I remember right.'

He patted the pockets of his cardigan and pulled out a packet of cigarettes.

'Anyway, I wasn't here when it arrived. I've been away in Germany, working for a private collector. He'd got a tiger he wanted preserving. A very demanding job, that.'

'And you live alone?'

'Yes, alone,' said Strangway, lighting up. 'It's a kind of lonely job, mine.'

He shut and repadlocked the door of his shed and held out an arm to indicate a move back to the house.

'So how on earth did my numbers come to be on this piece of paper? I can assure you this Cotswold News Agency is completely unknown to me.'

'Me too, Mr Strangway. I'm trying to find out who they are, but they seem to be rather elusive.'

Later, outside the office at Edge Farm, Annabel's mouth hung open as Jan related the story of her visit to Evesham.

'You should've seen the place, Bel. Honestly, I've never seen anything like it. There were cases of stuffed animals everywhere, birds, fish . . . And when he showed me into his shed, known as the studio, I bloody nearly threw up.'

Annabel giggled.

'Thank God you didn't. There's nothing more humiliating.'

At that moment a thought hit Jan.

'Just a minute, Bel.'

She darted into the office and Annabel followed to find her boss leafing feverishly through the 'T' section of Yellow Pages.

'Takeaway Food . . . Tank Cleaning . . . Tattooists . . . here we are, Taxidermists.'

She ran her finger down the short list of names.

'Here he is! "G.S. Strangway. Taxidermal services

by international practitioner" – don't laugh, he told me he'd been working in Germany – "Preservation and restoration carried out. All species considered. Evesham." Then it gives the phone and the fax number.'

'Jan,' Annabel said deliberately, 'are you thinking what I'm thinking?'

'Well, it's obviously no accident that Strangway's numbers were in that poisonous press release. By the fact that the numbers correspond. The question is, why?'

'I'll tell you what I think,' interrupted Annabel, 'it's clear they got the numbers from there.' She was pointing to the volume of Yellow Pages on the desk. 'And I don't believe Strangway had anything to do with it, beyond innocently placing the advert for his business.'

'But I still don't see why they used him.'

'I think they knew you'd try phoning the number, Jan. They were sending you a message.'

'Get stuffed you mean?'

'Don't, it's not funny. It all sounds too like that scene from *Psycho* – you know, in Norman Bates's office?'

'Oh my God, Bel! I never thought of that. "A man should have a hobby"!'

'Yes, that's it, Jan. Can you think of anything else in the film that fits? Maybe we can get a handle on the villain here, if there is one.'

Jan was musing, trying to remember the plot of a film she hadn't seen for years.

'A woman travelling alone, murdered in the shower by a motel guy who thinks he's his own mother . . . I don't think I know anyone like that, as a matter of fact.'

Suddenly Annabel gasped.

'Oh shit, Jan. I've just had a thought. A very, very nasty thought. Who played the woman?'

Jan clicked her fingers, trying to remember the name and getting it at just the moment Annabel herself pronounced it.

'JANET Leigh!' they both said simultaneously.

Twice Jan had left messages at Cheltenham police station for DI Hadfield. Now at last, after a fortnight, he returned her call.

'It's about time, Inspector Hadfield,' she said tartly. 'I've been trying to reach you for at least two weeks.'

'I'm sorry Mrs Hardy, but I've been on holiday. Didn't the office tell you? South Africa, actually.'

'No, they didn't.'

'I must say, it's been the trip of a lifetime. Me and my wife. Wildlife safari for a week, then the beach near Cape Town. Fantastic. Saw the lot, lions, elephants, zebra, wildebeest. I've got some incredible snaps . . .'

He paused expectantly, as if anticipating that Jan would suggest she pop round to view the photographs.

'I'm glad it was a good holiday, Inspector,' Jan continued, ignoring the silent invitation. 'But I didn't exactly phone you to get a stripe-by-stripe account of the zebras.'

'Oh, right, of course you didn't . . . so what can I do for you?'

'Well, I faxed you a poxy and damning press release

purporting to come from an outfit called the Cotswold News Agency. I wanted to know what you thought. Have you seen it yet?'

'No, er . . . I just got back today. It'll be in my in tray, no doubt.'

'Well it's already been circulated round the parishes in this area, community newsletters and that sort of thing. I see it as a poison-pen letter. But no one's heard of this Cotswold News Agency and the press release itself's completely unprofessional, badly put together. It seems it was just sent to spread nasty gossip, implying for instance that my stable is in crisis, and that Eddie was to blame for the crash.'

'I see. Does it identify itself?'

'Well, it's unsigned, but the phone numbers are those of a taxidermist in Evesham, would you believe?'

'A what?'

'Taxidermist. We reckon these people, whoever they are, want to send me a message of some kind – quite a nasty message, actually.'

'I see. Look, I'll go through my in tray and find it. I'll phone you back immediately.'

But Hadfield didn't phone back immediately and, as the evening wore on, Jan thought to herself he'd probably gone home to stick his safari photos into the family album. She decided to call him again in the morning and give him a piece of her mind.

Just after eleven, Jan was getting into the shower as usual, when she heard the phone ringing. She turned off the tap, quickly wrapped herself in a towel and padded through to the bedroom.

'Hello.'

The voice was muffled, like someone with a heavy cold.

'Hello, Jan. Or should I call you Janet?'

'Who is this?'

'Oh, a friend. Have you been in the shower, Janet?'

Jan shuddered and nearly dropped the phone.

'What?' she managed. 'What did you say? *What* did you bloody say, you bastard?'

But the line was already dead.

Jan ran downstairs, first bringing in the dogs, then after making sure with feverish, trembling fingers that every door and window was securely locked, she dialled 999. The squad car was with her in nine minutes and a sympathetic uniformed sergeant heard her out, nodding his head like a priest hearing a confession.

'Well, Mrs Hardy, I can appreciate this must have been an incident of some concern to you. You say you've had anonymous calls before?'

'Only twice, and no one said anything then either. But this was far worse. He knew I'd been in the *shower*, for God's sake.'

Jan did not mention the *Psycho* connection. Looking at the broad country face of the policeman, she did not think it would play very well with him, and she didn't want to get into convoluted explanations about Evesham and the poisonous press release. Not until she could talk to Hadfield at least.

When the sergeant completed taking his notes, he snapped shut his pocketbook and pushed it back into his breast pocket.

'Mrs Hardy, most of these calls come from lonely, repressed men who need an outlet for their fantasies. They generally come to nothing and stop quite soon. But some are more obsessive, and we do have to consider every possibility. Is there anyone else on the premises apart from yourself? Your staff maybe?'

'No, they're all living out at the moment. There's only the children.'

'OK, I'll arrange to have a car call round throughout the night, and then with your permission we might come back and install a recording device in the morning so we can monitor any more calls of this nature. But I'll have to talk to my inspector about that.'

'That's not Inspector Hadfield, by any chance?'

The sergeant clearly knew who she was talking about, but he shook his head.

'No, Mrs Hardy. He's CID. They may well get involved at some point, but for the moment it's Uniform you'll be dealing with.'

Knowing that there were two burly members of the Gloucestershire Constabulary keeping an eye on the place gave Jan the confidence to go to sleep that night. It was not a long-term solution, but for now it was better than a sleeping pill.

13

With surprising efficiency, Gloucestershire Police installed a device for automatically recording the telephone calls made to Edge Farm, as well as providing an emergency number for Jan. For several weeks neither was needed because there were no more anonymous callers and no unexpected visitors, so Jan was beginning to relax. They were coming up to the time of year, during June and July, when the horses would be turned out to grass and their empty boxes would be thoroughly cleaned by the skeleton staff and Gerry Harris, Jan's builder and handyman. Gerry had come to talk about the job with Jan, to discuss steam-cleaning and disinfecting the boxes and what equipment he would need. The two of them then toured the yard to note any repairs and repainting that had to be done.

As they came to Morning Glory's box, the horse was standing at the back and made no attempt to come and put his head over the half door as most did.

'He's staying in the yard all summer, is he, Jan?'

'Yes. It's a shame really, he's missing out on his summer break, but I'm having to work with him every day.'

Gerry looked serious.

'That won't be no hardship to him, I reckon.'

Jan smiled. Gerry's devotion to her was never expressed, except through oblique compliments like this.

'I bet if you asked him,' she said, 'I'm sure he'd say he'd prefer a bellyful of grass. But he's still as nervous and jumpy as a Jack-in-a-box, so I've got to persevere with him. Mr O'Hagan sees him as his star novice hurdler next season, but I'll have to get his head right first.'

'If anyone can do it, I'm sure you can.'

'Oh, Gerry, that's really kind of you to say that.'

One by one the horses still in training had their last racecourse outings. Even Russian Eagle, his off-hind leg fully recovered, ran once more and won, landing a nice gamble for A.D. – or Jan assumed he had. A.D. rarely discussed his dealings with the bookies, whether successful or otherwise, but he had phoned Jan about the animal's well-being every morning between the four-day acceptance and race day. Jan didn't think even A.D. would have been quite so interested if nothing except the prize money had been at stake.

During one of these calls he departed from his usual script.

'Jan, some policeman from Cheltenham's been trying to get in touch with me. Feller called Hadfield. Something to do with Eddie Sullivan's behaviour in my box on Gold Cup Day. What's going on?'

'It's about the accident we had on Cleeve Hill, I guess.'

'But that's ancient history, isn't it?'

'Yes and no. The police are still looking into it. Have you spoken to him?'

'No. I expect I shall have to eventually, though. 'Bye, Jan.'

A few days later, with a dozen of the yard's inmates already turned out in the fields, and several more gone home to their owners, Reg and Mary came over in the afternoon, Reg to tend the pea and bean rows he'd planted in a sheltered spot behind the house, and Mary for a chat. It was warm and sunny as Jan sat with her mother on the paved terrace that ran the full length of the house, drinking tea and sharing the home-made cake Mary had brought with her.

'How's Eddie?' asked Mary.

'Doing well. They say he'll be ready to leave hospital soon.'

'He must be delighted. It's been such a long time.'

'And how are you, Mum? How's the kidney problem?'

'Doctor says I'm holding my own. Anyway, I didn't come here to talk about myself. Are you OK?'

That was typical of Mary. She had never liked being the centre of attention, much preferring the subject of other people, which meant that she had a mild weakness for local gossip, and a subject she wanted to discuss a few minutes later.

'I've heard something about Virginia Gilbert,' she announced. 'I don't know if I should tell you.'

'Oh, Mum, please! You can't go all coy like that. What is it?'

'It seems she's seeing a lot of a certain estate agent.'

'Estate agent? Not Harold Powell?'

'Yes, that's the one.'

'As a matter of fact, I already know. I've seen them together at the races, they were as thick as thieves. I assumed he was trying to sell her a horse or buying one off her. I didn't realize people were talking about them. What's going on? Is she training a horse of his or are they up to something else?'

'They say the two of them are going together, you know, as a couple – if you see what I mean.'

'As a couple? Harold and Virginia, a *couple*?'

The idea seemed so unlikely that Jan almost laughed out loud.

'I shouldn't think the colonel approves at all,' Mary went on. 'His daughter must be fifteen years younger than that ghastly man, and he's married.'

'Separated to be fair – although I don't see why we should be.'

'Anyway, with you and her always being such rivals, and I remember what you went through with Harold Powell before, so I didn't think I should tell you.'

'Well, you have now and I'm glad you did. What's more, I think they deserve one another.'

As they went back into the house with their empty mugs, Mary spotted the black voice-recorder beside the telephone.

'What's that for?'

Jan had not mentioned the nuisance calls to her

parents, not wishing to worry them unnecessarily. But, given that the unit had a sticker identifying it as the property of Gloucestershire Constabulary, now she couldn't avoid it.

'It's just that I've been having a few anonymous calls. The police say it's not particularly unusual. Some sad git with too much time on his hands, probably.'

Mary put her hand to her mouth.

'Oh, my goodness!'

'Can't they trace these calls, then?'

It was Reg, coming in from the garden and pulling off his boots.

'Oh, hi, Dad. I've been told they're probably from a call box. It's nothing, really nothing. Happens to hundreds of women. The recording's just for evidence if they do happen to catch him. How are the peas coming on?'

'Well. You'll be able to harvest them soon.'

Later, Jan took her father down the yard to look at Morning Glory. She wanted his advice, and there was nobody in the world whose opinion she valued more when it came to problematic horses. But as they walked slowly towards the stables, Reg was still mulling over the conversation they'd had earlier.

'Are these phone calls worrying you, girl?'

'Well, yes. I suppose they are, if I'm honest. They're making me really nervous, particularly at night. But the police have been bending over backwards to give me protection.'

'Who d'you think's at it? Sounds like it might be the same folk who's sent round that letter about the yard being in trouble.'

'Yes, I know it does. And, obviously, I've got to suspect Harold Powell. That's even more sinister if he's really joined forces with Virginia Gilbert.'

'Virginia won't do anything against you, I mean not like that. For one thing her father wouldn't let her.'

'Dad, she can do what she likes behind his back. Though you're right about the colonel. He's been a proper ally of mine all along, in spite of Virginia's hatefulness. He doesn't let it affect our relationship one bit. He's even asked me to buy a horse for him at the July sales.'

Reg trudged on, still pondering. At the yard gate he stopped, then turned to Jan and said, 'I don't care for the idea of Powell having any influence on Virginia. She's a vindictive one when she wants to be. Always was, even as a child. And we already know what that man can do when he turns his hand to it, don't we?'

'You're not kidding. In fact, Dad, I think it was Harold Powell who deliberately tried to run me and Eddie off the road after Cheltenham. I think it was him in the Range Rover that overtook us.'

'Hmm, I wouldn't put it past him. He's a bad lot, that's for sure. But have you told the police about all this?'

'Well, I hinted at it, but it's a monstrous accusation to make. Of course I told them how he tried to cheat me out of Stonewall Farm, and they know all about his trial over the death of poor Olwen. They also know it was me that corroborated the evidence against him. Do you think I should actually accuse him of trying to kill me and Eddie? Won't they think I'm paranoid?'

Reg mulled over his daughter's concerns.

'I don't see why they should. It's their job to take all the possibilities seriously. You've got to make them do just that, else something far worse might happen.'

By now they had arrived in front of Morning Glory's box.

'Now, Jan, let's forget about these vile matters for the time being and have a look at Mr Temperamental, shall we?'

Jan's opportunity to make an explicit accusation that Harold Powell had tried to kill her came with unexpected swiftness. The next day Inspector Hadfield arrived at Edge Farm to check the voice-recorder, so he said, though Jan suspected that reason was something of a smokescreen. Hadfield was checking on her rather than on the equipment, she believed.

'Here it is,' she said, showing him the set-up beside the phone in the hall. 'We call it the black box – my own personal flight recorder. Has this now become a CID matter, Inspector?'

'The Uniform branch alerted us to the fact that you have been getting nuisance calls. They do that as a matter of course, Mrs Hardy. And, given that I'm already in charge of the team looking into the death of William Moorhouse, I've been wondering if there's any connection between the two.'

'Well, that's me and you both. I have told you about

Harold Powell already, haven't I? If you ask me, it's him behind it.'

'I've made some enquiries about Mr Powell since you suggested he might have been there on Cleeve Hill when Mr Sullivan's car crashed into William Moorhouse's car—'

'But I keep telling you, it *didn't*.'

Hadfield spread his hands.

'All right. Let's say it has been suggested by you that Mr Powell was there on the night of the road accident involving those two cars. He categorically denies it. He says he left the racecourse at least an hour before your accident, which I have confirmed independently, by the way, and that he was already at home in Hay-on-Wye by eight, which was just before the accident.'

'And have you confirmed that last bit independently?'

'No. It's not been possible because he lives alone.'

'Exactly. His wife's buggered off because he's such a toe-rag. He could easily have been waiting for us hidden in a gateway or something. It wouldn't have been difficult to spot Eddie's car.'

'All I can say is, we have no real evidence at the moment that Mr Powell was anywhere near Cleeve Hill at the time. Of course, I've been through his file and I can see he could have a grudge against you, after standing trial over the death of your mother-in-law. If we could establish it was him making the phone calls, that would make quite compelling evidence indeed.'

Hadfield sounded tired, distracted. Even his eternal smile was wilting.

'So what about the letter circulated by this Cotswold News Agency?' Jan challenged. 'Wouldn't you describe that as compelling evidence? The whole thing's a concoction. It's bogus. Tim Farr of the *Daily News* told me there has never been any call for an agency like that. He says the practice of sending news dispatches to parish newsletters and the like is unheard of in this area, and he should know.'

Hadfield gave her a sharp look.

'Has Tim Farr been sniffing around here?'

'Not specially. He's called in once and we've talked on the phone.'

'How interesting. He's been trying to talk to me, too. My sergeant says he's been sticking his nose rather deep into the circumstances surrounding your accident.'

'I know he has. He thinks the Range Rover wasn't just a reckless driver, but someone who deliberately wanted to do me and Eddie harm. Which is what I've been saying to you all along.'

'Well, frankly, if there's no evidence—'

Jan interrupted, pointing to the black box.

'Excuse me, but why is *this* here? And what about the Cotswold News Agency then?'

'Well, Mrs Hardy, it will do no good getting all wound up about this, but yes, I agree that's a very interesting development. It may be coincidental, we'll have to wait and see. I gather you went to see Mr Strangway personally.'

'Yes, I did.'

'If I may say so, that was rather a rash thing to do.'

'Oh, I don't know. It was obvious he had never heard of me before.'

'As a matter of fact, I agree this time, though you weren't to know that. You need to be more careful. But after speaking to him myself I'm satisfied he had nothing to do with putting his phone number on the circular.'

'Which is already known around here as the poison press release.'

'Ha! That's very apt. It's a rather clever tactic, I admit – I mean, as a way of spreading gossip. There's nothing illegal at all on the face of it. The writer was very careful not to print anything that's not already been printed, or could be printed, in the press. There's nothing prejudicial or obviously libellous.'

'But isn't it libellous to write that Eddie was drunk? They can't possibly know that for sure.'

'But, you see, it doesn't actually say that. It says he'd been celebrating and if anyone chooses to interpret that as being drunk, well . . . Had he in fact been drinking, by the way?'

'Now come on, Inspector Hadfield. We've covered that topic already. He had just enough champagne to make a toast. He wet his whistle and that was it. Let's get back to the poison press release. Are you saying that, even if you find who sent it out, you can't take any action?'

'Not directly, I fear. But, as you said, it might be used as circumstantial evidence.'

'It's a bit more than that, I think, with its dreadful innuendo about *Psycho*.'

Hadfield looked puzzled.

'*Psycho*? The Hitchcock film?'

'Yes. Didn't you hear what the anonymous shit said to me the other night?'

'I'm sorry, he said what exactly?'

'He asked if I'd been in the shower.'

'Did he indeed? I'm sorry, I didn't realize that.'

The Inspector was clearly put out that he did not know this important fact. He pulled a notebook and pencil from his jacket pocket.

'And you say there's a connection with this press release and *Psycho*? I don't think I follow you. Did he mention the film explicitly?'

'No, it's just obvious. He's wanting me to make the connection myself, which I have done. You see, it ties in with the taxidermist's phone and fax numbers being on the press release. You know what that was all about, don't you?'

Hadfield was staring at her bewildered. 'Hang on a second . . . taxidermy. I hadn't thought of that. *Psycho* . . . the room behind the office of the Bates Motel, full of stuffed birds . . . Janet Leigh saying, "A man should have a hobby." I must have seen the film ten times at least. I'm a big Hitchcock fan, you know.'

'So you'll know Janet Leigh played the victim. Don't you see the connection there?'

Hadfield seemed to flinch under the force of his realization.

'Oh my—! Yes, yes, of course. Jan, Janet. This is extremely interesting – *extremely* interesting, quite disturbing actually.'

'You can say that again.'

Hadfield shot a few more questions at Jan and jotted down some rapid notes. Then he made his excuses and, newly energized, retreated to the car. Now he had an unaccustomed spring in his step and at last Jan thought she was getting somewhere. Until this point in time, she was sure, he had not really believed in the third car on Cleeve Hill, and had been altogether too detached, reluctant even, about the crash, treating it as if he would much prefer to wrap it all up as a dangerous driving case, dump the blame on Eddie and go home to put his feet up. But now, at last, thanks to Hitchcock, Hadfield's interest had been whetted.

Jan continued to move the horses out into the paddocks, usually in pairs as they were less likely to fight. She only had space for half of them on her own pasture, but a neighbouring farmer was more than happy to host any spares in two of his fields, which meant she had the comfort of knowing where they were and easy visits.

Over the next three or four weeks, when they had settled, the horses would be caught and given their annual inoculations – something Jan preferred to do when they were out of training in case it affected their performance on the track. There was an art to this operation. She found that after a period of being footloose and fancy free, the horses generally became harder to catch. Every group developed a mini-herd mentality, a hierarchy in which most things were done in imitation of the herd leader. For Jan and her staff, the trick was to identify the leader in each group – the chief mischief-maker as they called him – catch him first and put a head-collar on him. They then led him into a corner and the others usually followed, after which it was relatively easy to catch and inject them. In most cases, it was Jan who enticed the gaffer into his collar.

They were in the middle of the inoculation procedure when Jan heard the parp-paaarp of a motor-horn coming from Edge Farm. Having successfully collared the lead horse in the field where they were working, Jan left Annabel in charge and drove home as fast as she could. There she found an ambulance waiting outside the house, as the attendant pushed a single figure in a wheelchair. She registered that the ambulance had the words Stoke Mandeville Hospital stencilled on the side and realized that Eddie Sullivan had finally arrived back.

She jumped out of the Shogun and rushed over to him.

'Hey! It's you. This is unexpected.'

'I went on and on and on at them until they had to let me go.'

'Well, it's fantastic, Eddie!'

'I don't know about that. I've nowhere else to go.'

She knew she should kiss him. If he had been standing, maybe she would have because it would have been the kiss of equals. But to go to him, bend over and place a kiss somewhere on his head or face, a helpless man in a chair with a rug over his knees, seemed awkward and false, it would be different from any kiss she had ever given him before. She recoiled, patting him on the shoulder instead.

'Welcome to Edge Farm, Eddie,' she said. 'Welcome back, Eddie.'

He simply nodded.

'I need to go in now,' he told her with matter-of-fact simplicity. 'I need the toilet, and you're going to have to help me. I can't even have a bloody pee on my own.'

14

'Oh, all right, Eddie . . . all right . . . if you need me to.'

But take him to the *toilet*. Could he still be as helpless as that? Jan was horrified until she saw Eddie's face. He was looking at her intently, studying the effect of what he'd just said. Then he laughed, not the old full-throated laugh that she used to find so attractive, but a more cynical one. Nevertheless, it was the first laugh she'd heard from him for more than two months.

'Eddie, tell me you can go to the loo by yourself, will you – please?'

Eddie shrugged and spread his hands innocently.

'You needn't worry, Jan. I can go by myself,' he said.

'Then why did you say that?'

'Just testing. You promised my mum you'd look after me – I was wondering how fair that extended.'

'That's not very fair, teasing me like that. You're a bloody disgrace, Eddie Sullivan.'

Jan laughed too, from relief more than anything else. Then one of the ambulance crew produced a pair of elbow crutches, which he handed to the patient.

Eddie took one in each hand and heaved himself out of the chair.

'As a matter of fact, I can do a lot of things by myself now – not everything, but we can't have it all, can we?'

Jan put Eddie in Megan's bedroom. The children were delighted to see him again, and happy to double up in Matty's room as they had done when Sue stayed.

But having Eddie around, with his crutches persistently lying in wait for the unwary to clatter into or trip over, certainly emphasized how small Jan's living space was. For the first time she found herself wishing for a bigger house – a feeling she resented because she loved the home Gerry Harris had built for her. One day, she thought, when she had some extra cash, she would get Gerry to extend it, so she could have a spare bedroom, at least.

Eddie got around well, manoeuvring himself through the rooms and up and down the stairs with surprising agility for someone who until recently had been claiming he would never walk again. But his legs were still too weak to support him unaided and they could not be persuaded to do precisely what he wanted. Sometimes, Jan thought, he exaggerated his helplessness, but then she saw him struggling to walk and saw too how quickly his energy drained away. At these moments she felt dreadfully sorry for him.

'Jan,' he said one night, soon after his return from hospital, 'can you talk me through the day of the accident? It's still a complete blank. I want to know everything, every detail.'

Patiently she traced what she knew of his activities that day. She described the race meeting, how the Gold Cup was won, Russian Eagle's success in the Cathcart and the celebrations afterwards. She told him how they had left the owners' and trainers' car park, driven up Cleeve Hill and been forced off the road by the Range Rover.

'And you think that car might have been driven by Harold Powell?'

'Well, yes. And even the police are beginning to get interested in the possibility. If only you could remember a bit more, Eddie. You were driving. You were in a much better position to see who the other chap was than me.'

Eddie gave a discontented grunt.

'Everything I've been saying,' Jan went on, 'doesn't it spark even the tiniest memory?'

'Not the tiniest. So the police are coming round to the idea of my innocence, are they?'

'A little. I don't think they're convinced yet, but certain things have happened. I wish they hadn't, but the plus side is that they support my theory of someone with a grudge against us.'

Jan told him, for the first time, about the poison press release and the anonymous phone calls she had received.

'It could be the widow Moorhouse, couldn't it? She has a grudge against us by the sound of it.'

'The last phone call was from a man. So, if it's her, she's got an accomplice.'

Eddie was specially intrigued by her visit to the taxidermist.

'Great movie, *Psycho*,' he said musingly. 'Do you know you never actually see her getting stabbed?'

Jan shivered. 'Ugh, Eddie, don't!'

'No, it's true. It's a cinematic illusion. You just think you see the stabbing from the way it's edited.'

Eddie relaxed back in his chair and focused on the wall, as if it was a screen. He began to quote, in the portentous voice of the psychiatrist who sums up the story of Norman Bates at the end of the film.

'*I got the whole story – but not from Norman. I got it – from his mother. Norman Bates no longer exists. He only half existed to begin with. And now, the other half has taken over – probably for all time.*'

Eddie turned back to Jan, who was impressed.

'My God, for a man with memory loss you've got amazing recall. And you've got something in common with Hadfield, by the way – he's another *Psycho* nut.'

Eddie shrugged.

'I admit I've seen the film two or three times. But I wouldn't call myself a nutter. To be honest, I didn't even realize I knew those words.'

Although there were evenings when Eddie and Jan talked together, they couldn't get back their old friendship, let alone the intimacy that had once been so special to them. There was a certain reserve now, a holding back, as if they were both waiting for the other to make a move. Jan could not make up her mind about Eddie. She was finding it extremely hard to get used to his different behaviour, with his unpredictable outbursts of anger and bitterness, particularly when they were aimed at her.

She was not sure how best to help him, and decided to telephone the consultant neurologist at Stoke Mandeville.

'I'm confident Eddie's on the mend, Mrs Hardy. It's still very early days,' said a reassuringly upbeat voice. 'But he's not so sure of that as I am, not yet anyway. He won't need a trip to Lourdes before he throws those crutches away, believe me.'

'He seems very depressed. Sometimes he's really volatile. Is this normal?'

'I've seen patients like that many times. It's really very complicated and can be hard to unravel. Depression and anger can often set in because of the slow progress of treatment and the fear of not regaining all one's functions.'

'You mean these dark moods will clear up when he realizes he's not going to be in a wheelchair for the rest of his life?'

'Well, that will help. But not necessarily, I'm afraid. The complication is that he had a severe knock on the head. That alone can bring on long-term depression, sometimes even personality change.'

'He still has amnesia about the day of the accident, Doctor. I don't just mean the crash – the whole day's wiped out.'

'And he may never recover those memories. That in itself can be behind a person's unhappiness. The recovery of memory is seen as important, as if it contains the only key to solving the problem. That's why a lot of uncertainty and anxiety can be focused on the memory loss alone.'

'So what can we do to help him?'

'Keep him busy. There's the programme of exercises he will have already learnt here; he should be doing those every day. And you should arrange regular visits from a physiotherapist through your GP. And if you can keep him active in other ways, that would be all to the good. Give him small tasks, play Scrabble, cards, anything that won't tire him out too quickly.'

At the end of June a fat A4 envelope arrived stamped with the logo of Tattersalls Sales. Enclosed was the catalogue for the auction at which Jan intended to find a horse for Colonel Gilbert.

That night she lay in bed, scrutinizing every page and marking the likely lots. After she'd read for twenty minutes, her eyelids began to droop. Sleepily she turned another page, the type dancing up and down as her sight blurred. She was just ready to let the catalogue drop from her fingers when Lot 214 came momentarily into focus. In an instant she was wide awake. Where had she seen that name before?

The pedigree described was of a well-bred four-year-old, whose sire had been a stayer on the flat, while the dam had progeny that included several National Hunt winners. The gelding's own exploits on the track, running for the Yorkshire flat trainer Clive Appleby, had so far been undistinguished. The description tried to make the best of his dozen or so runs, but to a pro it was clear this horse was considered a failure and

Appleby was well known for firing horses out of his yard if they did not live up to his expectations. This particular damp squib was called Velvet Dynasty.

Then in a flash Jan made the connection – it was the race she'd watched on television in Eddie's room at Stoke Mandeville, when she had fancied the prospects of the bay with the squiggly blaze. Velvet Dynasty, she'd said to herself, could make a very nice National Hunt horse some day. Now she pencilled in three thick stars against the horse's name and closed the catalogue. He just might be the one, and he would probably be sold within the colonel's price limit.

The next day she phoned Clive Appleby.

'I've got a client who may be interested in Velvet Dynasty. What can you tell me about him? Is he sound?'

'He's a decent horse, all right, I've always thought a lot of him. He's been catching pigeons on the gallops at home, but he's never come good on the track. We don't know why. It's probably nothing to worry about, a touch of immaturity more like, but my owner, he's the impatient type and doesn't want to keep him on the off-chance.'

And nor do you, I'll bet, thought Jan.

'Thank you, Clive. That's very helpful.'

'He'll make you a nice jumper, in my opinion,' Appleby went on. 'There's some class hurdlers and chasers in the family, as I'm sure you already know.'

For a more independent view Jan got the number of Froggie Whelan, the flat jockey who often rode for Appleby's yard. Froggie could not have been more helpful.

'Oh yes, I've rode him in a coupla races. They all had a great regard for him, you know, the way he went at home. But he's been a let-down on the course.'

'But does he have any specific problems I should know about, Froggie? He doesn't break blood vessels, does he?'

'No, definitely not, there's nothing you can put your finger on. Give him a change of air and he might be a different horse.'

Jan knew Froggie was right. Sometimes when horses had problems it was just boredom, or they didn't like the regime they were living under. Another regime, another stable, and they could be utterly transformed.

The sales, held at Tattersalls' Park Paddocks in Newmarket, stretched over three days, but Jan decided to attend only on the second, when Velvet Dynasty was coming up. As a precaution she had marked a few later lots as alternatives for the colonel, but in her mind she had already decided the bay gelding would be her primary objective.

Reg always went with Jan to bloodstock sales if he could. Father and daughter thoroughly inspected Velvet Dynasty in the morning, getting Appleby's lad to walk him out of his box. The quality of his conformation, which had first impressed Jan on the small screen, was substantiated, and the liquid movement when he trotted was a complete joy. Reg walked around him twice, then looked him in the eye. He could see plenty of spirit, but no roguery.

'He's bonnie, Jan,' was Reg's verdict. 'A real bonnie one.'

Threading their way back through the many would-be purchasers who were coming and going on the lawns that surrounded the stables, Jan suddenly drew her father to a halt with a violent tug on his jacket.

'Look! It's them!'

Walking in the same direction, a dozen paces ahead, she saw the backs of a man and a woman. Jan knew the man's angular boniness so well, the tall frame in the tailored country suit and dark hair beginning to turn grey.

'My God, they're walking hand in hand, Dad! With all these racing people everywhere. Do you see?'

'Yes,' said Reg, 'and why not?'

'It means they're making it official, public, that they're together. How horrible. "Harold and Virginia." Yuk! In fact it's worse than sickening, it's sinister!'

Jan had a chance to study the couple more carefully in the refreshment room, where she and Reg went for a ploughman's. Harold and Virginia were drinking wine with a group of Virginia's rich friends, whose booming public-school laughter echoed around the walls and off the ceiling. Harold Powell, she knew, was not from this social background. He was self-made, the son of a Herefordshire farmer. But he showed no sign of discomfort amongst these grown-up children of wealth and reputation, smiling at their jokes, even contributing a few himself, while constantly exchanging fond glances with Virginia.

'Is her father here?' Reg asked, noticing the object of Jan's frequent attention. 'Didn't he say he might be?'

'He rang this morning to say he didn't feel up to it. I had already faxed him the details of the horses I was interested in, stressing that I thought Velvet Dynasty would probably be the best of them—'

'Which he is, to look at,' Reg interrupted.

'He said the pedigrees looked fine and he trusted me to get him something he would be proud of.'

'And so you will, my girl. Only maybe he's sent Virginia just to make sure.'

'That would be a complete waste of time,' Jan replied dryly. 'She wouldn't know Arkle from a pantomime horse.'

Reg popped the last bit of his cheese into his mouth and stood up.

'I just need to pay a visit to the gents,' he said. 'Us old men, you know . . .'

Watching her father make his way slowly between the tables, Jan was startled by the male voice close to her ear.

'You and your mouth, Jan Hardy,' he growled.

She whipped round and saw it was Harold. He quickly slid into the chair Reg had just vacated.

'Been talking about me to the police, have you? You never stop, do you? Will you never learn?'

Harold was speaking in a low, menacing voice, his mouth hard set, his teeth clenched. Jan was too alarmed to say anything as he drummed his fingers on the table.

'That copper Hadfield's been making my life an effing misery, poking around, asking questions, thanks to you.'

Jan looked across to the group Harold had just left.

She saw Virginia take a sip from her glass of wine while, at the same time, shooting a swift sideways glance across the room at Harold.

'Look,' Jan interrupted, 'if the police are making enquiries, they must think they have good reason.'

'Yeah, because of your lies, you bitch. You destroy my reputation, my marriage—'

'Well, you seem to be consoling yourself on that score all right,' said Jan, tipping her head in Virginia's direction.

'That's none of your bloody business. Keep out of our way, or I'll see you crushed, you and your precious horses. Do you get me?'

With that parting shot he got to his feet and left.

An hour or so later it was Virginia's turn to have her say. Jan and Reg were sitting beside the sale ring, waiting for Lot 214, when she drifted by alone.

'I hope you're spending wisely,' she said in a sarcastic manner.

Virginia was smiling, but despite her pretence Jan caught the undertone of spitefulness.

'I always spend money wisely,' said Jan. 'I've never had enough of it to do otherwise.'

'But this isn't your money exactly, is it? It's my father's.'

'Your father has approved the lots I may be bidding for,' said Jan.

Virginia stood watching the horse currently being auctioned as it circled the ring, while the auctioneer called out the bids into his microphone.

'Six thousand, five hundred. Come on now, ladies and gentlemen. Who's going to say more for this attractive filly?'

'Oh yes, indeed, he told me,' Virginia said. 'He also told me what he was prepared to pay. It seems an awful lot . . .'

'*Seven* thousand. Thank you, sir. It's your bid. Who'll say seven five?'

Jan made a huge effort to control her increasing anger.

'It's about the right price for what he's looking for. I would have thought you knew that. Or, if you didn't, you must have twigged by now.'

'Well, yes, Jan, as a matter of fact I do know. After all it's why he has most of his horses with me, isn't it?'

The next lot was Velvet Dynasty. Jan desperately wanted Virginia to go away, but instead she sat down right behind her and Reg, literally breathing down their necks.

There were two early bidders. The auctioneer started at five thousand, while Jan stayed out of it until the offer rose past ten, then twelve. There was a pause after one of the bidders dropped out and the other, a well-known Lambourn trainer called Jamie Fuller, looked smug. His expression seemed to say that, at this price, the horse would be a bargain, but the smirk dissolved as Jan jumped in with a flick of her catalogue.

'A new bidder on my right! Twelve thousand five hundred. Thank you, ma'am. Do I hear thirteen, sir? Thirteen thousand guineas?'

Fuller looked pained. He raised his catalogue, then he and Jan batted back and forth in increments of five hundred until the bar stood at seventeen and a half thousand. The next bid was with Jan. She lifted her catalogue once more.

'Eighteen thousand guineas,' the auctioneer called. 'Now, sir, the bid is with you at eighteen thousand five hundred. No? This is your last chance. Won't you reconsider? You may regret it, you know.'

But the Lambourn trainer had had enough. He shook his head impatiently, clearly riled by Jan's unexpected intervention. The auctioneer looked around.

'Any more? No? Selling, then, at eighteen thousand guineas once . . . twice . . . SOLD to Mrs Jan Hardy.'

He banged his gavel.

'Thank you, ma'am, it's good to see you here,' he said, scribbling down a note of the price and the buyer. 'And now, Lot two hundred and fifteen is a four-year-old grey gelding by Shareef Dancer . . .'

As Jan watched her new purchase leave the sale ring, she turned to her father full of joy.

'We got him, we got him, Dad!' she whispered, forgetting Virginia's presence.

'Yes, and I don't think you'll regret it,' said Reg, equally pleased.

'Oh, but you will if what I heard this morning is correct,' said Virginia, leaning forward. Jan turned round.

'What was that?'

Virginia nodded to where Velvet Dynasty's rear end was disappearing from view.

'He's a whistler, so I've been told.'

Jan looked at Reg in alarm. A whistler was a horse with suspect breathing. It often followed an attack of pharyngitis, bronchitis, pneumonia, influenza or pleurisy and could seriously affect a horse's performance. Could Virgina be right? It wasn't something you could tell by just walking or trotting a horse up and down a stable yard at a sales complex. Only when the horse was galloping would the larynx make a high-pitched sound.

Reg just shook his head, as if to say he didn't think it a very likely story.

But on their way home the question of Velvet Dynasty's wind was still on Jan's mind.

'What if she *is* right, Dad? I'll have to return him.'

'Well, if he was, I don't reckon that Jamie Fuller would've been bidding for him. Didn't you talk to the jockey beforehand?'

'Yes, Froggie Whelan. He never mentioned it and he'd have had nothing to gain from keeping it from me, would he? I asked him if the horse was a bleeder and he said the horse was completely sound as far as he knew.'

'That's all right then,' said Reg. 'So stop worrying. You're not going to know for sure till you get him up on those gallops and the vet's had a listen to him. Virginia was probably just taking the Mickey. Like I said, she's got a nasty streak a mile wide, that girl.'

15

Jan couldn't stand the uncertainty of not knowing if Virginia's jibe about Velvet Dynasty was correct or not. As soon as she got home she rang Shirley the vet.

'Shirley, I need you here first thing in the morning to listen to a horse's wind. I bought him from Newmarket sales today and he had a clean certificate, but I've since been informed he's a whistler.'

Shirley detected the anxiety in Jan's voice.

'Jan, I'm operating on a horse in the morning, so I can't come then. You've got seven days to notify Newmarket, so surely it can wait a couple.'

'*Shirley!*' Jan said with an edge to her voice, 'I need to know. Not only for my sake, but I bought the horse for Colonel Gilbert and I need to let him know what's what.'

Shirley stood her ground. 'Well, as I said, Jan, I can't do tomorrow. But I do have a colleague over from America who's staying for a few weeks, he could come along instead. His name's Lance Clancy.'

'That's fine. Tell him to be here at seven-thirty, and by the way, Shirley, he'd better know his job.'

When he arrived to examine Velvet Dynasty in his stable, Lance Clancy first opened the horse's mouth and had a good look inside.

'Now then, little lady, everything seems OK in there,' he confirmed, letting go of the tight hold he had on the horse's muzzle, who snorted his disapproval. Lance then placed his thumbs and forefingers on the horse's throat in the area of his Adam's apple. 'Can't feel any problems there either. So we'll endoscope him now, then he can go out to exercise. I'll listen to him on the gallops and we'll endoscope him back here in his box afterwards.'

'Would you like a coffee while I tack him up?' Jan asked. 'Roz will get you one.'

'No thanks, little lady, we'll get the job done first.' The phrase 'little lady' was beginning to grate on Jan's nerves. Maybe it was just his southern twang. Other than that, she had to concede he seemed a very nice bloke.

'OK. If you go up the gallops in my Shogun with Annabel, my assistant, I'll let the horse stride on past you at the four-furlong marker and then I'll trot back to you.'

'That'll be fine, little lady,' said Lance.

OK, Jan thought, getting more irritated by the second, *just drop the little lady. It's worse than 'you know what I mean'*.

Jan eased Velvet Dynasty into a canter, steadily building up speed, until he zipped past the vet and Annabel. Jan listened intently to the horse's breathing as she eased him to a trot.

'That sounded perfectly clear to me,' she declared

as she reached the place on the gallops where the vet, equipped with his stethoscope, was waiting to continue his examination.

'Sounded pretty clear to me too,' Lance agreed.

As he finished the endoscopic procedure back at Edge Farm, he declared, 'Apart from a bit of mucus, I can see no problem at all. Little lady, you have yourself a fine young thoroughbred and I'm sure he'll win plenty of races for you. Now, you mentioned some coffee. I sure could handle one if the offer's still open.'

'Sure,' said Jan almost imitating the Yank, 'come on up to the house. Fran will have some freshly made.'

As she entered the house, the red message light was flashing on the answering machine. Jan pressed the play button and heard the voice of a worried-sounding Reg.

'Jan, it's your dad. Give us a call as soon as you get in. It's important.'

Jan dialled and Reg picked up the phone almost before the ring tone started.

'Dad, you sounded upset. What's happened? Is it Mum?'

'No, your mum's all right. It's Colonel Gilbert. There's been burglars at the Manor.'

'Oh, no! Is everyone OK?'

'No, at least the colonel's not. He was there on his own and heard glass shattering in the night, three a.m. or something. Anyway, he thought it was the storm, so he went downstairs without thinking and found two men in his dining room, so they're saying. Helping themselves to his silver, they were. The colonel shouted that he'd got a gun and they took off through the French windows. Apparently, the colonel ran after them shouting, threatening them and then he just collapsed on the lawn. There was no one to help him. So he just lay there.'

'Oh, the poor colonel! How *awful*. How long was he out there?'

'They didn't find him till morning, when Mrs Whatsername came in between six-thirty and seven.'

'Oh, Dad! You mean he was out in the open for hours, in that dreadful weather?'

'I don't think he was conscious, mind. They say he'd had a heart attack, on top of that there was hypothermia, as he'd been lying in the wet. They took him to hospital, but he was more dead than alive. They don't expect him to recover, that's what I've heard.'

'Well, *they* can always be wrong. We've got to hope for the best, Dad.'

'OK, girl. I'm sorry to be the bringer of bad news. I thought you should know, you having two of his horses.'

Lance sensed the tone of the conversation Jan was having with Reg and silently mouthed, 'I'll catch up with you later for the coffee. 'Bye for now.'

Jan held up a thumb and mouthed back, 'I'm sorry, thanks very much.' As the vet left, she turned her attention back to the phone and Reg.

'Yes, Dad, thanks. Speaking of which, I've only just come in from galloping Velvet Dynasty.'

'What was he like?'

'Like magic, and what's more the vet gave him a clean bill of health – no wind problems at all. He's going to be good, Dad, I just know it. He's very willing and really fast, with fantastic acceleration. Give him a bit of schooling and I reckon he'll take to hurdling like a good 'un – maybe a *very* good 'un.'

'Well, that's something anyway. We must hope the colonel will be here to enjoy it.'

'The first chance I get I'm going down to the hospital to tell him. It will do him the world of good to know we've bought him a future champion. It's the best possible medicine he can get.'

Annabel and Jan had coffee together in the office, as they did most mornings. Normally they would talk about possible races for the horses, training and veterinary problems, the staff, the feed supplies and the many issues that arise from day to day in a working racing stable. But at this quiet time of year, when most of the staff and horses were on holiday, there was little enough to discuss and Jan concentrated on describing the new horse's exciting gallop.

'Gosh, he sounds like a real prospect,' said Annabel.

'Potentially the best hurdler I've had,' Jan said. 'I can't think why he was such a flop with Appleby. He's got real speed. I haven't travelled so fast on a horse since MG carted me.'

'How *is* MG? From what I've seen at a distance he's still quite a handful.'

Jan sighed. 'No real progress, I'm afraid. God, it's frustrating. He's so tense, always keyed up. The enormous amount of energy he uses putting himself under pressure is such a waste. Once he sets foot outside the stable he's on such a high burn. I need him to trust me. But some days he won't do a single thing that I want him to do. The awful thing is I believe he could be every bit as good as Velvet Dynasty – maybe even better. But at the moment he's got about as much chance of going racing as a clothes horse.'

Annabel was sitting with her head and long neck bent back, gazing dreamily at the ceiling.

'But just think of it, Jan. If we can get him right, Edge Farm might have, not just one, but two brilliant novices. That would really bristle the moustaches of the tweed brigade. What a lovely thought.'

Jan drained her mug. 'There's nothing I'd like more, but there's a long way to go before that happens.' She chuckled, getting to her feet.

As the two women strolled into the yard to rinse their mugs under the tap, grunts and groans could be heard coming from one of the boxes on the opposite side, where Eddie's crutches were leaning against the wall. This was where Gerry, after consultation with Jan, had laid some threadbare carpet on the floor and brought in a couple of poles from the pony paddock, fixing them securely on trestles as parallel bars. Roz had borrowed a rowing machine from a friend in the village, while Declan contributed some old dumb-bells. Now it was Eddie's personal rehabilitation unit.

Jan and Annabel, like a pair of snoopers, peeped over the half-door of the loose box. Eddie was lying on the ground in his tracksuit, spread-eagled and breathing heavily, his eyes closed, sweat dripping from his forehead.

'Hi,' said Jan. 'How's the Arnold Schwarzenegger routine?'

Eddie opened his eyes. 'Bloody terrible. Help me up, you two. I've had enough.'

Jan unlatched the door and went in, followed by Annabel. Taking one arm each, with care they hauled Eddie to his feet. Once he was standing he shrugged off their supporting hands.

'Let go of me. I can walk to the door on my own.'

Grimacing at the effort, he moved with a drunken, dragging gait. The two women hovered nervously, one on either flank, ready to catch him should he crumple or lurch too far from the vertical. It was only half a dozen paces, but Eddie completed his task unaided.

'Eddie, you're so much better,' exclaimed Annabel.

'I don't know about that. I haven't noticed any improvement. It seems to me I'm just the same as when I left Stoke Mandeville.'

'No, you're not,' said Jan. 'You're definitely on the up.'

Eddie grunted cynically. 'On the up? If only you knew the half of it! Pass me those sodding crutches. I'm too knackered to go without.'

In the afternoon Jan rang Cheltenham General Hospital.

'I was wondering about Colonel Gilbert, and if I can visit him. He was brought in this morning.'

'Please hold,' said a female voice.

Jan was put through to someone else and repeated her enquiry.

'Are you a relative?'

'No, I'm a . . .'

What was she? Employee? Friend? Business associate? Not exactly any of these, and yet, in a way, all three. She settled for 'A family friend.'

'I'm terribly sorry, but I have sad news. The colonel died at about ten-thirty this morning.'

Jan gasped. Despite what Reg had said earlier, she was unprepared.

'I see. Did he . . . did he regain consciousness?'

'No, I'm afraid not. It was very peaceful.'

'I see. Thank you.'

Jan stood numbly by the phone listening to the tick of the hall clock. An airliner mumbled across the sky. Then, from what seemed like miles away, she heard a car draw up outside. She knew it must be Fran bringing the children home from school.

Now her feet felt as if they were glued to the floor. It was hard to believe that Colonel Gilbert was dead. She'd known him, as her parents' landlord, all her life, and though they were separated by both age and class she had respected and liked him enormously. All right, she admitted, he was a bit of an old codger, but a kind and loyal one, and he'd never been anybody's fool, that was for sure.

Jan was suddenly brought back to the present as the front door burst open and Megan raced into the house. She shouted a greeting and charged up the stairs.

'What are you doing?' her mother called after her.

'Changing, putting my joddies on,' came the answer. 'I want to put Monarch over a few jumps before tea.'

Monarch! He'd belonged to the colonel; he had lent him to Megan for her junior eventing. What would happen to the pony now? It would break Meg's heart if she had to part with him. And what about the other

Gilbert horses in her care – the racehorses, including Wolf's Rock and this brilliant new one Velvet Dynasty? Their training fees helped to pay the bills. If they left, she'd lose a crucial amount of her income at a stroke. Few businesses could take such a hit easily and certainly not hers.

Briskly pulling herself together, she went to the bottom of the stairs.

'Megan, you'd better come down. I've got something to tell you.'

Five minutes later her daughter was in tears. Jan explained that Monarch's fate would be decided by the colonel's heirs, his daughter Virginia and son Harry.

'But they won't take Monarch away from me, will they? They can't! They absolutely can't.'

'Sweetheart, they can. But that doesn't mean they will. We'll have to wait and see. I'm sure nothing's going to change for the time being. Anyway, this is no time to be thinking about ourselves. We must remember poor Colonel Gilbert, he's been so kind to us in the past.'

Megan pouted.

'I suppose so. But I *hate* those burglars – it will be all their fault if Virginia Gilbert takes Monarch away.'

A little later Matty came solemnly to his mother, who was sitting in the lounge, and crept onto her lap.

'Mum, is Colonel Gilbert in heaven? With Daddy?'

'Yes, darling,' Jan gulped, stroking his hair as he put his head on her breast. 'I'm sure of it. The colonel was a very good man. Daddy will look after him.'

The funeral was held a week later and, though Jan and her parents arrived in what they considered to be plenty of time, there was precious little room left in Riscombe's medieval church. The benches were packed with dignitaries and a high proportion of the village population, many of them tenants who depended more or less on the squire and his estate for a living. Harry and Virginia Gilbert sat in the family pew at the front. She was wearing a stylish black outfit with a string of pearls, while her twenty-four-year-old brother, her junior by seven years, wore an Italian-style black suit, the uniform of a young City slicker. But there was no sign of Harold Powell.

The colonel was dispatched according to the rites of the Church of England, with nothing added and nothing taken away. The hymns were sung, the vicar gave his eulogy and prayed over the body, and the coffin was carried out for burial in the Gilbert vault, which was surmounted by an ornate Victorian structure. Over the door the Gilbert coat of arms was flamboyantly carved in marble. Sniffles had been heard throughout the service, but there was no outpouring or other demonstration of grief even now as Virginia, dry eyed, followed her father's coffin down the aisle, though Jan thought she saw Harry surreptitiously wipe away a tear with a knuckle.

Outside, in a fine drizzle, the congregation watched as the colonel was laid to rest beside his late wife.

'I thought he was a lovely old gentleman,' said the postmistress later to a group of mourners, which included Jan. They were at the funeral gathering at Riscombe Manor in the already crowded ornate room known as the Great Chamber, which had been added to the medieval structure by an Elizabethan Gilbert four hundred years ago. Its walls were lined with linen-fold panelling, and the ceiling had a complicated patchwork design in highly decorative plaster, while the high mullioned windows were inset with coats of arms in stained glass. 'He liked to do things the old-fashioned way.'

You can say that again, thought Jan. Under Colonel Gilbert the Riscombe estate had in many ways been suspended in a time warp. The rent continued to be collected on the traditional quarter days – Lady Day, Midsummer Day, Michaelmas and Christmas. By modern standards the estate workers were poorly paid, but they received, in the colonel's opinion, considerable benefits in kind: free issues of scrumpy from the Riscombe cider press, fruit and vegetables from the kitchen garden and honey from the beehives, while the colonel played the part of country squire to the hilt. He had been very active in the community, opening the annual fete, judging dog shows, chairing the board of school governors and the parish council, acting as local magistrate and, from time to time, accepting various ceremonial county offices, such as the high sheriff.

'Yes, he was tradition-minded, was the old colonel,' said George Machin, the village butcher, whose sausages were famed for miles around. 'And there's gunna be changes all right, with these young 'uns in charge, that's for sure.'

There was a lot of speculation about Harry Gilbert. It was thought he had little appetite for playing the squire and would probably cling to his well-paid City job, leaving the estate affairs to Virginia. This idea was not universally popular as Virginia was regarded with some suspicion for her high-handedness and apparent meanness. On the other hand, it was felt she knew a great deal more about country life than her brother, who was seen as little better than a flash City boyo. Everybody remembered how he'd once killed a heifer on the Winchcombe Road in his Mercedes sports car, and offered the farmer a twenty-pound note by way of compensation. The matter had only been resolved by the colonel's intervention.

Jan noticed a group of Virginia's stable staff standing together in the large window recess and made her way over. The head lad, Scottie Venables, was a small easy-going man whose knowledge of horses would have commanded more respect had he not been so fond of the bottle.

'Mrs Hardy!' he said, tossing back his wine and reaching for another from the tray of a passing waiter. 'I hear good things about this new horse you bought for the colonel, but I reckon he'll be coming to us before too long.'

'In that case you know more than me, Scottie. Miss Gilbert's said nothing about it either. The colonel's will hasn't been made public yet, has it?'

Scottie nodded, swaying slightly on his feet.

'That's right. The boss has said nothing to me about it. But we'll have him back at Riscombe before September, mark my words.'

'It must be right if you say so, Scottie,' Jan said with a forced smile.

They continued to talk about more general racing topics until Jan noticed her father signalling to her that he and Mary wanted to leave. Jan crossed the hall to the cloakroom to gather their raincoats. She was searching through the damp, higgledy-piggledy pile when someone came in behind her.

Virginia shut the door and leaned her back against it.

'I'm amazed you've got the bloody nerve to come into my home and chat up my stable staff,' she said with quiet menace.

Jan found her father's coat buried on a hook under six or seven others. After a struggle, she unhooked it and turned to face Virginia.

'I don't know what you mean,' Jan said as coolly as she could. 'I came here out of respect for your father, not to chat anyone up.'

'You're a common, underhand, conniving bitch, Jan Hardy. I don't want you here. You're not welcome in this house and you never will be.'

Jan coloured.

'I may be common as muck in your eyes, Virginia, but when it comes to conniving, it would be impossible to beat you and your new boyfriend.'

'What's *that* supposed to mean?' hissed Virginia.

'You and Harold. These games you're playing. It'll all come out, you know. Because I'll make sure it does, however long it takes.'

'Fuck you. You'll make sure of nothing. I'll see you in hell first,' Virginia raged. She turned and grasped the door handle.

'Oh, one more thing,' she continued, speaking more

lightly, as if she had just thought of something juicy to hasten Jan's demise. 'You've got several horses you shouldn't have in your yard, including Wolf's Rock and Velvet Dynasty. They're *my* horses now and I'll be sending my transport to collect them the day after tomorrow. I'd be obliged if you'd have them ready to travel.'

'What about Monarch?' asked Jan, almost in a whisper. She wished she hadn't had to ask the question because to do so put her in a weaker position, almost like a petitioner.

'What?' Virginia sneered. 'That shitty little pony? What possible use would I have for him? Particularly since your daughter has no doubt been busy ruining him for the past year. My father, in his wisdom, realized this. He left the animal to her in his will.'

Virginia yanked open the door and marched out. As Jan searched on for Reg's tattered old golf brolly, she felt a bubble of relief rising inside her, which partially displaced the heavy black anger she felt towards Virginia. Monarch at least was staying.

'Thank you, Colonel,' she whispered devoutly.

16

Around the middle of July, Lady Fairford got in touch to say she was in need of six weeks' stabling for two hunters, and she wondered if Edge Farm could take them. It did occur to Jan that it was an unusual time of year for hunters to be exercised, but Lady F said they were youngsters and needed a bit more educating before she could go cubbing with them in the autumn. Jan thought it was more likely her ladyship had heard the rumours about Virginia Gilbert's treatment of her and wanted to apologize in a roundabout way. Though it meant exercising and schooling the new inmates, Lady Fairford paid generously, and this way Jan had a little extra money to help plug the hole and make good some of the training fees lost after Wolf's Rock and Velvet Dynasty's removal from the yard.

Most days Jan and Annabel had been taking the Fairford horses up to the ridge and onto the bridle path that ran along its length for four or five miles. It was a superb ride, which passed through a couple of small woods and gave them a chance to talk in the relaxed way that horse riders do when hacking through beautiful country. It was amazing that, however many problems you set out with, they soon got washed away, they agreed.

'But are you *sure,* Jan?' Annabel continued, as the horses picked their way along the sandy track that snaked through the first of the copses. 'There's so much going on at the moment and I'd feel a bit of a rat leaving you.'

Every year they had the same conversation about the pros and cons of Annabel taking a holiday in August.

'There's nothing going on I can't handle,' Jan said. 'It's the silly season. These two fellows are leaving next weekend. Most of the horses are turned out. The weird phone calls have stopped and no more nasty news bulletins have been sent out. I also think the police have Harold well and truly in their sights, and he's very unlikely to try anything on, not at the moment anyway. So I'll be all right, honest. You're entitled to a holiday, so get off and enjoy yourself while you can.'

'But what about you? How long is it since you went away with the kids?'

Jan sighed. How long? Actually, when she thought about it, she realized she'd never been away with the kids, not since John died. Not properly *away*.

'Well, we're all going over to stay a week with Mum and Dad at Riscombe. Gerry wants us out of the way as he's putting in a proper fitted kitchen. Ben's going to be home. It'll be great, all of us together.'

'Is Eddie going too?'

'Eddie? No. That'd be a bit too much for my poor mother. He'll be the caretaker at Edge. Gerry thinks he can probably make use of him, bending lengths of pipe or something.'

'They get on well, don't they? Surprisingly.'

'Why surprisingly?'

'Come on, Jan. You know how Gerry feels about you. You'd think he might be jealous, but not a bit of it. Since the accident he's been Eddie's best mate.'

'Not to mention his personal fitness trainer.'

They emerged from the wood to a place where the path followed the apex of the ridge. The views were sensational. From there they could see at least six counties. To the west was the lower Severn and beyond that the Brecon Beacons and South Wales, while, if they turned the other way, the fertile fields of Gloucestershire were spread out beneath them. They drew their mounts to a halt and sat in the early morning sun, breathing in the fresh, clear air, two silhouettes against the sky.

'So, anyway,' Jan continued after a few moments' silence, 'what are these holiday plans of yours?'

Annabel coloured slightly.

'I've been invited over to Barbados to do some scuba diving.'

'Wey-hey! That sounds sexy. Who by?'

'Johnny Carlton-Brown, actually.'

'Really? That's fantastic. Is it a big party?'

'No, it's not a party at all. Just me.'

'You mean just you and him?'

'Yes, I'm afraid so'

'No one else at all?'

'No. Not another soul.'

'Bel, is there something you haven't told me? Have you two been getting together on the sly?'

'Not on the sly. But we have been out a few times. I like him.'

'What happened to whatever her name was – Vanessa, that's it, the actress? I thought she was his girlfriend.'

'Not since she won that Oscar. She's dumped Johnny and decamped to Los Angeles. She's going out with some brawny action hero now.'

'So why didn't you tell me you were seeing JCB until now?'

'Oh, you know me. I didn't consider it was a big deal, and I don't want a big deal made of it.'

'Is it a big deal, though?'

'No, *definitely* not. As I said I like him – uhm, quite a lot, actually. But I'm not in love with him.'

'Not yet, but you wait till you get out there. Lightning can strike without warning, you know.'

'They say the hurricane season's over.' Annabel laughed. 'I expect I'll be safe enough.'

Jan started to give Eddie a briefing on everything that might occur during her absence at Riscombe.

'Yes, yes, Jan,' he interrupted. 'I know how it all works in the yard. Remember, I have worked here before. I've got your parents' phone number and anyway you're only a few miles away. Just leave everything to Gerry and me, we'll be fine. He's offered to stay in the house if I need him to.'

'It sounds like you'll be glad to see the back of us.'

'Rubbish. I want you to have a rest. You're going to need one before the start of next season. So I don't want you worrying about this place, or about me.'

'Well, of course, worry is something you can't control that easily when you have animals to deal with, whether they have two legs or four. Anyway I'm inclined to do it by myself, but you could help me out, maybe.'

Eddie shot her a warning glance.

'What do you mean, help you out?'

Jan sensed that they were swimming in deeper waters than they had been exploring recently, but she plunged on.

'It's just that . . . well, it's the way you are these days. You're so impatient, so critical all the time . . . so hard on yourself. I wish you'd ease up.'

'Ease up? I can't ease up or I'll be in that bloody wheelchair for the rest of my life.'

'Come on, I know you have problems. But you're not the only one. Everybody has them. I have stacks.'

'Yes, the most obvious being me, I suppose.'

Jan could not deny it.

'The point is, I expect you to get over your problems. You seem to feel that unless you are always fighting you will actually go under.'

'What do you expect me to think? I'm a sodding cripple.'

'That's crap, Eddie. Just look at the progress you've made. You were in a bad way, I admit. You couldn't speak properly, or take a single step unaided, or remember what year it was even, but look at you now. You have improved out of all recognition.'

Eddie gave a bleak smile.

'The trouble is I keep thinking of the things I still *can't* do four months on.'

He spread his fingers and counted. 'I still can't walk the way I could. I can't remember the accident, the worst day of my life. A man died and I don't even know for certain whether I was responsible.'

'Eddie, get a grip! You were *not* responsible—'

'Let me finish, will you? I can't ride or drive, play tennis, earn a living, sleep through the night, or have a bonk even.'

'*What* did you say?'

Eddie gave a tired shake of his head. Suddenly all the fight seemed to have gone out of him.

'You heard.'

'I've been wondering how long it would be before that subject came up,' Jan said gently, tears welling up in her eyes.

'Don't worry. It probably won't again. I'm not criticizing you, am I? It's not your fault.'

'Are you sure?'

'No, this is something I have to deal with alone.'

'Oh? And there's me thinking sex is better when there are two people taking part.'

'That's not funny. It makes no difference, Jan.'

'What's that supposed to mean?'

'It's supposed to mean I can't do it, not anyhow.'

He was staring fixedly downwards, apparently studying his shoes. In reality, he was unable to meet Jan's eyes.

'Tell me, Eddie.'

'All right. It's like this. I don't think I can have sex at all. It's a physical incapacity.'

Jan tried to hide her astonishment. It would explain a lot of his behaviour, but why had he not told her this before?

'Is that what the doctors are saying?'

'No, I haven't discussed it with them. Well, not since Stoke Mandeville, when it was mentioned as one possible effect of the spinal damage.'

'Temporary or permanent?'

'One or the other.'

'Why did you keep this from me?'

'I didn't, not deliberately. But it's not easy for a guy to confess to. It scares the shit out of me, if you really want to know. My eyes see you, I smell you, my mind wants you, but nothing happens.'

'So, it's this that's making you angry? I'm really sorry, Eddie, you should have said something before now.'

'Jan, I know I've been ratty, but that's because I feel so low. I can't seem to see any light or a way out of this black hole at the moment. I just wish we could, you know, get back to the way we were. As a couple I mean.'

'Do you, really?'

Eddie sighed and spoke very quietly. 'But anyway, it's just wishes, isn't it? And they don't come true very often, do they?'

The Pritchards had always been a close family, and Jan genuinely looked forward to returning with her children to stay in the house where she had spent the best part of her childhood. Particularly, on this occasion, because her brother Ben was staying too.

Jan felt Ben's life had something of the prodigal son about it. Years ago he'd left England as a mumbling nineteen-year-old with a backpack and a guitar, in flight from Reg's desire that he would knuckle down and they would work the land together. But Ben ended up in Australia, where slowly he began to fashion a reputation as a musician and songwriter. After four years maturing, Ben came back – a more complete, more articulate young man than seemed feasible – to land a job as a record producer in Johnny Carlton-Brown's rising company, Brit Records.

On their first evening reunited at home, the Pritchards had a big family meal, washed down with plenty of Riscombe cider. They played French cricket, then reminisced until late in the evening, when Ben got out his guitar and sang them half a dozen of his own delicate, bluesy songs. Halfway through one of the numbers, 'Wedding Tune', Jan found tears stinging her eyes.

'That's a beautiful song, Ben,' she sniffed as he played the last chord. Jan had to admit she was a little woozy from the cider. 'What are you doing writing about weddings, you sad old bachelor?'

'It's not about me, Sis. Actually, I was thinking of you when I wrote it, you and John, on your wedding day.'

It was then Jan burst into proper tears.

Next day brother and sister went off first thing to do their mother's big shop. When Jan returned, hauling in a cargo of bulging plastic bags, she knew instantly that something was wrong.

Mary was sitting at the kitchen table, her old face puffy from crying. Reg was on the phone, standing with the receiver jammed to his ear, his agitation visible in every action, by the way he held himself, tapping his foot, aimlessly fingering the telephone cord, and working his jaw as if chewing a bit of gristle.

'Mum? Dad? What on earth's wrong?'

Reg immediately hung up.

'They're just keeping me on hold until I give up, I reckon,' he growled. 'Bloody solicitors! Snakes in the grass I'd call 'em!'

Jan dropped the shopping and hurried to her mother's side. She took Mary's hand.

'Hey, Mum! Tell me. What's gone on? Why are you crying?'

Mary shook her head, her mouth twisted in anguish. 'You'd better ask your dad.'

'Dad, what is it? Please *say* something.'

Jan looked pleadingly at Ben, who was coming in behind her carrying the rest of the shopping.

'There's something wrong, Ben. Dad, tell us what it is, for goodness sake.'

Without saying a word, Reg picked up a piece of paper that was lying beside the phone. He handed it to Jan. The printed letterhead established it was from a legal firm in Evesham and it was dated two days earlier. Jan started to read the contents aloud, rapidly.

But then, as she realized the actual meaning, she slowed down in appalled disbelief.

Dear Mr Pritchard,

<u>Riscombe Vale Farm Cottage</u>

On the death of Colonel Gilbert, the legal title to the house and thirty acres of land, previously leased by you, at a peppercorn rent, from Colonel Gilbert, has passed on to his daughter, Miss Virginia Gilbert. As I am sure you are aware, the current lease is due to expire next March. I am writing to inform you of Miss Gilbert's intentions regarding the above property.

On the expiry of the lease, Miss Gilbert wishes to take possession of the land and the dwelling house for her own use and your lease will NOT be renewed. You will therefore vacate the property on or before the due date.

Not wishing to cause inconvenience, Miss Gilbert has instructed me to make the following offer. Should you wish to leave Riscombe Vale Farm Cottage at an earlier stage, all outstanding rent from that period to the date Miss Gilbert receives vacant possession will be waived. Only on condition that the property is left in a habitable condition, and that the land is fenced and similarly cared for, will the money be waived.

We look forward to hearing from you on this matter.

The letter was signed by one of the partners, Arthur Snodgrass.

Jan's first reaction of complete disbelief gave way to reality when she thought about the person who had instigated it. This was Virginia Gilbert's revenge against her. It had nothing to do with Reg and Mary, or Ben, or anybody else. It was directed at her and it came from envy, snobbery, callousness – the full battery of dangerous qualities that Virginia possessed and had always possessed.

Somewhere into her memory flashed a vision from years ago of Virginia, aged about eight, coming into the Manor kitchen hand in hand with her father. Reg had been asked in for a cup of tea and a friendly chat about farm business. But during the proceedings Virginia had pulled Jan, who was a couple of years older, to one side and whispered, so that her father would not hear.

'I don't usually play with children from the village, they are common. I much prefer playing with my school friends, only don't tell Daddy. He gets cross when I say things like that.'

Jan had looked at Virginia, puzzled, then said in defence of her friends, 'Well, I heard Lady Fairfax telling my dad she really liked her new horse and that he was a bit common, but he had a lot more substance than a thoroughbred, so you really should like them, Virginia.'

Unnoticed by Jan, Ben had taken the letter from her hand and read it through again.

'Is it true that the lease expires on the twenty-fifth of March?'

Reg nodded gloomily.

'The old lease, yes, Lady Day. It's been in force for forty years or more.'

'But Virginia can't do this!' Ben spluttered. 'Didn't

the colonel say you could live on the farm as long as you wanted to?'

Reg nodded.

'He did. He changed the lease, but I don't know exactly what it said.'

'You probably never read it, Reg Pritchard,' said Mary in an unnaturally high tone. 'You're far too trusting. I've told you that before.'

'I've got a copy in the bank,' Reg continued, ignoring the telling off. 'Anyway, whatever the colonel wanted, he's not here now. What a man does in kindness can usually be undone in spite.'

'Well, I'm not so sure,' said Jan grimly. 'And I'm not going to let her get away with it. Let's have that letter. I'm going to show it to Fred Messiter and ask him what the hell's got into Virginia.' *As if I didn't know*, she muttered to herself.

'Right. I'll come too,' said Ben, rushing after her. They jumped into his sports car and sped off to the manor.

Fred Messiter had been the Riscombe estate manager for a quarter of a century and liked to say he knew the colonel's land better than its owner did. He and his wife Gillian had always been good friends to Reg and Mary, and he was appalled when Jan showed him the letter.

'Oh my Lord,' he exclaimed, combing his hand through his thin hair. 'Look, I really don't know anything about this. It's . . . it's . . . well, I'm speechless.'

They were in the estate office, built into one of the

old coach houses at the Manor. It was an orderly room, with a row of metal filing cabinets along one wall and a desk under the window, where they had found Fred sitting. The atmosphere was pleasantly spiced with smoke from his aromatic pipe tobacco.

'Have any of the other tenants had letters like this?' Jan asked.

'No, Jan, not so far as I know. Miss Gilbert's said not a dicky bird to me about it. What do they mean by "wishes to take possession of the land and the dwelling house for her own use"? As far as I know she's got the Manor to live in. Harry's got the house in Fulham. He's not bothering with the estate at all. Though he got a half-share of it, I do know that much.'

'Then why do you think Virginia's doing this?' asked Ben.

'Well, I can only think she's meaning to sell it,' Fred answered in her defence. 'There'll be the bill for inheritance tax to pay, you know.'

'But it doesn't say she's going to sell the farm,' Jan objected. 'She wants it for her own use, whatever that may be.'

'Something sinister,' said Ben, 'knowing her.'

'I'm sorry. I wouldn't know,' Fred continued, turning the palms of his hands upwards as a sign of defeat.

'Perhaps she doesn't want anyone to know she's selling it,' Ben said, 'not for the moment. She won't have a clue how big the tax bill's going to be just yet, will she?'

'Anyway, all this is beside the point,' said Jan impatiently. 'The fact is, whatever the real reason, Virginia's had this letter sent. The important questions are: what about Colonel Gilbert's promise to let my parents stay as long as they wish? And can Virginia do this anyway? Can she take the farm over and dispose of it if our parents refuse to move out?'

Fred laid his smouldering pipe in an ashtray on the desk and laced his fingers together, placing them across his chest.

'The original lease was drawn up long before I started working here. I probably read it when I first came, while I was rationalizing the filing system, but I can't remember any details. About ten years ago I do remember the colonel coming in to fetch it because he wanted it revised, he said. That was when they reduced the size of Reg's acreage from a hundred down to thirty, at the same time as his retirement.'

'So-called retirement,' commented Jan.

The estate manager unlaced his fingers, rose slowly from his chair and went over to the three filing cabinets. He hesitated for a moment, then seized the chrome handle on one of the drawers and drew it towards him. He riffled through the hanging files with his thick, strong fingers.

'Of course I had nothing to do with the revising. The colonel had his solicitors in Broadway do it.'

'Evidently not the same firm as Virginia's been using, then,' observed Ben.

'They were probably too honest for her,' Jan put in sardonically.

Fred flicked a look of alarm in Jan's direction. For all his employer's faults, he depended on Virginia for his livelihood and was none too comfortable hearing her being maligned.

'Now,' he said, 'we'll be on better ground if we know exactly what the terms are.'

Having no luck in the first drawer, he clattered it shut and slid open another. It was from here that he fished out a card folder labelled 'Riscombe Vale Farm Cottage'.

'Got it!' he said triumphantly.

He laid the file on his desk and flipped it open. Jan and Ben stood on either side of him as he leafed through the contents, most of it sporadic correspondence about leaky roofs and water supply. At last he came to an envelope spotted with age on which was written: *RISCOMBE VALE LEASE*.

The original forty-year-old document came out first. It was typewritten on heavy foolscap paper, its pages held together by green ribbon looped through punch holes in one corner, with blobs of sealing wax at the bottom of each page. It contained screeds of detail, defining exactly the land covered by the lease, and giving a minute description of the house and farm buildings. Fred found the paragraph which laid down the lease's duration and put his finger on where the expiry date was given: the coming 25th of March.

Fred laid the old lease aside and fished inside the envelope again, this time drawing out a copy of the revised deed, which, like the other, was typed and sealed with wax, signed at the bottom of each page by Colonel Gilbert and Reg Pritchard. He turned the pages slowly until he came to a numbered paragraph, which he tapped with his index finger meaningfully.

Jan and Ben leaned over to read what it said. Once disentangled from the undergrowth of legal jargon, and all the 'aforementioneds' and 'notwithstandings', the meaning of the provision was quite clear.

The revised lease said that the leaseholders should have the right to use the dwelling house and land for as long as they might wish, without let or hindrance, only provided that they gave three months' notice of their intention to quit.

Fred looked up, his mouth hanging open in surprise.

'Well, what do you make of that?' He shook his head in bewilderment. 'Miss Gilbert can't have read this. They can't have been aware that the old lease had been superceded. She must have been working from a copy of the old lease that she found in the house. It's the only explanation.'

Jan and Ben looked at each other as smiles of relief and triumph slowly creased their faces. They could think of another explanation, but they decided not to stretch Fred's loyalties by sharing it with him. What did it matter, anyway? The newly found lease looked completely watertight. Virginia's little scheme had been blown right out of the water, smashed to smithereens, Jan thought with glee.

17

By the time Jan came back to Edge Farm, drought had succeeded the earlier storms. Even where race-courses were equipped to water the ground, the tracks became bone-hard and Jan was forced to put all her racing plans on hold. Use of the all-weather gallop was invaluable and helped to keep the string fit. Some trainers kept on racing despite the conditions, eager to snap up prizes in fields that were generally smaller and less competitive. But Jan had seen too many horses ruined by this kind of greed and told her owners it was in their best interests to be patient, the rain would come eventually and give the ground a 'cushion'.

Although he was supposed to have twice-weekly physiotherapy at the hospital – timed to coincide with the afternoon lull in the yard's activities so Jan could drive him there – Eddie used every excuse he could to get out of the appointments.

'Eddie, don't forget it's your physiotherapy today,' Jan reminded him over breakfast.

'I think I'm getting a cold. I'd better not go.'

'Don't be daft, a bit of a cold's not going to make any difference.'

'I can't go to the hospital and sneeze virus everywhere. It's completely antisocial.'

Three days later there were more excuses.

'I've got to skip physio again, I've done my shoulder. Ricked a muscle or something on the rowing machine. It hurts like hell.'

'So now you need the attentions of a good physio even more.'

'No, Jan, I don't,' he contradicted sharply. 'The advice on this kind of injury is to rest it, and that's what I intend to do.'

Jan decided to ask Tony Robertson if he would talk a bit of sense into Eddie.

'It's undermining his recovery, Tony. He does work out here, but I think he needs to see the experts to keep him concentrating on the most beneficial movements.'

Tony agreed to drop in the next day. When he arrived, he spent half an hour with Eddie in the living room and emerged with an amused smile on his face.

'How's his shoulder?' asked Jan.

'I gave it an injection. He didn't like it much – he's pathologically terrified of the needle – but he submitted in the end. I also told him he had to keep up the physio or his problems will only get worse.'

Later, when Eddie felt the coast was clear, he looked for Jan in the kitchen, his face like thunder.

'That bastard doctor of yours is a nutter, completely unethical,' he growled.

'Oh, come off it, Eddie. What the hell are you talking about?'

'I'll have you know he deliberately tortured me with that injection and I've a bloody good mind to report him to the General Medical Council.'

'Oh, grow up, Eddie, for God's sake. Like everyone else he's only trying to help. Stop whingeing, people are walking on eggshells around you. Well, enough is enough.' Jan couldn't believe what she was hearing and that *she* was saying it.

Eddie looked shaken.

'We've all done the sympathy bit to death, Eddie. Now snap out of it, or not only will you not get any better, neither will our relationship.' Leaving Eddie with his mouth open and plenty to think about, Jan got to her feet and stormed out of the house and down to the yard.

By the end of August, rain was cascading down on Gloucestershire, turning the ditches into streams and the streams into rivers. Gerry invited Eddie to the pub and took him in his van, leaving Jan alone with the children. It was about half-past nine when through the sheeting rain she heard a knock on the door. She put on the security chain and undid the latch.

'Yes?'

'I'm looking for Mrs Hardy.'

It was a young, male, Irish voice.

'You've found her. What's it about?'

'It's about a job.'

Jan stole a cautious look at her visitor through the gap between door and jamb. Under the porch light, she could see he was a thin streak of a child, carrying a sodden, yellow, dilapidated rucksack. His hair clung to his scalp like a bath cap and glistened like wet seaweed. Rainwater trickled like tears down his drowned face.

'My goodness, just look at you. You need wringing out.'

'I walked from the station. It's seven miles.'

Jan hesitated. Then, with a sudden impulse of concern, or intuition perhaps, she unhooked the chain and swung the door wide open.

'You'd better come in. Quick. Go through there and wrap yourself round the Aga. I'll find a towel and some clothes.'

Only then did it occur to Jan what a silly move she had just made. The pasty-faced boy could have been anyone, dangerous even, and he could have been *with* anyone, for that matter. She was alone in this isolated house, with just Megan and Matty upstairs asleep and below in the yard close on half a million pounds' worth of vulnerable, highly tuned horseflesh. What chance would she have?

But, by the time Jan had thought all this through, she was sure her visitor was alone and harmless. Puzzling, but innocuous, and looking in desperate need of help.

The boy was trembling as he shuffled into the kitchen. His grimy, torn anorak dripped onto the quarry tiles and the trousers of the blue suit that he wore underneath were drenched and plastered with mud. His cheap shoes squelched. Jan ran upstairs and fetched a towel, a clean T-shirt of her own and a pair of Eddie's old jeans.

'Get out of those clothes and dry yourself,' she said,

thrusting the towel into his arms. 'Then put these on. I doubt there's anything dry in that rucksack, is there!'

She dropped the clothes on the table beside the boy and smiled at his startled, unspoken question.

'Don't worry, I won't look.'

Turning her back, Jan hoisted the hob cover on the Aga. She unzipped a tin of tomato soup, upending it into a saucepan, then dropped two thick slices of bread into the toaster. Behind her, as she stirred the soup, she could hear her visitor laboriously exchanging one set of clothing for the other.

'You decent yet?' she asked with a faint smile.

There was a grunt and she turned. The boy looked more pathetic than ever, his black hair rubbed down and the clean clothes hanging off him, at least two sizes too big. He was just like a kid who'd missed his bedtime and was afraid of the dark, his eyes darting around taking everything in.

'Don't you know me, Mrs Hardy?' He turned a beseeching look up to Jan. 'That time we met . . .?'

Now, seeing him standing there clean and dry, Jan remembered. She clapped her hand to her mouth.

'Oh God, yes, of course! At Newbury. You did that thing with the horse. You're Patsy Keating.'

'Yes. An' you offered me a job.'

'I did what?'

'That's why I'm here. You said I could come and work for you any time.'

Suddenly she wanted to laugh, but stifled it because Patsy Keating was so plainly serious.

'Well, yes, I know what I said. But I didn't mean—'

She sat down at the table and scrubbed her face

with her hands. This was ridiculous. She looked up again.

'Anyway, you had a job. What happened to that?'

Patsy Keating shrugged and looked at the floor.

'I run away,' he whispered.

As he spoke the tomato soup boiled over with a furious hiss onto the hot ring.

On that day at Newbury, six months earlier, Jan had had a runner in the first race, Johnny Carlton-Brown's Supercall. As she stood in the paddock with Annabel and the owner, watching the gelding in his walking paces and discussing his future, the first of the jockeys appeared from the weighing room.

The day had started fine with long periods of sunshine and high silvery clouds, and warm air. But, as the runners for the first race circled the parade ring, storm clouds began to mass in the west and the sunlight lost its sparkle, dimming to glowering shades of old gold. In this hectic light the atmosphere began to thicken so that the thin file of brightly dressed jockeys glimmered like a string of coloured party lights.

As they entered the paddock, the riders fanned out to find their connections. Jan knew virtually all the senior members, at least by sight. But these were conditionals and only a small number would ever make the grade as professionals, though all were devoutly convinced they could. Jan was only able to name a few, but among the unfamiliar faces one caught her attention, a pinched, pale figure who seemed tiny even among these diminutive men. He was wearing the colours of one of Virginia Gilbert's notoriously demanding owners.

'That one looks like he's going to his execution, poor little sod,' she murmured to Annabel. 'Probably the first time he's ever worn Mr Kavunu's silks.'

Annabel nodded towards a large gelding, who was jigging round the ring. 'That's nothing to how nervous his horse is. Look at him, I wouldn't give him a snowball's chance, and he's fancied.'

Jan looked in her race card for the name of the horse, Canteloupe, and then read across to see who his tiny pilot was: *Patsy Keating*. She looked up again at the horse. He was still on his toes, yanking at the leading rein with repeated jerks of his head. His flanks foamed with sweat and his eyes rolled.

'Bel's right,' Jan murmured to JCB. 'I doubt we've got much to worry about from that one. He's boiling over.'

Virginia Gilbert, Canteloupe's trainer, was talking urgently to her jockey. Then she took Patsy by the elbow and began steering him towards their runner, apparently anxious to get him in the saddle as quickly as possible. Suddenly, as Jan felt Albert Mines, her jockey, tap her on the arm to get his instructions, a nerve-shredding detonation of thunder ripped through the air.

It spooked all the horses; some of them snorted and shook their heads, but Canteloupe was just as if he'd been ignited like a firework. With a whinny of terror he reared, his front feet jabbing the air like a shadow boxer. Virginia's lad was caught off guard. He panicked and let go of the lead rein, then tried to snatch it back but only snatched at air. Canteloupe was loose and had completely lost his head.

Snorting, he came back to earth and began to buck and kick ferociously, veering off the tarmacadam path surrounding the parade ring onto the grass, where the owners and trainers were gathered. Those nearest to him scattered in alarm, while the grooms leading the other runners stopped and tried to soothe their horses. Jan looked anxiously towards Supercall, who was being led by Roz. He remained typically unconcerned. But Canteloupe was beyond reason. He began to buck in circles, lashing out viciously before standing on his hind legs, rearing and squealing with fright. Suddenly the watching crowd gasped as they saw Patsy Keating stroll almost casually towards the frenzied horse. His tiny, brightly coloured figure stopped immediately under the forelegs of the huge, rearing animal. He opened his right hand, before raising it in the air beneath the horse's muzzle. Canteloupe's rage, or fear, or whatever it was, drained from him and he came back to earth instantly, planting his forefeet on the ground and standing absolutely still. He swished his tail once, nodded his head and flared his nostrils, but did not move one iota. Murmuring words that nobody could hear, Patsy rubbed the palm of his hand over the gelding's muzzle and Canteloupe, in a gesture that looked simultaneously grateful, loving and respectful, shoved his nose under his jockey's right armpit. Thunder cracked and echoed around the racecourse for a second time, more loudly if anything than the first. But it had no effect on the horse as Patsy took the leading rein and handed it to the groom.

Several members of the crowd broke into spontaneous applause.

Jan looked at Annabel. 'I can't believe what I've just seen. How on earth did he do that, Bel?'

Annabel shrugged.

'I don't know. But whatever that boy's got, if you could just bottle it . . .'

Virginia had checked the horse's legs and surprisingly – no doubt under pressure from Mr Kavunu – decided not to withdraw her runner. But word of the incident had reached the betting ring and Canteloupe's price drifted, so he started at relatively long odds. Meanwhile Supercall was shortened to second favourite.

The race took place in heavy rain. Jan was pleased with Albert, who gave Supercall a great ride, sticking to his instructions by keeping out of trouble on the outside of the field, and challenging with a smooth run from the two-furlong post. In truth, the horse was not really wound up for the race and, after clattering the last obstacle, finished not a bad third, ten lengths behind the winner. But the revelation was Canteloupe. Patsy Keating had him hacking round at the back of the field for most of the race, gently allowing him to improve his position as they reached the final bend. Weaving through beaten horses can be a tricky manoeuvre at the best of times, let alone on slithery ground. But horse and rider achieved it without fuss. As Canteloupe pinged the last two flights, he lengthened his stride to go past the favourite and won by three easy lengths.

An hour later Jan had run into Patsy Keating outside the weighing room. He was out of the riding gear and wearing his crumpled blue suit and cracked shoes.

'That was quite something what you did in the paddock,' she said. 'I thought the horse was going to have your head off for certain.'

Patsy gave her a thin, twisted smile.

'Sh-Jesus, he wouldn't do that.'

'How did you know he wouldn't? Weren't you afraid?'

The jockey looked up at her with big steady eyes.

'No horse would worry me.'

Jan laughed.

'Well, all I can say is, if you can do that, you can come and work for me any time.'

She hadn't meant it as a serious offer, of course. Poaching stable staff from any trainer, let alone Virginia Gilbert, was not the way to get on in the racing world. She had meant the remark as a compliment, a way of showing her admiration. But Patsy, it seemed, had taken her words literally. And now here he was in her kitchen.

'So why did you run away?'

'I couldn't put up with it no more.'

'With what?'

'Working for Miss Gilbert. They didn't treat me right.'

'Who didn't?'

'The other lads. They were always playing tricks on me.'

'How old are you, Patsy?'

'Nineteen.'

'Haven't you any family or friends that you can go to?'

'In Ireland, but I've no money. That's why I need the job, see.'

'Yes, I do see . . .'

Jan studied him carefully. He was shovelling the soup into his mouth hungrily, then snatching bites of the buttered toast she had placed on the table in front of him. He looked pathetic and vulnerable and suddenly, without quite knowing why, her heart went out to him.

When he'd finished, Jan gave him a slab of fruitcake and a mug of sweet tea. Patsy was terse and she couldn't get him to tell her in any more detail why he no longer wished to work in Virginia's yard. By ten-thirty she gave up.

'I really need to think about this, Patsy. The truth is, I don't need any more staff at the moment. But I'll tell you what I'll do. You can stay here tonight and I'll speak to Riscombe tomorrow. Will that be all right? They'll be wondering what on earth's happened to you.'

Patsy nodded. 'I don't mind if you talk to them, long as I don't have to go back.'

'OK. You can sleep in the caravan – did you see it down below? Come on, I'll take you.'

The old caravan, in which Jan and the children had lived for a year after first coming to Edge, was not particularly wholesome after its most recent tenants, Dec and Con, had vacated it, but at least it was weatherproof. Patsy appeared almost happy as he looked around, then dumped his sodden rucksack on the table. Jan found a stinky sleeping bag in the cupboard, but, as she left him, he gave her a wan smile, which she read as an expression of gratitude.

Jan walked across to the yard and let herself in, then went from box to box to check that all was well. When she came to Morning Glory the horse immediately backed away from the door, rolling his eyes suspiciously. She slid back the bolt and went in, talking to him in a quiet voice while stroking his silky smooth neck. MG had made painfully slow progress over the summer, but he had come to trust her to some extent. She had been riding him herself every day as no one else in the yard could get near him. That was a problem now since Jan had too much to do to devote herself to one horse. Tonight, no doubt, his emotional state was not helped by the storm, but Jan knew even on a quiet day his nerves were as tightly strung as a newly tuned piano. She also knew there was an awful long way to go before they could even begin to fulfil A.D. O'Hagan's ambitions.

Jan was still mulling things over as she locked the yard gate and made her way back to the house. She passed the caravan, its window now glowing with a pale yellow light, which seemed to wink in the rain. Thunder rumbled overhead and suddenly, as if it were a bolt of lightning forking from above, the thought hit her. She heard again the thunder of that afternoon at Newbury, saw Virginia's horse Canteloupe loose in the paddock, and Patsy's astonishing feat bringing him under control.

She remembered, too, Patsy's calm and utterly convincing remark to her afterwards.

'No horse would worry me.'

Next day Jan phoned Fred Messiter.

'I've got someone here at Edge Farm,' she told him; 'one of Virginia's lads from the yard – Patsy Keating. Do you know him?'

'I know of him all right.'

'Well, he just turned up here last night. He says he's run away.'

'Really?'

'You don't know what's been going on, do you?'

'No, I'm afraid I don't. I deal with their wages, but that's about it. You'll have to ask Virginia.'

'I'd rather not. Can you give me Scottie's number?'

A minute later she was dialling Scottie, who lived in one of the estate cottages.

'Patsy!' exclaimed Scottie. 'So that's where the little git is. We missed him at evening stables and he didn't turn in this morning. What's he bloody playing at?'

'I don't know the ins and outs of everything. He only told me he ran away because he wasn't very happy. Then he clammed up. He seems really upset. What's going on up there?'

The Riscombe head lad hesitated, while considering the situation. Then he cleared his throat.

'The lad's been with us since the New Year. Strange boy, fantastic with the horses, mind. In fact he's one of the best horsemen I've ever seen at that age. But he doesn't get on with people, if you get my meaning.'

'Go on, Scottie.'

'I don't know why for certain, but the rest of the lads took against him. I suppose that's why he says he's not happy.'

'But he seems harmless enough.'

'Oh, yeah, he's harmless. But he's a loner. Never joins in with anything.'

Jan could understand the problem. There was often a strong bond amongst stable staff, and they quickly came down on anyone who wouldn't try to fit in.

'So what would you like me to do with him?' she asked. 'Shall I run him back?'

'Oh, I don't know . . .'

Jan couldn't decide whether Scottie's caution was defensiveness or indecision.

Eventually he continued, 'What the hell took him to your place anyway?'

'He says he wants to come and work here.'

'Oh, does he now?'

There was a pause. She sensed Scottie taking a long draw on a cigarette.

At last he said cautiously, as if advancing a dubious proposition, 'Tell me, Mrs Hardy. How do *you* feel about the idea?'

Now it was Jan's turn to hesitate. She knew Patsy knew horses, but the worry was all the bits she didn't know about him.

'Well, I'm not really sure, Scottie. Are you saying Miss Gilbert would let Patsy go?'

'Yes, Mrs Hardy, I think she might. I'll have to talk to her, of course. But it'd be a weight off of my mind if she did, I *can* tell you that.'

'Scottie, there is just one thing – can you assure me that this boy is honest?'

'Oh, don't get me wrong, Mrs H. Patsy's straight all right, in fact he may be too straight.'

'Meaning?'

'OK. He's very religious. Catholic, if you know what I'm saying.'

'Tell me more.'

'Well, that's it. He's *very* Catholic.'

Jan could imagine why this might be a problem. Almost all the Irish lads had Catholic backgrounds, though it was not that often you saw them trailing off to Mass unless there was a particularly important religious celebration. Yet she could guess most of them had left home with the same parting words from their mothers ringing in their ears: 'Now promise me, Sean – Kieran, or whoever – you'll never miss Mass over there in England.'

Patsy's observance of his religion would be an uncomfortable reminder of their backsliding, and some of the more uncouth ones among them wouldn't like it.

'I'll need to think about this,' said Jan. 'Can you talk to Miss Gilbert anyway? In the meantime I'll have another chat with Patsy.'

The rain, for the moment, had cleared and the Gloucestershire air was breezy but warm. After breakfast Jan went down with a mug of tea to the caravan, where Patsy had yet to emerge, though she did find him up and dressed. He was sitting at the table with a book open in front of him.

'I've been talking to Scottie,' she said.

'D'he say I got to go back?' His voice quivered with fear.

'How would you react to that?'

As if tasting a foul medicine, he screwed up his face.

'No way. There's definitely no way I'm going there ever again.' Now a tear watered his eye.

Again Jan was touched by his vulnerability. She went on softly, 'Come on now, don't worry. Scottie was very understanding. And he thinks Miss Gilbert might agree to you coming here, at least on trial.'

Patsy relaxed and that wry smile, the boy's only way of showing pleasure, appeared on his face.

'So I can stay?' he asked huskily.

'I can't say for definite, not at this stage. I will need to get clearance from the Jockey Club and your stable pass, if you do, but I'm thinking about it. You can stay today and, if you want to show willing, there's some mucking out needs doing. So come on. Get your skates on.'

Before they left the caravan she glanced at the book open on the table. It was a prayer book.

Jan took Patsy and introduced him to Roz Stoddard, then asked her to find him some boots and get him going. Annabel, who was just back from Barbados, was already in the office looking through the next week's entries when Jan appeared.

'Thanks to the rain it looks like we'll be able to declare most of these.'

Two mugs of coffee steamed on the desk in front of her.

'Yes.' Jan nodded in agreement. 'It'll be a huge relief to get started.'

Annabel handed one of the mugs to Jan.

'Who was that kid? He looks familiar.'

Jan sipped from the mug.

'Don't you remember him? That's Patsy Keating.'

Annabel frowned.

'Not . . .?'

'Yup. From Virginia's. Remember Newbury, the conditional race? That's him. He turned up late last night, soaked to the skin, almost hypothermic, looking like a ghost. He said he'd run away and wanted to come and work for me.'

'No! Just like that?'

Jan nodded.

'Yes, just like that. Weird, isn't it? I've just spoken to Scottie Venables. Of course, he wouldn't say, but I'm pretty sure Patsy's been bullied at Riscombe. Scottie said Patsy was *very* religious, making it sound like he'd got a screw loose.'

Annabel wrinkled her nose.

'Perhaps he's a religious maniac. Do you think he flogs himself with thistles and thorns?'

'*Bel,* stop it, this is serious. Patsy's come here and thrown himself on my mercy. He's desperately unhappy and it's not his fault, I'm sure of it. Remember when we used to take in horses that were resting and we discussed how some of them were probably only depressed. And how later on we realized that it was literally true. We said then they deserved as much of our love and attention as the ones with sore feet. Well, it's the same with Patsy, and I really don't think I can turn him away. I just can't.'

A brief silence fell between the two women before Annabel, staring mindlessly through the window, continued, 'Speaking of disturbed animals, they seem to be Patsy Keating's particular forte, don't they?'

Jan was in the middle of taking a sip of coffee and looked up at her assistant, expectantly.

'Go on,' she said quietly.

Annabel carefully set her mug down on the desk.

'I wouldn't be surprised if you were thinking the same as me,' she said.

'And that is?'

The two friends looked at each other and spoke in unison.

'Morning Glory!'

18

Scottie Venables did not ring back until after evening stables.

'I spoke to Miss Gilbert about Patsy,' he told Jan.

'What did she say?'

'She's no very pleased. She doesna like the idea of Patsy pissing off to you like he did.'

'No, I can imagine.'

'So I claims if the kid's unhappy here, we won't keep him anyways. In the end she says, all right, Scottie, you handle it.'

'That's good,' said Jan. 'I've decided to take him on, anyway. Will you send over any paperwork?'

'I don't do paperwork, Mrs Hardy. That's Fred Messiter's department. I'll ask him to send you his P45, and all that kind of stuff.'

'Thanks, Scottie, I'm glad we sorted this.'

'Me too. You've got yourself a good horseman, that's for sure. I suppose you could call it a fair swap.'

'I'm sorry?'

'Patsy for this Velvet Dynasty we had from you. My God, Mrs H, that's a surprise package and I'm no joking.'

'What do you mean?'

Scottie laughed.

'No, no, you'll be finding out soon enough without me telling you.'

Jan was gutted by the way such a lovely, promising horse whom *she'd* picked out had been whisked away from her, not to mention the grievous loss of her old friend Wolf's Rock, who always managed to pull a race out of the fire when she most needed it. So she did not appreciate Scottie's crowing – if that's what it was.

Strolling out of the office a couple of minutes later, Jan saw Patsy's slight figure in the yard going from box to box talking to the horses, all of them coming forward eagerly to greet him and have their muzzles rubbed, even though he had no carrots or Polo mints as a bribe. She noted how confidently Patsy carried himself when he was around them, not with the bounce of a show-off parading his skill, but like someone relaxing amongst his own tribe. His mouth hardly moved as he whispered to them, but she was too far away to hear any magical words.

She smiled and went across to him.

'Patsy, I've got news from Riscombe. It's going to be all right. Miss Gilbert has agreed to let you transfer to Edge Farm, and I'll be happy to have you. So, is it a deal?'

She held out her hand and as Patsy shook it, his face lit up with pleasure and relief.

'Thank you, thank you, Mrs Hardy. That's great.'

'You can go on using the caravan for the time being. Is that OK?'

'Yeah, that'll be fine, I'll soon have it shipshape. It'll be like brand new, you'll see.'

'Now, about the horses, I thought I'd give you just the one to do for the time being. It's what you might call a specialized job, and Annabel and I have a feeling you're just the man for it. He's called Morning Glory and he needs some special TLC. He's from Ireland, so at least you'll be speaking the same language.'

'I seen him already, Mrs H, in his box,' Patsy said.

'What do you think of him?' Jan set off walking towards Morning Glory's box, with the lad stuck to her side like glue.

'I thought there was somethin' up with him, so I asked Roz. She said he's a bit mental. Well, I think he's just scared, but I let him know he could trust me. So I reckon we might work well together.'

For the monosyllabic Patsy, it was a long speech, but it was also just what Jan thought.

'Well, here he is. How are you, old boy? Meet your new lad. Patsy's going to be looking after you now.'

Morning Glory came cautiously to the door and as Jan raised her hand to stroke his muzzle he backed away, blowing sharply down his nostrils as he did so. She outlined the reasons for MG being at Edge Farm, as Patsy listened with close attention.

'Anyway,' she finished, 'whether he's a nutcase, a fruitcake or just a misunderstood genius remains to be seen. I want you to spend all of your time with him, ride him in his work and do him in his box. He's not easy, Patsy. He's even had the pluck to run away with *me*. Which was not very pleasant for either of us, I can tell you. But I did get a good feeling when he galloped, so he might just be the best horse we've ever had in this yard – with the right handling, of course. Do you think we can get him right for a novice hurdle in a few weeks' time?'

Patsy nodded, his face serious.

'It might take a bit longer,' he said, 'but I reckon we'll get there in the end, won't we, old boy.'

Once a week Jan had a half-hour conference with A.D. O'Hagan on the telephone. As usual, they went through each of his horses, discussing their general fitness and reviewing suitable races. A.D. always required a variety of options and made the final decision. It never ceased to amaze Jan how a busy international financier had time to study the conditions of a race at Fontwell Park or Newton Abbot. But A.D. was the consummate gambler, who never let the slightest detail escape his attention.

'Now what about Morning Glory?' he asked. 'I'm rather hoping he'll run before the end of October.'

'Me too, but I can't rush him,' Jan said. 'I've got a new lad, Patsy, working with him full time. He gets on with him brilliantly.'

'So have you marked out any possible entries?'

'There's a couple of novice hurdles at Warwick and Stratford that might suit.'

'And they are?'

Jan gave A.D. the details.

'Would you like me to enter him?' she asked.

'I'll get back to you on that. Now what about Russian Eagle?'

It was interesting that A.D. never put extra pressure on Jan by asking if she thought a horse would win a particular race. For that she was grateful. She knew what A.D. required of his trainers, which was to know how fit a horse was when it ran. Then it was down to him to decide what its chances were of winning.

Every year on the second Sunday in September a horse show was held at Cheltenham racecourse and this year both Megan and Matty were due to take part. During August Megan, with Monarch, had been at pony club camp in North Wales. By the time she returned home, her enthusiasm for junior eventing had been gushing. Matty, a beginner, and a great deal less confident than his sister, had at last started to enjoy his riding under the tutelage of his grandfather. He and his pony Rocket had already been entered in some of the mounted games. 'Then he'll have a target,' Reg had confided.

That morning the chaos at Edge Farm had been comparable to Grand National day. Reg and Mary had arrived early to help with final preparations and found the place in a state of high tension. While Reg worked with Matty, grooming Rocket and plaiting his mane, the keyed-up Megan rushed around, infecting everyone with her feverish excitement. Every detail had to be checked, every contingency allowed for. Mary, making sandwiches with Jan in the kitchen, observed it all with amusement.

'Mum,' shouted Meg breathlessly from the hall, 'I've checked the fuel in the lorry and I don't think there's enough to get us there. So we'll have to leave enough time to fill up on the way. And I *wish* people wouldn't go off with the clothes brush. I need it for my hat.'

'You used to be just like that,' Jan's mother said fondly.

'I still am,' Jan answered, grinning.

Despite Megan's anxiety, the party of five, with the two ponies, arrived at the showground in good time. Jan had tried to persuade Eddie to come with them, but he'd flatly refused.

'No way, Jan. I don't like going out while I'm like this. I don't want the sympathy vote.'

'You go out to the pub with Gerry.'

'That's different. Everybody knows me there.'

'Forgive me, Eddie, but that's pathetic. Until you're prepared to face the world, you'll never be able to consider yourself better.'

'I'm not better.'

'Please yourself, stay here, but you can't hide for ever, Eddie,' Jan responded, full of despair, then left without him.

Jan was making her way from the parking area to the secretary's tent, where she needed to confirm the children's entries, when Tim Farr came into view, striding purposefully towards her.

'Could I have a quick word, Mrs Hardy?'

'If you can walk and talk at the same time you can, but I'm on urgent business. What's it about?'

'I was in the pub in Stanfield, your local,' said Farr. 'And Terry the landlord was saying you'd just taken on a new lad from Miss Gilbert's yard.'

'And?'

'Well, according to Terry, this lad had been complaining about mistreatment by the staff at Riscombe. I was wondering if you could confirm that.'

'No, sorry, I can't. That would be confidential. Anyway, who told Terry this?'

'It seems to be pretty much common knowledge, actually.'

Jan knew this often happened in a village like Stanfield, which was small and intensely curious about any strangers that appeared.

'OK,' she said, 'I can confirm I *have* taken on a new conditional. His name is Patrick Keating and he has transferred to me from Miss Gilbert. That's all.'

'The thing is,' Farr persisted, 'I'm working on a story about stable lads' working conditions and I've been turning up more and more tales of harassment and bullying in training establishments. It seems this is a serious problem.'

'Not in my yard it isn't.'

'What about Miss Gilbert's?'

Just for a second Jan was sorely tempted. Then she saw, in her mind's eye, the likely headlines: HARDY ACCUSES GILBERT YARD OF BULLYING or even worse, in tabloid transformation, TRAINERS IN CAT FIGHT OVER STAFF. She shook her head firmly.

'Forget it. There's no way I can answer that because I honestly don't know what goes on in Virginia Gilbert's yard. You'll have to ask her. I'm sure she will be most obliging, she is with most people,' Jan added mischievously.

'I will, of course. But it would help if I'd already established some of the facts. Do you think Patrick would agree to talk to me?'

Jan stopped and turned to the journalist, raising her finger.

'No, Mr Farr, absolutely not. I won't have you pestering my staff just to feather your own nest, so stay away. Patsy's a very shy boy. You wouldn't get anything out of him anyway.'

'I could try . . .'

'I have already said it once, stay away. Keep off my property. If I catch you hanging around my place looking for a story I'll be onto your editor before you can say, "Hold the front page". Have you got that?'

Tim sniggered and ran to catch up as Jan strode off.

'All right, all right, you're the boss. But I'm not giving up on the story. It's a public issue, and important for the good name of the racing industry. If my editor agrees with that, why wouldn't you?'

'I would. But I'm not getting involved. My life's complicated enough as it is. Please just go away.'

By now they had arrived outside the secretary's tent. Jan turned to face Farr once more.

'Look, I've got to go and sign in, or my daughter will kill me. This is a very rare, but very important, family day for me, so please leave us alone.'

But Tim Farr hadn't quite finished.

'Oh, Mrs Hardy, there's just one more thing. On quite a different complication in your life, are you aware of any further developments in the case involving Eddie Sullivan? You know, the road accident?'

'No. Are you?'

'It's just that, well, I understand Inspector Hadfield is now preparing a case against him for causing death by reckless driving. It seems he's convinced Mr Sullivan had been drinking excessively. Apparently he doesn't believe in the third car that you and I have spoken about. Nor does he believe there's any evidence against that certain person who we both think may have had it in for you and Mr Sullivan.'

'More fool him then,' said Jan, trying to control her increasing anger and frustration. 'So who does he think's been trying to blacken our names all over the West Country? And how would Hadfield know about this supposed *excessive* drinking by Eddie? Eddie was unconscious for four days. He couldn't possibly give a sample.'

'I know that. But I'm told Inspector Hadfield has statements from others who saw him drinking at the racecourse.'

'Malicious gossip. That would be enough for a prosecution, would it?'

'I don't know. But I guess it might be.'

'Who the hell's been giving these alleged statements anyway?'

'Well, I only know of one for sure.'

'And that is?'

'Are you sure you want to hear this?'

'Yes, of course.'

'It's Virginia Gilbert's head lad.'

They returned to Edge Farm in moderate triumph. Jan had been determined not to let Tim Farr's unwelcome news spoil the afternoon, and had forgotten it completely when Megan and Monarch won the dressage class and came third overall in the working pony. Later

Matty and Rocket had a hilarious time, especially in the apple-bobbing contest, which involved riders trying to capture small russet apples floating about in buckets of water without using their hands. Matty had ridden Rocket to the bucket and stood him correctly beside it. Then, as the child struggled to get a hold with his teeth, his hair soaking, the pony decided to help him out. As quick as a flash, Rocket stuffed his head in the water right up to his eyes and drew the apple out in triumph, chomping on it with delight.

In the evening Toby Waller phoned to tell Jan that he had business commitments which meant he wouldn't be able to go racing on the Wednesday, when Flamenco was due to run at Worcester.

'Oh dear, I was hoping to have a chat, actually,' Jan replied. 'Did you know the police are still pursuing Eddie, the bastards? I thought the idea of getting him for death by reckless driving had gone away, but now it seems it hasn't.'

She passed on the information Tim Farr had given her.

'It still looks a bit thin, if you ask me,' Toby said, doing his best to reassure her. 'Is Eddie's memory still totally blank? Can't he remember anything at all?'

'He says he can't. Hadfield obviously doesn't believe him, though.'

'I know a good defence brief can try to convince a jury that the amnesia is genuine, and that Virginia's employee, the guy who made the statement, could be accused of acting against you maliciously, with some success, no doubt.'

'Well, he must be. Especially as his boss seems to be

going out with Harold Powell now. Can you *believe* that? Why can't we nail that skunk once and for all?'

'Because there are no witnesses to his presence on Cleeve Hill. No proof that he did anything. But there's still time, and while there's time there's hope. So hang on to that.'

'I wish Eddie could. He seems close to despair at times. It's really worrying and such a struggle.'

'Oh, Eddie'll come through. It's a difficult time for you both, I know, but he'll come through.'

A few days later A.D. O'Hagan was on the phone.

'How's it going with Morning Glory, Jan?'

'Patsy's doing wonders with him. He's been working him on his own, so at last we're getting him into some sort of shape. We think he's made real progress these last few weeks. But I'm still worried about his attitude to other horses around him. The only way to sort that out will be to try him, I suppose.'

'Exactly. I'm sure you know what you're doing. So that's settled then. We'll aim him for the Stratford race you mentioned in October.'

Jan knew she now had to get serious with Morning Glory. She had given Patsy enough time to get to know her wayward inmate. They walked and trotted then cantered the horse on alternate days, working him on his own after the rest of the string had come in. Then, in the third week of September, they tried him once more with just a couple of others. On the way to the gallops MG was fully charged, but Patsy held him together, constantly talking to him, reassuring him, stroking his neck until they reached the end of the track and the start of the gallop.

Suddenly the horse exploded, leaping in the air like a kangaroo. Patsy sat still, as cool as a cucumber, until he regained control. He turned the horse in a circle and headed off after the others, who were waiting for him. Two more huge leaps placed him between them, and as they set off galloping Patsy's pale cheeks turned bright pink. After four furlongs the horse pulled away finishing ten lengths clear of his rivals.

'He's a quick horse,' was all Patsy said after he had brought MG under control and walked him gingerly back.

Later Jan and Annabel discussed the fairly disastrous gallop with Patsy. Annabel suggested they should return to the citation bridle, but Patsy said definitely not.

'I'm thinking maybe the biggest problem is the other horses,' he said. 'He doesn't even try to run away when he's on his own. He's just sensible then and you can get some serious work into him.'

Jan had been thinking along the same lines.

'I agree with Patsy. I'm sure everything the horse does, he's telling us something. Maybe he's saying he's not the sociable type. If so, we'll just have to accept it and go back to working him on his own.'

'But if he can't cope with a couple of horses at home,' objected Annabel, 'how's he going to manage on a racecourse with twenty odd banging and crashing over hurdles?'

'We'll worry about that when the time comes,' Jan said. 'What's more, I don't even know if we can get him into the horsebox to get him there yet. Still, at the moment I just want to get him fit.'

But the looming problem of MG's reluctance to load would not go away and one morning in late September Jan decided they would put him to the test. She had Dec bring the lorry to the yard gate and lower the ramp. The interior of the vehicle was divided so that four horses could travel together, each in its own stall.

'Why don't we try taking out the dividing walls, Mrs H? Maybe he just wants more room.'

'That's a good idea, Patsy,' said Jan.

It only took a few minutes to realign the partitions, which created twice as much space for the tricky horse to stand in, and meant he would be less likely to be spooked by the stalls touching his flanks. Jan knew that cajolery and kindness would be the only methods to work long term as the use of force and the drug ACP had already failed with him.

Talking to MG in a continuous stream of soothing words – something he'd never have been able to manage with a human being – Patsy led the gelding gently up the ramp. MG moved forward cautiously as the handlers held their breath. First his head crept up the ramp, sniffing it as he gingerly moved forward inch by inch, then the withers and finally the quarters passed inside the lorry. Dec and Con raised the ramp swiftly but quietly and waited for the sound of kicking. Jan got into the cab and peeked through the sliding panel into the horse compartment. MG was standing patiently while Patsy held his bridled head and gently stroked his muzzle.

'You all right, Patsy?'

'Yes, Mrs H. He's as nice as pie now.'

Jan saw MG blink and for a moment his eyes rolled upwards, the pupils almost disappearing. But as Patsy rubbed his nose, the horse lowered his head with a snort of acceptance. As Jan turned the key to start the engine she looked back, expecting to see a reaction. There was none. She slipped the transporter into gear and drove slowly along the tarmac that formed an access road between the yard and the house. MG was still unfazed.

'Let's take him for a trip down the village and see how he reacts,' she said.

'Well done, Patsy, that was a relief. It was a brilliant idea, moving the partitions. I really think we might have cracked him at last,' Jan said when the experiment was over and MG was safely back in his box.

At that moment the sound of cars being driven fast up the lane from the main road could be heard. The bulky horsebox, still parked beside the yard entrance, masked the view so it wasn't until the two cars swept onto the forecourt that Jan and her staff realized they belonged to the police.

Inspector Hadfield stepped out of the first vehicle and carefully placed his trilby on his head. He then flicked his jacket with his fingertips – like a dog scratching at fleas – before taking a deep breath.

'Mrs Hardy,' he said, his serious voice belying that incessant milky smile, 'is Edward Sullivan here? I need to have a word with him.'

19

Eddie must have seen the police cars from his bedroom window and he appeared at the front door without being summoned.

'What the hell's going on?' he bellowed, holding on tightly to a pair of walking sticks, which were replacements for his elbow crutches.

Hadfield beckoned a uniformed constable forward and strode towards the house. Jan hurried to catch up.

'Mr Edward Sullivan?'

The policeman's voice was formal, without a trace of his concocted geniality.

'I think you know who I am, Inspector Hadfield,' Eddie snarled.

'Mr Sullivan, this is a warrant. I am arresting you on suspicion of causing death by reckless driving. I must warn you that you are not obliged to say anything unless you wish to do so. Anything you do say will be taken down in writing and may be given in evidence.'

Eddie's resentful attitude was instantly dispelled as he looked wildly back and forth between Hadfield and Jan.

'What? You can't. I don't get this, you're *arresting* me?'

Hadfield nodded.

'Yes. You'll be coming back with us now to the station for questioning.'

He beckoned to a second constable and the two uniformed officers stood on either side of Eddie. One of them gently touched his elbow and Eddie yanked it away.

'Get your sodding hands off me,' he yelled. 'I don't need your bloody help.'

The two constables flanked him as Eddie hobbled between his sticks, still protesting, all the way to the patrol car. Hadfield moved rapidly towards his own car, with Jan in quick pursuit.

'What the hell is this? You can see Eddie's disabled. He's in no condition—'

'He can walk, Mrs Hardy,' interrupted Hadfield, as he turned to face her. 'You needn't worry. I'll have a police doctor look at him when we get to the station to check if he's fit to be interviewed.'

Jan watched anxiously as Eddie clambered into the back of the second car. He gave Jan a look she had never seen before, an angry, glowering black look.

'Inspector Hadfield,' Jan pleaded, 'stop it. This is completely and utterly *ridiculous*.'

'I don't think so, Mrs Hardy. Now you can give the station a ring later on if you wish and I will tell you what has transpired.'

He opened the door, slipped into the passenger seat and motioned his driver forward as if he was mushing a team of huskies. The two cars took off at speed while

Jan and her team watched in complete astonishment. The whole affair had taken less than five minutes.

It was three hours later when Jan phoned the Cheltenham police station and spoke to the desk sergeant. She was told Eddie had been charged and put in a cell. She then asked if she could speak to Inspector Hadfield, but was informed he had already gone home to Mrs Hadfield.

'So tell me, what happens next?' asked Jan.

'I'm told he'll go before the magistrates in the morning,' the sergeant continued, in a practised and kindly tone. 'They'll consider bail favourably, I imagine, but of course you can never be sure.'

'But where? When? Do you have any details?'

She quickly wrote down the address of the court alongside the time: ten a.m.

Eddie's time in custody was brief. Following hurried discussions with Tony Robertson, Eddie's doctor, Jan contacted a local solicitor, Bob Warren, who went to see Eddie promptly and agreed to represent him. Jan watched from the back of the court as Warren, a small ginger-haired forty-something in an untidy suit, successfully argued for the prisoner to be granted bail on Jan's surety. Outside, on the steps of the court house, Jan thanked him profusely.

'I don't know how we'd have managed without you.'

'That's OK, Mrs Hardy. It's what I do.'

'What happens now?'

'You take Eddie home and give him a bit of TLC. This ordeal is bound to have set back his recovery. I'll go back to the office and put in an application for legal aid. The police and the Crown Prosecution Service will now start to prepare their case.'

'Their *preposterous* case,' Eddie called out truculently from several yards away.

'So there'll definitely be a trial?' Jan asked hesitantly.

Warren shrugged.

'Not necessarily. That's for the CPS to decide when they have reviewed all the evidence. Of course, while Hadfield will be trying to persuade them to proceed, my job at this stage is to see if I can get the charges dropped.'

'Is that likely?'

'No, not very, I'd say. The police have clearly been thinking about this for some time. They must be reasonably confident they have a good chance of it going to trial or the arrest wouldn't have taken place. But we'll see . . .'

It was still morning as Jan drove Eddie back to Edge Farm. He looked like thunder and was reluctant to discuss events in the police station, or the police questioning.

'I just told them the truth – I've got amnesia and can't remember the bloody accident. Hadfield didn't believe me, of course. What is it with that man?'

'Oh, Eddie, I hope you didn't lose your temper.'

'Lose my temper, I was spitting blood a couple of times. But I realized it wouldn't do any good in the end.'

'Well, it wouldn't. What do you think of Warren?'

'Don't know. He's all right, I suppose.'

Bob Warren turned out to be far more than all right. He was a bull terrier. During the next three weeks he drove over several times for consultations with Eddie and Jan. He also spoke to everyone else in the yard and to all of Eddie's medics. At Jan's suggestion, he contacted Tim Farr and on his own initiative looked into the background of William Moorhouse, whom he already had knowledge of through the legal network. Again at Jan's insistence, and with her help, he compiled what he called a narrative account of Harold Powell's ventures, beginning well before the auctioneer had attempted to defraud Jan over the sale of Stonewall Farm. He regarded the fake press release as extremely significant, and took affidavits from the Taylor-Joneses at the vicarage in Chiselcombe, and hunted down several other recipients of the offensive document.

As Warren often stressed, there was nothing else either Eddie or Jan could add while the wheels of justice slowly turned.

'Just get on with your lives,' Bob advised. 'Leave the worrying to me.'

In the midst of this upheaval, Edge Farm Stables was doing well. Over the next month Jan sent out fifteen runners, and carried home two trophies, as well as getting a second and three third places. One of the winners was for A.D., on a day when he could not be present. As usual on these occasions, the Irishman sent Jan a bottle of champagne with a note, written in his own rapid scrawl.

> Sorry to have missed Wexford Lad. Congratulations to you all. We are looking forward to Morning Glory at Stratford. A.D. O'H.

The Stratford race was now only a week away and this was A.D.'s way of letting Jan know just how keenly he was following MG's progress. Jan did wonder why this particular animal was so important to him. She knew he had paid a lot of money for the horse, but A.D. was a very rich man indeed. On the other hand, she also knew for sure that he didn't like the idea of being taken for a mug. Perhaps now, having shelled out far more than the horse appeared to be worth, he urgently wanted Morning Glory to prove him right.

The days preceding the Stratford meeting had been showery, but the day itself dawned under a clear sky. The beautiful crisp autumn morning promised perfect racing conditions. By ten they were ready to load Morning Glory and Jan seriously hoped he wasn't feeling as nervous as she was. It was a huge relief when he went up the ramp calmly into the enlarged stall and then travelled to the course without incident. His race was a novice hurdle that had attracted so many declarations it had been split, with MG in the first division, which was the opening event on the card.

Jan and Patsy were settling MG into the racecourse stable when Annabel brought Jan a race card.

'Have you seen the runners in the other division?' she asked, pointing her finger to a name halfway down the list, a name Jan knew only too well: Velvet Dynasty, owned by 'executors of Col. G. Gilbert', trained by Miss V. Gilbert and ridden by F. Howlett.

'Yes, I saw it in the *Racing Post* earlier this morning. It looks like we've been spared an interesting clash,' Jan said.

For the time being she was too busy concentrating on MG to think any more about Virginia's runner. At first MG was keyed up and suspicious of his strange new surroundings, but Patsy had stuck to the horse's side like a limpet and managed to calm him down by degrees. The fine weather only added to the optimistic gloss. And the Edge Farm contingent felt they had done everything they could to give MG his best chance. Now it was all up to him.

The parade ring at Stratford was sited between the racecourse buildings and the finishing post, so the entire stand had a good view of the runners. This could easily have added to MG's emotional state, despite the reassuring stream of talk Patsy was directing towards his left ear as he led him round.

At last the jockeys dribbled into the paddock and a

wave of anticipation swept through the crowd. A.D.'s usual jockey, Murty McGrath, had taken the ride. Although Jan had invited him to give MG a spin on the gallops a few days earlier, the champion jockey had other commitments and couldn't make it.

'Murty,' she said nervously, her mouth as dry as chipboard, 'you *have* seen this horse before, haven't you?'

Murty rode hundreds of horses every year but, like most successful jockeys, he had total recall.

'Yeah, I rode him OK, if you can call it that. He was headstrong all right and always wore a citation bridle. He fought me like a wildcat, but I never gave him his head until two furlongs out. But he didn't quicken, burnt himself out, I reckon. To be honest with you, I didn't take to him. I thought he'd a phobia with other horses. Something must have happened when he was broken, I'd say.'

'Well, he's *much* better now, different altogether, thanks to a lot of hard work by young Patsy. That's the lad minding him.'

Just then Patsy and MG came wandering by. Murty's eyes lit up as he looked at the horse's head in alarm.

'Where's the citation, Mrs H? Surely you're not running him without one?'

'Yes I am,' said Jan firmly. 'He doesn't need all that gear in his mouth. In fact, I'm pretty sure that's been a large part of the problem. That bridle hurt him and I've been weeks sorting out the inside of his mouth.'

Murty was looking volatile.

'Mrs H, I'd not expect you to put me up on that horse without extra precautions being taken, that's for sure.'

'Now look, Murty,' Jan persisted, 'it's no good you going on about this. Anyway, we haven't brought the equipment with us. So we haven't got a choice. He runs as he is and that's the end of it.'

'I've got two more rides this afternoon. If this one puts me in hospital because you sent him out with the wrong bridle, you'll have the other owners to answer to and they're not going to like it.'

'Don't be bloody ridiculous, Murty. Are you telling me the champion jockey's afraid of the horse? Is that the case?'

'Afraid? Course I'm not afraid. I'm just not a fecking eejit.'

The bell sounded, signalling the jockeys to mount and Patsy brought Morning Glory to a halt.

'Now, Murty, look,' Jan said firmly, 'I know the horse has ideas of his own, and if you try and dictate to him he'll expend all his energy fighting you – as you found out over in Ireland. So you've got to go *with* him to some extent. Understand? Let him run the race the way he wants. As long as he's not pissing off and he jumps over all the hurdles, I don't mind.'

'You're saying it's a steering job then, are you?' Murty growled. 'Jesus, the horse is a novice. He knows no more than a dead cat would know.'

'Well, let's just see, shall we, Murty? Let's call it an experiment. But the point is he has to go to the start without getting steamed up. Don't canter him down with the others. Take him out on the course last, and go very steady. That's essential. You'll be fine, you'll see.'

At the very moment Murty was getting a leg-up from Jan, A.D. hurried over to join them.

'All right, Murty?' he said.

Murty tipped his cap.

'He's on his toes, Mr O'Hagan. But Mrs H's been telling me to let him do it his way.'

A.D. patted his horse's neck.

'Off you go then.'

Murty checked that the last of the runners had already left the parade ring, and moved MG off at a sedate walk towards the exit and the course. Only the odd sideways jink of his quarters betrayed the horse's nerves. A.D. watched them depart, then looked sharply at Jan.

'Do it his way, is it? You're not forgetting this is his first race over obstacles?'

'No, A.D., I'm not,' said Jan, suppressing her irritation. 'Don't worry. I know he can jump. He's a natural, you'll see. I'm sure the obstacles will help settle him.'

But as soon as the words were out, Jan feared she had been overconfident. She didn't like being taken for a mug any more than A.D., but if MG didn't perform and her 'experiment' failed, that was exactly how she would look.

The opposition was more formidable in numbers than in quality, or so it appeared. The noughts in front of MG's name, denoting his unplaced efforts in his races in Ireland, were uninspiring to the punters, and he was quoted at long odds behind a group of fancied horses who had more useful, and more recent, form. But none of them, in Jan's eyes, could be seen as an overwhelming threat.

At the start, MG began to show signs of his old temperament, sweating and tossing his head from side to side, but the jockey's excellent horsemanship held him together. As the runners were called into line, Murty had MG poised slightly behind the rest, and timed his approach to the tape so skilfully that MG was already on the move when the elasticated tape flew away. The horse immediately lifted his head and, lengthening his stride, he glided into a three-length lead.

The first few hurdles presented no problem and he soared over them like a gazelle. Following Jan's instructions to the letter, Murty sat as quiet as a mouse, allowing the horse to find his own stride into the obstacles. It was obvious, even to the apprehensive jockey, that MG was enjoying himself out in front. The horse pricked his ears and looked confident as they came past the stands for the first time. He led the field around the tight left-hand bend which took the horses on towards the back straight, where halfway along they briefly met rising ground. Now the pace increased and they were galloping downhill towards the final turn.

Watching through binoculars from the stand, Jan's heart was thudding loudly against her ribs – she knew the race was reaching its climax. Morning Glory was handling the sharp bend well, but, quickly scanning the field for dangers, Jan saw two horses take advantage of the downward slope and career past the tired runners in pursuit of Morning Glory. By the time they turned into the straight, with just two hurdles to negotiate, the pair had forced their way into second and third places. They were still four lengths off MG, but it was obvious the race was going to be between the three of them.

Morning Glory got too close to the second last and hit it hard. All around there were cheers for the more fancied runners, as MG's advantage was reduced to a length. Murty responded by crouching lower in the saddle and seeming to raise his whip.

'Don't hit him, please don't hit him!' Jan said out loud, without realizing.

Murty didn't hit MG. He merely glanced to the side to check on the opposition. He pulled his whip through to his other hand and rested his knuckles either side of the horse's withers. Jan thought this was a breathtaking display. Most jockeys would have panicked, waving their whips, thrashing their horses' backsides. Murty did neither. He simply concentrated on making himself part of the horse's own flowing movement. But the two pursuers continued to close inch by inch. Approaching the last flight of hurdles, the three animals were almost level. Clearly galvanized by the sudden proximity of two other hard-breathing horses, Morning Glory stood way off the jump and executed a breathtaking leap. One of the challengers blundered and tipped his jockey over his ears. The other hopped over well enough but, by the time his jockey had shaken him up for a final effort, Murty McGrath had gone beyond his reach. On the run-in, as Morning

Glory extended his raking stride inch by inch, he won with seven lengths in hand.

In the unsaddling enclosure Murty was delighted as all his earlier anxieties were washed away.

'He just made monkeys of the lot of 'em! And he had a ton in hand. Mrs Hardy, you were right. No more citation bridle for this feller. He loved it out there.'

'Thanks, Murty,' said Jan, 'and you rode him perfectly. He obviously likes you better than he did.'

'It wasn't me that did it. It was the horse. Look at him. Just look at him now, he wouldn't blow a candle out.'

They all looked at Morning Glory in the golden afternoon sun. His breathing was already back to normal, and he was the picture of well-being.

So was Mr A.D. O'Hagan when he took the bridle and posed for the photographers, an unusually broad grin lighting his face.

Jan had no more runners and by now she'd have got her winner into the transporter and headed back to Edge as early as possible. But today she couldn't leave, at least not until after the sixth race. She wanted to see Velvet Dynasty run.

To lose horses to other trainers, especially ones with potential that she had spotted in the first place, ones that she had personally schooled over obstacles and taught the rudiments of the game, was a physical pain to Jan. And when the other trainer was Virginia Gilbert the pain was doubled. But today Jan felt compelled to watch, even though it was likely to add to her torture. The last time she'd seen Velvet Dynasty compete on a racecourse had been on the flat while she was watching TV. He'd been given a miserable ride, and made no impression on the result. Since then Jan had ridden the horse herself so she knew how misleading that form would be. Even more recently Scottie Venables had bragged to her that the horse was a surprise package. Now she was itching to know exactly what he meant.

Finbar Howlett rode Velvet Dynasty in quite a different style from the way Murty had handled Morning Glory. For half of the two miles he kept him under tight restraint, placed nearer last than first. But once they'd passed the stands and begun the second circuit Finbar gradually released him, letting him carve his way through the back markers. At the top of the final bend the horse was contesting the lead and, with two to jump, he was already a couple of lengths clear. His leap at that second last gained him another length in the air and, after that, there was not another horse to be sighted as Velvet Dynasty skipped over the last and won as he liked. Jan felt like spitting rust, but an image of the colonel came into her mind and she knew how pleased he would be. Jan's eyes welled up – it was hard losing such a dear and loyal friend as the colonel. Her only connection with him was the horses and now her old friend Wolf's Rock, not to mention Velvet Dynasty, had left. 'Life can be so unfair,' she sniffed, but she had to steel herself for what lay ahead, good, bad or indifferent.

The staff breakfast at Edge Farm the next day was a noisy affair. Annabel, who always collected the *Racing Post* from the newsagent's in the morning, had read aloud an inside story, printed under the headline,

HARDY AND GILBERT UNVEIL HOT-POT NOVICES AT STRATFORD

It made good copy: two female trainers from different walks of life, each possessed of a novice hurdler of exceptional ability. The paper had made no bones about how it saw things working out. No doubt Velvet Dynasty and Morning Glory were going to be intense rivals throughout the season but, more than that, they were going to embody a larger rivalry between their two trainers. Which horse, which trainer, was the better? On the evidence of their respective debuts, both horses ran enticingly over the same distance and under identical conditions, and they could not be split. The issue would remain undecided until they met, possibly at Kempton over Christmas.

At the moment Jan rarely made statements to the press if she could avoid it, so she was not quoted. Virginia Gilbert had been rather less discreet. 'Mine would beat hers doing handsprings,' she was quoted as saying. 'It will be no contest. We're ready whenever Mrs Hardy is. I can't wait.'

Jan's staff, on the other hand, were equally positive that MG, with his raking stride, would never be caught by the Gilbert horse. Jan said little, allowing them their effervescence. But as she left the table to answer the phone, she knew in her heart that a front-runner was always a big target, vulnerable to any particularly fast-finishing opponent, and Velvet Dynasty looked all of that.

She picked up the phone.

'Hello, Jan, it's Virginia.'

Jan almost dropped the receiver.

'Yes?' she said, trying not to sound too peeved.

'I take it you've read the *Racing Post*.'

'Yes.'

'They seem to think we're rivals. I really can't think where they got *that* idea from.'

'From you, I would think.'

'My horse will smash yours into the middle of next week, you do know that, don't you?'

'That's not a very pleasant way of putting it, and I doubt it's true either,' said Jan.

'Well, *we're* up for it at this end. Are you?'

'I'm up for most things, Virginia, as long as they don't harm my horses. But I'm not going to let you or the newspapers determine my horse's entries.'

'Oh no, of course not, but I do have other priorities, and one of them is to show you I've got the better horse. Another is to stop you spreading snidey rumours about my yard. Goodbye.'

A continuous tone cut in, so Jan replaced the handset. 'Right, if that's what she wants, so be it. I'll take you on Virginia,' she muttered, 'and I'll bloody beat you too.'

She didn't understand what Virginia had meant by snidey rumours until a few minutes later when, breakfast over, she was leafing through the pages of the *Post*. A small diary story caught her eye: 'Tim Farr's crusade against stable bully boys'. It appeared from what she read that Farr's investigation was shortly to be printed in the *Wessex Daily News*. Despite all its efforts, the *Post* had been unable to discover any details, except for one. Which stated that one of the stables being investigated was Riscombe Manor.

20

Before leaving the racecourse, A.D. O'Hagan had told Jan that he and Siobhan were staying overnight at Stratford, where they had tickets for a performance at the Shakespeare Memorial Theatre.

'But I have some people to see in Bristol tomorrow evening,' A.D. had continued, 'so Daragh and I'll be down your way in the morning. You won't mind if we call in, will you? I'd like a chat.'

'Of course not. Come to lunch.'

Jan was considerably more relaxed in her dealings with A.D. than she used to be, but the prospect of his visits still made her quake a little. Usually A.D. would come to cast a critical eye over the stable and his horses, but his stopovers had at times heralded a change in his racing policy.

It was well over a year since he had invited Jan to dinner at the Queen's Hotel in Cheltenham to outline his plan to set up an English training operation at a modern stable complex, with Jan as his private trainer. She had been bowled over by this show of confidence, but so far she had resisted the idea. She knew it would give her the kind of financial security most trainers only dreamt of, but she was unwilling to give up the independence she had worked so hard to establish. While she had not heard the scheme mentioned recently, A.D. was not the kind of man who let himself be thwarted. So she assumed it was not a dead duck.

Siobhan had gone straight from Stratford to Birmingham airport before flying on to Amsterdam, where she was due to give a recital, so A.D. arrived accompanied only by his driver, Daragh. Jan had fretted about whether to give them something out of a fancy cookbook, but in the end they sat down in the kitchen, herself, Eddie and the billionaire, to peas, mash and grilled sausages washed down with cider.

A.D. ate methodically, cutting the sausages into small rounds and carefully pasting the slices with Colman's mustard before putting them into his mouth. Eddie ate slowly and was almost silent, though he responded politely to A.D.'s enquiries about his recuperation. The court case, however, was not mentioned.

A.D. talked mainly about the horses and went through the list, paying particular attention to Russian Eagle, who in three weeks was due to run in the Mackeson Gold Cup, the first big chase of the season at Cheltenham in mid-November.

'He'll struggle to go the pace, I suppose,' A.D. said with a quizzical look. 'I doubt he'll be one of the fancies.'

'I don't know about struggle,' Jan countered. 'It depends on what he's up against on the day. You needn't worry about his fitness. He's really sharp and as keen as that mustard you're putting on your sausage.'

'Excellent. And so are the sausages, by the way.'

When they'd finished eating and Jan was making coffee, A.D. looked at his watch and said unexpectedly, 'Jan, would you mind putting on that radio at all? Just briefly. Siobhan's got a new recording out and they're playing something from it in a couple of minutes. She wants me to let her know if they give it any sort of review.'

'Oh great, I'd like to hear it myself. What's it on?'

Jan eventually found the wavelength of the classical station and the presenter was highly respectful towards Siobhan. A.D. nodded his approval at the words: 'One of Europe's top mezzo sopranos at the top of her game, with a coloratura technique almost comparable to Callas's.' Jan did not have a clue what this meant, except that to be compared with Maria Callas was obviously a hell of a compliment.

One of the tracks, an aria Jan decided, was sung in French, but she was at a loss to understand the words, though she fully appreciated the phenomenal control of the vocalist. She glanced from A.D. to Eddie, who both sat in silence concentrating, with their eyes cast down.

When the aria finished, A.D. switched off the radio and, for a few moments, no one spoke.

A.D. gave a contented sigh before suggesting that he and Jan take a tour of the yard, and then what he called a post-prandial walk through the pine trees above the house, as far as the top of the ridge.

'Your man, Eddie, has quietened down a lot,' he said on the way.

'Yes, I know, but he's a lot better physically, I think.'

Suddenly Jan decided she ought to broach a matter that, so far, she had been keeping from her patron.

'A.D., I hope you don't mind, but while we're on the subject of Eddie, there's something I ought to tell you. I wanted to give him something to work towards, some incentive, so I promised him . . .'

She swallowed hard. She had no idea how her 'boss' would take this.

'Well, you see, I promised him he could ride Russian Eagle in the National – if he made a full recovery, that is!'

A.D., possibly from complete surprise, said nothing. Jan hesitated, then carried on.

'I know I should have talked to you first, but it just came out, you know, sort of spontaneously. I didn't even ask your co-owner at the time.'

'And what does Annabel say now?'

'Oh, she thinks it's a great idea. She knows Eddie can, or at least could, ride the course, and he gets on with the horse really well.'

'Hmm. I suppose if the pair of them can virtually win the Foxhunters', then theoretically they can win the National. Is that what you're both thinking? Well, not if Eddie's in the state I saw him in just now he can't, that's for sure. He'll have to get rid of those sticks and prove he's completely fit, *completely* fit, mind, or I'd never agree. The National is not there for occupational therapy. And he'll have to sort out this police thing. He can't ride a horse from the jailhouse, can he?'

'Oh!' said Jan, surprised. 'It won't come to that, I'm sure. It's all going to be cleared up. Eddie's got a very good lawyer now.'

'Did you know that feller Hadfield came to see me at Aigmont?' A.D. went on. 'He wanted to know was Eddie drinking in my box during the afternoon before your accident.'

'Blimey! I hadn't a clue. Did he go over to Ireland especially?'

'He did. And I told him I didn't see the man take a drop.'

'Thanks, A.D. I appreciate that. So will Eddie, I know.'

'It was the honest truth. But there may be others that saw things differently. Anyway, I don't want to talk about that now. I wanted to have a word about Morning Glory.'

He explained that there was a race in Ireland, a good-quality novice hurdle at Leopardstown in early January, and he wanted the horse to run. As a successful poker player A.D. never liked to reveal his hand, but he dropped a broad hint that he had already backed the horse to win.

'I'll send you the details. It wouldn't do for you to be putting him in the wrong race. Now, the question is what do we do with him in the meantime?'

'We're all keen to take on that novice of Virginia Gilbert's.'

'The one she pinched from you after her father's death, who won the last race so handily at Stratford?'

'Yes, that's the one.'

A.D. laughed.

'I thought so. I saw the *Racing Post* this morning, so I knew it was on the cards you'd be thinking along those lines. What race have you in mind?'

'The obvious one's next month at Cheltenham, on Mackeson day.'

The Mackeson Gold Cup was the feature race of the season's first major meeting, and the two-mile novice hurdle on the same card was a prestigious event, worth four times the prize money that Morning Glory had collected at Stratford. A.D said nothing to Jan's suggestion at first, as he was concentrating on the track and maintaining his footing. As they came out of the trees and saw the crown of the ridge just above, A.D. reached the top before Jan with a final scrambling effort, and sat on the ground, breathing deeply, waiting for her to catch up. He gazed reflectively over at the wide spread of country on the other side of the hill, with the Welsh mountains in the distance.

'Will you look at that?' he said in wonder as she joined him. 'You could probably see the Wicklow Hills from here if you had the eyes for it.'

Jan flopped down beside him.

'So, anyway, what do you think?' she persisted. 'I'd say that's possibly the race Virginia will be going for as well.'

'Yes,' agreed A.D., to Jan's delight. 'That sounds fine, let's go for it.'

They absorbed the view for a few moments longer until A.D. broke the silence.

'There's one more thing I need to tell you, Jan. I'm

going to view a yard in the Lambourn area tomorrow. It fits the biography and it's what I'm looking for over here, at least on paper.'

He turned his head and looked steadily at her.

'So if I like it, I'm hoping you'll give it the once-over. It would be a great opportunity.'

Jan took a deep breath.

'Well, A.D., if you want my *advice* . . .'

A.D. chuckled.

'It's not advice I'm wanting. It's your agreement to come in with me.'

'But I've already said no to that. It's not that I'm not grateful or anything.'

'Well, the offer's still open, Jan, but it won't be for ever. As of this week, or this month, maybe this year, you can still change your mind. Now . . .' He glanced at his watch. 'I'd better be off to my meeting. I'll race you down, but no running, mind!'

That afternoon Jan completed the entry form for MG's next contest. Then, after a moment's thought, she telephoned Reg at Riscombe.

'That was a great win yesterday, girl,' her father enthused. 'He's maybe your best horse. I expect he'll need a few more races like that before he's proved it, mind.'

'Did you see the result of the other division?'

'Velvet Dynasty? Yes, won his by the same margin, didn't he? When do you intend taking him on?'

'Are you reading my mind, Dad? Virginia's actually challenged me, so I can hardly back down, can I? I'm well aware that hers is good too, but I do have the advantage because I've handled both horses. And we all think our chap's better.'

'So what's the plan?'

'I've entered him in a novice event on Mackeson day. I'm pretty sure Virginia will be considering the race, but it wouldn't go amiss if it got around Riscombe village that we were definitely entered. If you know what I mean.'

Jan knew her father well enough to know that he was smiling.

'Just leave it with me, girl. I'll make sure everybody knows, don't you worry about that.'

Tim Farr's story ran in the *Daily News* two days later. It was a subsidiary item in a small block on the front, but occupied all of the back page, under the headline: THE UNACCEPTABLE FACE OF RACING. Farr had secretly recorded conversations with stable staff from two different establishments. The piece detailed initiation rites and other humiliation games as well as sexual harassment.

The article ended with a ringing denunciation of the perpetrators.

> Of course, not all racing stables are like this. But it is an unacceptable fact that there are individual trainers, and senior members of staff, who allow such practices to continue. Many of the young men or women come into racing purely for the love of animals, their sole reason for working with them. It is shameful that such idealism is

> battered by workplace bullies to such an extent that some apprentices actually run away, abandoning their possessions. Which is already alleged to have happened at Virginia Gilbert's yard at Riscombe Manor, where a member of her staff was forced to 'bolt' after months of being harassed for his religious beliefs. There is no suggestion that Miss Gilbert knew what was going on at the time. But the point is she should have known.

'Wow, I bet Virginia doesn't like the fact that her yard was mentioned,' Annabel declared when she and Jan discussed the piece later.

'Do you think so? The snippet about Patsy looks just that – a snippet. But, God, I'm really uneasy about this kind of reporting. It smears the whole of racing and there are so many good people in the industry working their balls off for a pittance, including us.'

'Yes, I know, but Tim Farr's right about not betraying the idealism of staff. People do genuinely care and they are quite prepared to put up with the long hours and low pay. But to allow them to be bullied, that's despicable.'

'I agree. If I found out there was anyone here doing that kind of thing, even a hint of it, I'd have their guts for garters, believe me.'

The following Sunday afternoon Edge Farm was almost deserted. Eddie had gone off with Gerry, to support his friend in a stock-car race. Jan thought it seemed a strange therapy for someone who'd nearly died in a car smash, but now that Eddie had a macabre interest in it, Jan was even more afraid that his next step would be to get the Morgan patched up so he could race it himself.

Megan and Matty had disappeared with some friends from school for a ride on their ponies and none of the staff were around when Jan went down to the yard to take stock of the feedstore. She'd just made a note of what needed ordering, and was relocking the door, when she heard a man's voice behind her.

'All *alone*, are we?'

The menace in the voice was immediately recognizable and Jan knew instantly that she was about to come face to face with Harold Powell.

He was striding with grim purpose across the yard towards her.

'I hope you've got a very good reason to be here, Harold,' she said, trying to control her voice and stop it quaking.

'Oh yes, I've got a good reason all right. I've come to give you a final warning, Mrs bloody Busybody,' Harold spat out.

Jan did not feel the need to reply any more sweetly.

'Don't you speak to me like that. I won't take any warnings from you. Your threats won't work, so just sod off before I call the police.'

Now Harold was shaking his finger at her.

'I've got a lot more than threats, I've got actions. I've already done some things, and I can do more, you'll see. You'd better watch your step.'

'So tell me what you have done.'

Harold made quote marks with his fingers.

'"This press release is issued by the Cotswold News Agency as a service to the community." Remember that? "Have you had a *shower* lately, Mrs Hardy?" Remember that too?'

'I always thought it was only pathetic tossers like you who made anonymous phone calls, and sent unsigned letters full of malicious gossip. Well, now I know I was right, you jerk.'

'As a matter of fact, I did it for another reason. I did it to make you shit scared, you self-righteous little bitch. You've put the police on to me again, haven't you? Accusing me of things you have no way of proving, not ever. Now you're making allegations against Virginia's yard that are unsubstantiated. You won't be allowed to get away with all this. You will have to be *stopped*. One way or the other.'

'Are you going to try shoving me off the road again, is that it?'

'Next time there won't be a mistake. I'll make damn sure of it. That car put me off. If it hadn't suddenly appeared, I could have made a better job of you and *darling Edward*. I was hoping for a fire – in fact, an explosion would have been nice. Still, better luck next time, eh!'

Jan had been edging round, with her back to the line of boxes beside the feedstore. She maintained continual eye-contact with Harold, wondering if he had gone completely insane. His livid face had turned ghostly white, his eyes had become bloodshot and his lips were drawn tightly back around bared teeth. She felt that if she showed him a moment of weakness he would attack her with his clenched fists.

'Talking of which,' Harold snarled more gleefully as he jerked his thumb in the direction of the feedstore, 'that little lot in there would *burn* merrily enough, I dare say, along with your precious horses.'

'So you are going to turn into an arsonist now, Harold. Is that to go with the attempted murder?'

'Getting rid of you wouldn't be murder, Jan Hardy. It would be a service to humanity.'

He twitched and moved towards her. Jan felt perspiration on her brow and edged further along the wall. The horses looked curiously over their stable doors. Some pawed the ground and whinnied at this extraordinary confrontation.

Jan saw a muck fork that had been left against the wall just a few feet away, in the direction she was heading. Slowly she took a couple more strides. Grabbing it in a flash, she held it in the air, pointing the tines towards Harold.

'Go back,' she warned.

Making a gesture calculated to mock, he moved away, tut-tutting and shaking his finger from side to side in a sarcastic manner.

'Stick me with it, would you? Now what would your Inspector Hadfield have to say about that? He'd say you were conducting some kind of ruthless vendetta against Virginia and me, wouldn't he? And I think he'd be right, don't you?'

'Vendetta? That's you and your ghastly girlfriend. I was ready to forget that you tried to cheat me over that land. I was even prepared to accept that my mother-in-law had, in fact, died accidentally. But now you've admitted your crusade against me. I'm going to see you locked up. That's for certain!'

Harold seemed as though he was about to speak. But instead he took a deep breath and thought better of it. He looked at the horses ranged on every side; they looked back at him bewildered. Suddenly, for whatever reason – the staring horses, the brandished fork, the fact that he might have said too much – he unexpectedly lost his nerve.

'Well, fuck you,' he said contemptuously, 'you'll see where it all gets you!'

Harold moved swiftly towards the archway, and, as he reached it, he turned. Jan was standing in the same position, with the fork raised.

'I'll get you yet, Jan Hardy. You'll pay for this,' he hollered. Then he was gone.

21

Jan gulped in air, her heart still pounding. Gradually she lowered the fork, then finally dropped it to the ground as she sank to her haunches.

'*God, please help me!*' she said aloud, covering her face with both hands. 'Is this never, *ever* going to end?'

'It's all right, Mrs H.'

Jan snatched her head from her hands and looked up.

'Who's there?' she called to the voice coming from behind her. She turned and there was Patsy Keating, his moon face peering over the lower door of the stable.

'Patsy! Where in heaven's name did you spring from?'

'I was in here all the time. I heard everythin' that feller said, so I did.'

'You did?'

'Sure, I did so. He said he wanted to kill you.'

'You bet he did,' said Jan grimly. 'You sure you really heard everything?'

'Yeah. He said he made phone calls because he wanted to scare you shitless.'

Suddenly it struck home. This was it! The breakthrough she'd been waiting for.

'Patsy!' she cried, tears running down her face in relief, 'you clever, clever boy! I believe you're the answer to my prayers, I really do.'

Patsy was puzzled.

'Your prayers, Mrs H?'

'Come on, let's go in. We need to make an important phone call.'

She caught hold of Patsy's arm and ran with him into the office, where she immediately dialled Bob Warren's home number. The woman who answered said she was Nina Warren and sounded rather peeved when Jan said it was work, and an emergency, and please could she speak to Bob urgently.

'I'll have to get him,' said Mrs Warren primly. 'He's in the garden.'

Fretfully and unaware that she was doing it, Jan drummed on the table with her fingers until Bob came on the line.

'It's Jan Hardy. I'm sorry to ring you at home on a Sunday, Bob, but I thought you should know. Harold Powell turned up here. He's threatened me – again, viciously – though I suppose I should be getting used to it by now. But I'm still shaking.'

'Did he come alone?'

'Yes – at least, I think so.'

'How did he threaten you? Verbally? Or did he actually hit you?'

'No, yes, I mean verbally. But there's more. He admitted everything: it was him that tried to drive us off the road, and he made the anonymous phone calls, and he also sent out those fake news bulletins. And what's more he said he wasn't giving up and that he was quite prepared to kill me if necessary. For ruining his life, he said.'

'When was this? How long ago?'

'Not long. Ten minutes or so.'

'Well now, don't be too concerned about this, Jan. I've seen it all before, people lashing out in rage.'

'I'm not concerned. I'm delighted. Because we've got him, haven't we? Now we know for sure he was responsible for Cleeve Hill. Eddie's off the hook, isn't he, Bob?'

'I'm afraid not, Jan. Unless, by some crazy chance, you recorded Harold's remarks on tape. Otherwise he'll deny it, then it's just the same old story, your word against his.'

'But it's not. I didn't record the conversation of course, but somebody overheard it. Patsy Keating, one of my stable lads, was right here. He heard the whole lot.'

'Did he, by God? Well that certainly puts a whole different complexion on things. Is he with you now?'

'Yes he is. He lives here in a caravan by the yard.'

Bob covered the mouthpiece of his phone and Jan heard a muffled exchange between him and his wife. Then he was back on the line.

'Just give me a bit of time to get out of these gardening clothes and I'll drive straight over. I think it's important that I record what Patsy actually heard from his own lips while his memory's fresh.'

The solicitor duly arrived with a tape recorder and interviewed Jan and Patsy separately about Harold's escapade. Bob told Jan that he would prepare affidavits based on the recordings and inform Hadfield of the new evidence.

'And I'll certainly tell him that Powell admitted causing the crash on Cleeve Hill in front of a witness: and that the police have also charged the wrong man. Just for good measure, I'll lodge a complaint on your behalf against Harold Powell for threatening behaviour, just to show he wasn't here to play a game of pat-a-cake. All in all, I'm pretty hopeful this will be enough, particularly with the amount of circumstantial evidence we've already got about Harold Powell's animosity towards you. I can get the CPS to drop the charges against Eddie. Where *is* my client, by the way?'

As Jan told him, Bob burst out laughing.

'That man's something else, you'd think he'd have had enough of crashed cars by now.'

Bob Warren had left Edge Farm by the time the stock-car duo returned. Jan and the children heard Gerry's van drive onto the forecourt, pulling a trailer with an extremely battered car roped to it. The Hardys rushed out from the house to meet them.

Eddie stayed in the passenger seat as Gerry stepped out and came towards Jan. His face looked pained and anxious, a man bearing bad news.

'Gerry, what's the matter? Didn't it go well?'

'It's Eddie, Jan. I'm really sorry, I—'

'What about him? Come on, out with it.'

Gerry spread his arms wide helplessly to explain.

'I don't know how it happened. Well, I do. There was all this free beer, see, and while I was racing, well, he just went a bit over the top, if you know what I mean.'

'You mean he's drunk?'

'You'd better come and look.'

Eddie was slumped in the van with a stupid grin on his face. Over the past months Eddie had been temperate. He went to the pub regularly with Gerry, but actually drank very little. Today had clearly been a different story. There was no doubting he was completely plastered. With his shirt pulled out of his waistband, he was slurring his words and his eyes had that unfocused look of a man whose head was swimming in alcohol.

Furious, Jan yanked open the door and Eddie, whose head had been lolling against the window, nearly fell out.

'Hello, Jan,' he said woozily as he levered himself upright. 'How is the most beautiful racehorse trainer that ever lived? Are you all right, old girl?'

'Eddie, you're pissed!' said Jan, slightly amused by his comments. 'Get out. You can't sit there all night. Gerry wants to go home.'

'Good old Gerry,' said Eddie fondly. 'I've been telling him about my plan to ride Russian Eagle in the National next year.'

Jan took his elbow and gently but firmly pulled him out of Gerry's van. Eddie stood there swaying as she extracted his walking sticks from behind the seat.

'Come on, Gerry, let's get him into the house,' she said, beckoning Eddie's drinking buddy over. Cautiously they half walked, half dragged Eddie towards the front door, while he still rambled on about Russian Eagle.

'The Ger-rand *National*,' he was saying. 'The ambition of every jockey. C'mon, tell you what, let's go down and see my friend Eagle. C'mon, Jan, please. I want to pay a visit to my old friend Russian Eagle, future hero of Aintree.'

'No, Eddie, not now, for Christ's sake! You'll scare the living daylights out of him. I'm putting you to bed.'

They got into the hall and were manoeuvring Eddie up the stairs. Suddenly he wrenched himself free from Jan's and Gerry's guiding hands and spun around.

'But I don't *want* to go to bed. I want to see my *horse*.'

At that moment he reminded Jan of her five-year-old child whining close to bedtime. Then, all of a sudden, he seemed to step forward into the air and missed the tread, tumbling to the base of the stairs. He landed in a heap at the bottom in total disarray, in front of the horror-struck Megan and Matty.

'Oh God!' shrieked Meg. 'Is he all right? Is he dead?'

Jan had been a qualified first-aider for years and she had more than once tended fallen riders with broken bones – but most of those had been sober. Eddie would not respond sensibly to her questions about what hurt and what didn't and she was unable to see or feel a serious injury, so in the end she let Gerry carry him up the staircase and lower him onto the bed. Eddie did not seem to be in any pain and lay in the fetal position, already half asleep.

'Do you think he's hurt himself?' Gerry queried anxiously.

'I'm damn sure he has, going arse-over-tit like that. But he's so rat-arsed I really can't tell if it's bad. But it's his spine I'm concerned about. I'll just have to call the doctor.'

Tony Robertson appeared briefly that evening, behaving rather off-handedly when he realized why the accident had happened.

'Let him rest, sleep it off,' he told Jan. 'I expect he'll be pretty bruised and sore in the morning. Though I wouldn't think he's aggravated his spine. But you say he still had numbness in his legs – before this happened even?'

'He says so, he's still walking unsteadily.'

Jan lowered her voice.

'And he also told me – it's a bit difficult really, Tony – but he can't have sex, he said nothing's happening.'

Tony looked at Jan shrewdly.

'Is that so?'

For a brief moment Jan was worried that he was about to make a wisecrack, but he quickly pulled himself together.

'Eddie's a lot better now than when I first saw him, that's for sure, and he's well on the road to a full recovery. But one can't take any chances with spinal injuries like this. So he'd better have another assessment. I'll arrange for a visit from a physiotherapist I know. She specializes and lives in this area.'

'She?' said Jan.

'Yes, her name's Gloria Hooke.'

'And this Gloria, she specializes in sex, does she?'

For the first time since he'd arrived Tony relaxed and laughed out loud.

'No, silly. Spinal injuries and so on – which, of course, can include sexual dysfunction. In any case Ms Hooke is much better equipped to assess Eddie than I am.'

The next day, after they had worked the first lot of horses, Jan took Eddie a mug of tea in bed. He had evidently been awake for some time. She heaved him upright and packed a couple of extra pillows behind him.

'Does that hurt?'

'Everything hurts. I'm knackered, completely knackered.'

He was in a deep trough of gloom.

'Just look at me,' he went on. 'No good to anyone. Half-crippled, unemployable, *drunk* . . .'

'Eddie,' said Jan impatiently, 'we've been round this block before. Tony Robertson says you're probably fine, but you're to stay in bed for the moment. Anyway, he's arranging a home visit from a physiotherapist, who'll give you another assessment and work out the appropriate treatment. Tony is adamant you're making good progress and will fully recover. This is only a temporary setback.'

'A temporary setback before I go to jail, you mean,' Eddie reflected gloomily.

'No, Eddie,' said Jan, suddenly realizing she had not told Eddie about Harold's incriminating visit. 'There's really good news about that!'

She summarized the previous afternoon's events at Edge Farm.

'So you see,' she went on as Eddie listened without comment, 'Bob thinks the CPS will decide there's not much chance of a conviction, and Hadfield will be under serious pressure to arrest Harold Powell. If so, your problems will be over.'

Eddie let out a profound sigh.

'If only it was that simple.'

As Jan and Annabel stood at the yard entrance waiting for second lot to return from the gallops, a small hatchback drew up and out stepped a tall Nordic-style blonde, with a huge bosom that seemed likely to burst the buttons of her white tunic at any moment. Her left breast was adorned with the badge of the Chartered Society of Physiotherapy.

'Hi, I'm Gloria? The physio? I've come to treat a Mr Sullivan – right?'

Jan and Annabel exchanged bemused glances. From her accent, and the way she turned every statement into a question, she seemed to be a New Zealander.

'Oh, yes, right,' said Jan. 'Come this way. I'm so grateful you could give us a home visit. He's still in bed, I'm afraid. He had a bit of a fall yesterday and he's rather sore. Do you know his medical history?'

Jan explained the background of the road accident as she escorted Gloria up to Eddie's room. The physio was carrying a medical bag not unlike the one used by Tony Robertson, though Jan imagined it was packed with massage oils rather than drugs.

As they went in, Eddie was lying motionless under the duvet, his eyes still closed.

'Eddie,' said Jan brightly, 'this is Gloria, your new physio.'

Eddie groaned.

'Do I have to?'

Gloria looked at Jan and smiled sweetly.

'Mrs Hardy, I'm sure it would be best if you left me alone with Edward? You must have loads to do?'

With reluctance Jan left and made her way to the stable office, where she found Annabel.

'I think I can see why Tony said she was better equipped than him. The bastard! He's done this on purpose.'

An hour later Jan heard a voice calling 'Coo-ee, coo-ee?' She left the office and saw Gloria Hooke beckoning with one hand, medical bag in the other. Jan swiftly joined her and they strolled to the car.

'We've had a really good session,' said the physio. 'I'll send a report to Dr Robertson and call back in a couple of days?'

'Do you think Eddie's aggravated his back injury with that fall yesterday?'

'Oh no. I'm wondering if the acrobatics on the stairs have actually done some good?'

'What on earth do you mean?'

'Dr Robertson told me, in confidence, of course, that Eddie was reporting some dysfunction which he found a little er – embarrassing, shall we say?'

'Ye-es. I know about that,' said Jan cautiously.

'Well, it isn't uncommon for patients with spinal injuries to complain of these physical problems – or difficulties of a *sexual* nature?'

The physio sounded impeccably clinical. Reaching her car she slung the medical case across to the passenger side and settled herself in the driving seat. She shut the door, wound down the window and started the engine.

'But,' she went on, 'just to *reassure* you, in Edward's case I can positively confirm that everything appears to be in perfect working order now? Well, in *that* department at least?' She winked. ''Bye, Mrs Hardy.'

Jan stood with her mouth half open as Gloria drove away, shaking her head in disbelief. When she told Annabel about it afterwards the two of them cracked up.

'You mean falling down the stairs made him a bit stiff, and now he can—?'

'Yes!'

'When he couldn't before?'

'Yes! According to the Buxom Bombshell.'

'Oh dear, we shouldn't really be mocking the afflicted, should we?' said Annabel as she caught her breath between fits of laughter.

'I don't know that we are. Perhaps he's been mocking us,' Jan replied.

But over the next few days Jan began to appreciate

the more serious side of it all. What did it mean? Was it significant that she had joked about Eddie's condition? Did it mean she had abandoned, or lost, her desire to have Eddie as a lover? When she reflected more deeply she realized it wasn't about Eddie's lack of potency, or otherwise. It was about reality. Her attitude to him had completely changed in the last seven months. It was not physical at all. It was not his disabilities, but his personality – his new, far more aggressive and impatient personality – that had brought the change. How cruel was that? As soon as she told the man she loved him deeply, the *person* she loved was taken away, maybe for ever. It was like having her lover abruptly and unknowingly substituted for his twin – identical in outward appearance, but inwardly quite different and far less appealing.

For the time being nothing would change, Jan knew that. But Eddie was still her guest and another dependent. A discussion about their more intense relationship – a discussion she knew would eventually take place – would have to wait for now.

For two weeks there was no more news from the police regarding the case against Eddie. Meanwhile the business of racing and, if possible, winning had to go on. Jan's training fees were barely covering her costs and extra prize money was an important means of making up the deficit. Her personal target was to average a winner every fortnight; it had looked quite feasible in the first two months of the season, but suddenly they dried up. Jan had the whole string scoped by the vet, but there was no sign of virus. She made slight alterations to the feeding regime. But in the end, reminding herself of a few very near misses, she reasoned the element of luck was the one thing she couldn't control and that was now weighing against her. Soon the scales of justice would dip the other way, and if she kept the horses in good condition it was only a matter of time.

'Don't panic and lose your cool,' Reg had advised. 'You'll just have to sit it out.'

Many of the stable's hopes for a reversal of fortune would be riding on Russian Eagle and Morning Glory at Cheltenham. As MG's race approached, the sporting press began to hype it up even more. Several diary pieces appeared hinting at a grudge match between two ambitious neighbouring female trainers, though the main focus was on the rivalry of the horses, and the sense that the race would provide one of those climactic head-to-head contests that were the lifeblood of any sport.

On the morning of the race Jan's stomach was churning with nerves from the moment she woke. Riding Dingle Bay out at exercise, she could hardly concentrate, her mind was only half on the job in hand. Would MG load in the transporter? she wondered. Would he boil over in the paddock or down at the start? Was he fit enough to take first prize? Or would his run be jinxed by the unknown factor that had prevented her other horses winning for the last three weeks?

Annabel was equally nervous about Russian Eagle's tilt at the Mackeson. Realistic counsel did not see an Irish Grand National winner triumphing over the faster two-and-a-half milers, though Bel was more concerned about his safe return in what was probably going to be a fast and furious contest.

The horses travelled in the same lorry, with MG occupying his usual double stall, while Russian Eagle, uncomplaining, remained in the single compartment. Roz and Patsy had hardly left their charges' sides during the last forty-eight hours. Now, after decanting them from the transporter, they led them towards the security boxes at the course and tried to suppress their nerves, as they both knew their edginess could be transmitted to the horses.

The Mackeson was the fourth race on the card. Eagle was easily the pick of the paddock, and Roz was crimson with pleasure when he was awarded 'the best turned out'. Impeccably behaved as he went to the start, Russian Eagle under Murty McGrath ran, Jan thought, an excellent race to get third, making only a couple of minor jumping errors, and ceasing to be competitive only after jumping the second last, when his two faster rivals quickened away up Cheltenham's notoriously demanding hill to the finish. Even though Russian Eagle completed at one pace, he did so to the unrestrained cheers of his connections.

As Annabel pointed out to Jan, a third in the Mackeson was worth a great deal more than most wins. Things were looking up, they were sure of it.

But for Morning Glory, two races later, the preliminaries went rather differently. In the paddock, despite

Patsy's best efforts, MG grew more anxious by the second, and though it was a misty, cold November day, there were streaks of foamy sweat running down his flanks. His behaviour clearly affected the market. Overnight the two novices had been joint favourites, but now Velvet Dynasty edged ahead to be clear race favourite, with Morning Glory half a point behind him. The bookies, like the crowd, found it difficult to separate them.

The plan was for Murty to let him run exactly as he had at Stratford.

'Remember,' whispered Jan fiercely to him in the paddock, 'he's a free spirit. Don't cramp his style.'

'I'm hoping the hill doesn't do him,' said Murty pessimistically. 'I've seen it get the better of some real champions in the past.'

'No negatives, Murty,' warned A.D. O'Hagan, who stood beside Jan.

They looked across just as Virginia Gilbert was checking the girths of Velvet Dynasty. By contrast, the Riscombe horse looked cool and magnificent. As Jan watched Scottie Venables leg Finbar Howlett into the saddle, swarms of butterflies were fighting for space in her stomach. She told herself that MG's sweating was not too significant, that it wasn't necessarily a serious problem. In fact, she decided she would probably have been worried if MG had *not* sweated. It was just his way of behaving.

As before, Murty was last taking his horse down to the start, and stood him discreetly behind the pack while they jostled for position in the line-up. To begin with the race did not go well since Murty misread the starter's intentions and as a consequence mistimed his approach to the tape. He had just checked the horse's forward momentum the second the tape flew up.

Missing the break meant MG had to use far more energy to reach his preferred spot at the head of affairs. Murty had no choice but to accept the situation and let the horse's surging acceleration take him through the pack and into the lead. By the time the field streamed past the stands, Morning Glory was doing what he liked to do best, galloping and jumping, refusing to let any other contender claim equality.

As the horses turned left-handed and headed into the country, Jan was scanning the runners through her binoculars to check the position of Velvet Dynasty. Finbar had him sat at the rear, loping along. She searched for dangers. It was a big field, but nothing was travelling as well as MG and Velvet Dynasty; it was still, she thought, between the two of them, though the Gilbert horse was equally full of running.

Morning Glory's pace was breathtaking. He treated the hurdles as if they were invisible, taking them in his stride. The only problem with that approach was, no matter how confidently the horse was racing, she knew that if he hit one hard he would have the stuffing knocked right out of him.

Along the back straight Finbar Howlett started to drive Velvet Dynasty through the field. Blithely unaware, Morning Glory was still full of running as Murty let him stride on. MG was now seven or eight lengths to the good and, three hurdles out, Murty looked round. There were no dangers in sight, just a line of horses with their jockeys rowing away and getting little response. Murty turned back and, as he did so, Finbar drove Velvet Dynasty stealthily between two horses and emerged from the chasing pack. Slowly, relentlessly, unknown to Murty, he began to shorten the distance between them.

Watching Morning Glory's lead diminish, Jan told herself not to worry. She knew he had the ability to quicken and, as she watched him sweep over the penultimate flight two lengths ahead of Finbar and Velvet Dynasty, her belief in him was intact. Obviously still full of fight, MG hurtled towards the last. Suddenly, Virginia's horse found another gear and quickly reduced the lead.

It was not until they approached the final obstacle that Morning Glory sensed the other horse. Instantly he responded and pricked his ears. In a breathtaking show of defiance, he took off. It was brave, reckless even. But he was too low, far too low, and moving swiftly. His front feet ploughed through the timber frame and he was unable to get them back quickly enough to make a safe landing. He crashed into the ground on the landing side of the hurdle, crumpling and rolling, and torpedoed Murty McGrath like a bullet over his ears. The jockey hit the ground, bounced twice and instantly curled up to minimize the damage if he was trampled by the pursuing pack.

Jan felt extremely nauseous as she lowered her binoculars. At least half of the crowd were going wild as the favourite cleared the last with consummate ease and galloped to the winning line unchallenged. MG and Murty continued to lie on the ground, neither of them moving. She glanced at A.D. beside her. His binoculars still raised, he was staring grim-faced at his stricken horse.

22

'God, please let him be just winded,' Jan kept repeating to herself, her eyes filling with tears as she pushed her way from the crowded owners' and trainers' stand out onto the course, battling her way through the huge mob of racegoers who thronged the lawns in front of the stands. One group of men, dressed in tailcoats and T-shirts reading 'Kevin's Stag Party Boom-Boom' were doing a conga along the row of bookmakers' pitches.

Jan was in no mood for games and with the pressure soaring through her body she bulldozed her way past them and made it to the small gate leading onto the track, which was manned by a couple of security guards. As Jan tried to go through, one of them spread his arms to prevent her.

'Don't be a bloody *prat*,' she shrieked, blinking back her tears and waving her arm. 'I'm with that injured horse. Let me by.'

'Badge,' the guard demanded. Jan looked down at her shoulder bag and flicked it over. TRAINER the man saw and stood aside as she hurried through. Jan looked anxiously down the course towards the final hurdle, where she could see a St John's Ambulance Brigade vehicle and the horse ambulance. Men in green overalls were putting up screens around the stricken Morning Glory.

Jan's nausea was reaching a crescendo and the shoes she had chosen to wear for the races had raised heels – not pointed, but high enough to sink into the soft turf as she ran towards the dramatic scene. She stopped for a second and bent to rip them off her feet, taking the chance to gulp in some air. Members of the crowd who had anxiously remained in the stands, glued to their binoculars, as the horse lay still where he'd fallen, now urged Jan on as she sprinted down the track in stockinged feet, her shoes clutched in her hands.

As she got closer, she saw that Murty had hoisted himself into an upright position. He sat on the wet grass rubbing his arm, looking shaken but in one piece.

'Murty, you OK?' she called.

Murty nodded as he unfastened his helmet and smiled ruefully.

'Crashing fall,' he wheezed, stating the obvious. 'He took off a mile too soon. There was nothing I could do,'

'No, I could see that. Anyway, thank goodness you're all right. I'll catch you later. I must see to the horse.'

As Jan entered the circle of screens, she could see immediately that Morning Glory, though still lying on the ground, was breathing, his sides heaving up and down like bellows and his nostrils flaring. The duty vet, Peter Heaney, whom Jan knew slightly, was kneeling beside MG, his stethoscope on the horse's chest. He looked up and nodded a brief greeting. At the same moment, Patsy arrived, panting, his face a mask of distress.

'Will he be all right, Mrs H? He will, won't he?'

Jan shrugged, gesturing hopefully towards the vet.

'Are you the lad that looks after him?' said Heaney, rising to his feet.

'Yeah,' said Patsy. 'I do him.'

The vet motioned him towards the horse's head.

'Right, let's get him up then. I've checked him all over and he seems all right. Just winded, I think.'

MG struggled to his feet and stood looking rather bewildered. As Patsy stroked the horse's neck and whispered his magic, the animal soon regained his composure.

'He looks sound,' said the vet. 'You can walk him back, if you like.'

'Thank you, sir,' said Patsy. 'I'm really grateful.'

As the crowd saw the horse being led slowly towards them, they gave out a huge cheer and a round of applause. That, Jan thought, was what she loved most about racing: although many racegoers knew little about the ins and outs of a horse's life, they cared about the animals just the same. They were there for the horses, in the same way the horses were there for them.

The next day the hacks were reasonably encouraging. One headline simply read FIRST ROUND TO RISCOMBE. Another argued that Morning Glory's fall was not a result of tiredness, but that he was so full of running, he had been goaded into a disastrous take-off. There was no doubt in the reporter's mind that MG would have held Velvet Dynasty's challenge on the run-in. Most agreed that the fall had deprived the crowd of a pulsating finish and that the issue between the two talented horses was still open. Only a rematch would decide.

Virginia, of course, had other ideas. In her interview she said Jan's horse was already out on its feet coming to the last and would have had no chance, even if he had stood up.

'Mine's a superstar,' she claimed. 'As far as I can see, there's not another novice in the country that's capable of beating him. Mrs Hardy's horse certainly can't, as we've seen already.'

It was crystal clear MG was stiff through his loins, but he came out of the race well, considering, since he ate up his feed next morning. After discussions with A.D., Jan felt there was no need to alter the plan to go to Leopardstown in early January, but decided they wouldn't risk the horse in the meantime. Virginia, A.D. had heard on the grapevine, was aiming Velvet Dynasty at the Kempton Park meeting on Boxing Day, so a rematch would be unlikely until the Cheltenham Festival in March.

On the following Monday Inspector Hadfield telephoned. His voice was far more conciliatory than when he had come to arrest Eddie as he asked if he could come over to Edge Farm that afternoon. He arrived with a different female constable, who was introduced as WPC Kibble.

'I'm sorry we've not been in touch until now regarding your allegations against Harold Powell,' Hadfield began, as they sat round the kitchen table drinking tea.

'I haven't had time to think about it,' said Jan. 'I've

had such a lot on, I've been more than happy to let Eddie's solicitor, Bob Warren, deal with it.'

'We have, of course, been continuing our investigation on the basis of the sworn affidavits from yourself and Mr Keating. So we're here now, basically, to give you an update. But first, may I ask if you've had any other visits from Mr Powell since he made the original threats?'

'No.' Jan answered cagily, wondering where this was leading.

'Not seen him anywhere, or had any phone calls or other communication from him?'

'No, nothing. I've seen him at the races a few times with Virginia Gilbert – that was earlier, though – but I haven't seen him on a racecourse since.'

'When you say "with" Miss Gilbert, what do you mean by that exactly?'

'I mean what I said: *with* Miss Gilbert. Really, Inspector, that's a daft question.'

Hadfield coloured and his ever-smiling mouth twitched.

'Sorry. I meant, are you aware of any personal relationship between Harold Powell and Miss Gilbert?'

'I'm aware there's talk of one, and I've seen them holding hands in public, once. So I suppose so, yes.'

'You don't sound very convinced.'

Jan considered.

'Well, it just seems so unlikely. Virginia's boyfriends always used to be Hooray Henrys of her own age, not middle-aged psychos like Powell.'

Hadfield gave a small embarrassed cough at Jan's description of Harold.

'And did Mr Powell refer to Miss Gilbert at all, or his relationship with her, when he came here and threatened you?'

'Yes, he did. It's in my affidavit, isn't it? He accused me of slagging off Virginia's racing stables to the press, which is completely untrue. But it was obvious from the way he said it that he wanted it known he took it as personally as she did.'

'Suggesting there was still a personal relationship between them at that time?'

'Yes, definitely. But why don't you ask them?'

'I have already put it to Miss Gilbert, but she declined to comment.'

'Oh, does that mean she's off the hook? What about Harold?'

'Ah well, that's the problem. Mr Powell seems to have disappeared. Which is why I was wondering if he's been in touch with you in any way.'

Jan felt unusually thirsty all of a sudden. She offered more tea to the police officers and then poured herself another mug, which she drained almost immediately. She was thinking that, if Harold Powell had gone to ground, he might be capable of anything, including carrying out his threat against her.

Hadfield, good policeman that he was, had gone ahead of her.

'Mrs Hardy, I don't think we should take Mr Powell's disappearance lightly, so I am here to inform you that we would like to increase your level of protection. This time we'll post officers on the premises, twenty-four hours a day.'

Jan nodded her head in relief.

'Yes, good. Thank you, Inspector Hadfield. Me and my children will sleep a lot easier knowing there's someone keeping an eye out.'

'They will also follow you discreetly when you go out, Mrs Hardy. It will not only protect you, but it may locate Mr Powell, should he turn up. Now we need to interview him in connection with several possible offences, including the threatening behaviour which you and Patsy Keating have alleged.'

'Is one of the other offences causing death by reckless driving?' Jan asked cunningly.

Hadfield gave another embarrassed cough.

'Yes, I can confirm that is the case. In fact, since we are here, I need to see Mr Sullivan. Is he around?'

'Yes, he's down in the gym. It's in one of the stables. I'll show you.'

Eddie defiantly rowed away on his machine, his face unchanging, while Hadfield told him he was a free man again: all the serious charges had been dropped and the lesser offences of keeping an untaxed, uninsured car, had been referred to the magistrates' court, from whom he would be hearing in due course.

When Hadfield finished, Eddie stopped rowing, reached for a towel and mopped his face.

'So it was old Harold who dunnit and not me. Well, congratulations, Inspector. Now bugger off, will you? I've got another five hundred pulls to do before supper.'

The police took up their duties later that day, when an unmarked car arrived containing two young constables.

They backed the car into the old stone barn, where it would be less conspicuous, and settled down to their guard duty, consuming quantities of sandwiches, soup and tea provided for them by Fran, but otherwise causing little trouble. After eight hours each detail would be relieved by another pair, and so it went on. More than once Jan wondered if they were armed, but decided she preferred not knowing and so did not ask. At first she was obsessively conscious of their presence behind her every time she drove to the shops, to Riscombe or to the races, but after a week she became used to it. After two, she sometimes forgot they were there.

The only trouble the police presence did cause was when Bernie Sutcliffe came to visit, turning up without notice in the middle of one afternoon. Jan was vacuuming the sitting room and didn't know he was there until he'd come stomping in, breathing hard.

'Jesus Christ, Jan, what's going on? I've just been turned inside out by two coppers in your forecourt. Phew, bloody 'ell. I thought they were waiting for me. Why didn't you tell me they were 'ere?'

Bernie's Brummie twang always became more pronounced when he was upset.

'That's simple.' Jan grinned. 'I didn't know you were coming.'

Thankfully, Jan gave up the idea of housework and wound away the vacuum's cable.

'Why on earth would you think they were here for *you*, anyway?'

Bernie bit his lip, his reptile eyes swivelling evasively.

'Oh, well, you know what it's like – usual problems. Blokes like me are always rubbing the coppers up the wrong way . . . Anyway, what's going on? Them two wouldn't say a word.'

'I'm not supposed to say, but they're on surveillance, part of an investigation into someone I once knew as an owner, so you needn't worry; it's got nothing to do with you.'

'Good, that's a relief. Who're they after then? Not that chap Powell?'

Jan was surprised.

'What do you know about Harold Powell, Bernie?'

'Oh, I 'ear things. He stood trial for the death of your mother, right?'

'Wrong. It was my mother-in-law. But now Harold's made threats against me personally. So I've been given round-the-clock protection.'

This impressed Bernie.

'Threats, eh? You should 'ave come to me instead of that lot, Jan. I could do better than them.'

'I didn't know you were into protection as well as scrap metal.'

'Security, not protection. There's an important difference. It's a little sideline I developed after a gang of scousers nicked 'alf a ton of roofing lead off me.' Bernie chuckled.

'Well, thanks anyway, but I think I'll stick with the constabulary,' Jan replied. 'So, what can I do for you? Thinking of buying another horse by any chance?'

'No way. Two's quite enough, thank you, especially when neither of them's winning. I'm not made of money. No, I was in the area, so I thought I'd drop in for a gander at my horses. But if you're busy, I can come back another time . . .'

It was very unlike Bernie to be so considerate or to be in any kind of a hurry, for that matter. But today he was positively jumpy, and continually looking out of the window to check the whereabouts of the police. Jan enjoyed prolonging his agony by insisting he come down to the yard to inspect his horses. Bernie slunk past the police car almost on hands and knees and kept looking back over his shoulder as he crept down towards the stable block. Just for a moment, as the horses were led out, his old habits revived and, despite a complete lack of equine knowledge, he made his customary critical remarks.

'This one's a bit thin around his arse, isn't he? And I should 'ave that lump on his leg looked at, if I were you, Jan.'

'That's normal, Bernie. It's his hock,' Jan giggled, refusing to be provoked. She had learned to handle Bernie long ago, including his periodic attempts to cajole her into going out with him. She strongly suspected that the real reason for his appearance today had been to renew these attempts. But the police presence had made him so neurotic that, within just twenty minutes of his arrival, he had made his excuses and scurried off back to Birmingham.

During the last few weeks Jan had been seeing rather more of another owner than she was accustomed to. The three Barbadian weeks spent with Edge Farm's assistant trainer had clearly left Johnny Carlton-Brown besotted, and there was hardly a weekend when he didn't show up on Saturday morning to watch the gallops – or in reality, as Jan privately thought, to watch Annabel with her shapely rear raised, go past him on the back of one of his horses.

As she reflected, Jan realized it could present an insoluble problem. If JCB married Annabel, he would very likely want her to quit her job at Edge Farm. This would be a terrible loss to Jan, who depended on her friend for so much. On the other hand, if Annabel and JCB separated because she preferred the job to the man, he would, in all probability, take his horses away. Knowing men as she did, Jan reckoned it would be much too painful for him to keep a connection with a yard that maintained a stronger hold over his beloved's affections than he did. But the real problem was to know what was going on in Annabel's mind. She was so damned secretive and reserved about her love life that it was impossible to second-guess.

The only answer, Jan decided, was to face the dilemma head on. In early December, while travelling with Annabel to Warwick racecourse, where one of JCB's horses was running, Jan manoeuvred the conversation to the point where she could delve a little deeper.

'Bel, you and JCB – what's the story?'

'Oh, you know—'

'That's just the point, I don't really and I need to. He's absolutely crazy about you, that's obvious, and he'd whisk you off at a moment's notice to live with him, in Barbados or somewhere else remote. But what do you feel? Do you love him?'

'I feel . . . the same as I've always felt.'

'You've told me before that you liked him, but you weren't in love with him. Is that what you mean?'

'Yes and no, I suppose.'

'Bel, please stop being such a bloody pain in the arse. Yes and no what?'

'Yes I like him, no I don't *think* I'm in love with him.'

'But how can you not know? I would.'

'I never do know. That's my burden in life. I mean I know I love horses, and I love this life. But with men I can never seem to work it out. Of course, that's a different kind of love, isn't it? And scarier.'

'Scarier?'

Bel nodded slowly, then changed the subject. It was as far as Jan got in her attempt at plumbing her friend's romantic soul. They were as open and frank with each other as two women can be – about everything except Bel's romances. At times Jan felt slightly angry. Here she was, feeling wretched about the hopes she had had for herself and Eddie, which now appeared to be doomed. And there was Annabel, with men queuing around the proverbial block to take her out, and she had not the slightest idea what she wanted.

One morning the post delivered a letter with an Irish stamp. It contained a brief note from A.D., written as usual by his own hand.

Dear Jan,

You remember our chat at Edge Farm regarding my search for a property in the Lambourn area? I have

> taken the liberty to enclose the agent's particulars of one that has recently come on the private market. Could you possibly find the time to run your eye over it? If nothing else, I would value your opinion of the place.
>
> Yours,
>
> A.D.

He had added a PS:

> You should view the premises strictly on its potential. Though I gather it's in a bit of a state at the moment.

Jan unfolded the stapled sheets, which offered a 'unique opportunity to buy' Tumblewind Grange, near Lambourn, 'an estate of character'. She knew the property A.D. had looked at following Morning Glory's race at Stratford had been rejected because it was too small. Jan scrutinized the description of the new place and could see instantly, on size, Tumblewind Grange would pass muster. There was a large Jacobean house 'in need of restoration'. The outbuildings included stabling, six cottages and four hundred and fifty acres of land, mostly laid to grass and some woodland 'previously used for shooting'.

That particular day Edge Farm had no runners. So on impulse, and without telling anyone except her police escort where they were going, Jan loaded the children into the Shogun and drove down to Berkshire to take a look. She already knew what A.D. was contemplating when he requested her to make this visit. He was hoping, expecting even, that she would be seduced. Jan was equally determined not to be, whatever it was like.

Tumblewind Grange, though on a beautiful site in a fold of the Downs, was at first glance not very seductive. The young agent at the Lambourn office gave her the keys to the house and told her to be particularly careful upstairs as the floorboards were rotten. The police stayed in their car just inside the front gates, while Megan and Matty raced, like a couple of wild ponies, around an overgrown formal garden at the back of the house. Jan pushed open the dilapidated front door and was met by an overpowering smell of cats and damp. Fungus grew inside the hall and the walls were covered in mould. Cautiously she ventured further, and found several broken windows and fallen plaster. Water oozed from pipes onto mossy floors and the electric cables must have predated the war. Jan decided the claim that the house had 'until recently been occupied' was the best bit of fiction she had ever read.

On the other hand, the report stated that it was a house of character, which was undeniable. To Jan's unpractised eye there seemed to be two styles of architecture. One half was reminiscent of Riscombe Manor, with low ceilings, mullioned and leaded windows, wooden panelling and stone floors. The other wing had sash windows and sprung floors – where there were boards! – high ceilings and marble fire surrounds. In one particular room, the display of decorative plasterwork was quite spectacular, though badly ravaged by time and damp.

She tried to imagine living here, but couldn't. It was far too smelly, gloomy and draughty. More Tumbledown than Tumblewind Grange she decided.

As Jan went outside she could hear the children laughing. *At least they like it*, she thought. As she crossed the yard there was evidence that the outbuildings had at some time been used as a sawmill, with rusty woodcutting machinery lying about and a huge mound of rotting sawdust. She walked round the old stables and outbuildings; though well sited in relation to the house – not too close, like a farmyard – they were structurally useless and would have to be demolished.

Jan gathered the children and drove up one of the estate roads towards a group of three cottages. They seemed empty at first, but she saw blue smoke curling up from one of the chimneys and went and knocked at the door. A youngish man wearing a woollen bobble hat and dirty overalls answered. Jan pulled the estate agent's particulars from her pocket.

'Hi, I'm pleased to meet you. I'm looking over the estate on behalf of a friend.'

'Oh yeah?'

They chatted for several minutes on the doorstep. At first the man was not very forthcoming, but in the end he mellowed and Jan found him quite informative. Apparently he lived in the cottage with his elderly parents and worked on a nearby farm. He said only one of the other cottages was occupied but the land was leased to various local farmers, and there had been a lease on the shooting until two or three years ago. Old Mrs Trent had lived in the house until she died last year aged ninety-two. After her death the local authority had removed thirty-three cats for humane destruction.

Driving home, Jan was deep in thought about what she would tell A.D. The estate would need a huge sum of money spending on it. The stables and outbuildings could not be repaired and extended; they would have to be completely rebuilt. The house and cottages, while not absolutely falling down, were in a perilous condition. But with adequate funds the house in particular could be spectacular.

As far as the land was concerned, there was plenty of scope for the modern training complex that A.D. had been dreaming of. Jan knew he also had the money to bring it about. The chalky, undulating land was ideal for gallops, and there was plenty of paddock space available for turning horses out. All in all, she decided, if A.D. was prepared to lay out the money, Tumblewind Grange would do him well. Whether it would do her was quite another matter.

'Mum?' enquired Megan, from the back of the car. 'Are we going to live in that old house?'

'Tell me, what do you think of the idea, Megs?'

In the driving mirror Jan saw her daughter frown.

'It's got a lot more room for horses than Edge,' she said at last, 'but I think it's a lot less friendly.'

'I know just what you mean.' Jan laughed. 'What about you, Matty? What do you think?'

'Well, it has got a secret garden,' he said. 'And a troll lives there.'

When Jan got back, she went straight to the office and wrote a note to A.D. about what they had seen and found out at Tumblewind Grange. She decided, however, not to mention the troll. She put the note in the fax machine and dialled his number, then riffled through the pile of unopened mail that lay in front of her. Most were bills, or circulars, but one envelope was addressed by hand and locally postmarked. She grabbed the paperknife and slit it open.

She recognized neither the writing nor the address neatly inscribed at the top of the page. Flipping the sheet over, she looked at the signature in amazement. It was a letter from Rachel Moorhouse.

23

Dear Mrs Hardy,

I felt I must write to you. Yesterday the police informed me they had dropped the charges against Eddie Sullivan regarding the death of my husband. They said they are now seeking another man in connection with the crash, so it seems I was wrong when I accused Mr Sullivan, and you, of being responsible for my husband's death. I don't know what you must think of me, bursting into your house uninvited and accusing you like I did, and blurting on about my husband and his affairs. I was at a very low ebb, and I didn't have anyone to confide in or advise me. I was doing a lot of things impulsively without thinking about the consequences. Anyway, things are much better now and I am on a more even keel. I have met a kind-hearted man, who has done more to restore my faith in human nature than I would have thought possible. Even my kids like him!

I am sorry if my actions and words caused you distress. You too know what it is to be a widow. The difference between us is that I have been released by chance from an unloving, brutal marriage, while you probably lost the love of your life. Stupidly, I failed to appreciate that you had more to complain about in your widowhood than I did. Bitterness and envy I now know are a dreadful disease that can eat you alive. I hope you can find it in your heart to forgive me and wish you every happiness and success in the future.

Yours most sincerely,

Rachel Moorhouse

Jan read the letter through twice. It must have been hellishly difficult to write and Rachel Moorhouse had her wholehearted admiration for having the guts to do it. She did wonder, however, if it had been done at the prompting of some therapist or perhaps the 'kind man' the letter mentioned.

Jan opened the letters drawer of her filing cabinet. She had separate folders, which held the correspondence with each of her owners, and two for letters from members of the public, one labelled 'Fan Mail' and another marked 'Nutters'. The Moorhouse letter didn't fit either category, so she dropped it into a third file labelled 'Miscellaneous' and closed the drawer.

In early December, for no obvious reason, the fortunes of Edge Farm began to pick up when Supercall and Teenage Red both won at Wincanton to give Jan a double, while Tom's Touch found his form with a scintillating victory at Hereford and even old Arrow Star got his head in front in a mud-spattered four-horse finish at Leicester. Then A.D.'s hurdler Gyllipus travelled all the way to Ayr to record his first win of the season.

That night A.D., who usually combined his racing

in Scotland with a few rounds of golf on the Ailsa course, gave Jan dinner in the luxury surroundings of the five-star Turnberry Hotel, where he always stayed, and where Jan had dined with him nearly a year ago.

'It's almost déjà vu,' A.D. smiled, greeting her in the lobby with a light kiss on the cheek. 'Remember last year? Our horses had been going through a terrible patch, I was chafing about the results. Suddenly you pulled out a surprise hurdle win at Ayr, then we dined here. Snap.'

He clicked his fingers.

'The only difference being that this year we won't eat in the main restaurant, I think. The food's excellent, but on the rich side, and I've got my cholesterol to consider.'

They strolled through to the hotel's Terrace restaurant, where the cuisine was far less extravagant.

When they were seated, Jan told A.D., 'Gilly's by far the nicest horse to train. We love him to bits.'

'Yes, I admit those horses we took over from Gary West have been a success, or two of them certainly. When am I going to see Holy Mist on the track, by the way?'

Between ordering food and a bottle of Chablis, they talked horses and about their prospects for the big Boxing Day and New Year's Day fixtures. But Jan guessed her owner was skirting around the big issue and that it was bricks, mortar and green fields rather than horseflesh that A.D. really wanted to discuss. She had noticed earlier he had a large brown envelope with him. Now he drew out the estate agent's glossy prospectus for the sale of Tumblewind Grange estate and laid it on the table. He tapped the black rectangle representing the house.

'Thank you for having a look at this for me. On the basis of your report, I went down there myself last weekend.'

'And?'

'The buildings are, as you say, in a terrible state. But the land is very good indeed, which is the only thing that really matters.'

He traced some lines on the plan with his forefinger.

'I thought we would establish some gallops here and here, and possibly here, and an all-weather track over here. The stables and most of the outbuildings will come down and a new stable block will be built for a hundred or so horses on roughly the same site. I've also earmarked a place for an equine pool, and a horse walker just here, behind the walled garden. There's a lot of room for turnout paddocks on either side of the drive. Of course, I'd have the cottages renovated for use of the staff.'

Even though she knew A.D. acted decisively when his mind was made up, Jan was completely taken aback at the speed with which he had moved on this.

'Goodness, A.D., this is all very quick. Have you bought the place already?'

A.D. closed the prospectus, slipped it back into its envelope and turned his attention to the food in front of him.

'Not yet, though I have put in a bid.'

'I see . . . Well, it's certainly an exciting project. Something you can get your teeth into.'

Jan felt torn. The old nagging but crucial doubts

about her independence remained. And the still fresh memory of the big, smelly, decaying house at Tumblewind made her feel queasy. Yet she had seen the land for herself and she had to admit it really *was* an exciting location for a racing stable. Furthermore A.D.'s legendary acumen and thoroughness were not a myth. Jan knew, under his direction, all he had described was set fair to become a reality. She couldn't help it – her pulse had undeniably quickened during A.D.'s brief presentation.

His clear, steely blue eyes met hers with the focus and aplomb of a completely self-possessed man.

'Yes,' he said quietly. 'It *is* an exciting project. I myself would have around forty horses in situ, and we can make up the numbers to another thirty or forty from other owners on a commercial basis. But, with a hundred boxes, we'd always have the capacity to expand our business if we wished.'

He reached for the bottle of wine and refilled their glasses.

'You know it's been a dream of mine for many years, and I still want you to be part of it.'

Jan had just forked some seafood into her mouth. As it contained octopus, which required chewing, it gave her more time to think. She munched – for slightly longer than necessary – then said, 'A.D., you know my feelings about being my own boss, keeping my independence.'

'But now you've seen the potential of Tumblewind I find it difficult to believe you're not tempted. Just a little, perhaps?'

'I've already turned you down once.'

'And you may again, I know that.'

'And what then?'

'I'll have to find someone else.'

'Who?'

A.D. shrugged.

'No one specifically, not at the moment, anyway. It's you I want, Jan.'

'I suppose if I say no, you would withdraw your horses from my yard?'

A.D. nodded. 'Yes, I'm afraid that would be on the cards, but not until the new yard is up and running.'

'So how much time have I got?'

'Supposing my offer on Tumblewind Grange is accepted, it will take between eighteen months and two years to complete the makeover. I'd hope to appoint a resident trainer before we're into the latter stages of the work, let's say by the end of next year. There, you've got twelve months before you make a final decision. After that I will need to go ahead – reluctantly, of course – without you.'

Now Jan decided to put her own cards on the table.

'A.D., you're a hard man to say no to. And I must say it was a very smart move to get me to look this place over. I admit to being a tiny bit tempted. But there are so many other important considerations. I will probably need all that time before I'm really sure about this, one way or the other.'

A.D. sat back and took a sip from his wine.

'That'll be all fine,' he said, his eyes twinkling in expectation.

Edge Farm's run of success looked set to continue when Supercall made a quick return to action in the A. F. Budge Gold Cup at Cheltenham, destroying his field in a classy chase. So, after six victories in just over three weeks, Jan and her staff were on a high until – in spectacular fashion – Arctic winds brought wintry storms down from the north-east. The snow lay thick on the hills and surrounding fields, and drifted to clog the woods, fill the ditches and cover the hedgerows. Temperatures continued to fall and the air became still and cold as a very hard frost set in, making horse racing impossible anywhere in Great Britain. The National Hunt yards were all in the doldrums and bookmakers filled their empty satchels by taking bets from Australia and on whether there would be a white Christmas.

Everyone knew that racing would resume as soon as a thaw allowed and trainers like Jan, with their all-weather gallops, had a distinct advantage. For the rest, there wasn't much to be done except sit it out. Horses remained in their boxes or old bedding from the stables was used to make small exercise rings. A lucky few within striking distance of a beach could canter horses at the water's edge.

Just before Christmas, with frost still holding the landscape in its iron grip, a carol service was held in Chiselcombe church. This annual event, with mince pies and hot punch served afterwards in the village hall, was always supported by farmers and people from well beyond the boundaries of the parish. The proceeds were usually divided between local causes and the Injured Jockeys Fund.

Jan drove over via Riscombe, in order to pick up her

parents and a huge tray of mince pies baked especially by Mary for the occasion. Megan, as a member of the school band, was due to perform a carol and from the moment they set off she began to practise her recorder piercingly. Matty's class was scheduled to recite one of the lessons, and he had a few verses to speak solo. Not to be outdone by his elder sister, he started to rehearse his lines at the top of his voice:

'For UNTO you is born this day in the city of David a SAVIOUR, which is Christ the Lord.'

'Shut up, Matty!' said Megan. 'I'm trying to rehearse.'

'So'm I,' said Matty. 'And THIS shall be a sign unto you; ye shall find the babe wrapped in SWADDLING clothes, lying in a MANGER . . .'

Megan blew louder, and Matty shouted louder.

'AND SUDDENLY THERE WAS WITH THE ANGEL A MULTI—, MULTI—, MULTITUDE OF THE HEAVENLY HOST PRAISING GOD AND SAYING . . .'

Finally, Megan blew the recorder as hard as she could into her brother's ear, which made him scream in pain. Grimacing, Jan spotted a lay-by ahead and pulled in, checking in her mirror as she did so. Her police escort drew in behind her. Jan leaped out and yanked opened the rear door of the Shogun.

'Out! Out you get, young lady.'

Grabbing her arm, she dragged her daughter out, still holding the recorder, and marched her towards the 'escort'.

'Since you're going the same way,' she said, as the driver wound down her window, 'I thought you might like to make yourself useful, so can you give this one a lift? She's dying for a ride in a police car, aren't you, Megan? And she's driving the rest of us up the bloody wall.'

The young constable looked confused as Jan pulled open the rear door and pushed Megan onto the back seat.

'And don't forget your seat belt,' she warned, before turning back to the police officers. 'I hope you two like music. See you later. And thank you.'

Clambering back into the Shogun, Jan spoke soothingly. 'It's all right now, Matty darling, Megan's in the other car so you can practise without having her recorder blasting away in your ear.'

She heard Matty filling his lungs to capacity before belting out the last line at maximum volume.

'GLORY to GOD in the HIGHEST, and on EARTH PEACE, GOOD WILL TOWARD MEN . . . Mum? Why are you laughing?'

As always, Jan thoroughly enjoyed the service. The church was beautifully decked out with a crib and a tree, while a huge Christmas candle stood close to the altar. The congregation overflowed the pews and people were packed into the back of the nave. 'God Rest You Merry, Gentlemen' was as rousing as ever and the choir's rendition of 'The Holly and the Ivy' was sparkling. The instrumental music, though not always exactly in tune, was applauded and the reading from St Luke's gospel by Matty and his friends passed off without a hitch. By the time the vicar had spoken and offered up prayers, a warm Christmassy glow was felt by all and, as the choir slid quietly into 'Silent Night', Jan thought of the timelessness of it all. For centuries people, in many cases the ancestors of *these* people, had come to sing or listen to these carols, and to recite or hear these words and prayers.

After a finale in which everyone joyfully roared out the chorus of 'O Come All Ye Faithful', they crunched through the snow to the village hall, which stood across the road surrounded by its own car park. Jan had parked the Shogun there after offloading Mary's mince pies. Now the congregation made hungry inroads into the piles of country fare, with punch and orange squash in paper cups dispensed by the Women's Institute.

With the Shogun fully loaded, Eddie arrived in Gerry's van, and as Jan entered the hall she saw the two men already in conversation with a blonde girl. The woman turned her head slightly and revealed herself as Gloria Hooke, the pneumatic physiotherapist. Eddie was able to walk with the help of just one stick now, and they were obviously discussing this development since Jan saw Eddie raise the stick and point to it. Following Gloria's first couple of visits to Edge Farm, Jan had asked Tony Robertson to call her off, and a highly skilled male physio had taken her place. But the reunion tonight seemed to be warmly welcomed by Eddie, who was smiling and talking to her with considerable vigour, at least when compared to his recent standards.

Jan did not have much time to dwell on the matter as Viv Taylor-Jones, the vicar's wife, spotted her and came over.

'Hello, Jan. I thought you might like to know that we never had any more of those unpleasant news thingies.'

'I know, it just seems to have been a one-off. I think the police effectively put a stop to it.'

As they chatted, Jan noticed the ghastly Virginia Gilbert with a small group of her equally ghastly friends on the other side of the hall, knocking back the punch in large quantities. She kept glaring towards Jan, shooting her dark looks. When Viv Taylor-Jones had been gently detached by one of her husband's parishioners, Virginia seemed to make up her mind. She pushed through the crowd towards Jan, who was now standing on her own.

'I suppose you think it was pretty clever,' Virginia said venomously, 'getting Harold into trouble.'

'I don't know what you're talking about. I didn't get him into trouble. He managed that all by himself.'

Virginia was plainly inebriated. She drained her cup of punch and snatched another from a passing tray.

'Yes you did, you common cow. You bloody snitched on him,' she hissed.

'Virginia, please, not here. Take my advice . . .'

Jan found being anywhere near Virginia usually brought down a red mist, but tonight it seemed strangely easy to keep her temper under control. Perhaps it was the spirit of Christmas.

'You'll find Harold's got no principles,' Jan went on. 'He doesn't care who he hurts. He'll hurt you in the end, that's for certain.'

'Oh, your bleeding heart?' Virginia sneered, as she took a hefty pull from her drink.

'No, Virginia, this is a fact. He's no good, no good at all, not in *any* way – unless he's OK in bed, on which subject of course *I'm* not qualified to speak.'

Jan hadn't been able to resist the gibe, which instantly caused Virginia's expression to switch from sarcasm to outrage in the blink of an eye.

'How dare you, how *dare* you, you snidey, disgusting bitch.'

Virginia hurled her cup at Jan's head, spun unsteadily on her heel and walked away in a haughty fashion. One or two people in the immediate vicinity looked in consternation at Jan, who groped in her bag for a tissue. Luckily Virginia had already drunk most of the contents, and only a few sticky drops had reached their target. Jan wiped them away and hurried off in search of Reg and Mary before anyone could approach her.

After half an hour people started to drift away. Jan rounded up the children and her parents and headed for the car park. She had just loaded them into the Shogun when she remembered Eddie. If Matty sat on his grandfather's lap there would be room for him, and it would save Gerry the trouble of driving an extra six miles to Edge Farm before going home. She decided to return to the hall to see if the two men were still inside.

She was just crossing the deserted apron of tarmac in front of the hall, and had still not quite reached the circle of light made by the overhead lamp, when she heard the scrape of a footstep behind her.

'Don't say a fucking word, you bitch,' a man's voice growled.

A gloved hand had clasped her upper arm, as another clamped over her mouth. She could smell the man's sweat as she was pulled against him and then bent round in the direction he wanted her to go. Seconds later she found herself being forced towards the shrubbery that fringed the perimeter of the village hall's car park. She knew instantly it was Harold Powell.

Despite her struggles, he was far too strong. He had almost manoeuvred her, slipping and sliding on the underfoot ice, into the bushes. Suddenly they both became aware that someone was standing in their path.

'Hey you! What the *fuck* are you doing? Let her go. Let her go, *NOW*.'

It was Eddie. He had been coming out of the bushes, zipping up his fly. When he saw Harold and Jan he had stopped momentarily to assess the situation and shouted out his challenge. Then he charged forward, raising his stick for the attack. Harold was taken completely by surprise. For a second he slackened his grip on Jan's arm, and by twisting her body she was able to slip his grasp and duck to the ground, glimpsing, as she went down Harold's face, blanched white, his teeth set and the eyes narrowing.

Jan crawled out of the way as Eddie launched himself, thrashing wildly with his stick. Harold gave a cry and raised his arms to ward off the ferocious attack. Slowly, under the rain of blows, he sank to his knees. After several moments, as Eddie landed another three or four cracking shots, running footsteps were heard and Jan's guardian angels, the two police constables, launched themselves into the fracas, pulling Eddie away and helping Harold, bruised and bloodied, to his feet.

Jan struggled to her feet, her legs weak with fear. She dusted the snow from her clothes and continued to shake violently, but was otherwise unhurt.

'That's Harold Powell,' she panted. 'That's the man who threatened to kill me. Thank God you were here.'

24

It was much later that night as Eddie sat with Jan by the fire in the lounge at Edge Farm. They were drinking hot chocolate made with added cream and heavily laced with brandy, an Eddie special. The air hung heavy with the scent of pine from a tree the children had festooned with garlands and fairy lights.

'What were you doing in those bushes anyway?' asked Jan.

'Having a pee, what else?'

'Ah!'

'And it's lucky I was – the bastard – or God knows what might have happened.'

'Yes, I realize it could have been a lot worse.'

The fire crackled as a chunk of log fell into the grate.

'Thanks for saving my life, Eddie,' Jan said meekly. 'Or my virtue. Or from whatever Harold thought he was doing.'

'You've nothing to thank me for, but you can thank my stick.'

'Thank you, stick.'

A long pause followed as they sipped from their mugs and stared into the fire, which periodically flared up only to die away again. Both had a sense that they had turned a corner in their relationship, but Eddie was the first to say it, in his usual moody, despondent way.

'We haven't ever got it back, have we, Jan? Not since the accident.'

'I know. It's been pretty awful.'

'That's all I was thinking as I flogged that bastard. Not only has he put us both through nine months of sheer hell, but he's actually taken away what we had together and at that moment I honestly didn't care if I killed him.'

There was another long pause before Jan, staring into the dying embers and feeling close to tears, whispered, 'I did love you, Eddie. I really did. But you've changed so much.'

There, she'd said it. She looked straight at him to see how he would react.

'I know. The weird thing is –' Eddie sighed – 'I've even noticed it myself. I actually *feel* different and I can't fathom it out.'

'That can't be very nice.'

'It wasn't. It still isn't, but I'm getting used to it now – the new me.'

'Oh, Eddie! I just wish—'

But Eddie had pulled himself out of his chair. He came over to Jan and reached for her empty mug.

'It's late. I've got to go to bed.'

He limped out of the room. A moment later she heard him washing up at the kitchen sink. It was something he would never have done a year ago.

'Yes,' she thought to herself. 'It's late – probably too late.'

Christmas Day was getting ever closer, but the freeze did not relent. The whole racing industry held its breath for the big Boxing Day meeting at Kempton Park, where many National Hunt stars would be on show. By Christmas Eve the meeting was in grave doubt and it was eventually called off the next day. Ireland, on the other hand, had been largely clear of snow and ice, and Morning Glory's date in the Fitzpatrick Castle Hurdle at Leopardstown, on the Saturday after New Year, was still very much on the cards. Jan and Patsy – still the only human beings MG would trust – were working diligently to keep the horse fit and ready to run.

To avoid the long journey by road and ferry, A.D. had decided the horse should take the much quicker route via Dublin airport.

'But A.D.,' said Jan fretfully, 'I really don't think MG would travel in one of those horse crates, not if it's like the one we sent Russian Eagle across in for the Irish National. He'd probably be packed in a narrow stall with a lot of strange horses on board, both of which he hates.'

'OK, I'll find a way around that,' promised A.D.

What he found was a deal with a friend who owned an Irish freighting company that specialized in transporting livestock. A.D. wangled a flight for Morning Glory in a specially adapted TNT jet that would otherwise be flying back empty from Luton to Ireland on the day before the races. Jan, who planned to travel with the horse, along with the obligatory Patsy, spoke to A.D.'s friend and was assured all would be well.

A week before they were due to travel, as Jan scanned the *Racing Post*, she read an item that almost made her drop the paper. As everyone knew, Virginia Gilbert had originally intended to run Velvet Dynasty on Boxing Day at Kempton; now she had switched him to contest the Fitzpatrick Castle Hurdle. The Leopardstown authorities were delighted. As the *Post* put it:

> Virginia Gilbert's Velvet Dynasty and Jan Hardy's Morning Glory have already established themselves as two of the best novice hurdlers around. The resumption of their rivalry on Irish territory is set to capture the imagination, especially of the English fans, deprived by the weather of their usual racing programme.

This was a complete understatement. The rematch had become the talking point of racing folk from the Sussex coast to the borders of Scotland.

Later that day Jan took a call from Fred Messiter in Riscombe. He sounded embarrassed.

'Hello, Jan. Look, I hope you don't mind but I'm calling on behalf of Virginia. She feels she can't speak to you directly because of what's happened recently.'

'What does she want?'

'It's about getting to Leopardstown. The thing is, she can't get Velvet Dynasty on a transporter. Everything's full and she's at her wits' end. She's read you're taking your horse over in a plane on his own, so we were wondering—'

'If we can give hers a lift, I suppose.'

'Exactly.'

Jan's first inclination was to laugh at the cheek. Her second was to turn the proposal down flat. With difficulty she suppressed them both.

'I'll have to ask my owner,' she said cautiously. 'A.D.'s gone to a lot of trouble over this flight, so I couldn't agree without his permission.'

It took Jan several calls to locate A.D., who had been spending the Christmas break in Monte Carlo. He listened to Virginia's request without any show of surprise.

'I wouldn't say there was a problem in principle,' he said judiciously. 'But I wouldn't want to take the horse across only to be beaten by him. You are confident that won't happen, aren't you?'

Jan didn't think confident was quite the right word. Very hopeful would be nearer. But she'd already told A.D. that she considered Morning Glory the better horse, and wavering was not what he liked. Involuntarily shutting her eyes, she took the plunge.

'Yes, barring accidents, I am.'

'I gather there's a lot of interest over there in the two horses meeting again. Is that so?'

'All the papers are talking about it.'

'Then I think the sporting thing to do is to say yes to Miss Gilbert's request, don't you? I'll talk to my pal who owns the transport.'

'How much would we charge her?'

A.D. considered the question.

'I'd say a hefty fee would be in order, wouldn't you? At least that's one way of covering my bet.'

So it was arranged. Early on the Friday morning, the day before the Leopardstown race, Declan drove Jan, Patsy and MG to Luton airport. They drove straight onto the tarmac to where the plane was waiting. Another horsebox with *VIRGINIA GILBERT RACING* emblazoned on the side was already parked beside it. Scottie Venables was talking to a tall, silver-haired man, who introduced himself to Jan as Simon Lacey, the pilot.

Scottie invited Jan to load Morning Glory first as his own lad hadn't arrived yet. Jan climbed the steep ramp to inspect the interior of the plane's livestock compartment, where she found a stall had been formed for Velvet Dynasty, and a larger space, more like a loose-box, had been laid out for Morning Glory.

'I'd better warn you,' Jan said to Simon Lacey, 'my horse is very nervous and I don't really know how he'll react to being shut inside a roaring and throbbing tin can.'

'What I usually do is taxi to the end of the runway,' the pilot told her. 'If everyone inside's still smiling, I'll take off. Of course, if your horse throws a wobbly, I'll have to take *him* off.'

Jan had no choice but to agree to this alarming procedure and went back to her lorry to get on with loading.

No sooner had Jan and Declan lowered the horse-box ramp than MG – covered in a light sheet and already booted up for the journey – started to fret. As

Patsy led him out, he jerked at the lead rein and whinnied, hating the hard, unfamiliar surroundings of the airport, with nothing green anywhere in sight. The steep ramp that led up into the dark, cavernous belly of the aircraft seemed to have even less appeal. MG tossed his head and whinnied again. His skin shivered, rippling his rug.

Patsy hung on for dear life and continued talking to the horse, stroking his neck as Jan packed MG's ears with large chunks of cotton wool and placed a hood over his head to stop him shaking the wadding out. Then she fitted a piece of headgear, known as a poll guard, which made him look like a four-legged rugby player with a scrum cap. The device had a special function. It would protect MG if he reared up in a space with very limited headroom and the hood would muffle the sound of the jet engines.

Watched by Jan, Declan and Scottie, Patsy led him forward. As his hoof touched the bottom of the ramp, Morning Glory jinked and backed away. Patsy turned him in a circle and approached again. Jan was holding her breath with her teeth clenched, as this time MG inched further up the ramp, but the unfamiliar smell of the aircraft's interior overwhelmed him and he backed down again.

'Would you take him, Mrs H, and bring him up yourself?' suggested Patsy. 'I'm thinking maybe he'll come in after me.'

Patsy jogged into the plane and waited just inside the shadow of the interior. When Jan presented MG to the ramp, the horse hesitated and then walked onto it like a novice skater stepping onto the ice. A few feet up the incline he stopped again, dipping his head then stretching it forward. He knew Patsy was near. After making a few more hesitant steps towards the lad, he picked up the direction of his scent more strongly and immediately climbed on until he was inside the plane. Patsy retreated to the interior as MG advanced, almost casually now, into the loosebox. Reunited with his handler, MG gently shoved Patsy with his nose, asking for it to be rubbed.

'He's all right now,' said the lad. 'I'm only nervous about the devil getting into him when the engines start.'

Now it was Velvet Dynasty's turn.

'My bloody travelling lad's late, he's been in London for a few days off. The bastard promised he'd be here on time,' Scottie said.

'If you're sure he's coming,' Jan replied, 'Declan can help you load.'

Just then a young man with long black hair curling up at the back of his collar emerged from the terminal building. Lighting a cigarette, he began strolling nonchalantly across the tarmac towards them.

'Michael, put that sodding fag out and get your arse over here, ya bloody great lummox,' bellowed Scottie. 'You're late.'

As the Gilbert lad approached, Jan noticed that Patsy had left Morning Glory and was standing at the top of the aircraft ramp. When he saw who was approaching, his jaw dropped and his eyes widened. In a second he vanished into the belly of the plane.

'What's the matter with him?' Jan whispered to Declan.

'Shit, Mrs H,' said Dec more seriously. 'That's Michael Fahey. He's one of the lads who gave Patsy such a hard time when he was at the Gilbert place.'

Jan shut her eyes and held them shut for several moments.

'Oh God. That's all I bloody need.'

Though frightened initially by the engines' roar, Morning Glory did not go berserk as Jan had feared, and Simon Lacey radioed the control tower for clearance to take off. Patsy stayed with the horse throughout the flight, with Jan in the forward seating, and they landed in better order than any of the team had dared hope. At Dublin airport Patsy brought MG down the ramp to a gleaming modern horsebox, supplied by A.D. Entering it in much the same way as he had boarded the plane, MG seemed to be learning at last. Meanwhile the behaviour of his travelling companion was as sweet as a syllabub.

Leopardstown was about twelve miles from Dublin airport but, with most of the city lying directly between, the journey took considerably more time. So it was not until early afternoon, some six hours after they had left Edge Farm, that they finally settled the two horses in the stable block at the racecourse. It was not a race day and the area was quiet and businesslike, with horseboxes coming and going as some of the next day's runners arrived to be boxed, groomed, watered and fed by their attendants.

Jan was booked into the Shelbourne Hotel in central Dublin, where she was due to have dinner in the evening with her friend, the bloodstock agent Sean McDonagh. She had equipped Patsy with a flask of tea, three packets of sandwiches, chocolate and a bag of Irish coins for the phone. After giving him instructions for the horse's evening feed and the phone number of her hotel, she gathered her belongings ready to leave.

But Patsy was very quiet and looked anxious.

'You're sure you'll be all right? That guy from the Gilbert yard's not been bothering you, has he?'

Patsy hurriedly shook his head.

'Good,' said Jan. 'Phone me at the hotel at six. Don't you forget now.'

He assured her he wouldn't.

Leaving the stable area, she looked up at the sky, which was just beginning to darken. The wind had got up and a few black clouds had blown in from the west. Pulling her woollen jacket more tightly around her, she passed six or seven young men, obviously overnight stable staff, kicking a football between them. Seeing Jan, they stopped to watch her go by and she saw them nudging one another and passing remarks. They were too far away for the words to carry, but she could imagine the content. Fixing them with a defiant glare, she thought she recognized the mullet hairstyle of Michael Fahey amongst them.

Later, as she lay on her hotel bed, Jan dialled A.D. O'Hagan at Aigmont.

'We've arrived and the horse is safely ensconced at Leopardstown with Patsy,' she told him.

'Good, I'm glad to hear it.' A.D.'s voice sounded as calm as ever. 'You'd no trouble with the flight?'

'Not to speak of, thanks to Patsy. Without him I don't know if we'd have got MG on the plane even.'

'How's our rival?'

'Good as gold, like I knew he would be. But don't worry, A.D. I'm sure we can beat him. Ask Murty.'

'I have done and he's not as confident as you.'

'I didn't say I was *confident*. I am optimistic, though.'

'The forecast says more rain. I really don't want to see the ground softer than it is already.'

'No,' agreed Jan. 'That's out of our hands, but it wouldn't be ideal.'

'Well, we're committed now. I'll see you tomorrow. Perhaps it would help if you said a few Hail Marys.'

Jan hung up and lay still for a moment, wondering if A.D. had really meant her to pray. At first the only noises penetrating the room were the wind and Dublin's incessant traffic. But after a few moments she heard a new sound, that of the first spots of rain spattering against the windowpanes. Hoping this would be no more than a light shower, she closed her eyes and, without meaning to, fell asleep.

Jan woke with a jolt. What time was it? Her watch read five past six. She rubbed her face and grabbed her bedside phone to dial the stables office.

'Sorry, Mrs Hardy, your man's not about at the moment,' said the official who at her request had gone to look in Morning Glory's box. 'That horse of yours is all right, though. There's nothing to worry about.'

'Please would you tell Patsy he *must* call me,

immediately. I gave him the number, but I'll give it to you again in case he's lost it.'

Jan recited the number and hung up. Patsy had probably gone to the toilet or something. She decided to take a bath, but with the bathroom door ajar so she could hear the phone. It did not ring and twenty minutes later, still damp and wrapped in a hotel bath sheet, she called the stable office again. Patsy had not shown up.

Jan was due to meet Sean in the hotel bar at seven-thirty. As she dressed she tried to imagine what the hell Patsy was up to. She had given him specific instructions not to leave the horse for more than a few minutes. But, if the man in the office was to be believed, he had been away from MG now for at least an hour. By quarter past seven, as she took the lift down to the lobby, she felt a sense of dread. Before leaving the room, she had made a last-minute decision. Changing out of the dress she'd put on for Sean, she got back into her jeans, jumper and jacket. She would have to go out to the racecourse immediately and find out what was wrong. There was nothing else for it.

Recognizing the greying head of Sean McDonagh, as he stood with his back to her talking to the barman, she hurried towards him.

'Jan!' he cried, raising his glass of whiskey to salute her approach. 'Sure it's great to see your shining face.'

He lightly touched her upper arm and gave her a peck on the cheek, then looked at her clothes.

'Have you just arrived?'

'No, Sean,' she began, 'I'm terribly sorry, but I'm

afraid dinner's off. There's a bit of a crisis and I have to get back to Leopardstown immediately.'

The bloodstock agent's delighted grin dissolved into a look of concern.

'What sort of a crisis?'

'You know I've got this temperamental horse we're running tomorrow? Well, the lad who is supposed to be staying with him at the racecourse stables isn't coming to the phone or calling in even. He's usually so reliable, I don't know what's happened.'

Sean drained his glass.

'I can see why that would be a worry. Come on, I'll drive.'

'Oh no, I couldn't possibly impose—'

'Nonsense. Haven't I the car outside? And Leopardstown's on my way home anyway.'

Jan felt some of the weight lift from her shoulders. She looked gratefully at Sean's weathered, kind, dependable face. She had someone with her now and, whatever was going on at the racecourse, at least she wouldn't have to face it on her own.

The rain was still pouring down and the roads were slick, but Sean drove fast and skilfully. On the way Jan summarized the situation.

After hearing her out, Sean said, 'I saw the horse run on TV, at Cheltenham when he fell at the last. Looked all over the winner to my eyes, but I gathered from what the commentator was saying he's no Goody Two-Shoes.'

'That's one way of putting it,' Jan agreed.

'Anyway, I wouldn't be worrying too much about

your man at this stage. He's probably just gone off with the rest of them to the pub and forgotten the time.'

'I wouldn't have left him alone with the horse if I didn't think he was dependable. He loves that horse – in fact, I think he'd probably die for it. He's usually very serious about the job. He wouldn't just go off to the pub. I don't even think he drinks. He's a very devout Catholic.'

'Ah well, piety doesn't stop you drinking, unfortunately. Quite the opposite, some would say.'

Sean sighed and shook his head, as if he had privately decided alcohol must be at the root of the problem. Threading through the early evening traffic, he took the main Wicklow road to Ballsbridge, Donnybrook then Stillorgan, where he turned right off the national road towards Leopardstown itself.

'I only hope we're in time,' Jan prayed.

'In time for what?'

'In time to stop a disaster.'

'Ah sure, the horse'll be all right for a couple of hours, even if he is a bit lonesome. So don't you worry about that now.'

The racecourse stables were enclosed by a high mesh fence, with the stable office next to the gated entrance. Jan and Sean walked in to find the two security guards watching television.

'The horses have been a bit noisier than usual,' said the older of the two. 'But you'll often get that with stopovers. Otherwise it's been quiet enough here.'

'Have you seen my lad yet? Patsy Keating?' asked Jan.

'No,' the other one stated. 'But a lot of the lads went off in a gang to the pub down the road a while ago.'

'When?' asked Sean.

'About an hour or so, I'd say.'

'That's where he'll be,' said Sean. 'I'd bet on it.'

'But he can't be, that's *after* I phoned the first time,' Jan protested. 'And he wasn't here then. What the hell is he playing at? He's damn well supposed to be *here*.'

Jan produced her racecourse pass.

'I must go in and take a look at my horse,' she said.

'OK, Mrs Hardy,' said the senior man, after carefully scrutinizing the pass. Oddly, he made no comment when Sean, who had no pass, followed as she headed towards the row of boxes, each housing one of tomorrow's runners.

Patsy was not at Morning Glory's box and it was obvious to a blind man that the horse was distressed. He was continually calling out, walking round and round in circles, and in the process winding up the horses on either side of him. Jan examined the box carefully. Patsy seemed to have made a nest for himself in the corner. Jan saw an indentation on the bedding, and the sandwich wrappers and the tea flask were hidden in a corner behind the water bucket. But the tatty yellow rucksack that Patsy had been carrying with him was missing.

While Jan stood by MG's head, stroking his neck, doing her best to calm him, Sean offered to find the large group of visiting lads and see if Patsy was with them. Jan heard the tyres squeal outside as her friend turned his car and drove away fast in the direction of the bar mentioned by the guards.

Jan continued talking to Morning Glory. She knew she was no substitute for Patsy, but at least he knew her.

'Oh MG, MG,' she whispered. 'What's happened? Where on earth's Patsy gone?'

The horse blew down his nostrils, snorting loudly, and pawed at the bedding.

25

The rain had stopped by the time Sean returned to Morning Glory's box around twenty minutes later, where he found Jan sitting outside on an upturned plastic milk crate. But there was no sign of Morning Glory, who had turned to face the back wall in sullen fashion and was taking no interest.

'I don't suppose you found him?' Jan questioned, without much hope of a positive response.

'They say he's not been in the bar at all,' Sean said, breathing hard, 'but I spoke to some of them other fellas.'

'They haven't seen him?'

'No, and if they have they're not saying. I couldn't get a peep out of 'em, but I've a lead on him anyway.'

He pulled a crumpled, torn piece of envelope out of his pocket and showed it to her. Jan saw some scrawled details, and even made out the name: Michael Cusack.

'Who's Michael Cusack?' she asked.

'I believe he founded the Gaelic Athletic Association.'

'Sorry, Sean, I'm lost. I don't get it.'

'It's simple – they named a block of flats after him, and in that block of flats lives Patsy's family.'

'You mean this is the Keatings' address?'

'It is. How important is it that you find him tonight? I mean, do you need him right now?'

'Yes, absolutely. Without Patsy, the horse drops to pieces. Just look at him, he's already gone into an almighty huff. I doubt we'll be able to send him out tomorrow, not without Patsy being here, that's for sure. And if we did, it's highly questionable whether he'd run a worthwhile race. How far away is this place?'

'Not far. It's here in Dublin, just a few miles up the road.'

Jan sprang up, suddenly filled with renewed energy. 'Sean, can we go in your car?'

'But what about the horse?'

'He'll manage until we find our boy. Come on, big fella, you can't desert me now!'

'Tally ho!' said Sean with a broad grin.

They returned to the security gate, where Jan called in at the office.

'If Patsy Keating, the lad who looks after my horse, turns up, tell him I'll be right back.'

'Right y'are, Mrs Hardy,' said the guard.

As he drove, Sean explained what had happened in the pub.

'There was about a dozen of the boyos in there. I asked after Patsy, which they thought was quite amusing – I mean amusing that I was looking for him. "What would you be wanting with the quare feller?" said one and, "He's after going to confession," said another.

'It wasn't till I left the place that one of them came chasing after me in the street. He said he knew Patsy, they were kids together. I asked him where the Keatings lived and bingo! He gave me the address, simple as that. It's the obvious place for him, especially if he's been frightened off by those lads.'

'Unless he *is* at confession,' said Jan drily.

During the twenty minutes' drive, the cityscape changed to one of housing schemes and suburban squalor – grey blocks of flats interspersed with windswept and derelict open spaces.

'You have to be very careful driving on the roads here,' commented Sean.

Jan looked around. Compared to the city centre, there seemed relatively little traffic.

'Why?'

'You'll see.'

A few moments later the rump of a shaggy-coated grey horse, his long mane and tail matted and clogged with sludge, suddenly appeared in the car headlights. He was wandering along the road, totally unfazed, and appeared to be following the centre line. Sean slowed to a walking pace until they had passed the bedraggled animal, then accelerated.

'That's why,' he said. 'These estates are crawling with semi-wild horses, a lot of them owned by kids. Some are just abandoned.'

'Where do they come from?'

'The first Sunday of the month there's a horse fair at Smithfield Market, in the city centre, where the youngsters go and pay a few quid for a pony. They bring it back to whichever of these rackety estates they live on and either tether it or turn it out on some old patch of scrubland.'

Jan looked from side to side, and every now and then spotted the ghostly form of a horse or pony standing in the dark, cropping whatever grass it could find. She even saw a mare with a foal at foot.

'But why on earth do they do it?'

'Status. Excitement. In the evening they round 'em all up and go out and race one another. Dubliners call them the urban cowboys. I bet Patsy was one of them, in his early days. Many of them are travellers' kids, who at least have some idea how to look after a horse. But a lot are typical skangers, who haven't a clue, and don't even give enough water to the poor beasts. It's rumoured they actually keep them in the apartments, like you would a pet dog. Would you believe that? Apparently they take them up and down in the lifts, horse shit everywhere. I read about one kid that wanted a zebra, so he painted black stripes on his pony with some old paint he found. Of course the poor sod became real sick with the poisoning.'

'But it should be stopped,' protested Jan, horrified. 'Aren't there any controls?'

'This is Ireland. You need to get a licence for a dog, but even a baby in nappies can own a horse. They're talking about legislation now to bring in licensing and an age limit, but of course it'll take a few years.'

'Well, the sooner the better.' Jan sighed with relief.

At last they approached the estate, where the apartment blocks stood in line a little back from the road. Sean slowed right down to scan the names on the weather-beaten display boards. The dilapidated concrete structures were rust stained and densely scrawled with graffiti, each displaying a few boarded-up windows. Sean moved gently on, then pulled up.

'This looks like the place,' he said, squinting at the ramshackle building.

They left the locked car and approached a door, which stood half open. Jan led the way, reading the name of the block on the board above: Michael Cusack House. She pushed through into a damp, smelly hallway, from which a concrete stairwell rose to the upper floors. By the dim light of a single bare electric bulb dangling from the ceiling, they began climbing the stairs.

'I wouldn't fancy doing this on my own. Thank goodness you're here,' said Jan. 'Do you have the flat number?'

'Yes, it's thirteen.'

'It would be,' she answered grimly.

Standing outside the flat, they could hear the mumblings of a television. Jan tapped on the door, then hammered louder. Eventually a quavering voice was heard.

'Who's there?'

'It's Jan Hardy.'

She heard her name reverberate around the stairwell.

'I'm Patsy's boss in England. Is he there?'

They heard the security chain rattle and a second later the door jerked open. A watery old eye inspected Jan through the crack.

'I'm his grammah. What do ye want at this hour of the night?'

'I need to speak to him. I don't wish him any harm. We're friends.'

With a whumph, the door was shut. Jan grimaced and shot an anxious look at her companion.

'Shit!' she mouthed silently.

Then they heard the security chain sliding out of its groove and the door opened again, wider this time. A small woman with tangled grey hair gave them a fuller inspection. She pointed at Sean.

'Who's that?' she demanded gruffly.

'He's a friend. He drove me here. I don't know the area. I would never have found it on my own.'

The woman swung the door wide. 'You'd better come in.'

Compared to the grime of the stairway, the flat was pristine. The carpets and curtains, with their bright swirly patterns, were well worn, but immaculately clean. So were the holy pictures that seemed to cover every square inch of the wallspace, and the white lace doilies laid on the gleaming table and sideboard. The whole atmosphere carried a powerful smell of furniture polish.

'Sit down there.'

Patsy's grandmother gestured at the settee, which was placed against the wall opposite a television. A spaghetti Western was blaring from its screen.

Obediently they perched on the edge as the old woman shuffled out of the room. A moment later they heard her calling out, 'Patsy, Patsy, you there?'

Jan closed her fists and lifted them in front of her.

'Yeesss!' she whispered.

Sean jumped up and stationed himself by the door,

his face tilted upwards, listening. Elsewhere in the flat they could hear the sound of an urgent conversation, though the words were initially drowned out by a long burst of gunfire from the TV. Then the old woman came back in, followed slowly and reluctantly by a very hangdog, very nervous Patsy Keating.

''Lo, Mrs H,' he said.

'For Christ's sake, Patsy,' Jan exploded, 'what the bloody hell are you doing here? I need you, so get your things right now. You're coming back with us.'

Patsy knew he had a snowball's chance in hell of standing up to Jan that night. So he collected his yellow rucksack and mumbled something to his grandma. She kissed him and grunted a reply as she opened the door of the flat.

Jan sat with Patsy in the rear of the car while Sean drove back to Leopardstown, and gradually Jan extracted the boy's story. Michael Fahey had been his chief persecutor at Riscombe, and after Tim Farr's article in the *Wessex Daily News* he had been disciplined by Scottie Venables. Although Fahey already despised Patsy, the punishment had redoubled his loathing and, during the flight to Ireland when the two of them were alone in the horse compartment, Fahey had threatened all sorts of evil retribution.

But it was much later, when he met up with a few of the boyos at Leopardstown, that things became far more serious. They had already heard the rumours concerning Morning Glory and his total dependence on Patsy Keating. As they all liked a wager, Michael

Fahey had seen a way of discrediting Patsy, while at the same time making sure that Velvet Dynasty was an attractive betting proposition in Saturday's race. Backed up by his pals, he'd gone round to MG's box and told Patsy that the animal would be blinded if Patsy didn't scarper.

Jan gasped. Some of those lads had already been questioned by Sean in the pub. They knew a search was on. If they guessed Patsy would be found and brought back, would they carry out their brutal intention?

'Ah, don't you worry too much about that,' Sean reassured her. 'It's all cod. They wouldn't risk actually doing anything to the horse. There's too much security at that place. It's empty threats.'

'But I couldn't take the chance, mister,' said Patsy plaintively. 'I wouldn't mind what they did to me, but I had to save MG. Isn't that right, Mrs H?'

'I can see your point, Patsy,' said Jan. 'And I don't blame you for being frightened. But you should have told me instead of buggering off like that.'

It was almost midnight when they arrived back at the racecourse and Patsy was reunited with Morning Glory. The horse had come to no harm and was visibly delighted to see his lad, spinning round in his box and nickering with pleasure.

There was no way Jan could go back to the Shelbourne, not that night. After a big warm hug from Sean, who then left for his home in County Wexford, she dropped in to the stable office. There she found the two guards hypnotized by the same Western that Patsy's grandma had been watching in Michael Cusack House.

'I've had serious threats made against my horse,' she told them, raising her voice to compete with the volleys of frenzied shooting from the TV. 'You will be extra-vigilant, won't you?'

'Right,' said one of the guards, lifting a finger but not taking his eyes off the screen.

'Did you hear what I just *said*?' Jan shouted.

The two men turned to her, blinking.

'Sorry, what was it?'

'I said, I have reason to believe my horse may be got at. So I'm staying here tonight, with the lad, if that's all right with you. Is that clear enough?'

'Right you are, Mrs Hardy,' said the older man. 'No problem at all.'

For the next six hours Jan and Patsy were always near MG's box, taking it in turns hour by hour to keep watch while the other catnapped.

As she poured the lukewarm remains from the flask into a beaker at what seemed like their darkest hour, around three a.m., Jan asked, 'Was it your grandma who brought you up?'

'Mostly she did.'

'So where's your mother?'

'In England.'

'When did you last see her?'

'I dunno. Four or five years ago, maybe.'

'And what about your father?'

'I never seen him in my life.'

Poor little sod, Jan thought. She could only imagine how hard his life must have been.

After what seemed an eternity, daylight came and life resumed in the stable complex as more horses began to arrive for the day's racing. With plenty of people around, Jan thought it would be safe to return to Dublin for a quick shower and change while Patsy saw to the horse – a good lead-out, a ten-minute pick of grass, a sip of clean water, a thorough grooming followed by a small feed would set him up fine.

When Jan got back to Leopardstown around ten, she went straight to the stables, where to her horror she saw the Riscombe thug leaning over the open half-door of MG's stable with a cigarette in one hand, speaking to Patsy inside.

Jan stormed up to him.

'Get away from here, Fahey! Don't you dare hang around the box door with a lighted cigarette. You're not supposed to smoke in here anyway. Are you so thick you don't know anything about the rules?'

Fahey sprang from the loosebox door and jogged backwards away from Jan, showing her his open hands, shrugging his shoulders and grinning impertinently.

'You're a bloody disgrace,' Jan went on furiously. 'Don't think I don't know what you've been up to, because I do – everything.'

Fahey curled his lip and raised two fingers.

'Stuff you, you old bag,' he sneered, before turning on his heels and marching away.

Jan was crimson and shaking with rage. 'What did he want? What was that bastard saying to you?'

'Nothin', Mrs H,' said Patsy, who was polishing the bridle the horse would wear in the race. 'Just the normal gab he always gives me.'

'About what? Did he threaten to harm you or the horse again?'

'No, he said he was only havin' a dig, like.'

'What else did he say?'

'Same as usual, he took the piss out of me for going to church. And said I shouldn't be involved in racing because it was, you know, a sinful type of business, so.'

'Do you really think it's sinful, Patsy?' she said more calmly.

'A lot of it is so,' he replied with sincerity. 'But the horses wouldn't be, would they?'

Jan couldn't help laughing.

'No,' she agreed. 'Naughty, bloody difficult, sometimes impossible, yes; but sinful? I don't think so, not even nearly.'

Later, in the owners' and trainers' bar, Jan gave A.D. O'Hagan a summary of the previous night's drama, highlighting the role taken by Virginia's travelling groom. It seemed to give the great man less cause for concern than she expected.

'We do get these threats from time to time,' he said unflappably. 'It's usually just a blast of hot air.'

'You're taking it rather lightly, A.D. They talked about *blinding* the horse, you know!'

A.D. gave a wry smile.

'Ah well, *you* never take it too lightly. In my time I've had two of my horses threatened with being shot.

Here in Ireland, can you believe? So there it is, you just take the necessary precautions, as you did last night – very effectively, if I may say so.'

'But what can we do now? We can't just let them get away with it, can we?'

'What we do is simple,' said A.D. 'We go to the races and our horse gives theirs a good licking.'

For all A.D.'s apparent indifference, Jan could not restrain herself from tackling Virginia in person. Small clusters of owners and trainers were beginning to gather, as the runners for the Fitzpatrick Castle Hurdle circled the parade ring, still wearing their sheets. By sheer coincidence Jan happened to enter immediately behind an unaccompanied Virginia, and she increased her pace to catch up with Velvet Dynasty's trainer.

'Virginia, are you aware your lad threatened to blind my horse last night?' she demanded.

Somehow Jan prevented herself from raising her voice. On a racecourse, not just the walls, but every blade of grass could have ears, and she did not want this feud with Virginia to get more publicity than it already had.

Virginia smiled. 'Horrible sense of humour some of these young men have, don't they?'

'I don't think a criminal offence is a laughing matter. What are you going to do about it?'

Virginia looked at Jan with indifference.

'Well, I don't see why we should care what *you* think, so nothing. Now, if you'll excuse me, I have a horse to see to.'

As Virginia stalked off, A.D. appeared in the ring with his entourage, quickly followed by Murty Mc-

Grath and the other jockeys. Caught up in the vital business of last-minute preparations and racing instructions, for the time being Jan brushed aside Virginia and her cruel sarcasm.

Previously Jan had taken runners to the Cheltenham Festival, Aintree and Fairyhouse's Irish National and no one could describe the Fitzpatrick Castle Hurdle, with its 25,000 Irish punts in prize money, as being remotely in the same class. Yet she felt, if it were possible, even more tension now than on those distinguished occasions. Of course, the previous night had left her exhausted, but that didn't matter. It was how the horse came through it all that was much more relevant, and he seemed absolutely fine, although Jan wished Reg had been there to reassure her. In her experience, when it came to assessing a horse's well-being, Reg's keen eye was second to none.

Jan told Murty to ride Morning Glory exactly as he had done before.

'Only don't fall at the last this time,' she said with a twinkle in her eye.

The ground was a little sticky after the previous day's downpour, which would to some extent cramp MG's free-running style. But, on the other hand, it would also blunt the finishing speed of Velvet Dynasty and the other 'flat yokes', as A.D. so succinctly put it. The debates that raged on the course, as the horses made their way to the start, were as to whether this was going to be another duel between Jan's and Virginia's yards, or whether some other pretender would emerge to take them both on. The betting market at this stage suggested the former. MG and Velvet Dynasty were joint favourites at seven to four, with the next in the list standing at five to one.

The two-mile start at Leopardstown was a couple of furlongs away, to the left of the stands, and Jan and A.D. took up a position that gave them a good view of the line-up. Jan thought Murty handled MG beautifully on the way to the start, and once again she marvelled at his cool, controlled horsemanship. Now, through her binoculars, she could clearly see the O'Hagan colours moving around at the back of the pack as the champion jockey attempted to position MG so that as the tape flew up he would already be moving forward. She also caught sight of the Gilbert colours, worn once again by Finbar Howlett on Velvet Dynasty.

Murty judged the start perfectly and MG immediately pulled into a clear lead, his tail streaming proudly behind him as he surged up the incline. As the horses thundered past the stands, and through the flying divots, Jan noted that Velvet Dynasty had taken up a position nearer to last than first. Finbar was using his familiar waiting tactics.

The crowd let out a huge roar. They loved Morning Glory's devil-may-care hurdling, gasping and cheering when he skimmed over the obstacles at full speed. His jump at the fourth, around the halfway mark on the far side of the course, heralded a mammoth groan as he hit the willow, but this time he never even broke stride. All the way along the back straight Jan could see Velvet Dynasty and Finbar Howlett deftly picking their way through the field. As they swung round the long final bend and downhill towards the start of the home straight, he had moved into fourth place and was travelling better than any of the runners, with the exception of Morning Glory.

Jan's mouth was bone dry, her heart thumped like a jackhammer, and her teeth were clenched as Velvet Dynasty powered into second place and began determinedly to close on the leader.

Here we go again! she thought, her mouth too dry to speak. She flashed a glance at A.D. He had never told her the size of his bet, but she could see from the way the muscle in his jaw was twitching that, for him, a whole lot of cash depended on the outcome of the next few seconds.

This time, unlike Cheltenham, the horses rose to meet the last flight in unison, with Velvet Dynasty on the outside. As Morning Glory's forelegs touched the ground, he pulled his hind legs under his body to give maximum power to that all-important first stride away from the obstacle. At the same time, right alongside, Velvet Dynasty screwed in the air, landing at an angle. The two horses collided shoulder to shoulder.

Completely knocked out of his stride, Morning Glory came off far worse and Murty, for the first time that day, had to earn his riding fee. He yanked violently at the reins to avoid colliding with the rails, and to get the horse back on an even keel. For a couple of strides he let his mount regain his balance, before giving him a dig in the flanks with both heels to restart his run. MG responded wholeheartedly, though by now he had lost considerable ground. Even worse, he had conceded his position on the rails as Virginia's horse barged across in front of him.

MG acknowledged his jockey's desperate call and lowered his head to dig in, as Murty steered him away from the rails to tackle Velvet Dynasty on the outside. With the furlongs ever-decreasing to the winning line, MG began to make steady progress. It was agonizing. Step by step, with every reach of his forelegs, he took a few more inches off Velvet Dynasty's lead. As they raced past the stands both horses were at full stretch, their ears laid flat back as their jockeys pumped away like a couple of madmen. Morning Glory was edging closer to Velvet Dynasty. The crowd went ballistic as he reached the other horse's quarters, then his neck, both jockeys pushing, pushing, trying to lengthen their mount's stride, refusing to give in.

In the last few lung-bursting strides the horses' heads rocked back and forth, with first one and then the other getting his nostrils in front. Finally they flashed past the post and there was only a nod in it.

Jan went bright red, flushed with excitement and emotion. Not since winning the Irish National had she seen a horse of hers fight back so bravely. She looked at A.D., but he was still watching as the horses careered on round the bend, their momentum taking them several hundred yards further along the course before their jockeys could begin to pull them up. As they did so, A.D., slowly and deliberately, lowered his binoculars.

'Half a stride after the post, we were in front.'

'But . . .?'

'At the line itself, I just don't know, I couldn't be sure.'

Jan saw a microscopic bead of sweat nestling in the wrinkles of A.D.'s brow as they waited for an announcement.

'Photograph, photograph.' A voice bellowed over the loudspeaker a few seconds later.

Now the result of the race was in the hands of the judge.

There was absolutely no way of knowing which way it would go, who was the victor or who was the vanquished. The noise from the crowd had fallen away, but the course still buzzed like a gigantic hornet's nest as everyone debated the outcome. The bookies were busy quoting prices on the result of the photograph, with an apparent even split between those who thought Morning Glory had got up to win and those who maintained that Velvet Dynasty had held him off.

Jan pushed her way through the throng of racegoers moving around the stand, mesmerized and electrified by what they had just witnessed. She was halfway to the unsaddling enclosure when the announcer's voice boomed out from the PA again. She stood still to listen.

'Here is the result of the photograph. First number six, Velvet Dynasty; second number ten, Morning Glory; third number twelve . . .'

The lives of drowning victims are said to flash before their eyes. Now Jan had a similar experience. It was as if all the stress and problems of the last six months had come back to haunt her in a concentrated form.

Jan made her way to unsaddle her horse. She found Velvet Dynasty already standing in the winner's slot. His connections were triumphant, with Virginia already posing for photographs as Michael Fahey went about his business wearing the smuggest of smug smiles. Patsy, on the other hand, looked shell-shocked as he led Morning Glory into the number two position. Jan could find nothing to say as Murty slipped to the ground and faced her, his face grim.

'Did you see that at the last?' he growled. 'I'm fecking sure he did it deliberate.'

Murty undid the girth and removed the saddle and weight cloth before stomping off towards the weighing room. Then Jan saw her owner emerge from the crowd to intercept him. A.D. listened attentively as Murty talked, gesturing angrily. The owner nodded just once, before Murty touched the peak of his cap with the whip he was carrying and hurried off to weigh in. As Jan was about to fling a cooler across Morning Glory's steaming back, A.D. arrived to rub the horse's nose.

Jan swallowed the hard lump that was still lodged in her throat.

'A.D., I'm so sorry—' she began.

A.D. held up his finger.

'Shhh! Listen!'

The public-address system crackled and the announcer's voice was heard again.

'Objection. Objection.'

Instantly the crowd buzzed at the prospect of another twist in the tale. A hush descended and you could have heard a pin drop as the announcer continued.

'The second has objected to the winner on the grounds of bumping and boring and taking his ground after the last. Patrons are advised to retain all betting tickets until the stewards have made their ruling. Thank you.'

Jan's hand was over her mouth as A.D. murmured, 'It's not over yet, Jan. It's not over yet, my girl!'

When the stewards sat to adjudicate, they considered nothing but the video replay and the evidence provided by the jockeys concerned. So, although Jan went with Murty to the stewards' room, which was across a corridor from the weighing area, all she could do was stand outside. Finbar Howlett was already waiting at the door as they got there. To Jan's relief, there was no sign of Virginia.

Murty mouthed something uncomplimentary at Finbar as they lingered.

'McGrath, Howlett, come in!' the steward's secretary said as he opened the door.

At that moment Jan was reminded of a summons to the head teacher's office at school. She caught a glimpse of the scene inside. It was a large room, in which three male stewards were sitting behind a polished table. To one side, on a trolley, were a television set and video recorder. As the two jockeys entered, the steward's secretary marched to the far end of the table and stood to attention – it was his job to advise the stewards on the rules of racing.

There was a loud 'clunk' as the door closed.

The voices inside the room were audible, but not the words. Jan knew roughly what was going on. Firstly the tribunal would hear what the objector, McGrath, had to say, followed by Howlett's defence. Then they would all look at the video recordings of the race, most importantly the head-on, but also views from the side and rear. Jan had already seen a television replay of the two horses jumping the last and was in no doubt that Morning Glory would have crossed the line first if he hadn't been bumped. But was the bump deliberate or accidental? Murty was absolutely convinced of Finbar's guilt, and though Jan, in her heart of hearts, was not quite so sure, she knew the stewards would have to reverse the placings if they agreed with her jockey.

She wandered into the weighing room and chatted with the clerk of the scales, then wandered back. She chewed her lip, bit a fingernail, and studied the framed ancient sporting prints lining the corridor's walls. At last, after almost ten minutes, the door of the stewards' room opened again and the secretary ushered the jockeys out.

'Wait there a moment while the stewards deliberate. I will call you back when they have reached a decision,' he said.

Before closing the door firmly again, he gave Jan an icy stare, which did nothing for her confidence in the outcome. Finbar was glowering, and Murty seemed edgy as they waited by the heavy highly polished outer door. Jan looked at her watch. The next race was due off in twelve minutes. If the stewards didn't produce a verdict quickly, the session would have to adjourn.

Nobody wanted that, certainly not the punters who would be anxious to re-invest.

Suddenly the door swung open. It was the secretary dressed in his traditional tweed suit and bone-polished shoes.

'McGrath, Howlett, please come back in.'

It took the stewards less than a minute to deliver their verdict. Murty bounced out of the room followed by Finbar, looking decidedly sour, and the secretary, who strode off hurriedly with a paper in his hand.

'What's happened?' Jan whispered. 'What's the result?'

But Murty, with a mischievous smile quite different from the scowl he had worn earlier, was already off.

'I'll catch you later, Mrs H. I'm riding in the next. Listen for the announcement.'

Jan went outside, where a spell of watery sunshine had now brightened the winter afternoon. She stood with her back to the wall near the weighing-room door, content to be by herself. Then she heard the PA system crackle into life.

'Ladies and gentlemen, following the objection by the second to the winner in the previous race, the stewards found that Velvet Dynasty interfered with Morning Glory at the last flight, and thereby gained an unfair advantage. Finbar Howlett has been suspended for foul riding and number six, Velvet Dynasty, has been placed last. Here is a revised result: first, number ten Morning Glory, second number twelve . . .'

Jan felt very calm. She shut her eyes and rested her head against the brick wall of the racecourse building, as the sun's warmth bathed her face.

26

The trial of Harold Powell, on the double charge of attempted murder and causing death by reckless driving, was held in the second week of March before Judge Laurence Bancroft, sitting at Gloucester Crown Court. Harold's brief was Charles de Courcy QC, a well-known London silk, while the Crown was represented by Benjamin Jeffreys, a senior barrister practising on the Western Circuit. When the clerk of the court asked the defendant how did he plead, Harold said firmly, 'Not guilty,' to both charges.

As a witness for the prosecution, Jan was excluded from the early stages of the proceedings. Bob Warren had explained to her that a jury had to be selected, and then the preliminary submissions of prosecution and defence would be made before Jeffreys could open the case for the Crown. Which he did on the second day, when those waiting in the witnesses' room began to thin out as they were called to give evidence. One by one, the police officers, including Brian Hadfield, stepped up to the witness box to describe the scene on Cleeve Hill almost a year ago. A pathologist gave the results of his autopsy on the body of William Moorhouse. Members of the forensic science team provided details of skid patterns, impact analysis and paint fragments. As she and Patsy sat, awaiting their turn, Jan did not feel overly nervous, except on behalf of Patsy. He was clearly tortured, sitting there pale as a glass of milk.

Jan was called to the stand immediately after the expert evidence. She took the oath, then looked across to the public gallery, where Reg and Mary were sitting, so close together she knew they were holding hands. Nearby, she could see both Toby Waller and Annabel. There was no Eddie – he'd said he couldn't face it. But sitting detached from the others, Virginia, in a typical 'look at me' pose, glanced at Jan. Next, Jan looked across at Harold, who was standing in the dock. Flanked by two stony-faced prison officers, he was staring menacingly back at her.

After the preliminaries, Jeffreys courteously invited Jan to lead him through the hours preceding the accident on Cleeve Hill. She gave details of the race meeting and A.D.'s party, and of Harold threatening her. She went on to report how she and Eddie had left the course, and how they were being overtaken by a car on Cleeve Hill as another car was speeding towards them; how they had been barged off the road by the overtaking car, which sped away leaving mayhem in its wake. Finally, she detailed her injuries and Eddie's long and painful rehabilitation.

Jeffreys went on to ask about Harold Powell. How long had Jan known him? Would she tell the court how he had acted in the sale of Stonewall Farm? Did anything subsequently occur to suggest someone might have a grudge against her? What had happened when

Harold visited Edge Farm on that afternoon back in October?

'No more questions,' said Jeffreys at last. Jan was feeling relieved and rather good until she saw the figure of Charles de Courcy rising to his feet to cross-examine her. She steeled herself, remembering Bob Warren's advice: the man was a highly skilled advocate; she must keep her answers brief and be as decisive as possible.

'Mrs Hardy, I won't detain you very long,' the QC began suavely. 'Now I understand that, on occasions when one has had a success at the races, it is usual to celebrate with champagne and other alcoholic drinks. Is that so?'

'Yes,' Jan agreed, 'many people do.'

'Prior to your road accident, you yourself had been celebrating with your owners at the Cheltenham racecourse, after the win you so admirably described to the court. Is that so?'

'Yes, I had a glass or two.'

'In the hospitality suite of your horse's owner, A.D. O'Hagan?'

'Yes.'

'Was Edward Sullivan present in Mr O'Hagan's box?'

'Yes, he was.'

'And did he celebrate the victory?'

'Yes, of course. He was delighted.'

De Courcy looked at her over the top of his half-moon glasses.

'I mean, did he drink the champagne or any of the other alcohol on offer?'

'I didn't see him.'

'But he was with you, was he not?'

'Not all the time. When he was with me he didn't drink.'

'And when he offered to drive you home, did you ask him if he'd had a drink during the day?'

'Yes, I did.'

'What did he say?'

'He said he was fine to drive because he'd had no more than a gnat's bladderful.'

A ripple of laughter ran around the court, quelled by a glare from the bench.

De Courcy continued, 'Which means, I take it, that he *had* had something to drink?'

'Yes. It means a very little.'

'Indeed? Though a gnat's bladder is not, I think, a term recognized in the Weights and Measures Act.'

There was another wave of giggles. De Courcy was clearly enjoying himself.

'On that same afternoon at the races,' he went on, 'you allege that you met the defendant by chance and that he threatened to make sure that you would, I quote, "get what's coming to you". Is that right?'

'Yes.'

'Was anyone else present when, as you allege, he said these words?'

'No.'

'No witnesses at all?'

'No.'

'I see. Now, can we move on to the accident itself? Mrs Hardy, how well can you remember it?'

'I remember it well. I'm not likely to forget it, am I?' Jan responded, feeling a little flustered as the memories were brought back to life.

'How well did you remember it immediately afterwards – the next day, for instance?'

'Not very well, not then. I'd had a bang on the head, I was concussed. It was fuzzy, broken up, like a dream.'

'Were you suffering from what is sometimes called transient post-traumatic amnesia?'

'That's what I was told by the doctors, yes. It took time to get all my memory back.'

'How much time?'

'Days. A week or two.'

'A *week* or two, really? And did it all come back at once, in a complete picture?'

'No, it didn't. It was bit by bit.'

De Courcy glanced at the jury meaningfully.

'And when these fragmented memories of the accident *did* come back to you, was it only then that you remembered seeing the car that you say overtook Mr Sullivan's on Cleeve Hill?'

'Yes, it was.'

'Did you remember recognizing that vehicle at the moment it came alongside you?'

'Well, I saw what sort of a car it was.'

De Courcy consulted the bundle of papers in front of him.

'A four-wheel drive, yes? But you never at any stage during the recovery of your memory thought that you had recognized the individual car? Something specific – that you knew, for instance, who owned it?'

'No. I didn't, not then, but I—'

De Courcy cut in.

'Only that it was some kind of four-wheel-drive vehicle.'

'Yes.'

'What colour was it?'

'I don't know, it was dark.'

'The car was dark?'

'No, no . . .'

Jan was getting more flustered. She consciously pulled herself together.

'I meant the *night* was dark, obviously.'

'I see. And did you, when you recovered your fragmented memory, remember recognizing – in the dark – the driver of this vehicle, which you allege pushed Mr Sullivan and you off the road?'

'No, I didn't see him, I—'

'You didn't even *see* this driver, did you? Not at all, not even in silhouette?'

'No, because I—'

'Thank you, Mrs Hardy, yes and no will be fine, unless I ask for elucidation. I have just a few more questions.'

De Courcy adjusted his half-moons and turned a few pages of his bundle.

'You have told the court that things began to happen to you subsequent to the accident, suggesting that someone had a grudge against you – a few anonymous phone calls, and this mysterious press release that you have described. Was there anything in those reports that told you the defendant was their author?'

'I suspected him.'

'But there was nothing specific about them that told you that it could, in fact, *only* be him?'

'No, I guess not.'

'So the instigator of these unpleasant events might have been someone else entirely?'

'No, I don't think so.'

'Oh come, come, Mrs Hardy. Don't tell me public trainers of racehorses don't sometimes provoke the wrath of disappointed racegoers and gamblers – for instance when their horses unexpectedly lose a race.'

Jan glanced anxiously at the judge, who was busily writing notes.

'Well, yes, it does happen occasionally. But to my knowledge that was not the case here.'

'To your knowledge, to your *knowledge*,' de Courcy repeated, surveying the jury before going on. 'But you decided at some later point, did you not, that the defendant was responsible?'

'I began to suspect him, yes.'

'Even though you had no real evidence?'

'I had good reason—'

'But no hard *evidence*? No facts?'

'No,' agreed Jan reluctantly, 'I suppose not.'

Again the barrister rifled through the pages of his bundle.

'I turn to the episode you have described to the court when, as you allege, Harold Powell came to your stables and admitted responsibility for the accident, among other things. Apart from yourself and your employee, Patrick Keating, did anyone else actually hear him threaten you? Or see him even?'

'I don't know.'

'You did ask around, surely?'

'There was no one else there, except Patsy and myself.'

De Courcy asked a few more questions about the stable routine on Sunday afternoons – who wasn't there, who might have been there – then suddenly he snatched his glasses off his nose, rose to his full height, raised his voice and went on the offensive.

'Mrs Hardy,' he boomed, 'were you extremely worried at the time that your friend Edward Sullivan was himself being investigated by the police over the death of William Moorhouse on Cleeve Hill?'

'Well, yes, I was worried, but I—'

'I put it to you, Mrs Hardy, that Harold Powell was never at your stables on that day, any more than he had been on Cleeve Hill when the accident occurred.'

'No. He *was* at the stables.'

'And that you made up this story of his confession, and asked your employee Patrick Keating to confirm it, in order to get Edward Sullivan off the hook. That's it, Mrs Hardy, isn't it?'

'Mr de Courcy, Harold was *there*.'

'Mrs Hardy, would you tell the court why, after training my client's horses for several years, and with some success I might add, he removed his horses from your care and sent them to Miss Gilbert?'

'Because I asked him to remove them after we had a disagreement and I recommended Virginia Gilbert as an alternative,' Jan replied sharply.

'Why Miss Gilbert in particular?' de Courcy countered.

Jan was already getting irritated by de Courcy's

demeanour. 'Because I thought they were a pair of sh . . .' Jan choked back the expletive. 'Because I thought they would be a good match temperamentally.'

'Really!' de Courcy intoned. 'I put it to you, further, that you knew that Mr Keating had a grudge against the defendant's friend, Miss Gilbert, for whom he once worked. You yourself had a grudge against my client because you believed he had cheated you over a land deal. So, between you, you conspired to implicate Harold Powell and exonerate Edward Sullivan, your friend. That's right, isn't it?'

Jan knew she was red in the face, not from embarrassment, but anger. How dare this man call her a liar? How dare he accuse her of conspiring against Harold, when it was Harold who'd conspired against her? She took a deep breath. *De Courcy's doing this on purpose,* she thought. *He's hoping I'm going to lose control. I can't let them get away with it.* She inhaled deeply and knew it would be fatal to start shouting.

'No, no,' she continued as coolly as she could. 'It's me telling the truth and Powell who's lying. You've got it arse about face.'

'Now, Mrs Hardy!' said the judge sharply, looking up from his notes.

But her retort was enough to shut de Courcy up. He bowed and said, 'Thank you, Mrs Hardy, no further questions.'

Jan had not expected to be branded a liar by the defence though she realized it was the obvious tactic –

the best chance for Harold to win. Now, after de Courcy's vicious cross-examination, she began to appreciate how uncertain her entire future looked in the light of this case. Suppose Harold was acquitted. Would that mean she was in the frame for perjury? Or conspiring to pervert the course of justice? It didn't bear thinking about.

Once her evidence had been completed, Jan was able to sit in the public gallery. She was more concerned about Patsy than she had been for herself. How would he stand up to any rough treatment from de Courcy? Surprisingly Patsy was an effective witness, answering Jeffreys's questions quietly and with conviction. But when it was de Courcy's turn, he simply waved his hand.

'No questions, your honour.'

'Thank you, Mr Keating,' said Bancroft. 'You may step down.'

Harold's defence team had decided to rely on the argument that the Crown's case was too flimsy. Tellingly, they did not want to risk exposing their client, with his tendency to flip his lid, to Jeffreys's questions. So Harold did not give evidence and de Courcy confined himself to calling one of the drinks' waiters at Cheltenham, who said he thought he'd seen Eddie 'supping'. Then came two not especially persuasive character witnesses and a scientist, who stated in tortuous terms that anyone who'd had a head injury might not be all there, mentally, for several months after the event. This last evidence was an obvious attempt to back up de Courcy's attack on Jan, but the scientist was so circumspect, and used so many 'maybes' and 'possiblys' that, as Bob Warren said later, he tended to strangle his own theories at birth.

De Courcy's closing statement was short. He hammered home the fact that no one except Jan, the victim of a serious head injury, had seen the third car at the scene; that no one except Jan and Patsy had heard Harold Powell confess to being responsible for the accident; and that both might harbour grudges against Harold, either directly or because they didn't like Virginia Gilbert, who was Harold's closest friend. A much more likely explanation, the QC argued, was that Eddie Sullivan had been intoxicated, and had caused the accident himself. With that poisonous suggestion, he sat down.

Benjamin Jeffreys countered strongly with the fact that there was no evidence of Eddie's inebriation, that skid marks in the road and paint traces on the Morgan might have been from Harold's Range Rover, that Harold had made obvious and demonstrable threats against Jan, and what was more, he could produce no alibi for the night of the accident. It was a good closing speech, confident and uncomplicated.

By lunchtime on the third day the evidence and the judge's concise and impartial summing up were over and the jury retired to consider their verdict. During the recess, Jan had a light lunch with Bob Warren in the court cafe.

'Why did de Courcy not cross-examine Patsy?' she questioned.

'He didn't think it would help his case. He sensed that Patsy was a sympathetic witness, that the jury liked him – quite rightly, by the way – and wouldn't want to see him attacked.'

'What about me? Wanted to see me attacked, did they?'

Bob smiled broadly.

'They enjoyed that. You gave as good as you got, mind.'

'Did I? Bloody cheek, that man accusing me of lying.'

'De Courcy's been quite clever, actually, but I think he may be feeling he's met his match in you. And by the way all this about Eddie drinking is rather clutching at straws. The forensic reports make it virtually certain a third car was there, and the fact that Harold could produce no alibi is very damaging.'

'So what do you think will be the verdict?'

Bob sighed. Years of experience had taught him not to second-guess juries.

'We can only wait and see. Keep your fingers crossed.'

Jan was thoughtful, remembering how she had waited outside the stewards' room at Leopardstown for the verdict after a very different kind of trial. The outcome there had gone in her favour and now Morning Glory was due to contest the Supreme Novice Hurdle at the Cheltenham Festival in a couple of weeks. For the yard these were exciting times. But if Harold Powell got off they wouldn't be, that was for certain.

The jury were out for two hours before coming back to ask for clarification about the forensic evidence.

They then retired again and another hour dragged slowly by. Jan was sitting with Reg and Mary on a bench outside the court when they noticed the atmosphere had grown more hectic. Bob Warren bustled up to them.

'*Quick*, the jury's coming back,' he said. 'I think this is it.'

'All rise,' came the cry as Judge Bancroft entered.

Two minutes later they watched as the jury filed in. Jan squinted and tried to read the verdict in their faces but could see no clues. They all looked uniform and serious.

The clerk of the court cleared his throat.

'Would the defendant please stand?'

Harold did so, his eyes flicking from one member of the jury to the next. The clerk turned to the jury's foreman.

'Would the foreman please stand? Have you reached a verdict on which you are all agreed?'

'Yes.'

'Do you find the defendant guilty or not guilty of attempted murder?'

There was a minute pause as the whole court held its breath.

'Guilty.'

There was a loud whoosh as the onlookers breathed out and the tension was released. Someone in the public gallery blurted out, 'Yess, yess!' Jan closed her eyes from pure relief as Mary, sitting next to her, squeezed her arm. Jan slowly opened her eyes and looked at Harold. The muscles in his jaw had tightened, but he appeared otherwise unmoved.

The clerk continued, 'And do you find the defendant guilty or not guilty of causing death by reckless driving?'

'Guilty.'

'And are these the verdicts of you all?'

'They are.'

For several seconds Judge Bancroft allowed the buzz of the excited court to die away. Then he spoke firmly and without hesitation.

'Harold Powell, you have been found guilty of two extremely serious offences, the more serious of which is attempted murder. For this offence I sentence you to a term of imprisonment of ten years. On the charge of death by reckless driving, I sentence you to a term of five years. These terms are to run concurrently.'

Bancroft looked down from the bench at Harold Powell and his words rang out with crushing finality.

'Take him down.'

Epilogue

The short dark afternoons of midwinter were behind them now and there was still light in the sky as Jan, her family and friends emerged through the swing doors of the court house and gathered on the steps.

Jan felt totally drained after the emotional helter-skelter of the trial and closed her eyes as she breathed deeply. Even the taste of the traffic fumes, which hung in the cold damp air, was preferable to the musty atmosphere of the court room. Jan was still trembling as she thanked Benjamin Jeffreys for a job well done.

'Don't thank me, Mrs Hardy, that's the man you should be thanking.' Jan half-turned and saw a smiling Bob Warren walking towards her.

'That was a good result,' he said.

'Not in my opinion,' contradicted Toby. 'The sentence was too lenient.'

'Don't you worry about that: to a weak man like Harold Powell it will be more like twenty years; he'll suffer all right.'

'Good,' Annabel said brightly, 'I hope he does.'

'And so say all of *us*,' agreed Toby.

But Mary, usually a quiet presence in any group, put a warning hand on Toby's arm.

'No, Toby, we must hope he learns how much harm he's done, and how much suffering he's caused. Maybe he'll come out a better person then.'

'Not much chance of that,' growled Reg.

But Mary insisted.

'Reg, that's what we must hope will happen,' she insisted. 'Otherwise, what's it all for?'

Jan felt a sudden surge of love for her ever-optimistic mother, and a pang of regret that this strong-minded, yet gentle woman should have been put through the strain of this trial when her own health was not particularly good.

'Yes, Mum,' she said. 'I want him to come out a better person, too.'

But only after the bastard's been to hell and back was the thought she kept to herself.

'Well, is anyone up for a glass of something?' asked Toby brightly. 'I noticed a decent-looking little wine bar up the road.'

Jan made her excuses. Reg and Mary wanted to go home and she had to get back to the children and the horses. She was just guiding Reg and Mary down the steps when they heard a clatter of heels behind them. She glanced back to see who was coming down.

'I suppose you think you'll get away with this, you bitch!' hissed Virginia Gilbert from the side of her mouth as she swept past.

'What did that woman say?' asked Reg, as Virginia reached the pavement and stalked off up the road.

'It wasn't congratulations, Dad.'

'You'd better keep an eye on that woman, Jan. She's

not going to let this rest despite what your mother might think.'

'I always do, Dad.'

They had just reached the pavement and were turning towards the car park when they heard a shout from the road behind them. Jan turned. Belching smoke from its exhaust, Gerry's van drew up at the kerbside. Eddie climbed stiffly from the passenger seat and leaned inside to pull out a rather bedraggled bunch of flowers wrapped in cellophane.

'Just wait here for a moment,' Jan told her parents and went over to meet him.

'These are not much, but—' Eddie began.

'Garage, I suppose?' She chuckled.

Eddie gave her a slight, self-mocking smile.

'We stopped for diesel. What I'm saying is, I'm really sorry. I got them because I wanted to apologize for leaving you to sit through the trial, and all that. I know I should have been there. I was just being a sodding wimp.'

Jan gestured to Reg and Mary.

'My mum and dad were with me. So were Bel and Toby. I was all right really.'

Eddie took her hand and placed the flowers in it. All of a sudden, his eyes seemed larger and more tender than usual.

'I don't want to lose you, Jan,' he murmured. 'I know some things were said before Christmas, or implied, at any rate. But I've been thinking a lot in the past few weeks and I can't believe what has happened to us this last twelve months. I want to try again.'

Jan clutched the flowers with both hands. She shut

her eyes, squeezing the lids tight, then opened them again. He was still there in front of her, waiting for a response.

She sighed.

'Eddie Sullivan, you're bloody impossible. We've had one good result today. I suppose we'd better go home and get our lives sorted out, hadn't we?'